The Vast Southern Lands of
Ravi-shan
as set down by Fima
Lore-master of Mountain Home
R. Ambros
R. Dessa
Castalan
Upani
Neela-jul
Mumari
Plains of Dire Thirst
Fire Mountains
Dûn Arian
pass
T
A
D

Fire-heart

A Tale of Alterra: The World that Is

For Chris

BY

(welcome back!)

C.S. MARKS

PARTHIAN
PRESS

Fire-heart

Cover Art by John Connell

Maps and Interior Design by Carie Nixon

Interior illustrations by C.S. Marks

Edited by Leslie Wainger

Published by Parthian Press, all rights reserved

PARTHIAN PRESS

ParthianPress.com
ISBN: 978-0-9859182-9-3

The Author's Website: CSMarks.com

Table of Contents

Chapter 1: Gaelen's Vision 1
Chapter 2: The Company Travels South 19
Chapter 3: Dûn Bennas 27
Chapter 4: On the Ravani Road 51
Chapter 5: The Forsaken One 73
Chapter 6: The Voice of the Spider 97
Chapter 7: Sutherlings and Easterners 123
Chapter 8: The Festival 147
Chapter 9: Cuidag's Web 179
Chapter 10: Traps and Treachery 207
Chapter 11: The Sellers of Flesh 241
Chapter 12: Hallagond Proves Useful 269
Chapter 13: The Unlucky Moon 297
Chapter 14: Some Debts Repaid 319
Chapter 15: The Fire-cloak 345
Chapter 16: The Silver City 367
Chapter 17: The Crossing Begins 395
Chapter 18: A Savage Land 417
Chapter 19: Trials of the Road 435
Chapter 20: The Legacy of Salasin 463
Chapter 21: The War Council 481
Chapter 22: Ali's Folly 501
Chapter 23: The Enemy At the Gates 525
Chapter 24: The Battle Is Joined 555
Chapter 25: The Sons of Diomar 583
Chapter 26: The Company Is Reunited 601
GLOSSARY of NAMES 613
About C.S. Marks 633

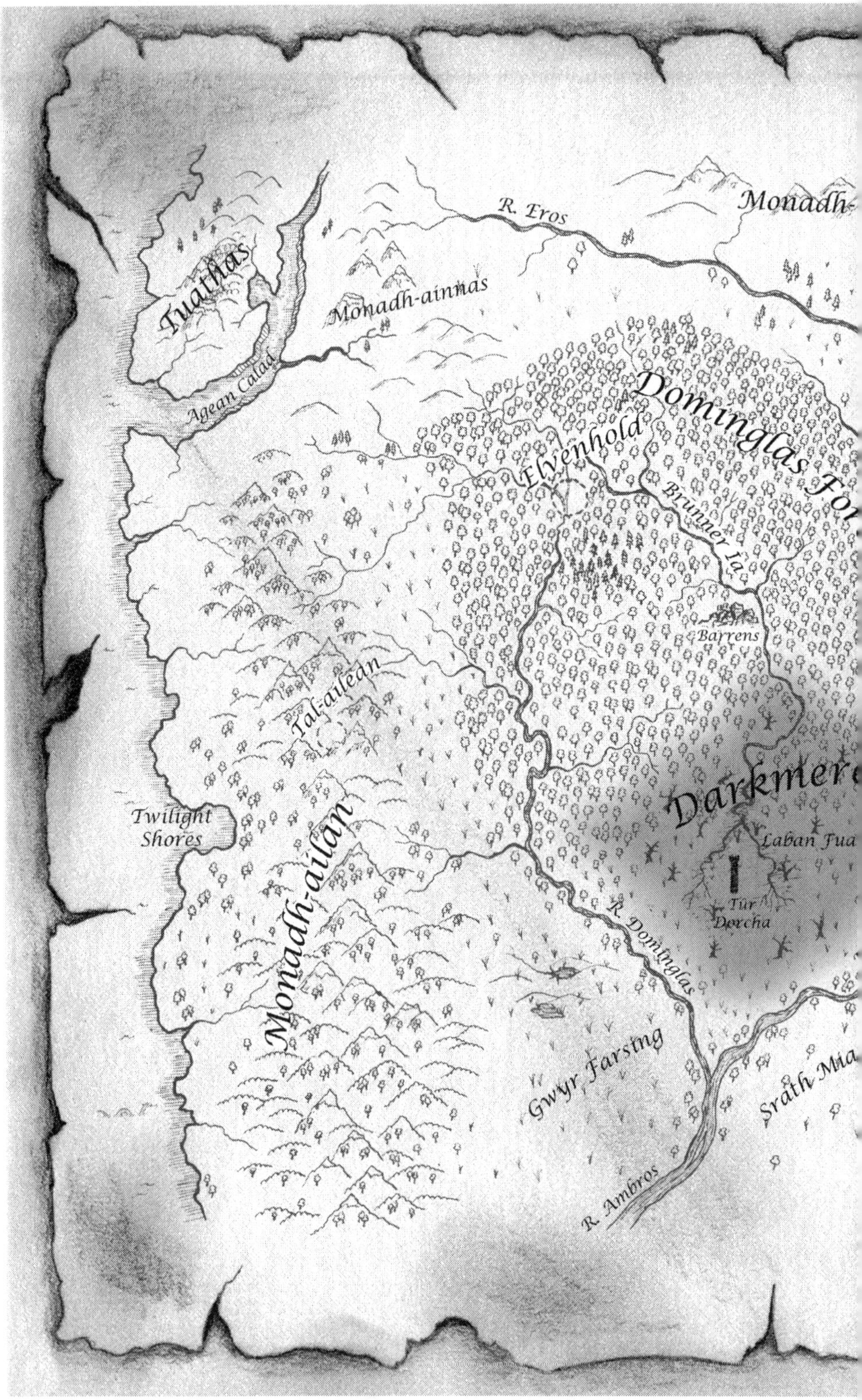
R. Eros
Monadh-
Tuathas
Monadh-ainnas
Agean Calad
Domínglas For
Elvenhold
Brummer Ia
Barrens
Tal-ailean
Darkmere
Twilight Shores
Monadh-ailan
Laban Fua
Túr Dorcha
R. Domínglas
Gwyr Farsing
Srath Mia
R. Ambros

Lands and Realms of
Alterra
(in part)
R. Brocca
Monadh-hín
High Pass
T
S
A
D
Monadh-talam
(mountain home)
Iolari Pass
East Gate
R. Artan
Lón Artan
Brunner Aigred
Cós-domhain
Linnefionn
West Gate
Tal-sithian
Falad Capell
N
100 miles

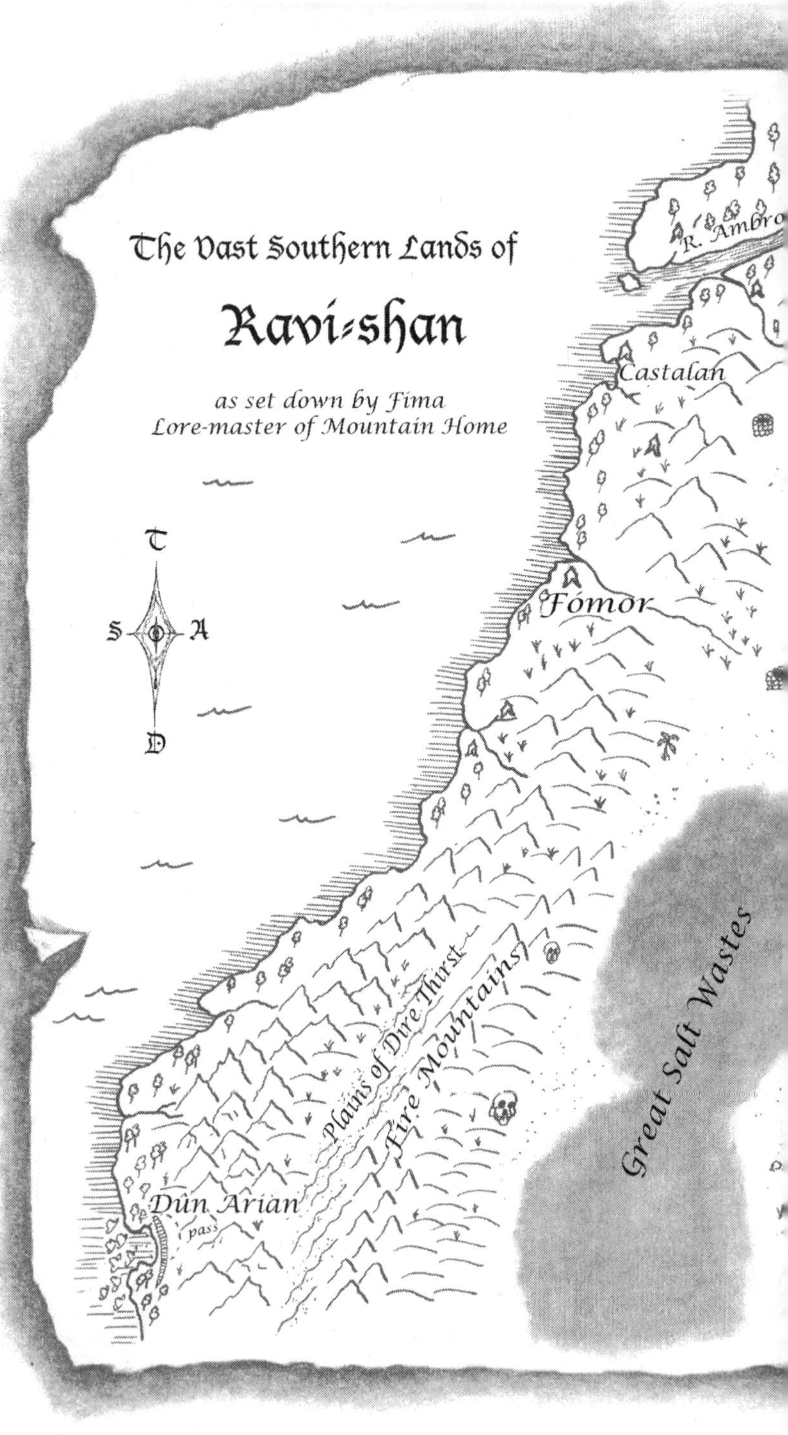
The Vast Southern Lands of
Ravi-shan
as set down by Fima
Lore-master of Mountain Home
T
S
A
D
R. Ambro
Castalan
Fomor
Plains of Dire Thirst
Fire Mountains
Great Salt Wastes
Dûn Arian
pass

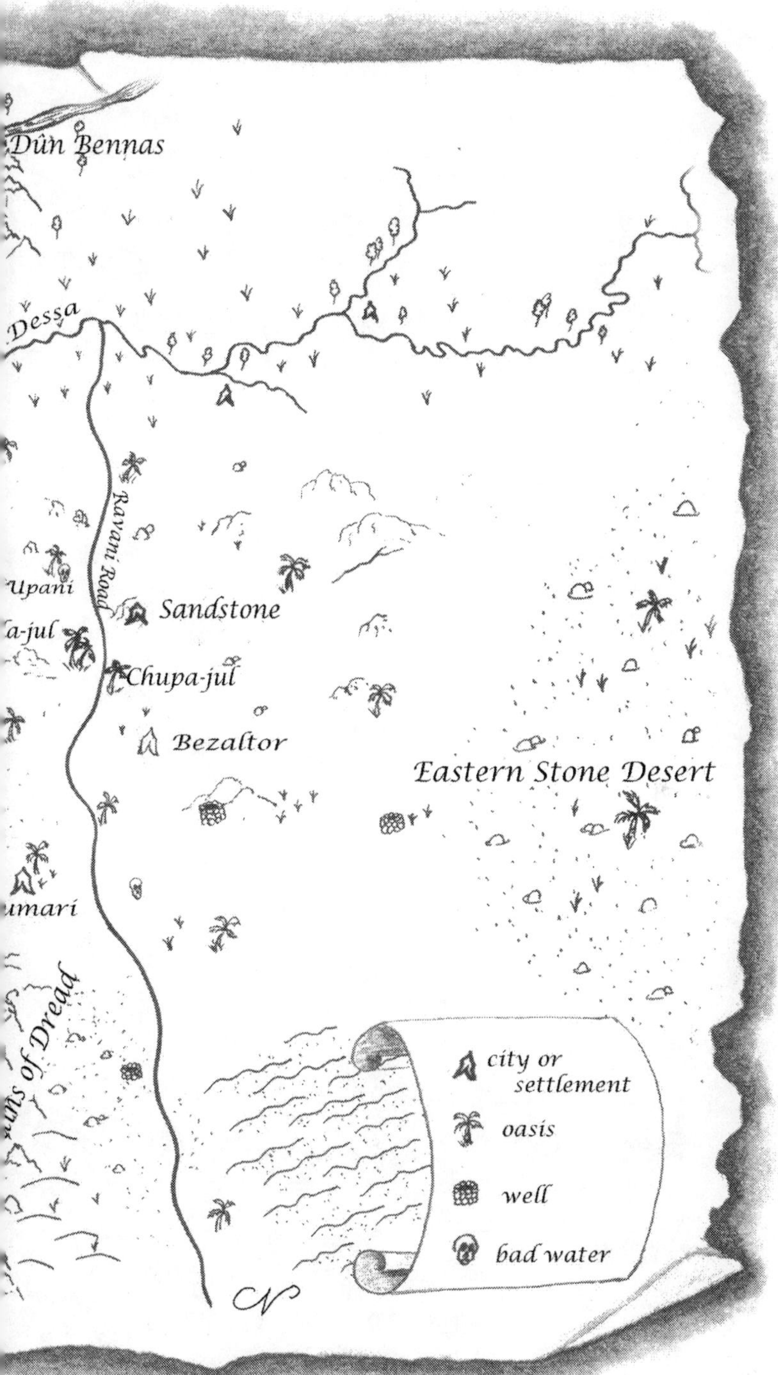
Dûn Bennas
Dessa
Ravani Road
Upani
a-jul
Sandstone
Chupa-jul
Bezaltor
Eastern Stone Desert
umari
ins of Dread
city or settlement
oasis
well
bad water

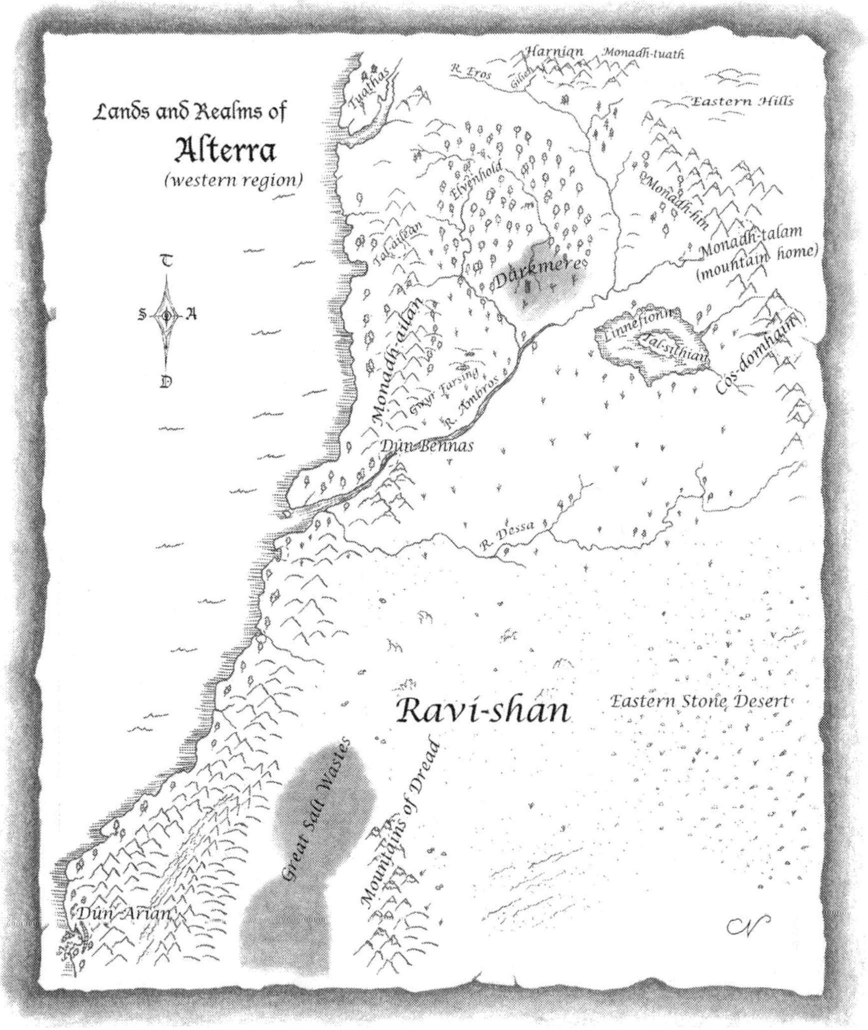
Lands and Realms of
Alterra
(western region)
T
S
A
D
Harnian
Monadh-tuath
R. Eros
Gilieh
Tuathas
Eastern Hills
Elvenhold
Monadh-hin
Tal-ailean
Monadh-talam
(mountain home)
Darkmere
Linnefionn
Tal-sithian
Cos-domhain
Monadh-ailan
Gwyr Farsing
R. Ambros
Dún Bennas
R. Dessa
Ravi-shan
Eastern Stone Desert
Great Salt Wastes
Mountains of Dread
Dún Arian

1
Gaelen's Vision

Gaelen had been blind for far too long. Her other senses were keen, certainly, in fact they were getting keener by the minute. She knew the Elven-hold so well that she managed without help, and thank the stars for that. But she had been forbidden to go into the forest, and that had distressed her. She had spent a good portion of her life perched in trees, alert for anything out of place, alone with her thoughts.

Will my thoughts ever be mine alone again, I wonder? She had not known the answer to that question since Gorgon Elfhunter had looked into his accursed mirror for the first time. *Well, I certainly gave him more than he bargained for. Unfortunately, he has done the same to me. Will I ever be free of him?*

They were still connected. She had taken the mirror, along with his left hand, but they were still connected. She knew it, and so must he. It wasn't anything obvious—a vague, oppressive feeling that came over her sometimes—and she knew the blindness made it worse, for she was always in darkness now. *But I'll heal...he won't. He has been in darkness his whole life.*

Gaelen also knew that she had truly laid Gorgon low. He was far away by now, no doubt holed up in some forsaken, lonely place where he could feel safe, trying to hide himself from her. *It will be awhile before he dares venture forth again,* she thought. *Yet he has lived a long time...one day, he will return for me.*

She ran her fingertips along the smooth, polished shaft of her bow in a loving caress. She had made it herself years ago, and she knew every contour. With a sigh, she raised it, took her stance, and drew it back, but there was no arrow fitted to the string. *I dare not lose strength in my arms and shoulders. Once I find him again, I'll need it.*

It frustrated her—she missed the sound of the swift arrow in flight, and the very satisfactory "thunk" as it hit the target. She would never be the archer Nelwyn was, but she held her own. *A blind archer is a bit of a hazard, though...one of these days I'll heal. Everyone says so.*

She hadn't heard Wellyn at first, but she caught his scent in the breeze wafting through the chilly corridors of the armory. She knew his scent anyway, but even had she not, the overarching smell of wormwood and camphor would mark him until his wounds healed and he could use his right shoulder again. Though the medicines would prevent him stiffening up, it was now impossible to approach without her knowledge.

"What are you doing, Gaelen? Drawing your bow without releasing it? For a moment there, I wondered..."

Well, obviously I can't release it without putting some poor innocent at risk, can I? "I'm just hoping to keep the strength in my arms and shoulders. It's easier to maintain than to regain," she said.

"Don't I know it," he replied, and she could imagine his rueful expression. "At this rate, I won't be able to draw without pain for quite a while. I miss the sound of the arrow, though, and the satisfaction I get when I place it just right. From the expression on your face, I see you share the sentiment."

"It's rare that I place an arrow exactly where intended, Wellyn, but yes...I do miss it."

"You're not the best target shooter, Gaelen, but I've seen you in battle. You shoot fast and you shoot well. I think your talents need purpose to awaken them."

Gaelen smiled. Her father had been the same way—always bested at target shooting, but rarely equaled in a crisis. He had made his name that way, earning the admiration of the King and a permanent place as his bodyguard.

Like all good archers, Gaelen never took her bow anywhere without the arrows that matched it, and she heard Wellyn draw one from her quiver.

"I swear, Gaelen, you must have the plainest arrows in the realm."

What he did next surprised her, and she startled at his touch. "Here. Take the arrow and fit it to the string," he said. "Now let me guide you, and we'll hear our favorite song today."

She drew a deep breath, fitted the arrow, and raised the bow. He gripped her shoulders gently—she could feel the weakness in his right hand—and turned her toward the target. He leaned forward, his face close enough for his breathing to lift the hair from her neck. *He has been chewing ginger root again. I gave him that habit long ago, and he has never given it up. The King hates me for it.*

"Now draw," he said. "I'll guide your hand."

She drew back with the fluid motion of the expert, anchoring her right hand just below her cheekbone. When released, this would be a powerful shot. He corrected her twice.

"All right…release!"

This really shouldn't work…it's a good thing we're alone down here. I suppose hitting the wall is the worst thing that could happen. She held her breath and released the arrow. It flew straight to the target, though only just barely, quivering just inside the outer edge. Gaelen knew it…she could tell by the sound it made, and it made her happier than she had been in days.

"Again!" cried Wellyn. "We hit the target, but we can do better."

As she practiced over and over with Wellyn that afternoon, her thoughts strayed into deeper waters. This sort of partnership was the way things were supposed to be when one lives a happy life. It wasn't just the presence of other people that made the difference, but whether the heart will let them in. *My heart knows what it wants, and cannot have. Does that mean I must live the rest of my life alone? And if I cannot accept love, does that mean I cannot give it?*

She knew where the thoughts came from. Wellyn guided her arm, but she kept wishing for Rogond. She longed for his strength and his steadfast devotion. She longed also for the sight of his thoughtful grey eyes, the turn of his jaw, the rugged shoulders and slim waist. When he was near her, she felt desires that she rarely experienced these days. *It would be wonderful to love again…*

But more than that, she wanted to care for him, to be there whenever he needed her. He was vulnerable in so many ways. *Why does he love me? I'm not sure why anyone would…I don't even like myself sometimes.*

She paused and looked around, blinking at the darkness. "Wellyn?"

"I've called a halt to our practice session, Gaelen. Your thoughts stray from the task. How weary you must be!" He embraced her, as he was one of very few who knew she would allow it. "It will be all right. Your eyes will heal…everyone says so. But we both need rest, I think." He took the arrow from her and placed it back in the quiver before retrieving the others.

He knows where my thoughts have turned—that he has been shut out of them. I can feel his regret, but I can't call them back now. "What you have done today is very kind, Wellyn, and I won't forget it," she said. "You have always been the best friend I could wish for. We'll practice again tomorrow if you'd like." *I still wish you were Rogond.*

"I would, indeed," said Wellyn. "And once your sight returns, and my shoulder is still too weak to hold a steady arrow, you'll finally best me. We'll drink to your momentary victory!"

To her surprise, Gaelen's head swam for a moment, and she grew pale. Wellyn, obviously alarmed, drew her to a bench along the wall, sitting down beside her. She shivered with a sudden chill, and he wrapped his cloak around her, settling her back against his chest, warming her. Again, she thought of Rogond. Though the chill worried her for a moment, she swept it aside. *It's not Gorgon. It's cold in the armory—it's always been cold in the armory. It's not Gorgon. You know what he feels like—it's not Gorgon. No cloak, no warm friendship, can make that chill go away.*

The chill did go away. She and Wellyn fell asleep in the solace of friendship, united by hardship, far from Gorgon Elfhunter and anything to do with him. But as she drifted off, Gaelen knew that she could no longer delay her decision regarding Rogond.

Lore-master Fima lay unmoving upon the bed in his private chamber, looking up at the intricately carved ceiling. Despite all efforts, Gorgon still lived. Of this Fima was certain, for he had held the mirror, and could feel the vitality of it. *The malevolence of that creature pervades it. The mirror seemed to warn me not to look into the glass...as if I would ever be curious enough to try such a foolish thing.*

Fima wondered what other powers Gorgon had been given. No one had reported signs of any other, but still he wondered. *As long as Gorgon is alive, the Greatwood is threatened. Surely the King knows it...though I'm sure the Woodland Elves are doing all that can be done.*

He had gone to see the King the day before, and had been somewhat mollified to hear the tales of those sent to track Gorgon, viewing the shame and frustration on their faces. *I didn't realize how impossible the task is. Gorgon has by now made his way deep underground, and covered his tracks so well that they'll never find him. They don't know the vast pathways beneath the Barrens—and they don't like walking in darkness. Small wonder their hearts quailed when they discovered Gorgon's sanctuary and realized that he had gone deep...we'll have to find another way. But for now, at least, the monster has been damaged. According to Gaelen, he isn't likely to bother anyone for a while. We have time.*

Unless Gorgon wanted to be found, his path would remain unknown. Those who had lingered long in his lair were nearly sickened by the remnants of his presence. *It will be up to Gaelen, then. She'll find him again one of these days, mirror or no mirror.* Fima sorrowed for a moment, wondering what the outcome would be. He was almost glad for her blindness. At least it slowed her down and gave her a respite.

He also knew that Gaelen's frustration grew by the day. This fettering of her freedom wouldn't stand much longer unless someone thought of a way to divert and channel her energies. Wellyn had been especially helpful so far. He gave Gaelen something to be concerned about besides herself. *And then, there's Rogond. He certainly won't stand by and let Gaelen's frustrations get the best of her. He'll think of something.* Just before the Battle in the Barrens, Gaelen had declared Rogond her protector, bestowing the banner of Ri-Elathan, her most treasured possession, upon him. Rogond had shown it to Fima before carefully folding it and placing it beneath his tunic, next to his heart. It rested there always.

Fima smiled at the thought of Gaelen's declaring anyone to be her protector—as if she needed one. *Ah, but we all need protectors, don't we?*

If I can do this, it will all have been worthwhile. Gaelen carefully placed her left foot among the rotting leaves and moss, easing her body forward, mindful of every twig and leaf. A leather visor covered her large, bright, useless eyes. Rogond was not far away—she could hear him breathing if she concentrated hard enough—but she would have to navigate through the understory of the forest without alerting him.

They had played this game every day for several weeks now. Actually, it was Rogond who had suggested it when Gaelen had grown bored and weary of confinement. She had taken to sneaking up on people as a method of entertainment.

"Could you do that in the forest, I wonder?" he asked.

"I would love to try," said Gaelen, "but the healers won't let me leave the Elven-hold until I can see again."

Rogond chuckled at her. "Since when do you do as you're told, anyway?"

"Since I promised Fima. He made me swear to behave myself and do whatever the healers asked." She sighed, twisting her restless hands in her lap. "I cannot deny the advantages of being blind. I have used this time to hone my other senses…it's amazing what you miss when you can see. The sounds, the smells, and you learn to truly *feel* things, too. I'll bet I can tell you what color your tunic is, just by feeling it. In fact, I might not even *need* to feel it. Let me try now." She concentrated, her brow furrowing, her expression deadly serious. "I sense…I sense the color of the sea at sundown," she said at last, smirking a little. All of Rogond's tunics were blue-grey.

"Impressive," said Rogond. "Perhaps we should try tomorrow. I'll borrow one of Galador's."

"Good idea, as long as it's a blue one."

Neither she nor Rogond could shake the idea of Gaelen's going out into the forest, and after a few days he had come to her with a very special gift. "I designed this with Fima's help," he said. "I call it a stealth suit. Here—let me help you put it on."

Gaelen was soon attired in close-fitting garments of soft dark leather. Stiff leather "feelers" projected from both shoulders, both knees, the back of the gloves, and the top and sides of the leather head-covering. A leather visor concealed and protected her eyes. Gaelen was delighted.

"Just like the whiskers on a cat!"

"Exactly. Now let's go and try it out. Fima has given his blessing."

Rogond had taken her out into the forest, very near the Elven-hold, and placed her among the brush and trees. Then he had gone a distance away—at first, only about thirty feet—and called to her to come and find him. Her task was to circle around and approach him without his being aware of it. He had obligingly blindfolded himself, as well.

At first, things had not gone well. Gaelen had some difficulty adjusting to the "feelers" and she made quite a bit of noise. All would be silent for a while as she eased her way through the thick foliage, then the rustling and snapping as she blundered into something, then the muffled cursing. But she rapidly became quite formidable, though he had always managed to detect her…until now.

Twenty feet of undergrowth stood between Gaelen and her goal. She waited for the breeze to pick up, rattling the aspen leaves, before she let out another long breath. *That's cheating. You should act as though you're trying to do this on a calm day.*

She approached Rogond from downwind, taking in the scent of him, which had been forever etched in her mind. He smelled musky, as did all men, but it was not unpleasant. She thought of it as earthy, especially when combined with the shaving-soap he used, which was heavy with juniper berries and wild mint, among other things. Another foot down, and a few more inches' advance. *He doesn't hear me. I'm really going to do it this time…*

Rogond had promised to remain alert, but it was late spring, the moss was warm, the smells of the forest were soothing, and he was drowsy. A thrush called in the deep wood, answered by another. The aspen leaves quaked, the pine boughs sighed in the wind, and he still did not hear Gaelen.

He owed it to her to be vigilant. He took off his blindfold, rose to his feet, stretched his arms and legs, and walked a small circle around the tree he had been resting against. *She will take advantage of that—I'll bet she advanced several steps while I was walking around.* He moved to the opposite side of the tree-trunk and sat down again upon the soft moss, drawing forth the flask from his belt. He had taken a long swallow of mead, and was rummaging for some dried venison to go with it, when Gaelen's booted legs appeared right next to his left knee. She startled him, and he jumped a little. He had heard nothing.

She laughed—a free, musical sound filled with delight—as he rose to embrace her. "You did it! You truly startled me, Gaelen. I hereby promote you to hunter-scout first class!"

"I would say blind hunter-scout *supreme*," she said. "I was already a first-class hunter-scout."

He took her in his arms, stroking her hair. He was extremely proud of her. Blindness would have depressed him, but she had turned it into a challenge.

"Now, if I can only do it on a dead calm day," she said. Rogond smiled and shook his head. Leave it to Gaelen to immediately raise the level of effort required.

"Let's just relax and enjoy the rest of this warm afternoon," he suggested, reaching up to remove her head-covering and visor. As always, she started back from his hand—Gaelen did not like having her head touched. "Easy, now...I just want to see your pretty face," he said, gently lifting the visor from her eyes, which were still clouded by an odd, silvery film, almost like mirrors. The healers had said this would lift and fade away, but it was rather eerie at the moment.

Soon Rogond had drained his flask of mead and eaten all of his dried venison and fruit. The warm sun made him sleepy, and he stretched out on the carpet of moss with Gaelen beside him. *We are quite safe here, so close to the Elven-hold. The woods are crawling with hunter-scouts. A wee nap won't hurt...* Soon, he was snoring softly.

Gaelen, who was still healing and, therefore, would actually sleep at times, preferred a quieter resting-place. She made her way carefully to a nice, comfortable spot some twenty feet away, where the rustling leaves would mask the regular, deep rumble emanating from her beloved Aridan. There she drifted, her eyes open but unseeing, as her thoughts strayed into the realm of dreams.

At first all was fair and pleasant, and her visions gladdened her heart. She walked alone in the stony forests above Mountain-home, hearkening to the sound of the wild waters cascading from tall peaks, breathing in the rich scent of pines and spruces as the sky gave way to a field of brilliant stars. Gaelen had not seen the stars save in her dreams for a long time, and they took her breath for a moment, but as she continued to gaze at them her vision blurred and her head swam. She could not take her eyes from the wheeling stars that turned with dizzying speed above her, until her vision went dark and she fell from the pinnacle of rock upon which she had been standing.

She came to herself almost at once, but she was now in a place she had never been before, even in dreams. Still, it looked familiar. *No...wait! I have seen it...in fact I stood in this very spot before, though it had looked very different in the Stone of Léir.* It was the Battle-plain surrounding the Dark Fortress in the northern waste, where Lord Wrothgar had been defeated long ago. When last she had seen it, this landscape had been filled with countless warriors of two great armies, engaged in a deadly struggle. In the center of all, Wrothgar himself strove with the High King Ri-Elathan—Gaelen's beloved life-mate, whom she called "Rain." Wrothgar had ultimately defeated him, burning him slowly to death in a nightmare of black flame, and the sight of it had horrified Gaelen almost beyond return.

She saw no fearsome Flame Lord now. Only one warrior did she see, lying alone upon the desolate, rocky plain. She ran to his side even as he lay dead before her, longing to contact him one last time, to tell him that he had not failed. *Rain...Rain, Wrothgar was defeated that day, though you did not live to see it.* But as she knelt beside him, suffering the heat of his ruined body long enough to turn his face to hers, she beheld a sight that froze her blood and nearly stopped her heart.

Ri-Elathan's eyes were closed, not open as she had seen them in the Stone. What remained of his once-handsome face broke into a familiar twisted, evil smile, and a cold voice rang in her horrified mind: *I am not yet vanquished, Gaelen Taldin, my sworn enemy. I will come for you and everything you love. Be ready, for this time I will stand before an army greater than any you have seen. When the time comes I will deal with you, and you will be alone...utterly alone! I will take your spirit with me into the Darkness, and there will be no returning from it.*

Malicious laughter assaulted her then as she tried to move away, tried to protect herself from what she knew must follow. He would open his eyes now, and she would not be able to bear it. She had to break free of him! As though sensing her desire, Gorgon gripped Gaelen's arms with Rain's hands, the heat still strong enough to burn her as she cried in pain and terror.

Look at me, Elf, for I would speak my piece. Your beloved has failed. The Black Flame grows again, and nothing the Elves can do will stand against it. I have escaped their pathetic attempts to destroy me, and will gather strength. When I have done so, I will come first for you! If you still abide in the Greatwood, I will sweep through as a great fire that withers all before it. None shall withstand my wrath. I will kill every Elf I encounter, even as I am searching for you. Their deaths—their pain—will be on your hands.

Gaelen longed to defy him, to speak of his defeat, but she could not. Her vision would not give way, and she was powerless. Ri-Elathan's eyelids opened, and she cried in revulsion as Gorgon stared at her, his cold, pale grey eyes filled with malice.

Now her right arm was free, for Gorgon held her, and he had no left hand. She wrenched her other arm from his iron grip, crying again, as her vision blurred and swirled and changed. Now she stood upon the plateau in the Barrens, where she and the Elves of the Greatwood had met and defeated Gorgon's army. The dead lay scattered around her—but not Gorgon. She had failed. The monster still lived, and he was gathering strength. When he was ready he would come for them all!

She turned and ran headlong, for she knew that she could not prevail, not in this place. Gorgon's horrid, oily laughter stung her ears as she fled in the dark, trying to escape her fate. Her eyes burned with tears of pain and revulsion as she careened into an unknown destiny, wishing only to escape the lingering sight of her beloved Rain's ruined face twisting into that of her mortal enemy. She ran as a terrified, blind deer through the Greatwood, and when she finally exhausted herself and fell senseless beneath the black canopy, no light would reach her sightless eyes.

When she awakened she would remember nothing for a time, not even her own name, until at last she heard the voice of Rogond. It drew her from her bewilderment, and she called out to him, clinging as a drowning person clings to the last rope in the world.

Rogond had awakened to find that Gaelen had gone. At first he wondered whether she was trying to sneak up on him again, but a brief examination of the area told otherwise. He found her water-flask beneath a nearby tree; evidently she had curled up there, probably for a nap. She had risen and wandered into the forest—her tracks indicated an aimless, but not panicked, course. *Sleepwalking, maybe? She almost never sleeps, and even when she does, she seems half-awake. This makes no sense…*

He continued to track her, though even when sleepwalking she was light-footed and difficult to follow. Now the signs became obvious—she had been startled by something and was running, almost blundering, through the forest. He found signs that she had torn her clothing in the brush...she was running headlong and blind, but there was nothing chasing her. *I don't understand. What is she running from?* Here was blood. Now he could panic.

"Gaelen? Gaelen! *Gaehhh-lehhhhn!*" He tried to keep the terror out of his voice as he called to her. He followed her tracks, still calling, until at last he heard her voice in the distance.

"Thaylon...Thaylon...I'm here..."

He came upon her at last, drawn to her desperate cry as she answered from the far reaches of the glimmering shadows. He ran to her as she reached for him, enfolding her in his arms, nearly overcome with relief that he had found her alive and whole. She did not weep, but simply clung to him, her eyes closed, breathing in his scent, reveling in the feel of his arms and the deep, soothing sound of his voice.

Gaelen realized that she could never face the trials ahead without him, though she had once thought to do so. Gorgon had prevailed, and she would not be free of him until he lay dead before her. Her heart would never survive without Rogond now—she knew it.

She remained still and silent for a few moments, her thoughts turning swiftly in her mind as she tried to make sense of them, but in the end, she simply listened to her heart. *Now is the time. He's ready... and I'm ready, too.* "Thaylon, I know not what fate awaits us, but if you are still willing to share it, I will bind my heart to yours. It loves you, and will bind to no other yet living. You have my answer."

Rogond held her to him as though he would ever remain in her embrace, her declaration of love still ringing beautifully in his ears. He was afraid to release her lest she relent, or this fulfillment of his greatest hope prove to be but a vision no less real than the one that had driven her to this place, and to this moment.

Gaelen Taldin, daughter of the Greatwood, returned his embrace, trembling as the terrible visions she had beheld faded from her mind. Though they still pained her, she could not see her wrists, the skin reddened and blistered as though they had been burned.

As the weeks wore on, Rogond noticed a few small things, indications that Gaelen's vision was beginning to come back. The healing was so gradual that she probably didn't notice it herself. The healers had examined her, declaring that she would probably be sound enough to travel within the fortnight. Rogond was glad not only for her sake, but also for his—he was about to undertake a great journey.

He had declared his intention to begin the search for his brother, and Gaelen, naturally, had offered to go with him. His friend Thorndil, who had survived Gorgon's defeat in the Barrens, had put forward a plan. It seemed a fair assumption that, should Rogond's brother have survived the Great Plague, those few Rangers who still roamed the northern wilderness would know most of him. If Thorndil inquired of as many as could be found, he might gain enlightenment. He would then send word to the Greatwood, so that Rogond could follow whatever trail was revealed.

Gaelen liked Thorndil, and she was concerned for him, for she knew he was an old man, and he had been wounded in the Barrens. She had asked Rogond about it as they lay together upon the riverbank. "You have sent Thorndil to the north, to inquire of your folk…I trust his wounds are healed?" she said.

"They were healed before he left. You should not worry so about him; he is as tough as thick leather and as hard as iron."

"When last I saw him in the heat of battle, the iron appeared a bit rusty," she countered. Rogond had to agree, for Thorndil had taken a few minor yet painful wounds, and his pain showed in his movement, which had no doubt seemed stiff and a bit ungraceful to Gaelen. She did not realize the extent of what he had endured in his life, nor did she comprehend the nature of ageing. Time had sat somewhat heavily upon Thorndil in recent years.

"He's getting old, Gaelen. There's not much we can do to stop the decline of our bodies with time. He has taken many hurts, some of which will always trouble him." Rogond knew that she understood this—some of her own old wounds bothered her on occasion, and would do so until the end of her life.

"Tell me of the Fate of Men, Thaylon. Do you face the same fate as Thorndil? Will you decline with time?"

"You know I will...I must," he said. "But not for a long while. I'm not rusted yet." He took her in his arms and tried to quell her restive thoughts, stroking her tangled, windblown hair with a large, strong hand. *She's holding something back. There's something she wants to tell me...I hope I will want to hear it.* He decided not to ask her about it, having learned that she would tell him in her own good time, and not a moment before.

"Now you should rest," he said. "I won't go looking for my brother without you, and you cannot go until you are healed. Let's speak no more of age and rusty joints and the burden of time." Despite his assurances, it took her a long while to settle down. He could feel the tension in her body, the energy in her beating heart. She was like a coiled spring, senses attuned to every sound, and would not relax. He took her left ear in one of his massive hands, stroking it gently until she gave in, stretched like a cat, and closed her eyes at last.

Gorgon Elfhunter celebrated the return of Gaelen's eyesight more fervently than anyone. He nearly wept with relief as the terrible white light faded slowly from his tortured awareness and he began to perceive with his own eyes once more. Though his chamber was so black he could barely make out the very faint outline of his own right hand, his pain finally diminished. He closed his eyes, and found only comforting darkness. *Her sight is coming back, and mine with it,* he thought. *May I never behold that terrible Light again! Now, at last, I can rest.*

Gorgon's pain had been assuaged, though it would never leave him completely. He was still connected to her, and the connection would not be broken until one of them lay dead before the feet of the other. Still, he rejoiced, because that very connection would one day mean her doom. *I will be able to find her, no matter where she runs to.*

He chuckled with malicious pleasure, though it pained and wearied him, and the chuckle soon gave way to a growl. He would never stop hating her...not should the stars go out and never shine again, and the mountains crumble into dust at the world's ending. But such black thoughts would not serve him now. First he would satisfy his thirst, and then he would rest and heal himself, retreating into his usual state of torpor. His mind, normally filled with the violence of his plans and emotions, would sink down into welcome sleep. *She will not sense me then—not unless she takes hold of the mirror. Surely she isn't that foolish.* He would sleep, and let her forget about him for a while. When he had healed, he would go forth again and exact his vengeance.

You have unwittingly allowed me to see into a world wherein I have never been welcome, no matter my desire. For the time being, that world is yours... enjoy it while you may. He lowered his scarred face to a pool of clear, cold water that had collected in his new sanctuary.

Well...maybe just one last fantasy. Let it never be said that I don't think often of you, you barren, wretched she-dog! His mind, so long fettered by pain and doubt, ran wild as he imagined what he would do to her.

On the first new moon of autumn, Rogond met with Thorndil and a Ranger named Turan near the gentle river Eros, the wide stream flowing into the Ambros south of the Northern Mountains.

Turan was one of a very few men who stood as tall as Rogond, but he was older—much older. Like Thorndil, he had lived through the horror of the Plague years. He sat on a flat river-stone, puffing slowly on a carved wooden pipe that had seen many, many years of service, as the Company gathered to hear what he could tell. He turned his flinty gaze to Rogond, who sat nearest.

"First, my friend, let me tell you that I do not know whether your brother still lives. Neither do I know for certain that he does not, and that's good news. So many of our folk perished during the Plague that your brother would no doubt have been among them, but we were far away beneath the Eastern Hills when the sickness came. At any rate, the first son of Rosalin was named Hallagond, which means 'tall stone,' though I don't recall him being quite as tall as you are."

"His name is much like yours," said Gaelen.

"A coincidence," said Rogond. The Elves named me 'treasure-stone' because they found me among the rocks. "I don't know what name my mother gave me."

Turan nodded. "It's an interesting coincidence that your names are so similar. You are much alike in appearance, with the same grey eyes and dark hair. He bore a scar across the back of his right hand from an Ulca-blade. His voice was not as deep, but was...rougher, somehow. You say you were raised by Elves, and it is evident in your manner of speech. Hallagond grew up in Dûn Bennas, among men."

"Hallagond," said Rogond, savoring the sound of his brother's name.

"When he matured he came to the northlands seeking adventure," said Turan. "He traveled with us, gaining renown as a skilled fighter. He showed great perception and intelligence, and we came to look up to him, for he was a natural leader. We took to wandering the region just to the north of where we are now sitting, convinced that the Dark Powers were trying to establish a new stronghold there. Hallagond befriended the Northern Mountain dwarves, often coming to their aid.

When the rumor of the Plague reached us, Hallagond wanted to return to Dûn Bennas to aid his family, but we convinced him that such an effort would prove futile. By the time we became aware of it in the northlands the Plague had already swept through that great city, killing nearly everyone in it, including the King. It was said that the pyres of the dead sent up smoke that could be seen all the way from heaven." Turan paused for a moment, his gaze distant, his eyes pained. Lightning flashed in the western sky, and the thunder grew louder as the storm drew nearer. Shaken from his private thoughts, he continued.

"The dwarves convinced us to retreat to the Eastern Hills, and to shelter belowground so that we might survive, for the pestilence had spread like a wildfire. I would expect Rosalin left Dûn Bennas in a vain effort to escape it, and it's a good thing you were found and fostered by the Elves. If your mother had not been set upon, and you had remained with her, there is little doubt that you would have died. It was not a good death, the Plague…"

Here he paused again, his brows drawing together above haunted eyes. Rogond knew Turan had lost friends, and perhaps family, in that dreaded scourge. Few living men were untouched by it. "At any rate," he continued, puffing once more upon his pipe, "the Rangers who fled to the Eastern Hills survived, for the Plague spread to the north and west. But the people of the southlands suffered great loss. Many settlements perished down to the last man. Hallagond and I longed to give aid to them, but we knew that to travel there would mean near-certain death, and it was necessary that at least a few of us remain to carry on the line. The blood of the Tuathar survives… barely."

"After two years had passed since the last rumors of the pestilence reached us, we decided to venture west again to see what could be salvaged. It was a grim journey. We looked to the dead as we could, burning the untended bodies, despairing as we found so few alive. Hallagond and I were separated; he and a group of Rangers supposedly became involved in some nastiness with a group of brigands, but none returned. I later learned that all save Hallagond had vanished, and I was somewhat surprised to hear that he had then fled back to the Eastern Hills. I have neither seen nor heard anything of him since. That was, let me see…perhaps five and forty years ago?"

Turan drew a long draught on his pipe, as though lost in thought. "We did not understand why he had gone from us, but we have received no word of him. We could not imagine what business he would have in the Eastern Hills, which are largely uninhabited, though dwarves have spoken of delving there. As I have said, we don't even know for certain that he still lives. What other course would have kept him from his duties here? We all wonder what became of his companions."

Turan looked into the eyes of Rogond, and his expression was grave. "Some have guessed that your brother has either gone mad, or has lost his honor somehow."

Rogond took in a sharp breath, for the loss of honor to a Ranger was a fate much worse than death. "You've guessed, but you don't know," he said to Turan with some fervor, for he would defend his brother despite never having met him. "There are many explanations possible. You have said that you don't even know where he is, or whether he has fallen. Why would you stain his name with such a speculation?"

"Because Hallagond would not abandon his people, nor would he fail to bring word of the fate of his companions unless too ashamed to do so. I knew him as well as anyone, and called him friend. He would only retreat to such solitude if he could no longer suffer our company, and there's only one reasonable explanation for that. But you're right…anything could have happened. It's possible that he encountered an evil so fearsome and terrible that it deranged him, though I think that unlikely."

"Do you know of my father?" asked Rogond. "Did Hallagond tell you his name, or his fate?"

Turan looked down at his feet. "He did not. He mentioned your father only with bitterness, and never by name. It would seem they didn't get along, which may have been why Hallagond left Dûn Bennas in the first place. I'm thinking he believed his father thought him unworthy, thus his seeming urgency to prove otherwise."

Turan looked earnestly at Rogond. "If you would learn more of Hallagond, you should go first to the dwarves of the Northern Mountains, for they knew much of him. It's my hope that he renewed his ties with them on his way to the Eastern Hills, and he may have made his intentions known. I have not inquired of them, as I found them somewhat difficult to deal with, but since you have brought a dwarvish guide with you, all may be well. I'm sorry that my tale does not gladden your heart."

Rogond nodded. "That it does not, my good Turan, but you undertook a long journey to bring this news, and I thank you. I must now continue my search. Hopefully I will find my brother and learn the truth. Perhaps he can be healed, and his honor restored, if indeed he thinks it lost."

"I wish you well in that endeavor," said Turan. "Hallagond was a good man. Be careful in the dwarf-realms." Then he fell silent, drawing his hood down over his face.

Gorgon Elfhunter stood alone under the brilliant stars, the east wind lifting silky hair that glinted like spun gold in the darkness. The trees of the Greatwood were stirring; he could hear them even from this distance, and he scented the air, sensing the change in the wind. His pale eyes narrowed, and he closed them for a moment, concentrating upon Gaelen, his mortal enemy. As he did so, he reflected on the gift she had unwittingly given him. He had never before seen the beauty of the night sky, not until he perceived it through her eyes. Now he was drawn irresistibly to the brilliant silver lights burning above him, as were all his mother's kin. But with that gift came the reminders of things he had never had, and would never be given. He had seen so much of her world—a world forever denied him—and he hated her for it.

His life had been simple before she came into it. He hated her for that, too…for making him think about the answers to questions he had never allowed himself to ask. Blood and pain had been his only friends, and now he wanted more—far more. This connection between them, forged by the mirror, was both a blessing and a curse. He was aware of her…if he concentrated hard enough he could almost see her face sometimes. As he learned to hone his sense of her, it would be increasingly difficult to hide from him. But he also knew that she was aware of him, too. He could feel the heat of her desire—the one he shared—to hunt him down.

I have the advantage. Her thoughts are complicated, and she has many others to turn them to, whereas mine have only one purpose. She will be distracted…I will not. She is weakened by love of that fool ranger and the rest of that sentimental, ridiculous clan. I can still guard myself from her, and follow after her. One dark night, I will take them all.

He ground his teeth and took a deep breath, filling his massive chest with clean, cold air. Winter would be coming on soon, and he had the sense that Gaelen and her friends were on the move. He resolved to follow her as soon as he could manage it. He also needed to ensure that Lord Wrothgar did not know of his whereabouts, and that would require some care. Gorgon would most certainly need to manage his vengeance alone; he would take no further aid from the Shadowmancer, of whom he was quite understandably fearful.

Now he looked once more upon the stars, his gaze softening with delight that filled a small corner of his dark heart in spite of himself.

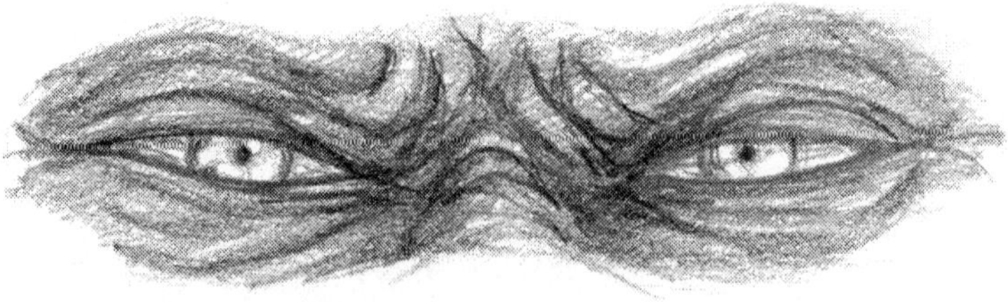

2
The Company Travels South

The trip to the Northern Mountains, though hazardous, had proved worthwhile, though most of what Rogond learned merely confirmed what he had already heard from Turan. His brother was now a man alone...alone and without honor. He had forsaken his people, running away to some far-distant southern land "where no one would know his name." The dwarves could give nothing more specific than that regarding Hallagond's whereabouts, but at least the Company now knew in which direction to look for him.

I do wish we had something more specific than "south," thought Rogond. *South is not much to go on, but at least we might actually be able to get somewhere before winter comes.* He sighed, glancing back over his shoulder at Fima. "It's a good thing you were with us. Your folk were most helpful, though far from encouraging. Thanks to them, we won't waste precious time traveling to the Eastern Hills."

Rogond drew a deep, sweet breath of air heavy with the scent of late-season flowers, and looked out over the wide grasslands stretching before him. *I will not rest until I either find Hallagond or learn of his fate. Perhaps I can help him regain his honor. Regardless, I will not relent until I have heard the tale from my brother's own mouth.*

Now that the Eastern Hills were no longer in their plan, the hearts of the Company grew lighter, as they were more likely to reach milder lands before the onset of winter. Yet the journey would take months, even mounted. There were many obstacles before them, and many ways they might have chosen, but in the end they decided to make for the River Ambros, which they could then follow to the southern city of Dûn Bennas. Once there, Rogond wanted to spend some time in the Hall of Records, for now that he knew the name of his mother and brother, he might learn a great deal more. They could spend the winter there, provisioning themselves for the journey.

Upon leaving Dûn Bennas, they would continue southward through the scrublands until they encountered the first of the desert. This stretched far beyond the borders of Fima's map, where it was labeled the "Ravi-shan", or Sun-country. From there they would take the Ravani road and begin the search for Hallagond in earnest. This made sense to Fima, who would not take one step out of his way if he could help it. He had never been to the desert lands, but he already suspected he would not like them.

"Are there Elves in the Sutherlands?" asked Gaelen, who had just been relieved from the watch. Rogond thought she was worried about leaving all that was familiar behind, and the thought of encountering other Elves along the journey would comfort her.

Rogond looked over at Fima. "I don't know how far south they may be found, but there are Wood-elves in the Verdant Mountains, and most especially in Tal-ailean, which is a beautiful country. Yet they were never many, and they keep to themselves. We are unlikely to encounter them."

Fima nodded. "Much of the land between the Greatwood and the mountains is under the sway of men, yet it is a fair land, Gaelen. You and Nelwyn will enjoy passing through it, from what I'm told. Our test will be in the southern desert, for in the Ravi there are no trees, little water, and men of strange ways and savage temperament. Not all are savage—the lore of the region speaks of several learned cultures that are, quite frankly, intriguing—yet the Plague wiped out many of the inhabitants. Those who survived were thrown together in various interesting ways; a lot of cultural barriers were broken down by simple necessity." He shook his head. "The kindreds of men suffered greatly in those years. What good fortune that our Rogond was in the arms of the Elàni."

"Well, should we encounter Elvish folk, I will warn them of Gorgon, and pray that he does not follow behind us," Gaelen muttered.

Rogond lifted his eyebrows at her, and then spoke in a low, gentle voice. "What brought him to your mind, little one? Do you have a sense of him now? Does he follow us? What do you feel?"

She closed her eyes for a moment, and Rogond saw the first three fingers of her right hand curl as though upon a bow-string. When she opened her eyes again, they were bright with loathing. "The Elfhunter is not hunting yet, but he soon will be," she said simply, and then left him, climbing once more upon the rocks to stand the watch beside Nelwyn and Galador.

Fima shook his head. "She is aware of the creature, and I suspect he is aware of her. He will find us again one of these nights. That's why she is willing to travel so far from her home, and why she asked about Elves in the south...she wants to lead Gorgon away from Elven folk. There is some insight that she has not shared with us—something happened to her in the Greatwood."

Thorndil had lit his pipe and was now puffing thoughtfully on it. "We must not press her about it, for she will tell us nothing until she is ready. That monster has wounded her…the wounds are deep enough that even I can see them."

They sat in silence for a while, Fima joining Thorndil in lighting his own pipe. Rogond heard a small rustling from above, just before they were all startled abruptly by Gaelen, who sprang down from her stony perch.

"Have you taken leave of your senses? Evil creatures do not partake of that leaf. The scent of the smoke will draw them here! Have you both gone mad? Put them out!"

She disappeared as suddenly as she had appeared, leaving them blinking at one another in surprise. She had frightened Fima nearly to death once again.

Thorndil looked annoyed. "I will smoke if I please," he grumbled, though, after another moment's thought, he put out his pipe.

"She's right, and you both know it," said Rogond. "Yet this was most unlike her. She is not herself…the mention of Gorgon has unsettled her. We must try to be understanding."

"I will be dead if she does that to me but once more," said Fima, obligingly putting out his own pipe. "I would not want to make her my enemy."

"That you would not," said Rogond. "Just think of this as a way to aid you in sharpening your alertness. I heard her before she appeared; soon she will not be able to startle me anymore."

Fima snorted. "A fine job you did of not showing it. Your entire body jumped, your eyes were as wide as ours, and I saw your hand dart for your weapon. Save your breath."

Thorndil settled back against the stone, drew down into his warm cloak, and was soon asleep. Rogond and Fima remained awake until dawn. "I wish that none of us had ever heard of Gorgon Elfhunter," said Fima. "The violation and torment of Gaelen is the worst of all his foul deeds, in my humble opinion."

The first of the late autumn gales found the Company sheltering near the foothills of the Verdant Mountains. They had come straight south, turning westward from the River Dominglas, skirting around the fens and marshes that dotted the lands near the river. The journey had taken them through wide, rich grasslands, and the horses had enjoyed the grazing there, though it was diminished by the imminent onset of winter.

"It's a good thing they're putting on some flesh," said Galador as he appraised their plump, glorious mounts. "They will soon face deprivation in the southlands. I worry especially about Eros—he is not of the type that will fare well in such conditions. With such a thick coat, the heat will surely tax him."

Rogond patted Eros, feeling the nice layer of flesh covering his ribs. "Yes, he has always grown plenty of hair. From what I hear, the nights can be cold in the desert, so he may yet do well. He has always taken care of himself, this one. If I have to, I will clip his heavy coat." Eros seemed to take his meaning, snorting and lifting his proud head at such a ludicrous suggestion. Clip him, indeed!

A storm came upon them in late afternoon. It blew down out of the mountains, and the winds in the wide lands were terribly fierce with little to block their way. The rain lashed the travelers until they found makeshift shelter within a ring of stones; even Eros' thick coat was soaked to the skin. The horses put their tails to the storm, crowding together with their heads down, ears flattened against the rain. The two-legged members of the Company huddled among the stones, thoroughly wetted, but at least protected from the biting wind.

Rogond marveled as he sat between Gaelen and Galador, for it seemed they were always warm to the touch. He envied them their efficiency, for they ate much less out of need than he, and they kept warm on very little. Their energy seldom waned, and they suffered less from the weather. He looked over at Thorndil, who sat by himself, probably out of pride. He would not want the others to know how miserable he was, shivering and trying to keep his teeth from chattering.

Rogond reached into his pack and extracted two lovely honey-cakes that he had been saving for himself and Gaelen, should she ever need her spirits lifted. He moved to sit beside Thorndil, noting the pain in his eyes. The old Ranger had taken many wounds, and the weather played havoc, especially with his gnarled hands. Though they were still strong, the swollen joints and crooked fingers ached and throbbed.

Rogond offered him one of the honey-cakes, and they sat quietly together, enjoying the sweet taste and the renewal of vitality. Thorndil's shivering grew less, and he smiled at some fair thought that crossed into his mind. Rogond wondered whether he should suggest that his friend remain in Dûn Bennas, for he would be most useful to the people there, but he thought better of it. With luck, Thorndil would come to this conclusion himself.

"When we get to the city there will be plenty of food, drink, and warm fires. It will be a fine place to spend the winter," said Rogond. "I, for one, am looking forward to some new garments. These have about reached the end of their usefulness."

Thorndil snorted. "You still retain your fondness for new clothing. The Elves have influenced you beyond recovery...even when we were in the northern wilderness you bemoaned the fact that you could not wear fine new things. You're forever hopeless." He chuckled at Rogond. "We could never reckon who you were trying to impress."

Rogond regarded him with a wounded expression. "Why do you disparage me? I merely wanted to ensure that our enemies could not track us by scent alone. It makes hunting Ulcas so much easier when you don't need to worry about always approaching them from downwind."

"That sounds like something a certain She-elf would say," replied Thorndil. "And speaking of She-elves, I believe I shall try to light my pipe, if you will assist me." Rogond nodded. This thought had occurred also to him. In spite of the wind and rain, they managed to strike sparks while sheltering under their cloaks, and soon they were both drawing contentedly.

Fima, alerted by the faint whiff of smoke wafting on the wind, was drawn to the Rangers at once, and the three of them were soon quite happy with life. The Elves looked curiously at the indistinguishable mass of dark, soaking wet cloaks, out of which blue smoke and laughter were drifting. Rogond, Thorndil and Fima weathered the storm together, reveling in their glorious leaf, telling jokes and tales, still shivering but warm in spirit, sharing in their mortality.

It's good to have friends, thought Gaelen, hunkering down in her cloak, *except when we must leave them behind.* She drew a wistful sigh, remembering the day Wellyn had come to see her in the stables before she left the Greatwood. He had appeared in the doorway, flushed and breathless, having run all the way as though he feared she had gone already.

He came straight to the point. "You're preparing to leave us again, aren't you?"

"Yes, I'm leaving. Rogond is traveling north the day after tomorrow, and I'm going with him," said Gaelen, taking notice of the look of dismay on her friend's face. *This isn't like him… he is generally quite used to my being away.* "Why are you thus distressed? I leave the fortress often and long…it is not usual for me to be here unless reporting to the King or receiving orders. This has long been my habit."

Wellyn stood for a moment, his eyes wide with anxiety, then his face flushed and he tried to turn from her. She gripped his arm, staying him, and forced him to look into her eyes. "Tell me what has unsettled you. I know you would not be grieved without cause. Tell me."

Her insistence was genuine and he responded to it, drawing her to him and embracing her. She returned the embrace, for she could feel his urgency and would calm his fears. She also wanted to know the nature of them…it truly wasn't like Wellyn to be afraid. She knew that he sometimes had difficulty revealing his thoughts and concerns, and she waited patiently for him to begin.

He drew a deep sigh, his breath warm and comforting on the nape of her neck. "I know that you are seldom in the Elvenhold for long, and I'm quite accustomed to your leaving me, but this time is different, for…you will not return. I have seen it."

Gaelen pulled back from him and looked into his anxious face, her own expression shocked and saddened. "Of course I will.

What have you seen that makes you doubt it? It's my greatest wish to return and never leave again, but I must wait until certain things are resolved. I must leave the Greatwood, Wellyn. I must leave for now, no matter my desire. I cannot be here if…" Her voice trailed off. She did not wish to upset Wellyn further by the mention of Gorgon, and she knew that she could not return until he lay dead before her at last. Her promise to Rogond was only one of the forces driving her.

Wellyn found no comfort in her assurance. "Gaelen, I have foreseen your fate…you and I will never meet again in Alterra if it comes to pass. Please do not go from here—not yet. I'm not ready to give up my friend when I have only just recovered her. Please stay your flight from the Greatwood, or at least allow me to go with you for a time."

She knew that he would never even suggest such a thing had he not held a very disturbing premonition, and he trembled as she drew back from his embrace, saddened by the despair in his eyes. "You know better than to try to avert the course of your fate, or of mine," she said. "It's not your destiny to be bound to me or to my task; that much I know. And you know the futility of such a hope. I would take great comfort and courage from your presence, for you are a stalwart friend and I love you, but your destiny lies not with mine. It has ever been so."

"If you are my friend, then let me do as my heart directs," he said. "Let me protect you. I know your heart is no longer yours to give…I have known it since I was young."

Gaelen smiled at him, though there was sorrow in her eyes. "You are yet young, my dear Wellyn—obviously young enough to believe that you can deny the directive of destiny, or that the King would ever allow you to leave the realm. Visions may not come to pass, and I shall live forever in the hope of seeing you again. For now, let's enjoy the time remaining to us."

Even as Wellyn resolved to go to his father and beg leave to travel with Gaelen, he knew she was right. He would not be allowed to leave the Greatwood, for his duties lay within it. He had not come to see her again—not even when the Company departed—and Gaelen thought to have seen the last of him until they made their way beside the rushing waters of the Brunner Ia, when she beheld a shadowy figure in the mist. She gave a cry, handing Siva to Nelwyn, and ran toward it before anyone could stop her.

Wellyn emerged from the mist to stand before her, clasping her hands in his own, looking earnestly into her eyes. "I did not attend your departure because I could not say what needed to be said. You are ever my friend, Gaelen, and I love you dearly. I would have you stay in the Woodland, where you are sorely needed, but since you will not, I must now bid you farewell."

She could see the distress in his eyes, and tried to reassure him and herself. "I will miss you. I'm glad you came to see me…I was afraid that I would not be able to bid you farewell. Don't fear, for I shall do all I can to return home. I have long known that a great destiny awaits you; one day you will rule this realm. Therefore you must not try to find me, or follow me, for I must not divert you from your appointed path. I believe that we *will* meet again, and then I will hear all you have to tell. Think of those long and happy hours, and be comforted.

But Wellyn was not comforted, as Gaelen spoke to him then for the last time ere she departed: "Remember our friendship and be glad. I shall always love my friend, though we are parted. Farewell!"

He released her, their hands lingering for just a moment, and when she turned from him, he did not follow. He would grieve in silent solitude for many days, knowing in his heart that he had seen the last of her. Gaelen was not yet certain, for she knew that she would remain true to her word, and would try to reunite with him in spite of what his vision had foretold.

3
Dûn Bennas

The Company met no enemies on the way to the White Fortress, and despite low provisions and occasionally immoderate weather they reached the banks of the Ambros in good time, turning westward to follow it to their destination. During one of their rest stops, Nelwyn approached Fima as he sat upon a comfortable pile of dry leaves at the base of a large oak. "Will you tell us about the men of Dûn Bennas?" she asked. "We have never before traveled so far to the south."

"They are of the same line as our hardy Rangers," said Fima. "The King in Dûn Bennas knows Thorndil, and I actually met him once—we should be welcome there. It might be another matter in the Ravi-shan, where you will find races of men in great variety. We do not really know much of their history or culture…especially since the Plague has mixed everything up and thrown everyone together."

"The kindreds of men vary greatly in their appearance, stature, and temperament," said Galador. "Anori-folk and sutherlings, for example, have little in common, and they have no love for one another. Neither is much like the northmen. To be sure, they are all men, and all are mortal, yet in other respects they are very different. We will see many wonders in the southern desert lands."

Gaelen was disquieted, glancing over at Nelwyn, who was already gazing back toward the familiar lands of the Greatwood. She had imagined most men to be like Rogond and Thorndil. What if the men of the southlands were fierce and foul? She didn't relish the thought of traveling to such a place, where it might be difficult to tell enemies from friends. She looked over at Rogond, hoping for reassurance.

"Don't worry," he said, "I will make certain that no harm comes to you or to Nelwyn. For every enemy, there will also be a friend. You'll see." Even as Rogond spoke the words, Gaelen hoped they would prove true. Fima and Galador were looking at him with raised eyebrows, as though they doubted him. The people of the Ravi-shan were strange, and reputedly savage. Friends might be in short supply in those lands.

"So long as we remain together, I will not fear," she said, with a dismissive attitude she didn't truly feel. "Nelwyn and I have had some experience with Anori-folk, and they are of little consequence...they spend much of their time fighting amongst themselves. I will admit that we never tried to befriend them; there's no love between us."

"Gaelen, there are many tribes of men known as Anori-folk," said Fima. "Those encountered by your people are quite different from those who roam the lands to the south and east of here. Some are far more organized, and vastly more dangerous. Do not take them lightly. I don't mean to frighten you, but I fear your irrepressible confidence. I want you to walk with your eyes wide open."

"I will not take them lightly, Lore-master," said Gaelen. "Nor will I allow myself to hold any arrogance before the people of the southlands. If this place is as strange and forbidding as you have described, we shall need their aid. I hope Rogond is right about the likelihood of finding friends among them, for none of us has the slightest idea of how to survive there, and we shall be completely dependent upon their hospitality. We are all walking into this desert land in relative ignorance. Let's hope her lessons will not be taught with too hard a hand!" The entire Company nodded gravely at her. They could not have agreed more.

They drew near Dûn Bennas after about another fortnight. Gaelen, as usual, was the first to notice. "We will approach the City soon," she said, turning to Rogond. "I can smell the rapids and see the distant mist." She pointed to the southwest, indicating a very faint halo in the air over the foothills. "What can you tell us about it?"

"I know some of the history," said Rogond. "It's known as the White Fortress, and it came to glory after the destruction of Tuathas. It is now the greatest remaining realm of men in the west of Alterra, so far as is known. Dûn Bennas was colonized and enhanced by enlightened men of Tuathas—my ancestors—and is still inhabited by their descendants."

"That realm has not fared well in recent times," said Fima. It spans both sides of the Great River, united by seven mighty bridges which, I may point out, were designed by dwarvish folk."

"Yes," said Rogond. "The people suffered great loss during the Plague years…four out of five fallen, they say. Not even the Royal Family was spared—King Hearndin, who was the only male survivor, rules it now." He shook his head. "I cannot imagine the sorrow and darkness that fell upon the people of the White Fortress…I only pray that some record of my heritage survives there. I may learn much, if luck is with me. It's a strange path that has led me here. If we had not become lost in the Great Mountains, I would not have learned my mother's name. If it were not for Farin in Cós-domhain, I would not have learned of my brother. Now, in the home of my family, I hope to find out all I can."

Gaelen wanted Rogond to learn as much of his heritage as he could, so that he would know from whence he came. She could trace her own ancestry all the way back to the beginning of the First Reckoning, and that was a comforting thought. It helps to know who you are. She rode ahead, as usual, scouting the way.

The Verdant Mountains had loomed to the north and west of their path for quite some time, and as they approached Dûn Bennas the peaks appeared also on the south side of the river, shrouded in white snow and grey mist. When the sun hit the slopes of the mountains, the Great City gleamed as a jewel with bright waters flowing right into its heart, and it was among the most beautiful sights they had ever seen.

Galador winded his silver horn as they approached, announcing the arrival of friends. Soon a small but well-armed party of men appeared, riding proud horses.

"Please identify yourselves and declare your intentions," said one. "What brings you to the White Fortress?"

Fima bowed low. "I am Fima, Lore-master to Lady Ordath of Mountain-home, and no stranger to the City," he said. "My friend Rogond is descended of the White Fortress. Thorndil is known to King Hearndin already. This is Gaelen of the Greatwood, her cousin Nelwyn, and this is Galador, who hails originally from the Realm of Light. Last I knew, Elves were always welcomed among you. Is that not so?"

"In general, it most certainly is" said the tall man, removing his elaborately tooled leather cap with a flourish. "Welcome to Dûn Bennas."

The ragged and travel-worn Company met with a warm reception, since Thorndil and Fima were already known to the King, and Elves were always welcome in a city founded by Tuathar. Fima, as Lore-master to Lady Ordath, would be treated as a visiting dignitary.

Dûn Bennas was built on high, rocky bluffs on both sides of the river, united by the seven bridges, five of which remained passable. The River Ambros was wild and swift in this place, and the City could not be gained by water except from upstream, foiling Corsairs and other enemies who would try to invade by coming upriver from the sea. There had been a settlement here for ages, on the northern side, but it had been overrun many times in its history. When the Tuathar came, they built the mighty fortress that had withstood all enemies save one...the Plague had found the citizens despite all efforts.

The City was arranged in three levels, and the highest of these, on the northern bank, was the abode of the King. The Company would be conducted there eventually, but first they were shown to quarters and given food and drink, as well as the opportunity to make themselves clean and presentable. This was welcomed especially by Rogond and Thorndil, who languished in the embrace of hot, soapy water for as long as they could justifiably do so.

They were all offered fine new clothing, and by the time they had made themselves ready to be taken to the King, they looked magnificent. There were plenty of rooms and garments to be had, and Rogond despaired as he thought of the grave loss of life that had resulted in such a surplus. He wore a high-necked black-and-silver velvet tunic, dark indigo velvet breeches, and his old black boots, which had been cleaned and polished. He looked like a courtier of the King.

The Elves were resplendent—even Gaelen, once she had been persuaded by Nelwyn, had donned new raiment. "There is nothing wrong with what I'm wearing," she had insisted, shivering in her sleeveless green jerkin.

"Look how beautiful and warm these are. They might have come from Elven-realms, they are so fine. I'm wearing them, for I wish to be warm and comfortable," said Nelwyn, who had outfitted herself in her favorite colors—green and gold.

Gaelen was convinced when she put on a thick, soft velvet tunic of a red so dark that it was nearly black. With it went a dark grey woolen cloak lined with the same velvet, the neck trimmed in soft, black leather. She wore her own brown doeskin breeches and her old brown boots, though they were clean, and she had turned the tops up, lacing them above her knees. Weapons would not be permitted in the audience hall, yet she wore them anyway. They could take them from her at the door...if they could find them.

Galador, Thorndil, and Fima had also found glorious new attire, and they all sat down to a simple but fine meal that seemed like a banquet after so many weeks on the road. There was white bread and honey, thickened cream and roasted pork, and dark red sweet tubers laced with butter and nutmeg. There was wine and ale, and a warm fire burning. Several of the folk of Dûn Bennas joined them, as Rogond told the tale of their journey.

Gaelen commented that she had rarely tasted a better meal, even in Mountain-home. The serving-women were delighted, favoring her with warm smiles and extra-large helpings. They were intrigued and somewhat awed by the Elves, and were a little surprised when Gaelen rose and bowed before them.

The plates and cups had been cleared away, and evening pipes drawn forth, when a tall, well-dressed man of proud bearing came in, stating that he was to conduct them to the King when they were ready.

Rogond looked around at his companions. "We are ready now, if it please the King."

They strode forth from their warm chamber into the early evening twilight, and then made the long, circuitous climb to the uppermost level, where Lord Hearndin, the fourteenth King of Dûn Bennas, awaited them.

The Great Hall was not like any other place they had ever seen, though Gaelen was strongly reminded of Cós-domhain. Much of the same skills had gone into the carving of the huge, marble archways and columns. None of the Elven-realms she had visited compared with it, for they seemed to rise from the woodlands in harmony with the trees and growing things around them. Their design was more delicate, taken from those found in nature. This structure, an imposing, formidable edifice of stone, was more like the surrounding mountains.

Impressive, yes, but cold, thought Gaelen. *Not alive, like the halls of Mountain-home or the dwellings of Tal-sithian, or even the Elven-hold.* The enormous carvings of dead kings did nothing to diminish this feeling of coldness. This would be a place Gaelen would need to endure, and after standing before Lord Hearndin she would look forward to escaping back to the warmth of her chamber, or better still, to sitting atop the wall under the stars.

Gaelen knew that King Hearndin had not expected to occupy the throne, but he had ruled wisely and well. He faced a great task, for the strength of the City had been lost to the Plague along with her people, and it would take a strong ruler to regain it. Her enemies had tried to take her while she was thus weakened; two of the seven bridges had been breached and were not as yet rebuilt, but Hearndin had kept his realm safe, calling all folk of good will to shelter within its walls. Dûn Bennas, though still diminished, was rebuilding. Hearndin had lost his beloved queen to a winter fever, but not before she bore him two fine sons.

He sat upon a magnificent throne of polished marble in his main audience hall as the Company was brought before him. Brown eyed and dark haired, his strong, well-chiseled face was solemn beneath his fine, dark beard. He was tall and of regal bearing, with a strong frame, for he was still relatively young. He regarded his guests with a keen glance.

"Fima Lore-master is known to us, and welcomed here, as is Thorndil of the northland. Perhaps you would favor us by introducing your companions?"

Fima bowed low, and introduced the members of the Company, who stood forth one by one. Each time the King inclined his head courteously, as a scribe wrote the names upon a parchment. When Fima had finished, he turned to Rogond. "Perhaps you should tell the King why we have come."

"It would be my pleasure," said Rogond, stepping forward and bowing. "We have come here to rest and provision ourselves for a great journey to the south. My friends and I are on a quest to discover what is left of my family, and also to learn more of my history. Therefore, I would be most grateful if you would allow me to examine the records of your citizens, as my mother and father were denizens of the White Fortress when the Plague came…in fact, I was born here."

"Then by rights, you are a citizen as well," said the King. "You shall be taken to the Hall of Records in the morning. Our lore-master will assist you."

"Begging your pardon, my lord," said Fima, "but I would also ask leave to avail myself of your stores of knowledge, as I greatly desire enlightenment wherever I travel. Will you permit me?"

Hearndin smiled. "Anyone who has earned the trust of Lady Ordath is worthy in our sight. Our halls are open to you."

He turned then to Gaelen, Nelwyn, and Galador. "It has been long since we have been blessed by the presence of the Elàni. What would Elves ask of the King?"

"Only leave to wander in your wonderful realm," said Galador. "We are here to aid and support our friend in his quest. We require no favors, yet any aid you may give to Rogond is much appreciated."

Hearndin smiled at them. "We are honored to have you," he said. "I would hope to be favored with Elvish songs and tales before you depart from us. You may wander anywhere in our realm as you will… but there is something I would ask of you."

Galador bowed. "What does the King require?"

"It will wait until you are settled," said Hearndin. "But know that I am very, very glad to see you. You may help us solve a problem that has been troubling us for some time. I will say no more at present."

Gaelen stepped forward then. "In my own country, I am considered a fair singer," she said. "I will gladly sing for you whenever you like."

The King chuckled at her. "Be not so quick to promise, for we may be so fond of your singing that you shall have little rest. Of course, you should sing at our feast of welcome tomorrow, but I would so enjoy a taste of things to come. Will you favor me now?"

Gaelen bowed, closed her eyes for a moment, and then began to sing, her rich, haunting voice echoing in the polished marble halls. None of those folk had yet heard the song of the Greatwood, and their hearts were rent by it. When the song ended, the people stood as though entranced for a moment. "Thank you for that," said Hearndin. "Elven song is of rare beauty, and you have exceeded my expectations tonight. We look forward to more song tomorrow. We trust you will remain throughout the winter with us?"

"If it please you, my lord," said Rogond. "We are at your service until the spring rains come, and we must then leave for the far southland."

"Then let us hope for a peaceful winter," said Hearndin. "May we count on you to aid us in defending the City should need arise?"

"As I said, we are at your service," said Rogond. "We shall make every effort to earn our keep."

"Say nothing of earning, for you are our guests. Should enemies threaten, we are pleased that you will stand beside us, but let's hope it will not come to that. For now, return to your quarters and take rest. Tomorrow night we shall feast, sing, and tell tales. We look forward to our next meeting."

The Company bowed and took their leave, but as they were escorted from the hall, Gaelen turned back for a moment to look once more into the eyes of the King. She wondered what task he had for the Elves to perform. *Ah, well...he said we would find out later.* She inclined her head respectfully, turned from him, and thought no more of it.

Rogond, Thorndil, and Fima slept better than they had since leaving the Greatwood. The Elves walked quietly through the empty streets, observed only by the sentinels who manned the tall watchtowers. The wind had risen a bit by midnight, and an early snow began to fall, settling briefly upon their woolen cloaks before their warmth turned it back into rain. Gaelen, who in general disliked tall walls blocking her view of the world, soon stood upon the battlements of the third level, turning her bright eyes homeward. She was taken with a sudden urge to call out to the Greatwood, and though her sweet song did not awaken anyone, those in hearing experienced dreams of tall trees and deep green glimmering forest light. All who were favored with that song were comforted; even the grim sentinels relaxed their vigilance, and felt safely at peace until the dawn.

On the following morning, Hearndin's folk conducted Rogond and Fima to the Hall of Lore, a storehouse of the written knowledge of the realm of Tuathas with many levels and chambers. Here, also, was the Hall of Records, housing the annals of the citizens of Dûn Bennas. Fima, who was familiar with the organization of such documents, was most helpful.

He and Rogond were both saddened as they turned page after page of names, so many of which bore a red mark indicating death by the Plague. Rogond trembled as he read, for the first time, the name of his father, spouse of Rosalin, taking notice of the red mark beside his name. Diomar had fallen while still in the City.

The records listed four children of Diomar and Rosalin, three sons and a daughter. Hallagond, it seemed, was born to them in the year S.R. 7188. Then there were two who had died when only a few days old—a son, Aranor, born in 7194, and a daughter, Vana, born 7201. The youngest son was born less than four months before the Plague came to the City. Rogond's eyes grew bright with unshed tears as he learned for the first time the name he was given at his birth; the word swam in his vision for a moment. *Ah, Gaelen…you are indeed perceptive,* he thought, as he beheld the neat, dark letters upon the parchment: **Man-child, born 17 January 7216, given name Thaylon.**

The wealth of knowledge held in Dûn Bennas was impressive, and to one such as Fima, it was irresistible. The dwarf was unusual in many ways, the two most noticeable being his appreciation for and tolerance of the Elves, and his insatiable desire to learn and know all things. He fully intended to spend all of his time in the labyrinth of chambers and passages known as the Halls of Lore and Learning, having his meals brought to him so that he would never need to leave it. When his presence was commanded elsewhere, he grumbled under his breath until he was allowed to return to whatever manuscript he had been reviewing. He confided to Rogond that he was envious of the Elves' ability to forego sleep, for he would waste no time with his eyes closed.

Gaelen laughed when Rogond told her of this, for she loved Fima, though she could not truly understand his obsession with the written word. Gaelen and Nelwyn could read, and enjoyed doing so as opportunity arose, yet they could not imagine preferring constant study indoors to wandering under the sun, or beneath a veil of starlight. They had learned much of what they knew directly from the mouths of wiser and more learned Elves of the Greatwood, for it was their custom to impart knowledge directly from one generation to the next. The study of scrolls and parchments was left to scholars such as Fima, and the lore-masters of Dûn Bennas.

Chief among these was a man named Astor, who was of great age, with a white beard as long as Fima's and deep-set, coal black eyes. He stood tall and strong among his folk, and was greatly respected. He intimidated the lesser lore-masters, gliding silently about in long robes of a dark indigo. He wore no ornament save for a silver seven-rayed star bound to his brow, the mark of his position.

He and Fima barely tolerated one another at first, for Fima was accustomed to having free rein of the libraries of Mountain-home, and Astor was not in the habit of allowing visiting dwarves to take such liberties with his precious parchments. Fima shrugged off Astor's disapproving glares with nary a second thought—Astor needed to develop a sense of humor, and to accept the fact of Fima's presence, for the right had been granted to him by the King. Once Astor witnessed the care and reverence with which Fima treated the manuscripts, his opinion changed. They were kindred spirits, after all. As Fima was unique among dwarves, Astor was rare among men.

He reminded Gaelen of a large, upright vulture, with a thin blade of a nose that, while noble and handsome, resembled a beak in her opinion. His eyes bore down without mercy on anyone who, in his estimation, lacked the proper respect for his hallowed domain. Yet Gaelen could see the humor behind them. She, of course, drew his scrutiny immediately as she roamed through the halls searching for Fima, for she was of light and cheerful temperament despite the bitterness of the weather.

The snows had come down from the mountains, and Dûn Bennas was now veiled in white. Gaelen the hunter-scout had taken a practical view of snow in the past; it made tracking at once easier and more difficult, and it made small quarry that were still clad in brown or grey coats easier to see. It dulled the sound of approaching enemies, and made it difficult to see for long distances when it fell heavily. Gaelen the Elf thought it beautiful, loving the feel of the soft, cold caress of the flakes on her upturned face.

She suffered less from the cold than did the people of the City. They would often wonder at her strong, graceful form standing motionless upon some tall battlement in early morning, the wind whipping her hair back from her face, her eyes trained on some distant sight, as a statue of marble impervious to the biting cold and whirling snow. She seemed at such times to give off a sort of inner light, and those of mortal race who beheld her were at once comforted and disquieted, for an ancient power lay within her. Then she would shake the snow from her hair, and draw her cloak about her, and the moment was broken. She was only a Wood-elf, after all.

Said Wood-elf had just availed herself of breakfast, including a rather large portion of toast with honey, and she was in quite a light-hearted demeanor. She moved quickly through the dim, silent halls, her bright eyes reflecting the glow of candles and sconces along the walls, searching for her friend Fima. She found him at a study-table with his head on a great, open volume, snoring softly, candle melted down to the brass holder.

Contrary to his belief, she did not wish to startle him, and she prodded him gently. This did nothing to rouse him, so she tried harder, calling into his ear. He stirred, but his snoring only grew louder, and Gaelen grew impatient. Now was the time for major measures. She drew forth a crockery bowl covered with a cloth, and held it before Fima's bearded face. Removing the cloth, she revealed several plump, brown sausages on a bed of mashed, buttered turnips, which Fima relished. A nice chunk of hard-crusted bread added its aroma to that of the wonderful sausages, and Gaelen knew that Fima would not long sleep through such promise of pleasure.

He stopped snoring, his nose twitching ever so slightly before drawing in a long, deep breath. One bright blue eye opened, and he smiled at the sight of Gaelen, who then drew his breakfast away from under his nose. "A fine awakening," he said, raising his head from the table and yawning. "I'll be having that sausage, if you don't mind."

"Naturally," she replied, placing it before him and moving to the nearby window, where she settled contentedly. Fima truly loved a good meal, and he dove into his breakfast with enthusiasm. Gaelen looked out of the leaded-glass window onto the wide courtyard below, where the snow drifted ever deeper, sitting upon the ledge with her feet drawn up before her. Her attention was drawn back to Fima when he suddenly stopped eating, and she looked around to see what had diverted him.

Astor had approached in silence, and now stood beside the table where the dwarf was sitting, looking with some disapproval on the remains of his meal. Fima had moved every parchment out of harm's way, yet there were a few crumbs on the table, and his fingers were oily from the sausages. The dwarf shrugged, brushing the crumbs back into his now-empty bowl, wiping his hands on the cloth that had covered it. Astor then turned his piercing gaze to Gaelen, staring rather pointedly at her feet, which were drawn up before her on the window-ledge. She bowed her head in acknowledgment, and courteously placed them back on the floor.

Astor then sat down opposite Fima, and they began to discuss some matter of debate that had no doubt begun long before, as Gaelen regarded them curiously. She thought it somewhat rude that neither had deigned to involve her in the conversation; perhaps they thought such matters were too weighty for her comprehension.

Well, that might be true, thought Gaelen, who considered herself unlearned, *but at least they could acknowledge my existence before dismissing me*. She trained her attention to their discussion, and after a time she managed to catch the gist of it, or so she thought. In fact, she was drawn in before she realized it, and when Fima and Astor had reached an impasse on a point of disagreement, she suddenly spoke up without really meaning to, offering her own viewpoint.

They turned to her as though only just aware of her presence, surprise on their faces. Astor spoke first to her. "I was not aware that you were learned in such matters, Gaelen Taldin," he said, "or I would not have excluded you from our debate. Come, then, and join us if you would." Fima winced, for Gaelen was not learned in the matter of their debate, and she would no doubt resent having to admit it. But she simply cocked her head to one side and regarded Astor with a raised eyebrow.

"If being learned is necessary to join the debate, then I shall forego it," she said. "I should not have forgotten my place before such scholars as yourselves. It just seemed to me that, if the Asari had wanted to involve themselves more directly in the affairs of men, they would have traveled more widely, and not relied upon others to spread their teachings for them." Here, she paused and looked away as though chagrined. "Of course, had Shandor not left Monadh-talam, all would have...been lost..." Her voice trailed away as she realized that this discussion was quite over her head.

"How know you of such things? Have you read the accounting of the First Reckoning?" Astor's face was stern, but his voice was kindly. He rose and moved to a tall shelf, reaching up to take a large, heavy volume bound in worn, scarlet leather. He invited Gaelen to sit beside him, and placed the volume before her, opening it to a beautiful engraving showing the artist's depiction of the twelve Asari as they might have appeared when first they were sent to Alterra.

"You can read?" asked Astor, for it was not so with all the citizens of Dûn Bennas. Gaelen nodded; she was not offended by the question, and looked upon the book with wonder. "Then I will leave you to enjoy this wonderful way of passing time, Gaelen of Greatwood. You will be certain to let me know if any of this accounting does not agree with what you have been told, won't you?"

Gaelen nodded, turning the page carefully to reveal yet another beautiful engraving. She then began to read the words, falling into a deep realm of learning and mind-pictures. The story was timeless, the words poetry, and they captured her utterly. The tales and recordings of Elves and men were laid before her, and, though she would never pursue them with such fervor as Astor and Fima, she would always remember her sojourns and explorations in the Halls of Learning.

King Hearndin summoned Rogond and the Elves on the following afternoon. "It seems you have all settled in nicely," he said. "Now I'm afraid I have a favor to ask of you—and it may well turn out to be a difficult one to grant. My people will conduct you." With very little explanation, they were taken deep into the Healing Halls to a quiet chamber. The attendants unlocked the door, shaking their heads. "We need your aid," they said. "Our scouts found her and brought her here...she has been here a long time. We have not been able to reach her. She has spoken no word, and has never allowed any but the most minimal care. She is wasting away…we have no doubt that she'll die unless someone can draw her out. Please, if you will, try to aid her."

To the astonishment of the Company, they beheld a strange She-elf cowering on her bed inside the chamber. Her blue eyes held no light, yet they were bright with the terror that comes of madness. Her hair, a dark, warm brown, was matted and tangled. She had been in Dûn Bennas for over a year, and in that time had spoken not a word.

The scouts of Dûn Bennas had found her wandering in late autumn, shivering and senseless. They knew her to be at least partly Elven, for her features were Elven, yet they had not seen one of immortal race so beleaguered, and her trials showed upon her face and body. She had aged, as Elves will appear to do only when they endure tribulation so great that their very spirit is diminished. Though that spirit may be recovered with time and healing, the mark left behind fades but slowly, and she would never again appear as she had before her time of trial.

The hearts of the scouts went out to her, and though they dreaded whatever seed had been planted in her, they could not leave her to her fate. They brought her back to the City, where the people tended her with difficulty. She would not eat, and was terrified in the dark, but quailed and wept at the sight of open fires such as those used for heat and light during the winter months. She cowered in a corner of her chamber as the healers tried to comfort her, noting the myriad of scars upon her body with dismay.

The Company now gazed upon her with a mixture of pity and horror. "Who has done this to her, Galador?" whispered Nelwyn, who had never before seen an Elf so degraded.

A tiny spark flickered in the She-elf's eyes. She turned slowly toward Galador, making a small, strangled sound in her throat as though trying to speak.

Nelwyn took a step back. "Galador…"

The mad She-elf struggled to her feet, to the astonishment of everyone in the room. She took a few tottering steps toward Galador, her arms outstretched, tears of pain mixed with relief standing in her eyes. The strength went out of her legs, and Galador caught her as she sank to the floor, whereupon she wrapped both arms around his neck, clinging to him as though she were drowning and he could pull her from the waters of terror and despair. "Can it be that you have come for me? I have forgotten my name, but I remember yours, my beloved. Can it be that you have come? Take me home, oh, please, please take me home."

"What is your name? Where is your home?" Galador asked her, but she would only weep and cling to him. At last she stopped weeping, seeming exhausted. Galador gently freed himself from her embrace. "Help me get her back to her bed," he asked Gaelen and Nelwyn, who stepped up to assist him, whereupon the mad Elf lashed out at both of them with surprising strength, knocking Nelwyn to the floor and cutting Gaelen's cheek with one of her long nails.

"Keep away from me," she spat at them. "You will not take me from Galdor. None of you shall lock me away from him. Keep away!"

Despite her obvious weakness, she looked quite capable of defending herself, and they backed away. Galador did not know what to do, and he said to her, "Come, come, do not lash out at these good Elves, who only wish to aid you. They are my friends and companions, and will do you no harm."

The feral Elf's eyes narrowed as she looked over at Nelwyn, who had regained her feet and was now staring wide-eyed at her cousin Gaelen, slowly shaking her head. Gaelen's cheek was bleeding, and her bright eyes glittered.

"This one is fey, and no mistaking it. She has obviously taken you for one of her own folk. See if you can calm her, and then perhaps she will have peace for a while. It seems only you will be able to approach her safely."

The mad Elf had gone back into her shell, sitting on her bed, arms wrapped about herself, rocking slowly back and forth. "Take me home, Galdor, please take me home," she muttered, over and over, in the voice of a small child. Her haunted blue eyes filled with tears that spilled down her pale, scarred face, as Galador sat beside her and gently wiped them away. She leaned against his side, still rocking. Galador looked helplessly up at Rogond, who had stood aghast through the entire confrontation.

When next he stood before the King, Rogond told of the encounter. Hearndin shook his head. "It is as we suspected—the She-elf will find healing only among her own people. It would seem that Galador is the only person who can comfort her, at least for now. If she has not come to herself by the time the spring rains fall, it may be that you will need to take her with you. Her survival in Dûn Bennas is unlikely. I would beg you—do not make us responsible for her death."

Rogond's heart was in conflict. *One should not refuse such a heartfelt, well-meaning request of the King, particularly when one is standing before him, yet can we give this mad Elf the aid and comfort she requires?* "Let's see how things progress, my lord," he said. "The decision must rest with Galador, for he will bear the greatest responsibility, and the greatest burden." He bowed and took his leave, his friends in tow, wondering whether they would end up being saddled with this strange, sad little soul, and what her fate would be.

The remainder of the winter passed pleasantly enough for the Company, and the early spring rains would be upon them before long. Galador had taken up with a scholar, a man named Chamberlin, whose special interest lay in the history and lore of the Eádram. A rare find for such a scholar, Galador provided many details that had not been known.

He made sure to spend part of each day with the feral She-elf, for under his coaxing she had been able to eat with some regularity and at least take marginal care of herself. He typically went to see her just after sunrise. Though Nelwyn often went with him, she would wait outside the chamber door, for they had learned early on that the She-elf would not eat if Nelwyn was there…she would respond only to Galador.

Hearndin's people had been most appreciative of Galador's efforts. "At least she will have a chance now," they said. "We didn't want to watch her starve...we have been quite helpless in dealing with her," Galador bowed, acknowledging their gratitude, but he knew full well what it would mean: the Company would have to take the She-elf with them. She would surely die without him. He had spoken to Rogond about it.

"I suspect you would rather not be burdened with her…I don't even know if she can travel. I do know one thing, though. If I leave her behind, she'll die."

Rogond pursed his lips and drew a deep breath. "I believe you. I saw the change in her when she first heard your name. I have no doubt that she will burden us, but her caretakers say that she has improved already under your ministrations. Maybe she will improve enough to travel without being too burdensome."

"I don't minister to her," said Galador. "I sit with her while she eats."

"You calm her and bring her back into the daylight," said Rogond. "I'm afraid this task has fallen to you. Sometimes we are afflicted with such things—they seem to be like stones in our path—because they have been ordained. Things happen as the Fates intend. If they have sent you to save this lost soul, who am I to object?"

"I really don't see how we can leave her. Not unless she comes around to the point of trusting other people…and I really don't see that happening. She still has not told me her name…if indeed she even knows it herself." Galador shook his head ruefully.

Rogond clapped a friendly hand on his friend's shoulder. "We'll do what we have to do, and face what we must face when the time comes," he said. "In the meantime, what do you plan for today?"

"I thought I'd spend a little more time in the Library. I promised Chamberlin I would look over some of his drawings."

"I have been promised a trip across the bridge. They say they will show me the house where I was born," said Rogond. "My father and mother lived there, though it is long abandoned. I have been warned that it is in disrepair."

"Well, take care, and do not expect too much," said Galador. "I will be here later, if you want to talk about it."

It was a good thing Rogond had been warned about the state of his father's house. He stood in the doorway, wondering how anyone could have lived there, taking notice of the holes in the roof, the smell of mildew, the crumbling plaster—this part of Dûn Bennas had made but small recovery in the past fifty years. Rogond saw many, many empty dwellings there. He stooped to examine an object long-forgotten in a dusty corner of the former bed-chamber. It was a comb of tortoiseshell, probably his mother's. He picked it up, tenderly dusted it off, and tucked it away. "I've seen enough," he said to his guides. "Will you show me where the dead are buried?"

They took him to the mound that covered the burned bodies of the dead. It was a large mound, now snow-covered, with a simple monument of marble inscribed in an ancient northern tongue:

"In this place lie those taken cruelly by the Plague, fathers and sons, wives and daughters, fair and enlightened children of Tuathas. We are lessened by their passing, but vow that our City shall live on, ever-mindful of their memory."

Rogond bowed his head, bending down upon one knee. His father's ashes lay beneath this mound. "I will find my brother, and restore him if I can," he said in a quiet voice, eyes closed against the sorrow that threatened to come forth. "His honor, and that of our line, shall be recovered. I wish I could have met you and known you...I hope to make you proud." He turned from the mound and left that place without realizing that his deeds, and his character, would already have made Diomar very proud.

The first of the spring rains had begun to fall when Rogond came into the library, bringing the news that Thorndil had taken seriously ill. He had been out on the eastern battlement with a few companions when the the color had gone out of his face and he had nearly passed out, slumping against the wall. He vomited, and at first they all thought he had eaten something bad and would now feel better. But after retching painfully for a few minutes, he suddenly doubled over in pain, falling to the stone floor, shaking and sweating. Understandably wary of any sign of illness they had backed away from him, calling down to Nelwyn and Galador, who happened to be within sight in the courtyard below. They knew that Elves would not suffer illness and could safely approach Thorndil.

Though she knew little of the frailties of men, Nelwyn could see that Thorndil was in a bad way—heart racing, pale, and shuddering with pain. She tried to calm him, but he did not seem to know her. Galador lifted him and bore him to the Hall of Healing as Nelwyn went in search of Rogond.

At first, even the healers were reluctant to approach. Then the chief among them came forth from his chamber, and drew nigh to Thorndil, examining him. "This is not the Plague," he said with relief, turning a withering glance upon the apprentice healers. He was the only one among them who had witnessed the devastation; he had been a young apprentice himself then, but he knew it well and would never forget it. His face grew grim as he made a more thorough study of his patient. "What is his age?" he asked.

"I don't know," said Galador. "Nelwyn has gone to find Rogond. He will know more of Thorndil than anyone."

When Nelwyn found Rogond, he had gone first to the library to fetch Gaelen. He still remembered her aid when he lay near death of fever. It was his opinion that she had saved his life—whether true or not, it would always be his belief. Fima joined Rogond, Gaelen, and Nelwyn at Thorndil's side.

Rogond knelt beside his friend, who had by now regained his wits, though his face showed the pain he bore. Rogond then asked that he be allowed to question Thorndil alone, a favor granted by all save the Chief Healer, who insisted upon remaining with them.

At last the doors opened, and the Elves were allowed to join Rogond inside the chamber. Thorndil had been given something for his pain and was now resting, his grey eyes relatively calm. Rogond drew Galador aside. "His ailment is not one that will run its course. This is serious, and they will need to cut him open."

Galador nodded grimly, though he found the prospect horrific. He had spent enough time among men to know that such efforts rarely succeeded, though they were never attempted unless the patient was certain to die otherwise. He had seen this done but once, in the wild, when one of Rogond's other companions had taken deathly ill. The unfortunate man had died in agony several days later. Galador shuddered. At least Thorndil would have a better chance here in the City, but the outlook was not a hopeful one. "When?" he asked.

Rogond's face was grim. "As soon as can be arranged. I have been asked to assist. Lady Ordath taught me a few things, and the healers apparently believe that I will be of use. I might not be able to do any more than hold him down, but at least I can do that." He looked away for a moment. "They will work on him as soon as they can make ready. I wanted to ask you to take Gaelen with you and distract her…she is not taking this well."

Galador nodded. "I will if I can," he said.

Rogond and Galador returned to Thorndil's chamber, where the healers were making ready to begin the difficult task of saving his life. "Come on, Gaelen," said Galador, nodding also to Nelwyn, who was holding Thorndil's hand. "The healers have said that only Rogond may remain."

Gaelen looked up at Rogond. "Does he know what they are going to do to him?" she asked.

Rogond nodded. Thorndil had been told, and though his eyes had filled with dread, he knew there was no other way. His pain would end this night, one way or another.

"Then I will speak plainly," she continued, looking back at Thorndil, taking his other hand. "They will cut him open, and he will know it. He will need aid…aid that I can give him. I need to stay with him."

Rogond dropped his gaze, considering her words. It was true that Thorndil would be able to feel the pain as they worked on him. Though there were herbs and extracts that would render a man insensible, as though in deep sleep, their use was tricky; one might find that breathing suddenly stopped, with death coming soon after. No…they could dull the pain, but they could not take it away. A small moan from Thorndil caused Rogond to look down at his friend. The healers were binding his arms and legs to the table with heavy cords, and Rogond saw the terror behind his eyes.

Gaelen soothed Thorndil's brow, promising to sing for him, and his fear grew less. In spite of the healer's decree, she would remain.

Several hours later, Gaelen and Rogond would emerge to be greeted by their anxious friends. Fima was first to speak. "Were you successful? Does Thorndil still live? I cannot tell it in your faces!" The dwarf was nearly bursting.

"He lives, at least for now. We shall know in a few days," said Rogond. His weariness was graven into his face, and he appeared to have lost years in a few hours. Gaelen was unmarked, save for the haunted look in her eyes, and she would speak no word of what she had witnessed—not then, not ever. As soon as she saw Rogond at rest, she would return to Thorndil, who would no doubt have need of her.

Thorndil spent several days in doubt of recovery. He had seen one hundred thirty-six years in Alterra, and for a while it seemed he would see no more. Yet he rallied at last, his pain and fever lessened, and some of his strength returned.

Gaelen hardly left his side in that time. She and Nelwyn sat ever beside him, aiding the healers as they could. Gaelen sang to him and soothed his fevered brow as Nelwyn held his gnarled hand, giving him what strength she could. Thorndil would recover from his ordeal, and he would always carry love for Gaelen and Nelwyn in his heart.

It was a good thing the healers had been willing to take such drastic measures, for Thorndil would surely have died had they not. He felt much improved after a few weeks of rest and care, yet it would be a long time before his recovery was complete. He would not be at full strength for some time, and this was difficult for him to hear. It meant that he could not go with the Company.

Rogond told him so on a grey, rainy afternoon as he listened with a heavy heart. "If you remain here until your healing is complete you will be as strong as ever, but the journey will tax you such that you may not survive if you attempt it now. I have sworn to leave at the coming of the early spring rains." He looked Thorndil in the eye, though he spoke softly. "I intend to do so."

Thorndil returned Rogond's steady gaze, for he knew that his young friend would not be dissuaded. He also knew that Rogond was right, and he nodded slowly. "Then be on your way with all speed. I know you are anxious to find Hallagond. I pray that you will find him, and that you will not be too dismayed by what you find. I will remain here in the service of the King." He sighed and turned his head to the window, where the rain was sheeting down the leaded glass. "I regret your setting forth without me, as I would not abandon you. I especially regret leaving Gaelen and Nelwyn…I shall miss them. If fate permits, perhaps one day I will find you again."

Rogond stood and placed a hand on his friend's shoulder, then turned to leave. "May it be so, my friend; we will miss your stout heart and your keen blade, not to mention your knack for striking a spark to a pipe in the pouring rain! We shall say our farewells in a few days. Keep well."

The Company left in three days, having gathered provisions and made their farewells. They stood at the last before King Hearndin, who sorrowed at their going. "We shall miss your singing and dancing, and your fine tales, as well as your keen presence on the watch-towers. May your journey be fruitful, and end well. May you keep safe, for you are the friends of the King, and you are ever welcome in Dûn Bennas. I would hope that you return here when your task is done. Thank you, also, for your help in dealing with…what did you name her? Was it Dona?"

"We had to have something to call her, my lord," said Gaelen. "The name Dona means 'one who is miserable.' It seemed fitting."

"Perhaps one day she will not be so miserable," said Hearndin. "If so, she will have your Company to thank for it."

They bowed before him, and turned to leave. They had already received many fine gifts from the King and the people of Dûn Bennas, but Hearndin called out to them at the last, for he had forgotten something. "Gaelen Taldin, singer of renown! I have one last token for you. I nearly forgot, and I should not wish to have you leave without it."

Gaelen stood before him and bowed, as the King handed her a small, worn leather volume with a faded gold inscription: 'Doom of the Wind-Lord."

Her eyes opened wide with delight as she opened it, finding page after page of a beautiful poem copied by the scribes of Dûn Bennas and still in fine condition. Most of the wear had come from Gaelen herself over the winter, for it was one of her favorites. There was a small parchment enclosed, with a written inscription: *I give this volume to Gaelen Taldin, that she might remember the Lore-master of Dûn Bennas, whom she calls Death-eagle. Treat this well, and it will ever bring you joy.*

Gaelen dropped her eyes. This was a heart-felt gift, and Astor would relinquish it not lightly. She had occasionally referred to him as death-eagle, though she had thought him unaware of it. It may have been that he was even more silent and stealthy than she! Her ears reddened at the thought.

"Astor reminds you to take care of his gift," said Hearndin, smiling at her. "He would have given it himself, but he has other business this day. He bids you farewell." Gaelen bowed again and turned to leave, but the King called after her:

"Don't be dismayed—I have also noted the resemblance of Astor to a vulture. You are not the first to draw that comparison. Sometimes I think he actually works at it—he seems to find it amusing. Farewell!"

Dona rode beside Galador, for she would speak only to him, and that rarely, on a gentle black horse named Malvorn. Nelwyn rode upon Galador's other hand, as Gaelen and Fima rode at the fore with Rogond.

Gaelen missed Thorndil already. *How did we come to be saddled with her? We might as well have waited until Thorndil was healed, for she will slow us down so much that the same end will be achieved. At least Thorndil could ride, and think, and fight…and I liked him.*

Thorndil had not been present in the Halls of the King when the Company said their farewells, nor did he attend their departure, for he was not yet strong enough. He resolved that one day he would try to find his friends again, for he worried that they would have need of him. The healers had taken him to a small balcony near his chamber, from which he could sit and observe their going, and he raised his right arm in farewell. It seemed to him that both Rogond and Gaelen turned back for a moment, though they were nearly too small to be seen clearly. Then he saw Rogond's right arm raise high in the air, followed by Gaelen's, and he felt a pang of longing, despairing at the thought of never hearing her song again.

4
On the Ravani Road

The Company drew southward through the scrublands south of the Ambros, making their way slowly toward the Ravani Road that would lead them into the northern desert. The north of the Ravi-shan was still considered part of Hearndin's realm. Rogond hoped that Hallagond had remained there, for if he had gone into the deep southern desert, finding him would be difficult at best. None in the Company knew much of that distant, reputedly savage land. They would not be able to speak the tongues of the desert peoples, nor would they know any of their customs. Elves did not venture there, and were largely unknown except through stories brought down from the north. What would the desert people think of them?

Rogond knew his hope that Hallagond had remained in the lands nearer to Dûn Bennas was probably in vain. He tried to put himself in his brother's place, imagining that, if he would run to lands so distant that his very existence would be forgotten, he would almost certainly travel beyond the lands of the King. In order to find his brother, Rogond suspected that he would need to lead the Company into the strange and dangerous lands of the Ravi-shan. The name, in the sutherling speech, meant "sun-country," but the Elves called it Tal-fásath, which meant "wasteland, realm of great loneliness." Rogond shook his head, considering the prospect. Perhaps he should take on this task alone, and keep his friends from harm.

He looked over at Gaelen and Nelwyn, who were busily currying the horses, swirling clouds of long winter hair flying before their practiced hands. He shook his head again. His friends would never allow such a course to be taken; they would all insist on going with him. He caught a whiff of fragrant smoke as Fima approached him from behind, his long clay pipe in his hand.

"I see you shaking your head, Rogond. I trust you're not thinking any foolish thoughts, such as leaving your friends behind and going into the southlands without them, are you?"

Rogond smiled. "I wonder whether you actually know my mind sometimes. You are absolutely correct about my foolish thoughts. Yet I know them for what they are…foolish."

Fima nodded in agreement. "Gaelen has given her heart to you, Thaylon. Remember that it was not given lightly. She will die rather than allow you to walk alone into peril. I believe the same may be said of Galador." Fima chuckled. "He thinks you need him to protect you from Gaelen, if nothing else."

"Yes, I know what he thinks," replied Rogond. "Yet I wonder now which of us needs protection? This strange Elf who has so attached herself to him…what will become of her? I wonder how Galador will fare as the journey grows longer, and he cannot free himself from this unfortunate burden."

"Hmmm…" said Fima, puffing on his pipe and looking back over his shoulder at Galador, who was even now sitting at a distance from the fire, looking rather dejected. Dona was beside him as always; at the moment she appeared to be resting, curled up beside him with one hand clutching the fabric of his cloak. Galador sat away from the fire because Dona was terrified of it. They had discovered this early in their journey, when she had cowered away from the fire, yet if Galador left her to warm himself she would cry for him until he returned.

"Do not leave me, Galdor, please do not leave me here alone. The dark will come—the terrors…terrors with *teeth!* I shall die if you leave me!" Poor Dona would become more and more unbalanced until Galador returned to her side, reassuring her. The longer he left her, the greater the effort required to calm her, until finally he simply resigned himself to his task and stayed always at her side. Already he grew weary of it.

Poor Nelwyn was having some difficulty with this arrangement. Dona no longer looked at her with menace in her eyes—in fact, she would not acknowledge Nelwyn at all—but Nelwyn could not be alone with Galador, in fact she was uncomfortable even speaking to him when Dona was listening. They could not really blame Dona, for they did not as yet know or understand her pain, but she burdened them and slowed their progress, for she was weak and unused to traveling. She could only make about ten miles a day, even mounted. And she would not travel at speed, for she was no longer a skilled rider.

Gaelen still did not trust her. Though even she could not reconcile leaving her behind, she would have given a great deal to be rid of her. By the second week into the journey they were all thinking it, though none would say so.

A glimmer of hope came on one beautiful night, as Gaelen lifted her voice to the stars in song. Dona stared at her with wide eyes, rose to her feet, and took a few tentative steps away from Galador. She closed her eyes, listening, with a serene smile on her ravaged face, as some of her torment fell away. Nelwyn and Galador watched her in wonderment, and when the song ended she stood as though transfixed. Then her eyes snapped open, darting left and right as the shadow of her fears returned.

"Gaelen…sing something else. *Anything* else!" said Nelwyn, who had already sat down beside Galador, free to be alone with him for the moment.

Gaelen, who understood her friend's urgency, began to sing a song that she called "The Hunter's Heart," a stirring chant she had composed herself. She liked to sing it as she ran through the Greatwood in pursuit of game for the King's tables. It was the first song that came to her mind, and she hoped Dona would be lulled by it, yet the response to this new song was quite different. Dona did not close her eyes, but instead she moved to stand uncomfortably close to Gaelen, staring intently at her. Then she began to sing along with her, her voice faltering, tears welling forth, singing no words but tones only, as Gaelen looked at her with pity in her eyes.

Gaelen continued until she finished the chant, hoping that Dona would at least gain some joy from the toneless, broken attempt at joining her. Yet it was not so, for Dona grew agitated at once, looking around for Galador. When she did not immediately see him she turned on Gaelen. "Where is Galdor? What have you done with him? You have lured me from him with your dark song, and now he has fallen! This is *your* doing!" She sprang at Gaelen with a cry like that of a wounded animal, her eyes at once desperate and murderous, but she was weak, and held no weapon. Gaelen, who had once held the mighty Gorgon Elfhunter at bay, had little difficulty subduing her.

Galador leapt to his feet as Gaelen cried out to him for aid, and he rushed to her side, trying to calm Dona, who was now crying and clutching at him. Gaelen left him to his task, backing away and shuddering with a combination of pity and disgust. How would they ever deal with this mad Elf, who even now spoke to Galador in a panicked voice: "Do not let her sing again, Galdor! Her song will take you from me, and you are my only light! Hers is the voice of evil!"

"It's not *my* voice that is of evil," Gaelen growled, taking note of the scratches on her arm. Yet when her blood had calmed, she was troubled. What had caused Dona to try to sing the hunting chant? It was almost as though there was something in "The Hunter's Heart" that had called to her...that she wanted to be a part of it. Perhaps she had been a hunter in whatever realm she hailed from.

Whatever her origins, Dona had left Gaelen with a chill, uneasy feeling that starlit night. It seemed almost as if her lips were trying to form the words to Gaelen's hunting chant, though she could not have known them. Gaelen had returned to the watch, shrugging off the uneasiness, for she must have imagined it. Yes, she must have... but on the next morning she suggested that at no time should Dona be left untended, for had she acquired a weapon, she would no doubt have used it. *Well, that's the first time anyone has actually wanted to kill me for singing,* she thought. She looked out over the empty plains, and sighed. This was going to be a very long journey.

The spring had come with a vengeance, and for the next few days they were lashed by storms that brought fierce winds and driving rain. They weathered these as best they could, seeking shelter among the scrubby trees or under overhangs of rock, listening to Dona's incessant crying as she clung to Galador in panic.

The lightning and thunder apparently dismay her. Everything seems to dismay her, thought Gaelen as she sat beside Nelwyn, thinking rather dark thoughts. She could see the same weary sentiment on Nelwyn's face. "Perhaps Thorndil seeks us even now, and will blunder on us in the dark, accidentally running mad Dona through with his sword," she said.

"Gaelen…how horrible of you!" Nelwyn whispered in a shocked voice. Gaelen was chastened, and hunkered down into her cloak. After a few moments of silence, Nelwyn spoke again. "Do you think Fima would allow me to sharpen his axe for him? My hand could…could slip! Who knows? It might just accidentally take her head off. The axe would be slippery with the rain, and all…"

"Or perhaps one of those big rocks over her head might happen to fall. You know, that has been known to happen. A tragic end, to be sure, but not painful," said Gaelen.

"Well, maybe a *little* painful," said Nelwyn, and that set them both to laughing as quietly as they could into the folds of their wet cloaks. They leaned against one another, side by side, trying not to let anyone hear their laughter at Dona's expense. They reveled in the moment, like so many in their past, such as they had not shared in a long while.

Then Gaelen noticed the long, booted legs standing in front of her, and her gaze was drawn upward into the glowering face of Rogond.

"Ill-natured Wood-elves," he muttered. "One day your cruel joke will turn on you. I am disgusted." Then he turned as if to leave them, but looked back to meet their round-eyed stares. "Thorndil would never be so clumsy as to run her through accidentally, but after a few days with her you might be able to convince him to do it on purpose." Then he left them to the agony that comes with trying to control uncontrollable laughter. They gave up after a few moments, causing Galador and Fima to wonder if they had lost their wits.

Another two days brought the Company within sight of the River Dessa. Fima drew forth a wonderful new map showing the Ravani Road; they could already see it winding like a dusty brown ribbon beyond the river banks. "There it is!" Fima declared in a hearty voice. "There is the way to our next adventure. See how it stretches out before us, just inviting us to see what lies beyond! It makes me young again." He puffed out his chest, drawing in a great draught of air, and then blew it out enthusiastically through his fine, white beard. "This is a perfect morning for an adventure. Let's be off at once!" He started down into the valley, walking swiftly and tirelessly on his short, sturdy legs.

Gaelen and Nelwyn smiled. Fima's enthusiasm was infectious. "Too right!" they shouted, and raced after him, Siva and Gryffa leaping down the gentle slope with their tails in the air. Gaelen called back to Fima as she passed: "We are going ahead to scout the ford. We will return when we are satisfied that it's safe."

This "scouting" turned into a horse race, with little Siva battling the mighty red Gryffa, two happy Elves bending low over their necks with the wind in their hair, reveling in their freedom. Gryffa was first to reach the ford, but only just. The horses stood panting in the shallows, for the day was warm and they were winded, so the Elves sluiced water over their necks and splashed it up under their bellies. They drank gratefully as Nelwyn and Gaelen played in the chilly water, making a great deal of noise. Just as it seemed they would surely drown one another, the rest of the Company arrived. Rogond sat tall upon Eros, looking at them with a slightly jaundiced eye.

"Well, my fine scouts! Is the ford safe?"

Gaelen shook her wet hair from her eyes. "Safe? Oh…oh, yes! Yes, it certainly appears to be safe. We would have warned you otherwise."

Rogond smiled at her. It was good to see the Elves so light-hearted. "Well, enjoy the river, for such opportunities to drown your cousin will be quite rare the farther south we travel. We should fill every available water-vessel before we leave this place." He dismounted from Eros' back and turned him loose to drink, an act he soon regretted, for Eros walked placidly into the shallows and, without warning, dropped to his side, rolling in the water, soaking Rogond's gear.

"He is taking your advice, I see," said Galador with a lopsided smirk. Rogond scowled. He really did not care for riding on a soaking wet saddle. His wayward mount regained his feet and shook his powerful frame, sending water flying in all directions.

Fima preferred to stay dry, so Gaelen led him across on Siva.

Galador dismounted, thinking that he would have to lead Dona across. To his surprise, she slid down from Malvorn's back and handed him the bridle-reins, wading into the water until she stood waist-deep in it. Finally, it seemed they had discovered something which brought her joy. Far from being afraid of the river, she bent over, soaking her brown hair and combing though it with her fingers, then raised up and snapped it back over her head. It was the first thing they had seen her do that indicated she was actually capable of taking care of herself, and they were encouraged. Sound came from her, and at first they wondered whether she was crying again, but then they realized that she was singing. As before, her song was toneless and no words came forth, but she seemed happy for the first time since leaving Dûn Bennas.

She remained in the river until the rest of the Company had crossed. Galador went to her and took her hand, and she followed him with some reluctance onto the Ravani Road. She turned back once, and whispered something to the river that Galador could not understand.

The River Dessa marked the boundary of the King's realm to the south, and they had traveled well over a hundred miles to reach it. Now they were in foreign lands, on the road leading southward through the desert. As the sun rose high they took their first taste of what was to come; the heat would eventually tax even the Elves. They decided to do much of their traveling at night, when it was cooler. This suited everyone except Dona, who feared the darkness. She rode with Galador upon Réalta, and he led her mount as she clung to him, eyes closed, muttering in what sounded like gibberish.

As they continued to travel southward, the land changed. The grass diminished, and the soil turned dry, stony, and poor. There were plants here that even Nelwyn had not seen, and did not know. Some of these had spines or thorns, or thick, leathery leaves to store water. The grazing was not too bad—not yet—but many of the plants here were not fit for the horses to eat.

"Rogond...why are we attempting this desert crossing in summer?" asked Gaelen one dark, breezy evening, as the last of the sunlight disappeared over the western horizon.

It was a fair question, and Rogond had no answer. He turned to Fima, who usually had something to say. "There is little difference in the seasons here, except at night. It is always dry, and the heat of the day is little less in winter, but the winter nights are quite cold. You will be glad we travel as we do, little Wood-elf. Tonight, I believe you will be treated to the first of the desert stars, for the high clouds of the past few nights are clearing. Look to the heavens!"

Gaelen did so, and nearly fell from her mount. She gasped, open-mouthed and wide-eyed, as an incredible array of sparkling stars burned brilliantly above her, with no clouds or heavy air to obscure them. She had not seen anything like these stars, as there was nowhere in the North that so many could be seen, save for perhaps the summit of the tallest mountain. She was completely transfixed, and drew Siva to halt, sliding down from the saddle and sinking to the stony ground, staring at the lights.

Galador and Nelwyn reacted in the same manner, and Rogond and Fima knew they would go no farther this night.

Galador set Dona down, encouraging her to lie with them and gaze at the stars, but she curled into a ball would not open her eyes. Galador coaxed her, almost tenderly. "The stars are bright, and their light keeps us from harm. Fear no darkness, gentle maiden." He looked over at Nelwyn and drew a deep breath. "I will protect you. Do not fear."

Dona opened her eyes, moaning a little in dread of what she might see. Then she beheld the innumerable, brilliant lights, and she was amazed. Her doubt gave way to joy, and she laughed for probably the first time in a long while, rising to her feet and taking Galador's hand. She pulled him upright, then began to dance under the stars, still laughing, beckoning him to join her. She had no strength, and soon grew weary, sinking back down upon the ground as he sat beside her. Dona would now travel willingly in the darkness, so long as the skies were clear and her "Galdor" was at her side.

They encountered the first of the people of the Ravi on the following afternoon as they sheltered from the heat of the day, resting among the rocks. Gaelen and Nelwyn were on the watch, nearly invisible in the pale dust-colored cloaks given to them by King Hearndin. Nelwyn saw the caravan first, and she called to Gaelen, who was watching out to the north and west. The Wood-elves alerted their fellow travelers as the strangers approached: five men, about a dozen horses tied head to tail, and three peculiar-looking animals, obviously akin to horses but with very long ears. At the fore went the most peculiar creature of all, much taller than a horse, striding along placidly on long, knobby legs and huge, flat feet. A warm, light brown in color, its long neck undulated like a serpent with a strange, ungainly head wobbling about on the end of it. It moved with deliberate grace.

"What *is* that?" asked Gaelen, incredulous.

"I think it's called a dromadan," said Fima. "But I have never seen one until now, except in pictures."

As the men drew nearer, Gaelen caught their scent on the wind. They were unwashed, but had tried to mask it with musk and spice, which would have been pleasant if not for the foul undercurrent beneath. Water was precious in these lands, and Gaelen expected to encounter many unwashed bodies here.

One of the men, richly dressed, led the caravan astride the strange animal. The others were most likely his servants. Their task, apparently, was to follow along with the horses, encouraging the reluctant ones with their whips.

Gaelen loved horses, and she knew these men for what they were. She gritted her teeth as she stood beside Rogond and Fima, her eyes drawn to one poor, lame fellow with a dull bay coat, thin and wasted, trailing the line. He struggled to keep up as the richly-dressed man called a halt.

"These are horse-merchants. They will have nothing we want, but you might wish to inquire after Hallagond," said Fima. "They probably speak some form of Aridani."

Rogond approached the caravan with Fima and Gaelen, while Galador, Nelwyn, and Dona remained hidden.

"Hail, wayfarers. What is your business here?" asked the man on the dromadan. Rogond and Fima bowed, but Gaelen stood erect, looking squarely into his eyes. He would not long meet her gaze, and pretended to ignore her.

"We seek a man named Hallagond, and are traveling to the southlands, where we have been told we may find him," said Rogond. "He is tall, and grey-eyed, and probably resembles me, for we are brothers. Have you heard any tales of such a man? "

The horse-merchant considered, looking at Rogond with some suspicion. "If he is your brother, then you should know whether or not he resembles you," he said at last. "I know of no Hallagond. We are here because these rocks collect water; there is a tiny seep that flows from beneath them. Surely you have found it already."

"We have," said Fima. "You are welcome, and your animals as well. Three of our companions still shelter among the rocks, but they will not harm you."

Gaelen's gaze was torn between the man and the horse. The man was a sight to behold, with raiment of many beautiful bright colors and fantastic, woven designs. He wore a full, black beard and moustache, into which many tiny golden beads were plaited. Several gold rings dangled from his large ears, and a silken cloth was wrapped about his head to keep the sun off it. He was not especially tall, but was of considerable girth. Gaelen did not care for his eyes; they shifted and changed expression to suit the moment. *False, inside and out*, she thought.

The horse was shaky and weak, and bore the scars of many battles. It stood with its head down and eyes closed. As Rogond and the strange man continued their parley, Gaelen cautiously approached it. The servants drew near to her, warning her to keep away. "That one is worthless, and will soon fall to the ravens," they said. "He is treacherous, and will bite and kick. Keep clear of him."

As though he knew the men were speaking of him, the little bay horse opened his eyes and raised his head, laying his small, neat ears back flat against his skull and baring his teeth, swiping at one of them. He was rewarded with a crack of the whip across his scarred face, and he blundered back against his tether, a large welt already forming between his eyes. "Another lesson wasted on you," the man growled, but his satisfaction gave way to fear as he stared down the shaft of an arrow. Gaelen's hood had blown back, and she was angry.

"Throw down that foul whip," she commanded, "for you are not even-tempered or skilled enough to wield it. Throw it down!"

Rogond was at her side at once, the tension in his voice obvious. "Put that away. You are in their lands now," he urged.

"They are cruel and dirty! That animal has suffered enough—I will not stand for it to be beaten." Gaelen kept her bow trained on the man. Her eyes narrowed, and her fingers tightened on the bow-string. "Are you deaf? *Drop it!*" The man did so, and only then did Gaelen lower her weapon.

"Forgive our excitable friend," said Fima, bowing before the horse-trader. "She has been long in the wild, and knows not the proper decorum. We will explain this to her. Please, help yourselves to the water. There is more than enough for all."

The horse-merchant stared at Gaelen, who stood before his servant with her chin in the air, as though daring him to pick up the whip again. Then, he began to laugh. "She must be stupider than she looks, to risk death for the likes of that animal."

Several of the trader's men had drawn their long daggers to hurl at Gaelen, not realizing that the bows of Nelwyn and Galador had been trained on them unaware. Now they sheathed their weapons again, laughing along with their master. Gaelen took no notice. She had approached the bay horse, who stood glaring with pinned ears, threatening to bite her.

"Let her do as she will," said the trader. "On her own head be it if the wretch takes the meat from her arm." Leaving one of their number to restrain the animals, the men went to fill their water-skins.

Rogond and Fima stood watching Gaelen, who was now trying to lay hands on the little horse. He took several vicious lunges at her with his mouth open, and she was taken aback, for he was quick. But something in his eyes told her that she would be rewarded for her persistence, and after a few moments of this hostile dance, she managed to place a hand upon his neck.

He threw his head in the air, squealing and tossing his long forelock, but as he felt the touch of her hand he seemed to calm, knowing she would not harm him. Warmth and power flowed from her hand into his scarred neck, and he dropped his head, though his eyes were still fearful at first. She broke down the last of his resistance, stroking his neck and shoulders with both hands, and he nickered at her, trembling with pleasure at her soothing touch. He had not felt such a hand in a long time.

Once he had been a proud war-animal, the favored mount of a prince. The last battle had gone ill, his master had fallen, and he had been wounded and taken by the enemy. At first they had thought to kill him, but instead they traded him off to any who would give a few coppers for him. He would not suffer himself to be ridden, and was beaten nearly to death a number of times as he passed from one set of hands to the next. He learned to hate men and everything about them, for they had taken his prince from him, and treated him cruelly ever after.

Gaelen was not a man. She neither smelled like one, nor sounded like one, nor acted like one. She was kind, but proud and skilled, like his lost prince. He sensed no evil in her heart. The little horse, whose name had once been "Rama," had been battling demons for a long time. He longed to have peace again, and even more he longed for his lost prince to take him and ride him into battle once more. Perhaps then he would fall with honor, and his misery would end. He looked into Gaelen's eyes and nickered softly. *Will you take me there?*

Gaelen knew that he had once been a fine animal despite his poor condition. *He was made to be swift and strong, and to turn on a hair. Such battles he must have seen! Large eye…deep and soft, and wide nostrils—good for stamina. Refined, chiseled face that speaks of good breeding. His coat is terrible, but that can be changed…*

He was quite lame, and as Gaelen examined him she did not know if she could make him sound again, but she wanted to try. She would free him if she could.

The caravan spent the remainder of the sunlit hours sheltering among the rocks, though the horses were made to stand in the heat of the sun. They were apparently on their way to a market held many days west. Gaelen overheard Rogond asking if the Company could or should follow them, for he might gain news there. The response of the horse-merchants, apparently, was not encouraging, and Gaelen felt a brief pang of guilt—perhaps her actions had ensured that they were not welcome.

She shook it off, taking water to the small bay horse, that she had called "Finan" in honor of his beautiful, long forelock. When she offered him a full water-skin he took the small end in his mouth, sucking with care, for he knew to waste not a drop of it. He drank about half, then stood dozing with his head down as Gaelen lay in the shade created by his body. The men all thought her mad.

As the sun went down, the men of the caravan prepared to move on. Gaelen stood by, trying to catch as much of their conversation as she could. Their eyes darted toward her, and they forsook their own tongue, speaking so that she could understand.

"There's only one fate awaiting that scrawny devil. The meat buyers will give a few pennies for him, though he will be tough and stringy."

Gaelen was horrified. *Finan sold for meat? That must not happen!* She ran to Rogond and Fima, nearly breathless, so agitated that she had lapsed back into her own tongue. "Are they speaking the truth? Will they sell him for meat? It's *unthinkable.* Horses should not be eaten, especially…especially *that* one."

Rogond tried to calm her. "They probably just said that to upset you. You did not endear yourself when you drew your bow on them," he said gently. "Look at how thin that animal is. They would get very little out of him from a meat buyer."

"They will get nothing for him from anyone else," Fima countered. "I'll wager that the only use he has left to him is for meat. Don't worry, Gaelen. At least he'll be out of his suffering then. He is not destined for a pleasant ending, but his life has been hard for a long time, from the look of things."

The bells on the harness began to jingle as the horse dealer's strange mount rose to its feet, signaling their departure. Gaelen watched as they turned westward, filing slowly away from her, Finan limping dispiritedly at the end of the line.

Gaelen could not let them take him. She called for Siva, and before her friends could stop her she had ridden out to intercept the slow-moving trader. Rogond and Fima rode up behind her on Eros, for they knew how foolhardy she could be.

As she approached him, the horse trader regarded her with a smug expression—he knew why she had come. His voice was silky as he addressed her:

"How may I serve you, little archer?"

"That horse…the bay at the end of the line...I wish to buy him from you," she said, before Rogond and Fima could stop her.

"Ah! That was a fine animal once—a war-horse, the favorite of a prince, I was told," said the trader, rubbing his hands together before commanding his tall mount to kneel so that he could dismount from it. "I'm afraid he will need to bring a dear price."

Fima laughed. "You refer to the scrawny, lame bag of bones at the end of the line? The one you said would go only for meat? There's hardly any meat on him. Let us be clear!"

The trader looked down at his hands. "Ah, yes, he may very well go for meat, unless…" He looked sidelong at Gaelen through half-lidded eyes. "...Unless someone skilled enough to heal him should acquire him. That would be his only hope, I'm afraid. Alas that no such person sees his hidden potential." Then he regarded Gaelen as though seeing her for the first time. "Of course, if this worthy person should buy him, he might have the chance to be whole again, but I don't know what she has to offer." His eyes wandered to Siva. "Will you trade that mare for him?"

Gaelen snorted. "I think not," she said. "Your animal is so weak that I would not get far trying to ride him. Siva is not for sale."

"A pity," sighed the trader with a dramatic shake of his head.

"That animal is practically worthless," said Rogond. "Whatever price he would bring for meat—which cannot be much—we might give. It would save you the trouble of dealing with him."

The trader looked into Gaelen's wide eyes. He knew she would give anything to save the animal; he could read it in her face. "You have some fine weapons…will you trade them?"

"I need them. I dare not part with any of them," she replied. Gaelen had very few possessions of worth, and she knew it.

"This is ridiculous!" said Fima, his blue eyes blazing. "You are trying to take advantage of her. Take your nag and go. Rogond's offer is more than reasonable. We turn our backs to you! Come on, Gaelen," he muttered. "We don't need this animal. You will forget about him soon enough. Walk away."

Gaelen's ears reddened and her face flushed. She had nothing else to give for Finan.

"That is an interesting trinket you are wearing on your cloak," said the trader, eyeing the silver brooch Gaelen wore always. It had belonged to Ri-Elathan, and was given by the Lady Arialde herself. "Will you trade it for the animal?" His greedy eyes rested on the beautiful piece of silver with its pattern of stars. "I will trade even for that brooch. What say you?"

Gaelen's hand flew to her cloak, fingers covering the small silver token. She could never part with it. "May you lie forever in darkness," she muttered, turning Siva and riding back to where Nelwyn waited anxiously for her. Fima and Rogond tried once more to bargain for the horse, but the trader merely looked at them with a smug smile.

"I know what is in her heart," he said. "She will come to me, and I will own whatever she has to give. Wait and see!"

Fima was dangerously close to drawing his axe, but he took a deep breath and mastered his anger. "Here are five pieces of silver," he said, drawing them from his purse, "which is an absurdly high price to pay for an animal that you yourself admitted is worthless! Just take it and go."

Rogond was amazed at Fima's offer, as it is not in the nature of dwarves to part with riches for worthless, broken-down war horses.

"I would let him go for eight gold pieces, my good dwarf," said the trader. I'd reckon your foolish little friend's sword is worth that, and she will give it to me...wait and see."

Fima reached for his axe, but Rogond stayed him—they could not shed blood over such matters. "Come on, Fima," he growled, throwing a disgusted look at the trader. "I hope you receive a princely price for that animal from the meat buyers, for it is all you will receive."

"I am just a humble man trying to earn an honest living," he called to their backs, as he and his men burst out laughing before going on their way.

Gaelen was being comforted by Nelwyn, who knew well what she was feeling, when Rogond and Fima returned. "I'm sorry, little Wood-elf," said Fima, patting her shoulder. "They just wouldn't be reasonable. We should make ready to leave, and never look back."

Gaelen looked over her shoulder at Fima, and nodded. She packed up her gear and swung aboard Siva, trying not to look at the long line of dark figures diminishing against the western sky. Then she heard the sound of Finan as he called to her—one clear, loud whinny that said all that needed to be said.

Gaelen rode up to Rogond. "I can't let this happen," she said, eyes blazing, jaw set. "If I let them take him, I will regret it for the rest of my days."

"But, Gaelen…you can spare no weapon! You have nothing to give for him," said Rogond. "And you don't need a broken-down animal to burden us and slow our progress. Think about what you're doing!"

"I am," she replied. "I'm thinking quite clearly. Dona is not the only burdensome soul in need of healing." She touched Ri-Elathan's brooch, pain in her eyes. "This is only a piece of silver. It is not Rain. Finan is a living soul, one that I can save from torment. If I don't turn the balance in his favor, what does that say of me?" She wheeled and galloped off before Rogond could stay her.

It took her quite a while to return with Finan, for he was very lame and she had to go carefully. Rogond and Fima looked in horror at her unadorned cloak—the brooch was gone. Gaelen's eyes were full of pain; Rogond knew she would ever regret losing this token, and he sorrowed for her. Yet it was her choice, and there was nothing for it now.

She busied herself with tending to her new horse. She massaged his injured limbs that night and again in the morning, singing to him as she did so, and provided as much feed as she could safely give him. She curried his coat, moving gently over his bony body, as he stretched and shuddered with pleasure. He wouldn't leave her until the last breath left his body, and he once again found his prince.

Siva, disgruntled that Finan was receiving so much extra attention, expressed her displeasure by turning her head and nipping Gaelen's leg. Gaelen patted her affectionately. *I know. I have been neglecting you. I shall try to do better.* Siva was only mollified after Gaelen spent an extra-long session grooming and currying her.

They camped on the banks of a small spring whose name they did not know, where there were small, shrubby trees and even a little grass, to the delight of the Elves and the horses. They had made a small fire, and Gaelen sat tending it as Rogond kept watch.

Fima approached, and sat beside her, the firelight flickering in his white beard. He turned his weathered face to her, blue eyes full of warmth. "You did the right thing, Gaelen. I didn't think so at first, but I'm beginning to understand now." He patted her arm. "I would cheer you if I could. I know you are missing your token."

Gaelen sighed. "I told myself it was only a piece of silver," she said, "but I do miss it. I thought I could feel something of my beloved whenever I touched it...it was always warm. I don't know why." She stared into the fire, remembering the touch of the silver and the feel of the pattern. Her fingers had known it well.

"Perhaps this will cheer you then, though it was dearly bought," said Fima. Reaching into his tunic, he drew forth Gaelen's brooch, pinning it carefully to her cloak. "There we are...much better!" he said.

Astonished, Gaelen couldn't even breathe for a moment. "How? *When?*" was all she could manage to say.

Fima chuckled. "Rogond and I went back some hours after the caravan left us. You were scouting ahead, and we rode back. Eros had to make all speed to get us there and back before you returned, but he did." He spoke to her under his breath "I'll have you know that brooch cost me eight gold pieces. The humiliation was almost too great to bear. Don't you ever tell anyone!" He smiled at her. "It is not in the nature of my folk to part with gold for broken-down war-horses, but for the heart of a friend, they might."

"Oh, Fima…I can never repay you. I don't know what to say," she cried, embracing him.

"Please, please, my good Gaelen! You forget yourself. If you will loosen your grip on my neck I will consider it payment enough. Just fix that animal! If anyone can bring him back to life, it will be you." She released him and he smiled at her. "It might help restore at least some of my self-respect," he said. "In future, allow me to do the bargaining; you wear your feelings far too plainly. You may be swift, agile, clever, and capable, and sometimes even show a *little* wisdom, but you are not in the least bit shrewd!"

"But…eight gold pieces! That's a small fortune, Fima, more than I have ever possessed. I don't know what to say in the face of such a sacrifice." Gaelen's voice quavered a little as she fought the urge to embrace him again.

"You need not say anything," said the dwarf, as they sat side by side, staring at the fire. "After all, they were only pieces of metal," he said gently, "nothing more."

Gaelen was unusually attentive to Fima for some time after, though she had long been fond of him. He enjoyed her attentions for the most part, until Rogond and Galador suggested that perhaps he was going soft with Gaelen attending his every need.

"Ah, my friends, you can't be envious without showing it," replied the dwarf. "But don't fear. This will wane soon enough. I intend to make the most of it in the meantime."

Galador turned to Rogond. "I believe our good dwarf has regained his investment already, yet he still accepts her services. Always she ensures that he has the best provender, the softest sleeping place, and she fetches whatever he needs. She'll be combing and plaiting his beard next!" He winked at Rogond.

Fima stretched and yawned. "She has done so already, my good Galador," he said, as though it were of no consequence. Gaelen, who could not plait her own hair, was nonetheless quite skilled; her agile fingers had woven Nelwyn's hair for years.

Rogond knew that there was now an even stronger bond of friendship between Fima and Gaelen. He often observed her fingers straying to the silver brooch, as though to ensure that it was still there, her eyes peaceful the moment she touched it. He did not begrudge her this token, this memory of her beloved. Her most precious talisman, the tattered remnant of Ri-Elathan's banner, she had passed on to Rogond, who carried it always beside his heart, for it was the symbol of her faith in him. Gaelen sang now mostly for Rogond, though he suspected that she occasionally sent a song heavenward, to the One who waited for her.

In truth, Fima would be justified in having his beard plaited many times over, for his investment had been greater than Gaelen knew. The recovery of the brooch had been far more difficult than a simple exchange of gold for silver. Fima and Rogond had ridden hard to catch the trader, for they did not want Gaelen to know of their plan until it was accomplished. As they drew nigh, they saw the trader's men draw their weapons, for they had taken advantage of tender-hearted Gaelen, and they feared the wrath of her friends.

Eros halted before the trader's strange beast, and as Rogond and Fima dismounted and held their empty hands before them, palms upward, the men relaxed. These two had come to bargain, not to exact revenge. The trader smiled inwardly, though he kept his face expressionless. His profit would increase a bit further by the look of things. He commanded his animal to kneel, though he did not dismount from it.

"How may I be of assistance? I had thought our business completed, but I see that there is yet some service I may provide."

"You know well why we have come," said Rogond. "Gaelen should never have traded that brooch, for it is of great sentimental value. It has little worth otherwise, for it is a small piece, and only of silver." He looked sidelong at Fima. "We are prepared to part with gold, which is of the greater value, to restore our friend's token to her."

"I might consider parting with it," said the trader with a glint of avarice in his dark eyes. "What have you to offer?"

"I will give five gold pieces," said Fima with obvious reluctance.

"The price was eight," said the trader, "and that was for the horse, not the brooch."

Fima struggled to keep his emotions from showing. "This is a small piece of silver. It is of little worth to anyone save Gaelen, who treasures it because it belonged to…a dear friend, who was killed in battle. Why not do something kind and considerate for once? Since you are determined to take advantage I will meet your original price of eight gold pieces for the horse. I would then appreciate the return of the brooch that should never have come into your hands." He patted his axe-haft in a meaningful manner, his blue eyes smoldering.

The trader drew himself up and looked down upon Fima with disdain. "You are in my land now," he said, "and you seem to believe that we know nothing of affairs in the north. I recognize the design on this trinket—it was worn by someone of great importance, perhaps even the High King himself, if I am not mistaken. Its like will not be made again. Try to deny it! It is worth far more than its face value as a piece of silver, and you know it. *Now* let us be clear!"

Fima's white beard bristled as he struggled with his temper. "Do you work the northern trade route to Dûn Bennas?"

The trader's eyes narrowed. "Why do you ask?"

"Well, *do* you?"

"Occasionally, though it is of little consequence in my affairs. The King's men sometimes desire horses of the kind I can provide. Desert-bred animals are unmatched in agility and hardiness, and can travel farther and faster through barren lands than your larger northern animals, hence you favor them as mounts for scouts and messengers."

Fima examined the fingers of his right hand. "It may interest you to know that our Company travels in the service of the King. He will not take kindly to it, should you treat us ill. No animal will you or your sons barter in the north, not ever again. You will be turned away from the White Fortress and her markets. Meet your original price of eight gold pieces." He looked hard into the trader's eyes. "Or you will regret it."

For the first time since their meeting, the trader took Fima's words to heart. Yet he would not give in so easily, for trading was his livelihood, and he was skilled in it. "Your gold pieces are like a thousand others. This brooch is one of a kind, and it is of hard silver, a rare and precious metal. It is worth at least ten gold pieces. Your Elf traded it. No one forced her."

"She had nothing else to give," said Rogond, his grey eyes hard. "You took advantage of the regrettable bond she made with that worthless horse. You are certainly not leaving my Elven friends with a favorable impression of humanity!"

The trader was not chastened in the least. "Your Elven friends need to learn how to survive in the Ravi, if that's where you are going," he said. "And they will need to learn to stay their hands upon their bow-strings, for they will see far worse than whips being used on horses." He looked at Fima again. "Against my better judgment, I will part with the brooch for ten gold pieces, though it is probably worth more to the right person. You, for example, would give more if I insisted—your heart is open for all to see. In return for this sacrifice on my part you will not interfere with my trading rights."

Rogond smiled to himself. Fima's words had been taken to the trader's heart.

Fima then surprised himself by drawing forth his purse. "Done," he growled, reluctantly removing ten heavy gold medallions and handing them to the trader's man, who stood by. He would forego the courtesy of handing them directly to the trader himself. The trader then reciprocated, giving Gaelen's brooch to his assistant, who handed it to Fima. All parties bowed, signifying the end of the transaction.

"May you find prosperity sending these nags to better treatment in other hands," Fima said with mock politeness. "I doubt there will be any tender-hearted Elves to save them, alas!" Rogond lifted him onto Eros' broad back, then swung up behind him. As they turned to leave, the trader called out to them.

"Wait one moment! I would favor you with some advice, and a warning," he said, an undercurrent of menace in his voice that they could not dismiss. Rogond turned Eros about, facing him once more.

"Well?" growled Fima, who was anxious to be on his way. "What have you to say?"

"Only this. You had best look after the Elves, for they are not safe in southern lands. There are many who will covet them, especially the golden-haired one. Some might even try to take her, and do harm to the others. She would bring a great price." He shot a meaningful look at Rogond. "Before I became a dealer of horses, I traded in slaves. It was highly profitable, but slaves are much more difficult to manage, and since the Plague few can afford them. Slaves are a luxury, but all are in need of horses."

Rogond's lip curled with disgust, and the trader smiled. "Oh, don't worry, for your excitable little friend would not likely be taken. None would want to deal with her; they will simply cut her throat. No, it is the golden-haired one they will desire. Watch after her, my friends. None of you has even a glimmer of a notion of how to survive in the southlands, and I fear you will not live long. I expect to see that brooch at market one day, when your reckless, annoying She-elf lies dead."

Rogond's blood rose to his face, and his grip tightened on his spear. The trader looked into his eyes and was afraid, dropping his gaze for the first time. "I mean only that you will need aid to remain safe in the deep desert. Do any of you speak our tongue? You need a guide to conduct you safely, and I would suggest that you acquire one as quickly as you may. Take this advice—or leave it—it matters not to me. You and your friends must suppress your proud natures, for they will not serve you here. That is a lesson you had best take to heart." With those words, he commanded his animal to rise. He would say no more.

Rogond and Fima rode with all haste to rejoin the Company. "Remember, Rogond," said Fima in a worried tone. "I gave eight gold pieces for the brooch. Not ten, only eight. I don't know if I could admit to having given ten…"

Rogond nodded; Fima's secret was safe. As he rode, he considered the advice they had been given, doubt growing in his heart. The

Company had received their first taste of life in the southlands, and the taste was still bitter in his mouth.

5
The Forsaken One

Far to the south of the place where the Company now rested, a tall figure prowled quietly along paths twisting between rows of colorful, desert-worn pavilions. Such places were now fairly common in these lands, for wherever there was water, there would be men. They were a varied lot, congregating in these "tent cities", building nothing of permanence. Should the water supply be exhausted, the city would simply disappear, and the people would move to the next known water source. The tent cities served as stopping-places for caravans of merchants who would replenish their supplies and trade some of their wares before moving on. They were also frequented by bandits and brigands who needed water and provisions, though they were less willing (or likely) to pay for them.

Because the denizens of the tent cities were mostly temporary, and because they were made up of many tribes and cultures, Hallagond considered them to be perfect dwelling-places for one who wishes to remain unnoticed. His group of unsavory companions had purchased a rather large quantity of liquor, together with a small amount of rather potent leaf known as "dream-weed" in the common-tongue. The sutherlings simply called it "marwani", which meant basically the same thing. Hallagond's companions had persuaded him to join them in partaking of both, but he had done so only minimally. Now he was the only one among them still able to stand on his legs. He left them passed out on the floor of their tent and went out into the city, as was his habit. He would spend no more time among them than he needed to.

Still, he was glad of them. A lone traveler brought forth too many questions and aroused suspicion, for none would travel alone in the Ravi if they could help it. Hallagond had no other need of them. He had become quite capable of looking after himself, even in these hard lands.

The marwani had left him with a pleasant heightening of his senses. He reached into his small pack and extracted some dried figs wrapped in leaves, placing one in his mouth and chewing slowly, savoring the incredible sweetness. As he did so, he looked up at the stars...even after all these years they still amazed him. The folk of the northlands had no idea how bright and clear a night sky could be, and unless they traveled here they never would know, for Hallagond did not intend to return there to tell them of it.

He still stood tall, lean and leathery, browned by the desert. His eyes were not dark like those of the desert peoples; they were grey, like those of his mother and father, and of the brother who was not yet known to him. His strong arms bore several elegant, multicolored designs. He had paid dearly for them, but they had been done by one of the greatest artisans to be found in the Ravi-shan.

He remembered well the willowy, hooded figure bending low over his outstretched right arm, studying it with grave intensity. The artisan, of whose gender Hallagond was at first uncertain, had looked into his eyes, whispering words in a tongue that had not reached his ears in many a year. "This is a sword-arm, of late unused except in need of survival, though it was once mighty. It will need protection in the trials to come. Do you wish my aid?"

Hallagond did not reply in the Elven-tongue, though he spoke it well enough. "If you ask whether I want your services in decorating my arm, then the answer is yes, or I would not be here. If you ask whether I need your protection, the answer is no. I need no one but myself for that." Then he added, "But if you would place upon my arm designs that you feel will aid me, I say, what can it hurt? Do as you will." The artisan had smiled, revealing perfect white teeth—a rarity in these lands.

"Are you of the Undying Folk, artisan? You are said to be of great age, yet your eyes and your smile suggest otherwise," asked Hallagond, at once regretting the question, for the artisan said no more to him. When the work was done, Hallagond was very pleased. He had little doubt that the artisan was of Elvish race, though he never lowered his hood to reveal his face. He had adorned Hallagond with runes traced in elegant, swirling lines of indigo and purple, spiraling up and down both forearms. Their nature would not be known to many in the Ravi, and the tongue was High-elven, which even Hallagond did not know well. Yet he could make out some of it—one word in particular was repeated several times.

"Why does the word 'tréiga' appear so many times? I know what that word means...why do you refer to me as forsaken?"

The artisan's eyes glittered under the dark folds of his hood. "Is that not who you are? Have you not forsaken yourself and your heritage, man of the north?"

Hallagond had tensed his arm, thinking to deny it, but he could not. The artisan knew him for who he was. He remained silent through the rest of the session, which would be the last. After Hallagond had paid the artisan—and the work had cost much of what he owned, for it was of fabulous quality—he took his leave. Yet he could not dismiss the Elvish words that had appeared like a vision of his past life, as though sent to guide him. *Forsaken...yes, that is who I am. The word in the sutherling tongue is "amand". From now on, I shall be Al-amand, the Forsaken One. Hallagond is no more. I am Al-amand.* He smiled a grim and humorless smile. "Should I ever need reminding, I need only regard the runes upon my arm."

He had since acquired other designs interspersed among those of the Elvish artisan, as well as a few in places on his body that are best not described. He had not borne sober witness to any of them. There was a red-and-gold dragon in flight that was actually quite beautiful, and a nice rendering of a rearing horse, but then there was the lopsided skull with a red rose clenched in its broken teeth. It could have been worse, he supposed. He had known of men who had gone to some inept artisan in a semi-drunken state, only to wake with something truly ridiculous permanently affixed in their flesh. Learning from their example, Hallagond had lately stayed away from the artisans.

The careers and the lives of such unfortunate lesser artisans were often quite short, as disgruntled customers occasionally exacted harsh vengeance when they became sober. Hallagond remembered one poor, trembling artisan trying to explain to one of his companions that he actually had requested the name of a certain well-known harlot be inscribed across the back of his right hand, together with a somewhat unseemly and amateurish rendering of her. It had taken Hallagond plus two others to drag their enraged companion away.

Hallagond had called back over his shoulder, offering advice: "Never again give in to such a request by a drunken man, no matter what he offers you. You will live longer!"

That was long ago, and Hallagond, known now as Al-amand, bore many marks upon his flesh other than the designs graven there. He had lost his left earlobe, bitten off during a brawl, and there were at least a dozen other scars that he had acquired since leaving the northern lands. Yet the scar on the back of his right hand, a jagged, ugly brown mark, had come from an Ulca blade. That was the only obvious physical reminder of his former life as Hallagond the Ranger, save for the scar that he most detested—a rather extensive burn mark on the front of his right leg. The circumstances surrounding it had turned a part of his heart forever to stone.

His handsome face was relatively unmarked, at least what one could see of it through his luxuriant beard, which had recently been streaked with silver. Some men of the southlands grew their beards long, for they were a mark of male prowess in certain cultures. Yet other races were beardless, growing facial hair only with great difficulty. These were those of eastern descent, or so Hallagond had been told. Their eyes were dark and exotic, and their smooth skin tended toward a light, warm brown. They were attractive people. So were the darker tribes of the far southern coasts, where the unrelenting sun had formed men whose skin was nearly black, like polished mahogany. Hallagond found them fascinating as well as comely. They had interesting ways and unique and beautiful speech that he could not begin to understand, yet those who spoke Aridani had revealed their engaging good humor. They seemed generally content with the state of their lives, describing the beauty of their homeland. Hallagond could not help but envy them.

He had actually befriended a few of them as they came northward to trade their ivory and rare essences in the markets of the great coastal cities of Castalan and Fómor. Since the Plague, none of the trades were especially prosperous. Not only had the number of buyers diminished, but so many producers of goods had perished that there was less offered for sale. What goods there were commanded high prices. Not many could afford such luxuries as slaves and ivory, yet a few were relatively prosperous, having taken advantage of the riches left behind by the dead.

With so few customers, the slavers had needed to cut back considerably, and many had gone into other pursuits. This was just as well in Hallagond's opinion; he detested the very thought of people of any race being used in this manner, bought and sold and traded like cattle, cast aside or killed when they displeased their masters or outlived their usefulness. Though much of the Ravi-shan was wonderful, like a sweet, ripe fruit, there was also much that was rotten.

His friends in the ivory trade had offered to take him to their southern lands with them, and he had considered it, but at the last declined their offer. No...this seamy, disreputable place was more befitting of Al-amand. He did not deserve a life of pleasant comfort, surrounded by gentle people. Who knew what evil he would bring among them? They did not understand his reasoning, but they accepted his choice, reminding him that he would be welcome among them should his heart change.

As he stood alone in the dark, he heard the sound of unpleasant laughter and cries of dismay coming from a nearby tent. There was apparently some activity going on inside, and he was drawn to investigate. Hallagond possessed an inquisitive nature, with a knack for discovering mischief. He smiled when he he realized that the tent was a gambling-den, for he had not seen a good game of chance in a while.

As he approached the entrance, a man was flung through the doorway to land in the dust at his feet, crying out in dismay. Hallagond stared at him for a moment, as the man began to weep, clutching at the dust with both hands. He was nearly naked, and evidently had been beaten. He was so wretched that Hallagond was taken with a sudden urge to aid him.

"What happened? How did you get yourself beaten? Did you wager beyond your means, or try some trick that failed you and was discovered? Speak, if you would have aid."

The man tried to gain his feet, but could not rise above his knees without help. Hallagond offered his hand, and the weeping man took it. "Thank you," he said, "but I must now go and climb to the tall rocks yonder, then throw myself from them."

The man began to weep again, as much with shame as with pain this time, as Hallagond continued to question him. He had indeed wagered beyond his means, but he had done so because his family was in need, and this was the only way he could think of to gain enough wealth to feed them. Hallagond looked at him and shook his head, for the man was clad only in a loincloth. Obviously, the other gamblers had taken everything else. He looked into the man's eyes, and saw no lie behind them.

"Gambling is a very poor way to provide for your family," said Hallagond, who had no family to provide for. He had found himself in the same position on at least one occasion, having lost nearly everything, including his sword, at the tables. He knew how easily this could happen.

"Do not cast yourself from the rocks just yet," he said, after conducting the man to an empty stall in the nearby bazaar, giving him his cloak to ward off the chill of the desert night. "I'll see what I can manage." Hallagond loved games, and now he had an excellent excuse to join in this one, if they would have him. If not, he would find another way.

"Take care, stranger," the man whispered as Hallagond turned to leave him. "They are treacherous, and your own wealth may be taken. It was so easy for them…so easy!" The man shook his head as though he still couldn't believe he had lost everything with no effort at all. Hallagond smiled a grim smile. Truthfully, he had been looking for a diversion from the tedium of the past few days. Here was a challenge to which he could rise, while telling himself that he was only doing it to increase his own wealth, and because he enjoyed the gambling tables. He would not admit to any loftier motive.

He entered the tent, hands empty, palms outstretched before him to show that he held no weapon. The men at the gambling-table looked up as though expecting no one of consequence, and their eyes widened when they beheld a tall northman standing before them. Hallagond spoke quickly. "I came to play, and would join the game. I have gold," was all that he said.

They regarded him for a moment, then smiled at the thought of acquiring Hallagond's wealth, becoming very solicitous. One rose and offered him a seat beside him at the table. "Forgive our lack of warmth," he said. "We half expected the last wretch to return with a weapon, for he was…unbalanced. We had no idea that one of your obvious stature would grace our tables. Please, by all means, join the game."

They would prove to be adversaries of average skill, playing as dishonestly as most in Hallagond's experience, but he would more than match them. He had learned much from his many disastrous defeats, and it was difficult for them to read his northern features. When all was ended, Hallagond was a great deal richer.

He had needed to draw his blade upon finally rising from the table, as they were reluctant to allow him to leave with his newfound wealth, but he cautioned them: "Be thankful I leave you with anything. You are outmatched! If I stay here any longer, you will all be in the same condition as that poor wretch you cast out earlier. Be thankful."

He somehow managed to make it to the doorway alive, and once outside he disappeared utterly. Disappearing was something else Hallagond was good at, and his pursuers had little hope of finding him. Muttering to themselves, they returned to their den. The sun was rising anyway, and all were weary. They looked forward to finding the northman upon another time.

Hallagond returned to find the small man still in the empty stall in the bazaar, which was now coming to life with the rising of the sun. Trading would begin and continue until late morning, then resume in early evening and extend until dark.

The man rejoiced to see Hallagond still alive. "Thank the sun-and-stars you have not been killed," he said. "Were you successful?"

"How much did you lose at their hands?" asked Hallagond, who would keep his successes hidden for the moment. When the man told him, he was surprised. It didn't sound like very much at all, and if that was all this man had, with a family to raise, it was small wonder he had tried such a foolish plan.

"What number are your children?"

"Six, my lord, but only two are sons."

Hallagond shook his head. "Then take what you lost, plus some for each of them," he said, giving the man a purse more than three times as heavy as the one he had lost. "Buy yourself some clothes, and stay away from the tables henceforth. You have not the skill. The rest I will keep, for I need provisions." He remembered the murderous looks he had left behind in the gambling-tent. "I believe I shall be moving on before long." The man was speechless, and offered Hallagond's cloak back to him with reverence.

"Keep it. I will buy another," said Hallagond, smiling.

"Why did you do this? Were you sent from heaven?" asked the man.

Hallagond laughed. "Most assuredly not! I enjoy the games, and excess wealth makes one a larger target, so I kept only enough to share with my companions. The wine will flow with abandon tonight."

"You were sent from heaven, whether you know it or not," called the man, drawing Hallagond's cloak about him. He turned and went in search of new garments, as well as food and a few small gifts for his wife, his sons, and, most especially, his four beautiful little girls.

"By the Beards of my Fathers, Gaelen, can you not move that animal any faster?" Fima, obviously irritable, had not endured the sort of deprivation the Company was now experiencing.

Gaelen was unruffled. "Don't blame Finan for the heat and the lack of water. Those things are not of his doing. It's not Finan's fault that we have found no shelter, and so must travel under the sun until we do. The faster you travel, the hotter you will get, and the more water you will need."

They were still traveling what they thought was the Ravani Road. Rogond hoped there would be many wayfarers and merchants coming and going, for they might bring news of Hallagond. But as he looked at the vast and barren lands that seemed to stretch forever before him, he wondered whether finding his brother would even be possible. He had known from Fima's maps that the Ravi-shan was a vast, largely uncharted and inhospitable place, but now, when faced with the reality of it, he knew he had underestimated his task.

He looked back toward his companions, doubting yet again the wisdom of his choice to lead them here. The Elves, save for Dona, seemed to be faring well enough. But the mortal contingent, including Fima, the horses, and himself, were less resistant to the heat and lack of water. Rogond marveled at Gaelen, who walked in the full sun wearing her sleeveless green jerkin, yet showed no effect other than a slight browning of her shoulders. Fima, who was of ruddy complexion, bore little sign even after he had removed his helmet (his hair was a bit thin on the top of his head). After so many generations working in forges of fire, the skin of dwarves would not burn easily. Still, the heat taxed him, more likely due to his advanced age, and he had learned to wear his hood to shade his head and face.

Rogond had worn his hood from the first day that he traveled under the desert sun, and he sweated profusely in his dark garments. He was getting weaker by the day, for the water supply was dangerously low and they had been rationing it. This road took them through lands where there was no shelter of any kind, nor was there much sign of other travelers having passed this way in recent memory. The dust and sand made it difficult to even find the road sometimes, though it was wide, and had been marked with stones on both sides. Rogond was worried, and rightly so.

Dona could not keep up with the Company unless mounted, so Galador led her on Réalta. Nelwyn walked beside him leading Gryffa and Malvorn, who was now carrying most of their gear. Rogond smiled—this pleased Nelwyn, as she could converse quietly with Galador and, for the moment, forget that Dona existed. He looked back over his shoulder at Gaelen, who walked behind him leading Siva with Fima in the saddle, the dwarf staring glumly at the never-changing horizon. She had already turned Finan loose to follow along as he could, knowing he would not leave her.

Rogond led Eros, striding along with a confidence he did not feel. At least the sun would be going down soon, and some relief would come. Then they would shiver through the cold desert night, and in the morning the sun would find them again. *Surely there will be water along the road...*

Darkness found the Company wondering how much longer they could continue on this path. The Elves sat together, looking at the stars, as Fima and Rogond rested for the moment. They would need to continue on, making as much distance as they could while the blessed darkness held.

Rogond noticed that the water had been diminishing more slowly these past days, and he asked Gaelen about it, bidding her to come and sit beside him. "Have you and your friends been foregoing your share of water? If so, you must not continue. You may be immortal, but you still need water. Fima and I will manage, and we're sure to find water soon. I simply cannot imagine that the Ravani Road would stretch for too many days without passing a water source."

Gaelen drew Rogond's hood back and looked into his worried grey eyes. "I cannot offer comfort, Thaylon, for my imagination has already reached its limit with respect to this place. Yet I have been thinking…are you certain that we are still on the Ravani Road? There has been no sign of other travelers. Perhaps this is a lesser road that was abandoned for lack of water? We have found neither water nor shade for days now. How certain are you that we have not missed the path?"

Rogond shook his head—he was not certain at all. He had learned to navigate by the stars, and he had kept his sense of direction, but he did not know the lay of these southern lands, and he could not trust himself. Fima was a lore-master, not a navigator. It was quite possible that they had somehow diverted from the main road, and were now on a path long abandoned. Rogond could not bear to think of that now.

"The marking-stones are still there," he said, "though they are smaller and farther apart than before. Regardless, we must find shelter and water, and soon." He looked hard at Gaelen. "What would the hunter-scout suggest?"

Gaelen pondered for a moment. "I could ride back the way we came, and see whether I can find the Ravani Road again," she said. "But first we must find shelter, as you suggest...find it, or make our own. Perhaps our cloaks might be fashioned together to provide shade. Then we might rest under the sun, though that still does not address our lack of water. As to that, the hunter-scout has no suggestions. I have not caught even the slightest scent of water, though I have been vigilant." She sighed, drawing against his side to warm him.

Rogond considered. "What of Nelwyn? She can sometimes provide insight from examining the things that grow. Has she any ideas?"

"As you can see, Thaylon, there is almost nothing growing here," said Gaelen. "And Nelwyn has seen no green thing indicating the presence of water nearby; I have asked her." She squeezed his upper arm affectionately. "Sorry to bring only ill news. Perhaps we'll find water tomorrow. Rest now, my love."

Rogond drifted into sleep, the beautiful words "my love" fading slowly from his hearing. If he died of heat and thirst tomorrow, at least he would have lived long enough to hear those words, and he would not say that he had gone to his death an entirely unhappy man.

Gaelen added her cloak to his, covering him gently against the cold. Then she stood, stretched, and shook the dust from her breeches. She breathed the dry air in all directions, taking in a few scents wafting upon the wind. There were none of real interest—a faint hint of old carrion, and a sort of musky scent common in the desert air—but not even a hint of water. Gaelen sighed. Rogond was right; she and her companions needed water, no matter the cost.

The horses suffered as well, especially Malvorn, whose burden had not been lessened and who was black in color. He was not desert-bred, and, like Eros, he had a thick coat. It wrenched Gaelen's heart to see him so deprived. He followed without complaint, for he trusted her, and that pained her heart all the more.

She felt eyes upon her, and turned to regard the little bay horse, Finan. He was still very thin, as they had nothing to feed him, and he was also lame—the rocks and sand were not his friend. His presence had slowed them, for Gaelen had insisted that they allow him to catch up when he fell behind. Though they would not have admitted to it for her sake, she knew that some in the Company resented Finan, and she felt a pang of guilt. Perhaps they would have found water by now had she not slowed their progress to wait for him. Yet, as she looked into his fine, intelligent face, she knew that somehow his fate would be tied with hers. She had known it from the first time she had laid hands on him.

He took a step toward her and nickered, dipping his proud head, his long forelock blowing back from large, bright eyes. There was a sort of expectation evident in him, as though he wanted her to do something, but she did not know what it could be. "I'm sorry, Finan, I have neither food nor water to share with you tonight. Tomorrow will be better." In truth, she had been giving half her own water-ration to Finan and Siva, saving the rest for Fima and Rogond. Gaelen had not had any water in two days.

She tried to stroke Finan, but he stepped back from her. This puzzled her, and she tried again. Again, the horse stepped back.

"What do you want of me?"

Finan did not answer her, but turned and limped off toward the east, making his way slowly away from the Company as Gaelen called after him. "Finan! Come back, do not go so far astray…I cannot waste energy finding you in the morning. Come back!" In answer, he turned his head back over his shoulder, calling softly, then continued painfully to the east. Gaelen did not know what to do; she was beginning to weaken from lack of water and she was confused. "I can't leave my friends for you, Finan, come back...please come back!"

Her cries alerted Nelwyn, who was at her side in moments. "You dare not risk the energy to pursue him, Gaelen. Perhaps he has gone because he has lost his sensibilities due to thirst and starvation. You can't risk yourself any further for him. He will either return or not, but you must not pursue him. Come now, and sit with us. Fima has promised to tell us a tale before we move on." There was sadness in Nelwyn's eyes as she looked upon Gaelen; her cousin was conflicted, in despair, and most probably dying of thirst before her eyes.

"Fima needs to save his breath and his strength, as do we all," Gaelen replied. Then, as she looked back toward her distant, wayward horse, a thought struck her. Finan wanted her to follow him. He was possessed of some knowledge that she lacked, and he would lead her; all she had to do was listen to him. She embraced Nelwyn, and when she drew back her eyes were bright and full of hope.

"Finan would not leave me without cause—he wants me to follow him, I just know it. Don't tell the others, but I am going after him. Do not fear…I'll find you again before the sun rises."

Nelwyn knew better than to try to dissuade her, though she thought the idea bordered on suicide. To leave the Company and set off alone following a lame, starving horse seemed less than sensible. "You should not go alone…I'll go with you," she said.

Gaelen quirked a half-smile at her. "Do you actually think you will escape the vigilance of Galador? We would all be going if that happened, for he would try to leave Dona, and her cries would awaken Rogond, and we would all take the risk. Either that, or Rogond would throw a sack over my head and sit on me until morning to keep me from leaving. He will not understand. You, on the other hand, know I'm right."

Nelwyn nodded, though she didn't like the idea of Gaelen leaving without her. "Take the water-skin with you. At least do that much to safeguard yourself," she said. After taking the nearly-empty vessel, Gaelen bowed, turned to follow Finan, and rapidly disappeared from sight. Nelwyn returned to Galador and Dona, settling against her beloved, sharing in his warmth.

"You astound me, Nelwyn," said Galador. "I heard much of what was said. Gaelen truly intends to follow that worthless animal into the desert in the dark of night? I have been watching her; she has been giving her water-ration to the horses for two days. She is probably confused from thirst, and her judgment is poor. How could you let her go?"

But Nelwyn only sighed and shook her head. "I did not try to prevent her because I believe she's right. She has some special insight with respect to that animal. My love, if someone doesn't find water, we'll all die in a few days. Gaelen knows it, and she took the risk to prevent it. I trust her. How could I stay her?"

Galador shook his head. "I trust her less, Nelwyn, and I do not look forward to telling Rogond that his beloved has left us. Yet I will trust you and hold hope in my heart, though my own sensibilities would deny it. We must rest and save our strength, for tomorrow I suppose we'll need to go after her. Let's hope it won't mean the death of us all."

"Trust her, beloved. She will not fail her friends. Her instincts are seldom wrong, and neither are mine. Trust us both, and rest well."

Galador would trust Nelwyn until his last breath left him. As for Gaelen, well, that might take a bit more doing, but as long as Nelwyn held such faith, he would try not to doubt her.

Hallagond's companions were pleased when he revealed his winnings. They immediately ordered several casks of decent wine, knowing the word would soon spread that a night of merriment was forthcoming. Sure enough, the visitors began arriving as evening fell, bringing with them food of various kinds, and Hallagond soon found himself in the middle of a lively gathering which, as with many in the tent city, soon turned to widespread drunkenness and debauchery.

He had hired musicians and dancers for the evening; they would work for nearly nothing so long as they were given food and drink. Several of the "guests" had brought weed with them, and the smoke filled the tent with a choking sweetness. This, combined with the influence of the wine, put Hallagond into such a relaxed state that when one of the dancers, who fancied him, asked him to attend to her alone, he agreed. This was not typical of Hallagond, who was more in the habit of disappointing those who would lie with him, rarely assenting to any but the most superficial display of affection. Tonight his defenses were weak, and he followed the dark, lithe dancer into the alleyway behind the tent.

In a moment he realized his folly, for two men leaped upon him as the dancer ran off into the shadows. He knocked one cold, then drew his curved dagger, just managing to fend off a killing thrust from the other before burying it in the man's belly. Hallagond recognized him as one of the men from the gambling-den. Apparently he could not wait long to try to reclaim his wealth, even though Hallagond had won it in a fair game. Hallagond had considered it a fair game because all the participants were cheating at the same time.

There did not seem to be any others lurking to take him, so Hallagond bent over the man he had knocked senseless, judging that it would be some time before he awakened. *I'll just relieve him of any valuables for my trouble,* he thought, just before his head suddenly swam and his vision blurred. *Mother of Mayhem! I hadn't realized I was this drunk...* He called out to one of his companions just before his eyes rolled back and he fell to the ground in a dead faint. When they found him, they thought he had been killed.

"No, he's still breathing," said a broadly-made man named Azori, who was the closest thing Hallagond had to a friend. He shook his head, sniffing at Hallagond as he examined him. "He's out cold, but unhurt—obviously got the better of these two. Ah, well, too much weed and wine will do that to a man. Take him back inside, but feed these reprobates to the vultures. I don't know why they attacked Alamand, but it's always better to be cautious. They who make trouble once will make trouble again."

Hallagond lay unresponsive and unseeing, but in his mind he regarded the visions before him with curiosity. Surely he was dreaming, or having some sort of drunken hallucination...certainly not his first. But this was more vivid, and somehow more real, than any drunken vision of his experience.

A very tall young man, dark-haired and grey-eyed, stood before him, his gaze reproachful. Beside the tall man stood Hallagond's father, Diomar, looking on him with dismay. Diomar shook his head. *See what you have become…you have squandered the blood of Tuathas, and now you languish in the pit of your own despair. You could have been as worthy as any of our line, yet you deny your heritage. If you cannot climb from the pit, then you may as well have died, Forsaken One. Your mother weeps from shame, for she loves you. Your brother likewise searches for you that you may be redeemed. I know you will try to thwart him—I blame myself for the curse of your stubbornness. Take warning! Your path leads only to despair. Turn from it, or be dead to those who love you.*

Hallagond's heart and his gaze grew hard, and he tried to answer his father, but he could make no sound. The vision shifted, but not before Hallagond looked intently at the man he supposed must be his brother. He could see it in the man's eyes…grey eyes, like his own eyes and his father's. Well, what of it? He needed no one, he answered to no purpose any longer. Diomar faded from sight, a look of immeasurable sadness on his grim face.

Now Hallagond saw other strange sights shifting and changing before him. He saw a small but beautiful city, with spires of gleaming silver, poised on the sea with its back to the desert. He had never seen the like of it before. He saw a She-elf, dressed as one of the Ravani, save for a cloak that seemed to be woven of living flame.

Then he beheld a vision that truly frightened him—a huge warrior clad all in black armor, radiating power and malevolence. It turned to him, and he heard a voice from beneath the black helmet, chuckling in an ill-natured way. *Stand not in my path*, it said in the Elven-tongue, pulling off the helmet in one smooth, elegant motion to reveal pale, malevolent eyes. Hallagond tried to turn away, but he could not. The hair was long, and silken gold...Elven hair. What sort of abomination was this?

Hallagond then looked behind the creature to behold an army clad all in red and black. The monster laughed, throwing its head back and raising its arms. In one hand it held the severed head of Hallagond's brother which opened its dull, dead eyes and, to Hallagond's ever-growing horror, spoke to him: *I have found you at last, but too late. You ran from your destiny, when you could have turned the tide. Look now, on that which you have wrought.*

Hallagond heard the dying screams of his company of Rangers. The Silver City in his vision was burning, and the people were screaming—he had failed them as well. He could not bear it, not another moment, or he would scream himself. This he did, coming to his senses at last, soaked with sweat, crying out in horror and grief. As the vision faded from his inmost sight, he shuddered and wrapped his arms around his knees, closing his eyes against the torment until it cleared like smoke that is blown away. The next voice he heard was Azori's. "You aren't just drunk…you're fevered. Here, this will put you right." Azori offered him a full goblet of wine laced with bitter herbs, and he drained it without a breath, then fell back into a deep sleep. His consciousness had already decided that he would not remember this dreaded prophecy; it had already faded into the realm of forgotten dreams.

Far to the north, Rogond, brother of Hallagond, was deeply involved in his own dreams. At first they were dark and frustrating; there was water, but he could not reach it, and there was food, but he could not take hold of it. He was lost in the vastness of a dark and barren waste, and he could hear his friends calling to him. They were in desperate need of food and water, and they cried for aid, yet he could neither find them nor aid them.

He wandered this way and that, chasing the elusive water that always seemed to disappear when he drew near enough. He told himself that he should ignore the sight of this phantom water. It was not real, and he only wasted precious time and strength pursuing it, but he could not help himself. *This time there will be water*, he told himself, over and over, only to be disappointed. His thirst was nearly unbearable. *This time there will be water…this time…*

He heard his beloved Gaelen laughing, and he tasted water on his tongue. Though it was gritty and impure, he had never tasted anything so sweet. "There IS water, Rogond! Open your eyes and see!" Gaelen laughed again, and he smiled. She held a half-full water-skin before his grimy, sweat-streaked face. "Have all you desire, my love. There is enough that we may all drink our fill, and more besides!"

"What miracle is this?" he stammered, looking around and squinting into the rising sun.

Gaelen was elated. "Drink, bold warrior, and make ready, for we travel to the east. There is shelter there, and water aplenty, yet we would not have found it without Finan. Come!"

She had returned just before sunrise, charged with hope and energy, running lightly back to her friends with the news that water and shelter had been found. "We will be able to replenish our supplies and our strength," she said. "Though there is little to eat, at least we'll have water and shade."

That was enough motivation for the Company. They packed up, following Gaelen's lead, and after a journey of nearly six miles they came to an interesting formation in the rocky landscape. Though there were no tall rocks that could be seen from the road, there was a small canyon sinking down into the earth, perhaps twenty feet deep and two hundred feet long. In the bottom of it there was water—brown, gritty water to be sure, but plenty of it. It was wonderfully cool. There would always be shade here, and the Company could take rest.

Finan stood placidly, calling to Gaelen as she approached with her friends.

"He found it, not I," she told them. "I just had to listen. These are his lands, after all."

Finan would prove to be a very worthwhile investment. They all learned to watch him, for he knew which sights and sounds were of consequence, and which were not. He would display an uncanny talent for finding water.

Fima's good humor returned with cool shade and the slaking of his thirst. "I was wrong about that animal," he declared. "He is worth every bit of ten gold pieces." At this, Gaelen and Nelwyn stared at him, as Rogond chuckled and shook his head. Fima gasped. "Eight, I meant *eight* gold pieces! Yes, eight. How could I have forgotten, of course it was only eight. Only a fool would have given ten! Yes, he is certainly worth eight. Wouldn't you agree?"

Galador stood with Rogond, a knowing smile on his face. "He is even worth ten, my good dwarf. In fact, I would have given all the gold in Alterra for this water, and so would you."

The Company rested in the canyon for two days. There was plenty of water, and once it was strained through tightly-woven silk it tasted fine enough. There was even a little grass—dry to be sure—but to the horses it was most welcome, for they had been maintaining on very little feed for some time. Réalta, in particular, was beginning to show it; the faint outline of his ribs was always visible.

Finan seemed to know that he had proven his worth in the eyes of the Company. He amused everyone by dropping at the edge of the water-hole and sinking down onto his side, wallowing contentedly and rolling over so that both sides were equally muddy. Then he rose as Gaelen went to fetch him, shaking his bony frame and sending wet muck flying in all directions, covering her with brown globs and flecks. Gaelen shook the mud from her hair and approached Finan, bidding him stand knee-deep in the water while she massaged his lame leg carefully. She found the wet silt around the water-hole perfect for applying as a poultice, and Finan was obviously improving under her careful attention.

Nelwyn knew that Gaelen's touch with lame animals bordered on the miraculous, but neither she nor Gaelen could say whether Finan would ever be sound again. It didn't matter. Sound or not, Finan was one of the Company now.

Gaelen made sure to spend time with Siva, and she asked Rogond if she should scout the way back and try to find the Ravani Road again. "It cannot be too far behind us. If I take plenty of water for myself and Siva, I will surely encounter it in a day or two. We will then know how far we must travel to return to our course. What say you?"

"I say we should not separate in these hostile lands," said Rogond, packing up his gear. "I would advise that we not break the Company apart. If you encounter trouble there will be no one to aid you, and we will wait in vain for your return. Better we should all go back together." Even as he spoke, he wondered how difficult it would be to find the road again. How had they been waylaid in the first place?

He had thought he was paying careful attention, and remembered no diversion. He sighed. "It may be farther than you think, Gaelen. Let's speak no more of it."

Gaelen turned from Rogond, her attention drawn to Finan. He stood alone at the south end of the water-hole with his head erect, ears pricked forward as though listening intently to something. He gave a low chortle and took a step forward, his body quivering.

Just then Galador, who was keeping the watch, called down to them. "There is something in the distance, Rogond. It appears to be a caravan…I counted many animals and men among them. Come up and have a look."

Rogond did so, thankful for Thorndil's glass. His friend had given it ere the Company departed Dûn Bennas. *Take it, so that I may have yet another reason to find you and retrieve it one day. You will have greater need of it than I.* Rogond smiled as he thought of Thorndil, hoping that he was well. He raised the glass and focused it on the tiny dark specks that had appeared to the south. It was somewhat humbling to be in the presence of sharp-eyed Galador.

Gaelen stood beside him, shading her eyes with her hand. "You may have seen them, Galador," she said, "but Finan heard them first. I would imagine no one thinks me foolish for wanting him now!"

As the caravan drew nearer, it became clear that they were heading for the canyon where the Company was now sheltering. Rogond looked hard at the strangers through the glass and saw nothing threatening; they seemed relaxed and in good spirits, the harness-bells of their beasts announcing their approach. He could hear the men singing, the one in the back keeping time by clapping his hands.

As the only man among the Company, Rogond was elected to greet the caravan. He stood tall upon a rock with his right hand raised in a gesture of welcome. The man in the front of the caravan raised his right arm in return, and called out to Rogond in a strange tongue.

"Hail, worthy travelers," replied Rogond. "May your journey be without hardship, and increase your wealth. My name is Rogond. I come from the far northern lands, and I do not understand your speech, yet I see that you are not an enemy. My comrades and I welcome you to the water, and we hope to gain enlightenment from you."

The man halted his dromadan, bidding it to kneel so that he

could dismount. There were twenty of them in the caravan, nine of which were ridden, the rest laden with various goods. Their harness was colorful, clean, and in good repair.

The leader smiled, showing brown-stained teeth, and returned Rogond's bow. Then he spoke in heavily accented Aridani. "Hail, man of the northlands. May you find sweet water whenever you thirst. How many are you, and what brings you to our beautiful desert?"

"We are but six, and we have come searching for one of our family who is lost," Rogond replied. "We have been waylaid from the Ravani Road, and were hoping you could redirect us and set our feet back upon the right path."

At this the man laughed. "Ah! Well, it is easy to understand how that could happen, after all, the Ravani Road is only the most well-traveled in all these lands, and is wider than a brace of dromadin. And how, my friend, did you lose the road?"

"I honestly do not know," Rogond replied, smiling with good-natured humility. "Somehow we found ourselves lost and without water, until we discovered this place. It's well that we did, for we would no doubt have kept to the lesser road, and our journey would have ended badly."

"Indeed," said the man, "but you did find the water, which proves that you have some ability in our hard but wonderful land. Ah…but my manners are lacking! Forgive me. I am known as Hamir, son of Hamidir." He bowed again, dropping his hood back to reveal a white silken head-wrap beneath it. Rogond returned the bow, taking notice of the other eight men, who had dismounted and turned the beasts loose so that they could make their way down to the water-hole.

"We shall speak at length when we are fed and rested," said Hamir. "This is a fine place to spend time, so long as no enemies approach. But, where are your companions?"

"They have been instructed to remain in hiding until I call them," said Rogond. "We were not certain of your intentions, and I fear you may yet find them somewhat, ahh…somewhat different from the folk you normally encounter here. I assure you that they will harm none of you so long as your intentions are honorable."

Hamir laughed again and clapped Rogond on the shoulder. "As if encountering a lone northman isn't strange enough! We shall look forward to some fine stories tonight. My companions are of my family—five are my sons, two are my brothers, and one is the son of my sister. We shall make merry and have a fine feast with our new friends, and you shall tell us of your people and your lands. When all are rested, we will lead you back to the Ravani Road."

After Hamir and his fellows watered their beasts and made camp, Rogond asked if he might summon the rest of the Company. Hamir called his kinsmen together. They were travel-worn, but they were reasonably clean and courteous, inclining their heads to Rogond as he bowed before them. They sat cross-legged upon small mats of felted dromadan wool.

"Please, my new friends, give welcome to our Company," said Rogond, summoning the Elves and Fima to stand at his side.

"What strange folk are these?" they asked, looking especially upon the She-elves and Fima. The Elves all wore their hoods, concealing their elegant ears, but the light in their eyes and in their faces could not be hidden. Fima, with his very short, stout frame and long, white beard, was likewise strange to them, but they were quickly put at ease by his open, good-humored expression. Fima knew a friend when he saw one.

The Elves, on the other hand, inspired awe rather than fellowship. They seemed distant and unapproachable to Hamir and his kin, who had not beheld the light of an Elven face before. Dona stood as ever beside Galador, clutching his arm, her face mostly hidden by her hooded cloak. She would not look at the men, which was just as well; they would no doubt have frightened her. There was no light in her face, and the men dismissed her, for she did not inspire the same awe.

As Rogond made introductions, Gaelen and Nelwyn stood with their chins lifted, weapons slung at their backs and their belts, their bright eyes looking directly into those of the sutherlings, to whom they seemed proud and immodest. Neither Gaelen's bare arms and shoulders nor her short mop of windblown hair would have been tolerated among females of Hamir's tribe. Their women went about their daily lives covered from head to foot, and their hair was never cut, as it was a gift from heaven and the mark of their womanhood. A woman's husband was the only one allowed to touch it, apart from the other women of her immediate family. The men shook their heads—they were not quite sure what to make of Gaelen and Nelwyn.

"I see that you travel with women-folk, Northman…at least, I *think* the little one is a woman," said the elder of Hamir's two brothers. "You must have great patience as well as boldness. At least it explains how you lost your way. Women-folk are forever talking, and they must have distracted you." The men all laughed at this; apparently females in these lands were not so independent as in the Greatwood Realm. Their scorn toward Gaelen was obvious.

She flushed, staring hard at the one who had spoken. Fima muttered under his breath, still smiling. "Take no offense, little Wood-elf. They have different ways from your own, and I'm sure he meant nothing by it."

Gaelen did not smile back. *Different and strange ways indeed, for in the Greatwood we do not insult strangers, especially when they are bristling with weapons, no matter their gender.*

She flexed the fingers of her right hand, suppressing the urge to send a shaft into the sand a hair's breadth from the man's naked toes. She would not suffer scorn when she had done nothing to earn it. Hamir seemed a friendly, helpful man, at least on first meeting, but she was not so sure about the others.

They talked among themselves, looking sidelong at her, occasionally chuckling and shaking their heads in evident disdain. Though she did not comprehend any of their speech, Gaelen took their meaning. She responded by smiling and bowing, speaking the Sylvan tongue, which she knew they would not understand.

"You are made uncomfortable, and so you disparage me because I am different. Your discomfort is understandable, for right now I would so enjoy removing those smiles from your faces by demonstrating how the past thousand years have improved my skills at archery."

Nelwyn moved to stand beside her, for she had likewise felt discomfited. "I would join you in that demonstration. I expect we could change their expressions very quickly in a few seconds. Alas that we cannot." She sighed and shook her head, then settled down beside Galador.

One of the younger men approached Gaelen and offered her one of the brown woolen mats, inviting her to sit. She looked around, noting the rest of the Company already sitting cross-legged as the sutherlings did.

Rogond rose and stood beside her, entreating her with his eyes, placing a gentle hand upon her shoulder and whispering in her ear. "Sit beside me my love, who is at least my equal in all things. Do not feel slighted; only remember that we are in their lands, and must learn their ways. They are what their land and their people have made them, even as you are. Sit beside me now, please, and be content."

Gaelen drew a deep breath. "Merchants and shopkeepers," she muttered. Then she sat beside Rogond and prepared to learn as much as she cared to of these strange people, with their strange ways.

6
The Voice of the Spider

Hamir and his folk proved to be generous and entertaining, especially once Rogond revealed the nature of his quest. Finding a lost brother was a thing they could well understand. They shared their food with the Company, who were by now in serious need of it, and promised to provision them for their journey southward. Hamir was going north and then west when he reached the Ravani Road, for he had spices and silks to trade.

"Are you making your way as far north as Dûn Bennas?" asked Rogond, who would convey a message to Thorndil.

"No, my friend, we will venture only as far as the lands near Castalan. There is a fine market there." Hamir considered for a moment. "Why did you not go there seeking your brother? There are some folk of good will who would carry back the news that you are searching for him...the only way you will have a hope of finding him is through such a web of words."

Rogond looked down at his feet, abashed. "The truth, Hamir, is that I did not know of such a marketplace. Nor do I know anything of these lands, or how to go about finding my brother. I am beginning to realize the folly of my quest, for I don't have the slightest notion of where to begin. I managed to lose my way even upon the Ravani Road, which, as you kindly pointed out, is the best traveled of all the thoroughfares through these lands." He sighed and shook his head. "I would not lead my friends into peril, but it seems I'm incapable of keeping them from it. I did not find the water; Gaelen's horse that was born of the desert did so."

Hamir shrugged. "At least you had the good sense to follow him. You seem a fairly bright fellow, and you will learn quickly. Yet I must caution you that your search will indeed be difficult. Folk in these lands seldom remain in one place, save for those in the permanent settlements, and those are nearly all along the coast. Your brother may indeed be there, but he will be a challenge to find, even so. Why did you ask if we were going to Dûn Bennas? Is there some message that you wish carried?"

"I left a comrade there; he was too ill to accompany us further," said Rogond. "I merely wanted to assure him that we are well, and I was hoping to gain news of his recovery, for he was none too hale when we left him."

"Why did you not wait until he was healed? Is your brother in some danger? Is that the reason for your urgency?" Hamir, as with many folk of the Ravi, rarely considered anything to be of great urgency. Haste and lack of foresight often resulted in death in these unforgiving lands.

Rogond flushed, realizing that Hamir was right. It probably would not have made any difference to wait until Thorndil had recovered, but Rogond had worried about Thorndil's age and ability to cope with this difficult journey. Once he had recovered, there would be no way to leave him in Dûn Bennas without hurting his pride, but this was not the only reason for Rogond's reluctance to remain longer in Dûn Bennas. He looked levelly at Hamir.

"I stood before the grave of my father, whom I have never met, and swore to him that I would find my brother, who is lost. I sense that he is not just lost to me—he is lost to himself, and if I do not find him soon, I will never be able to bring him back. Does that make any sense to you?"

Hamir looked away for a moment, as though lost in thought. This strong, tall man, so full of good-humored intelligence, had never known his father? Hamir had difficulty imagining it. "Yes, north-man, it does indeed. Far be it from me to disparage the actions of one acting on such a promise. Yet, I fear for you. You must acquire a guide as soon as you may."

Rogond smiled. "And where would you suggest I find such a desperate soul, who would guide six inept fools for little pay?"

Hamir placed a hand on Rogond's shoulder. "You may be inexperienced in the Ravi-shan, but you are not a fool. Still, it will not be easy to find a guide. We'll see what may be done…I will do what I can to aid you. The way to Castalan is long, but there is another settlement to the south of here where folk of many races gather for news and trade. It is called the Sandstone. You should probably head there if you don't want to spend months traveling to Castalan.

"My brother was said to be going south, to a place where no one would know his name," said Rogond.

"Ah. Then the Sandstone might suit him better than Castalan would, anyway. One more word of advice—you will soon learn that women-folk in these lands do not act in such ways as your proud She-elves. They need to be covered and taught to be silent, especially in the Sandstone. That may be the most daunting of all the tasks before you." He bowed before Rogond, then turned and went back to the water-hole, where his brothers and sons had prepared a fine meal for all to share.

The Company tried to gather as much familiarity with the ways of the desert-folk as they could in those few days with Hamir, and they learned many things of interest. For example, the sutherlings did not like or trust the anori-folk, and the anori-folk trusted no one, and the dark-skinned folk of the far southern coast were likewise not trusted by anyone, and so on.

Worse than Elves and dwarves, thought Gaelen as she sat listening to their tales. Since the Plague, temporary alliances had formed between certain tribes and families, but Hamir predicted these would most likely break down as the numbers of men swelled again. They would be fighting over territory in no time. The Ravi-shan was a colorful mosaic of Peoples, but there was little blending between them.

The Company also learned that the Elves would best be concealed from many of the Ravani-folk, particularly the sutherlings. Although their beauty and strangeness would inspire awe in some, they would be feared and even demonized by others. In some cultures, Elves were known only in legend, and were presumed to have never really existed. They were known as "Avinashi," the immortal ones. If certain groups among the sutherlings learned that such beings not only existed but walked among them, it would challenge their system of beliefs, engendering suspicion and fear. They might likely wish to re-establish the belief that Elves didn't exist by simply eliminating them. They would not be so open-minded as Hamir and his people, who were well-traveled merchants, and therefore better informed and more tolerant.

Hamir drew Rogond aside. "Conceal the nature of your Elven friends until you learn who you are dealing with," he said, looking pointedly at Gaelen and Nelwyn. "Be especially cautious of them. There are those among the Ravani who will despise them for simply daring to speak their minds in the presence of men, never mind that they openly carry weapons and go about uncovered. They must both be instructed well, especially the smaller one. She is not so wise as the other, and her temper is high. You must be firm with her, Rogond."

Rogond took Hamir's point, but he could not resist saying a few words in defense of Gaelen. "She is wiser than you know, and will learn quickly. She may not like it, but to preserve the Company she will do whatever is necessary…have no fear."

Hamir snorted. "She cannot alter her nature, Rogond. That is my only warning. Remember it."

Hamir's words troubled Rogond for the rest of the afternoon. Perhaps these southern lands were truly too dangerous for Gaelen to share with him. Perhaps he should convince her to return to Dûn Bennas, or even to go back north to the Great Forest with Nelwyn, and await him there. He did not have the slightest notion of how he would do that.

Later, as the sun set and the sky turned to sparkling indigo, Gaelen's clear voice rose in song as she stood on the rim of the canyon, looking northward. She sang a song Rogond had not yet heard, written in both Aridani and Sylvan Elvish. It had come forth from her very soul, reminding Rogond of the reason she had left the Greatwood in the first place:

I am of the Woodland, ruon-an daras a d'oro
My heart in the Greatwood ever abides,
The Light of Creation we never beheld,
But the light of the Forest lives ever in our eyes.

Oh, long have we roamed where the swift arrow flies,
Defending our home and singing to the night,
We are thought by many less fair and less wise,
Yet the hope of the woodland rests in our sight.

Away from the Forest my path takes me now,
The Shadow is growing, and yet I must fly,
And though my heart yearn I forsake Tal-aruinnas
The Greatwood shall not hear my last Battle-cry.

Ai, canta-ainye ruon-dara, canta-ainye éarran,
Canta-ainye samratha, samratha éna Tal-arruinas.
Ai, canta-ainye fomyhar, canta-ainye geamrath,
Canta-ainye magláin, magláin éna Tal-aruinnas.
Am-ailges mair sàite-ath
Chon gorgon-deian, chon gorgon-deian.

O, sing swiftly of autumn, sing swiftly of spring,
sing swiftly of summer, summer in the Greatwood
O sing swiftly of harvest, sing swiftly of winter,
Sing swiftly of awakening, awakening in Greatwood
For I shall not abide here again until the Dark Horror ends,
Until the Dark Horror ends.

Where this path will lead me I cannot yet say,
Though I know that in darkness is where it will end,
If by taking this path I will safeguard the Greatwood,
Only out of darkness will I see her again.

I am of the Woodland, ruon-an daras a d'oro,
My heart in the Greatwood ever abides,
The Light of Aontar we never beheld,
But the light of the Forest lives ever in our eyes.
The Light of Elysia we have not yet beheld,
But the light of the Forest lives ever in our eyes.

Rogond knew that she welcomed the search for Hallagond, for it would draw Gorgon away from the Elven-hold. Once they had found him, she would return to the task that still lay before her. She would not allow foolish pride or impulsiveness to threaten her survival, for if she did, she would never see to the death of Gorgon.

Hamir and his family had not yet heard the song of the Woodland, and they became still and silent as it filled their hearts with yearning for their own homelands. When the song ended and faded away, tears stood in the eyes of Hamir and at least three of his sons.

In the morning, Hamir approached Rogond as he made ready to set forth again. "You say that you have little pay to give your guide, my friend, yet the song I heard last night would be payment enough for me were I not bound to my present path. Her song will prove to be of great value, for none will have heard its like. She is a stubborn, difficult, beautiful treasure…guard her well."

It took several days to return to the Ravani Road, though the caravan moved with steady efficiency. The long-legged dromadin moved in a deliberate and stately manner, but the Company soon discovered that they could also move with speed if they wished, surpassing even the swiftest horse over short distances. In addition, they required less water than the horses, and were virtually tireless provided they were not overburdened.

The Company and Hamir's folk each took advantage of the opportunity to learn as much as possible from their new companions. They sought shelter during the heat of the day, resting and conversing quietly together. The men marveled at the tales of the Elves, and their respect and wonderment grew, especially when they learned of Galador's great age. They gained a better understanding of Gaelen and Nelwyn when they realized that, in Elven cultures, females could be hunters, even warriors, enjoying the same freedoms as males.

"It is indeed strange to us," they said, "That you would risk your women in warfare, and allow them an equal share in the management of your affairs. Yet we respect your ways, which you are free to follow in your own lands."

Hamir addressed Gaelen and Nelwyn, both of whom had warmed considerably toward him. "Here, my friends, you would be better served to conceal your fierce independence. Keep it in your heart, but do not wear it openly. I will give you gifts that will serve you well, if you will accept them." He drew forth well-made garments of fine black silk, carefully showing Gaelen and Nelwyn how they should be worn, and they were soon attired in the manner of women of the southlands. "Now at least you will attract less attention," he said, looking upon them with satisfaction.

Gaelen did not care for this attire, as it restricted her movements and limited access to her weapons. Though the silk was fine and would be both warm and cool to wear, she felt as though she had been wrapped in a black shroud. She looked over at Nelwyn, whose expression told of similar mind. Yet they could both see the sense of it, and the need for it.

Hamir patted Gaelen's shoulder. "Wear them when you are among the Ravani. When you are traveling, you may do as you please. I suspect you will learn even to fight while wearing them if need be."

"Why are they *black*?" asked Nelwyn. "Black is the warmest color…and the men are dressed in white."

Hamir crafted his response carefully, for in this case the truth would not do at all. Women wore black because they were thought to be unclean. At last he simply said, "You ask too many questions."

"I shall be dead very quickly if I try to fight in this bolt of loose cloth," Nelwyn grumbled. "If I tried to draw my bow, I would become so entangled that I would fall to the ground in a heap."

"You had best not be carrying your bow among the Ravani, Nelwyn," said Gaelen with a wry look. She turned to Hamir. "Am I correct, O Teacher of Difficult Desert Ways?"

Hamir smiled at her. "You are correct. It's better that you limit yourselves to weapons carried in concealment."

"Ah! You mean weapons like these?" Gaelen leaped suddenly into the air and drew both of her long knives from beneath the silken wrap, casting them with unerring precision into one of the strange, tall plants that grew in that part of the desert. Festooned with spines that were like daggers themselves, they stood as tall as Fima; some even as tall as Gaelen. They bore no branches or leaves, just a plump stem covered with wicked barbs.

Hamir laughed, as did his youngest son Lamas, who admired Gaelen and had become fond of her. "Look here, and see what you have discovered," he said amiably, withdrawing her knives from the strange plant. "You can get water from these. Come and see!"

Gaelen did so, and once she worked her slender fingers around the fierce thorns she felt the moisture around the wound. "Cut off a bit of the flesh, like this," instructed Lamas, handing her one of the knives, while he demonstrated with the other. He took a section and squeezed the sweet juices into his mouth, then smiled with satisfaction. "Ahhh! The desert provides well for those who know her secrets."

Gaelen and Nelwyn followed his example. The wonderful, slightly sticky juices would nourish them as well as cure their thirst. "Don't count on finding many of these, for they are uncommon," said Lamas. "You will need to leave the road to find them, for those that grew near the main thoroughfares were taken long ago. Oh, yes, and I should probably mention that some varieties will make you quite ill if you consume them. If I see any, I will point them out."

"That makes me feel so much better," muttered Nelwyn. "Why does there always need to be an 'oh, yes, and I should probably mention…'"

Gaelen chuckled at her. "Stop complaining and pay attention, for we all rely on you to advise us with respect to herb-lore. It will be up to you to know the good from the bad."

She turned to Hamir. "We thank you for your gifts, but I would repay you. How may I serve?"

"You may sing again for us tonight. My sons will teach you a song of our land—Lamas is a fine singer, aren't you, my son?"

Lamas blushed and dropped his eyes. "I am unworthy to sing in the presence of the Elves, father. You know it. Please do not ask it of me."

Gaelen tried to reassure him. "It would please me greatly if you would sing for us, Lamas. I have heard the songs of men, and delighted in them. Your voices are fair, though different from ours. I thoroughly enjoyed listening to the warriors of Dûn Bennas as they performed their battle-chants while practicing in formation. I must insist that you sing for us, as I would not be deprived of hearing you. Until tonight, then?"

She turned and made her way back to find Rogond, intending to show him her new raiment. Lamas looked after her, his expression indicating that he would rather trip and fall on his own blade than sing in front of her, for it would probably be less humiliating.

When they finally gained the Ravani road, it was easy to understand how the Company had lost its way. The main thoroughfare had been blocked by boulders and debris, around and over which sand and loose gravel had drifted. The marking-stones had been moved, no doubt with the intention of diverting travelers onto the lesser road. This appeared to have been in place for at least a year, and Hamir shook his head. "We have not traveled this way in the recent past; someone has taken great pains to obscure the way. This trap was well laid; a stranger would not notice anything amiss, especially by dark of night. Bandits will sometimes use such deception to waylay travelers by turning them onto a less-traveled road. The bandits could then lie in wait…recall the point at which we passed between those rocky cliffs? If I were a wagering man, I would expect to find evidence of bandits there. They could remain concealed, and there was water within a days' ride. Apparently the road didn't provide enough victims, as we are still alive and were not attacked."

Rogond was chagrined at having missed the deception. The Company had come upon it in the dark, and turned neatly onto the lesser path exactly as intended. "I was taken as easily as a lamb to the slaughter," he said quietly. "It was fortunate that the bandits had given up their game, otherwise we would have been slain. I have not exactly distinguished myself as leader of our Company."

Hamir nodded. "You are not prepared to lead them in these lands. I say once more—you need a guide. My folk will remain with you until tomorrow, but then we must continue on to the west. We do not begrudge you the provisions we have given, but it means we must reach the marketplace all the sooner. Otherwise, I would see you farther south."

He looked to the east, and the rising sun. "My youngest son, Lamas, has asked if he might go with you as guide," he said, "but I have forbidden him. He is not as adept in the deep desert as you will require, and he is barely into his young manhood. He has not yet taken a wife." He shook his head. "I'm certain you've noticed his attentions to your Elven friends, particularly Gaelen. He is enamored of her, I believe. And she did not make things any easier when they sang together under the stars. I must separate him from her, and quickly, otherwise he may earn your wrath!" Hamir smiled as he said this, for he knew that Lamas was no threat to Rogond.

Rogond understood Lamas' feelings quite well—it was Gaelen's song that had doomed him to love her. "Indeed, you must separate him from her, lest his heart be broken. She and Nelwyn are very special, and it's small wonder he admires them. Yet their hearts have been given, and his hopes are in vain."

Hamir snorted. "As if anyone of my household would consider either of them as fit and proper wives for my son! I would have to disown him if he brought Gaelen into our tents. Such a proud, vain creature would be unthinkable. Make no mistake, my tall friend—I admire your companions and have enjoyed their company, but I would never consider either of them as suitable life-mates for a gentle soul such as Lamas. Why, they would be running his affairs in no time! Thank you, but I prefer my own wives, who exist to love and serve me and my children. Perhaps they are not as exotic, but neither are they of such high temperament. Keep your Gaelen, worthy northman."

Rogond smiled back at him, though there was a slight edge to his voice as he spoke. "That I will, Hamir, until my last breath leaves me."

"Fair enough. Let's prepare to go 'round and set your feet once more upon the right road. You have a long journey ahead." He clapped Rogond on the shoulder before going forth to gather the caravan.

As Rogond prepared the Company for departure, he reflected on Hamir's words. He watched his beloved Gaelen stroking Siva, speaking to her in a gentle voice, before swinging gracefully astride. She turned the mare to the south, the hot, dry wind fanning her hair back from her face, bright eyes looking out to the horizon, as Nelwyn rode up beside her. They stood together—two beautiful, spirited, and thoroughly dangerous creatures—and he and his good friend Galador owned their hearts.

"I'm sorry, Hamir," he muttered, "but you truly do not know what you're missing."

They first heard the wailing cries drifting on the wind when they passed the barrier and found the Ravani Road once again. It was a sound of abandonment and despair, of a lost soul in fear of death, and it had a chilling effect on all in hearing.

Dona, in particular, was dismayed; she was no stranger to such cries of desperation. She wept and clung to Galador, her wide eyes glazed with terror. "Do not go there, Galdor! It is a place of torment…*do not go there.* They will take you, and hold you in darkness, and there will be no one to aid you. I could not bear it; I will die before I let them take me again. Do not go there!"

Hamir's folk regarded Dona with a mixture of pity and curiosity, and they had given her a wide berth. They did not know quite what to make of her.

Galador shook his head. "She has been like this, or worse, since she was thrust upon our Company," he said. "She is in need of healing, but I don't know what healing we can provide. At any rate, I had best stay here with her while some of you investigate the source of that wailing. She may become unbalanced, and she can be dangerous at such times." He turned back to Dona. "Hush, little one…I will protect you and keep you from torment. Do not fear."

She did not stop weeping, though her eyes grew calmer and lost some of the panic behind them. Galador wondered what had befallen this poor creature, once a proud maiden of immortal race, to turn her onto such a course of madness and despair. He embraced her, genuinely overcome in that moment with the desire to make her whole again. She closed her eyes, and he sang to her so that she would not hear the pained, helpless cries upon the wind.

Nelwyn and Gaelen looked into the distant south, along the side of the road, and soon located the source of the wailing. "There is…a man. Actually, it is only the head of a man…but he is alive. He appears to have been buried up to his neck. He is making the sound, though he grows weaker by the moment," said Gaelen.

"He must have heard the bells on Hamir's harness, and is hoping for rescue. We must go quickly if we would aid him," said Nelwyn.

Hamir's eyes narrowed. "We must be cautious; someone left him there to be found. Most likely he is a villain, and this is his punishment. Perhaps harsh, but probably deserved. On the other hand, he may have been set there to lure the unwary. We must be cautious."

"But there is no cover, father," put in Lamas. "Where could enemies be hiding? There is no place of concealment. I agree with the Elves…we should be quick!"

Hamir cast a withering glance at his son, who flushed and looked submissively down at his feet. "Well, since my youngest son agrees with the Elves, then most certainly we should do as they suggest," he said, with obvious sarcasm. He turned to Rogond. "You see why I would not allow him to go with you? He would certainly not make a suitable guide, as he forgets all I have taught him, seeking instead to impress you and your friends."

Lamas appeared to want to sink into the ground, as his elder brother Hamad laughed ill-naturedly under his breath.

Gaelen tossed her hair from her eyes. "Fine, Hamir. I will take the risk, and approach this man, for I agree with Lamas—there is no place of concealment. I believe your first instinct is correct, and he has been left as an example, not as bait." Without waiting for permission, she mounted her horse, and she and Nelwyn rode toward the dark speck in the distance.

Rogond looked at Hamir and shrugged. Then he mounted Eros and followed them. Lamas made as though to pursue Rogond, but Hamir shook his head, making a clucking sound with his tongue. Then he and his sons sat quietly down, and waited.

Gaelen and Nelwyn had dismounted, carefully approaching the man. He was in a bad way, having been buried up to his neck in the sand for a day and a half with no shade or water. His head was uncovered, his skin blistered from the unrelenting sun. His red-rimmed eyes peered through a filthy mask of sweat and grime. He stared at Gaelen and Nelwyn as they approached, not knowing whether they were real or merely products of his fevered imagination. His gaze was drawn especially to Nelwyn, whose golden hair and green eyes seemed to have come straight from a beautiful dream. He had seen an engraving of a creature very like her in one of the sacred books once—yes, he was dreaming, and soon he would be dead. The ravens had already begun to gather.

"Are you a spirit sent to conduct me to the Eternal Realm?" he asked Nelwyn in a croaking voice. She did not understand his speech, which was of his own tribe.

Gaelen then spoke to Nelwyn in the Elven-tongue: "He is near death. We must give him water, and free him, for the weight of the sand must make it nearly impossible to breathe."

To the dying man's ears, the speech of Elves was lilting and beautiful, especially when spoken in Gaelen's voice. Here, surely, were the minions of heaven, sent to deliver him. *I had never dreamed I would go to paradise...*

Gaelen knelt beside him, offering him a swallow of water from her water-skin. He sucked greedily at it, but she pulled it away. "Not all at once," she admonished him in the common-tongue. "I'm told giving too much water to a man dying of thirst will sicken him. This you can ill afford. Have patience." She offered the water-skin again, but this time he grabbed the small end between his teeth, and before she could stay him he had taken several great gulps. His eyes rolled back into his head, and the color drained from his face, just before he brought up most of the water onto the sand in front of him. He moaned miserably and his head lolled over.

"We had best begin the task of trying to free him," said Nelwyn, obviously alarmed. "Otherwise he will die very soon." She looked over at Gaelen, who simply stood staring at the man, her nose wrinkled in distaste. "I know he is foul, but we cannot leave him to die. Someone has done this to him...for what reason I can't imagine. He must have made some very cruel enemies. Help me, now!"

Rogond had come up from behind and now stood with them, taking note of the wet sand in front of the man's mouth. "Gaelen... you know better than to give too much water to a man dying of thirst. You've made him ill, plus wasted the water. We must revive him in the hope that he will be able to take more...slowly this time."

"I did not intend for him to take so much, but somehow he managed it," Gaelen replied. "What's done is done. Do we dig him out, or do we revive him with water? I leave his fate to you, who are so knowledgeable. Command me as you will."

Rogond nodded in recognition of her sarcasm. "Very well, then make yourself useful. Ride back and tell Hamir what we have found, and ask him what should be done. Nelwyn and I will work to free him, but it will take time, for he is buried deep. Quickly, now!"

Gaelen bowed, mounted Siva, and galloped back to meet Hamir, who had become curious and was already approaching with Hamad and Lamas. When she described the man, Hamir became concerned.

"Do not dig him out yet; wait until I have examined and questioned him. It's likely that he is a villain, and that this is a doom appointed as punishment for some vile deed. If so, then I'll know it. Ride back, and stay your friends from their labor."

Rogond and Nelwyn had succeeded in uncovering the man's neck and the top of his shoulders by the time Hamir approached. He stooped beside the man, pulling aside long, stringy hair to reveal an oddly-shaped burn mark on the side of his neck. Then his face hardened as he rose to his feet and nodded, his arms folded in front of him. "This man has been branded as a thief and a brigand," he said. "He must have stolen from the wrong person. I'll warrant his villainy is responsible for at least one death, or he would not have merited such severe punishment. Leave him for the ravens! We should not interfere."

Rogond considered Hamir's words. "He may be a thief, but he is also a man. We cannot leave him here to die. He is already in agony, and things will get worse before the end. In my world we do not leave even our enemies to suffer, we kill them quickly. Thieves are certainly not dealt with so harshly…we must release him."

Hamir shook his head. "In doing so you will earn the wrath of whoever placed him here, and you will then be held responsible for his future misdeeds. Better to kill him quickly, if you would aid him. Even so, you will not gain the favor of those who deemed this fate appropriate for him. Best that you walk away."

Rogond looked at Hamir as though seeing him for the first time. "You surprise me, my friend. I had not thought you capable of abandoning a soul in need…luckily you did not do so to us."

"You are not criminals under the hand of justice. In our lands we do not interfere, for there are so many different people with different ways and laws that we simply cannot. The peace between us can only be kept if we allow others to mete out justice as they see fit."

Rogond considered, taking Hamir's point. "Let's question him, at least," he said, turning to Nelwyn. "Have you had any luck in reviving him?"

"Indeed," answered Nelwyn, "he is stirring even now, but I am uncertain of his strength. If you want to question him, we should probably free him first."

Nelwyn could not help but feel pity for the helpless man. He moaned in pain and misery, opening his dark brown eyes to gaze at her with desperate hope. She offered him the water-skin again, and he took a few slow, deliberate swallows of water, having learned from his earlier experience. His eyes were reasonably clear as Hamir knelt upon the sand in front of him.

"What is the reason that you are tormented, thief? Speak, if you would convince us to free you. What was your crime that warranted such a harsh sentence?"

The man immediately began to weep, his red-rimmed eyes gazing up at Nelwyn. Gaelen brought forth a spare cloak, draping it over the man's head so that it blocked the sun. He muttered words of gratitude, still weeping, but could not look into her bright eyes. From that moment, Gaelen mistrusted him.

"I am here by ill fate, for I have done nothing to warrant such a terrible death," he said.

Hamir scowled at him. "Oh, and I suppose that brand upon your neck simply appeared by mischance? Do not lie to us, or we will simply leave you to your judgment. I ask you again, what was your crime?"

The man seemed not to hear, and began to babble aimlessly, as though nearly hysterical. "What sort of crazed behavior is this?" said Hamir. "The heat and lack of water have deranged his mind."

Gaelen watched the man's eyes. He was far more aware than he would have them know, for though he appeared confused and addle-brained, she saw his sly eyes narrow and his expression change to suit the moment. She knelt before him and, as he continued babbling, slapped him hard across the face. "Save it," she spat. "You had best start providing us with truthful answers. Your false derangement isn't fooling anyone. Speak, and the truth this time. I grow weary of you already."

The man's eyes narrowed again, and he shot a vicious look at Gaelen, who had made a lifelong enemy in that moment. Then his expression changed as he began weeping and pleading for his life once more. "Please, fortunate ones, release me that I may tell my sad story. If you have any compassion at all, give me freedom and shade and water, and a few moments of peace. Then, if my tale does not convince you, please kill me quickly. I am too weak to try to escape or do harm to anyone. May the Almighty shrivel my tongue forever if I speak falsely! Please, my friends, help a soul in need. In return, I promise to serve you until the end of my days."

A thought struck Rogond, and he addressed the weeping man. "Do you know these lands, and know them well?"

The hair on the back of Gaelen's neck stood straight up—she knew what Rogond was thinking. "No…beloved, this is a snake," she whispered. "You cannot trust him! I have seen it in his eyes."

The man stopped weeping, and as he looked upon the pale-skinned, grey-eyed Ranger, he knew the truth. *He is not of the Ravani…he needs a guide! My fortunes are changing—I can feel it in the wind.* "Yes, Blessed Rescuer, I do. I was born and raised in the Sutherlands, and have wandered them all of my life. Why do you ask? Is there some way I may serve?"

His face twisted into a fawning expression that filled Rogond with disgust. He did not trust this man any more than his companions did, but the Company needed a guide. This man had promised to serve them. At least he could aid them for a time, until they found someone more trustworthy.

"Let's release him, and hear his tale."

They dug the man from the sand with difficulty, and discovered the secret to his survival. He should have suffocated from the weight of so much sand compressing his chest, but he had been fitted with a wine cask placed over his torso and bound arms, such that he could still breathe. Apparently, whoever had done this wanted him to remain alive and suffering.

The man muttered his thanks over and over as they cut his bonds and gave him fresh clothing to wear. He was given food and drink, and allowed to rest under a silken shade until he was strong enough to speak. He would give his name only as "Sajid," and would tell nothing of his family history, for he claimed not to know it. He did have a sad story to tell—of poverty and desperation.

"I admit to being a thief, but I stole only enough to survive. Any of you would have done the same when faced with the poor choices

I was given. I am now so thankful for my life that I would serve you unconditionally, until my death. Please allow me to aid you in whatever small way that I may. Allow me to earn an honest living, for as I lay near death I was shown the folly of my dishonest ways. The Almighty sent you to save me, that I might prove my worth."

"Indeed," said Hamir frostily. "We shall meet and decide your fate. In the meantime, do not move from this spot. If you do…"

"If you do, you will take one more breath before you fall," said Gaelen, who sat smiling coldly at him with her bow in her lap. She turned to Rogond. "We'll await your decision," she said. "He will not move from here, never fear." *You know what I think in the matter…*

The debate over what to do about Sajid lasted over an hour, and at the end of it they still had not decided. Nelwyn and Lamas were in favor of releasing him; Hamir and Hamas were far less generous. Galador was not inclined to trust any thief of the Ravi, and Fima couldn't make up his mind. It would fall to Rogond, as leader of the Company, to decide the fate of the wretch.

"I will not interfere," said Hamir, "and your point is well taken… he probably could guide you, until he stabbed you in the dark, perhaps."

"I'm weary of this," said Rogond. "We will watch him tonight, and decide tomorrow. But I would ask this question of you all: if the decision is to take his life, which of you will have the soul to kill him as he stands helpless before you? Think on that…and sleep well."

They did think on it. Not even Gaelen had such a cold heart, despite the ominous feeling that the Company had just invited a deadly spider among them, and Sajid was spared. Hamir and his family departed for the far coastal markets with some reluctance, having left their new friends in the care of a guide who, while better than nothing, could easily prove treacherous rather than true.

The Company made their way ever southward, their progress steady and sure, for Sajid knew where water and food could be found, as well as what was safe to eat and what was not. He also made it known that he spoke several of the common languages of the Ravani, even a bit of the Anori-speech, which was both odd and difficult.

"Surely it could not be as difficult as Rûmhul," said Gaelen, who had tried to learn the complex dwarvish tongue with limited success.

Fima chuckled. "I'm not so certain of that, Gaelen...I have tried my hand at the eastern tongues, and they are quite a challenge. It will be interesting to see if you find them so, as they are almost sung rather than spoken."

Gaelen was fascinated. "Will you speak some of it for me, so that I may hear?" she asked Sajid. He obliged her, a false smile on his face, eliciting an astonishing reaction from Fima. He drew his axe almost without thinking and placed it at the frightened man's throat.

"I understand enough of that speech to know what was being said," he growled. "He who insults my friends insults me. You will now apologize to her at once!"

Sajid stammered an apology, saying that he meant nothing by his words. "I chose that phrase just because it is very musical, and for no other reason."

Fima was not convinced. "It seems more likely that you wanted recompense for the humiliation you suffered when she slapped your face. I know all about it! You'd best put your ill feelings toward Gaelen behind you…you wouldn't want to make an enemy of me."

Sajid was suitably intimidated, but that didn't prevent him from glaring at Fima's back. If he had possessed a dagger and a bit more nerve, the dwarf might have been in peril.

"What did he say?" asked Gaelen, drawing Fima aside.

"It's not a phrase that is normally applied to one such as you," Fima growled. "In fact, it's not a phrase that civilized folk would hear at all. I will say no more."

Fima left Gaelen to wonder what had been said of her by this strange little man, in whose hands the fate of the Company now rested, as they regarded one another with barely concealed contempt.

"You're making it ever more difficult to prove your worth," said Gaelen in a chilly voice, whereupon Sajid simply smiled one of his falsely ingratiating smiles.

"You are proud, and ignorant. My chance will come soon enough, and then you will understand the nature of my worth. Your lives will depend on me one day, and then may I have the grace to forgive your insolence."

"May you, indeed," said Gaelen smiling back at him. "And may I have the patience to wait until the day after to place a shaft between your worthless ribs. Do we have an understanding?"

Sajid nodded as Gaelen stared hard at him. As before, he could not endure her gaze, dropping his eyes before retreating to his own affairs.

Rogond had observed that all was not well within the Company, and he was becoming concerned at the ever-growing tension. There was some enmity between Sajid and nearly everyone else; only Nelwyn seemed not to mind him. Rogond admired her for it. *She always tries to see the best in everyone. The rest of us are quite the suspicious bunch. I'm sure it can't be easy for our oily little guide...perhaps I should try to be more like Nelwyn and give him the benefit of the doubt. After all, he did suffer mightily for his crimes. Perhaps he has turned a new leaf. He has done nothing to harm us...so far.*

Sajid had responded to Nelwyn's gentle, friendly nature by spending quite a lot of his time with her, teaching her desert ways, imparting some of the sutherling tongue to her, and asking her to tell him of her world. When he really worked at it, he could be almost charming. This worried Rogond, as Galador positively bristled at such times. *Since the advent of Dona, he has spent virtually no time alone with Nelwyn. This can't be a good thing for either of them.*

Indeed, Nelwyn's resentment of Dona grew by the day. Sajid was friendly enough, and Nelwyn tolerated him, even enjoying his company at times, but he was absolutely no substitute for Galador. Gaelen still resented Dona for, among other things, making Nelwyn unhappy. Besides, she was sincerely tired of Dona's incessant crying.

Dona, who, unlike Nelwyn, distrusted everyone except Galador, would not suffer Sajid to be anywhere near her. At least she and Gaelen agreed on something.

"She is mad, that one," said Sajid. "Her soul is filled with demons, and they pursue her day and night. She will bring nothing but trouble among you."

Gaelen bristled at him. "You would know all about afflictions of the soul, though I expect yours is so small and shriveled that demons would not even bother to torment you. I will not suffer scorn of any Elf from your lips. Take heed, and be silent."

Sajid favored her with an ill-natured look, then dropped back beside Rogond. "I sense you are a man of valor and worth, so how is it that you allow your women to speak thus to their betters? Were she in my tent, she would know her place and learn proper manners!"

"Ah! Well, you are welcome to teach them to her," said Rogond. "Shall I call her over so that you may begin your instructions?" Sajid did not reply to this, but was quiet for a moment. Then, to Rogond's surprise, he laughed.

A few days later, the tension that had been building between Dona and Nelwyn finally erupted. Dona had fallen asleep, for she was weary; the demons that afflicted her heart would not allow her to gain strength, and she would never be strong until they were vanquished. Galador had taken advantage of the opportunity to spend time with Nelwyn, holding her at last, embracing fiercely in the shade of the rocks among which they were sheltering. There was water here, and all could drink their fill. The ground was stony rather than sandy, and the going was less tiring. Nelwyn had never been so glad of an embrace, and she loved Galador in the cool darkness of their sanctuary.

Gaelen was attending to Finan when she first heard Dona's cries, followed by Nelwyn's. Rushing to defend her cousin, Gaelen found her locked in hand-to-hand combat with poor, mad Dona, as Galador tried in vain to come between them.

Dona had awakened, and been dismayed to find Galador gone from her side—her eyes searched frantically for him to no avail. Then she heard Sajid's silky, menacing voice from behind the tall stone at her back.

"Your beloved has gone to lie with another," he said. "Surely you have seen the way he looks at the golden-haired one; her beauty is so much greater than your own. You have lost him to her. Search for him...I know that you will find him with her. Always she has tried to steal him from you." Dona nodded, eyes bright with tears. She didn't trust Sajid, but she knew he was speaking the truth this time.

"Go now, little flower, and reclaim your own. You must not harm the golden-haired one, for if you do, your beloved will resent you for it. But you must teach her to stay away from him…can you do that?"

Dona nodded again, her terrified eyes resolute. Then she rose and went in search of Galador, only to find him locked in loving embrace with Nelwyn.

"You will not take my beloved from me!" she cried, attempting to pull Nelwyn away. Nelwyn's suppressed anger and frustration overcame her gentle nature, and the two of them were now fighting fiercely, each desperately trying to reclaim her own.

When Gaelen appeared, Galador shouted to her: "Gaelen, take hold of Dona—I will handle Nelwyn! Be quick, before they truly hurt each other!"

Gaelen leaped into the fray, wrestling Dona away from Nelwyn with some effort. Dona's madness had made her strong, and she fought like a cornered animal. Gaelen was hard put to defend herself, for she was constrained not to hurt Dona, whereas Dona had no such compunction.

They strove for several minutes as Galador held onto Nelwyn. Then, just as it seemed the struggle would end, a blade suddenly appeared in Dona's hand. She swiped at Gaelen as the smaller Elf drew back in alarm. The blade sliced through the skin and into the muscle of her left arm, and she cried out in pain and surprise.

This changed everything, and the terms of the battle were now far more serious. Gaelen grabbed Dona's wrist and twisted hard, disarming her. She picked up the blade and tossed it away as Dona wept, for she was now too weak to prevail, and she knew it. Gaelen drew herself up, raising her right arm to strike her adversary, fury in her eyes.

Then, to the astonishment of Galador and Nelwyn, Gaelen's expression changed. She lowered her arm, and the fury drained from her face to be replaced by an expression of incredulity. She was staring at Dona's neck, normally hidden by her tunic and her hair. She released her grip on Dona's arm as her fingers searched, pushing back Dona's hair to expose an oddly-shaped purplish mark. Dona had surrendered, for her strength was gone, drained by the ferocity of her emotions.

Gaelen's anger fled, her discovery filling her heart with grief and remorse tinged with horror. She knew that mark, even as she had once known the one who bore it. Dona was an Elf of the Greatwood. Both Gaelen and Nelwyn had called her "friend."

Elraen? Is it really you? We thought you lost, we searched for you to no avail. "Elraen…it's Gaelen! Do you not know me?" Dona stopped crying, and her eyes grew wide. Gaelen tried again.

"Elraen…your name is Elraen. You are the daughter of Elandor and Elraeth. You had a brother, Alroth, who was slain. You are of the Greatwood Realm, where Ri-Aruin is King. Elraen…come back to us! Draw back this dark curtain, and return to the Greatwood. Oh…Elraen, my friend!"

Tears of pity and remorse stood in Gaelen's eyes. Galador released Nelwyn, who had gone to sit beside her. Rogond and Fima had heard the commotion, and were now witness to an incredible transformation. Dona, once known as Elraen, had not heard her name spoken in untold years. It was as though she had forgotten that she once had a life—a happy life, with friends and kin, and her beloved Galdor.

Gaelen and Nelwyn looked at each other, their faces full of pain. This mad She-elf, whom they had regarded as a burdensome nuisance, had once dwelled in the Greatwood. Were it not for the birthmark upon her neck they would never have recognized her, for she no longer resembled the Elraen they had known, she had looked almost like an old woman. It had not occurred to them that "Galdor" was not simply a mispronunciation of "Galador." Both Gaelen and Nelwyn had known Galdor, though not well, and it had been a long time indeed since they had thought of him.

Gaelen looked now upon her ruined friend, her eyes wide with sudden understanding.

"She has been to Tûr Dorcha," she stated softly, her voice full of dread. "The Shadow took her, even as it tried to take you, Nelwyn. Do you remember? You escaped that fate, but Elraen…" She reached out with a gentle hand, smoothing Elraen's hair as Nelwyn helped her to sit, speaking calming words. Elraen appeared to be a different person. Some of the years fell from her face, and a flicker of light kindled in her eyes.

"Yes, I'm Elraen…Elraen of the Greatwood." She looked around behind her to regard Galador sitting quietly, his face calm and gentle. "You…you are not Galdor! But I thought…I saw my beloved in your face! Where is he? Where is my love?" She looked over at Gaelen, and read the despair in her eyes. "Say not that he has been taken into darkness! I could not bear it…tell me the grief in your eyes is not for Galdor!"

"It is not for Galdor, but for you," said Gaelen, her soft voice breaking. She vaguely remembered Galdor, a fine strong Wood-elf who very much resembled Galador. He had died only a few years after the disappearance of Elraen. Everyone said that his grief made him unwary, and he fell to enemies as he wandered alone at night, singing of his pain at the loss of his love. They killed him with arrows, stripped him of his possessions, and left his body for the scavengers. His friends had found him, drawn to his sad remains by the harsh cries of ravens.

Elraen read the truth in Gaelen's eyes, wrapped her arms around her own shoulders, and began to wail.

Gaelen understood her pain, and she wept as she embraced her former friend, who was lost. Nelwyn wept also, for she had known Elraen and Galdor, though she had not thought of either of them in many a year. Galador was now at her side, offering comfort.

Elraen cried until she was spent, as Gaelen held her. Finally, she sank exhausted into sleep, but although the healing of her spirit could begin at last, her dreams were dark. She saw Sajid, and heard his honeyed voice speaking venomous words. She tried desperately to reach out to Galdor, to find him again, but she was denied. When she awoke, Gaelen was still at her side.

"You have found yourself again…there is light in your eyes once more. I'm sorry for my ill thoughts of you; I did not know you then. I know that does not excuse my actions." Gaelen felt guilty enough to be truly miserable, and it would take some time ere it faded. Eventually she would tell Elraen of the fate of her beloved, but for now she kept silent.

Elraen would begin to fight back the demons that had robbed her of her sanity, though they would always leave their mark upon her face, and upon her heart. She held no enmity toward any in the

Company any longer, save for Sajid, whom she named "Cuidag the Spider." Gaelen and Galador used it at every opportunity, to the annoyance of Sajid, who did not understand Elven-tongues, and thus did not grasp the meaning of it.

Radeef the horse-trader led his travel-worn animals into the bazaar, where a number of other traders, some legitimate, others as unscrupulous as himself, displayed their wares. He spent a rather disappointing day, selling only one animal, and it was the best he had. It brought a fairly good price, but he could not expect to gain much from the others, who had not borne the journey well. Thankfully, there was always the meat market. He would not run upon an opportunity again like the one involving the She-elf and that sentimental dwarf, in which he had traded a worthless, broken-down horse for ten gold pieces. That horse would never have survived the long journey, that was certain, and here he was ten gold pieces to the good! If only soft-hearted She-elves were more abundant, Radeef could afford to retire.

What he needed was a night of entertainment. He left the horses in the care of his lackeys, going at once to the gathering-place at the edge of the bazaar. A group of large, colorful tents stood in a semicircle, and one could obtain nearly any comfort here. He first made his way to the place where he could wash the dust from his feet, don fresh robes, and have his hair and beard combed and refreshed with scented oil. After paying a small amount for this convenience, he went to the tent where most of the drinking was going on. Here he could obtain nearly any sort of liquor, and he chose a sweet red wine. There were several acquaintances in attendance, all former slavers no more appealing than Radeef, swapping tall stories and drinking heavily.

Radeef regaled them with the tale of his encounter with the Company, having bilked a dwarf out of ten gold pieces. None of Radeef's companions could match this, and they were most suitably impressed.

"What was such a group doing in these lands?" asked one, who could not imagine such a thing.

"They were looking for some northerner named, ahhh...Hallagond, I believe. Yes, that was the name. The tall one who rode out with the dwarf is his brother, as I recall. Supposedly this man is now somewhere in the Ravi, and is tall with dark hair and grey eyes. A pity I did not have news of him, there's no knowing what they would have given for it."

"Hallagond, you say?" said another, his dark eyes widening in recognition of the name. "I'll warrant that is the true name of the Forsaken One, Al-amand. I know him. He is a scoundrel and a thief, but he is a northman with grey eyes and dark hair. Alas that I am traveling to Castalan, and not to the south! Yet there may still be some profit to be had, if I can get a message to Al-amand. He'll pay dearly to throw this brother off his trail, if I am any judge. He has made it quite clear that he doesn't wish any contact with his past life in the northlands."

"Truly?" said Radeef, his black eyes glittering. "If that is so, it may well be worth sending a message. If Al-amand will pay to ensure that his brother never finds him, we have ways of doing that, don't we?" He chuckled under his breath, imagining the money he would make at the expense of that ignorant northerner. It would not be all that difficult, as such an honest man would easily be led astray.

7
Sutherlings and Easterners

One of the more useful services provided by Hamir and his brothers was their examination and correction of Fima's map. They had added to it considerably, including the last-known locations of water holes, settlements, and lesser roads. The map would now prove much more useful than before.

After consulting with Sajid, Rogond elected to set out for the settlement known as the "Sandstone" in the common-tongue. There would be folk there of various origins, but primarily those akin to Hamir's family. These were generally good people, and Sajid explained that they would probably be of help. "Aid will be found where news abounds," he said, smiling at the cleverness of his rhyme. "In the Sandstone you'll find news of every kind."

The Sandstone was at least a week's journey away. Elraen still preferred riding behind Galador, and so Sajid was free to ride Malvorn once the gear was distributed among the other animals. Sajid had at first cast his eye upon Finan, whose lameness was no longer apparent.

"He is thin, but he was a fine animal once," Sajid observed, earning the first appreciative look from Gaelen. "Where did you acquire him?"

Gaelen described the horse-dealer and his men in great detail, whereupon Sajid smiled and shook his head. "That would be Radeef, from the sound of it. I hope you did not give too great a price, because if Radeef owned him, he will be lame. I'm afraid you will find he is not of much worth, my friend."

Gaelen's eyes glittered. "First, *Cuidag*, I am not your friend. Second, I knew Finan was lame from the first. Third, it's none of your affair what was given for him, and fourth, he has proven his worth a hundredfold, even if I never put a leg over him."

Sajid bowed and smiled a cold smile at her. "Most assuredly, my sharp-eared vixen. He must be worthy, if one as perceptive as yourself has chosen him, yet Radeef is not known for the quality of his livestock. That is all I was saying, and I meant nothing by it. Please, in the hope of a tranquil journey may we not try to get along? I have sworn to serve Master Rogond, and I will do so. Truly, I meant no offense, and my name is Sajid, not Cuidag."

Gaelen read the chill in his eyes rather than the smile on his face. She returned both the smile and the cold gaze, saying: "Of course. We certainly would wish for a tranquil journey. By all means, let's pretend to get along. That will be easiest if you refrain from speaking to this vixen, for she sees what is in your heart. I will have a great deal of difficulty trusting you, and I shall be ever-watchful." With that, she turned and left him to his own thoughts.

They were three days into the journey when Galador first sighted a plume of dust on the horizon. He called it to the attention of Nelwyn, and the two of them stood upon a small ridge of rock, training their sharp eyes to the east, from whence rode a group of nearly fifty brown-clad horsemen. They rode at a ground-covering trot, occasionally breaking into an easy lope, leading many pack horses. Galador and Nelwyn called to Rogond and Sajid, and the four of them were soon looking intently at the horsemen, who appeared to be heading straight for the Company.

"They have broad, brown faces and dark eyes," observed Nelwyn. "They wear little ornament, and they ride well. The horses are small, even for desert-bred. Sajid…what sort of folk are they?"

Their guide marveled at Nelwyn's keen sight. "Your eyes are as sharp as they are comely," he said. Rogond felt Galador stiffen beside him, but he said nothing. After all, he could not disagree with Sajid, who was now squinting into the distance.

"I cannot see them well enough to tell as yet, but they sound like Kazhi, and if so, then fortune smiles on us. They are friendly folk so long as one does not offend them."

"Try this," said Rogond, handing Thorndil's glass to Sajid, who looked through it with wonder.

"Ah! They are indeed Kazhi, from the great Stone Lands to the east. They travel westward sometimes, but since the Plague they rarely venture here. I do hope nothing has happened to drive them forth." Sajid lowered the glass, knowing that he and Rogond held the same thoughts, for the threat of pestilence was still very much in their minds. Not so long ago, the Plague had decimated the Ravi. It was not beyond possibility that these men now fled their homeland, hoping to escape some doom.

Gaelen climbed the ridge to stand beside Rogond, training her own sharp eyes on the approaching horsemen. "They do not appear anxious or beleaguered, and they seem to be in full vigor. Do not fear, Thaylon. I sense no darkness at their backs." She turned to Sajid. "What sort of folk are they?"

Sajid sniffed. "They are barbarians...unlearned, with crude and uncivilized ways; heathens that are not inclined to mingle with sutherling folk."

"Must we conceal ourselves, or do we risk an encounter?" asked Rogond. "Speak quickly, as they are approaching fast and will soon come within sight of us."

Sajid considered. "With me as your guide you need not hide, though it's wise for the Elves to conceal themselves. I would not fear the Kazhi, though I do not know how they will react to such strange folk as you. Galador should disguise himself until we know more. The dwarf truly cannot conceal his nature, but he appears harmless enough. The women-folk should shroud themselves, at least in the beginning. We may obtain news from the Kazhi, and though they are barbarians, they are not known as wicked folk. I would risk an encounter."

Gaelen, Nelwyn, and Elraen were instructed to remain concealed among the rocks as Rogond, Fima, Galador, and Sajid arranged to attract the attention of the approaching Kazhi. Sajid took a mirror-bright silver medallion, holding it so that it caught the sunlight. He flashed it over and over, sending a bright beam that would be easily noticed.

The lead horsemen swerved toward them—the signal had been seen. The riders soon surrounded the Company, their weapons clearly visible but not yet drawn. Rogond and his companions stood in the open, their empty hands held out before them. They bowed their heads in deference to the Kazhi, who reined their horses to a halt, effectively walling them in.

These men were unlike any Rogond had beheld. Short and stocky with brown, sun-weathered faces, their bright, dark eyes peered curiously at him. Some had long mustachios into which were plaited tiny beads of amber and gold. Their almond-shaped eyes held some distrust, but no malice. They seemed more inquisitive than anything.

They wore brown felted wool that turned the sun aside, over light under-layers that could be seen at the sleeves and collar. Their round hats were of the same brown felted wool, and a few had a band of black-and-white fur running around the edge. One of the men, who appeared to be of great importance considering the size of his hat and the length of his moustache, approached and held up his right hand in greeting while speaking in a strange tongue. Sajid bowed and replied, eliciting chuckles from the horsemen; apparently his mastery of their tongue was rudimentary at best.

"What brings you to this place?" asked the leader in common-tongue that was so thickly accented Rogond could barely understand him. "Who among you leads, and to what end?" He was trying to appear stern, but they all saw the good humor behind his eyes.

Rogond stepped forward. "I lead the Company," he said, bowing low. "I am called Rogond, this is my friend Galador, my friend Fima, and our guide, Sajid. Our purpose is to find one of my family who is lost, and was said to be somewhere in these lands. Would you care to linger awhile? We would be glad of your company, and of any news you might bring. We will be pleased to share what we have with you."

The leader looked back over his shoulder, spoke a few words to his companions, and then turned back to Rogond. "We will not linger here, northman. Instead, why not come with us to the next oasis, where water and shade may be found? I am Makita, chieftain of the black-tail tribe, and I would hear your stories, for we have rarely encountered northern folk. If you are mounted, why not ride with us?"

Rogond bowed again. "Hail, Makita of the black-tail tribe. We shall be most pleased and honored to join you. Shall I summon the remainder of our Company?"

Makita assented, inclining his head, and the horsemen parted so that Rogond could go and fetch the three She-elves, all of whom were shrouded in black silk. When all were united, they left with the Kazhi, riding southward along the Ravani Road for a time before turning west. Soon they came upon the oasis, a small but inviting pond fed from an underground spring. It was surrounded by strange trees bearing foliage only on the tops; the trunks were smooth, with transverse ridges. They displayed huge, multi-veined leaves that were tough and waxy to turn back the sun. The sight of them thrilled Gaelen and Nelwyn, for though they were not as tall or grand as the trees of the northern forests, they were still trees.

"They look like giant cane," Nelwyn observed.

Small, shrubby cedars surrounded the pond, their soft, green foliage exuding fragrance nearly intoxicating to the Elves, who had not had a whiff of anything green in a long reckoning.

The Khazi dismounted from their small mounts, who looked like ponies next to those of the Company, and turned them loose. The horses went immediately to the water with much squealing and ear-pinning as they jockeyed for position. Eventually they all drank deeply and were content. They had, however, stirred up the pond. Sajid was disgusted, and he said so.

"We will allow this to settle again before we fill our water-skins," said the Kazhi. "Our lives depend on our mounts, so we allow them to drink before satisfying our own thirst. We have learned that this is wiser, as the horses lack our patience and may be difficult to control should we deny them. They have done far more labor than we this day."

Gaelen liked this viewpoint. In fact, she liked everything about these apparently pragmatic people. They didn't seem haughty or pretentious, being plain-spoken and dressed for simple practicality. It was obvious that they didn't just depend on their horses—they actually cared for them. She noticed that they did not seem to like Sajid, and she smiled, remembering his description of them as "unlearned barbarians."

The Kazhi unpacked their mounts, explaining that they would remain at the oasis for a few days, resting and sharing tales. They quickly set up camp, unrolling large cylinders of brown felt that they erected into shelters. Despite their resemblance to huge mounds of dragon-dung, the shelters were quite practical, turning aside sun, wind, and rain. The largest one was set in the center of the oasis for Makita's family and their guests, which now included the Company.

When the sun had set, and the chill of the desert night returned, Makita's folk sat in the shelter, which they called a "yurut." They soon had a fire going, using dried dung-patties as fuel. Once one became accustomed to the smell, their usefulness became clear. The dung would burn for a long while, was very light to carry, and generated considerable heat. On the other hand, it gave off quite a lot of smoke that smelled of burning dung.

Gaelen was further impressed with the Kazhi when several of the "men" removed their round felt hats to reveal long, elaborately plaited hair and broad but very feminine features. The women of the Kazhi rode as the men, carried weapons, and apparently enjoyed the same liberties for the most part. At this juncture, Gaelen removed her black shroud, for she sensed that she need not conceal herself from these pleasant, relaxed people. Nelwyn and Elraen did likewise.

Their Elvish nature was not yet fully apparent, as Nelwyn and Elraen wore silken scarves tied around their heads, and Gaelen had taken a strip of linen and fashioned it into a headband that effectively concealed the shape of her ears. Still, the Kazhi regarded them with wonder, for they had not seen the like of them before.

Food that has been cooked over smoke from burning dung-cakes is apt to pick up a unique flavor, but the Company did not wish to offend their hosts, so they ate and drank with them to their mutual delight. The Kazhi introduced them to kumri, a beverage made from fermented mare's milk. Nelwyn struggled to control her facial expression as she forced herself to swallow it. It would definitely take getting used to.

Then she beheld a sight to bring tears to the eyes of a Wood-elf. The Kazhi possessed a large supply of dark, wild honey, and they were not at all shy about sharing it. "This more than makes up for the kumri," said Gaelen, dipping into her share with three fingers.

It would be a night to remember. The Kazhi-folk danced, sang, and told tales, which one of the older men translated. Fima, ever the lore-master, did his best to record the tales on scraps of parchment.

Finally, after many entertaining hours, Makita rose to his feet, stretched, and yawned. "It is late, my friends, and we have ridden long and hard today," he said. "Tomorrow it will be your turn to favor us with stories. Until then, please rest well in our hospitality." Then the Kazhi lay down on the floor of the yurut, some alone, others in pairs or small groups, and were soon asleep. Sajid and Elraen slept along with them, for both were weary.

Rogond and Galador stood together beneath the moon and stars, looking to the treetops where their beloved Gaelen and Nelwyn were happily keeping the watch. They felt at home for the first time since entering the desert, and were talking and laughing. Apparently, the honey had not yet relinquished its hold on them. Rogond reflected that such moments of friendship were meant to be savored, for they were sweeter than any honey could make them.

The next few days were among the most enjoyable of times. The Kazhi way of life depended and centered upon their horses. They used their hair, their dung, their milk, and sometimes even their flesh, bone, and sinew. They did not make permanent settlements, but roamed about their lands, thus they were superb riders.

The Company entertained their hosts with tales and songs. The Kazhi were especially amazed at the lithe grace of Nelwyn as she danced before them.

Sajid had coveted Nelwyn since he first beheld her, and now, as he watched her rather provocative dance, his eyes lingered too long upon her. This earned him a stony glare from Galador that said all that was needed. *Look on her again in that manner, and it will be the last sight you see, I warn you!* Sajid took the message and looked away, but he smiled and licked his lips. Galador could threaten all he liked; the Company needed Sajid's services, and he could bide his time.

No doubt the most enjoyable experiences for the Company were the mounted games, which lasted two days. At the end of it, they were in awe of the skill of the Kazhi-folk and their mounts. The little, plain-headed ponies were incredibly maneuverable, and the larger horses had no chance. Siva fared about the best, being smallish and finely made.

Not even Nelwyn could best the Kazhi at mounted archery—though they could not vie with her when she stood upon her own feet—and few could rival Rogond's skill with the javelin as he skewered target after target from an incredible distance, whether mounted or not.

Gaelen was allowed to try one of the Kazhi-horses, and she managed to pick up a tiny copper ring from the ground while galloping at full speed. *Ah! So that's why these horses are made so close to the ground,* she thought. In truth, their environment had made them so, for in the eastern Stone-desert food and water were scarce. Small horses kept far more easily than large ones.

The Kazhi-folk played their games, laughing and smiling whether they won or lost. These games were actually quite hazardous, and injuries occurred, but they served the purpose of sharpening skills needed both in peace and in war. Gaelen would have wished for these fifty Kazhi at her side when she and her folk had faced Gorgon's army in the Barrens of the Greatwood!

Rogond questioned Makita and his family at length, but alas, they could offer no enlightenment concerning Hallagond.

After a few pleasant days, the Kazhi made ready to depart, for they were continuing west, and the Sandstone lay to the south. The Company bade farewell to their new friends, promising to be at their service should the need arise. Gaelen and Nelwyn were thankful to know of the existence of such a people, who respected the capabilities of others regardless of size or gender.

Makita had given one of the little brown ponies to the Company to bear their gear, and the other horses were now burdened much less. Parting with a horse was the height of Kazhi generosity.

"Will this fellow be able to keep up with us, do you think?" asked Galador, eyeing the raw-boned little animal with doubt.

Gaelen smiled. "Small things may be mighty, Galador. He will outlast Réalta, and he should have no trouble with the pace we've been setting. Have no fear."

"Indeed," said Galador, eyeing Gaelen's own slight frame. She was a shining example of just such a point. Even though the Kazhi had not directly aided in the quest for Hallagond, it was a very glad thing to have met them.

The Sandstone, a permanent settlement carved into tall stone cliffs and ridges, rose abruptly from the floor of the desert as a major landmark that could be seen for miles. Sajid had explained that they need not be wary in approaching, as wayfarers were always welcome, especially if they brought goods to trade or tales to tell. They could replenish their supplies, and hopefully gain some word of Hallagond, for the Sandstone was an excellent location for news.

Sajid spoke to Rogond as they approached the outer boundary of the settlement. "There is one problem that you will face very soon if we do not find a remedy—you have nothing to barter or trade for supplies. You must find a way to earn wealth to pay for what you will need. Once the word gets out that you are seeking information, you will only get it if you can pay for it. That is the Ravani way, especially in a settlement like the Sandstone. If you cannot pay, you are sent away."

Rogond smiled, for he had noticed Sajid's tendency to rhyme, usually when he was trying to sound especially wise. Gaelen, in particular, found this annoying.

In truth, Sajid's words worried Rogond—what skills did the Company have that would be valued here? He told himself to wait and see; he would know what to do when the time came. He remained worried, in spite of having given himself such excellent advice. It was all very well to wait for an opportunity, but Rogond preferred having a well-laid plan, with advance knowledge of how he would direct his fortunes. He had not had this comfort in a long while now. So he worried, thoughts turning in his mind, as he led his friends into the thriving center of activity that was the Sandstone Settlement.

There were literally hundreds of dwellings carved into the cliff-faces. Inside it was cool, though dark, and the people were well protected. There were three very deep wells in the settlement; how they had come to be was uncertain, as they had been there since before the first records were written. The market on the central plateau was the place of gathering, and wayfarers pitched their tents in an area near one of the three wells there. The Kazhi had given a small yurut to the Company and had taught them the method of erecting it, so they soon had a comfortable, if crowded, shelter. On Sajid's advice, Gaelen, Nelwyn, and Elraen had donned their black garb, and they saw many women attired in similar fashion.

Gaelen wandered alone through the market, marveling at the variety of goods and people. The myriad of strange scents fascinated her; some were fair, others foul, but all were interesting. There were strange beasts as well, including what appeared to be very wooly cattle with oddly-shaped horns. Colorful birds abounded, many in cages but some flying free, filling the air with their cries. She saw mostly sutherling folk, the men wearing loose-fitting garments of white with white head-wrappings. Some sported colorful vests or trousers.

Gaelen saw also Anori-folk, the easterners, whom she had learned to recognize by their almond-shaped eyes and golden features. Both men and women were attired in very elaborate and colorful garments that would rival those of Elven princes. Their embroidered robes were among the most beautiful Gaelen had seen. Yet many wore plain garments of white or black, with sandals on their feet. These appeared to be laborers, for they all bore some burden and none were pausing to inspect the goods in the markets. Gaelen could identify with them, as she spent much of her time in the service of the King and did not dally among the courtiers.

Most of the sutherling women wore black, and only their eyes were visible. They stared at Gaelen, for although she had donned her black garb on Sajid's advice, they knew there was something odd about her. She did not carry herself as they did, but strode proudly and with purpose. Her eyes were unnaturally bright and clear, and enough of her face was exposed that the color of her skin could be seen. She dropped her gaze to no one.

If only her folk could see her now, browsing a market in the Tal-fásath! Then she reminded herself that she did have a purpose here, and that was to obtain material to repair one of her boots. To be honest, they had just about outlasted their usefulness.

As she approached one of the market-stalls, Gaelen spoke to one of the sutherling men, pulling the black silk away from her mouth so that she could be clearly heard. "Good day to you. Do you know where I might find a seller of threads and leather? It seems my boot is in need of some repair, and I find myself with a needle and no thread." Gaelen's question was honest, warm, and friendly, but the man's response was not at all as she expected. His eyes widened as though shocked, then filled with disgust as though Gaelen had said something very discourteous. Then his disgust turned to anger as he began yelling and gesturing with both hands, nearly alarming her into drawing a blade. He was obviously furious, but she did not understand what she had done to make him so.

Suddenly, Sajid was at her side, bowing and gesturing, speaking in his own tongue. The man fell silent, but the look on his face was almost murderous. He wore a curved blade at his side, and his hand strayed toward it. Sajid grabbed Gaelen by the arm and nearly dragged her away, still muttering apologies to the man, who gave a sort of self-righteous snarl before turning away.

"What did you think you were doing, speaking to a man with your face uncovered?" snapped Sajid. "You offended him severely, and he would have thought little of striking you, or perhaps even cutting your throat. He was of the Balalli—those folk will brook no violation of custom. Never speak to any sutherling man here again, especially without your veil. In fact, you should remain silent and allow men to speak for you."

"But why?" asked Gaelen. "What's so terrible about speaking to a man?"

Sajid ignored the question. "You must learn our ways, or you will not long remain here." He looked hard at her. "I fear your fate will be raven-bait."

Gaelen's lip curled. She would rather have gone with the Kazhi; the sutherling customs were too strange and restrictive. She was not accustomed to such a lack of freedom, and it perturbed her to no end. Not only that, she suspected that Sajid had purposefully neglected to tell her of this taboo beforehand just to get her into trouble and allow him to swoop in and "save" her. *Well, you've had your fun at my expense, but no more.*

"My thanks, Sajid, for your help in need. Yet this rhyming game is really quite lame. In future, please, spare us this disease."

She turned on her heel and went in search of Rogond, muttering under her breath. Perhaps it would be permissible for *him* to inquire as to the whereabouts of a leather-vendor.

She returned to the yurut to find Rogond napping in the shade. The journey had wearied him, and she did not wake him. Nelwyn and Galador had gone into the markets, and she did not know where Fima was. Elraen was sitting in the corner, rocking slowly back and forth, as Gaelen approached her.

"Elraen, would you like some water, or perhaps some bread and honey? I will bring it for you." Gaelen so wanted to help Elraen, but the depth of the hurt done to her was just too great. She did not respond until Gaelen touched her shoulder, whereupon she started back as though she was being attacked. "Elraen, do not fear…it's only your friend Gaelen. I was asking if you wanted water or bread, nothing more." Elraen calmed, smiled slightly at Gaelen, and shook her head. Then she began once more to rock gently, humming tunelessly to herself.

Gaelen's melancholy was interrupted by Fima, who had just come from the markets and was now in a state of happy excitement. "Gaelen! I'm so glad to find you here…I have interesting news," he said.

"Indeed?" she replied, all melancholy gone from her mind. It was very difficult to remain in a dark mood in the presence of her friend Fima.

"You know that Rogond has been wondering how we will gain wealth to provide for our needs here? Well, I may have found a way, but I shall need you and Nelwyn for it."

"Tell your tale, most helpful and enterprising dwarf," said Gaelen, sitting down in front of him. When he had done so, Gaelen was as enthused as Fima. She would go and find Nelwyn, and then they would see whether his idea would bear fruit. But first, she thought, she would remove the black garments. *I saw plenty of women in the market, dressed in all sorts of ways! Why do I need to pretend to be a sutherling, when other folk walk freely here? Sajid is just trying to keep Nelwyn and me under his thumb, and I expect she's as fed up with it as I am.*

Despite Sajid's advice, she would go forth as herself from then on, wearing only her linen headband to conceal her nature as the daughter of Elves. She shuddered with relief as the shroud fell to the floor, and she donned her quiver, bow, and blades, shaking her tousled head, her ginger-brown hair fanning around her face.

"Are you sure of this, little Wood-elf?" said Fima with a rather worried expression.

"I am," she replied. "I will get into far greater trouble trying to be something I'm not, and I am most certainly not a sutherling woman. Anori women wear the same clothing as men, and so do the Kazhi—I saw them in the market. The sutherlings may not know what to make of me, but at least now it's clear that I'm a stranger here, and they will not expect me to behave otherwise. Let's go and find Nelwyn."

They didn't need to go far. Nelwyn appeared in the doorway, having come back to see to Elraen. She took one look at Gaelen's lack of black shroud and removed her own at once, breathing a sigh of relief as she slung her beloved bow across her shoulders.

"Fima has hit upon a way that we may earn money to pay for our needs. He told me only a little, but it sounds intriguing," said Gaelen.

Nelwyn, who had brought some honey-cakes for Elraen, instructed her to remain inside in the cool darkness, away from prying eyes. Then she set off with Gaelen and Fima to the south end of the plateau, Fima explaining the plan as they went.

It seemed that one of the regular denizens of the settlement had been a horse-breaker who had recently found himself on the wrong side of a gambling debt. Because he could not pay, his legs had both been broken, and it would now be a long while before he would sit astride a horse. Yet there were nearly twenty young horses in need of training, and the horse-breaker's apprentices had abandoned him lest they be held responsible for his debts. The only way the unfortunate horse-breaker could pay was to ply his trade, which he could not do until his legs were healed. The horses languished in their paddocks, for none in the settlement had the skill to tackle them. Several had tried, for the owner would pay for each animal that was tamed and trained, but so far the horses had decided that they preferred the life of leisure, and no one had succeeded.

"The horse-merchant is practically begging for help," said Fima. "He has put the word out that he will give ten pieces of silver for each animal that is tamed and ridden. You two have such a knack for this, it should be no problem. We could earn two hundred pieces of silver if you are successful! What say you, my fine Wood-elves? Are you up to demonstrating your skill?" Such a question was, of course, entirely unnecessary.

The horse-merchant was in a bad way, for none would buy untrained stock, and he had to feed all twenty of these wild, head-strong animals. They had little to occupy their attention and had turned to mischief—the merchant had needed to repair his corrals twice in the past three days. He had not the skill to break them; he had relied on his now-crippled horse breaker for that. If he did not find someone fairly soon, he would be forced to sacrifice them at meat-market price.

When he looked up and beheld three strange folk approaching the compound, he was unsure of what to think. There was a very short, stocky fellow with a long, white beard; he was barely chest-high to the horse-merchant. He carried a broad-bladed axe slung at his back, and two smaller ones tucked into his belt. He was flanked by two tall, willowy females attired as men in boots and breeches; with bare arms and windblown hair. One wore a silk scarf tied around her head, and the other wore a linen headband. They were confident and purposeful in their approach, and they bore various weapons. The horse-merchant was afraid of them on first glance.

As they drew near, the very short stocky one spoke to him in the common-tongue: "I understand you are in need of a horse-breaker? Well, my two friends might be interested, if the pay is sufficient. We are travelers from a distant land to the north. I am Fima, son of Khima, of the Deep-cavern realm. This is Gaelen and her cousin Nelwyn, of the northern Greatwood forest. Tell us what you need, and we will see if it is worth our while. My friends have rather amazing abilities, and when we heard of your predicament they expressed the desire to be of aid."

The dealer bowed, introducing himself as Hari, the horse provider. "I breed and purchase untrained stock, and then sell it when it is trained and useful," he said. "But these have proven particularly difficult. Come and have a look at them."

Gaelen liked Hari from the moment she viewed the sleek, well-kept stock in the paddocks. He had freely admitted that these horses were being difficult; he had not tried to deceive her. She looked over at Nelwyn, who obviously was of similar mind. They would aid this man if they could.

The young horses regarded the newcomers with a haughty air. So, here were more to try and tame them, well, let them try! They turned their tails to Hari and pretended to ignore him.

"You see? Bad attitudes, the lot of them. I believe they've grown used to their easy, comfortable lives, where they drain my pockets every day, and are reluctant to learn to do an honest day's work." He looked at the Elves. "If you can get them to the point that they can be ridden, turned left and right, stop and stand, I will give you ten pieces of silver for each. In addition, I will add both your names to my prayers." He shook his head. "My horse-breaker has a gambling problem, and I must now suffer for it. Will you aid me?"

Gaelen looked over at Nelwyn. What did they have to lose? They nodded and bowed, placing their right hands over their hearts. Then they spoke words that Hari thrilled to hear: "We shall give it our best effort."

A considerable crowd had appeared around the stock-pens by the time the Elves began their task. Word had spread that two strangers from some far northern land were going to try their hand at breaking Hari's upstart animals. The horses had already placed several would-be horse-breakers in need of healing, and men were gathering to see this undoubtedly entertaining sight for themselves. Ordinarily, young horses are not especially dangerous provided they are given time and care, but groups of them can be deadly; an unwitting man could find himself amid a storm of flying hooves with little hope of escaping injury.

When Gaelen and Nelwyn appeared, there was laughter from many of the onlookers. Surely these two women did not think they had either the skill or the strength for this task! Horse-breaking was a man's profession.

Gaelen and Nelwyn ignored the laughter, and they did not take the ropes and bridles offered them by Hari, but simply entered the enclosure with empty hands. The young animals regarded them suspiciously, with proud heads in the air and mischief on their minds.

"They will have ridden all twenty before sundown," declared Fima, who immediately found himself in the center of a storm of wagering. Soon a considerable fortune rested on the abilities of the two Elves, and Fima kept all his fingers crossed, for he would not be able to cover the wager should they fail. He was not truly worried, for Gaelen and Nelwyn had learned from Capellion, the Master of Horse in the Greatwood, and they had been among the most eager of his apprentices.

"The dark grey colt and the bay filly lead the others," said Nelwyn. "Bring them into line, and the others will follow. You take the colt...I will handle the filly."

Gaelen nodded, and wandered in an indirect line to the group of horses, not looking directly at any of them. Rather than running blindly around as they had with past attempts, the horses simply stared at her in confusion. These would-be usurpers of their freedom did not appear threatening, as had the others.

The grey colt was the first to approach, and Gaelen knew that Nelwyn had given her the easier of the two herd leaders. He trotted toward her, stiff-legged, his knees breaking unnaturally high. He stopped and snorted, tossing his head, his long black forelock flying back around his shapely ears. He pawed the ground, trying to intimidate her, and several observers were speculating that she would soon be trampled if she did not retreat. She lifted her chin and turned to face him, looking directly into his eyes, meeting his challenge. He took two steps forward, tail in the air, and struck the ground hard with one foreleg, squealing. Gaelen did not move. One more step forward, and another strike. This one was close enough for Gaelen—it was time to begin.

"Aiyah!"

Gaelen spoke the word in a loud, commanding voice, and the colt snorted in surprise, throwing his head in the air, taking a step back from her. He regained his composure—she had startled him… that was all. He would soon put things right. He raised his body up, forelegs leaving the sand for a moment, shaking his head again.

"AIYAH!"

Something in her voice could not be denied. The colt stood on all his feet once more, looking quizzically at her as she approached him. She reached out to place a hand on his neck, whereupon he gave a half-hearted squeal and swung his teeth at her.

"Attend me, now," she said in the Elven-tongue. "Look to me, and be still. Be still and be silent. Attend me!"

She placed her hand again on the colt's neck, and he shivered and dropped his head. She spoke to him in a soothing but assertive tone, telling him that she would hear no argument, nor would she allow him to be harmed. It was best if he gave himself to her, for then they could be great friends and share adventures together. She spoke to him in this manner for several minutes, as she ran her hands over his entire body while he stood as still as stone.

When she massaged his ears, he shuddered with pleasure, and she knew then that he would suffer her every whim. She swung onto his back without another word, and he walked placidly as though in a pleasant dream, turning left and right, stopping when she wished it. Then she trotted and cantered around the enclosure, all the while stroking him with both hands, speaking to him in her gentle voice. When she finally swung down from his strong, grey back, he stood as though disappointed that the ride had ended, and he followed her all the way to the rail where Hari, provider of horses, stood with his mouth open.

Elves, Wood-elves in particular, have such a way, and Fima smiled. He knew that none of these animals would present any great difficulty.

Gaelen bowed before Hari. "Is that sufficient for your purposes? He will now suffer himself to be ridden anywhere that I desire. Will that serve your needs?"

Hari nodded, for he was speechless. He had reckoned the grey colt would be one of the hardest to tame, and now this same fearsome colt stood with his head bowed, asking Gaelen if she would please rub his ears once more. She smiled and bowed again, then led the grey colt into a neighboring paddock so that he would be out of the way of the others.

Nelwyn, meanwhile, had approached the filly. She was a beautiful bay, more intelligent than the colt, and she would be much more difficult to win over. The other horses crowded together behind the bay filly, for she led them, and with the help of the grey colt she had managed to thwart all previous attempts.

The filly sensed that she had more than met her match in Nelwyn. She tried to avoid her, wheeling on her hind feet, and began to run around the yard with the herd behind her, raising a choking cloud of dust. Faster and faster she flew, occasionally changing direction so that Gaelen and Nelwyn were hard put to stay out of the way of trampling feet.

At one point, the horses seemed to run right over Nelwyn; it was impossible to determine through the grey, swirling dust. But then they slowed, first cantering easily, then trotting, and finally coming to a halt in the center of the enclosure. The men shook their heads, expecting to see Nelwyn's broken body trampled flat into the sand, but there she was, astride the bay filly, speaking in a strange and beautiful tongue as she stroked the glossy neck. The filly turned and trotted quietly around the enclosure, then cantered smoothly as the other horses watched in obvious confusion. Once she tossed her head and squealed, pinning her ears and leaping to the side. Everyone thought Nelwyn would be unseated, but she hung on and rode through this disobedience. It was the last; the filly now stood as placidly as had the colt. Nelwyn dismounted, bowed to Hari, and led the filly to the holding-yard.

The onlookers had never seen anything like it. Gaelen and Nelwyn caught and tamed each animal in turn, as Hari rejoiced. Fima was likewise quite happy with life, as it appeared that he would be a great deal richer provided they could tame just one more animal each before sundown.

The sun was still visible over the rim of the Sandstone when Gaelen and Nelwyn approached the last two horses. Both Elves were weary, for taming horses in this manner requires more strength of spirit than of body, and they had each ridden nine animals in a little more than two hours.

Gaelen approached her animal, a grey filly. But as she did so, the filly took a tentative step…she was lame. She stopped with one foreleg off the ground, and was reluctant to even place it down. Gaelen shook her head. "I am sorry, but this one is lame. I dare not ride her; it will only make her worse," she said. Upon hearing those words, every man who had bet against Fima relaxed.

Fima heard chuckles coming from behind him as he sat on the fence-rail. "Remember, my stout friend…all twenty must be ridden before sundown, or you will lose the wager. I surely hope that you will be able to cover your debt. Your friend will not ride the lame one."

"Excuse me for a moment," said Fima, hopping down and approaching Gaelen and the filly. "Gaelen…please, may I speak with you? It's…it's very important." He looked nervously at the ridge, where the sun was beginning to set.

Gaelen ran her hands over the filly's leg, trying to calm her so that she could be examined. The filly started back, and Gaelen glared at the dwarf. "Stay away from her. She is not ready…keep your distance."

Fima was literally dancing, shifting from one foot to the other. "Gaelen…you need to get on her back. Don't ask me why, but if you care for me at all, *get on that horse!*"

"She's lame. I cannot ride her until I know why," Gaelen replied simply, lifting the mare's leg and examining her foot with interest.

Fima looked into the grinning faces of the spectators. They were counting their money already. "Please, Gaelen. You said once that you could never repay me for the…ahhh…the eight gold pieces I gave for Finan. Now you can! Just get on that animal and ride it, for the love of heaven!"

Gaelen looked at him, seeing the panic in his face. Then she turned back to the filly, and pried a stone from her foot with strong fingers. When she set the foot back down, the filly was still lame, but at least she would now bear weight upon it.

"I don't know what sort of mischief you have gotten into here, my good dwarf, but I do owe you a great debt, and for your sake, I will ride."

The sun was still visible, but barely, when Gaelen climbed aboard the grey filly, turning, stopping, even trotting a little. A great cheer went up from the observers that had not wagered against the Elves, and even from a few that had. They had not seen such a feat before, and most likely never would again.

Gaelen and Nelwyn dismounted and led the last two horses to their holding pen. Gaelen returned to stand before Hari. "That filly has a stone bruise; she will need a good soaking for many days. We will return tomorrow to collect our fee, if it please you."

Hari did not know what to say. "You are entitled to 200 pieces of silver, my friends. But, will you remain in my employ? Together we could turn such profit that we could all retire wealthy in a few years. Will you not stay?"

Gaelen and Nelwyn smiled. Hari was quite likeable, and it was no surprise that he wanted them to stay and aid him. "We cannot, O Provider of Horses. Yet we will be in the Sandstone awhile, and until we leave, we are at your service. We shall come tomorrow for our payment."

In answer, Hari handed them a heavy bag of coins. "In the southlands we learn that tomorrow is uncertain. Here is your promised payment…in case you wish to make merry tonight. You will have earned it!" He smiled broadly at them. "I believe folk would come from far and wide, and pay a great deal just to watch you two break horses. If only I had thought to charge them for the use of my fence-rails today!"

Nelwyn looked thoughtful as she held the heavy bag of coins in her hand. "Will these coins absolve your horse-breaker from his debt?" she asked.

"Ah! You mean my former horse-breaker, the one who cannot seem to stay away from the gambling-tables? In truth, he owes more...fifty gold pieces that will take months to earn, and the interest mounts. I doubt he will ever repay it." Hari shook his head. "He has finally learned his lesson, but too late. I would pay it for him, but I cannot afford such a sum and stay in business. It is a shame."

Gaelen looked sidelong at Fima, who was even now collecting the profit of his wagering on their abilities. "We know of one who might be able to aid him," she said. "Allow us to speak with our friend for a moment."

"Fima, when you are quite finished collecting from your associates, will you please come and parley with us?" said Nelwyn in an unassuming tone. Fima had suffered considerable anxiety and doubt of his future health in acquiring this gold, and he would not relish parting with it. Finally he nodded to the last disappointed victim, shoving coins into his already bulging pockets. He approached Gaelen and Nelwyn with seventy-four gold pieces, two beautiful jeweled daggers, and the papers declaring him to be the owner of two dromadin. He beamed as he showed them to the Elves. "See, my friends, what your skill has earned!"

Gaelen held up the heavy bag of silver. "No, Fima. *This* is what our skills have earned. This other is ill-gotten, and you must not keep it, for it will only encourage you to risk again, and you may not be so fortunate. Better you should remember your panic when it seemed that you would lose the wager." She quirked a sly smile at him. "Did you think I did not know? You were in fear for your very life! That is what you should remember."

Fima held a blank expression for a moment, as this revelation made its full impact. "So...you toyed with my life just to teach me a lesson? You...you insufferable *Elf!*" He began to growl and bluster. "Fine. I go to all the trouble, plus risk my very neck just to provide wealth for our needs, and you think it necessary to increase my anxiety! Well, I shall need to think harder before I part with my gold on your behalf the next time. Don't count on me to get *either* of you out of your difficulties!" Fima meant only about half of what he was saying, but he was annoyed at having been frightened nearly to death.

Nelwyn shook her head. "Small wonder that gambling is such a disease, when you can gain so much in such a short while without earning it! And then, you turn on your friend, regretting the most decent thing you have ever done for her. Do you see what this does to people? Why not learn from your near-disaster, as Gaelen suggests? You will be happier."

"I very much doubt it," Fima replied, though he had lost some of his bluster.

"Do you know how our friend can now be truly made happy?" said Gaelen.

"I do," said Nelwyn. "We must take fifty of your gold pieces, Fima. Please hand them over, so that we may absolve another poor soul lost in the mire of debt, one who has now learned his lesson. We may only hope that you will learn the same."

"I thought you were seeking to make me happy," said Fima. "Taking fifty of my gold pieces will not make me happy. That will, in fact, sadden me considerably!" He drew back, his hands over his pockets.

"Ah, you may not think so now, but think of the good feeling you will get each time you remember the man that you saved from terrible trial, while at the same time relieving yourself of ill-gotten wealth that will bring naught but trouble," replied Nelwyn with a rather impish smile.

"Come on, Fima, hand it over," said Gaelen. "You know that Nelwyn is right."

"I know of no such thing," grumbled Fima, reaching into his pockets. "I have enjoyed the fruits of wagering many times in my life, and only rarely have they brought trouble. Generally they bring food, and drink, and entertainment, and fine things. Yet I know that I would not have gained this wealth were it not for the two of you, so if you feel compelled to pick my pockets I must comply. Here!" He counted fifty heavy gold pieces, the majority of his winnings, into a bag and handed it reluctantly to Nelwyn. She practically had to pry his fingers from it. He was still upset with Gaelen and would not look at her. "I despise you," was all he would say.

Gaelen was not dismayed, for she knew this would not last. Fima was a beloved friend and always would be. He just did not like being outsmarted.

The Elves now approached Hari and handed the gold to him. "For the horse-breaker," said Nelwyn, bowing. "May he soon break horses once again."

"And may he have truly learned his lesson, and not inconvenience our new friend Hari by getting himself into further difficulty," said Gaelen.

Hari bowed. "And how shall I explain his good fortune to him? I should probably not say that his debt was paid with money gained from wagering, after all."

"Say only that the gold was given by those who wish for him to be able to earn an honest living," said Gaelen.

Hari bowed solemnly before the Elves. There were no words to reply, and none were needed.

Gaelen and Nelwyn bowed in return and then made their way back toward the now-quiet marketplace with Fima in tow. The dwarf, though still smarting from the loss of his wealth, admired the Elves for their consideration of Hari and the horse-breaker. Besides, he still had twenty-four bright gold pieces, two dromadin, and the jeweled daggers. He would offer these to Gaelen and Nelwyn, and he had already decided that when the markets opened in the morning, he would go to a honey-vendor and purchase the finest, largest container he could find.

Although most of the men who had witnessed the Elves' display of skill were filled with admiration, there were those now mired in darker thoughts. These were of the Ballali, and they of all the Ravani-folk were the least tolerant of strangers and strange ways. Grim and forbidding, they accepted nothing outside their own narrow system of beliefs, which they defended with a fervor bordering on fanaticism. This had worsened since the Plague; the survivors had been taught that they had only been spared because they carried the "pure faith," and any who strayed would be stricken down.

They were not liked by any of the other Ravani-folk, therefore they kept to themselves, ever on the watch for unbelievers and those they felt would bring evil among them. They now had seen two females, uncovered, besting men in a profession reserved only for men—there were no female horse-breakers—and there had been wagering, probably at their direction. The Ballali considered gambling to be evil, and naturally no woman was ever allowed to expose herself or parade before men in such a manner. These newcomers were the embodiment of demons in their opinion. If everyone in the crowd had been of such mind, all three would have been stoned to death.

Now the men made their way to the tent of their High Holy Man, the spiritual leader known as Asaad. He was very old and could no longer walk on his feet, but was borne on a litter on the rare occasion that he ventured outside his high sanctuary. He lived as did all the Ballali, spending much time in prayer, foregoing worldly pleasures, handing out judgment. The Plague had increased his power and influence considerably. He led his people in prayer thrice daily, his deep, rich voice speaking words both comforting and controlling. His followers both loved and dreaded him.

They bowed before him, prostrating themselves on the stony floor, and begged leave to tell what they had seen. Asaad extended his right hand, bidding them sit and give their news. When they had finished, Asaad's black eyes were stony in his ancient face. *What sort of evil has come among us? One of the men heard the white-bearded one referring to one of the women as "insufferable Elf." What can it mean?* Asaad had already been told of the bright-eyed stranger speaking so brazenly in the marketplace, dressed in black but with her face uncovered! Now the men before him declared that it was likely these were of the same folk, for their eyes had seemed unnaturally bright.

"Bright with hell's fire," said Asaad. "Obviously, they bewildered those animals with dark powers. Yet we should wait for a time to be certain, as they will have gained allies in the settlement. We cannot allow them to remain long, for they will infect the people with their unseemly ways."

"There are many who dislike them, for they lost much in wagering," said one of the followers.

"As they should have! Only evil folk gain from wagering. It is further proof that these newcomers are of evil," said Asaad with an all-knowing smile.

One of the men nodded. That made perfect sense to him.

"But, if they are of evil, why did they return their winnings in defense of the horse-breaker?" asked another.

"Because they wanted to encourage him to remain evil, and not receive his just punishment for gambling," replied Asaad. "The poor man is now lost, for this ill-gotten gold will allow him to wager again, to the further detriment of his soul. These devils know what they are doing." He looked at his followers with hooded eyes, daring them to disagree.

Of course, no one did. When one was in the presence of Asaad, all things became clear. He was surely the wisest man in all the world, and the one who would save his people from evil in this life, that they might enjoy divine pleasures in the next. They would do whatever he asked.

Asaad dismissed them to sit alone in the cool, candle-lit darkness. "Avinashi," he muttered to himself. "I am nearly certain of it." He had not really thought them to exist, except in tales, but these strangers fit the description. If they were Avinashi there was no knowing their age or their origins, but Asaad knew they would bring nothing but trouble to his controlled, orderly world. Avinashi would not die naturally, but they could be killed, oh, most certainly! Yet these had made allies, and rumor held that they were merely passing through these lands. So he would wait for a time, relying on his minions for news. If these Avinashi brought strife and dissention among his folk, the Balalli would eliminate the evil from their midst. Asaad had many righteous assassins at his command...the unwitting fools would never see them coming.

8
The Festival

"I would say our fortunes are improving," said Fima, lifting his ale tankard against Rogond's. "Just compare them to those of yesterday, when we had almost no money, few friends, and our Wood-elves going about in black shrouds. We now have enough money to serve our needs for a fair while, provided we are frugal, and we have our Gaelen and Nelwyn back. They have many new admirers, and even a friend or two. Nearly everyone was dreadfully impressed with the skill of our comely horse-breakers."

"And why not?" put in Galador, raising a glass of dark, sweet wine. "Even I am impressed, though Nelwyn never fails to impress me in all things." So saying, he gave Nelwyn an affectionate embrace with his left arm.

"Are you all quite finished congratulating yourselves?" said a voice from behind them. "I would warn you that not everyone witnessing the afternoon's horse-breaking incident was impressed in the way you would desire. There were undoubtedly some who were most *unfavorably* impressed." Sajid emerged from the shadows, a grim smile on his narrow face.

"I have heard many things already concerning this matter," he said. "There are those in the Settlement who have not taken kindly to your Wood-elves. They should never have gone against my advice and removed their proper clothing. They went about shamelessly, uncovered, in front of sutherling men. Then they engaged in horse-breaking, which is most unseemly for a woman—unheard of, in fact. Some folk have accused them of using dark magic to subdue the animals. Beware! Next they will think you are all in league with evil forces. If that happens, they will kill you before you can even react."

"We are not of the Ravani," said Gaelen. "I can hide my ears, but I cannot pretend to be what I am not. More folk were offended by my trying to pass as a sutherling woman. Why can I not simply mingle among these people as myself? I have seen such great variety here, and not all women are shrouded in black! The eastern women dress as the men, and they are accepted without question. What is so offensive about a simple Sylvan hunter-scout?"

Sajid's eyes narrowed. "I have neither the time nor the patience to explain the intricacies of our beliefs and ways to one so obviously single-minded, Gaelen Taldin. Just be warned, all of you. There are folk here who are very, very dangerous. The man known as Asaad, for example—he who leads the Ballali people—you risk grave peril in offending him. Supposedly he is a very spiritual man, spending much of his time in thoughtful meditation, but the truth is that he cares only for controlling the minds and hearts of his followers. He won't take kindly to your unseemly antics at all.

"It seems they would control or exterminate anything that threatens them," said Galador. "Otherwise, why would they suppress their women-folk as they do? Only so that they need not fear losing control of them, or being controlled by them…at least, that is the way it appears to an outsider."

"Again, I will not defend our ways to you," Sajid replied. "You are a guest in our house now, Tall One. These are sutherling lands; even the Anori-folk know that they must take care not to offend one such as Asaad. The peace between our peoples is uneasy at best. Please, my friends, take care that you do not tweak the tail of the tiger while you are inside his cage. If you would not fail, our ways must prevail."

"I thought I asked you not to do that," Gaelen muttered as she stiffened beside Rogond. The jubilant mood had quite gone from the Company, as they were all wondering about Sajid's warning. "You Ravani-folk confound me…I would have thought that, with so few spared by the Plague, you would place less importance on your differences, and be less easily offended by them. I would expect you to value your women all the more, for without them, you will not increase. One thing is certain—I will leave this place before I put on that horrid black shroud again."

Sajid knew that Gaelen would never understand his view of the world. Many of the desert folk cherished their women. Their laws were in place to protect them from harm and temptation, to keep them from straying into peril. Yet Gaelen had seen only frightened, submissive creatures who were afraid to lift their eyes to men. It was no good trying to convince her. He shrugged his shoulders and glanced sidelong at her. "Just be careful, little flower. Hide your light from Asaad and his folk, as they will not be at all shy about extinguishing it forever. Do you take my meaning?"

"I do," Gaelen replied, "Though they may find the task more difficult than that of beating their wives or their daughters. This flower has thorns!" She drew one of her throwing-knives and cast it into the floor a hair's breadth from Sajid's crossed legs before he could draw his next breath. He jumped, startled and fearful, then threw an angry look at Rogond.

"Were she in a tent with the Ballali, she would be dead now! They would not take the humor in this gesture. You had better control her, or you will lose her."

Gaelen rose to her feet and went to retrieve her blade, pausing to look Sajid in the eye as she did so. "There was no humor in the gesture. I am going out into the air, for you are unwashed and you have the reek of fear about you. I have never found that scent appealing." She bowed to her friends and disappeared into the dark.

Rogond turned to Sajid. "You should know better than to suggest that anyone here would control Gaelen, or anyone else in this Company," he said. "You will get on better with her if you persuade, rather than demand or insist."

"I think it's too late for Gaelen to get along with Sajid, no matter what he does from now on," said Galador. "Don't feel bad…it isn't easy to get along with her sometimes, especially when she has decided not to trust you, as I fear she has done."

"I don't feel bad at all," replied Sajid in a false, soothing tone, "for it will not be me who lies dead at the hands of the Ballali. My survival doesn't depend upon whether she lives or dies by ignoring my advice."

"Ah! But that is where you are wrong. Your survival depends *very much* upon it," said Fima, resting his hand upon the broad axe that lay at his right side. "If I were you, I would do all I could to ensure the safety of everyone in the Company, even those you dislike the most. Make no mistake about it." Then he chuckled, looking over at Rogond. "Oh, yes, Aridan, you had better set yourself to the task of controlling Gaelen at once. As *if!*"

Rogond, for once, did not smile back at him.

Nelwyn had noticed the looks on some of the spectators at the horse-yards. They were, as Sajid had said, most unfavorably impressed; the black looks on some of them could only be described as murderous. Nelwyn was suddenly afraid for Gaelen; she excused herself, and went in search of her.

Gaelen was not difficult to find, as there was no mistaking the mellow, thrush-like quality of the voice rising above the Settlement until it mingled with the countless stars. She sat near the well marking the center of the plateau; it was the Sandstone's main water source, and the supply was so rich that it actually flowed, cold and clear, into a pool that had been lined with marble and planted about with flowering shrubs and trees. No doubt the sound and smell of the water and growing things had drawn Gaelen there, and now she sang in a voice that might have come from the Eternal Realm.

Nelwyn was suddenly overcome with the desire to leave all their adventures behind, and to see the Greatwood again. She sank onto the soft sand beside the marble pool, weeping quietly. A child of the forest, she found these strange desert lands counter to her nature in nearly every respect.

Gaelen stopped singing, and Nelwyn knew that she had been heard. She wiped her tears away, trying not to weep again, and faced Gaelen with an expression of false cheerfulness, but it was too late. Gaelen wrapped her arms around her cousin in the embrace of a loving friend, as Nelwyn wept anew. "It's no good trying to conceal your thoughts from me, for they are my thoughts as well. This is altogether a wretched place, but we must endure it until it is safe to return home. I promise you that I will do all in my power to hasten that day."

That would be the day Gorgon Elfhunter lies dead, thought Nelwyn with a shiver. *It could just as easily be Gaelen, or Galador, or even me who lies dead before that monster.* The two cousins sat together, both of their spirits taken with a sudden chill.

Gaelen began to sing again, hoping to calm herself. Folk began to gather, drawn to the song, for it was a fine night to be out walking. Gaelen did not appear to notice them as they stood mesmerized by this stranger with the eyes and voice of an angel. She had spread her cloak on the ground beside her, and was somewhat surprised when people began to drop coins onto it, smiling at her and bowing. She sang softly until nearly dawn. When she finally grew weary and made ready to return with Nelwyn, she had collected twenty silver pieces, as well as about fifty of copper. There was also a finely-made brooch of copper in the shape of a running horse, and three strips of parchment inscribed with some strange symbols Gaelen did not recognize. She pocketed them, intending to show them to Fima and Sajid, when she looked up to behold Rogond standing before her.

"Gaelen…soon the sun will rise, and I would speak with you before then. There are some things that I must say."

She could see in his face that he was troubled, and she went to him, placing a hand on his arm. When she looked into his eyes, she knew why he had come. "You think I am being foolish with respect to Sajid's advice," she said. "You think I should shroud myself and be silent so that I may stay safe, isn't that right? I thought you would understand the importance of remaining true to your nature."

The disappointment in her voice stung Rogond's heart. She had not expected anything but support from him, and now he would need to tell her things that she wouldn't want to hear. *She needs to be told them, nonetheless.*

He guided her back to the edge of the marble pool, and they sat down together. "Gaelen, please know that I *do* understand the need to remain true to your nature. In truth, I would rather die defending you than have you resemble the Ballali in any way, but we must survive for a while in this place. I am very much afraid of this man, Asaad. Sajid says that anyone who threatens his beliefs, or the power he has over his followers, will simply disappear."

Gaelen's eyes narrowed at the mention of Sajid, and Rogond was forced to defend him again. "I know… Sajid is a loathsome wretch, but he has sworn to serve us, and as of this moment he has not led us astray. He is the voice of experience in these lands...the rest of us have none. I don't expect you to be courteous, but could you at least try not to threaten him so?"

"Can we not acquire another guide?" she replied, as though she had not heard him. "What advice has Sajid given that could not be given by someone trustworthy? I know we needed him to guide us to the Sandstone, but may we now release him, and find a guide who is not as closely acquainted with snakes?"

Rogond was becoming frustrated—she wasn't listening to the warning he was trying to give her. "Hamir mentioned that I would have trouble with you, but I defended you. I told him you were wise enough not to place yourself or the Company in jeopardy because of your pride and stubborn will. Was I correct, or no?"

Gaelen did not appear to take offense, but simply lifted an eyebrow at him. "You have not yet answered my question. May we not release the spider, and acquire another guide?"

For the second time since he had known her, Rogond spoke to her with an edge in his voice. "For once in your life, stop and think that there might be something more important than your prideful opinion. Galador is joking when he compares you to the Fire-heart, but right now your actions make the comparison quite an apt one!"

He knew she would not be able to ignore this—to be compared with Aincor Fire-heart in terms of willfulness was an insult of the highest order. She drew a deep breath and set her jaw. "I have not suffered as much humiliation in all the long years that I have been alive as I have since meeting Hamir," she said, her words like measured bits of ice. "I am certainly not used to being subjected to scorn simply because of a fact of my birth that I cannot change. My gender is a part of my existence…it is not something that I wished for, or brought upon myself through my own actions. I have never been belittled or dismissed because of it...until now. These people would take away my most basic freedoms: the freedom to express myself, to be who and what I am, to be respected because of what I can and have accomplished. Here, you are free to walk about and do and say what you like. You may wear your normal clothing and carry weapons. You may speak and have your voice heard…you cannot know what I am feeling!"

Rogond placed his hands upon her shoulders, entreating her to look at him. "Do you think a man who was raised among Elves doesn't know what it's like to be looked down upon and underestimated? Your people do not hold the same regard for men…you do not consider us to be your equals. Try to deny it! They meant well, but they could not hide their desire that I should be more like them. I was always a disappointment. And do you think I was ever asked for my opinion? It was only when I was taken to Mountain-home, and met with such folk as Lady Ordath and Fima, that I began to acquire a sense of my own worth. You cannot disparage the sutherlings entirely, for your folk are just as guilty of prejudice as they."

Gaelen looked at him with wide eyes. "It must have been difficult," she said gently, "but it is hardly the same. I know all too well the haughty and judgmental natures of certain Elves. I have been disparaged by them; even my mother looked on me in disappointment each time I cut my hair. I am considered undersized, and to be undersized among Elves is to be of lesser purity…of lower heritage. I have heard the words "eccentric" and "feral" used frequently in reference to me. The King would rather have locked me in prison had he known of the depth of feeling I held for his son—I know the taste of Elvish scorn! Yet I suffered no loss of freedom, and I was given the chance to prove myself worthy. There are few now in the Greatwood who would hold me inferior."

Here she paused, fire flickering in the depths of her eyes, remembering the self-righteous rage of the man in the marketplace when she had merely dared to speak to him. "This…this is different. It is darker, and uglier, and comes from the desire to control and suppress. It is not worthy of respect."

"Is it so different?" said Rogond in a quiet voice. "Perhaps few in the Greatwood would hold you inferior, Gaelen, but you are an Elf, not a man."

Gaelen looked away. "The distance between our kindreds was made in ancient times. Elves distanced themselves from men long ago, mostly because friendships are too painful—we could not bear the loss of our friends to sickness and death after so few years with us. Our hearts were broken many times over, and so we began to keep to ourselves. We did not make this distance out of scorn. And we have never sought to control you, but have ever allowed you to see to your own affairs."

Rogond nodded. "An attitude for which we are ever grateful. I only wanted to point out that prejudice is often based on things over which we have no control—your gender, for example, or my race.

"Those who would harbor such prejudices are not worth your consideration," she replied. "That's my opinion of those of the Ravani who would take my self-respect. Some are more enlightened, and they have learned to appreciate Nelwyn and me. I would spend my efforts on folk like Lamas and Hari, and not hide and cower in dread of the evil ones." She looked meaningfully at him, and her eyes were hard. "I know enough to be wary, Thaylon—I will not be easily taken."

He wanted to weep as he looked into her resolute face, for he knew that she had no concept of just how easily taken she would be, and he knew that he would not convince her of it. If they were in a city infested with Ulcas, it would not be so, but Gaelen held men in higher esteem. She could not even imagine the evil of which some were capable.

"Just think on it, my love, and remember that we answer to a higher purpose. We are only here for a short while, and we must still defeat Gorgon Elfhunter. You know it. Do not allow your pride to set him free. If the Ravani take you, he will rejoice. Just think on it."

"Not a day passes that I do not think on it, Rogond. And though this thought may not comfort you, know that Gorgon Elfhunter will not rejoice in my death at the hands of some narrow-minded sutherling, for it is his desire to achieve that death himself. Yet we must turn our thoughts elsewhere for now...tomorrow will you try to gain some news of Hallagond?"

"I will," he replied, "and do not distract me. I will not turn my thoughts without first exacting your promise to safeguard yourself while we are in the Settlement. If that means occasionally following Sajid's advice, will you not do it for my sake?"

Gaelen struggled for a few moments, her eyes distant. Rogond knew this would be a very difficult promise for her to make, and even more difficult to keep. Her hands clenched and unclenched several times as she fought with herself. Finally, she looked him in the eye. "For your sake alone, Thaylon, I will do as you ask. Just keep Sajid as far from me as possible. If he has advice to give, he can give it to you." She let out a long breath, as though what she had just said had taken great effort.

Rogond embraced her, though she was at first stiff in his arms.

"Our time together will be brief enough without my taking foolish chances," she said. "I will do all in my power to keep my promise, yet you need to know that there may come a time when I cannot. If that should happen, I will ask for your forgiveness in advance." She was silent then, as Rogond held her for a few moments before releasing her.

They spoke no more until they were on their way back to their encampment. Gaelen wanted to turn Rogond from his fears, so she showed him the profits she had made just from singing. "They give money for everything here, and they expect to be paid for every service," she said. "It's a strange concept, at least in my world. What I cannot make or provide for myself is freely given to me without payment. I'm a valued hunter-scout, and the King makes certain my needs are met. I have only to serve him in return, performing my duties faithfully and well. Giving and receiving little pieces of metal have never been required of me."

Rogond's expression was difficult to read as he walked beside her. She had thought to entertain him by showing him the proceeds from her performance, but he seemed conflicted. "You and Nelwyn and Fima have certainly advanced our fortunes in the past few days," he said. "A good thing, for I certainly could not have done the same. Folk would never pay me to sing for them."

Gaelen smiled. "Yet, if they could hear you sing, they might pay you to stop!" Singing did not number among Rogond's talents, and he was well aware of it. Yet, to Gaelen's surprise, he remained serious, and did not smile back.

He needed rest after his watchful night, so he lay upon his woolen mat with Gaelen curled up beside him. She rested her head upon his arm and, as she gently caressed his strong chest and shoulder, she thought she knew the source of his concern. Tomorrow would begin a time of celebration in the Settlement. There would be games and a festival in the marketplace. Nelwyn and Galador were hoping for an archery tournament, for they would almost certainly win prizes, adding to the Company's now comfortable coffers.

Rogond had not thought of his youth in many years, and he had just spent time recounting the tale of being raised among folk who might have considered him to be of lesser worth. He had not contributed anything to the Company's wealth as yet. Now he was having difficulty sleeping, as his thoughts turned in his mind. Perhaps he truly *was* of lesser worth. What skill would he have that would be of value in this place?

Gaelen sensed his insecurity, and her words soothed his heart. "Thaylon, do not be troubled. You do not need to prove yourself to me, or to anyone. You lead the Company, and you have led us well. It is we who must provide for you. Do not be troubled, for you have my heart. You have exacted a promise from me that no living Elf could have done. Is that not enough?"

He turned to meet her gaze, his grey eyes soft with affection. "It's more than I could ever have hoped for. Yet I still must contribute something…perhaps the games will provide an opportunity."

"If there is a spear-throwing competition, I will need to restrain Fima from wagering his entire fortune on you, for you will be certain to win and it will only encourage him," said Gaelen. "Tomorrow, we shall see. I'm certain you will find a way to show your worth if you feel you must, but I need no further proof of it." With those words, she gave herself to him in loving embrace, transporting him to a realm where he could forget all about his uncertainty.

Hallagond and his companions had made their way to the Upani oasis, known in the common-tongue as the "Darkwater". There were actually two water sources at the oasis, and it was wise to know which was safe and which was not, for to drink from the wrong one was most unwise. The water flowed from deep below ground, and was wholesome both to the eye and to the taste, but it contained a poison that would bring slow death. If men or beasts drank of it, and then filled their water-containers such that they continued for several days, they would sicken and eventually die. It was called the Darkwater because it blackened the inside of the mouth if taken in enough quantity. Such a sign meant death would soon follow unless the counter-agent was given immediately, and even then, the outlook for any but the strongest men was not hopeful.

The other water source flowed from nearer the surface, warm and murky. It needed to be strained through silk to be drinkable, yet it would not sicken provided the fine particles were removed. Hallagond knew the peril of drinking unfiltered desert water over time; sand would collect and settle in a man's entrails, causing great pain. If a remedy was not given, the man would die, for he would not be able to eat or drink for the pain, and he would die of thirst and starvation with a swollen belly full of sand. Hallagond had learned this lesson the hard way. Fortunately, one of his companions knew the signs and rode a great distance to acquire the remedy, which was rare and very expensive. It was also most unpleasant! Now Hallagond carried a large square of a very close-woven silk with him always, and would never willingly drink unfiltered water again.

His associates had done well for themselves in the tent city. Several had enhanced their personal wealth through thieving and pick-pocketing, and they could now purchase what they needed. Hallagond still had the remainder of his winnings, and had purchased a quantity of inexpensive wine.

He and his companions were in the process of drinking themselves into a stupor when a strange man approached, bowing, with his empty hands in plain sight. Azori and Azok, the two brothers who led Hallagond's band of thieves, were immediately suspicious, and their hands strayed to their weapons. The Darkwater was known as a den of vipers; wayfarers who knew the Upani would stop only long enough to water themselves and their beasts before moving on.

Hallagond looked up through the choking cloud of smoke that filled the tent, as the man addressed him. "I came to speak with Al-Amand," he said, "for I have news of great importance." It was then that Azori beheld four others standing behind him, obviously there for protection. Their eyes darted around the tent, and they were well armed. Azori and his brother Azok cast meaningful glances at their other companions, and those who were still relatively sober were now watchful of the strangers, though they feigned nonchalance.

"If I see Al-Amand, I will inform him," said Hallagond, his grey eyes cool. "Perhaps you will tell me the nature of your message so that he may decide whether it's worth making the effort to hear it."

The man smiled a knowing smile and bowed again. "Most assuredly," he said. "You may inform Al-Amand that my news will be quite meaningful to a man wishing to remain hidden from his past life.

There is one seeking him now, and we know his name, his nature, and his last known whereabouts. We would also offer our services to Al-Amand, should he wish to avoid being discovered by said person, for we have ways of laying a false trail so that Al-Amand will not be found. But we must speak with him, and our services will not come without cost."

Hallagond looked over at Azori, who was making a subtle gesture indicating that he could cut the man's throat quickly if Hallagond wished it. He considered for a moment. "And what is your price for the information, and for the deception thereafter?" he asked, his voice soft and menacing.

The man leaned toward him and whispered something in his ear, an act that caused Azori's hand to tense upon his weapon. Hallagond's eyes widened as he heard the proposed cost, and he chuckled, nodding to Azori. "That seems a bit steep, yet the information will be of importance as you guessed, and I don't mind paying. What say you agree to half that amount, and my associates allow you and your friends to leave with your lives?"

The man knew that Azori and his bandits were more than capable of making good on this threat. "Perhaps when Al-Amand learns of my news, the value of our service will be clearer," he said. "I will accept one-fourth of my fee for the news—the other three-fourths will ensure that this news has no impact on the future. For a greater fee we could make the problem disappear entirely, if Al-Amand wishes it."

"I grow tired of this game," growled Azok, whose temper was quicker than his brother's. "Tell us the name of the one seeking Al-Amand, and he will then decide what that news is worth. Otherwise, prepare to explore the Hereafter." In an instant, all four of the stranger's companions were struggling with Azori's men, and now stood with eyes wide, bright daggers at their throats. Azori himself was looking down the shaft of his crossbow at the stranger, who was fighting to maintain his look of confidence. He would have to reveal the name to Al-Amand, or be killed.

"I trust you will honor your agreement once the news is given," he said, trying to control the fear in his voice. "We have ridden long and through hardship to deliver this message, and should not be turned away without payment. I agree to one half of my proposed fee, though that is a bargain, and you wound me to the heart."

"Don't tempt me!" said Azori, sending a bolt whistling under the man's very nose, barely missing one of his companions to rip through the canvas wall, eliciting a few frightened squawks from outside. The man went very pale and began to tremble; his thoughts now turned to escaping with his life. "Speak!" said Azori. "We will not bargain until we know the name. Then Al-Amand will decide. Speak now, for you are trying my patience."

The frightened man turned back to Hallagond. "Am I addressing the Forsaken One?"

"You are."

"Then hear my news, Al-Amand. The one seeking you is your brother. He travels from the northlands with several companions—a dwarf and four Avinashi. He has sworn to find you and return you to the northlands. His name is Rogond."

Hallagond felt the blood drain from his face as he heard the stranger's words. Somewhere, buried in his thoughts, he had known of this. He did not yet remember the vision in which his father and brother had appeared before him, but he knew it nonetheless.

"Where did you encounter him? How came you by the knowledge that he is searching for me?"

"He makes no secret of his quest. The horse-trader Radeef had dealings with him along the Ravani Road. He was most forthcoming about his desire to find you and bring you back among your folk. Radeef has many associates, and they can keep a watchful eye for him. He will never find you if you do not wish it. I see in your face that my news is of considerable worth, even as I promised."

Azori growled at the man. "How do we know that you speak true? Radeef is not trustworthy… perhaps he has invented this to enhance his own wealth. I certainly would not put it past him."

The stranger considered. "Radeef noticed a golden ring upon your brother's right hand, with a black stone. He wears another ring of gold upon his left, with a multicolored stone. Does this aid you?"

Hallagond nodded. His mother had owned a golden ring with a black stone that was given her by the dwarves of Cós-domhain. She would never have parted with it, save upon her death, and then who else would have gained it if not her son?

"It does," he said solemnly, turning to Azori. "He speaks true. Lower your weapons and release them."

Azori's men did so, earning several black looks from the strangers. Hallagond then drew forth his purse, saying: "Here is your promised reward for the information. I will give my remaining assets to compensate you for throwing my brother off the trail. It is my last wish in this world to be found by him. Do what you must short of harming him. Do you understand?"

The strange man emptied Hallagond's purse into his hand. "This is not much payment for such a service," he said, sniffing at the gold. "It would be easier to just kill him."

"Yet surely your lives are worth something," said Hallagond, indicating Azori, who was now grinning wickedly at the stranger. "If not, I will take back my gold, for you will certainly not have the opportunity to spend it. And do not fear—I have one other asset that I will give to make certain my brother's quest is in vain."

He reached down into a hidden pocket of his leather vest, revealing a precious keepsake that not even Azori knew he possessed. It was a single bright stone of adamant set in hard silver, meant to be worn on a chain around the neck. It had been given to him long ago, and it was of Elven make. The one who had given it was long dead, and Hallagond had grieved for her, but his heart had hardened with time in the Ravi-shan. This was the only reminder left to him; he had not been able to part with it until now. It would buy his continued freedom from the past, ensuring that he would never need face his brother and reveal what he had become. He handed it to the stranger, who nodded in approval. Hallagond was now quite safe. The one who had given the stone to him would have wept, but she was far away, beyond the reach of sorrow.

The festival of Ujaala marked the longest day of the year, at the end of seven days of celebration. Among many folk of the Sandstone it was a time for merrymaking, but for the Ballali it was a time of fasting and contemplation, and numbered among their High Holy

Days. Long ago, Elves and men had discovered the nature of the seasons, where daylight waxed and waned in summer and winter. Although the seasons were much less variable in the southlands, still the days grew shorter after midsummer. Among primitive men, this had been a source of concern…would the light continue to wane?

According to the Ballali tradition, Ujaala was a time of foreboding, for the sins of every man were noticed and counted, and the light would now diminish until the Day of Undaala, the Day of Darkness, when the sun rose for the briefest time. Until then, the people would spend part of each day reciting the prayer of forgiveness, and only if they achieved it would the light slowly return.

Those of the Sandstone who were not of the Ballali had been busily preparing for the festival; there would be feasting and games as the people celebrated the turning of the sun. The Elves held a very different view of the events in the heavens, but they, too, rejoiced at midsummer, which they called Ri-solas.

The dwarves were less concerned with celestial happenings, but Fima never missed a good celebration when he could help it.

"Do you think Elraen is strong enough to join us in the marketplace?" Nelwyn inquired of Gaelen, who was in the process of stitching her boot. "She has remained inside for many days now… should we not encourage her to enjoy herself among these good-hearted folk? Sajid tells me that the Ballali will be inside, praying for themselves and meditating. It might be a good time to risk it."

Gaelen considered, but she remembered too well the actions of Elraen when she had taken fright, and was less inclined to take the risk. She could think only of the screaming, raving Dona with a blade in her hand. "I know the festival would be enjoyable for her, so long as she is not fearful. Yet if she takes fright she can be dangerous, and may harm others, thus bringing harm upon herself. I sense that these folk will not take kindly to her if she loses her composure. Better she should remain here with one of us. We can take turns in safeguarding her."

"She is perfectly capable of following our instructions," said Nelwyn. "We have left her alone many times. It's unlikely that she will venture outside the shelter…we need not worry. I only wanted to get her out among folk of good will, that she might see happiness and joy. It would benefit her after so much time in sorrow and darkness. Yet you're right; if she takes fright she may become unmanageable, and any benefit will be lost."

After promising to bring back goods from the festival, they reluctantly left Elraen in the shelter, though she was not unhappy about it. She sat alone on her woolen mat with her hood drawn around her face, rocking and humming to herself as though trying to ward off some dark memory. At times she seemed almost normal, but then there were times, like this one, when she appeared to draw into herself. Gaelen had hoped that she would heal quickly upon remembering her name and her history, but it was not so. This hurt would take far longer to heal, assuming it ever would.

The festival and the games were enjoyable as well as profitable for the Company. Nelwyn and Galador competed at archery, and Nelwyn bested all others, though there was one in addition to Galador who came close. For her effort she was given a beautiful prize of a golden arrow with a point and fletching of silver; it appeared to be of great age and its make was unknown. Fima expressed the opinion that such an example of craftsmanship could only have come from the hands of dwarves.

Nelwyn did not desire to keep the golden arrow, and she traded it to a dealer of antiquities in the marketplace for thirty gold pieces. She managed this with Sajid's help, as he was adept at bargaining and he spoke the local tongue fluently. Nelwyn decided to share her newfound wealth with Gaelen, so they each pocketed six of the shiny medallions, giving the remainder to Fima and Rogond for safekeeping.

The marketplace was calling to Gaelen and Nelwyn, and their gold was simply crying out to be spent, so they headed for the bazaar in high spirits. A marketplace is ever so much more wonderful when one has money to spend, and they spent several pleasant hours taking everything in. Because of the midsummer festival there were even more vendors than usual, and Gaelen and Nelwyn marveled at the variety of goods offered for sale by the colorful people of the southlands.

There was music, song, and dancing in the marketplace, and wonderful smells drifted from the stalls. The Elves sampled many foods and various sorts of drink from vendors of many races, even one or two who appeared to be Kazhi. They were selling beautiful garments of felted wool, dyed in many bright colors, with tiny beads woven into intricate patterns and embroidered upon them. "These would keep the rain off, that is certain," said Gaelen as she examined them, for they were thick and filled with natural wool-fat that would turn aside all but the heaviest downpour. Gaelen and Nelwyn each purchased a plain, unadorned hooded cape made from the wool in the hope that they would someday return to a land where hard rains fell.

The most attractive vendor to Nelwyn was also a wool-seller, a representative of a tribe of folk that hailed from some faraway mountains, and he was selling the finest wool the Elves had ever seen. Gleaned from very special goats, it was the softest in the world. Nelwyn sighed as she held it next to her skin, but alas, it was very costly, and she could not reconcile parting with such a large amount of gold. The vendor was no stranger to his art, and he saw the longing in her eyes as she replaced the creamy cloud of spun wool, her hand lingering upon the softness of it.

"There has never been one so fair that has ever worn such a garment," he said. "How it would become you! The chill of the desert night would vanish, for it is warmer than wool of three times the weight. I know you do not wish to leave it here, and so I will part with it for only five gold pieces."

Nelwyn smiled at him. "My thanks for your unwarranted praise, good wool-seller, but five gold pieces is still too dear. Since my other purchase I have only four pieces of gold and five of silver." She bowed briefly before turning to leave.

"Wait, wait, good maiden, for I would show you a wondrous sight! Only look at what I have to offer," said the vendor. Nelwyn turned back to him as he called over his shoulder to a young man, no doubt a son or an apprentice. The young man disappeared into the tent, and in a moment he brought out a bundle wrapped in gauze, handing it to the vendor, who revealed it with reverence. Nelwyn could understand when she beheld it, for it was a singlet made of the same creamy wool, only double layered. The outside was covered with fine golden embroidery in an intricate pattern of leaves and intertwining vines, but the wearer would feel only the soft wool under-layer next to the skin. It was a piece of artwork, and Nelwyn greatly desired it.

"What is the cost?" she murmured in a small voice, her eyes round and wide, long fingers straying to the beautiful singlet.

"For this, worked by hand by my own wives and daughters, I should have no fewer than twelve gold pieces," replied the vendor. "Yet I have been saving it for one worthy to wear it. Now I believe I have found her...see, how the fine gold thread matches your hair? How it catches the light in much the same fashion? To you, and only to you, the price is ten. If you would buy it, I will save it until you can afford it. I would honestly like to see my family's finest work adorn such a beautiful buyer." Nelwyn looked sharply up into the man's face, for she thought he was trying to flatter her into spending beyond her means, yet her gaze softened, for she saw only sincerity in his eyes.

Just then Gaelen came up from behind her, happy and excited. "Nelwyn! Wait until you see what I have found. It's the most wondrous..." Her voice trailed off as she beheld the beautiful singlet. "How beautiful! I didn't notice it earlier...this wool is softer than the finest velvet." She looked to the vendor. "It must be very costly."

"It is," sighed Nelwyn. "Ten gold pieces."

"For a *singlet?*" Even to Gaelen, who was unlearned and inexperienced in such matters, the price seemed high. "Still," she said, examining the fine embroidery, "it is of very fine quality. The color suits you."

"You're a fine lot of help, Gaelen," said Nelwyn, who was sorely tempted. Yet she still could not bring herself to spend so frivolously. She bowed to the vendor, noting the disappointment in his eyes as she politely declined.

"Are you sure?" said Gaelen as they turned to walk away. "You're going to regret this, you know."

"Yes, I know, but it's my choice. We will have need of the gold, and besides, it's too warm here for such things." She sighed. "It would have been oh-so-nice in the Greatwood, though."

"Never mind," said Gaelen. Come and see the other wonders of this place. We'll return home one day, and our folk will hardly believe what we tell them!" Gaelen led Nelwyn away from the wool-seller, but not before she looked back over her shoulder, speaking to him with her eyes. She would be back, and Nelwyn would own the singlet ere the day was out. The seller smiled and nodded, wrapping the beautiful garment carefully so that it would be ready when Galador came to claim it.

They found Rogond and Fima a short while later, and displayed their purchases. Gaelen had found a wondrous wax made from boiling the outer skin of one of the varieties of thorny desert plants. She had treated her old boots with it, and now showed how a very thin layer would turn water aside, reputedly for weeks. Gaelen was quite excited about it, and rightly so, for her old brown boots now looked almost new, glowing with mellow softness. The leaf-tracings upon them had been nearly worn away, but they were now visible again, for the wax had revealed them. "You can wax anything with it, including bowstrings!" she said.

Nelwyn had bought a container of the wondrous wax, a new flint, and her woolen cape. She could not bear to part with any more of her gold for anything other than the fabulous singlet.

Fima took note of the wistful longing in her eyes and wondered. "Well, my beautiful Nelwyn, have you had your fill of the marketplace?"

"Yes, Fima, I suppose I have," she replied. "I will go now and see to Elraen. Gaelen, why don't you go and tend the horses? They will be in need of water by now."

"That was my plan," Gaelen replied, but then she was distracted by a commotion coming from the north end of the market, where quite a large crowd was gathering.

"I wonder what the excitement is about," said Rogond, as the four of them made their way to investigate. When they arrived they learned that the games had resumed, and there would be a particularly difficult test beginning at any moment.

Apparently it was a sort of race, with the participants running as fast as they could to the base of the rocks, then climbing to the top where a tall pole had been mounted. The pole had been covered in thick, black grease, and the men would need to climb it and gain the top to win. It would take skill, speed, and agility, plus a hardy constitution. The competitors would not hesitate to thwart each other, even to the point of injury. The greased pole was a challenge in itself; most of the men had formed alliances, for it would almost require a team effort to scale it.

"I will go and fetch Galador, for he might want to watch this contest," said Gaelen. In truth, she wanted to tell him of the wonderful singlet, adding her three remaining gold pieces to the effort so that Galador could make a present of it to Nelwyn.

Rogond, Nelwyn, and Fima watched the men lining up for the test, clad only in cloths wrapped about their heads and their loins. They noticed Sajid standing in the front of the crowd; he no doubt wanted to wager on the outcome. In truth, their guide was planning to work his way among the preoccupied spectators once the contest began, for he would pick several pockets and increase his own wealth. Then he beheld Nelwyn and his plans changed, for there was a greater treasure to be gained.

"Look…that is Sajid, and it appears that he is entering the contest," said Nelwyn. Sajid had approached the entry table, paid his modest fee, and taken off his robes. He went to stand beside the other competitors, his head held high. He did not appear to take notice of the Company, yet he occasionally shot a furtive look at Nelwyn to make certain she was watching. He threw out his slight, rather bony chest and stretched his arms and legs, warming to the task before him.

At that moment, Gaelen reappeared beside Rogond. "Galador has some brief business to attend to, and then he has promised to join us." The field of contestants caught her eye, and she drew back in surprise. "What is Sajid doing? Has he entered the game? Well, that would make sense, for he is certainly adept at slithering. Half a moment…I would actually place a wager on him."

"Gaelen…you will do no such thing," said Fima. "She who admonishes others to forego the gambling-tables had best stay away from them herself!"

Gaelen did not seem to hear him, as she disappeared into the crowd, seeking out men who would wager on the games. Fima waited for another moment, looking anxious, then he started after her, calling: "Wait for me! I would join you in that wager." Rogond and Nelwyn simply shook their heads.

The men lined up for the start of the race, crouching like cats ready to spring. There were some fine, fit young men among them; sutherlings, Anori-men, even a few dark-skinned folk of the southern coast. There was one unsavory looking pale-skinned fellow, red and peeling from the hard Ravani sun, with hair the bright copper characteristic of some of the men of the north. He was scarred and fierce-looking, a veteran of many battles, with only one remaining eye. The others gave him a wide berth at the line as he dropped onto one knee, snarling and flexing his enormous, powerful shoulders. Other than the use of weapons being forbidden, there were no rules in this contest. Sajid would have his work cut out for him.

The starter held a white silken banner in his upraised hand, and then dropped it abruptly. All the men leaped forward, running as fast as they could toward the rocks. The long-strided, lithe ones reached them first and began to climb, but Sajid, who was small and wiry, was not too far behind them; his desire to impress Nelwyn gave wings to his feet. He scrambled up the rocks as though born to the task, and Gaelen and Rogond shared the same thought. He truly did resemble a spider as he scuttled unerringly up the difficult cliff-face.

There were those who did not make the climb successfully, especially when the other competitors had their way. The red-haired fellow managed to throw three of them off as he climbed slowly and deliberately toward the summit. There were no deaths, but there were several broken bones and bruises both to the body and to the pride. As the Company heard the unpleasant and painful sound of the unlucky ones striking the rocky bottom, they hoped that the prize would be worth the effort.

Sajid, meanwhile, had managed to gain the top. There were eight men ahead of him, but they were struggling unsuccessfully with the greased pole, unable to climb more than a few yards before sliding back down upon those below. The red-haired fellow charged up from behind, and Sajid leaped back out of the way, for he knew better than to stand before this roaring mass of muscle and sinew. The northerner, whose name, apparently, was "Olaf the Unfortunate," began to climb the pole by grabbing onto the other competitors. They were clinging for dear life, as he gained purchase by treading on their heads or their shoulders. He struggled briefly with one of the dark-skinned southerners, kicking him hard in the side of the head before climbing over the top of him.

Olaf was now only a few feet from the top of the pole, and Sajid saw his chance. He scrambled up the living chain of grease-covered men, several of whom tried unsuccessfully to grab him. When he reached Olaf he clawed his way up, balancing precariously on the shoulders of the man below, and then leaped like a cat onto Olaf's broad, muscular back. He was rewarded with a bellow of rage, but Olaf could not let go of the pole, and was momentarily helpless. Sajid took advantage, his eyes alight with savagery, his tight, sallow face twisted into a grimace as he whipped his head around on Olaf's blind side, grasping one scarred ear in his strong teeth. Olaf bellowed again, but with pain this time as well as fury, and let go of the pole with one arm, trying to strike Sajid. The smaller man then dug three fingers into Olaf's remaining eye.

Meanwhile, one of the easterners had grabbed one of Olaf's legs and one of Sajid's. He intended to use them to gain the top; Sajid in particular was still relatively clean, for he had only contacted the other men, not the pole. Olaf kicked the easterner in the face hard enough to rattle his teeth; he cried out in pain and let go of Sajid, but not Olaf. Sajid placed one foot on top of the easterner's bald head, springing with all his might toward the small banner at the top of the pole. He grabbed for it, snagging it with clever fingers. Olaf, however, would not be denied.

Sajid was now within his reach, and was grabbed from behind before he knew what was happening. He wriggled free of Olaf's greasy arm, the banner still in his hand, battling to keep hold of it as the beleaguered pole swayed under the weight of the chain of men clinging to it. Olaf swung wildly, trying to knock his rival from his perch, but this proved to be a mistake. The pole could not withstand the great unbalanced mass of Olaf lurching about on the top of it, and suddenly it tottered and gave way. As it fell, Sajid swung around onto the topside of it, leaping off just before it hit the ground. Most of the men let go, but not Olaf, whose name "The Unfortunate" was well earned as the stout pole crashed down on top of him. Sajid was victorious.

The Company had observed all this from their place among the spectators, Fima and Rogond making good use of Thorndil's glass. What they saw did not really surprise them, but the savage behavior of their guide was unsettling nonetheless. As Fima left to go and collect their winnings, Gaelen spoke grimly to Rogond. "Another guide, Thaylon, as quickly as may be found."

She turned to Galador. "He is capable of anything when he decides he wants something badly enough. I have seen the way he looks at Nelwyn. I fear we shall need to cut his throat some dark night."

Nelwyn had overheard this comment and started to suggest that her cousin's humor was in poor taste, but then she realized that Gaelen was serious. "You are as bad as Galador," she said. "He also thinks that Sajid is enamored of me. Believe me, if that were so, I should think I would know it. I have merely shown him courtesy, and he appreciates it...nothing more."

"I would keep away from him if I were you," Gaelen whispered. "You don't want to encourage him. I tell you, I have seen the look in his eyes. You always want to believe the best of people, but one day you will be disappointed. He is a viper…beware of him!" She stood silent for a moment, lost in thought. Then she spoke again to Nelwyn. "Observe him closely when he comes forward to claim his prize. He will look to you for approval. See if I am not right! He has done this only to impress you."

"Surely not," said Nelwyn, who was beginning to be unsettled by Gaelen's admonition.

When Sajid came forward to collect his winnings, he stood proudly, searching the crowd. When his eyes found Nelwyn he stood tall, smiling at her, lifting his chin. He brought his right hand to touch his forehead, bowing slightly, his eyes never leaving hers.

Galador stepped forward, looming beside Nelwyn, his eyes like black ice, and Sajid looked away. Galador and Gaelen were definitely in agreement—if Sajid did not turn his attentions elsewhere they would indeed have to cut his throat some dark night. It could not come soon enough for Galador, who looked over at Nelwyn and saw confusion in her eyes. To Nelwyn, the thought of Sajid being enamored of her was so preposterous and unseemly that it did not even warrant consideration, yet he had done exactly as Gaelen had predicted.

Gaelen looked over at her. "I told you so."

Nelwyn shook her head. "Must you always think the worst of people? Rogond and I are the only ones among the Company that have been even the least bit courteous to Sajid, and he has simply responded to it. You and Galador have made no attempt to hide your contempt for him—is it any wonder he shuns you? Now if you don't mind, Galador and I are going to take our goods back to the shelter and see to Elraen. Are you going to look after the horses, or not?"

Gaelen nodded and headed off in the direction of Hari's yards, after handing her goods to Nelwyn and Galador. Poor Nelwyn had been dismayed by the savagery she had just witnessed, and even more by Sajid's attention, but Gaelen did not know whether she truly grasped the seriousness of it. It was true that Nelwyn always wanted to believe the best of people, and that was a wonderful quality, but in this case it might have been a mistake. Gaelen loved Nelwyn, and would not change anything about her; she only hoped that Nelwyn's optimism and kind heart would not be her undoing. Gaelen would keep a very watchful eye on her cousin, just in case.

She waved to Hari as she arrived at the horse-yards, greeted warmly by Eros, Siva, and Finan, and her thoughts were soon diverted as she set herself to the task of caring for them.

"That animal has certainly seen his share of hardship, for the scars on his body tell the tale," said Hari, referring to Finan, who stood placidly in the corner of one of the holding-yards. He was not sociable with other horses, and thus had been placed in a small pen by himself. Hari, who usually housed several horses in such an enclosure, gave this as a courtesy to Gaelen. She had returned several times to ride the grey colt, the first that she had tamed, and it appeared as though Hari's fortunes were turning in his favor. The colt was swift and sure, and very powerful. He was tireless even in the heat of the day, and there was nothing he would not do with Gaelen astride him. There were many watchful eyes appraising him from afar, and Hari knew it.

Hari turned to her now. "I should make a present of him to you in exchange for that scarred war-horse, but I need to keep possession of him, for there are those who will pay dearly for his offspring. He is destined to sire my next foal crop and will serve well for many years. It would take a mountain of gold to buy him."

Gaelen smiled and bowed. "Your thought is indeed generous, Hari, Provider of Horses. Yet I could not part with Finan. He saved all of our lives, you see. One day, he will be whole again. Who knows... he may even see a battlefield, though I would not wish it."

She drew a deep breath. It was still too early to tell whether Finan would be truly sound again; his injuries had been very serious. He still favored one foreleg occasionally, though it was difficult to see, and he was reluctant to move in deep sand at speed, which was just as well.

"Ah, Gaelen my friend, I believe you've got it wrong. You saved his life, from the look of things. Your friend Fima told me the tale."

"Did he, indeed?" said Gaelen, smiling. "I am surprised...I'll wager that he left certain details out of his accounting."

"Details such as what? And I thought you did not approve of wagering," said a deep, growling voice. Fima was blustering up from behind, moving with surprising speed. He drew Gaelen aside. "I have been sent to collect you, for Rogond will not sit down to a meal without you, and both he and I are hungry! Come along, won't you? There's a good Elf."

Gaelen laughed. "Your stomach can speak to you for a bit longer, Fima. I must see to the other horses first."

Fima growled into his beard, knowing it was pointless to argue. He was so obviously crestfallen that Gaelen took pity on him, turning back to Hari. "Will you please check and make certain that the others are well, and that they are watered?"

"Of course," Hari replied. "And you will be happy to know that the wretched dun fellow has finally stopped trying to dismantle the fencing. I have never known a horse to set himself so to a task...I shall be glad to see the back of him."

Gaelen nodded in sympathy. Because of the terrain, which was both rocky and sandy, it was not possible to put up permanent fencing. Posts were set in a very clever pattern on top of the ground, with interlacing rails that defied all but the most determined animals. Woven ropes were also used, and Eros had managed to meet every challenge; he had set himself loose four times already. Finally, Rogond had suggested that Hari tie Eros on a short tether overnight, a nearly unbearable indignity.

Réalta had taken advantage, floating majestically back and forth as if to say: "How wonderful to be free to move about, so sorry you cannot."

Eros was often too intelligent for his own good, but after his night of confinement he seemed to have learned his lesson. He was still shunning Rogond, as though he understood that the intolerable tethering had come at his suggestion.

"Come Gaelen, before I shrink away to nothing," said Fima. Gaelen bowed to Hari, and then turned and followed her friend back to the festival so that they all might partake of some of the bazaar's exotic and excellent fare.

As Gaelen and Fima made their way back from the horse-yards, Sajid was deeply engaged in blunting all his senses with the most powerful drink he could find. He sat in the shade of stones, nursing a few bruises but still elated from his victory, smoking a small quantity of weed while drinking strong liquor made from grain and flavored with blackroot, which gave it a pleasant, musky aroma and taste.

His thoughts had turned dark in these past days, darker even than usual, as his unwholesome desire for Nelwyn had grown in his heart. He was uncertain now whether he drank to try to blunt his desires, or to bolster his courage to act upon them. He only knew that whenever she appeared before him, his thoughts turned to forbidden paths.

He shook his head, overcome with self-pity for a moment. What chance would he have of ever achieving his desire when Galador stood in his way? And why should he not have that chance? He was not tall, or especially strong, or particularly handsome, but he was certainly clever. He could be most winsome when he wished. Nelwyn, of all the Company, had been kind and considerate of him. He had desired her from the moment he first beheld her angelic face as he lay helpless, dying of heat and thirst.

He continued drinking, and the more he drank, the clearer his argument became. He swallowed another gulp of liquor, wincing as it burned his throat and made his eyes water. Perhaps now was the time to tell Nelwyn of his desires, and see whether her heart could be turned in his favor. Of course, he could always see to the death of Galador, but he was afraid to try. He had killed many times before to gain something he wanted…the first when he was only nine years old.

But he did not wish to earn the wrath of Rogond, Fima, or Gaelen, and he did not want Nelwyn to lose her lightness of heart in grief for Galador—better she should forsake him.

At last, Sajid came to a decision. He knew that Nelwyn had gone back to see to Elraen. He would make himself clean and polished, and go to her, and ask her to meet him by dark of night under the stars. Then he would declare his love for her, and see what the fate of his desire would be.

He drank the rest of the liquor; it was just enough to bolster his courage. If Nelwyn assented to his wishes, he would take her into the desert, vowing that he would spend the rest of his life in trying to make her happy. If not…if she spurned him, then he would take her into the desert for a different purpose. When the sun rose tomorrow, he would be gone; no one in the Company would ever find him again.

Nelwyn sat quietly inside the yurut with Elraen, sharing some honey-cakes with her and telling her of the sights she had seen at the festival. "There was a very large bird with brilliant red and gold feathers--red, gold, and green...even blue! It actually spoke. It answered questions. I would never have believed it. Perhaps I will ask the man to bring it here that you might see it for yourself."

Sajid could not understand Elvish speech, but he knew that Nelwyn spoke with tenderness and concern for her friend, and his heart ached with desire for her. He had rarely held such feelings; normally his attractions were of the baser sort. He cleared his throat, announcing his presence to Nelwyn, who looked at him with an open heart. When Elraen or Gaelen beheld him, their eyes held nothing but distrust and disdain. Even now, Elraen's eyes glittered as she drew back against the brown felt wall.

Nelwyn soothed her, and then turned to Sajid. "Is there something you need?" She was pleasant enough, though she could probably tell that he had been drinking and it disquieted her. He knew she did not like being around drunken men.

"I would speak with you, fair flower," he replied, his words thick in his mouth. "Please, will you hear me? It concerns a matter of importance, and I shall never find this courage again."

Nelwyn was puzzled, wondering what Sajid could say to her that would require courage. "Of course I will hear you," she replied. "What do you have to say?"

Sajid looked over at Elraen, his dark eyes half-lidded. "I would rather speak with you alone. It is an important matter that should not be shared. It might unsettle your excitable friend."

Nelwyn was now becoming concerned. What could he have to say that could not be said in front of Elraen? Perhaps he wanted to warn the Company of something dire; she knew that he was not always comfortable speaking his mind. She looked into his eyes, trying to read them, and saw no malice there, though they were clouded by drink. He swayed a bit as he stood before her, and she knew that his wits were likely clouded as well. She would do as he asked, hear what he had to say, and then suggest that he find a shady spot and sleep until he regained his sensibilities.

"Very well," she said, turning back to Elraen. "I will return in a little while. Do not try to follow me, and do not be concerned. Why don't you eat the last of the honey-cakes?"

Elraen shook her head, her wide eyes fearful. Nelwyn was so accustomed to this behavior that she barely took notice, yet now, to her surprise, Elraen actually spoke to her in earnest. "Do not go with him. He will have nothing to say that you wish to hear. Beware the voice of the Spider!"

Her warning was evident, but Nelwyn discounted it, for Elraen had always been distrustful of Sajid. "Don't worry. I will come back soon, and I will be wary. Remain here, and finish the honey-cakes. When I return, I will tell you a tale to gladden your heart."

Elraen wrapped her arms around her knees, and began to rock slowly back and forth, her face drawn into an expression of pain. When Nelwyn and Sajid had left the shelter she began to weep, for she knew that nothing good would come of it.

Sajid was now alone with Nelwyn; he had taken her to the green glade surrounding the central well. No one disturbed them, for the people were at the festival, and the Ballali were involved with their afternoon prayers.

Nelwyn regarded Sajid with some suspicion as she sat before him. *Why did he need to bring me to this place? Why not simply move outside the shelter, where Elraen cannot hear?*

Without any further entreaty, he began. "Nelwyn…I…I know that you and Galador are fond of one another, and rightly so. He is a fine companion, handsome and strong, yet I sense that he has grown distant from you of late."

His drunkenness had slurred his speech somewhat, but there was no mistaking his tone, and Nelwyn recoiled as she now knew that Gaelen and Galador were right—he was enamored of her. She shuddered at the very thought, yet she would still spare his feelings if she could. "Sajid, Galador and I have not grown distant. You are mistaken. Please, do not say any more...it will bring nothing but pain."

Sajid did not appear to hear her, but drew uncomfortably close, gazing into her eyes. "Of course, you would deny it, yet the pain in your heart is evident. Please, lovely woodland flower, let me fill the emptiness within. I have loved you from the first, and I will protect you from all dangers. Let me take you into the desert and show you the true wonders of our land, and of my heart."

She saw his resolve waver—no doubt he had read the dismay in her eyes. His gaze flickered left and right as he tried to think of something…*anything* to convince her. "I have heard Galador speak of Elraen. He desires her in his heart, and takes her to himself when you are unaware. Did you not know it? His love is false! I will never treat you with such disregard. May I be forever blinded and my hands wither if I should ever look with desire upon another."

The image of Sajid, blind and with withered hands, disgusted Nelwyn. In addition, she was shocked and angered at his suggestion that Galador's love was false. "Do not say any more, please! You are obviously desperate to speak so of Galador, and your drink has unbalanced you." She turned away from him, color rising in her face. "Do not speak to me again…ever."

He grabbed her shoulders and turned her back to face him, not gently. "You dare not turn from me," he said, "for I will not suffer your scorn. There are those here in the Settlement that would as soon see you and your companions dead. I can protect you from them. Only say that you will love me, if just for this one night, and you and they will be forever safe. Is it such a price to pay?"

He attempted to pull her to him then, an unhealthy lust glowing in his eyes, but he was unsteady and she easily rebuffed him.

She broke free of his grasp, furious, and drew her blade without thinking.

"Get back, Cuidag, or taste of your own death! You dare to imagine that I could ever, *ever* love one such as you? You threaten me and my friends, thinking that will win my heart? Gaelen was right about you. Nothing you can say to me now will allow me to trust you again. I am truly sorry for you, for you are pitiable, but I will waste no more time being civil to one who would speak falsely of my beloved and threaten my friends. How wrongly you interpreted the courtesy I have shown you! You will never have me…you *disgust* me! I would die by my own hand first."

Sajid obviously realized that all had gone as wrong as it could have, that he had no chance, and that he had misjudged her. He needed to salvage what he could, and try to placate her, for it now seemed that she would bring the wrath of the Company on his head. His expression changed to the familiar pathetic cringing.

"Please forgive me…I…I didn't know what I was saying. It was the drink. My thoughts were muddled…I didn't mean what I was saying. All is becoming clearer now…I didn't mean it. Please believe me…I would never harm you."

Nelwyn stared at him in disbelief. She did not truly understand the nature of men and drink. Did liquor so rob them of their judgment that they would lose all sense of reality, or had the drink simply caused Sajid to reveal what was truly in his heart? One thing was certain—there had been no mistaking the menace in his voice.

"You dare to suggest that you should be forgiven for attacking my beloved and threatening my friends because of *drink*? It was your choice to drink. Don't expect to be forgiven for your despicable words, for they can never be undone."

"I know," whined Sajid, "and I deserve some of your scorn. Yet I also deserve your pity, for I truly love you." He noted the look of revulsion on her face, and despaired. "Am I so vile that you would tear my heart so? Was there never any hope for our love?"

Nelwyn laughed at him in disbelief. "You're vile and deluded to think that I could ever love one such as you. You know nothing of me or my people if you do. Get from my sight, Sajid, and never again speak to me directly, for I will not answer. The one gift I will bestow on your scaly head is my promise that I will not tell the others of this...*regrettable* incident. Galador would most likely drag you out into the desert and leave you there if he knew of it, and he'd have Gaelen's help. They have already seen you for what you are, and now I see it, too."

Sajid did not know how to react. He had doomed himself from the moment he falsely accused Galador. He reverted to his fawning, cringing self, bowing before her. "I know...I know you're right. You are indeed fair and just, to spare me from death because of my drunken stupidity. I pray that I may repay you one day. You have shown me my place."

She sensed his humiliation, and she knew enough to recognize that he might indeed be dangerous, for she had wounded him. Yet he would not meet her gaze, denying her the chance to read the darkness in his eyes. If she had done so, she would have been unsettled enough to gather the Company and leave the Sandstone at once. As it was, she would suggest to Galador and Rogond that they acquire a new guide, knowing that she would receive no argument from Gaelen or Elraen on that score.

"Remember what I told you. Never speak to me again," she said, looking down on the top of his bowed head. Then she was gone.

Sajid remained in the glade, weeping with humiliation and loss. In truth, it was far from the first time he had suffered such scorn, but it still stung his heart. He truly did not know where to turn, for he had expected a very different outcome. Not only had she spurned him, she had laughed at him!

Though he had vowed to take her out into the desert and send her into darkness, he could not have done so, for his pride had been shattered. Still, for a while, Sajid held hope in his heart. Perhaps Nelwyn would come around; perhaps in time he could try again. He could wait a long time, gathering strength, and Galador would not remain watchful forever. Perhaps he could arrange a mishap that would take Galador from Nelwyn, and he would still be waiting to comfort her with open arms.

Unfortunately, he would soon realize that she had meant every word. She would not speak directly to him, nor would she acknowledge his presence. Though she was not obvious about it, he could feel her cold disdain whenever he drew near her. He took to watching her from the shadows, aching for her, knowing that he could never have her. His frustration grew and festered.

As the days passed, his thoughts would turn. If he could not have Nelwyn, no one would. He both desired her and grew to hate her, and his hatred gave rise to thoughts of vengeance. *She led me on... she is no different from any of the others; haughty and proud, thinking herself superior. She needs to be taught a lesson.* He sat once again in the glade by the well, remembering her shocked, revolted expression, nursing his wounded pride. *This is exactly why they should all be covered up and taught their proper place in the world, so they cannot tempt and humiliate us!*

When the plan came to him, his small, black heart was gladdened. Should it succeed, Nelwyn would suffer unimaginable hardship and degradation. Sajid would not need to worry about reprisal from her friends, either—not if all went as expected. He had work to do. Tomorrow he would go and seek out those who would aid him. Then he would make sure that the Company was driven from the Sandstone with no chance of acquiring another guide. They would be forced to endure him for just a bit longer, and then he would gain his revenge. *Who knows? There might even be considerable profit in it.* He now wore a sinister smile quite unlike the ingratiating, false one he normally displayed, and the true nature of Cuidag the Spider was revealed.

His dark thoughts were soon woven together into a well-conceived plan, like the strands of a web.

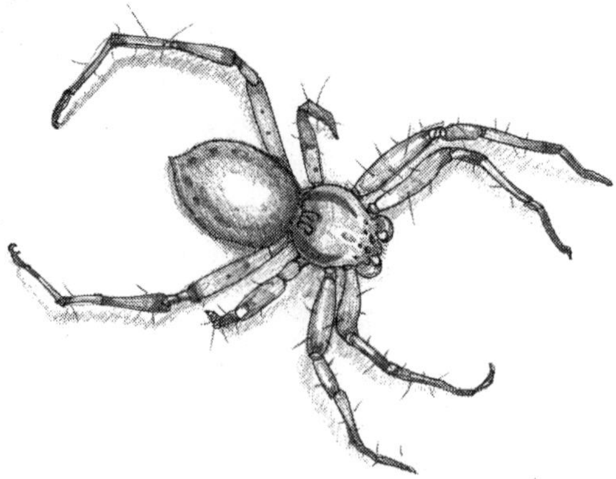

9
Cuidag's Web

Rogond spent as much time as he could in conversation with any who might aid him in the search for Hallagond, and he learned a number of interesting things. Hallagond would no doubt be traveling in disguise, for to do otherwise would place him at a potentially lethal disadvantage. Rogond knew of the enmity between certain tribes of Ravani-folk and the men of the North, but he had not realized how deep this enmity ran, nor the peril that he would risk in traveling these lands openly. He had now taken to wearing garb of the Ravani, and had grown his own beard to hide his northern features. His brother would have done the same.

Elves, Rogond was told, did not exist in the southlands. He had inquired as to whether any might be found, hoping to cheer Gaelen and Nelwyn, but he came away with a sense that their identity would need to be concealed at all cost. Known as "Avinashi" (Immortal Ones), Elves were portrayed as beautiful-yet-evil beings who would lure the unwary in an attempt to claim their very souls. Rogond did not doubt the origin of these tales; many sutherlings had lost their lives at the hands of the Elves when they had dared make war to the north in ancient times.

It would be much safer and simpler to employ a translator who did not know of the existence of Gaelen, Elraen, Nelwyn, or Galador. Besides, Rogond was reluctant to rely too heavily on Sajid, who had a habit of disappearing whenever he pleased.

Fima soon located and compensated a translator, a pleasant young fellow named Rashid. The dwarf had become well known since the wagering incident at the horse-yards, and as Rogond beheld some of the venomous looks thrown at Fima's back, he wondered whether his friend should have hired a bodyguard rather than a translator.

Fortunately, there was a code of conduct among the sutherlings, whose beliefs warned against the evils of gambling. Losses from wagering were assumed to be one's own fault. No retribution would be taken against the winner, for to do so would bring shame. Instead, those who had lost their wealth would need to be content in the knowledge that Fima had, by winning, doomed his own soul to the depths of evil deeds, and the inevitable punishment that would one day find him. Though they would much rather have tied Fima to a stake atop an anthill, it was better than nothing.

Because Hallagond had effectively disguised himself, and not been known by his given name in many years, Rogond learned almost nothing of him. Just as he was wondering whether the quest had been in vain, Fima bustled up to him in the market-place.

"Rogond, my friend, I believe we may have found someone who can be of aid. Rashid is with him already."

They made their way to the market, and the palatial stall of a wine-seller known as Harsha, of the city of Castalan. Rogond entered the tent to behold a richly dressed older man seated on a pile of cushions. Apparently his wines were of excellent quality and in high demand, for he was obviously prosperous.

A haze of blue smoke clouded the tent, and Rogond noticed a water-pipe on the floor, as well as several small clay vessels from which the sweet smoke emanated. It stung his eyes for a moment, and he blinked rapidly, knowing that he would need to be on his guard. He feared the smoke would muddle his wits, but in a few moments he did not seem to care.

Harsha gestured for Rogond to sit as he opened a bottle of fine wine, pouring some for himself and his guests. It was excellent, and Rogond complimented his host on its quality. Harsha was pleased, and for the next several minutes he gave Rogond more information than he had been able to gather in many days.

"I am only in the Sandstone on account of the Festival, expecting to do a brisk trade. My caravans often travel far and wide; in fact, my agents buy, sell, and trade wines as far north as Tal-ailean, though I have never gone so far. Yet I am well aware of the goings-on in the northern lands, and am quite familiar with the existence of Elves, although, to my knowledge, I have never met one.

What is undoubtedly of greater interest to you is the tall, grey-eyed man I met with in my home settlement near Castalan. He was traveling with a group of thieves and brigands, a well-known band led by two brothers, supposedly Fomorians, named Azok and Azori.

Their gang included criminals of many races—some sutherlings, at least one easterner, and several Corsairs."

Rogond knew something of the Corsairs. A varied folk, not truly a race, they were defined by their location and their profession. They lived in and around the southwestern coasts of Alterra, and they were shipwrights and sailors of renown. Fómor was their capital city, hence they were also known as Fómorians.

"What can you tell me of the Corsairs?" said Rogond. "I've heard many uncharitable opinions of them."

"That isn't surprising," said Harsha, exhaling a plume of blue smoke. "Pirates and brigands, living in lawlessness and squalor, and no right-minded folk venture near them if they can help it. Some of them look like you—certain families descended originally from northern outcasts, and they retained some of their stature and stamina. Most of the ones I have dealt with possess a sly, cunning sort of intelligence that is sometimes remarkable. I can say very little else of good about them, except for their unrivaled seamanship."

"I can trace my family directly back to Syrus the Mariner," said Rogond with some pride.

"Really?" said Harsha, his eyes wide. "If you run afoul of the Corsairs, tell them that. They might just respect you enough to let you keep all your body parts attached."

Harsha was an observant fellow with an eye for detail. He provided Rogond with a thorough description of the grey-eyed man, including the scar on the back of his hand, his missing earlobe, and the designs inscribed upon his arms. Harsha had seen Elven script before, and knew it as Avinashi.

"His name was given as Al-amand. That name, in our tongue, means 'The Forsaken.' Does this have meaning to you?"

Rogond nodded slowly. It would make sense, for his brother had forsaken his home and his heritage, perhaps even his honor. The scar was of significance to Rogond, although he had not known of the missing earlobe. When he drew back his hood so that Harsha could get a proper look at him, the older man's eyes grew wide, and then he smiled.

"There is no doubt that you are brothers. You have the same eyes, though there was more of pain and betrayal behind your brother's gaze. He only wore bravado on the outside…inside, I sensed he was troubled by shame and doubt." Harsha shook his head. "A pity, for he had a strong mind and heart upon a time. Now he is lost. You have a task before you...if he wanted to be found, he would not travel with Corsairs."

"You see much for a wine-vendor," growled Fima, yet Rogond knew Harsha's words made sense.

Harsha smiled at Fima. "When you have lived the sort of life I have, you learn to read people and see what is in their hearts. This is a talent I have long possessed. It is one of the reasons I am so prosperous—I am very difficult to deceive." He laughed good-naturedly. "You, on the other hand, have obviously not acquired this ability. How in the name of your fathers did you find yourself guided by one such as Sajid? I cannot imagine his words to you. Did you rescue him from some terrible fate, staked to an anthill, no doubt? His treachery is well-known to many here. It is to your credit that he has not betrayed you already."

Rogond's face reddened slightly. Harsha was indeed perceptive—the circumstances under which Sajid had joined them were almost exactly as he had just described.

"I see that I'm right," continued Harsha. "Do not be ashamed. Your kind heart has saddled you with Sajid, but that is easily remedied. I will give you the name of one who will agree to guide you if the price is right. Your kind heart, once lost, will be difficult to regain. Guard it well, for it will soon be tested. I will favor you with a gift of some of my wine as well, for I would improve your estimation of me and my folk. When you drink of it, remember that not all sutherlings are like Sajid."

"Never had I thought so, Honored Host," said Rogond. "Your gift is much appreciated, but I do not know how to reciprocate. I must confess to being unaware of proper custom in this matter. How may I repay your generosity?"

"No payment is asked or desired, my friend," said Harsha. "You will find the wine in your tent when you return there. But I do have some advice to be given at our parting. See if you cannot restrain your women-folk, as they are quite the topic of discussion here in the Sandstone." He shook his head in mild disgust. "People here are so…provincial! If you come to my home you will not find it so. You are ever welcome in the house of Harsha, as are your fair friends." He looked knowingly at Rogond, who realized that Harsha was well aware of the nature of his immortal companions.

Harsha then lowered his voice, speaking the common-tongue. "Your translator is true to his craft, Rogond, yet he was not needed here. If I have perceived certain…facts, there are others who have done likewise. Beware of Asaad! The Ballali will kill the Elves if they feel threatened by them in any way. They will kill you and the dwarf, as well. The name of the man who will guide you is Sundahi. I know him well. He was married to my eldest daughter, and he is a good man."

A cloud came over Harsha's warm, brown eyes, and Rogond knew that his daughter had suffered an ill fate. He nodded, casting his eyes downward in sympathy for a moment. "I cannot thank you enough for your aid, Harsha. You and your family are ever the friend of our Company. We thank you for your princely gift of wine, and hope that someday we may assist you. The folk of the Ravi-shan are indeed generous, such that few in the northlands can match them."

Harsha laughed. "You are eloquent, my good Rogond. Alas that my business takes me elsewhere, or I would invite you to join our caravan. Yet I know you will pursue your brother, though I have no idea where he might be at present. Don't waste your time looking in Castalan; my folk drove his companions from our midst, and they are not welcome there. It does not do to pick too many pockets."

Both men rose to their feet, and Rogond bowed once more to Harsha before taking his leave. They clasped hands, sealing their bond of friendship, Rogond being very careful of the old man's gnarled fingers until he felt the strength in them. This man would live long and well.

"Farewell, and may the Light shine upon your journey. I truly hope you find your kinsman," said Harsha.

"Indeed, my friend," Rogond replied. "May you and your family prosper. I shall remember your kind words and your wise advice. Farewell."

As he went out into the light and made his way to rejoin his companions, Rogond's thoughts began turning swiftly with the return of fresh air. This was the final day of the Festival—Midsummer's

Day. Before the evening feast he would seek out this man, Sundahi, requesting that he guide the Company henceforth. He would release Sajid, telling him that he was free of any further obligation. If Sajid resisted, Rogond supposed he would have to pay him to leave the Company in peace, but he was prepared to do so.

Tomorrow they would leave the Sandstone and continue southward to the next settlement, now searching for news of the band led by Azori, and a man named Al-amand. It would be good to be free of Sajid, for Rogond had never really trusted him.

The final night of the Festival would see the climax of the celebration of Ujaala, and at midnight there would be fireworks over the city. The Ballali would emerge for the first time since their period of prayer and fasting began, and they would gather together to beg forgiveness for the sins of men, beginning a long period of supplication until midwinter, when the days would begin to grow longer again. This was a solemn occasion, one of the most holy. Asaad would tolerate no interference, for at such times his power was greatest.

When Sajid was brought before him, shaking with fear, Asaad was inclined to disregard him at first. When he saw the resolve in the little man's eyes, he agreed to hear him. "I will hear you, unbeliever," he said, "and if what you say pleases me, I will spare your life. If not, if your intent is to be blasphemous or to deceive, I will take your head. Do you still wish to speak?"

Sajid wanted to turn about, but Asaad was essential to the plan, and to his credit he overcame his terror enough to remain. "Very well, then, tell your tale," said Asaad, as Sajid knelt before him, eyes downcast, two guards with very sharp swords at his back.

He stammered a little at first, but when no one struck him dead and he warmed to the tale, he grew bolder. Asaad listened with interest, and by the time Sajid had finished detailing his plan, the black eyes of the Holy Man were glittering, especially at the mention of the Elves.

Avinashi. So, they still exist, even as I suspected. Yet they are not so fearsome as our people believe, not if this sniveling little villain has traveled with them and lived.

"I only want the northman and his companions to be driven from the Sandstone," said Sajid, conveniently omitting the fact that Rogond planned to leave of his own accord.

"It shall be so," said Asaad, regarding Sajid, who was by now prostrate before him with his forehead on the floor. Sajid raised his eyes to meet Asaad's, but the coldness in them sent a chill through his body, and he looked away.

"Remember, Benevolent One, they must be driven forth tonight, before they have the chance to corrupt your most High Holy Day. I have it on good authority that the Avinashi plan to reveal themselves at midnight—to defile your ceremony. I would never want such a terrible thing to happen, so I have come before you. The Lord of Light has shown me this path that I might make up for my misdeeds."

Asaad's black eyes glittered with menace. "Do not speak of the Holy One in my presence, for you are unworthy, and I know you have a dark purpose to your mischief. Your heart is as black as any I have met, yet I will see your plan done and your end achieved. But do not delude yourself! If you remain in this settlement for one moment beyond the exile of your companions, or if you ever return, you will not long draw breath." As he said these words, one of his henchmen placed a cold steel blade on the back of Sajid's neck. "If things do not go as planned, and I must slay the Avinashi, I will slay you as well. Your feet are not set upon a righteous path. Get now from my sight, and do not ever speak to me again."

The blade was withdrawn, but as Sajid rose and looked into the face of this very dangerous man, he beheld a cold, humorless smile that would haunt his dreams to the end of his days.

After Sajid had gone, Asaad called together his most loyal followers. "I have been alerted to the strangers' intention to defile our midnight devotions. You, my trusted servants, must stand ready to drive the unbelievers forth. None will defend them, for none would stand in my way if they wish to remain alive. The infidels may have had acquired friends and admirers in the Settlement, but few, if any, will be ready to die for them."

It was essential to the plan that the entire Company be present at the evening feast, which would be held in a large, open area near the fireworks display. For one price, the people could eat and drink as much as they liked, so the night would be festive and merry. Asaad had instructed Sajid to ensure that the Company joined in the festivities, and this would not be difficult, with the exception of Elraen. Neither Asaad nor Sajid had taken her into their plan.

In preparation for departure in the morning, the Company had packed up their few belongings. Fima had reluctantly parted with his two dromadin, for they were young, and he did not know how to properly care for them. He sold them for much less than their true value, which pained him until Rogond pointed out that he had done nothing to earn them in the first place, and so should be thankful for what little gain he had made. This earned Rogond a look that could have melted glass.

The feast promised to be enjoyable, so the Company would attend, but they would take turns standing watch over their belongings. Such festivities made easy pickings for thieves, who would relieve absent owners of their valuables.

Elraen was told that she could join them at any time. "If you wish to come and feast with us, Elraen, please do so. Gaelen and I will watch for you," said Nelwyn, as Gaelen finished brushing and plaiting her hair. Alas that the evening was so warm, for Nelwyn would have worn her new singlet. Still, they donned their finest garments, hiding their elegant ears with scarves and headbands.

They had been invited to sit with Hari and his family, who had been told all about them and greeted them warmly. Hari had but one wife, and no sons, yet his daughters numbered three. They were lovely young maidens. They stared curiously at Gaelen and Nelwyn, to the displeasure of Fayalah, Hari's wife.

"You forget your manners! Keep your eyes where they belong," she admonished them. "Forgive our children, for they will not have met any such as you," she said. Yet Fayalah's eyes also roamed frequently toward Gaelen and Nelwyn, taking in their strangeness, though she was much less obvious about it.

Hari's eldest daughter, it seemed, was quite taken with Rogond. "They do not understand our tongue, do they?" she asked her father. Hari raised an eyebrow, shaking his head, and the three girls then proceeded to speak among themselves in hushed tones, declaring Rogond to be the most unusually handsome man they had ever beheld. They giggled musically until their mother silenced them with a withering look, informing them that any further unseemliness would banish them from the feast. They behaved with the utmost respect after that.

Rogond smiled, for he understood the message behind the words. Gaelen looked sidelong at him. "Rogond Thaylon, stealer of hearts!" she said with a good-natured smile, earning an affectionate squeeze of her arm.

Fima had offered to take the first watch, remaining in the shelter with Elraen. He had opened one of the bottles of wine sent by Harsha, intending to have a small feast of his own. He had brought plenty of food with him, for he would stand the watch for at least two hours, and his appetite was impressive. Elraen had never trusted Fima, and she would not speak to him, so he sat alone on his soft bedroll, eating and drinking and in general amusing himself. He did not begrudge this duty; he would be back among his companions in time for the fireworks display, since Galador had offered to take the watch at midnight.

Fima continued to drink the very potent wine, and soon found that he was nodding a bit. Well, it wasn't surprising, as he was warm and content, with a full belly. Perhaps a wee nap was called for; after all, Elraen would alert him if anything went amiss. As it turned out, Fima couldn't have stayed awake if he had wanted to. Harsha's wine put him into a deep sleep before he even realized it, his head dropping forward onto his chest, his breath whistling through his fine, white beard.

It was a beautiful, warm evening, and the desert breezes brought with them the scent of high summer. Flowers bloomed around the central well, where the fountains flowed into the marble pool. Elraen's head lifted into the wind, her body stiffening as she took in the scent of flowers, and...and water! Now that nearly everyone was at the feast, the settlement was very quiet. Elraen crept to the doorway, for she could hear the water flowing from the central well, and her heart rejoiced. She loved water more than nearly anything else, and she had not heard the sound of flowing waters since crossing the river Dessa. Though still fearful, she was also entranced. Without too much hesitation, she left the yurut with only one backward glance at the slumbering Fima, making her way toward the source of the crystal waters.

Only a few people observed her going, and she was shrouded and hooded, arousing little suspicion. When she arrived at the central well, her breath was nearly taken by the beauty of it. She shyly approached the fountain and the marble pool, tears of joy welling in her eyes. No evil thing would dare to intrude upon such a magical place, a haven in the heart of the cruel desert. The flowers were unlike any in her experience. Large, brilliantly colored blooms from the lands near the coast, they had been imported at great expense. Their scent was intoxicating.

Elraen shrugged out of her black shroud and tossed her long hair free. Clad only in silken undergarments, she stepped quietly into the pool, immersing herself in the clear, cool sweetness, feeling all her fears and cares wash away with the soft caress of the water. It had always been so.

She didn't even notice when the two serving-women, who had been sent to fetch water for the midnight rituals, dropped their long-handled water jugs in consternation and ran to raise the alarm. Apparently, Elraen had committed a sacrilege of the highest order.

She had no idea what she had done, standing waist-deep beneath the fountain, running her fingers through her hair. Her ears were uncovered, though she had lost part of the left one in Tûr Dorcha, but it didn't matter. It would not have mattered were she a mortal woman, or an Avinasha, or the foulest Ulca to come out of the darkness. She was female, and therefore unclean, and to defile the well on the Day of Ujaalah carried a sentence of death.

News of the catastrophe carried quickly, and the Company wondered why so many had risen from the tables in dismay. Gaelen and Galador looked at each other, sharing a sudden dread. Hari and his family were excited and flustered, and Gaelen grabbed Hari's arm. "What is it, Hari? What has happened?" He shook his head.

"I am uncertain, but they are saying that someone has defiled the central well—a very serious crime. I could not imagine what would drive someone to such an act. I expect we should go and see what may be done."

Gaelen was confused. "How does one defile a well? Have they poisoned it, or something? That would make no sense."

"Nothing so obvious, but all the wells in the city are blessed by the High Holy Man, Asaad, at sunrise on Ujaalah. To defile them, a woman only need touch the water directly. That is why the water jugs have such long handles. Women are never permitted to touch the water—not today!" His eyes grew wide. "Were you not told of this?"

Gaelen and Nelwyn looked at each other in horror, as a sudden intuition took hold of them. Elraen loved the water. They turned to Rogond. "We must go at once! Elraen…we have felt disquieted… there's trouble. We must fly, or she is lost!" Rogond, who had learned long ago not to question the intuition of Elves, followed them in alarm.

Quite a crowd had gathered around the central well by the time Rogond and the Elves arrived. People were chattering and muttering with dismayed excitement, for they all knew the consequences of this act. Those nearest the pool were staring at Elraen in disbelief. She had withdrawn into the center, and was now looking around with the eyes of a frightened doe. She had no idea of what she had done.

"She is one of our folk…let us through, please…please pardon us. Thank you," said Rogond, pushing his way through the crowd with the rest of the Company behind him. As he towered over most of the sutherlings, this was not difficult.

Galador's voice rose over the angry muttering. "Elraen…don't be afraid. I have come for you. That's right…come to me now. I will protect you." Elraen waded toward Galador's outstretched arms, and he gathered her in, lifting her as Gaelen, Nelwyn, and Rogond did what they could to keep the crowd back. No one had yet drawn weapons, but many of the Ballali had picked up stones from the ground, and one flew without warning, striking Galador's arm.

"That's *it,*" growled Gaelen, and the crowd abruptly fell silent, as they now faced two drawn bows and one glittering blade. The Company surrounded Elraen, shielding her.

"Please, good people, our friend meant no harm," said Rogond in a clear, commanding voice. "She is not of sound mind, and does not understand what she has done. We are strangers in your land, and do not understand your ways. We will make amends for her mistake, if you will allow it. We do not wish to harm any of you, but if you attack our companion we will have no choice. Please, put down the stones."

This seemed reasonable to most, but the Ballali were outraged and would not be placated. "She must face judgment, northlander! What she has done is a crime of great severity. The well is now unfit for anyone to drink, and it will be so for many months until our Holy Man can cleanse it of its impurity. She not only touched the water, she dared place her unclean body in it! This, on our Highest Holy Day…we must now use the other wells, which were of lesser purity. She must be held accountable."

Other unpleasant cries came forth from the crowd. "She is a devil-woman! She has ears like a beast! See the scars on her body? She is unclean and evil…she must die!" Another stone flew at Elraen, but this one was deflected by Rogond's blade.

Gaelen and Nelwyn were rightfully afraid, but their blood was aroused and their eyes were bright. Gaelen had taken about all she intended to—in the Greatwood, being female was not a crime. Yet she knew to hold her temper, lest she doom herself and her friends. *If only I could send this arrow straight to the heart of the next one to speak ill of Elraen…these wretches would not have lasted a day in the depths of Tûr Dorcha!*

The Company was now surrounded by a throng of black-clad Ballali, several of whom began to surge forward. They thought better of it when they saw the cold look in Nelwyn's eyes as she sighted down the shaft of her arrow.

"The next one who takes a step forward will fall before me," she said. "Try it, and see!" No one dared breathe for a moment.

"Step back, my people," said a soft, menacing voice, and the Ballali dropped their eyes as Asaad himself was carried forward on a litter. "Lower your weapons," he said to the Company, "for you are outnumbered. This is a matter for debate and judgment. I will hear your defense, and then I will decide. Lower your weapons, or die now."

Rogond spoke softly to his friends. "They will kill us all at a word from him. Lower your weapons. We cannot prevail here." The Company did so, but a stone flew from the crowd, striking Nelwyn.

"No more!" yelled Asaad in a voice that could not be denied. This man had power—one could hear it. "The next one who disobeys will be punished. Take the strangers to the place of judgment, and there we shall hear their defense."

"Shall we take their weapons, Wise One?"

"Naturally. And then set them all in bonds." He looked into the eyes of the Elves, knowing that he would spare none of them. He had thought to simply drive them out, but now he had an excuse to kill them, for they would not suffer harm to come to Elraen. They would no doubt go down fighting, sharing in her fate.

Gaelen looked directly into the eyes of Asaad, and as she beheld the malicious smile on his face and in his eyes, she knew the truth. They were all doomed…he would suffer none of them to live. She read this as plainly as if he had spoken the words. As his men came forward, she spoke to her friends in her own tongue. "They mean to kill us. If we surrender our weapons, all is lost. There is no hope in debate—he has decided already what our fate will be. It's time for desperate measures. I will die on my terms, not his!"

She waited until Asaad's men had moved away from him, then with blinding speed she drew her bow, aiming at his gloating face. "Don't move, any of you, or *he dies!*" she said. "Do you care for your High Holy Man? Do as I command, or say farewell."

Most of the Ballali could not imagine their leader being taken from them. The prospect was unthinkable! They would surely earn the wrath of the Powers of Heaven if they failed him now. For a moment, everyone froze, and dared not even breathe. Then Asaad rose with difficulty to his feet, though the sight of Gaelen's eyes glittering from behind her lethal arrow-point chilled his blood.

He approached her with halting steps, speaking in a voice that only the Company could hear. "I promise to hear your defense, Avinasha. Would you truly kill an unarmed old man? That is not usually in your nature, is it? Only I can secure your release from this place, and know this—it will be by my words that you live or die. My people will take you the moment I fall to your arrow. Show mercy, and it shall be given to you."

Gaelen knew he was trying to beguile her. His eyes told a different tale from his voice. She tightened her grip on her bow, answering him in a voice filled with cold loathing.

"Save your promises. I would sooner trust a snake than believe any words issuing from your forked tongue—I can read your thoughts in your eyes. Come no closer, or so help me, I will take you into darkness. Then long may your people grieve for you!"

"Asaad...she will do as she says. Make no mistake about it," said Rogond. "I believe she's right. You have no intention of allowing us to leave."

"So what, then, must we do?" asked the Holy Man, spreading his hands as though to say, "I'm a reasonable man, and here you are making things difficult and not allowing me to be reasonable."

"Order your people to allow us to leave," said Gaelen. "When we are safely away, you may return to your detestable way of life. You needn't worry about any of us again."

"Ah, but I will need to worry about you, for you see, if I let you leave, then you will have committed a high crime against the Powers of Heaven, and escaped punishment. I must be prepared to die rather than allow that to happen, for my power rests on it." His eyes grew cold as his lip curled into a snarl. "You should never have come into lands where you are not welcome. Now you will leave, for you will die."

These words were his last.

To the horrified surprise of nearly everyone in the crowd, Asaad stiffened, his eyes bulging with pain and astonishment, and then fell forward, a bright dagger buried between his shoulders. It had come from someone in the crowd. The Ballali stood in silent shock for a moment, and then gave a great wail of grief and anger. Many ran to their fallen leader, while others searched from where the dagger had flown, momentarily distracted from the Company.

"Come on!" called a voice from behind them. "Fly while you can!" Hari and Fima had pushed through the startled Ballali, who fell back, for without the guidance of Asaad they were unmanned and fearful. "They will soon regain their wits, and you must be gone when they do," said Hari. "Your horses are ready. *Come on!*"

The Ballali were in chaos, trying to discover who had taken Asaad, until one shouted: "The assassin was no doubt in league with the strangers...his evil deed has distracted us and allowed them to escape! Find them, and bring them to justice!" The angry crowd now turned to pursue the Company, who had made their way to Hari's yards. The horses were waiting, and Fima had already secured most of their belongings.

Sajid had followed them, for he would not be abandoned. None of this had been in his plan, and now he had to salvage what he could. "You cannot leave me here. They know I was your guide—they will kill me slowly and painfully. Please, I have served you well. You can't leave me here to die!"

Rogond looked around at his friends, knowing their thoughts concerning Sajid. "What is your will?" he asked them.

"Oh, let him come. We have no time to debate the matter. He can ride with us for now," growled Fima.

Hari urged them forward. "Quickly…they're coming now. They will kill you all! Leave while you can, and may the Blessings of Light go with you. You will need them."

"Farewell, Hari, Provider of Horses," said Gaelen. "Never was there a better friend."

"Never mind," said Hari. "I have always hated Asaad. It is good to be rid of him!"

"Who took his life, Hari? Do you know?" asked Gaelen.

"You are too curious," he replied, his dark eyes glittering. "It's best not to ask too many questions. Let's just say it was…a friend. Fly now...fly while you can!"

The Company rode from the Sandstone, escaping for the moment with their lives, but the Ballali had set archers upon the ridge-tops, and they sent forth a storm of arrows. One of these struck the gallant Réalta, and he fell hard as Galador cried in dismay. Elraen turned Malvorn, for she was nearest, riding back to where Réalta lay with Galador who, thankfully, had fallen clear. She swept up to him, leaping from her mount and grabbing his arm. "Galdor! There is no time!"

Galador could not see whether Réalta was still breathing, but he lay unmoving on the sand, and Galador could not delay. He swung aboard Malvorn, his eyes burning with loss. He had truly loved Réalta. He pulled Elraen up behind him, and urged Malvorn to follow the Company with all speed. In a few moments, they were out of range. The Company had escaped the Sandstone, but a part of Galador's heart still lay on the sand, his silver mane glittering in the light of the rising moon.

They kept going until the horses, exhausted by the deep sand, began to flag. They saw no riders pursuing them, at least not yet, and they drew to a halt. Rogond, who bore Sajid behind him, turned to regard Galador cantering toward him on Malvorn. Elraen clung to him, her eyes closed, her face pale and drawn.

Galador spoke softly over his shoulder. "Elraen…Elraen, it's all right. We're safe for the moment."

Gaelen had set Fima down, and now she rode back with Nelwyn. As they passed behind Galador, their eyes grew wide. Nelwyn gave a cry of dismay as Gaelen rode forward. She leaped from Siva to run to Malvorn's side, reaching up to Elraen. "She cannot hear you," she said to Galador. "One of their arrows found her. Get down, Galador, and help me!"

Galador swung his long right leg across Malvorn's neck, but Elraen's fingers still gripped his shoulders tightly, and as he slid down, she came with him into Gaelen's arms. A black-fletched arrow shaft protruded from Elraen's back, and she moaned as Gaelen and Galador set her down gently upon the sand. She shivered with pain and cold, so they wrapped her in their cloaks, setting Sajid to watch for pursuit, as Fima and Nelwyn examined her.

"We must draw forth the shaft, but it is buried deep," said Nelwyn. "I fear it may have been poisoned. Withdrawing it will do more damage, yet we must, or she will die very quickly now." *Her lips are blue, and her skin is cold,* she thought. *We may be too late already.*

"We will need to push it through and break the barb free before withdrawing it," said Rogond, who was experienced in such matters. He then set about the very painful task of pushing the arrow through the skin of Elraen's belly, so that Gaelen could cut the barb free and withdraw the shaft from the back without tearing her up inside.

Elraen scarcely reacted to any of this, to the dismay of Nelwyn, who sat holding her hand and speaking comforting words. She looked up at Gaelen, her eyes filled with tears, and saw that her cousin also knew the truth…no matter what effort they expended to save her, Elraen had seen her last sunrise.

The moon gave plenty of light, and it shone in Elraen's eyes as she opened them at last. Gaelen had removed her flaxen headband, dampened it with water, and was cleaning Elraen's face. "You are here with your friends. Don't be afraid…we will take good care of you, and you will heal quickly. You did a very brave thing going back for Galador…I had not even noticed that he had fallen. He owes you his life. When we return to the Greatwood, the King will have a feast in your honor, and you shall sit beside him. We will all drink to your courage."

She saw the familiar confusion in Elraen's eyes for a moment, and then, all at once, they cleared. For the first time since Dûn Bennas, Gaelen truly looked into the eyes of her friend. Elraen's eyelids fluttered for a moment, as though she would fall into sleep, but she marshaled her strength and kept them open, though she grew weaker moment by moment.

"Gaelen, it's all right. I will lie here under the moon, and I will leave you. I truly don't mind…I am no longer pained, and my thoughts are clear at last. The darkness has left me…the…the dark horrors have fled before the Light. Can you see it?"

Gaelen fought back tears, for she knew her friend was right, that she would leave them. Nelwyn was weeping already, her gentle spirit overcome.

"I see only moonlight, yet if the Light has driven the darkness from your heart, I rejoice that you have seen it at last. Stay with us, and be whole again, that we might return together to the Greatwood."

"I would love nothing more than to see the forest again, but that will not be my fate," said Elraen, her voice diminishing as her strength left her. "To you, and to your Company, I give my gratitude. You brought me out of darkness, and aided me when I needed you. You and Nelwyn have always been so…do you remember the fawn that we found, the one with the broken leg? I am like that fawn. You couldn't heal it, but you made certain it did not die alone in terror and darkness. I will go now to my beloved, who waits for me. I see in your eyes that you understand. Let me go in peace, and do not grieve for me, for I shall know joy again."

Elraen shuddered and closed her eyes. She was still in pain, and Gaelen and Nelwyn sat beside her, hoping either for a miraculous healing, or at least an easy release. This came a short while later, as Elraen opened her eyes again, her face shining briefly with the light of joy.

"Galdor? Galdor…you have come for me, and I shall go."

She released her last breath, her face peaceful and contented, as Nelwyn looked back expecting to see Galador, for Elraen had surely mistaken him.

Galador wasn't there; he was standing with Rogond. Gaelen, who looked now into the dead eyes of her friend, knew the truth already. Galdor had come for Elraen, and she was at peace at last.

The spirits of the Company were as low as they had ever been. They were alone in the desert with very few provisions. They had been driven from the Sandstone without their new guide, and would need to continue to rely on Sajid. Galador had lost Réalta, his favorite mount; both Siva and Eros would need to bear two riders. Eros grieved for Réalta, who had been his friend, and would not even take food from Rogond's hand.

The loss of Elraen placed the greatest hardship on the Company. Gaelen and Nelwyn were inconsolable for a time, especially Gaelen, who still felt shame at her earlier treatment of Dona. Her grief soon turned to smoldering anger, and she took to spending time alone, brooding under the stars, not speaking to anyone. She would not even respond to Fima's good humor.

They moved slowly, still bearing Elraen's body with them. Gaelen insisted on heading directly toward a distant stony ridge that would provide a suitable place to lay her to rest, over the protestations of Sajid, who was of the opinion that they wasted precious time.

"We need to find water, and soon," he said. "We have no time to wander about in search of rocks to cover your friend. She has gone from her body, and no longer cares." He looked directly at Gaelen. "You will not assuage your guilt this way. What has been done is done. She would not want you to risk yourselves for her. Leave her. I know where water may be found."

He realized that his words had fallen on deaf ears, and shook his head. "Elves never listen to the advice of others, do they? No matter how inexperienced they may be. In the desert, pride should be laid aside, or the desert ways will end your days."

"We cannot bury her properly in the sand," said Gaelen through clenched teeth. "I don't want some wretched sutherling defiling her bones just because the wind uncovers them." Then she turned her back on him, leading Siva toward the rocks to the southwest.

That night, Gaelen stood alone under the stars, so focused on her own thoughts that she did not hear Rogond coming up behind her.

"Gaelen, my love, I would speak with you. May I stand beside you for a while?"

Gaelen nodded, but she did not speak. She had not spoken to him all day. Rogond feared that her suppressed anger would consume her from within. He wanted to draw her out—to help her express what she was feeling.

"You must not blame yourself for what happened to Elraen. She is at peace now, and happy. This burden is not yours to bear." He put his arm around her shoulders. She stiffened, her chin raised, her eyes hard and distant, and he patted her gently, trying to reach her. "You need to let your feelings loose, Gaelen, and not keep them within yourself. Please tell me what troubles you."

Gaelen did not move, but she did speak. "I do feel guilt concerning my treatment of Elraen, but that is not what troubles me. I deeply regret her death, but it isn't just the fault of the sutherlings—she was lost long before. Terrible, horrific things were done to her, things you and I cannot even imagine…and for what purpose? What enjoyment did the Shadowmancer derive from her suffering? How is it that he goes unchallenged? Will he not pay for what he did to her? *He* killed her, or might as well have, for he took her very essence away. Only at the end did she truly regain it. I…I would see her avenged! If I stood before Wrothgar at this moment, I would try to slay him for what he did to her. That's why I'm angry!"

Rogond was shocked at her words. "Gaelen, don't be foolish! You could not hope to challenge Lord Wrothgar…you would not take one step before you fell. What happened to Elraen was tragic. The Black Flame is foul, the very epitome of evil, but he is far beyond you! Keep no such thoughts in your mind…they can only cause frustration. This sort of venom will poison you. Say goodbye to your friend, and move on."

"What of the other handiwork of Wrothgar? Shall I put aside my dark thoughts of Gorgon Elfhunter, as well? Will his victims ever be avenged?" Here, she looked into Rogond's eyes, as her own filled with tears of shame and frustration. "Is there no way to end this?"

"There may be no way to end darkness, for it is a part of this world," said Rogond. "It's up to each of us to choose whether we will embrace it, or turn from it. The more we turn from it, the less its power becomes."

He knew that Gaelen's view of the world was a simple one—there was that which was good, and that which was evil. Evil must be vanquished, not just forsaken. Yet Lord Wrothgar, with his great power, could never be conquered by one such as Gaelen. She had lived her long life in relative simplicity until her recent travels; they had opened her thoughts to many questions.

"Cannot evil be driven then from the world if all right-minded folk stand against it?" she asked hopefully.

"One evil might be vanquished," said Rogond, "but it would be replaced by another. The end of evil is a thing none of us will live to see, alas."

"Perhaps not," said Gaelen as he took her into his arms. He felt her sorrow, as well as her helplessness.

"In the end, evil did not conquer Elraen; she left this world in her right mind. Rest and be comforted," he said, secretly breathing a sigh of relief. Thankfully, Tûr Dorcha was far enough away that he would not need to prevent her riding forth to the challenge, standing before the dread gates, striking them again and again until the Black Flame came forth.

"You might as well try him, Gaelen, what can it hurt?" Nelwyn regarded Finan, who stood before them, shaking a fly from his ear. "The horses are overburdened since the loss of Réalta. If you could ride Finan, then Sajid could ride Siva. It is difficult for her to carry both you and Fima all the time, and Sajid has been riding double on

Eros. Eros is far better suited to carry Rogond and Fima. The only way you will know if he is sound is to try him."

Gaelen considered. "I suppose it couldn't hurt much…if he is still lame, I can always back off. I wonder if he will suffer himself to be ridden."

She approached him, stretching out her hand, and he walked forward willingly, dipping his head so that she could more easily rub the top of his neck. She moved around to his left, stroking his back and shoulder, speaking softly to him: "*Ehhhhya*…steady my friend. Let's see whether you will allow me to ride, all right? Steady, now."

She swung lightly up onto Finan's back, and he did not move, but shook his long forelock as if to say, "It's about time."

"It appears he will suffer me on his back, now let's see about moving him," said Gaelen, and she patted his neck, sending him forward. Finan stepped out willingly, breaking into a trot, gradually lengthening his stride before moving into an easy canter. Gaelen was delighted. He was smooth and easy to ride, had been trained very well on a time, and gave no argument. Her efforts had paid off, for he appeared to be sound. She was happy for the first time in many days.

They had buried Elraen among the stones, erecting a cairn over her body so that no beast or evil thing would touch her. Sajid moaned that they would surely die of thirst, for their water supply was low and they had gone miles out of their way. Gaelen and Nelwyn had learned that things were often not as they appeared in these lands, and the tall rocks that had seemed so near were a lot taller and more distant in reality. Gaelen had actually apologized to Sajid, yet she kept her course, and would not turn from it until Elraen was properly tended to. "Sajid, you were right," she said, then thought for a moment.

"You were right, worthy guide, concerning my pride,
For these unending sands are your native lands.
As such I should heed the words of Sajid,
Yet at risk of bad end I will see to my friend.
Though it may cause hardship, I will not leave her.
Look you now upon Gaelen, and believe her!"

She truly laughed then, and for a moment he almost found himself liking her. Then she turned back upon her course, her eyes bright with resolve, and he was more afraid of her than ever.

That night a very strange thing happened, one that not even Sajid could explain. As the Elves sat under the stars, they began to sing together. It was a song of grief and sorrow for the torment and loss of Elraen, and also a song of joy that her spirit had finally found release. Gaelen, Galador, and Nelwyn stood together, singing in beautiful harmony, and it seemed that all the desert creatures came forth and were silent, so that they could hear.

Clouds had gathered over the tops of the tall stone ridges where they were sheltering.This generally meant nothing, as clouds in the desert almost never bring forth rain, but merely tantalize and move on. Yet, on this night, in the midst of their song, the Elves felt droplets of rain begin to fall. The cold droplets turned swiftly into large, heavy drops that fell hard, soaking the dry ground, collecting in the hollows of rock, making fine, shallow pools of unsurpassed sweetness.

The Elves finished their song, the rain mingling with their tears, as Sajid capered ecstatically about. "Praise the Lord of Heaven, we are saved!" he cried. He continued capering like a child released from lessons, as the Elves looked on in wonderment. "Rejoice! Rejoice," he cried, approaching Galador, taking his astonished hand and pulling him around in a circle before letting go and leaping away, still laughing. The Elves and Rogond looked at one another and shrugged. Then they also began to dance in the rain, laughing in spite of their sorrow, as the puzzled horses looked on.

It rained nowhere else in the Ravi-shan upon that night. In the morning, as the Company prepared to leave, the very stones gave forth a bright array of color. This delighted Nelwyn most of all, for she had never before seen the wonder of the desert in bloom.

Their spirits lifted as they rode back the way they had come. They would intersect their prior course before turning southward again, for Sajid had informed them that they would now need to make for the next oasis, a place known as the Chupa-jul, translated as "hidden water." It was well that Finan was sound, as they could now make better time with only Eros double-mounted.

Fima sighed as he was lifted onto Eros' back behind Rogond. It was so much more pleasant riding with Gaelen, but Finan would not suffer anyone save Gaelen to ride him. In fact, he would not even suffer himself to be handled, for he had given his loyalty to her alone. Fima would now cling to Rogond's midsection and suffer in relative silence. Rogond and Eros were not happy about it, either.

Sajid had a bit of difficulty with Siva at first, and the suggestion had been made that Galador should ride her rather than Malvorn, but Siva was small, and Galador's legs were long. He missed his beautiful silver Réalta, who had been so tall and swift, yet he patted Malvorn and praised his strength, trying to make the best of things.

They had been two days on the track to the Chupa, having regained their southward course by half a day, when Eros began to hang back. He had been whinnying periodically since leaving the Sandstone, probably trying to call to Réalta, but it was unusual for him to lag behind. Rogond patted him, calling to Gaelen. "Is he moving well? He seems reluctant. Perhaps he is pained, or weary, yet I did not feel it so. What can you determine?"

Gaelen studied Eros intently. "I see no sign of pain, but you're right; he is reluctant. Perhaps we should stop and rest a while. We cannot afford to tax him, for we are not equipped to heal him out here."

Rogond agreed, and they stopped for an hour or two so that Gaelen and Nelwyn could tend to Eros. Fima was only too glad to have a respite from riding, and he stretched his stiff legs thankfully. Eros had learned to travel quite softly indeed when Fima was aboard, for the less he jostled the dwarf the more comfortable his loins would be at the end of the day.

The Elves could find nothing wrong with Eros. He was a bit dry, but so were they all. He nuzzled Gaelen affectionately as she knelt to examine his legs one by one.

"I can find no sign of ailment, Rogond, and in fact I wondered whether he is simply grieving. Yet I do not think so, in fact his attitude seems brighter than before. It's a puzzlement."

"Indeed," Rogond replied, stroking his lengthening beard.

Sajid wanted to move on, and they needed to pay attention to him, for he knew the distance to the Chupa oasis, and they did not. Fima drew him aside. "Why do we not make for this place, the one shown here?" he asked, pointing to the map. "I have some difficulty with Hamir's handwriting, but it looks like it says 'Neela-jul.' What does that mean?"

In truth, it meant "blue water." Sajid paled when he saw the map, for Fima had indeed pointed out a much more suitable stopping-point than the Chupa, but it was essential that they not go there. Sajid had made a plan, and that plan had not included the Neela. He had to bypass it in favor of the Chupa, whatever the cost. He appeared to study the map intently, considering, before he answered.

"We cannot go to the Neela. The name means 'dead-water.' The water there is not suitable, as it contains salt. The Chupa oasis, which is only a bit farther, will satisfy your every need. He looked at Fima with a wounded expression. "Do you not think I would have guided you well, and directed you to the Neela, if it would serve?"

"I would not ask that question of many here, Sajid, if I were you," said Fima with a chilly smile. "Yet I suppose you would have done, for your own survival depends on your ability to guide well. I will trust you for the moment." He stroked his axe-handle with a callused, almost loving hand, and Sajid took his point.

He smiled and bowed, but his darting eyes would not meet Fima's directly. "Please, Lore-master, it will be best not to mention the Neela. I will grow weary trying to convince the Elves that it is not in our best interest to go there. We will waste precious time in debate. If the stubborn She-elf decides to go off on her own despite my advice, the rest will follow her. We will be in quite a bad way if that should happen. Pray, do not mention the Neela—the Chupa is not far away." Fima agreed, and Sajid smiled. Another strand of his web was glued into place as they turned back southward, toward the Chupa oasis.

They had gone about another hour when Gaelen heard Rogond's distressed call from behind her. Eros had stopped, and was now refusing to move. He stood in the glow of the rising sun, his golden body aflame with reddish light, looking as though he were carved of marble.

Rogond patted Eros' strong neck. "Come on now, there's a good fellow. Why will you not move on?"

Eros lifted his nose into the wind, turned his proud head, and whinnied so loudly back over his shoulder that Fima was nearly deafened. Then he shuffled his forefeet restively, and whinnied again, as Rogond steadied him. "Easy, now...easy. What is it? What have you heard?" Eros tossed his head, circled twice, and abruptly dropped to his knees as Fima let out a sort of startled squawk. Rogond dismounted quickly, bringing Fima with him, as the rest of the Company gathered.

"Perhaps he has been drinking too much sand-water," said Sajid with a worried look. "If so, then he is doomed."

"But he doesn't seem to be in any pain," said Nelwyn. She was correct; Eros was not in physical discomfort. He was, in fact, quite excited as he sprang suddenly to his feet. He jerked backwards, pulling free of Rogond, and ran as fast as he could to the north, calling loudly.

"*Eros!*" Rogond called after him, panic in his voice. "What's gotten into him? We can't afford to lose him!" He turned to Gaelen. "Where has he gone?"

Gaelen smiled. "Don't worry, Rogond. I believe I know. Allow me to follow him, and all will be made clear."

Rogond looked curiously at her. "All right, but don't go too far!"

Gaelen released Finan's head and he sprang forward like an arrow, galloping after the now-distant dust plume that was Eros. Soon the terrain obscured them, and there was nothing to do but wait.

As the time passed, Rogond progressed from being concerned to being very worried. He paced back and forth as Nelwyn and Galador attempted to calm him. "Don't worry about Gaelen," said Nelwyn. "She possesses uncanny insights into the minds of horses, and she will return with Eros. Have no fear."

"But why is it taking so long?" said Rogond. "Eros is swifter than this. If she had caught him quickly, they would have been back long ago, unless they met with some peril, or something happened to Eros or to Finan. Perhaps Finan has gone lame again. If so, then Gaelen is in need with no one to aid her. We must go after her."

Fima, who was not patient by nature and who had been pacing along with Rogond, agreed. At least they would be doing something.

Galador, who had been keeping constant watch on the northern horizon, suddenly gave a cry and pointed, his face alight with uncharacteristic excitement. Everyone looked to the north to behold the beautiful sight of Gaelen, Finan, Eros, and one they had thought lost to them forever. Réalta's beautiful silver coat glinted in the sun as he made his way slowly toward them. Eros walked close by, urging him gently, following Gaelen and Finan.

Galador cried out again in joy, mounting Malvorn and flying back to meet them. The rest of the Company followed as they could, and Gaelen needed to suppress a smile at the sight of Rogond's long legs dangling below Siva's belly as he approached. Their little pack horse, the one that they had gotten from the Kazhi, was still with them, and was now demonstrating his uselessness as a riding animal by dumping poor Sajid onto the ground.

Réalta was in a bad way, but Gaelen had removed the arrow from behind his shoulder, where it had miraculously missed any of his vital organs. Galador had not known how badly he was hurt after his hard fall, but the Company had no time to find out. In truth, the fall had stunned him, and he had remained senseless for a time, coming to himself at last and struggling to his feet. Fortunately, he regained his wits before the scavengers got to him...almost. Someone had cut off his beautiful, long tail already.

Once aware, he struggled to rejoin his friend Galador, guided by scent and Eros' calls. Fortunately, his loyal friend had not given up on him.

Gaelen's face was alight as she waved to Galador. "See what our most perceptive Eros has found!"

Galador leaped from Malvorn's back and ran to his mount, embracing him and patting his neck. The shoulder-wound was painful, but it would heal if it did not fester.

Even Sajid was happy to see Réalta, for he had not been looking forward to the prospect of losing Eros, and thus having to ride the pack-horse. He smiled, congratulating Galador on the return of his friend. "At the oasis we can obtain ointments and herbs that will heal him quickly," he said.

Galador nodded, still stroking Réalta, who nickered at him, nuzzling the pouch at his belt. This was too much for Galador. He turned away, fumbling for some dried figs, tears filling his normally stoic grey eyes. He gave one to Réalta, causing Eros to toss his head indignantly and demand the same of Rogond.

"For the love of heaven, Thaylon, reward him!" said Gaelen. "Without his devotion and attention, poor Réalta would never have caught up with us. Now I am even happier that we diverted to tend to Elraen, for we bought time for Réalta to reach us. Devotion to a friend is always warranted, and is its own reward." She looked meaningfully at Sajid, who lowered his eyes and bowed.

"Too bad about his tail," said Fima. Réalta's tail, formerly long and lush, now barely extended past the bone.

Sajid shrugged. "Someone in the Sandstone will have a fine new fly-whisk. Our friend Galador will need to purchase one, for poor Réalta will be at the mercy of the flies until his tail grows back. He's lucky they didn't just take it off, bone and all."

"Ah, well, a small price to pay," said Galador. "There, there, Réalta. It will grow back. You are the most beautiful horse in all of Alterra in my eyes."

It was nearly two weeks before they reached the oasis, and it was indeed fortunate that Hari had provided them with many water-skins. They blessed the rain that had fallen so unexpectedly, for they had obtained enough water to survive the journey, but only just enough. Réalta drained three water-skins when Gaelen found him, for he had been subsisting on what he could sniff out from beneath the sand, and that was precious little. He had learned this trick from Finan.

The others of the Company were afforded the luxury of chewing the succulent desert plants for moisture, for they could circumvent the sharp spines. Sajid had taught them which were wholesome and which would poison them. "Oddly, some of the poisonous ones taste the best," he said.

"That does not seem at all odd to me," Nelwyn muttered. "That which seems helpful may hide poison beneath the surface. Though it may seem fair, it brings only evil."

Their guide seemed detached from them of late; he would not speak directly to Nelwyn, which concerned her not at all. This was remarkably different from his former behavior, when he would seek out her company and converse with her for hours as they rode. Nelwyn, who was very courteous and always wanted to believe the best of people, had seemed to enjoy his company, for he could be very charming when he wished to. Now she would not even look at him.

Something had happened. Nelwyn was not forthcoming, and when Gaelen had gently attempted to draw her into revealing it, she simply turned from her, saying, "I would not care to discuss anything of Sajid."

Gaelen stood watch on that evening and, as Sajid drew near her, she spoke quietly so that only he could hear. He was rummaging in his pack when her voice, as clear and cold as the ice that hangs from the dark limbs of trees during a late winter freeze, drifted into his hearing. "I do not know what has passed between you and Nelwyn, but know this: whatever loathsome deed you have done, whatever unwholesome thought you have expressed, whatever unseemly sentiment you have conveyed has done more to open her eyes than all of my warnings concerning you. Look not upon her again as I have seen you do in the past, for Galador and I are ever watchful."

She turned toward him, her bright eyes hard. "You truly confound me, Cuidag. At times you seem trustworthy, yet I cannot escape the notion that you are simply waiting for your moment to strike. To what end, I do not know, yet you are waiting…I can feel it. We Avinashi are not easily beguiled, and we can see into the hearts of men. Do not make the mistake of doubting it."

She turned back to the watch, satisfied that her warning had been conveyed. She had thought to cast enough doubt in his heart that he would give up whatever mischief he was planning. Yet she could not imagine the darkness that ruled him, or the degree to which Nelwyn's scorn had injured his pride.

The Company would soon face great hardship in these hard lands, for Sajid would not be turned from his course, despite his fears. As the Company approached the oasis, a slave-trader named Castor took up his position at an appointed meeting place, for he had been promised a great prize. Sajid would deliver to him the most beautiful creature imaginable, all wrapped in silk, and both of their fortunes would be assured.

10
Traps and Treachery

"There is the Chupa oasis. You can just make it out there, to the southeast. We are about an hour's ride from it." Sajid shaded his eyes against the rising sun and pointed toward what appeared to be a collection of shrubby trees surrounding several low, white dwellings. Smoke curled from one of these, probably from someone's morning cook-fire. "The oasis is larger than it appears—almost like a small town. There will be plenty of water, and we still have enough wealth to buy all that we will need for the next phase of our journey. Rogond, you should ask after your brother, for there are those who dwell in the Chupa who keep their eyes and ears open for news, and you may learn much."

Rogond nodded. "We should go there at once," he said, "for we must replenish our supply of water. Yet I worry about the people, and the manner in which we will be received. Is it possible that our troubles in the Sandstone have preceded us? We didn't exactly take the shortest way here, according to the map."

It was a valid concern, and Sajid appeared to take it to heart. "That's right...we were diverted from it by Gaelen, therefore it's possible that word of our difficulties might have spread," he said. "I will take the pack horse and fill our water-skins. When I return, I will have a better idea of whether your concerns are warranted. I am known here, and they will not object to my presence. I will learn what I may."

Gaelen turned to Nelwyn, speaking in the Elven-tongue. "If they know of him, and do not object, then the place must be a den of darkness. I don't trust him to go alone. One of us should go with him to make certain he does not get into mischief."

"A good notion, and I agree," said Galador. "Which of us is best suited to the task?"

Rogond turned to Sajid. "The others seem to think you should not go alone. You may meet with peril and need protection," he said. "Which of us would arouse the least suspicion traveling with you?"

Sajid's lip curled into a sort of sneering smile. "It really is most impolite of the Elves to speak in words that I cannot understand," he said. "I know better. They are not concerned for my welfare; they believe I will betray your interests. Try to deny it!"

"I won't deny it," said Rogond. "But my question remains. Which of us is best suited to accompany you?"

Sajid thought for a moment. "As much as it pains me to say it, probably Gaelen. She can be almost completely hidden by garments, and it is not unexpected that a man will travel with his wife. Gaelen is closer to me in height than Nelwyn is. If you insist that I not go alone, I would choose her."

"What say you, Gaelen? Will you go with Sajid and aid him?" said Rogond.

Gaelen looked levelly at him before turning her gaze to Sajid. "I will," she said, "but only if I may bear my weapons beneath my garments. I will not go unarmed into such a place."

Sajid nodded. "You should take your weapons in case of difficulty, but you will need to observe our customs, and stay quiet at all times. The moment you speak you will be known as a stranger, and not of these lands." He looked over at Rogond. "Being silent does not appear to be one of her virtues," he said.

Galador and Rogond both smiled. Sajid had a point. "She will do what is necessary, do not fear," said Rogond.

Soon Gaelen and Sajid were on their way, and Gaelen's abilities would be sorely tested. She was required by custom to follow Sajid, and to allow him to lead her mount, as women of Sajid's tribe were not allowed to ride freely. "Remember, you must never walk before me, and you must remain at least five paces behind when we are in public," Sajid admonished her. "And never, ever open your mouth to speak, at least not until I'm certain we will be safe. Do you understand?"

Gaelen gritted her teeth and nodded. This would not be easy for her. She mounted the little Kazhi pack-horse, who had been well trained to follow behind. He would suffer her to ride him after only a few moments of her touch and her voice—it was the Elvish way. Sajid rode Siva, who looked thoroughly confused at the sight of Gaelen trailing behind on the little brown pack horse. Gaelen and Nelwyn had named him Faladinn, meaning "hill pony." Finan was most unhappy with this arrangement, and had to be tethered to prevent his following Gaelen, for he would ever remain with her. He shook his head and squealed in frustration as she was led away behind Sajid, twenty empty water-skins dangling from the pony's harness.

Gaelen turned back toward the Company, concealed once again by her black shroud, and raised her right arm in farewell. Then she reached down and felt the comforting touch of the long knives tucked into her tall boots beneath the black silk. "Laugh if you will, Cuidag, only give me a reason to use these," she muttered. It would be a long and difficult morning.

They returned with full water-skins as the sun rose high, having spent only enough time to make certain of their welcome. This, as it happened, was not certain at all, and Sajid had learned that the incident in the Sandstone had become known to the inhabitants already.

"Ill news flies fast on the desert winds. Many would still have you pay for your sins."

"And what sins are those, I wonder," said Nelwyn to Gaelen, for she would not speak to Sajid directly. "Perhaps he refers to the unpardonable sin of escaping with our lives."

"No doubt he does. Yet not all of us were successful," said Gaelen, whose sense of humor had evaporated long ago. "Elraen most obligingly died anyway, and thus would have been absolved in their eyes. I'm sure that would have brought her great comfort."

She turned to Rogond. "We did bring back plenty of water, but I cannot vouch for Sajid's trustworthiness, as I could not understand him. Of course, I was forbidden to speak and gain enlightenment for myself. He could have told them anything. My effort was largely wasted."

"Not entirely, little flower," said Sajid with a smile that was genuine, but mean-spirited. "I derived great enjoyment from your silence for those few hours. I expect they will be the last afforded me."

Gaelen smiled back at him as she removed her black garb. She crossed her arms, reached down to her boots, and drew both of her bright blades, twirling them expertly. They glittered in the sun, singing ominously as they spun and flashed. "Sometimes," she said, "words are not needed."

The Company decided to make camp where they were, on the far outskirts of the oasis, in the shade of tall rocks. Fima could not venture into the settlement, for it was well known that a dwarf traveled with the fugitives from the Sandstone. Rogond, Galador, and Sajid would go back to buy more provisions and learn what they could of Hallagond while Fima, Gaelen, and Nelwyn remained in the encampment. Gaelen was not anxious to return to the oasis, forced to behave as a woman of the Ravani, forbidden to speak.

In truth, Sajid had spoken falsely. There were many women of the southlands who enjoyed most of the freedoms afforded men, but Sajid had delighted in inflicting as many restrictions as possible upon Gaelen, who, of course, knew no differently. So she had sat with eyes downcast, listening to Sajid ramble on and on in his strange tongue as he laughed and joked with the men of the oasis. A couple of times he had addressed her in a commanding tone, and naturally she did not respond, for she did not understand him. He would then mutter under his breath in the common-tongue, telling her to fetch him water, or to wait outside, or to see to the horses, and be quick about it! "And don't forget, you must always bow before me whenever I address you, and wait until you are dismissed," he had whispered through his sly smile.

Gaelen had complied for the most part, for she did not wish to disappoint Rogond by removing Sajid's liver on the spot, no doubt earning the suspicion of the local inhabitants. There would be time for this activity later, she told herself. For now, let him enjoy the illusion that he held dominion over her.

"One thing I will not do, web-weaver, is allow you to leave my sight," she had said. "Ask anything but that. My only purpose here is to ensure that you do not stray, and this I shall do. If you would have me see to the horses, you must go to them first yourself. I will not allow you so much as a breath outside my watchfulness." She had bowed before him then, as would a submissive wife.

Fima looked forward to spending time not on the back of a horse, as well as relaxing, eating and drinking, and sharing stories with Gaelen and Nelwyn.

Sajid, Rogond, and Galador left just before the next sunrise, taking all the horses save Gryffa, Finan, and Réalta, who was still healing. Galador would ride Malvorn until his favored mount was sound again.

Eros had been unusually solicitous of Réalta since his return, allowing him to stand beside his hindquarters so that he could wave the flies away with his tail, since Réalta's was nearly useless. He even stood back from the best fodder so that Réalta could eat of it first, to the amazement of Rogond. Normally, it was unwise to stand between Eros and a meal if one wanted to remain un-trampled.

Gaelen and Nelwyn had done what they could to heal Réalta, and he responded well to their experienced hands. Yet, as with Finan, this healing would take time. For now they would enjoy relaxing in the shade with Fima, who had expressed proper indignation at the manner in which Sajid had forced Gaelen to behave.

"Never mind, little Wood-elf. One day we will be rid of that weasel, and will all return home to where the soft rains fall upon our faces. With luck, Rogond's brother will be with us. You will never need bow to anyone again."

Gaelen and Nelwyn both turned away, and Fima realized that the mention of the soft rains made them both miss the Greatwood so much that they were overcome for a moment. He cursed his lack of sensitivity, and tried to cheer them at once. "Come, then, and let us play a game. Who enjoys guessing at riddles?"

Naturally, they all did. For the next hour, they attempted to confound each other with the most challenging riddles they could remember. Fima was quite good at this game, for he was very learned, and Gaelen and Nelwyn could not best him. "I can't think of anything more," said Gaelen. "It's as though my memory has deserted me."

"Well, you'll have to think of something," said Nelwyn. "It's your turn."

Gaelen thought for a moment, her eyebrows drawn toward each other in concentration.

"This loathsome creature is not as it seems,
It is the stuff of frightful dreams.
As slippery as an oily snake,
Casting sticky threads in its deadly wake.
With words of honey from a poisoned tongue,
It beguiles enemies and friends as one,

And when it believes it has earned their trust,
It lays them low with a venomous thrust.
You may think the answer has come unto you,
But instead of eight legs, this one has but two."

Rogond had promised to return before sundown, but that was many hours away. It would be a long day for those left behind. Gaelen held a feeling of foreboding that simply would not leave her, though she tried to dismiss it. She did not want to upset Nelwyn; after all, Sajid had been given plenty of opportunity to make mischief at the oasis already, should he have wished it. Gaelen did not understand his words, but she was very perceptive as to meaning and intent, and she had detected nothing dark in them. It seemed that Sajid had done exactly as he promised.

There was nothing for them to do now but rest in the shade of the stones, for they had left the yurut behind. Hari the Horse Provider had given them a silken drape that could be suspended with cords to form a sunshade; it was of a practical golden-sand color, and had proven very useful. They sat together beneath it, sharing a water-skin that had been filled with water from the Chupa. This water was clouded with mineral and held a strong taste, so Sajid had mixed a quantity of honey in it for flavoring.

As the faint sweetness filled her mouth and soothed her throat, Gaelen relaxed a little. A dark thought crept into her mind concerning the water, and she shook her head to banish it. After all, Sajid had drunk of it—she had seen him. She settled beside Nelwyn as Fima began a new riddle. They would spend several pleasant hours playing games and telling tales before the pain took them.

"Where is Sajid?" asked Galador, as he returned from seeing to the horses.

"I thought he had gone with you. I have been right here, enjoying the shade and the conversation." Rogond possessed a great gift for languages, and the longer he remained in the Ravani, the more familiar he was becoming with the difficult sutherling tongue. He had spent enough time in sharp observation of the people, listening intently to their speech. He could probably get along well enough to survive, though he was still a long way from truly mastering it. He sat now in one of the better gathering-places of the Chupa oasis; a tidy, white dwelling where they served food and drink, but no liquor. It smelled wonderful, and the few patrons appeared to be clean and well-mannered.

He reassured Galador. "Sajid has no doubt gone to see to affairs of his own. I expect this establishment is too respectable for his liking. The oasis is not all that large, and he should be easy to find. In the meantime, relax and try some of this…I have never had the like of it." He held forth a clay mug filled with a strong, dark liquid. Steam rose gently from it, carrying an enticingly rich aroma.

Galador inhaled the steam, and his face softened with pleasure. "It smells marvelous, but it's hot! Who would drink hot things in the desert?"

"I would," replied Rogond, "if they had the same effect as this. Try it!"

Galador raised the steaming mug to his lips and took a small sip of the dark fluid. For a moment his expression was difficult to read. "This is another one of those acquired tastes, isn't it?"

"Keep drinking," said Rogond. "You'll warm up to it soon, trust me."

Galador took Rogond's point a short while later, as he had finished his first mug and started on the second. He was brighter and more energetic than he had been in days; all the weariness seemed to flow away, and he was replenished. "Small wonder you are so cheerful," he said, looking appreciatively at Rogond. "What is this called?"

"The sutherlings call it 'kaffa.' It comes from very tall mountains far to the southeast of here, where they say it rains every day." He called to the proprietor, a friendly man with dark hair and a dark moustache. "If it please you, El-morah, will you tell my friend the tale that you told me earlier?"

El-morah was only too happy to oblige, after refilling Galador's mug and offering a fresh one to Rogond. He wore black robes with just a small bit of golden embroidery on the left breast, in the shape of a spreading fig tree, which was the emblem of his house. As with most merchants he was fluent in the common-tongue, and in a warm, gentle voice he told the story of how men came to drink of the kaffa.

"Kaffa is a divine gift, but because it was bitter no one would partake of it. So Aontar sent goats to eat of the fruits and leaves, and they began dancing happily. When the men saw this, they knew that the fruits were blessed, and they learned to roast them and brew them into drink, so that they might also dance."

El-morah smiled at Rogond and Galador. "I can see that you now appreciate the dancing goats," he said. "Do you travel with women-folk? If you do, then please accept this gift from my wife. Women find this irresistible…it will cheer them when nothing else can."

He looked back over his shoulder to make certain that he was not heard by the small, neat woman who was bustling about preparing food and drink. Apparently, she was his wife. "Believe me, this has saved my life on more than one occasion," he said under his breath, with a knowing look at Rogond. "One day it might save you as well. I will say no more." He placed a small package on the counter and returned to his duties.

Galador placed the wax-wrapped package in the pocket of his robe. "That fellow is very intuitive," he said to Rogond. "He must have met Gaelen already."

Rogond smiled. "Or someone very like her," he said, casting an eye toward the capable woman behind the counter. She was comely, with dark eyes and hair and a beautiful white smile, but her expression indicated that she would brook no foolishness. There was little question that she had an equal share in the governing of that household.

Rogond and Galador rose and bowed to El-morah before going in search of their guide, who, as Rogond had predicted, was not difficult to find. Sajid had gone straight to the seamiest tavern in the place, and was already in a drunken stupor. He would be of no help to them for a while.

"It's only mid-morning," said Galador in disgust.

"Apparently, in Sajid's world it's never too early," said Rogond, prodding Sajid's limp, senseless body with his toe.

The proprietor, a short, beefy man with a scar across his nose, bustled up to them, stating that Sajid had run up a considerable debt in his establishment over the past several years. He had been allowed to drink today only because he had assured the proprietor that he had friends who would pay.

"What will it take to absolve him of his debt?" said Rogond with a weary sigh. The dancing goats were fading from his mind already, to be replaced with the normal sinking feeling associated with Sajid.

The proprietor growled . "That man has not paid for his drink in a long while, and he always seems to disappear at inconvenient times. It will take five gold pieces to absolve him. He has sworn that you will pay, but in return, he has charged me with giving you some of the information you require. Does that make parting with your gold easier?"

"Five gold pieces! I suppose I should thank him, for I now have another excuse to wring his neck," said Galador with a venomous look at Sajid. Rogond held up a hand to silence him.

"Never mind. Let's just pay it and hear what this man has to say." He drew forth the coins and counted them into the proprietor's hand. Sometimes it was just wiser to give in.

The proprietor, named Haifa, was familiar with Hallagond, who had in fact been a frequent patron of this very establishment. Yet he had not been seen in this place for years. Rogond's heart sank, for his hopes had risen that his brother might not be far away.

"You should speak with a man named Kamal. He has traveled here from the City of Fómor, and has seen Al-amand there. Kamal will be here, probably before long. In the meantime, why don't you go to the market and replenish your supplies? They will be open for a few hours yet, though, naturally, they will close during the heat of mid-day. That will be the best time to return here and speak with Kamal. I warn you…he will want payment for the information. I hope this has been of help to you."

Something in Haifa's sly smile made Rogond uncomfortable. Galador, whose entire body had tensed from the minute the proprietor approached, shared the sentiment. With a last look of disgust at their drunken guide, they left for the marketplace.

As soon as they had gone, Sajid roused himself. He was, in fact, quite sober. He turned to Haifa. "Do you see how easily they are beguiled? When they return, merely tell them that your patrons found me offensive, so you dragged me away to sleep it off somewhere. They will not doubt you, as they always find me offensive."

Haifa laughed and nodded. "I will not find you offensive, Sajid, so long as you allow me to collect payment for liquor that you did not even drink," he said. "Where will you go now?"

"Ask me no more questions, and you need not conceal the answers," Sajid replied, leaving the establishment without another word. He stole quietly away, unobserved by anyone in the market-place. *Search for me all you like, you fools,* he thought. *You have seen the last of me...except in bad dreams!*

When the markets closed for mid-day, Rogond and Galador returned to Haifa's tavern. "We took Sajid to a place where he can sleep it off," said Haifa. "He smelled rather strongly." He ushered Rogond and Galador into a small antechamber, instructing them to wait there for Kamal.

Soon, a tall man with a greying black beard entered the room to sit before them. He was dark-skinned, but his eyes were an interesting shade of light green. He introduced himself as Kamal, lately of the city of Fómor.

"I understand you are seeking news concerning a man named Al-amand," he said.

"We are," replied Rogond. "What can you tell me of him, and what is the price of your aid?"

"First I will tell you what I can, and then you will decide whether my words have worth," said Kamal. "Haifa tells me that you are trustworthy. Take some wine, Northman, for you may have need of it. This is not a happy tale."

Kamal spoke for a long while. He told Rogond that his brother had gone to Fómor, had fallen in with pirates, and was now living as one of them. He had lost himself in drink, and in other things that were far worse. "You had better travel there at once if you want to aid your brother, for life among the Corsairs is short and violent. I heard rumors that his band of pirates were planning a raid on the city of Castalan in the autumn. If Hallagond refuses they will almost certainly kill him, if they haven't already."

"How long ago was that?" asked Rogond.

Kamal shrugged. "I'll admit, it's been awhile since I heard the rumors. Let's hope you still have time, as this will be a difficult journey. It's a long road to Fómor from here; it will probably take you at least two months to accomplish it. And you will not make it using horses only. You will need dromadin to carry enough water to survive. I know that you expected to pay only for information, and not for advice, but if I were you, I would reconsider. I cannot even say for certain that your brother still lives, though he was alive when I left him in late spring. But I might ask myself whether I should not go back to my homeland, and save the lives of my friends."

He looked pointedly at Galador. "None of *his* race will be welcome among the Corsairs, that's certain. Save your friends and yourself. In so doing, you will increase the chance that the more worthy son of your father will live to carry on his name."

Rogond listened to Kamal until he had finished speaking, and then gave him three pieces of gold, which was all he had remaining to him.

Kamal seemed satisfied. *After all, Radeef will pay me again for the same service.* He pocketed the gold with a cryptic smile before taking his leave.

Rogond and Galador sat for a while in silence. This was grim news. If Hallagond had fallen in with Corsairs, it was likely that he was either dead or beyond redeeming. At last, Galador spoke. "Rogond, I am your friend and shall ever be so…do not resent what I must say to you now. Is this a fool's errand?"

"So it would seem," said Rogond with sorrow in his eyes. "Still, I must try. I made a promise upon the grave of my father. This is *my* destiny...you must follow your heart. I will not blame you if you choose to take another path."

"Gaelen will go with you, no matter your choice," said Galador. "Nelwyn will not leave her. She also loves you, even as I do. We are inseparable, like it or not, and so we must prepare to follow you into peril. A promise is a promise, after all."

Rogond looked gratefully into the eyes of his friend, but he didn't know whether the unshakable friendship of the Elves actually made him feel better about the situation, or worse.

They decided to return to the house of El-morah, and to remain there until the afternoon waned, for inside it was cool and pleasant. "I suppose we should go and find our guide. He will surely have regained his senses by now," said Galador.

"He will have, provided he has not returned for more drink," replied Rogond. "Yet you are right. We need to return to the encampment before sundown. Will you go and make ready while I locate Sajid?"

Galador agreed, and they said their farewells to El-morah and his wife. Galador had purchased a quantity of the precious kaffa, for he was thoroughly enamored of it by now—it would taste so wonderful should one be forced to weather a cold rain. He smiled at the thought of huddling with Nelwyn under one cloak, sharing the warmth and cheer of the dark drink, and his heart was light as he left to prepare the horses.

Rogond received little aid from Haifa, for he claimed not to know of Sajid's whereabouts, even as Rogond pressed him about it. "Haifa, you said your men dragged him off…where did they take him?"

Haifa continued wiping down the counter and would not look directly at Rogond. "I sent them to fetch him and they said he had gone. He must have come to his senses and left. I do not know where he is at present, and I can't waste time over him." It was apparent that Rogond's welcome had run out. "Ask me no more questions, northlander. Look for your guide as you will, but don't bother looking for him here. You will upset my customers."

As Rogond turned to leave, Galador appeared suddenly in the doorway. He had been running, and was obviously agitated. "You have not located Sajid, have you?" he said. Rogond shook his head, a cold feeling creeping into his heart. "Well, you may as well stop searching. He's gone. He has taken Siva, and the provisions she carried, and has left the oasis. The stable-man said he has been gone for hours. We have been deceived!"

Galador's strong face was pale with dread, and the two of them shared the same thoughts. They needed to get back to the encampment at once! It was not long before they rode within sight of their friends, but to their dismay their greeting-signals went unanswered, for Gaelen and Fima lay still and silent upon the sand, and fair-haired Nelwyn, beloved of Galador, was gone.

Sajid had come upon the encampment earlier in the day to find that his plan had succeeded. Gaelen, Nelwyn, and Fima were in no condition to thwart him, for they had consumed a poison that he had placed in the water, and it had rendered them helpless. They would all die if the counter-agent was not given, but Sajid possessed only enough for Nelwyn and himself. He had placed the poison in the water before sunrise, and then added honey to disguise it. He had made a point of drinking some of it himself to allay suspicion, knowing that he could take the remedy at once, and had kept hold of it so that neither Rogond nor Galador would partake of it. Then, just before departing for the oasis, he had left it where Gaelen, Fima, and Nelwyn would be sure to find it.

He approached cautiously, for he feared the wrath of his victims, and if they were in the least bit capable, they would know of his guilt. Yet he found them as he had expected. Fima was curled up beneath the sunshade, his eyes open, looking as dead as Sajid had ever seen anyone look. The poison allowed him to see and hear, but not to move. Gaelen and Nelwyn lay where they had fallen—they had apparently been trying to get to the horses. Sajid was most impressed, for they would both have been in agony by then. Gaelen might actually have managed it, but she had not been able to ride. Finan stood protectively over her body. Sajid approached, and Finan stepped back, believing that he would aid Gaelen. But instead, Sajid bent over her, a wicked, triumphant smile on his face.

"Ah, little vixen! I see you've been laid low. Not so confident or capable now, are we? You'll wish you had never threatened me before this day is out. And your lovely friend, who spurned my advances...I will take her to a man named Castor, and she will fetch a great price. She will never know freedom again, but will be under the domination of men for the rest of her life. You are perhaps the more fortunate one; the poison will kill you before the sun sets. I know you can hear me, and you can see me. Look upon my face, Elf, and remember it in the hereafter. I am the one who bested you!"

Sajid went then to Nelwyn and tended her. First, he gave her just enough of the remedy to spare her life, but not enough to revive her.

Then he lifted her, gazing upon her beauty, marveling at the touch of his flesh upon hers. This was something he had greatly desired, but she was cold now—cold and without feeling. At first he nearly wept for her, but then he remembered her scorn, and grew stony again. "You should not have trampled my heart," he whispered, knowing that she could hear everything that was said, but could neither move nor react to it.

He wrapped her in the silken sunshade, securing her with a beautiful silver cord he had purchased earlier, and placed her carefully across Gryffa's back. He then ransacked the encampment, collecting anything of value that he could find, for he was a thief, after all. He took Fima's purse, which was heavy with gold and silver coins. He also took the silver medallion that Fima wore about his neck, the gift of Lady Ordath for his services as Lore-master, and the two jeweled daggers he had won from wagering.

"I should make haste," he muttered, "for I will need to be far away by the time the others return. I will be pursued, but there will be no success in tracking where I am going." He took Siva's bridle-reins and made ready to mount, but as he looked back upon Gaelen's sad, still form a thought struck him. *What if she manages to survive, somehow? She will hunt me down until the end of her days, as will they all, and I fear her…* He had not been able to resist gloating over her, and now Gaelen knew too much. She knew where Sajid was taking Nelwyn, and why. If they managed somehow to revive her, they might actually succeed in finding him.

He led Siva and Gryffa over to where Gaelen lay unmoving in the sand. Finan threatened the other horses, but even though he was suspicious, he allowed Sajid to approach. He truly thought this man would aid Gaelen as he knelt beside her.

Sajid spoke in a soft voice filled with malice. "I'm sorry, little vixen, but you must die now. You know of my plans, and I cannot suffer even the remotest chance that you will live to tell others of them. I have great faith in my poisons, but…well, you never know." He placed his hand on her forehead to steady her, intending to draw his dagger and cut her throat. She looked into his eyes, knowing that he would kill her in a moment. The poison had dulled them, yet her spirit shone forth as she focused on him: *No! You cannot take my life now…not until Gorgon Elfhunter has fallen!*

Sajid started back, for he read these thoughts as clearly as if they had been shouted in his ear. He was shocked, and even more afraid of her. As he drew forth the bright dagger, Finan abruptly came to life, lunging toward him with teeth bared, as another thought burst unwanted into his mind:

You dare not take her life! You cringing, pathetic creature... that privilege is reserved for the Elfhunter alone! Stay your hand, you miserable excuse for a descendant of worms!

Sajid did not know how to react, and as he looked into Gaelen's now-bright eyes they seemed to change. The pupils, which had been widened from the poison, constricted into tiny black dots. An evil power suddenly seemed to radiate from her, and Sajid gave a startled cry as the hand that held her forehead burned with it. He drew it back quickly, dropping the dagger. The horses screamed and ran back from her, Finan shaking his head in confusion.

Sajid gasped, weakened by the power that had flowed into him. He tried to stand, but he was dizzy and sick for a few moments, so he just closed his eyes, trying to breathe slowly until his head cleared. What in the name of all that was holy had just come over her? He had never before experienced such pure, raw hatred. He staggered to his feet, turning away from her, nearly retching with terror. He would not touch her again, and for a time his dreams would be haunted by visions of a huge, terrible, dark creature, powerful and vicious, laughing as it swung a bright sword to take his head.

By the time Rogond and Galador arrived, Sajid and Nelwyn were long gone. Galador searched frantically for Nelwyn, but when Gryffa and Siva were both missing, he knew the truth. Rogond had carried Gaelen into the shade. She had been lying in the open for hours, and was now in desperate need of water. Had Finan not been standing over her, she would have died already. Her body was cold despite the afternoon heat, and Rogond at first thought her dead, crying in grief as he knelt beside her. She did not appear to be breathing, yet his fingers searched her throat and found the faint fluttering of her heart. He held her close, trying to warm her, nearly weeping in fear for her.

Sajid had thought both Gaelen and Fima would be dead by sunset, but he had underestimated both of them. Fima was also stone cold and barely breathing, but dwarves resist poison even better than Elves, and both races are hardy when compared with men. Still, the poison was stronger than they were. The only thing their hardiness would gain was a longer time spent in dying.

Rogond knew that somehow Fima and Gaelen had been poisoned, as neither had sustained any wound or injury and they obviously suffered from the same affliction. He picked up the water-skin, which lay forgotten in the sand, and held it to his nose, detecting the scent of honey.

His eyes darkened as he thought of Sajid, who had apparently poisoned all three of his friends, and then had deceived everyone with false drunkenness so that he could return unaware and take Nelwyn away…to what end? Rogond did not wish to consider it. He heard Galador preparing to ride; obviously he wanted to go after Nelwyn at once.

He left Gaelen for a moment and approached Galador, whose expression told that he was both frantic and furious. He was barely rational, and Rogond would need to speak softly, controlling his own panic. "Galador, we cannot go after Sajid. He has been gone for hours, and we will not be able to track him in the sand. We must get Fima and Gaelen to the oasis, where they might be healed. They will both die if we do not…Nelwyn is in no danger, for if Sajid meant to kill her he would not have taken her. Please, my friend, I know you are distraught, but I need you…Gaelen and Fima need you."

Galador stopped moving as he listened to Rogond's words, standing still and silent until his friend had finished. Then he turned toward him, and Rogond could see the terrible mix of emotions welling within. "How can you say she is in no danger? I must go after her! She is my only love, and he has taken her. Do you not understand? I will die rather than let him take her. You would do the same had Gaelen been taken. I…I'm sorry."

He vaulted onto Malvorn and charged from the encampment, turning a deaf ear to Rogond, knowing he had to save Nelwyn whatever the cost. The former pack-horse did his best, legs churning in the sand, but he was not made for speed. As Galador rode, the realities of his situation began to creep through the panic that had obscured them. He would never catch Siva, who was far swifter than Malvorn. There had been tracks leading from the encampment, but, as Rogond had predicted, these had faded once the winds blew across the open desert.

Sajid could easily evade him, for he knew the land, and he was clever enough to lay a false trail. He was hours ahead, on a swifter horse that bore a lighter rider and more provisions. Galador carried very little with him, and he would not long survive should he lose his way.

His quest for Nelwyn was doomed to fail, and while he ran off blindly into the desert, Rogond was contending with Gaelen and Fima, who were barely alive. Rogond would never forgive him if they died, and for that matter, neither would Nelwyn. Galador pulled the sweating, panting Malvorn to a halt, and stood still for a moment. The sun had set and the moon was rising; if he was not careful he would lose his way completely. He cried out with grief and frustration as he turned Malvorn back, knowing that Rogond was right. They would save Nelwyn, but not on this night. Galador vowed that Sajid would suffer the most painful death at his hands should Nelwyn be harmed, and it was these black thoughts that filled his mind as he rode back to the encampment.

Rogond was trying to secure Gaelen and Fima so that he could take them back to the oasis. Finan, who normally did not suffer the touch of men, seemed to know that Rogond was trying to aid Gaelen. He stood placidly while Rogond lashed her to his back. Fima had been secured upon Eros already, and now Rogond mounted with some difficulty, holding Finan's tether. Eros and Finan were not friends, and they pinned their ears and lashed their tails. "Stop it, Eros! This is not the time," said Rogond. Eros quit fidgeting and lashing his tail, but kept his wrinkled nose in the air.

"Here. Give him to me," said Galador, as he approached Rogond unaware.

"Galador! Thank the stars you have returned! I really cannot manage this task alone." Rogond handed Finan to Galador. Malvorn, who was a gelding, had no difficulty with Finan.

"I regretted leaving you, though I know you would have managed somehow," said Galador. "But you are right. I…I just had to realize it myself."

They started back toward the Chupa with all the speed they could safely manage, releasing Réalta so that he could follow them as he might. Rogond turned to his friend, tears of gratitude standing in his eyes. "What convinced you to come back?"

Galador's face was stony. "I realized that I could not prevail, and that Sajid held the advantage. I would have run off blindly and gotten lost, and I cannot help her if that happens. And…I came back for you, and for them." He indicated Gaelen and Fima.

Rogond saw the pain in his friend's face, and he tried to reassure him. "There will be time later to find her. The horse-trader said that… that many would covet her. No one will want to kill her, Galador. We will find her, I swear it!"

"What horse-trader? What did he say about Nelwyn?"

Rogond realized that Galador did not know of Radeef's warning, and he was abashed. "When Fima and I rode out to recover Gaelen's brooch, the horse trader warned us that many would covet Nelwyn. He said that she would bring a high price in the…in the slave-markets. He told us then to keep watch over her."

"Why did you keep this from me?" cried Galador in indignation. "Perhaps I would have been more vigilant! Are you my friend, or no?"

Rogond replied, "I am. You have been most vigilant. The trader did not tell us anything that you did not know already, and you have safeguarded Nelwyn faithfully. You left her in the encampment with Gaelen and Fima because you thought she would be safe. You did nothing to further Sajid's cause. I, on the other hand…"

Rogond could not speak further. He felt a terrible responsibility for all that had befallen. This entire quest was undertaken on his behalf, Sajid had joined them on his approval, and he had fallen easily into the deception. The warnings of Radeef, and of Hamir, echoed in his mind, filling him with guilt. He was as unhappy in that moment as he could ever recall.

Galador took a deep, shuddering breath. He had not considered Rogond's feelings, in fact he had thought of no pain but his own. He tried to look into Rogond's eyes, but Rogond stared fixedly ahead as he rode. Galador knew what he would see in them. There would be guilt, desperation, and fear for Gaelen and Fima. If any of the Company died, there would be no forgiveness.

Galador nodded grimly and put his own pain aside, turning all his efforts to the aid of his friends. In truth, Galador wanted Gaelen at his side when he finally went in pursuit of Nelwyn, for she would hunt Sajid without rest, even as he would, and in the end the wretch would wish that they had left him to die in the desert so long ago.

Many miles away, the aforementioned wretch had dismounted from Siva and was now attending to Nelwyn. He carefully drew the silk back from her face, noting with some regret the dullness in her beautiful eyes. He had given her more of the remedy, but he had combined it with a sleeping-draught. Sajid had learned from the apothecary in the Sandstone that if one wished to save the life of someone who had taken this poison, it would be a courtesy to add something to dull the agonizing pain of recovery. Nelwyn had been in considerable pain for several hours now, but she was only able to make small sounds, and she still could not move, for she was restrained. The sleeping-draught had dulled her awareness, which was fortunate. Sajid knew that restraining her would be beyond him if she regained her senses, and in spite of his resentment of her, he did not wish to see her in agony.

He poured a tiny amount of the elixir down her throat, absently stroking her silken hair, gazing into her beautiful eyes. She stirred, trying to resist, but her movements were feeble and her eyes could not focus on him. He perceived confusion in their depths. He could only hope to make the rendezvous with Castor ere he ran out of the sleeping-potion, for once Nelwyn came to herself that confusion would be replaced by hatred, and then he would most likely need to kill her to save his own life. There would be no profit in that.

Gaelen had not been given a sleeping-draught, and in her eyes there was no confusion. She knew that Rogond had come for her, and she knew that she was being carried, secured to Finan. She felt unbalanced and awkward, as though she would slide off at any moment, and this was disquieting, but she could not move any part of her body to remedy it. Sajid had chosen his poison well if he wanted to claim revenge, for Gaelen had not experienced physical pain that could rival it.

The day had begun pleasantly enough, and when they grew weary of riddles, Gaelen and Fima had decided to try another of their favored pastimes. They enjoyed holding mock battles, sparring with their weapons, honing their skills. Gaelen held great respect for Fima in this regard, for he was a skilled adversary, and he was likewise hard put to defend himself from her.

The pain had come first upon Gaelen, as Fima drew back in horror, thinking he had injured her. He dropped his axe and knelt beside her, for she had doubled over and fallen to the ground, gasping. It had started as a vague tingling in her limbs, and she had paused in her sparring, staring curiously at her own right arm. This had turned rapidly into a burning pain that seemed to consume her entire body in flame. She had cried and dropped her weapon, staggering back and holding her hands before her face. Then she had dropped to the ground with her knees drawn up toward her belly. Nelwyn, who had been keeping watch, had fallen in nearly the same moment.

Fima, who could not imagine what was happening to his friends, felt the first unsettling sensation in his hands and feet as he tried to lift Gaelen and carry her into the shade. She was stiff and unyielding, shuddering with pain as he tried to calm her. Her eyes at first were wide with terror and confusion, yet Fima saw her slowly master herself, and she pulled back from him, rising painfully to her knees, her teeth clenched, blood flowing from her lower lip where she had bitten it.

All at once the pain came over Fima, and he was seemingly set aflame, reacting in much the same manner as the Elves, doubling over and sagging to the ground. What was happening to them? Gaelen knew that Fima would never survive lying helpless in the full sun, and she aided him in gaining the shelter. Dwarves are among the hardiest of folk, but Fima's age was against him, and he curled up into a ball of misery.

Gaelen and Nelwyn knew that they had to get help, and they would need to ride back to the oasis, where the only help would be found. They tried to gain the horses, sharing grim thoughts as their eyes met, but their bodies betrayed them. Nelwyn fell just short of

Gryffa, giving a sort of strangled moan that was very distressing to hear. Gaelen managed to wrap her arms around Finan's neck, for he was not tethered and came to her straightaway. She gave a feeble cry of frustration, for she could not mount him. Finan was very perceptive, and he dropped to his knees. Gaelen sort of fell across his back, but when he tried to rise again she could not grip him, and she slid to the ground like a sack.

All the strength had flowed out of her body, and it would no longer answer her commands. Thankfully, the pain was abating, and soon she could feel nothing. She lay with her eyes open, seeing and hearing all around her, perfectly aware, but otherwise completely helpless. Finan, greatly distressed, called softly to her, trying to rouse her, prodding her with his muzzle. When she did not move, he stood over her, shading her with his body, doing all that he could to aid her.

The next sight Gaelen beheld was the sneering face of Sajid the Spider. She could do nothing to respond to him, forced to listen to his vile words. When she realized what he would do to Nelwyn, she was nearly overcome with outrage and helplessness, for she could do nothing to stop him. As he knelt beside her, drawing his bright dagger to take her life, she knew that she could not prevent that, either, and she would never live to see to the death of Gorgon. That was unthinkable!

The hatred and indignation rose so strongly within her that Gorgon actually perceived it, though he was over a thousand miles away. He sat bolt upright, perceiving the situation as clearly as if he were there himself, taking in a startled breath, realizing that, if he did not do something, this little toad of a man would take Gaelen's life, denying him what would someday be his greatest pleasure! He focused all his dark power of thought upon Gaelen, channeling his malice through her, hoping that Sajid would perceive. The result was more than satisfactory, for Gaelen was so focused on her own hatred of Sajid that she was a perfect vessel, and thus did nothing to guard herself. Gorgon's thoughts flowed effortlessly through her bright eyes.

As soon as Sajid had drawn back from her, the contact had been broken. Gaelen had been helpless to prevent it, horrified at the surge of black hatred that had come not only from within herself, but from her mortal enemy. As Gorgon channeled his thoughts through her wide-open and utterly vulnerable consciousness, he learned several things of interest. She appeared to be in some vast, desert land, rendered helpless for some reason. And she appeared to be alone, save for the pathetic thief that would have taken her life. It made Gorgon wonder briefly whether any of his other foes had fallen already. Well, that did not truly matter, so long as Gaelen remained. He looked forward to the time of their next meeting, as he prepared to move forward again.

Upon reflection, he did hope that at least some of the others remained, for he had a score to settle with them as well. The Aridan, who had been instrumental in his defeat, would grieve bitterly at the sight of Gaelen before Gorgon took him. This vision was pleasing, and he was diverted for a moment, smiling unpleasantly before returning to his dark business.

Gorgon was not the only one who had learned things of interest. Gaelen had already known that Gorgon pursued her—she had felt it on occasion—but the quest for Hallagond had diverted her attention. This moment of uninvited, intimate contact had brought everything back into focus for her, and she resolved to return to her own quest as soon as she could manage it…if she lived.

It would be a very long night for Rogond. He and Galador had gained the oasis and had taken their friends to the house of El-morah, who was most helpful. He sent his wife, Mohani, to fetch a man named Shiva, who was said to have great wisdom in matters of healing.

El-morah had never before seen a dwarf, and Rogond knew that he would need to reveal the Company's history to their kindly host. This he did, to the wonder of El-morah, while they waited for Mohani to return.

Shiva, the healer, spoke only the sutherling tongue. El-morah would serve as interpreter, and after introducing himself and explaining their need, Rogond gave Shiva the water-skin that Sajid had poisoned. Shiva examined it, pouring a few remaining drops of the poisoned water into his hand, touching his tongue to it. "Someone has gone to the trouble of disguising this," he said, spitting upon the clean tile floor. "We must make haste…how long since they took the poison?"

"Many hours, I fear," said Rogond. "You can heal them, can't you?"

Shiva started back. "Many hours? They should both be dead then. This poison kills some folk in a matter of minutes. Surely, you are mistaken."

"They are…special," said Rogond. "I don't have time to explain. But the one who did this to them has taken one of our other companions. We must heal them as quickly as we can."

Shiva placed his hand upon Rogond's arm, his eyes full of concern. "You do not understand. You speak of healing them quickly, but I do not know whether I can heal them at all. This night will be a long one for all of us."

They bundled Gaelen and Fima against the chill of the desert night and carried them to Shiva's dwelling, taking only El-morah with them. Shiva needed his remedies, and Mohani did not wish for their children to witness what would surely be a night of suffering. This, as it turned out, was very wise, for as the remedy began to work, reversing the effects of the poison, the pain returned.

"I have heard it said that it is kinder to let death take you than to put you through the recovery," said Shiva. "Some have suggested giving also a sleeping-draught, but unless you give it immediately I have seen that go very wrong. It has been too long now for them, and they are too weak. I would prefer to not risk it."

As they set Gaelen down upon the floor of Shiva's dwelling, one of the little strips of paper she had received in the Sandstone fell from her jerkin. Shiva picked it up and examined it, as Rogond explained that it had been given in appreciation of her fine singing. The healer smiled grimly. "Give it back to her, northlander. It is a prayer for her safety, written in eastern tongue, and she will have need of it." He looked hard at Rogond. "She will scream before this night is out. Are you prepared?"

"What choice do I have?" Rogond answered, as Shiva nodded and prepared to administer the remedy.

Gaelen and Fima were by now so weakened that they were unable to fight the pain and control it, so they were both transported into a terrible realm. Fima lay with his blue eyes open, but glazed and unseeing, as the pain welled up from within him and he groaned with despair. El-morah and Galador tended him, cooling his brow as they could.

Gaelen lay shuddering in Rogond's arms, her body aflame, her eyes wide with pain and terror, seeing nothing around her and hearing nothing but her own cries. She could not hear Rogond's words, intended to comfort her, spoken in a voice charged with desperation. He wept as he held her, silent tears streaking his dusty face, rocking her gently as she rode through the next several hours.

Outside, Finan screamed incessantly, pacing back and forth to the limits of his tether, for he could hear Gaelen's cries. He broke into a hard sweat, for he could not break free, and the sound of Gaelen in such pain tore at him.

Quiet! You will bring the wrath of the whole settlement on our heads, said Réalta, his nose in the air. *You needn't make such a fuss, for there is nothing you can do about it.*

Eros, who was also tethered, did not attempt to break free, for he had no need. He simply untied the rather hastily-secured knot and then wandered over to stand beside Finan, for he understood his distress. *Stop fighting. I know you are unhappy and you wish to aid her, but you cannot. None of us can.*

I will not stand here to allow her to be taken into darkness by…by men! They cannot be trusted, they are cruel, and they took my Prince from me. I will not stand for it! Finan tried to rear, sqealing and lashing out with his forefeet at Eros, who easily avoided him.

The Warrior is a man, and he is most kind and worthy. It is wrong that you should have such an opinion, and I sorrow for what you have endured. Only listen to me…trust the Warrior. He will not let harm come unto the Soft-Singer. He loves her, and he will safeguard her. Turn your hatred upon men as you will, for many are treacherous and cruel, but not all. Eros approached Finan, nickering to him, reaching out to take the base of Finan's neck between his teeth, gently scratching it.

Finan dropped his head, submitting to Eros, for he was exhausted. He gave one half-hearted whinny in response to another heart-wrenching cry from Gaelen, but he knew that Eros was right. Rogond was not cruel, and not all men deserved to be hated.

Trust him. He will put her right, or die himself, said Eros, knowing the truth of it.

Gaelen finally regained her senses as the sun rose, opening her eyes to look into the face of her beloved. Rogond had spent most of the night with her in his arms, trying to comfort her, even as she had done as he lay dying of fever when first they met. She looked into his worried face and managed a wan smile. Then she remembered the flames consuming her body, and she grew terrified as she raised her hands to look at them. She expected them to be blackened from the fire.

"Peace, little one. You're safe now. The worst of the pain has passed, and you will be all right...don't be afraid," said Rogond, his voice strong and soothing.

Gaelen tried to speak, her voice coming forth in a sort of croaking whisper. "Am I whole?" Rogond nodded gently, smiling at her.

"But, I was engulfed in flames...how is it that I am not burned?"

"There were no flames...only in your mind. The poison that you were given made it so. You are whole, and beautiful as ever, though you have been through a terrible ordeal and you need to rest. Lie back now, close your eyes, and heal yourself."

Gaelen grew agitated and struggled against the weariness that threatened to claim her, for the mention of the poison had brought back all of Sajid's treachery against herself and her friends. "Sajid... he has taken Nelwyn. He has taken her, and she was given the same poison. And Fima...Fima was laid low as well. Say that he has not left us, please!" Her heart hammered inside her chest at the memory of her friends in such distress, recalling the words of Sajid as he gloated over her. *And there is something else*...she thought, remembering the dreadful intrusion of Gorgon Elfhunter.

Rogond grew alarmed, as she began to tremble in his arms. "Easy, now...you're spending your strength. Calm yourself, beloved. Fima is recovering, as you are. He is sleeping, which is what *you* should be doing."

Gaelen would not be calmed. "Sajid could not resist gloating, and he told me his detestable plan. He has taken Nelwyn to a man named

Castor, saying that she will bring a great price, and never be free again. I fear he is a dealer in slaves. We must aid her, for if she is sold we may never find her again. We must aid her! I am well, Rogond…my strength will come back quickly. We should find out where this Castor may be found and go after Nelwyn at once!"

Rogond's heart sank, though he tried not to show it. "Yes, yes, Gaelen. You're right. I will inquire as to the whereabouts of this man, Castor. We have made some friends here, and perhaps they will aid us. But for now, you must rest, and no arguments. I will return when I have learned all that I may."

This seemed to satisfy her, for she knew that Rogond would have a better chance of getting information, and that she was in no condition to accompany him. She nodded solemnly and closed her eyes. "Do not fail her, Thaylon," she whispered, as her body relaxed into sleep. Her heartbeat slowed back into its normal rhythm, and her face grew peaceful.

Rogond brushed a few damp locks of hair from her forehead and covered her with woolen blankets. Shiva, the healer, had been standing by, and he came forward to examine her. El-morah had gone home to his family, but Rogond had learned enough of Shiva's tongue to understand much of what he said.

"She will recover, northman, as will your other companion. I fear he has not fared so well…because he is old, he will not fully regain his strength. This will leave a mark on him. I'm sorry."

Rogond struggled with his reply, trying to make his words understood. "Thanks immeasurable...it is not sad so long as my friends live. It is…it is well."

The healer smiled a warm but gap-toothed smile. "You need practice in the use of our tongue, northman, yet you are learning. Well done."

Rogond bowed in respect. "I must now go and seek knowledge of a man named Castor. Do you know of him?"

Shiva shook his head. "I do not, but there are those here who might. Go to the tavern and seek one named Haifa. He is the proprietor. He may tell you much if you can motivate him. I heard that your wealth has been taken...a pity, for it will be gold that will best motivate one such as Haifa."

Rogond's face grew as dark as a storm-cloud and his grey eyes glittered with ominous intent. He had not forgotten the treachery of Haifa, who had surely been in league with Sajid.

"There will be other ways of motivating him, never fear. In the northlands we have special ways of motivating those who would bring harm to those we love." He caressed Gaelen once more with a reassuring hand, turning to Shiva before taking his leave. "Will you watch over her until I return?"

Shiva agreed, and Rogond went out to collect Galador. The time for courtesy was past. It was time now to see about "motivating" Haifa and his unsavory companions, and though Rogond did not speak their tongue fluently, he had no doubt that they would understand the language he was planning on using.

They went first to see El-morah, for they would thank him for his aid. He met them with a steaming mug of kaffa in each hand. "Rogond…you have not rested, and you look as though you could use some of this," he said. Neither Rogond nor Galador needed urging, and they drank of the wonderful drink, recharging their spirits. El-morah refilled their vessels without a word. This they drank more slowly, explaining their intentions to their new friends. Mohani served them lovely, sweet cakes, asking after Gaelen and Fima.

"They will recover," said Galador, to her great relief.

"Our children and I have been very concerned," she said. "What will you do now?"

"We must learn all that we can of a man named Castor, for one of our companions has been taken there by the one who betrayed us," said Rogond. "When we have learned all that we may, we will set off to recover her. I need a favor, though it pains me to ask when we have already been such a burden to you."

"Ask, my friend," said El-morah. "I will grant your favor, if it be in my power to grant."

"The She-elf, Gaelen, is already gaining strength. She will be ready to ride very soon, for she is of a race that heals quickly. She will ride swiftly and well, and will aid us in our endeavor. But our other companion, the dwarf, will take longer to recover. He is old, and though he would rather die than admit it, he will be forever marked by this ordeal. The healer has stated that he will not regain full strength. He cannot ride swiftly, and…"

"Say no more!" said Mohani, her dark eyes at once anxious and comforting. "He will be welcome to share our house. I know he will rest well here, and our children will enjoy his company. They speak the common-tongue, even as we do. Rest your minds, my friends." She looked over at her husband. "Is this not so?"

"Of course it is so, beloved wife," said El-morah. "But, thank you for asking."

Rogond knew there would be a large crowd in the tavern during the heat of the day, but when the afternoon waned, only those without work or family would remain. He did not wish for a crowd to be present when he and Galador went to speak with Haifa, and so they waited, drinking kaffa with El-morah and Mohani, mulling over their plan. It was a simple one: they would ask Haifa about Sajid and Castor, and if he was not forthcoming they would force the information from him by whatever means necessary. They would no doubt need to contend with Haifa's cronies, so Galador's primary task would be to protect Rogond. If all went as planned, no blood would be shed, though Rogond and Galador were more than ready to do so.

Rogond reflected on the situation, wondering just how far he would be willing to go. He was very angry, he had taken quite enough from untrustworthy folk, and his blood was hot within him. Yet he was not a killer, and never would be unless he had little choice.

Always before, that choice had been easy—there was no alternative to killing Ulcas. But these were men, and though they were enemies, men they remained. Rogond knew how different they could be; men like El-morah, who were intelligent, trusty, and courageous, stood beside men such as Sajid, who at the present moment was more loathsome to Rogond than any Ulca.

It was easier for Galador, for although he held a greater empathy toward men than did many of his race, he would have no trouble whatsoever with the thought of killing anyone who held Nelwyn against her will.

They would need to be cautious. They had already made enough enemies, and dead men have brothers, fathers, and sons. Haifa was no doubt on his guard, for he would surely know of the Company's plight.

El-morah agreed. "Haifa has many ears listening for him," he said. "If he was anywhere near the House of Shiva, he would have heard your friends crying out in the night. I know it was a sound I will not soon forget."

"Nor will I," said Rogond with a growl, his eyes flashing. In that moment he truly hated Sajid, Asaad, Haifa, and all others like them. Asaad had already met with his Day of Reckoning. If he had his way, Rogond would see to it that neither Sajid nor Haifa would profit from their evil actions. He gripped his sword-hilt, the color rising in his face, as El-morah removed the half-filled mug of strong kaffa, stating that, in his opinion, Rogond should drink no more of it.

"Do you want me to accompany you, my friends?" he asked, as Rogond and Galador rose to their feet and prepared to leave for the tavern. "You might need another set of eyes watching your backs."

"You will do no such thing," said Mohani, her face pale. Rogond could hardly blame her.

"I will decide my own actions, if it please you, my wife," said El-morah, his face darkening a bit beneath his good humor.

Galador stepped in quickly, for neither he nor Rogond wanted to cause an argument between these good people. "El-morah, we give you our thanks, but I believe Rogond and I can manage; we would not involve our friends in conflict with their neighbors. We will return when we have learned what we want to know." They bowed and said their farewells, stepping out into a late afternoon sun that had washed the white dwellings with gold.

The tavern was unpleasantly smoky, and smelled of strong drink and unwashed men. Rogond and Galador peered inside. They had no intention of entering by the front door.

Shiva had told them of a rear entrance. He knew it well, for when the drunken brawling got out of hand, and men were injured, he would be called there. Often, he came too late. Now Rogond and

Galador beheld about a dozen armed men in the tavern, including Haifa, who was behind the counter where the liquor was kept.

"You are certain of this?" said Galador, as Rogond gripped his spear-shaft in one hand and his sword in the other.

Rogond looked down at his tunic, at the small, faint stains left there by Gaelen's soaking-wet form, remembering her anguish as he held her. "Oh, yes, my friend," he said quietly. "I have never been more certain of anything. Let's show them how we deal with rats in the north!"

Galador nodded, and the two of them crept quietly in, Galador nocking an arrow to his bow. Rogond drew himself up and took a deep breath, his hands clenched upon his weapons. Then he suddenly strode forward, approaching Haifa from behind before he was even aware, slamming the sword on the counter and grabbing him by the collar of his robe before he could react.

"Let us counsel together, you and I," he said in a soft, menacing voice.

Haifa's eyes grew wide. There was a spear-point at his neck, and a very tall, strong, enraged man holding him by the collar. He swallowed in a dry throat, his eyes darting toward the knot of men seated at a table in the corner, who had drawn their weapons and half risen to their feet.

One of them raised his right hand to cast a bright dagger at Rogond, but cried in astonishment as Galador's arrow pinned his sleeve to the wall. The Elf had thrown back his hood and now moved into the open, bow drawn, speaking to them in a voice charged with power. "Don't move, any of you! The next one who raises a hand to my friend will never move again. Doubt me, and die. I have many arrows!"

These men had not looked upon an Elf before, but they had heard the stories, and Galador was no longer concealing his nature. "Raise a hand to him, or to me, and I will take your lives…perhaps even your souls! We Avinashi are deadly foes. Leave now, while you may!" The light radiating from his face and the menacing tone of his voice convinced them—they ran from the tavern as Rogond forced Haifa down onto the counter, the spear-point still at his throat.

"Where is Sajid, the serpent? Where has he gone? We know that you are in league with him. Speak quickly, or I swear you will never speak again." There was no doubt of Rogond's fury, yet Haifa underestimated him.

"I know nothing of Sajid. He is a drunken villain, and a fool. I am not such a fool, and would never throw my lot in with one. You are no killer, northman. Think about what you're doing."

Rogond's face twisted into an expression of pure ferocity, as he drove the spear-point into Haifa's neck just enough to break the skin. "Are you willing to wager your life on that opinion, you loathsome wretch? I detest you and everything you represent, and your lies have harmed my friends. I should kill you right now, but I will wait until you have answered my questions. If what you say pleases me, I will spare your life. If not, you will pay a high price for your reluctance. Do you take my meaning?"

Haifa did. "What do you wish to know?"

"Tell me of a man named Castor. Tell me where we may find him, and waste no time in doing it. When I grow impatient, my hands are unsteady." He dug the spear-point into Haifa's neck, bringing a trickle of blood onto his robe.

Galador called to Rogond in his own tongue: "Make haste, for those men will soon return with more of their fellows. We have caught them off guard, but they will recover quickly. We had best be gone ere they do!"

Rogond tightened his grip on Haifa, as the frightened man told of Castor, the slave-dealer, and where he might be found. When he had finished speaking, Rogond looked into his eyes. "Tell me why I should believe one word of what has just been told to me," he said, "and I will refrain from choking you to death on the spot. Ah. No answer? Well, I'm not surprised. Now, Haifa, we will begin again. You have ten fingers, but you have certainly told more than ten untruths. I will break one of your fingers for each lie you have just told, unless you replace it with the truth. I will break one of them now, just to show you that I am quite serious."

He looked over at Galador. "If he tries to escape me or screams too loudly, shoot him, please." Galador nodded, drawing silently upon Haifa, who began to whimper as Rogond gripped his right hand tightly, bending the index finger almost to the breaking point. Haifa gave a fearful wail, but Rogond was impassive.

"I have no sympathy for you. Think of this as a lesson in the rewards of honesty. Is there something that you wish to tell me now, or shall I bend this back just a little more? He continued bending Haifa's finger back uncomfortably in his iron grip.

"You wouldn't dare!" gasped Haifa, and then spat at him. There was a wet snap, and Galador winced as Haifa cried out.

"I have no time for your lies or your defiance," said Rogond. "When I run out of fingers, I shall break your miserable neck. Are you certain there is nothing you would recant?"

"Yes, yes…I may have been unclear," said Haifa. He looked with fear upon Rogond, whose eyes were like stone. For the next several minutes, he told quite a different story from the first, and Rogond listened intently. At last he was silent, save for moans of pain. Rogond looked over at Galador. "Was he truthful this time, do you think?"

Galador considered. "If we had believed him the first time, we would have no hope of finding Nelwyn. I think you should break at least one more of his fingers, just in case."

"No, no…I swear to you on my life, you will find Castor at the slave-market of Bezaltor. He will most certainly take your friend there to be sold, and then, who knows? If you hurry, you will get there in time to prevent it. Please…I cannot ply my trade with useless hands. Release me, if you are a man of honor. I have done as you asked."

When he was satisfied that Haifa had told the truth at last, Rogond released him. "I want you to know that it took all restraint within me to not shake you like the rat you are and break your miserable neck, or choke the life from you just now," he said.

"No doubt, northman," Haifa replied, still shaking with fear that was evident in his tear-streaked face as he cradled his right hand, hunching his shoulders protectively over it. His eyes narrowed with hatred of Rogond and Galador as he looked up at them. "You got what you came for. Now I would advise you to leave this place and never return. This is my establishment, and I decide who is allowed here. Return at your peril."

"Your threats didn't worry me," said Rogond. "You are a small man, and only of small concern. You needn't worry—we have no desire to set foot in this den of vipers again. But if I hear that you have sent warning to Castor, if you interfere in any way, I will return and finish you! You will have no chance to speak in your behalf, for you will not see from where my blade falls. The vipers will need to find another den. Remember that we have shown you mercy, and do not interfere. We take our leave of you."

Once outside, Galador addressed Rogond as they made their way back toward Shiva's House. "I can't believe you actually broke one of his fingers! I had not seen this side of you before. You will ever be his enemy, Aridan. I know that grieves you to no end, yet Haifa is indeed a rat, and rats like to strike from dark hiding places. We had best be cautious."

Rogond nodded as they walked along in silence. "We've known one another for a long time, yet there are still things you don't know about me. Sometimes rats just need to be spoken to in a language they can understand. It's not the first time I've used such tactics, and they are remarkably effective. I'll admit—I was angry…in fact I am still angry, and we didn't have time to waste in courteous debate. At any rate, I am glad I have a ferocious Avinashi for a friend. They will surely fear to attack me lest you take their souls!"

They both chuckled at this, entering Shiva's dwelling to find Fima and Gaelen still sleeping. Galador kept watch while Rogond sat beside her; his anger had left him weakened and drained. This was not yet ended. Rogond knew the vipers wouldn't allow some upstart northman to best them without attempting retribution.

He sighed and stroked Gaelen's hair, whereupon she stretched somewhat stiffly and opened her eyes. She smiled when she saw him, and he read her message clearly. *You have done what you must, and now we move to the next step in the journey. I will aid you, whatever happens. You have done well.* The trust he saw in her artless face moved him such that he embraced her, feeling life and vitality flow back into him. Though Gaelen was not yet strong, she apparently still had enough strength to share.

11
The Sellers of Flesh

At dawn the Company made their final preparations to leave the oasis so that they might find Nelwyn before she could be sold. Fima was unhappy at being left behind, but he was of a practical nature and understood the need for it. He was still very unsteady on his feet, and he grew weary at the slightest exertion. Rogond noticed that his normally ruddy complexion was pale, and there were more lines in his face than before. His eyes, formerly bright and sparkling with good-natured energy, now were slightly dull, as though still struggling beneath some burden that drew the life from them.

Fima knew that he could not ride with the Company. They would go as swiftly as their mounts would allow, and he would burden them, for he was no rider. He therefore agreed to stay in the House of El-morah, where he would be well looked after. The children, in particular, would grow to love him. Fima told the most entertaining stories, and even though the younger children would not easily understand him, Mohani could translate for them. Fima was so expressive that they were all rapt as he told tales of dwarves and dragons; in this alone he seemed inexhaustible. Yet he would spend much of his time sleeping, trying to regain his strength. He prayed that the Company would return for him, as Rogond had promised.

Gaelen had fared much better, but even Elves cannot heal fully in so short a time, and she would be taxed for a few days yet. It would have been quite pointless to suggest that she remain behind. Finan had been overjoyed to see her, nickering softly as she stroked his neck. He dipped his beautiful head down so that she could rub his black-tipped ears.

I tried to aid you, but I could not. I would fall protecting you. Please do not let them tether me ever again! He jostled her gently and she patted him before turning back to prepare her gear, leaving him untethered, for she knew he would not stray from her. This irritated Eros and Réalta, who were both tied securely to the rail. Rogond could tie knots that not even Eros could undo.

Malvorn, who was also tied but did not see the sense in objecting to it, was amused. *Stop complaining, you two. It's not so bad being tied. Perhaps they have left him loose in the hope that he will run off, and we'll all be rid of him and his bothersome screaming. Obviously, our folk intend to return for us!* Malvorn would have smirked if he could have.

Finan lifted his head high, tossing his long, black forelock from his eyes. *Tell yourself whatever you like, Servant of Men! The Soft-Singer has placed her trust in me...she leaves me free so that I may come to her in need. You're just too thick-headed to know it.* He turned his hindquarters toward Malvorn in a gesture of contempt.

Eros then aimed both hind legs at Finan, deliberately kicking him with only enough force to startle him. Finan leaped forward, snorting, as Eros, Réalta, and Malvorn shook their heads in amusement.

And you are apparently too thick-headed to know to place yourself out of range of my hindquarters. Soft-Singer left you untethered, but I still managed to put my feet to your hide!

Finan turned and struck hard at Eros, snorting, his flinty black foot raising a small cloud of dust as it slammed into the ground. Eros was not impressed. *Save it, O Mighty Battle Mount, for you do not intimidate me in the least! Come now, and let us be friends. You still have not rested well, and you are high-tempered. You had best save your strength, for today we ride, and we shall all be tested.*

This was very true. The Company would need to ride as fast as they could manage, and they hoped that the information given them concerning the likely location of the slave-dealer was correct. If they lost their way, they would not be able to aid Nelwyn. No one wanted to imagine her fate if they should fail her.

Galador had already made his intentions known—anyone who touched her in an unseemly manner would suffer, and anyone who harmed her would die.

He had been plagued with dreadful imaginings of what might be happening to his beloved. Normally grim and silent, he was now restive and given to outbursts of temper. Once, with no provocation at all, he reached out and grabbed Rogond's arm, his grey eyes wild, saying: "If they kill her, I shall not bear it. I will send my own spirit to the Far Shores rather than live without her. I will follow her as quickly as I can set my blade to my own throat!"

"Peace, my friend," said Rogond, who was concerned and even a little alarmed. "Let's trust it will not come to that. Nelwyn is of too great a value to them...they will not harm her. And rest assured we'll travel much more swiftly than a slaver's caravan. We will find her."

As the Company made ready to depart, Rogond kept a watchful eye, for he wondered whether Haifa might attempt retribution for the damage done to his hand, and to his pride. By now it was likely that everyone knew he had been forced to give information betraying the location of Castor to this northern stranger. Haifa had lost face, and might even face the wrath of Castor one day. Even though Rogond did not consider Haifa to be much of a threat, he would sleep lightly until they were far from the oasis.

His fears were not unfounded. There were those in the oasis to whom the lives of others were valueless, whose services could be had for a few pieces of silver. But Haifa had been advised otherwise by Kamal, who had explained that his "employer" had insisted that Rogond not be harmed.

"If you have him killed, I will be blamed for it. I have little doubt these strangers will meet with their doom soon enough. And I doubt they will come back here, for I have set them on the path to Fómor." Kamal then laughed ill-naturedly, pressing a few gold pieces into Haifa's hand. "A little something for your pain," he said. "And if that pain is too great, just think of those fools attempting the wide crossing for absolutely no reason at all! Even if they survive the journey, the Corsairs will have them, and they will not be at all considerate. That should ease your pain."

Haifa smiled and nodded. "You are not wrong. In fact, I feel better already." Both men laughed, raising their ale-tankards to drink to the downfall of the Company.

Rogond, Fima, Gaelen, and Galador sat for the last time that morning with El-morah and Mohani, sharing kaffa and conversation. El-morah turned to Rogond, for he would ask a question of him. "You were forced to leave the Sandstone settlement, and you came directly here, is that right? Why did you not go to the Neela oasis? It is nearer to the Sandstone, and the water there is of excellent quality.

In fact, we import water from the Neela to make our kaffa, as the water here would ruin the flavor."

Fima's eyes widened, and then narrowed as he listened to the question. "You say that the water in the Neela is of fine quality? I was told that it contained salt. Sajid wanted us to come here, and, like a fool, I trusted him."

"But you must trust your guide, Fima," said El-morah. "You really have no choice, when he knows the lands and you do not. It's natural to rely on his advice."

"It is not natural to rely on a serpent for anything," growled Gaelen, regretting her remark at once, for it obviously made Fima feel worse. She offered him her last honey-cake in an attempt to cheer him.

"Fima, why didn't you share this with us before the decision was made? Should we not all have had a voice in it?" said Galador.

Fima looked downcast. "I was asked not to by Sajid. He said that, if you knew of the Neela, we would waste precious time in argument. He expected Gaelen to do exactly the opposite of what he advised, and he thought she might...you know...go haring off anyway, forcing us all to follow her. He was rather insistent, and I was taken in by it."

Gaelen might have taken some offense had she felt stronger, but she merely shook her head. "It's obvious that Sajid has friends here. In fact, I believe he formed this dark plan while we were still in the Sandstone. I sensed that something happened between Sajid and Nelwyn, and I'll warrant he laid out her doom even then. This rendezvous with the slave-trader was planned long ago, and we had to be in the Chupa so that he could make the meeting-place on time—it's that simple."

Galador could not hear any more. He rose and went out into the early morning light, muttering something about looking to the horses.

Shiva had proven invaluable in the healing of Réalta; he had a marvelous salve that seemed to close wounds as if by magic. He had given a container to Rogond, asking no payment of him. "Take this, northman, and pray that you do not have need of it," he said. "It will burn when applied, but the wound will not fester and will heal quickly. I offer this to raise your opinion of my people. We are not all like Sajid."

Réalta would keep up with the others provided he was not ridden, and Malvorn would continue to bear Galador until Réalta was sound. The little Kazhi horse would bear much of their gear.

Gaelen had neither saddle nor bridle, for Sajid had required both to ride Siva, but this did not dismay her. Finan wore only a head-collar woven of fine black cord festooned with tassels to keep the flies away. Gaelen had bought it for him in the Sandstone marketplace, and it fitted his fine head beautifully.

Rogond followed Galador, for he would make certain that all was well with him. Mohani clucked softly and shook her head. "I am concerned for them," she said to El-morah. "I know they have been told where the market is, but can they find their way well enough? Gaelen is not yet strong…does it not make sense to wait until a guide may be found?"

"It does make sense," Gaelen replied, for she had been likewise concerned. "Yet we cannot wait—Sajid has a two-day head start on us already. We will need to be swift!"

"The swift may lose their way, for signs may be missed…I will worry constantly about you, for to bypass the market would mean disaster for all."

Gaelen sighed. "Galador will not wait, and neither will I. We'll just have to trust to luck, and pray that it does not fail us. If Sajid is still with Nelwyn, I will find him, for I will track his stench on the wind!" She quirked a wry smile at Mohani.

Fima was far more pessimistic. "Trust to luck? Good idea. Our luck has been fabulous so far."

"Yet we are not dead, Fima, and that must count for something. You will remain with these good people, in this fine place, drinking kaffa and eating…Mohani, what is this called again?" She indicated a dark block of bittersweet, waxy material sitting nearby on a salver.

"It's called koka. It will cheer me when little else can. Do you find it appealing?" Mohani broke a bit off and popped it into her mouth, allowing it to melt slowly so that she could savor it. Gaelen observed this behavior with interest, placing a small piece in her own mouth, trying desperately to control her facial expression as the bitterness of the koka took hold.

"For some reason, I do find it appealing, though it does take a bit of getting used to. I wish I could take you to my home in the Greatwood, Mohani, for there are some interesting flavors to be sampled there. We brew aromatic roots, and flavor the broth with fruits and with honey. I had grown fond of chewing ginger root—if you can do that without flinching, you have a strong constitution!"

"We have ginger root brought in from the coast," said Mohani. "We use it only for flavoring, and that sparingly. I cannot imagine chewing it!" She wrinkled her face and shook her head.

Fima was still unhappy. "I know I will be well looked after, but I will fret over you and Rogond and Galador until you return. Though I know I must remain behind, it pains me." A very dark look came over his face then. "I have a personal score to settle with Sajid, you see."

"Don't fear, my friend. I will take enough of his hide for both of us," said Gaelen. "And I will make certain that he knows his pain comes also from you. I now understand why he was left buried up to his neck."

"Well, don't you make the same mistake," Fima growled. "Some other kindly soul may take pity on him."

"Don't give it a thought," she said, her eyes flashing. "I intend to see him quite thoroughly, absolutely, irrevocably dead. I will tell you the tale when we return. Now, I must ride." She rose and bowed to Mohani. "May I take some of this…for Nelwyn?" she asked, indicating the koka.

"Of course. I have already prepared a package for you," said Mohani, handing her a sizeable chunk wrapped in waxed paper. "Be careful, my fierce Avinasha. Return soon, that your friends may be reunited."

Fima raised his clay vessel of kaffa. "I will drink to that day."

Five horses put their tails to the oasis, heading for the market at Bezaltor. El-morah had drawn the approximate location on the map, though he had never been there himself. He estimated it would take about five days' swift ride.

"One of my brothers found it once," he said. "He told me later that it was indeed a seamy and disreputable place. He also stated that he would never go back, as he was afraid for his life. Be very, very cautious, my friends."

Galador's face was stony. There would be no need for caution if he had his way; anyone who stood between himself and Nelwyn would regret it.

Even Gaelen was worried by the cold fury in Galador's eyes, though she shared some of it as she rode beside him. He looked over at her. "I shall be glad of your company, daughter of the Fire-heart. We shall need all of our determination to win this battle, and bring back my beloved. I trust your blades are sharp?"

"They are sharp," Gaelen replied. "And, just this once, I wish it were true, but I am no daughter of Aincor. As I have said many times, I am only a Wood-elf. Yet you may be glad, for we may accomplish more with cunning and stealth than with recklessness. For that, you need a Sylvan hunter-scout! Now, let's make time ere the sun rises too high."

She sent Finan into a canter, which delighted him, as he was eager to test his abilities and prove himself to her. He lifted his tail high over his back and leaped forward, easily passing Rogond, who led the Company. Eros flicked his tail once in disapproval. *So foolish*, he thought, *to waste energy*. Rogond placed a hand on his neck to steady him, but there was no need. Eros was not prideful, and had nothing to prove to anyone.

They would rest during the heat of the day, sheltering beneath the white silken shade that El-morah had given them. It was quite large; even the horses could fit beneath it if they stood close together. They would all be glad of it, for they would be in the open for much of the way, and it was not long past midsummer. Although they would travel mostly by night, they would need to make some distance under the sun to catch up with Nelwyn. They carried enough water for a week's journey, but Finan again showed his usefulness on the third night, insisting that they divert from their course to find a hidden water-hole.

They decided their course as they rode; when they arrived at their destination they would shroud themselves, refill their water-skins, and scout the market, hopefully locating Nelwyn. Then they would form the plan to recover her.

Poor Malvorn was worn thin by the morning of the third day. He was not designed to travel swiftly in the heat with little water, and Galador was becoming frustrated with him, though he gave his best effort. "Come on, Malvorn. Even the pack horse is swifter," he grumbled, as Gaelen looked over at him with a disapproving eye.

"He is making a grand effort, Galador. Do not disparage him. I have been watching Réalta…perhaps he could bear you for a while. He is moving well with no sign of pain. I believe that Shiva's wonderful ointment has healed him, so why not try him?"

Galador needed no urging, and neither did Réalta. Though he was perhaps not up to bearing a rider all day and night, he could carry Galador for a few hours. He was bred from ancient stock, and his bloodline was known for stamina as well as swiftness. The desert wind blew through Galador's fine, silken hair as he sat once more upon his silver steed, whose magnificence was diminished only a little by the stub of a tail that he now raised high into the air.

Eros snorted at the two of them. *What a pretty pair they make! If you didn't know it, you could always ask Réalta, who would be happy to remind you.* Though Eros liked Galador well enough, his heart was given to Rogond, with his understated ways and mortal weaknesses. Rogond had never failed him, and in that regard they were just alike, for Eros would serve his Warrior until his dying day.

The Company made excellent progress, as they had learned much from their time in the desert, and they were determined. They drew near the market by sunset of the fourth day. Smoke could be seen rising from it, and as darkness grew, the light of fires and torches appeared as a faint glow against the sand. They made ready to approach, Gaelen and Galador wrapping themselves in desert garb, as Rogond spoke quietly to them.

"My friends, I know you are anxious, and when we find Nelwyn you may become wrathful, but I would caution you that we will only achieve our goal if we all remain calm and clear of thought. We cannot prevail in open battle, not against so many. We will need our wits to free her." He looked pointedly at Galador. "I do not know how we will find Nelwyn, or whether she is even in this place. You must trust to hope, my friend, if we are to succeed."

Galador and Gaelen understood him, though their faces were grim. Rogond could see only their eyes from beneath their garb. They held no humor in them, glowing like embers amid the folds of black and white silk. Rogond was also robed in white, but he trusted his beard to hide his facial features, and of course, Galador had none.

They entered the settlement, going first to the well, where Galador filled the water-skins as Gaelen tended the animals. Rogond was appointed to scout the market, as he would arouse the least suspicion.

He went first to a large tent that seemed to be a center of activity, with folk of all descriptions coming and going, and many voices within. The air was thick with smoke, and he tried not to react as it stung his eyes and strained his breathing for a moment. Approaching what appeared to be a seller of drink, he ordered a flagon of wine and sat thoughtfully in the corner, drinking and listening to all around him. It was well that he had picked up some of the sutherling speech, for he was able to glean some useful information.

Though a variety of goods and services could be had at Bezaltor, its main trade was in slaves. It was, in fact, one of the few such markets remaining in the Ravi-shan. Few could afford such luxuries, yet there were those who could afford them, and they had sent representatives to the market to purchase only the very best. The auction began at midnight, and continued until dawn. Rogond and Galador would need to buy their way in; none were admitted without paying for the privilege. It apparently kept the beggars away.

As Rogond looked out over the crowd, his attention was drawn to one man in particular, who was sitting with a half-full vessel of wine. There was something undeniably familiar about this man, though Rogond was certain they had never met. Though he appeared to be of desert heritage, with brown skin and a full beard, one could see that he was taller than was usual in the Ravani- folk. There was something in his bearing that drew Rogond's gaze, though the man did not appear to take notice of him.

Remembering that he had promised to return and report what he had seen, Rogond finished his wine and took his leave, paying no more thought to the strange man for the moment.

He found Galador and Gaelen anxiously awaiting his return, and they were quite eager to be informed of what he had learned.

Castor was here; Rogond had heard his name spoken several times. This both cheered Galador and worried him. What if Nelwyn had already gone up on the auction block? What if Sajid had met with trouble, and had missed the rendezvous, so that Nelwyn was never here at all? Gaelen had said that Nelwyn had been poisoned—what if Sajid had failed to revive her?

Rogond could feel the uncertainty and distress emanating from his friends. "We will know soon enough, for the auction begins at midnight. It may be that Castor will wait until the time is right to present Nelwyn; he may be awaiting a certain buyer. Who knows? You and I will be there, Galador, and perhaps I can make inquiries. For now, let's go and pay our fee that we may be admitted. Gaelen cannot come with us, for only men are allowed in such places."

"Why am I neither shocked nor dismayed?" said Gaelen, who found the very thought revolting. "Yet you will have need of me if things go awry. Rescuing Nelwyn from this place will be difficult. If we cannot spirit her away before she goes on the block, it will be easier to retrieve her once she is sold, and leaves with her buyer. We can follow her, and liberate her at a time of our choosing."

"I will not stand for my beloved to be taken by any buyer…sold for pieces of gold!" Galador was bristling, and when Rogond tried to calm him he backed away.

"Hush! Lower your voice," said Gaelen, looking furtively around her. "You will gain nothing for Nelwyn if they hear you."

"They will not understand our tongue. Do you not realize what terrible things might happen to Nelwyn if she is sold? They will put their hands on her, and force her to do their bidding! You would actually stand by while your cousin bears the indignity of being traded like some common beast? I could not bear it...not for an hour! We will need to liberate her before she is sold." He threw a venomous look at Gaelen.

"It will not be the first indignity she has endured, Galador," was the cool reply. "What *I* will not stand for is failure to free her at all. We must do what is necessary to ensure that her captivity ends, even if it means that she must bear indignity. I would assume that you will see reason, and not end your life tonight with a blade between your shoulders, cast by a sutherling who happens to understand Elven speech."

She turned to Rogond with an expression of complete trust. "Order me, Thaylon, and I will follow. You know the ways of men far better than we. We await your direction." She looked over at Galador. "Is that not so?"

"It is so," said Galador, who dropped his eyes, momentarily chastened. He did trust Rogond. "I will yield to your direction, Rogond, for my judgment in this matter is clouded by passion." He looked from Rogond to Gaelen. "It appears that some of your good sense has rubbed off onto her—I expected her to be the difficult one. I'll try my best to follow her example."

"If I fall tomorrow, at least I will have lived long enough to hear that admission," said Gaelen. "I do not begrudge you your passion, Galador High-elven! Only trust that Nelwyn will be returned to us if we keep our heads, and strike when the time is right."

Rogond and Galador paid their fees, and they each received a card with a symbol identifying them as potential buyers. Rogond's card bore a picture of a raven, and Galador's was emblazoned with a scarlet sword. "May it prove fitting," he muttered as they entered the auction-tent, which was already packed nearly full with buyers. The turnout was much better than usual, for it was rumored that something quite rare was in the offing.

They had already been informed that weapons were not allowed, and had left their blades in Gaelen's keeping. She waited nearby, guarding their goods and their horses from thieves while keeping a sharp ear on the auction-tent. If things went awry, she would ride to the aid of her friends. In preparation, she had prepared her bow and quiver, and they stood ready beside Finan.

One furtive passer-by appeared a little too interested in their belongings, for they were guarded only by a woman. One glance from Gaelen's bright eyes, and he changed his mind, dropping his gaze as she drew herself up, her power radiating from beneath her black garb. Their belongings were quite safe.

Neither Rogond nor Galador had ever been in such a place before. They stared in disbelief as one unfortunate after another was put up for bidding. The auctioneer stood beside each frightened soul, while the seller extolled his or her special virtues. The block was surrounded by large, burly men with whips in their hands, and they were highly skilled with them; their task, apparently, was to prevent the crowd from getting too close. A tall pole stood in the center of the block, and some of the more difficult individuals were tethered to it to keep them from leaping into the crowd. Several appeared to have been given some elixir that rendered them dull and listless. They stared blankly at the jeering spectators, slack-jawed and unseeing.

Galador was revolted; Rogond could feel him trembling as the highly distasteful scene unfolded before them. This was an evil of the highest order, and Rogond forgot for a moment that some of these terrible folk were men—this was more reminiscent of Tûr Dorcha. Ulcas were bred to be enslaved and knew of nothing else. Men were destined to be born and die in freedom. To see the wretchedness of these was disheartening, no matter which side of the bidding they stood upon.

Rogond noticed that the tall man he had observed earlier was now present in the auction-tent, seemingly quite occupied with the goings-on. He turned his eyes toward Rogond once, as though he felt his gaze, but did not see him, for he was apparently bidding on the elderly woman who stood miserably on the auction block.

Things were apparently approaching some climax—one could feel it in the air. The crowd was becoming excitable, as though they had been awaiting some special event that was about to unfold. Rogond looked once more toward the tall man, who had raised his bidding card high over his head, causing the sleeve of his robe to drop back, exposing his right arm. This was not an unusual act, but as Rogond looked upon the man's arm he beheld the swirling designs graven there…the beautiful, flowing Elvish script was clearly visible, though only for a moment. And on the back of the right hand—a scar, dark brown, as from an Ulca-blade.

Rogond could not breathe. He barely felt Galador's arm as it gripped him, and he swayed as a wave of dizziness threatened to take him to the floor. Why had he not known it earlier? His brother was here…*here* in this dreadful place, apparently bidding for slaves. His father would weep if he knew it, but Hallagond was indeed the tall man who now lowered his bidding card, turning his penetrating grey eyes to meet those of the brother he had not yet known.

When their eyes met, and each realized the truth of the other, they stood frozen in disbelief. Hallagond's sun-weathered face went pale, and his eyes at first grew wide with wonder, then narrowed with dark dismay. How could this have happened? He had paid Radeef's associates very well to divert his brother, and yet he was *here*? Hallagond spat an oath and tried to turn and disappear before Rogond could think to make his way toward him, but the crowd pressed in as the voice of the auctioneer announced that the event they had been awaiting was at hand.

Galador gripped Rogond's arm more tightly. "What's the matter?" he hissed in his friend's ear. "What have you seen that has unsettled you? Turn your attention back now, for I have just heard the name of Castor from many in the crowd. Please, Rogond, your attention!"

As Galador looked into the face of his friend, he could see that all was not well. Rogond was now standing rigidly beside him, trying to pull away from his grip so that he could make his way toward the tall man who shared his father's grey eyes and brown hair. Hallagond had been trapped by the crowd, and was now making a point of not looking in their direction. Rogond turned to Galador.

"My brother, Hallagond, is here in this place…I have just seen him. Galador, my brother is *here!*"

"What? Are you serious? How can you be certain?" said Galador, scanning the crowd.

"He is standing over there—no, *there!* That tall man who is presently trying to hide himself from our gaze. I must go after him, Galador, before he can slip away. I won't be long…I promise."

"You dare not leave now...remember your purpose in being here. We are here to find and restore my beloved! There will be time later to find your brother again." He looked back toward the auction block, and his blood froze in his veins. "See, now, why you cannot turn from your purpose!"

Castor, the slave-trader, had brought in his wares, and they stood in a miserable line behind him. There was nothing remarkable about most of them, but there was one, tall and lithe, apparently none too hale, who sagged against the one who stood beside her. She was wrapped in sand-colored silk so that you could not see her features at all, but both Galador and Rogond recognized the remains of their gold silken sunshade. Nelwyn was here, and from the sound of the crowd she would be the climax of the night's dark business. Neither of her would-be rescuers could move for a moment as they realized the extent of the task before them.

There was nothing Rogond could do about Hallagond now. At least he knew that his brother still lived, but to find him here, in this place…it might have almost been better if he had not known. For now, he could not leave Galador, for his friend was rapidly losing control. Color had risen in his face, and Rogond could feel the heat of anger and grief radiating from him. He trembled slightly, and there was conflict in his eyes, as though he warred with himself. Rogond could not blame him—Nelwyn was in a bad way. She could not stand firmly on her own feet, but needed support from Castor, who had left the selling of his other "wares" to his subordinates. He would allow no one but himself to touch Nelwyn.

When the time came, Castor stepped forward—a tall, powerful man dressed in garish red and gold flowing robes. His full beard was neatly trimmed, his dark eyes cold and glittering with the promise of profit. He placed an arm around Nelwyn's waist to support her, and the restive crowd grew silent.

Castor announced to the buyers that what he was about to offer them was so rare and beautiful that its like would not again be seen. Slowly and with great ceremony, he removed the gold silken wrap from his precious jewel, and the crowd gasped and muttered as Nelwyn was revealed. Galador swayed beside Rogond, crying out in a broken voice at the sight before him.

Her graceful form was covered only by the barest of garments, sequined and embroidered, with many glittering medallions and bells tinkling musically with the slightest movement. Her wrists and ankles were bound with silken cord, but there was truly no need, for she was largely unaware of anything going on around her. Her green eyes were open, but they were glazed over and unseeing. Her beautiful hair was immaculate and held in place with combs made of pearlescent shells. Castor had done everything in his power to enhance her beauty, yet none of his efforts would have made the slightest difference, for Nelwyn's beauty was plain to all who beheld her, even if she wore garments made of cobwebs.

Such a large crowd in so small a space had made the auction-tent uncomfortably warm, yet Nelwyn trembled as she stood before them on unsteady feet. When the drape was removed, the crowd gave a collective gasp, followed by a brief moment of total quiet. Then a great cheer went up, indicating that the crowd was very pleased and excited.

Galador did not understand the sutherling tongues as well as did Rogond, but he knew from the expressions and gestures of those around him that there were things being said of his beloved that were most lascivious and unseemly. He ground his teeth together in silence.

Castor held up his hand, signaling that the bidding would soon begin. Many reached into their robes to take count of their coins, for hope of acquiring this beautiful creature surged in their hearts. Galador would not be able to bear this for long, and Rogond gripped his arm.

"Steady, now. At least we know that she is alive, and they have not truly harmed her. Steady, my friend. They hold the mastery for the moment." He had not seen this level of white-hot fury in Galador's eyes ever before, and it worried him.

The crowd was relatively quiet as Castor began to speak. "Ah, my fine friends, I have brought before you tonight the rarest of jewels. You will never find another like her! She is of an ancient race, and will never sicken, age, or die naturally. Just think of it—here is beauty immortal and unending, eternal perfection, and she is yours for the taking! But I must warn you that the price will be high, for I will not part with her otherwise. Free your gold, if you would have her!"

As Castor continued to describe the virtues of his fine offering, one of the men standing nearby turned to his fellows, and, with a look of unbridled lust on his sneering face, he began to describe the many uses to which Nelwyn would be put should he acquire her. His companions leered and laughed as he continued; regrettably, his descriptions were punctuated by hand gestures that did not require a translator to understand.

Gaelen shivered in the chilly night air as she stood watch over the horses, trying to perceive the goings-on inside the auction tent. Alas, it was difficult to hear over the crowd, but when the cheer went up in response to the unveiling of Nelwyn, a feeling of unease took hold of Gaelen. Her slight frame trembled and she suddenly grew tense. She missed her weapons and decided to make no further attempt to disguise herself, for she would soon go into battle—she could feel it. She pulled off her black garment and replaced her blades and quiver, relaxing slightly as she felt the comfort of cold steel against her leather jerkin.

She was observed only by a single onlooker, and she drew her blades quickly, daring him to say a word about it. He did not do so, but dropped his eyes and backed away, for the light in her face left no doubt that she was not of his world. Later he would tell his companions of her, and they would laugh, telling him that he should not drink so much.

Gaelen's intuition that she would soon do battle was correct. When Galador beheld the leering, unseemly expressions and gestures going on around him, knowing they were directed at his beloved, he could no longer keep silent. He gave a cry, lunging toward the worst of the offenders, as Rogond tried to restrain him. Galador wrenched free, falling upon the surprised men in a rage, attempting to throttle the one who had made the obscene gestures.

The man's fellows were quick to defend their comrade. They wrestled with Galador, and it was a good thing weapons were not permitted, for the Elf would have been taken quickly. Yet they now had to contend with Rogond, who leaped forward in defense of his friend. Galador fought with the strength of twenty men; he had injured several of his opponents, including the one he had grabbed initially, who lay unmoving upon the dirt floor. Yet he could not hope to prevail against a tide of outraged sutherlings.

In a shadowed corner of the auction-tent, Sajid the Spider lurked quietly, witnessing both the uprising and the suppression of Galador with satisfaction. He was in disguise, but had come to the auction because he wanted to witness the humiliation of Nelwyn for himself. Not even Castor knew of his presence, but he had no difficulty gaining entrance, for he was much wealthier than he had been, oh, yes indeed. Now, as he learned that the Company had discovered his plan and followed Nelwyn to the market, his heart was filled with fear. He could not risk being seen, for surely Rogond and Galador would want to avenge the deaths of Gaelen and Fima.

He would not wait now until Nelwyn was sold...better to make his escape while Galador and Rogond were restrained and helpless. He slithered through the crowd to the side doorway, bowed to the attendant, and handed him his bidding card. Appropriately, it was inscribed with the image of a yellow serpent.

The auctioneer bellowed over the din. "To disrupt the bidding is strictly forbidden. You all know it!" He looked over at the men restraining Rogond and Galador. "Drag the offenders outside, and make certain they remain there. Punish them as you see fit, but they will not be allowed back inside on this night."

The men did so, snarling at their captives. Many were also laughing ill-naturedly at them. "The slave auctions are no place for sentiment," they said. "If you would defend the honor of a maiden, better to make certain she does not come here. Once she is here, better you should stay away!"

Galador cried out to Nelwyn, and she perceived his cry, turning her blank eyes toward him, but she could not respond. The men laughed and dragged him from the tent along with Rogond. Once outside, where weapons were permitted, neither would live long. Sajid shook his head as he made his escape. He almost felt pity for Galador, but at the same time, better that the Elf should be dead than witness Nelwyn's fate.

Gaelen had heard the melee inside the tent, and she heard Galador's impassioned cry. She grabbed the weapons and sprinted to the aid of her friends, only to behold a shadowy figure slinking from the side entrance. Something made him turn toward her, and, as their eyes met, they both froze in astonishment. "Deceiver!" yelled Gaelen in a loud and terrible voice. "Betrayer and murderer! Your hour is at hand!"

Mother of Mercy! The Vixen is alive...how is it possible? And how in the name of heaven can she have found me already! Sajid panicked, knowing that he would never evade her unless she was diverted. He ran as fast as he could around the back of the large tent, toward the westward entrance, where even now Rogond and Galador were being dragged to an uncertain fate. Gaelen gained ground rapidly, for she was swifter and very, very motivated.

Yet as she rounded the corner, she beheld her beloved Rogond with a dagger at his throat, and her friend Galador, forced to his knees, a bright blade aimed at the back of his neck. She could do nothing but turn from the pursuit, hissing under her breath and skidding to a halt so that she might draw her bow. Sajid would not fall this day.

One of the men raised his curved sword to take Galador's head; he struggled against his captors, but the light had gone from his eyes to be replaced with resignation. He seemed to know that his hour had come, and that he would not be able to aid Nelwyn. He had failed her—his lack of restraint had come at a terrible cost.

Rogond was trying to stay the men from killing Galador, but to no avail. Apparently, one of their friends had died at Galador's hands, for his strength had been guided by a terrible rage, and he had broken the man's neck unaware.

The swordsman stood with raised blade, but he did not lower it to cleave Galador. Instead he staggered back, staring in dull confusion at the arrow-shaft protruding from his chest before he fell.

"There are more of them! Kill these at once!" cried the man who held Rogond. He pulled the Ranger's head back, intending to cut his throat, but dropped his blade as a tall, bearded man leaped into the fray. He had cast a bright dagger into the throat of Rogond's would-be executioner. Rogond was now trying to avoid being grabbed by the other sutherlings, while looking around in confusion.

"Thaylon! Your blades!" cried Gaelen as she dashed in to aid him, cleaving any who stood in her way. Their eyes met briefly; Gaelen's were bright with the heat of battle and Rogond could tell that it was not just Galador and himself that she would fight for this day. She would cleave sutherlings as long as any stood before her, to avenge Nelwyn…and Elraen.

The sutherlings had recovered their wits, though the sight of Gaelen and the sudden appearance of Hallagond had startled them. Gaelen had returned Galador's blade to him, and he now fought with new hope. None would stand before him for long, yet the tide of numbers was still against the Company, and they were beleaguered, especially Hallagond, who was fending off three enemies by himself.

Meanwhile, inside the tent, Castor ground his teeth in frustration, knowing he would be disappointed this night. The bidding had been disrupted, and many of the bidders had gone outside to witness the excitement. Others had fled, for they did not truly know or understand the cause of the confusion, but they could hear the cries of men dying, and they did not wish to learn any more.

The auctioneer turned to Castor. "How do you wish to proceed?"

"I will not offer her in the midst of this uproar," he said. "And I fear someone may try to take her from me. She is withdrawn until further notice." He wrapped Nelwyn once more in the gold-colored silk and lifted her in his arms. She was light to carry, and he made his way to his own encampment, his well-armed henchmen clearing the way before him. Rogond saw them leave, but could not break free of the melee to pursue them.

The battle was not going well. One of Hallagond's opponents had managed to slash him across the right shoulder, and he was in a bad way. His sword-arm now hung at his side, for there was no strength in it. The sword was his preferred weapon, and he was not as adept with his other arm. His enemies stood ready to take him, until a smallish, bright-eyed She-elf (*was* it a She-elf?) leaped in front of him, blades flashing. She cast them with deadly precision, and two enemies fell. She drew her bow without thinking, sending three more to the Eternal Realm as her hands blurred with motion.

She called back to him. "I know you understand Elven-speech, Hallagond Tuathan! Get ready to run, for there are too many of them! You must flee with us!" She then whistled as loudly as she could for Finan.

Rogond likewise called for Eros, and in moments the horses appeared, bearing their gear. "Fly, all of you!" cried Rogond, leaping onto Eros' back.

"Not without Nelwyn!" cried Galador, who still stood firm, defying any to take him who wished to meet their fate. Hallagond needed no urging, for he saw that he was outnumbered and could not prevail. He swung onto Malvorn as Finan rushed toward the surprised sutherlings, striking at them with his deadly forefeet, swinging his powerful jaws, his mouth open, teeth bared. Gaelen had retrieved her blades, and now leaped astride him as he charged forward, not caring what unfortunate stood in his way. He was indeed a war-horse, and his skills were apparent to all. He swept the enemy back like a tide.

Rogond rode up behind Galador, leading Réalta and calling frantically: "There's no time! We don't even know where they have taken her! You cannot prevail alone. Look beyond your madness… you cannot help her if we are all dead!" He looked into the eyes of his friend. "They will not harm her."

Rogond's voice somehow made its way through the haze of despair that had clouded Galador's reason. He sent two more of the Ravani to their eternal reward, fending off a killing blow from one of them, before mounting Réalta and turning to follow his friends.

The Company had ridden many miles beyond the borders of the slave-market, and it did not appear that they had been pursued as yet. Now they could regroup and decide what their next course would be. The sun would soon be rising, and many wounds needed tending, both of body and spirit. Rogond sat with Galador, who stared stonily into the distance and would neither speak nor make eye contact with anyone.

Hallagond's wound was potentially quite serious, but at least it did not appear to have been poisoned. Gaelen tended him, observing him with wonder, for he truly did resemble Rogond. She placed a quantity of Shiva's healing salve on the wound, and Hallagond cried out as if it burned him.

"Leave me in peace, Elf. I need no cure that is worse than the affliction, and I certainly did not need to have my life disrupted by the likes of you!"

Gaelen regarded him calmly. "Your brother would not make such a fuss, but would submit gratefully to my attentions. You obviously do not possess his forbearance. Keep still and be silent!" She examined his arm with practiced hands. "This will heal, but it will be a while before you wield a blade with it."

She looked into his eyes, though he tried to turn from her. "I am grateful for your aid in saving my beloved, and I'm very thankful to have found you at last. His search has been long and difficult. Perhaps now you will come to know one another."

Hallagond sniffed. "That man is your beloved? I'm less surprised than you might think. It would be typical of my brother to give his heart to an Elf, as from what I have heard, he is something of a fool. If you wish to speak with me in future, please do so in the common-tongue, for the sound of Elven-tongues is unwelcome to my ears." He then spat an oath in High-elven, his contempt evident. Gaelen was unmoved.

"If you find it more pleasing to hear the common-tongue, then I shall oblige," she said, "but I will hear no ill spoken of Rogond."

"Fine. Then let's not speak of him at all!" said Hallagond. His arm pained him a great deal, he had been driven from his companions, and he did not know how he would rejoin them. He had paid to ensure that his brother never found him, yet here he was, and it looked as though Hallagond would now have to face him. *Worse, this is all my own doing. I had to be noble and leap in to save him. When will I ever learn?*

Gaelen shook her head. "I'm certain you have quite a sad tale to tell...I can see it in your eyes," she said. "Yet your brother is my beloved, and I will safeguard him. Do you understand?"

"Ah. You mean that you will shoot me with arrows or cut my throat if I am unkind to him?" said Hallagond. "Well, then let's begin at once! I might prefer death to dealing with him. Do you not know that the reason your quest has been long is that I did not wish to be found? I would now take my leave of you, except that your foolhardy behavior has made that impossible! I risked my life for him, to what end I cannot know."

Gaelen's smile was cold. "Yet you made that choice," she said. "And now you must remain with us, for you owe me the debt of your life. I did not know you, and I could have let the sutherlings take you. You owe me your life. Now be silent, and live with it!" She looked at his arm again. "This will be less likely to fester now, but we will need to watch it for a few days. Rogond is better equipped to tell the signs than I; you should have him look at the wound each morning when we change the dressing."

Hallagond gave her a wry look. "Do you not see the scars I bear? I am quite capable of looking after my own wounds. I need no younger brother as a nursemaid."

"Yet, if you had been more adept at looking after your wounds, perhaps you would not bear so many scars," she replied. "For now, I will leave you to nurse your ill temper."

She rose and left him, her gaze drawn to Galador, who sat alone and miserable under the early morning sun. Rogond had gone to tend the horses and to keep watch for pursuit. Thankfully, there was still no sign of any—at least not yet. Gaelen sat quietly down beside her friend Galador, her heart grieving for him. She knew what he was feeling, for she felt some of it herself. Nelwyn was beloved of both of them, and she was still lost. How would they find her, and recover her, when they did not dare venture back into Bezaltor?

As if he sensed Gaelen's thoughts, Galador turned toward her, speaking for the first time since their flight from the marketplace. "This is my doing. Do you recall the night that Nelwyn lay dying in Mountain-home? The way I held you to blame for it? Now you shall have the chance to turn those same thoughts upon me, for I failed her. My lack of composure has cost us the hope of rescue."

"Only for the moment," said Gaelen. "We simply need to regroup and try again. I don't hold you to blame—I would be the last to blame anyone for lack of composure. Now we simply begin again. You will not help Nelwyn by sitting in despair."

"What do you think they are doing to her at this very moment? From what I have seen, many of those people have no vestige of honor or decency in them. What will they do to her?" The horror in his face was evident.

"I do not know," said Gaelen, and she meant it. "But what they will *not* do is harm her. She is of far too great a value to them. I know you can't put your mind at rest, but you must try. Only with clear thinking will we be able to restore her. We must turn all other thoughts aside for the moment."

She was thinking of Sajid, and the fact that he had escaped her vengeance. She had wanted to pursue him, but she simply could not. Now she had to come to terms with it, lest it consume her from within. There would be another day; his hour would come. This thought did not exactly assuage her frustration, but it was better than nothing. With a sigh, she placed a comforting hand on Galador's shoulder before moving to join Rogond on the watch.

There had been very little clear thinking in Nelwyn's mind in many days. She had drifted in and out of a dream-world, as Sajid and then Castor had given her a potion that blunted her senses, taking away both her awareness and her reason. She was adrift with no way to ground her thoughts, and they rambled in many strange directions. She did hear Galador's cries, and they dismayed her, but she heard his voice often in her mind. The feeling of dismay passed quickly. She did not see the unpleasantness of her surroundings, and she did not feel the hands of Castor and those others set to tend her. Yet every now and then a tiny spark of awareness flamed, giving rise to unpleasant and frightening thoughts. At such times she would fight, trying to ward off the hands and the visions until more of the potion was given to quiet her.

Castor was very unhappy at the outcome of the auction. He had sold his other captives, but he had expected Nelwyn to bring a very high price, and he truly did not want to be saddled with her. He knew how dangerous she would be when she regained her senses, and he wanted her to be someone else's problem by then.

Though morose and dejected for the moment, Castor had apparently been born under a lucky moon. As he sat in his tent, thinking of the riches that still lay beyond his grasp, one of his servants informed him that a man had come to speak with him concerning Nelwyn. Castor was on his guard—perhaps the man was up to no good, and would try to take her from him. But on the other hand, he might be the agent of a wealthy buyer, and Castor could conclude the transaction tonight, in private.

A man in fine robes of dark red was shown into Castor's tent. Well-spoken and of proud bearing, he introduced himself as the representative of the most honorable Chieftain Al-Muniqui. He had been sent to acquire the finest offering from Bezaltor, and he had seen Nelwyn on the block before she had been withdrawn. Castor rubbed his hands together and called for some wine, bidding the man sit down with him that the bargaining might begin.

Al-Muniqui was the eldest of four brothers, the ruler of a small but very wealthy clan that lived within close proximity of the Neela Oasis. His family had prospered because they were weavers of great renown, and their silks and brocades were among the finest to be found. Al-Muniqui himself lived in a beautiful stone dwelling, ornately carved and gilded, surrounded by his many relatives. Yet he had no heir, and two of his three brothers often turned a covetous eye toward the wealth and power of their elder. Al-Muniqui feared that one day they would rise up and claim leadership. Naturally, this could only happen upon his death, and he never passed a shadow without fear of lurking assassins. His other brother, the third-born, was feeble-minded, and no threat to him, but the others bore sinister thoughts behind their smiling faces.

Al-Muniqui's lack of an heir troubled him, for he despised his brothers, and did not wish for his wealth to pass to them. After all, a man's worth was measured by the number of sons he produced. Al-Muniqui had many wives, and they had given him three daughters, but he did not care for them. He let it be known that, should his next child be born a daughter, all of his wives would suffer the penalty. Surely, it was not he who was lacking. His wives conspired against him, and had been deemed unworthy by the powers of heaven.

Small wonder, then, that all of Al-Muniqui's wives awaited the impending birth of his next child with apprehension. The one who would bear this child was young and in good health...perhaps their daily prayer for a son would be answered. In the meantime they kept busy at their weaving, knowing that should a girl be born, they would all be beaten nearly to death. It was into this world that Nelwyn, daughter of Turanen, was sold.

The Company broke bread together as the evening drew down around them, prepared to mount their horses and ride…where? They had spent much of the day in debate over what their course should be, but they were no closer to agreement now than they had been in the beginning. Gaelen wanted to ride back to the market and disguise herself, hoping to hear news of Nelwyn. Rogond thought this a fair plan, except that it would be difficult for a lone female to lurk at the market without arousing questions, and Gaelen knew little of the sutherling tongues, so she would be unlikely to pick up news. Neither Rogond nor Galador could risk returning to Bezaltor, for they would likely be recognized, even in disguise. It was difficult to conceal the identity of one so tall. Hallagond was already fairly well known in the slave markets, so there was no use sending him. In addition, there was always the possibility of someone's recognizing their horses.

Gaelen was concerned for Rogond; he had not as yet spoken to his brother, other than to offer him food and water, as Hallagond had made it plain that he wanted nothing to do with him. He would not look Rogond directly in the eye, and would turn his back to him whenever possible. In Gaelen's opinion, he was behaving in a manner most childish. She sat beside Rogond now, tending his bruises, soothing his spirit as she could.

"Don't worry, my love, he will come around. I know he's being disagreeable, but that is only because he did not expect us to find him, and he was not prepared. Remember your promise to your father—you knew it would not be an easy task, and it will test your resolve. Steel yourself, for he will not open his heart quickly or willingly. His spirit is wounded...I can see it in his face. Yet there is still a kind heart beneath the thorny veil."

She began to rub Rogond's shoulders, and he relaxed slightly as some of the tension left him. "But, why does he not want to know his own kin, unless he is so ashamed that he cannot face me? I have set myself in judgment of him already, for he was engaged in a practice most horrific and evil. I knew his tale was not a happy one, but I never expected to find him involved in the buying and selling of flesh!" Rogond shook his head and drew a deep breath. Hallagond's presence as a bidder in the auction-tent had shocked him. It was the last place he had expected to find his brother, formerly a man of the highest character.

"Do you mean he was actually…actually *bidding*?" Gaelen had not realized this, and she threw a quick glance at Hallagond as though she expected to see scales covering his body, or perhaps horns sprouting from his forehead that she had missed earlier.

"He had a bidding card, and I saw him hold it up during the auction," said Rogond. As he thought of it, the tension returned to his shoulders.

Gaelen drew a deep breath. *It's obvious that we don't know what forces drive this man, and until we can learn more, it's better to reserve opinion.* "Calm yourself, beloved. We may not know everything yet. Don't judge him too harshly…there is something about a man who would own slaves that doesn't match what I have seen in Hallagond. Let's wait and see."

Rogond would take this advice for the moment, but he knew that if his brother had his way there would be very few words exchanged between them, and he would never know or understand Hallagond's motivation any more than he did right then.

The Company was still no closer to an acceptable plan, and each minute spent in fruitless debate distanced them from Nelwyn. Galador, in particular, looked haggard and grey-faced. They had to take action soon.

Hallagond had remained outside their discussions, stubbornly refusing to take part in them, sitting alone with sullen eyes turned toward the deep desert. Gaelen knew that he longed to escape their company, to run from Rogond, but she had reminded him that he owed her a life-debt, and until it was repaid he would be compelled to remain.

She knew that Rogond wanted to converse with his brother so that they might each learn and tell of their history, but he did not yet know how to approach. Gaelen did not understand Hallagond's reaction to Rogond, but she knew it pained him, and for this reason she went to speak with Hallagond aside.

She knew he didn't care for Elven-speech, so she addressed him in the common-tongue. He would not meet her eyes, but that didn't matter—she knew he could hear her. She told him of Galador, and of the importance of finding and restoring Nelwyn to him. She told him of their quest, and why Rogond had wanted so desperately to find him. She also told him that she respected his wish to remain alone, and at this he turned and acknowledged her, looking for the first time into her eyes.

"If you respect my desire to remain alone, why do you not release me?" he asked.

"Because that is not your destiny," replied Gaelen. "Rogond was told by a man named Kamal that you had gone to Fómor, and that was where you could be found. That has never been so, has it?"

"Most assuredly not. I would not live long there, regrettably. No right-thinking man of northern heritage would take such a risk.

I have been to the City of the Corsairs only once, years ago, and I quite had my fill of it." He paused for a moment. "Kamal had been paid to put you off the trail, but he should not have directed you to Fómor; you would not have survived the crossing."

Gaelen's eyes widened with sudden understanding, and then narrowed as she addressed Hallagond in a chilly voice. "No, you would have preferred that your brother not be harmed…it was you that paid Kamal, wasn't it? Your gold paid him to lie to us. Yet it was not the lie you would have wished for; I hear it in your voice. Even so, you would have seen us dead in the wastelands rather than face the only family you have left?" She shook her head in disbelief.

"You know nothing of destiny," said Hallagond, his voice bitter and dark. The color had risen in his face and his eyes were bright with the realization that Gaelen had guessed the truth; it had indeed been his gold that had paid for Kamal's lies.

"I know this much," she replied. "Your destiny lies, for the moment, with us. It should be obvious to you by now…for what other reason could you be so impossibly unlucky? In spite of your detestable plan you have been foiled, and Rogond has found you. You owe me a life-debt, and until you repay it, I will not release you. If you aid us in freeing Nelwyn, I will hold your debt paid, but don't think you will escape Rogond. He will continue to pursue you until there is no hope. Do you understand?"

Hallagond nodded, fixing her with piercing grey eyes that were nearly identical to Rogond's, but harder. They had seen things Rogond would never see…not if Gaelen could help it.

"I will aid you in freeing your friend, if you will then release me," he said. "But I will hold no love or regard for my brother. Do you understand?"

"No, I do not understand," said Gaelen, "but for now, I will accept your aid. That will mean that you must hold some regard for Rogond, at least. You will need to work with him if you would aid us. And know this, Tuathan…I will keep a tally of each hurtful thing you say to him, of each time you wound his spirit. These things will not be forgotten." She rose and went back to join Rogond and Galador. Hallagond hesitated for a few moments, and then he turned toward the Company, setting himself to the task of rescuing Nelwyn, unwittingly taking the first steps toward an unforeseen destiny.

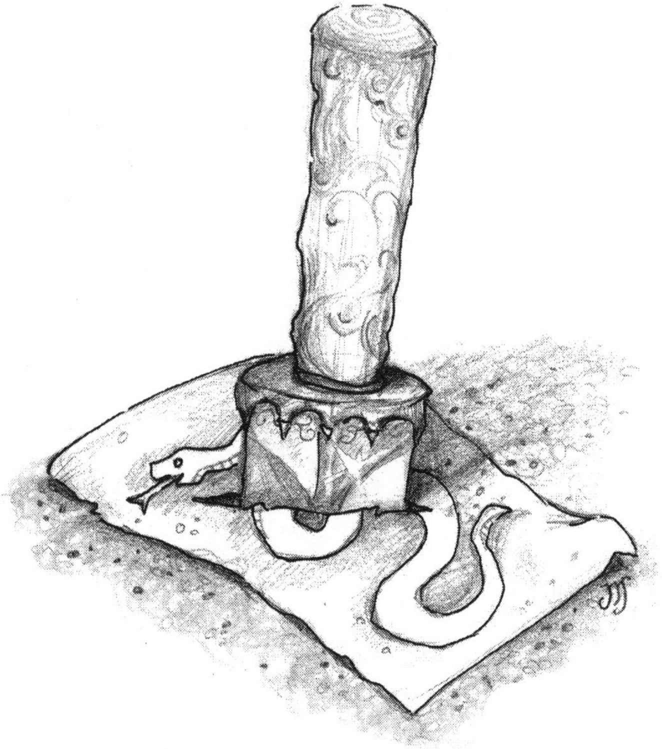

12
Hallagond Proves Useful

"I might be able to guess where your friend has been taken," said Hallagond at last. He had spent some time in consideration, having listened to the tale of the auction at Bezaltor. Gaelen noted that he still would neither look at nor speak directly to Rogond, and that both brothers were ill-at-ease. This would have to be mended, and soon, otherwise it might interfere with their rescue efforts. Gaelen's heart went out to Rogond; she could imagine the conflict of his thoughts. They had undertaken a long and arduous quest, only to find his brother bidding for slaves. A less honorable activity would be difficult to imagine. Thankfully, Rogond had not yet come to the realization that his brother had paid Kamal to mislead him.

Gaelen also knew that Hallagond was not as he appeared. He was trying to behave counter to his nature, and he was as conflicted as Rogond. Rogond's disappointment was matched by Hallagond's denial, and Gaelen did not wish to think too long upon either, for it made her weary and confused.

Even Galador could see the tension between the two brothers. He wondered whether this rough-looking man could aid them in finding Nelwyn. "You know these lands and the people in them. Even your guesses will be better than our meager knowledge," he said.

Hallagond looked into Galador's eyes, realizing that, if they failed, he would never survive. His spirit would waste away, and his body would follow it—he would die rather than return his heart to cold isolation. Hallagond had known relatively little of Elves, and he had never before seen sorrow that was thousands of years old. Galador's very life depended upon Nelwyn now. Everyone in the Company knew it.

Hallagond drew a deep breath. "We know that Nelwyn was withdrawn from the general auction last night—you effectively disrupted things before bidding could even begin. But I overheard a couple of very wealthy buyers discussing what they would give for her...they were representatives of a local Chieftain named Al-Muniqui. Nelwyn will command a price that few can pay, but Al-Muniqui is one of them. That's where I would look for her."

"Did you see this Al-Muniqui at the auction?" asked Rogond.

"No, only his agents. They were the ones in scarlet robes, extremely fine brocaded robes. Al-Muniqui and his family made their fortunes as providers of fine cloth, and his wares are highly sought after. I'll warrant even the Elven-realms have traded for some of it—none can match the quality of his silks. The weavers use pigments found only in the southlands to dye their fabrics. If she has gone to Al-Muniqui, then we are fortunate. His tribe lives near the Neela oasis."

Gaelen scowled. "Isn't that the place Sajid warned us away from? The one with the supposedly bad water?"

"That's the one," said Rogond.

"Who is Sajid?" asked Hallagond. "What 'bad water?'"

"Oh, never mind!" said Galador. "That is not so far away. I saw it on Fima's map!"

"Indeed, it isn't far," said Hallagond. "Yet Al-Muniqui will fight to keep his prize, and he's known to be a hard, ruthless man. You will need to make your plans carefully, or you will not prevail."

"You mean *we* will need to make careful plans, or *we* will not prevail," said Gaelen. "You are included in our Company now, Hallagond. We will depend on you to guide us." She chuckled at the brief look of dismay that came over his face. "Don't worry...once Nelwyn regains her senses, they might not fight so hard to keep her! There is a reason that Castor kept her bewildered. I would not want to be the man who first tries to lay hands on her."

Galador's eyes flared with rage at the thought of it. "No, I would not want to be that man either."

Gaelen nodded in agreement. "I don't yet know how we will rescue Nelwyn, but at least we now have some idea as to where to look for her."

They all hoped that Hallagond's guess was right—none more so than Hallagond himself. Rescuing Nelwyn was the only way to be free of the life-debt that bound him to all that was left of his old life.

Al-Muniqui stood before his new acquisition, his eyes half-lidded, as his agents prepared to reveal her. She had been placed amid cushions of multicolored brocade and covered with a veil of golden silk. Most men would have been tantalized at the sight of her lithe, graceful form, but Al-Muniqui was well accustomed to having the most beautiful women provided to him. He stood with his arms folded, daring the agents to impress him.

When they removed the silk, Al-Muniqui's reaction was quite satisfactory. His entire body tensed and he drew in a sharp breath. His eyes grew bright and warm as he gazed now upon a creature of such ethereal beauty that he was rendered speechless. He took a tentative step toward her, stretching out one hand toward the silken hair that lay like a river of precious gold on the pillow beneath her head. Her eyes were closed, her features relaxed and peaceful, but cold. She was an impossibly fair, wild creature from the far northern forest, and Al-Muniqui was pleased.

He touched her face, so smooth and clear, the color of cream and roses. He traced one of her strange ears, knowing that his agents had indeed acquired something of great worth.

Neither Al-Muniqui nor his agents truly understood the nature of Elves, or they would have left Nelwyn in the tent of Castor the slave-dealer. She would never submit to the attentions of Al-Muniqui—or of any man—for her heart was given, and there would never be another who would claim her. She would see to her own death first. Al-Muniqui would come to know this in time, but for now he expected this lovely, immortal bird he had trapped in a cage would agree to be his consort, and would one day provide him with many sons. He looked with approval at his agents.

"You have done well, and I am pleased. Take now your reward." He brought forth a silken bag of gold coins and handed it to one of the agents, who bowed respectfully before taking his leave.

Al-Muniqui was now alone with Nelwyn, save for the bodyguards who never left his side. He stood over her, a dark desire growing in his heart. She was his property now, and he would have her. "Sleep, little bird," he muttered. "Soon you will awaken, and then we shall come to know one another. I shall care for you if you please me… you will want for nothing." He leaned down toward her, taken with a sudden desire to caress her, but something stayed his hand. Somehow he could not bring himself to touch her again—it was as though he had been warned to stay away.

He decided to leave her in peace for the moment, his thoughts just a little unsettled, draping her once again in golden silk before turning to leave. When he stepped out into the gathering twilight his feeling of foreboding faded, and he thought no more of it.

After he had gone, two women crept quietly into Nelwyn's chamber, approaching to look upon her with wonder. One of the women was the youngest of Al-Muniqui's wives. The other was his most talented weaver, and though she was a slave, she was held in very high regard. The guards set at the doorway to the chamber allowed the women to enter, for they would surely do no harm. They stared at Nelwyn in silence.

"What sort of being is she?" asked the younger woman, whose name was Sari.

The weaver, a middle-aged woman named Bint Raed, shook her head slowly. An enlightened woman, she could read and write. She knew of the existence of Elves, for she hailed from a land where lore and learning were of value. "This is one of the Immortal Ones, whom the Sutherlings call Avinashi, unless I am mistaken," she said. "If that is so, then Al-Muniqui has indeed found himself a prize. Yet I wonder how she will fare…Avinashi are not known to submit to the desires of men. There will be trouble before all is ended." She stepped forward, still shaking her head. "I expect your exalted husband does not know what he has acquired."

Sari was very respectful of Bint Raed, for she was known to be both learned and wise. "Tell me of the Avinashi," she asked, for she had never even heard of such things before. "Are they truly immortal?"

"They may be slain, but they will not die naturally or suffer pestilence," said Bint Raed. "This one may be very, very old."

"She doesn't look old. Why have we not seen one until now? I've never even heard of such beings." Sari wasn't certain whether to believe in Nelwyn or not.

"They do not usually venture into these lands. How has she come to be so far from her home, I wonder?" Bint Raed felt a pang of sadness as she spoke, for, like Nelwyn, she was far from home. She had been captured and sold into bondage many years before, and had given up all hope of ever seeing her own lands again. She was always under watch, and there was nowhere to escape to. Al-Muniqui would have her killed rather than allow her to leave.

She looked into Sari's large, soft brown eyes, so wide with wonder. Sari had been born in the Neela and promised to Al-Muniqui at only nine years of age. He came for her when she was twelve. It was hoped that she now bore a son in her womb; she would give birth very soon now. This would be her first child, but if it was a daughter, it might well be her last.

Bint Raed looked down upon Nelwyn with sadness, but there was a small spark of anger growing as well. She had seen the manner in which Al-Muniqui broke the spirits of those who displeased him. This beautiful Avinasha would not survive long in this place, for she would never submit to captivity. One such as Sari had known of little else.

Bint Raed was among the most talented weavers ever born. She had come from a fair, white city that stood poised on the far southern coast, with its back to the desert and its face turned to the sea. The people of the city were educated and diverse; there were many races there, and they often intermingled. Bint Raed was the product of a sutherling father, who served in the city as a builder and maker of stone carvings, and a mother who was a fine weaver and carried the blood of the original city founders. These were men of the lost realm of Tuathas, and Bint Raed was proud of her heritage. Her mother's name was Raenien, hence her father named her "Bint Raenien" (daughter of Raenien), shortened to Bint Raed.

She remembered well the great City, with its gleaming white spires topped with silver, and the high sea-cliffs on which it stood. She remembered the clear, cold water springing from beneath the earth on which the city was founded, and the tall trees growing everywhere within its walls. But mostly she remembered the people, who prized learning and knowledge above all else. They were all free people, yet they did not often leave their enlightened realm. They feared that, should outsiders discover the City, their way of life would be lost. Bint Raed had longed to escape and see the wide world for herself, and this longing had made her feel trapped within her beautiful home.

Thus, she left the Silver City when she was five and fifty, traveling for a time with a caravan of merchants, later taken by bandits and sold to Al-Muniqui. When her weaving abilities were discovered, she gained favor in his household, but no liberty. He would never release her. It was ironic that she left her home seeking freedom, only to have it taken from her utterly.

She sat down beside Nelwyn, who stirred and moaned as though in the grip of an unhappy dream. *She does not yet know how unhappy she can be*, thought Bint Raed, taking Nelwyn's hand in her own. There would be no freedom for Nelwyn, or for herself, in this place.

Sari sensed the hopelessness welling in Bint Raed, and it frightened her. She knew the fate that awaited her should she displease her husband with a girl-child. She had always taken comfort in the strength of Bint Raed, who had seemed almost as a mother to her, and to see such resigned melancholy in the older woman's eyes was disquieting. She squeezed Bint Raed's shoulder, hoping to comfort her.

Nelwyn, still restive, moaned softly, then her eyelids fluttered open. Sari had never seen such a beautiful, clear green.

"Can you hear me?" whispered Bint Raed. Nelwyn closed her eyes again, for her head swam and her vision blurred, but she nodded slightly.

"Rest and be still, and hear my words. You are in the house of Al-Muniqui, and we will not harm you. Yet there are things you should know. Do you understand me?" Nelwyn's eyes opened wide, for this stranger had spoken in Elven-speech!

Bint Raed turned to Sari. "You should leave us now, little one. There are things that I must tell her that you should not hear. If you have not heard them, then your husband cannot force you to reveal them. Better you should leave now...return to your own chamber and rest for a while. I will come to you later."

"But…what was that strange tongue you were speaking?"

"Never mind. I learned it long ago, and I'm thinking Al-Muniqui will soon want to make use of it. Go on, now!"

Sari's eyes grew wide with confusion, but she agreed, embracing Bint Raed briefly before leaving her alone with Nelwyn.

Bint Raed explained many things, for Nelwyn would need to know of them. Though Nelwyn was disheartened upon learning that she had been sold into bondage, Bint Raed reassured her. Their hearts surged in the midst of their hopelessness, for each knew that she had found an ally, and neither would rest until both were free.

Hallagond called the Company to a halt just as they drew within distant sight of the Neela oasis. It was much larger than the Chupa, for the water was plentiful and of better quality. There were growing things here, and Gaelen's heart was glad, for she missed the cool, green tranquility of her woodland home. Her eyes were weary of the desert tans, greys, and browns.

Galador seemed less edgy as he looked out upon the oasis; at least Nelwyn was not being held in some terrible place. Her comforts could be attended to here, and Hallagond had assured him that, should Al-Muniqui have acquired her, she would want for nothing.

"If I know Castor, he will have demanded a small fortune, and Al-Muniqui takes good care of his possessions, for he values them. He has many wives, I expect, but none will have required such an investment."

Galador looked away, his voice cold as he spoke: "If he touches her, he will die for it. Should I ever encounter Castor or Sajid again, they will fall before me as well. I don't care what we have to do."

Hallagond, who was uncomfortable with strong emotion, was chilled by the murderous resolve in Galador's voice, knowing it could mean trouble for the Company. When Galador turned back toward him, his gaze was softer. "Thank you for your aid and reassurance. It has been of great help to me."

Gaelen, who had lately become protective and watchful of Galador, approached silently from behind Hallagond, startling him. Apparently, she had overheard. "We will first need to learn that Nelwyn is truly here," she said. "I have always had some awareness of her, and I sense she is not far away."

Hallagond considered. "I doubt that she is actually in the oasis, but the house of Al-Muniqui is not far from it—it draws from the same system of wells. I have never been there, and so we must learn where it may be found."

"I will go at once," said Galador, who was understandably anxious.

"I think not," said Hallagond, who would have been amused at the absurdity of such a suggestion had he not seen the menacing gleam in Galador's eyes. "You do not understand the sutherling speech, and you cannot be relied upon to hold your composure should you learn things that unsettle you. You're too bound up in this web, my friend. Not to mention the fact that you do not exactly blend in."

Gaelen smiled at this, for it was true that Galador's tall frame and beardless, ageless face made it difficult for him to escape notice. "Hallagond is right. You should not go among these folk in your present state of temperament," she said. "We need someone well versed in the ways and speech of these lands, and that would be Hallagond. I will go with him, for we shall need his skills and my stealth. I will disguise myself as a youth of the Ravani. At least then I may carry weapons openly, though I trust we won't need them…not yet."

Rogond, who had been tending the horses, approached in time to hear the plan. "I'm uncomfortable with your venturing alone into such a place," he said. "It will not be easy to pass their scrutiny, and your disguise must be very convincing."

"I won't be alone, I'll be with Hallagond. His task will be the harder one. I will act only at his bidding—it will be up to him to actually learn where Nelwyn is. I go only because of the possible need for stealth."

Hallagond was not concerned, either. "It will not be that difficult to disguise her. Your difficulties have come from attempting to put her in female garb; her proud bearing and attitude make her much more believable as an impetuous, prideful youth. Leave it to me."

That same afternoon, Hallagond and Gaelen rode together to the Neela. Hallagond was not well known among these folk, and his sun-browned face and full beard would serve to conceal him. Gaelen wore a loose-fitting robe of off-white with a head covering made of the same material, such that neither her hair nor her ears were visible. They had bound her chest with linen, and browned her face and hands with nut-oil. Hallagond had instructed her to look as few people directly in the eye as possible. She resembled a fit, willowy youth, and she took great comfort from the short sword hanging at her belt. Her long knives and throwing-daggers were hidden, but she could easily reach them. She rode happily beside

Hallagond, as Finan lifted his tail in the air and literally ran circles around Malvorn.

"Stop playing about and pay attention," said Hallagond. "This is a serious task, and here you are showing off. It's enough of an indignity for me to have to ride the pack horse without your pointing out his inadequacies."

Gaelen laughed musically at him. "First, O Expert Concealer of Elves, I do not see Malvorn as inadequate—he is an *excellent* pack horse. Second, I am supposed to be impersonating an impetuous youth, and I'm simply getting into character."

Hallagond scowled at her. "You can't allow yourself to be impetuous...this is serious. If you are discovered, there will be dire consequences. You must try to make yourself as small and beneath notice as possible. Do you understand?"

"I understand," she said. "My apologies. I follow wherever you direct me." She reined in Finan, to his displeasure, and trotted sensibly behind Hallagond into the heart of the oasis.

Azori and his brother Azok sat with their unsavory comrades, drinking kumri and shaking the desert sand from their boots. By now, the whole of the Chupa knew of Haifa's encounter with the strange northman, and though his broken finger would heal, it would be some time before he was comfortable. The worst of it was that he had needed to hire and pay someone to manage the bar for him, as he found handling heavy jugs and pouring drinks to be difficult with a clumsily-bandaged right hand.

Hallagond's companions were becoming concerned for him. Usually he returned promptly from the auction at Bezaltor, yet he still had not appeared. Azori's half-sister, Estle, was especially dismayed, for she was fond of Hallagond and would know what had befallen him. She asked Azori about it, but he could not enlighten her.

A comely woman, she had the same dark hair as Azori, but her complexion was very pale, like ivory, and her face freckled in the sun. Her eyes were grey, like Hallagond's, indicating her own northern heritage. She was a hard-bitten woman who had only been made stronger by deprivation and disregard.

Estle had lived in the Ravani for all of her life, the daughter of the same Corsair who had sired Azori and (reputedly) Azok. She had known her mother only briefly, as she had died when Estle was young, yet when she was alone and tranquil she often recalled her mother's face and gentle words.

Estle knew that Hallagond was not as he appeared, and that the cynical words he so often spoke were not from his heart. She hoped that he would one day come back to himself, for she loved him, and watched over him when she could.

He did not know that she cared so for him. He saw her as a friendly face, a worthy ally, and the half-sister of Azori and (probably) Azok. Hallagond would not have looked with longing upon her even had he known of her desire, for he would not have wished to earn the wrath of her two half-brothers, who tended to take any would-be suitors out in the desert and leave them there.

Estle doubted that Azori would have killed them (although she was not as certain of Azok), but she held little doubt that they had been instructed to put their tails to the oasis and never return. She did not wish for Hallagond to be banished, so she kept her distance.

She didn't know of his whereabouts at present, for Azori's band spent little time in the Chupa, in fact they had not seen the oasis in several months. By this time, word had spread of Rogond and his companions, and of their search for Hallagond. It had also been made known to the darker element in the oasis that Radeef and his associates, including Kamal, had been well paid to divert the Company toward Fómor, where Hallagond most certainly would not be found. Estle shook her head, and her cool grey eyes were sad. It would do Hallagond good to know that he still had family who cared about him. After all, she took comfort in knowing that her admittedly unsavory half-brothers cared for her, even though they were occasionally inconvenient.

Estle did not care for Haifa; she took her leave of the choking, smoke-filled dwelling full of unwashed, drunken men and ventured out into the desert evening. The sunsets here were spectacular and she was treated to an especially brilliant one of fiery red and orange; the high, wispy clouds appeared as flames in the deepening sky. Estle knew that such brilliant sunsets were often the result of terrible windstorms raising so much sand and dust that to be caught in one unprotected would likely mean death. The people of the Chupa would now be on their guard, for this was the season in which such storms occurred.

Where are you, Hallagond? Why have you not returned? Estle did not wish to think of him caught in such a storm alone. He was experienced in desert ways, but even experienced travelers could die, especially if they were caught alone on the open sands. Sometimes they simply disappeared without a trace, as though the desert had swallowed them whole. She gazed out at the sunset, the darkness at her back, her long, curly hair stirred by the wind. *I pray you are well. Keep safe, and may no evil befall you.* She noticed the first bright stars appearing, as the darkness slowly overcame the blazing sunset. She closed her eyes and spoke the words that Hallagond had taught her; words that came from fair, immortal beings who had walked in Alterra since the beginning of time. "Isa-i réaltae annachtim, Tréigam," she said, delighting in the beauty of the Elvish words and the sentiment they so eloquently conveyed. "May the stars watch over you, Forsaken One."

Hallagond and Gaelen returned to their anxious friends with good news. They had learned where Al-Muniqui could be found, and that Nelwyn had indeed come to dwell there. Hallagond's instincts had proven true.

Galador had spent the past few hours sitting atop a tall stone, his eyes closed, chanting quietly. Now that he knew for certain that Nelwyn was at Al-Muniqui's, he was anxious to mount a rescue, but Hallagond had set out food and drink, and would not be moved.

"I have brought a feast from the Neela at great trouble and expense, and I intend to partake of it. You will not be strong enough to aid your beloved if you don't eat," said Hallagond through a mouthful of bread and meat. "Besides, we can't afford to be in a hurry. This is going to take some planning."

Gaelen gave Galador's shoulder an affectionate squeeze. Hallagond was right. They did need to care for themselves first if they would aid Nelwyn. Besides, the smell of the wonderful meal was so intriguing that even Galador could not help himself, especially when Hallagond brought forth the wine to go with it. Galador drank quite a quantity of it, and soon he was considerably more relaxed.

Rogond was still uncomfortable around his brother, and spoke to him only when necessary. There were some difficult questions that he wasn't quite ready to ask. Why had his brother so wanted to avoid him? Why had he been trading in slaves? Rangers were sworn to defend the Light…why had Hallagond forsaken his sacred duty? The answers to these questions would have to wait.

"I trust your journey was uneventful?" he asked Gaelen, who was savoring a slab of fine flatbread soaked with honey. She lifted her bright gaze to his, nodding in response to his question, and he smiled at her unnaturally brown face surrounded by a windblown mop of ever-lightening hair. She was turning quite golden in the sun, the brown turning to silken copper strands that flashed and glinted as the wind stirred them. Hallagond had informed her that the nut-oil with which he had browned her face and hands would not wash off; it would need to wear away. Now her eyes glittered with suppressed mirth, and Rogond knew that she was not being entirely forthcoming.

He glanced over at Hallagond, who smiled and shook his head. Something amusing had happened in the oasis, and Gaelen was at the heart of it, but she did not seem inclined to tell the tale. Rogond raised one eyebrow at her. Perhaps the honey would loosen her tongue.

A few minutes later he invited her to share the joke with him. "Come, Gaelen—it's obvious that you have an amusing tale to tell. Will you not share it?"

Hallagond chuckled quietly as he finished his meal, rubbing sand between his hands to clean them. "Ah, yes. Gaelen Taldin, shameless breaker of hearts and raiser of false hopes!" he said, as Rogond lifted a curious eyebrow. Gaelen's bright eyes and impish grin told him that the honey was having its usual effect, and soon his curiosity would be satisfied.

Apparently, there had been an incident involving three young maidens. Gaelen had been left to watch the horses while Hallagond entered the local tavern to learn what he could of Nelwyn. The three maidens had been returning from the marketplace, and they did not recognize the slender "youth" standing outside the tavern entrance.

They could not help but notice "him," and the nearer they drew, the more intrigued they became.

Gaelen was tall enough by their standards, appearing as a beardless, very beautiful young man of perhaps fifteen years. With the sinewy, well-muscled shoulders and arms of a life-long archer, she was lean and lithe and put forth an air of power and grace.

The three maids had never beheld one such as Gaelen, and the light of her spirit was mesmerizing. They were neither frightened nor threatened, for Gaelen simply looked upon them with an impassive, mildly superior expression.

They were of a people who were much less constrained in their behavior than many of the sutherlings of Gaelen's acquaintance, and they began to blush and giggle as they whispered among themselves. It was plain to Gaelen that they were enamored of her. Despite her amusement she kept her expression dispassionate, pretending to take no notice.

They approached her, bowing and extending their hands palms upward in a gesture of greeting, addressing Gaelen in their own tongue. She did not understand them, and decided that perhaps it would be best to discourage them, but her indifference to their questions only intrigued them further. Hallagond, meanwhile, had emerged from the tavern and now stood quietly in witness, his arms folded, obviously entertained. He could understand their speech, and he would later translate, to Gaelen's amusement.

Gaelen wanted the maidens to understand that they were wasting their time trying to speak with her; that she did not comprehend. So she spoke to them in the Elven-tongue, using a deep, melodic voice. "I do not understand your words, but I take your meaning. Your efforts will bear no fruit, for I am a maiden even as you are, and your charms are somewhat wasted on me."

Hallagond pretended to gag himself with his own finger at the maidens' reaction to Gaelen's beautiful speech. They were all blushing furiously, their dark eyes glowing. They spoke among themselves, approaching her and smiling. Gaelen knew that they were flirting shamelessly, and she returned the favor, bowing her head to them and closing her eyes for a moment in acknowledgment. Then she drew up her lithe frame and reached behind her back, drawing her long knives. The three maidens at first started back in alarm, but Gaelen simply twirled her blades expertly—she had over a thousand years of practice—tossing them from hand to hand as they glinted in the sunlight. She flung them aloft, executed a graceful turn, and caught them before re-sheathing them. The maidens stood open-mouthed as Gaelen once again folded her arms before her, looking down at them with an expression of mild disdain. They were surely unworthy of her magnificence!

This, apparently, was too much for them, and they backed away from her before turning to leave. At the last moment, one lingered, turning back and running forward, removing her multicolored scarf and laying it at Gaelen's feet. Gaelen bowed, picked up the scarf, and reached out to take the hand of the maiden, bowing again and touching the hand to her forehead as she had seen the Ravani-folk do. The maiden gasped, turned even brighter red than before, and nearly tripped over her garments in her haste to retreat after her companions.

Hallagond was now laughing out loud. "You are truly shameless, to toy with them in such a manner!" he said. "She will dream about you tonight...they all will. If only they understood Elvish!"

"If only I understood their tongue," replied Gaelen. "I'll warrant there were some highly entertaining things being said. Alas that I do not."

"Oh, no doubt of it," said Hallagond. "Allow me to enlighten you. Let's see...ahhh...they asked your name and where you came from, and whether you intended to remain in the Neela. They told you their names and that they were sisters. But it was when they realized you didn't understand their speech that things got truly interesting. They began to comment upon the appealing nature of your shoulders, wondering whether your posterior was likewise alluring. They were quite smitten with your potential, although they did note that you are not yet grown to full manhood."

"My...my *posterior*? Oh, my!" said Gaelen, so amused that she could not speak for a minute or so. Her ears were as red as the deepest blush on the cheeks of the three hapless maidens, who had unwittingly fallen into a deep pit of foolishness.

Rogond examined the silk scarf; it was beautiful and of very fine quality. "Ah, Gaelen...you are the breaker of hearts," he said. "This is an admirable token; alas that it was given in vain."

Gaelen took the scarf and tied it around her head, binding her ears. She had removed her desert garb and stood now looking out at the beautiful, fiery sunset. "It was indeed given in vain, Thaylon, for you hold my heart. Yet I will keep it in remembrance of three maidens with spirits refreshingly free enough to court my affections. I am uplifted!"

"You see, Gaelen," said Hallagond, "not all women of the south-lands are suppressed. Giving you that token was a rather serious gesture…you might have acquired three wives all at once!"

Gaelen shook her head, for the concept of having more than one other living soul in possession of one's heart was difficult for her to fathom.

Rogond placed an arm about her shoulders. "Come, then, let us proceed to the house of Al-Muniqui. When we have seen the lay of things, we'll make our plan to free Nelwyn." The Company agreed, stowing their belongings and mounting their horses, and they were soon on their way.

"Most High, your treasure has awakened."

Nelwyn could hear the voice of her guardian through the locked door of her chamber, and she knew her captor, Al-Muniqui, would soon appear. She caught sight of him as the door was opened; he paused before a looking-glass in the hallway, surveying the condition of his magnificent robes and impeccably-trimmed beard. Few Elven-lords could match the quality of his raiment. *What a vain creature,* thought Nelwyn. *He probably thinks I'll be impressed…*

He entered her chamber as she sat upon a pile of cushions, prevented from rising to her feet by the silken cords that bound her. She had decided to remain passive, and not struggle, as Bint Raed had warned her of the futility of it. *Better to bide our time, and lull them into believing that I have accepted captivity. Then we'll make a plan to escape.*

Nelwyn was a gentle-natured spirit, but her wrath had been aroused. The more Bint Raed told her of the ways of Al-Muniqui and his brothers, the angrier she became.

Sajid had told her over and over of the deaths of Fima and Gaelen, and he had also told her that Galador and Rogond had been slain at his bidding. She had despaired in the midst of her bewilderment, thinking that no one would ever come for her, and she would never see her beloved again. Yet as her senses slowly returned she knew that this was not so, for she could sense Galador. She also could feel the presence of Gaelen, as she had done since they were young. Of the others she did not know, yet she sensed no grief in her cousin, and that was encouraging. Gaelen was drawing nearer—Nelwyn could feel it—and Galador was with her.

Her eyes glittered as Al-Muniqui approached her, a haughty smile on his face that was intended to be endearing, but failed. *Let him think himself worthy. Let him believe that he holds you in thrall.* She looked into his eyes as he drew nearer. *Soon he will learn otherwise, and then he will come to understand the folly in attempting to imprison the daughter of Turanen.* She smiled a cold, faint smile, and Al-Muniqui paused in his approach, as though suddenly afraid of her.

All right, you wretch…you haven't tried to harm me. Let's hear what you have to say. Her cold smile faded and he resumed his approach until he came close enough to touch her; he reached out and stroked her hair with a manicured hand. *Are his nails…actually painted? Ugh!* She held her breath and her body went stiff, but she bore it without complaint. *This time…*

"Welcome to the house of Al-Muniqui," he said. You belong to me now, and I shall provide for your every need. If you please me, you need not fear. Come now, and feast with your lord. My servants will prepare you." He clapped his hands twice, and two serving-women appeared, bowing so that their foreheads nearly touched the ground. "Prepare her at once, and then bring her to me." He turned back to Nelwyn. "You will please allow them to prepare you. If you comport yourself well, you will be unbound."

Her expression was impassive, concealing her dark thoughts. *Yes, you bushy-faced, pathetic man, unbind me. Then I shall strangle the life from you. Touch me and see!*

He left her to the attentions of the serving-women, and her thoughts were turned elsewhere for the moment. She had already been bathed and combed, but now she was given beautiful robes of green brocade that matched her eyes. She was scented with fragrant oils and brought to Al-Muniqui's chamber, her wrists still bound.

A comely young maiden sat beside her, offering to feed her, but Nelwyn refused.

Al-Muniqui, who had already begun his repast, lifted a disapproving eyebrow. "Come, come! You must be hungry, for you have not eaten in many days. It will do you no good to resist my hospitality, for there is no escape from this place. We are surrounded by deep desert; even if you could escape my realm, you would not survive. Why not make the best of it?"

Nelwyn lifted her chin and looked levelly at him. "I will eat only what I can place in my own mouth. I will not be fed like a child."

"Fair enough," said Al-Muniqui, "but I will not yet unbind you. You will need to make do with your hands as they are. Eat as you may."

Nelwyn could not deny that the feast set before her was nearly irresistible, as she had not truly eaten in a very long time. She had been kept in a sort of half-waking stupor, and as such had needed very little to sustain her. She was still in reasonable condition, but her hunger awakened as she regained her senses. Fresh fruits, soft breads, and tender meats were set before her, and despite indignation at having to try to feed herself with bound wrists, she suppressed her pride. Everything tasted wonderful, especially the fruits; she closed her eyes with pleasure as the sweet juices filled her mouth and throat. Al-Muniqui watched her with obvious fascination. He ate and drank, finishing his meal with a loud, resonant belch that, evidently, was the sign of approval among his folk.

The serving-maid was obviously relieved. She dipped a cloth into a bowl filled with lemon-and-herb scented water, wiping Nelwyn's face and fingers, removing all traces of the meal. Then she took her leave, and Nelwyn was left with Al-Muniqui. His bodyguards stood watch by the door, but they were well trained to take no notice of what was said in their presence. If they reacted at all, they would be punished. It was as though they were made of wood.

Al-Muniqui leaned forward, his dark eyes glowing as he met Nelwyn's proud glance. "Though I do not speak the common-tongue as well as I would like, I believe I can provide you with a clear understanding of what your fate will be. You will tell me of your race, and how I may please you, and I will do all in my power to ensure that your needs are met beyond all expectations. In return, you will submit to my bidding, and if you are pleasing to me you shall bear my sons. It is my hope that they will then be immortal, even as you are."

Nelwyn's eyes widened with incredulity at the notion that she would bear this man's children. *You have no idea what you're suggesting... how impossible it is!*

"This is your destiny, fair one. It is folly to deny it, for your fate turns by my will alone. Best to simply accept it...you will be happier. I can be a generous host, or a bitter taskmaster. The choice is yours."

Nelwyn fixed him with cold eyes that matched the chill of her thoughts, every hair on her body standing erect. *I will not speak to you, for I cannot defend myself from your wrath as yet. You are deluded, and know nothing of my race if you could even have such thoughts. She-elves cannot bear children of men. You don't understand what you have done, what folly you are pursuing. You may overpower me, and violate me, but no children will ever be forthcoming. I fear you have spent a great deal of your wealth for nothing.* She smiled the same cold smile she had given him earlier, and simply shook her head. *If I were you, I might try to recover some of my investment. You have been sold useless goods.*

Al-Muniqui did not care for that cold smile at all. He was not used to being denied anything he wanted. "I see that you do not care for the notion, my proud golden bird. But I will have my chance—you will share my bed before all is ended." He reached out to stroke her hair, but his hand was stilled by the look in her eyes.

If you would have me share your bed, you had better bring many of your minions to subdue me, for I shall die fighting you. If it truly is my destiny to remain here, then I shall remain a wild bird trapped in a cage. I shall neither sing for you nor bring you joy. Do you take my meaning?

To her surprise, Al-Muniqui smiled. "You think not speaking to me will cool my desires? You are all the same—at first proud and defiant, but your spirits are always broken in the end. I will allow you some time to adjust to your new home, but if you continue to defy me I shall have no choice but to allow fear and pain to sway your thinking. You'll speak to me then, when I will allow it. Count on that." He reached out to touch her golden hair. "Until our next meeting."

Nelwyn was left alone in her chamber, bound hand and foot to a post set in the center. She could recline on a soft bed, and there was food and water as well as some wine, but she would neither eat nor rest. She sat with her face buried in her arms, weeping quietly, her wounded spirit calling to her beloved. She had never desired to see his face so much as she did in those moments.

Bint Raed crept quietly in, for she had been assigned the task of watching over Nelwyn after sundown, having let it be known that she knew much of the Avinashi, including some of their tongue. She heard Nelwyn weeping and approached her cautiously, placing a comforting hand on her shoulder. "Hush, fair one," she said in the Elven-tongue. It will be all right. You will not long remain here, and neither will I. We will both be free, one way or another."

Nelwyn lifted her head and looked at Bint Raed with renewed hope. *She speaks Elvish, and she wants to escape captivity even as I do.* "Can I trust you, woman of the southlands?" Bint Raed nodded, her eyes and face guileless. Nelwyn read no deceit in her. "Then you are not wrong, for my beloved is nearby, and he will work to free us. I have very capable friends, and they will not rest until this wrong is undone. I promise you—I will make certain we are both set free."

Bint Raed took one of Nelwyn's hands. "We shall make a pact that neither will leave without the other, agreed?" Nelwyn nodded. Everything would be all right. She and her new friend would soon be leaving this place, and, if her cousin Gaelen performed up to her usual standards, Al-Muniqui would be left to wonder what offense he had committed against heaven to bring such a disaster upon his house.

Galador and Gaelen had despaired at the sorrow they felt in Nelwyn as she called out to them, yet they took heart, for she was alive and aware. The Company laid their plans to free her, the first of which would involve getting inside the compound and determining the lay of things. Their previous successful foray into the Neela had encouraged them.

"We will need to go in as traders of something they need or want," said Hallagond. "Yet I fear we have nothing to trade. We cannot give any hint of Elvish ties, so none of our personal belongings will do. What thoughts do you have?" He looked hopefully at Gaelen and reluctantly at Rogond. He had learned that his brother was thoughtful, and rather surprisingly clever.

Rogond considered for a moment. "We do have El-morah's wonderful kaffa…we purchased a healthy supply of it," he said.

"What if we were to go as representatives of El-morah, offering to provide a sampling of his wares so that Al-Muniqui might purchase a quantity to be delivered later?" asked Gaelen.

"Indeed, that might be believed," said Hallagond. "El-morah has never been generous about selling his kaffa in any quantity, and he is very secretive about where he obtains it, though many have sought to learn. He must be your friend, to have sold you a supply. I'll warrant Al-Muniqui and his brothers would love to lay their hands on a large amount of it."

"Perhaps we would be more believable as competitors of El-morah rather than as representatives," said Rogond. He looked over at Gaelen. "There will be trouble before this is ended," he said. "We should not bring El-morah into it as an unwitting participant. He and his family must be safeguarded from the wrath of those we are about to deceive."

"If I have my way, I plan on doing a great deal more than deceive them," growled Galador.

"Which is precisely why you are not going with us," said Hallagond. "Al-Muniqui's folk are many, and they have done nothing to violate the customs of these lands. Though you may find it contemptible, slavery is widely accepted here. Only by deception will we prevail."

"It would seem that only some of us find it contemptible," muttered Rogond under his breath, remembering the disquieting sight of his brother holding up a bidding card in the auction-tent at Bezaltor.

Gaelen looked Hallagond in the eye. "Indeed," she said quietly. "I don't suppose you would care to explain why you were seen trading with the flesh-peddlers. You do not seem to me to be a man who would own slaves. There must be some other explanation…pray, enlighten us?"

Hallagond shook his head. "I have learned at least one thing in my short association with you, Elf, and that is that a question, once asked, will not be forgotten until you receive an answer. Therefore, to save myself the pain of your persistence, I will tell you. I loathe the very idea of keeping slaves, and I could never sanction the thought of taking a man's freedom for personal gain. Yet I find myself in a land where this is not only acceptable, but commonplace. I'm forced to remedy it as I can, in my small way. I sometimes purchase inexpensive, broken men that they may be made free, for once I own them this is my right. It has cost me quite a lot over the years and my friends think I'm mad for doing it, but there you are. If you really thought I was an evil slave-trader, I'm surprised you waited so long to ask me about it."

Gaelen smiled back at him, and then turned to Rogond, who was staring at Hallagond with an expression of relief. "You see? I knew it. He has not declined anywhere near so far as anyone would believe." No one could say "I told you so" like Gaelen.

"Indeed," replied Rogond, who still could not get his brother to look him in the eye. "Only an honorable man would follow such a course." He turned and walked away, knowing that his comment would not be acknowledged.

Hallagond and Gaelen rode forth at dawn. They took the kaffa with them, as well as any weapons that could be concealed, as traders did not usually approach with weapons in plain view. Hallagond had admonished Gaelen that no blood was to be spilled, and no foolish rescue attempted.

Gaelen had bristled at this. "You insult me, Tuathan," she said. "It is as if you think me an incapable and undisciplined fool. How came you to hold such a view?" Then, she muttered under her breath: "As if I didn't know."

"Galador warned me of your impulsive nature, and I have seen the fire in your eyes," he replied. "So don't try to deny it."

"I can't deny it, but I would remind you that it was Galador who nearly got us all killed at Bezaltor. At least allow me to prove him wrong ere you judge me. I am bent on rescuing my cousin, I am not a fool, and I know what I must do." She looked into his eyes, and he read something in her expression that he did not like.

For the first time since they had met, he opened up to her. "You have asked me not to judge you, yet you are judging me now. You say you know what you must do, and you will not turn from it. Then you look upon me in the knowledge that I turned from my heritage, and you disparage me. You do not know what has befallen, and you are in no position to judge me!"

He regretted the statement at once, for Gaelen's eyes widened in surprise. "You read far too much in my declaration. I held no such thoughts. Yet you went there because you know it's true…you did turn from your heritage. And you know you were wrong to have done so, otherwise you would not be so defensive about it. Am I wrong?"

He did not reply to her, riding beside her in silence for several minutes. Finally, he seemed to put it behind him, for denial was a thing in which he was very experienced. "You will need a name, something that I may call you. You are to act as my assistant and apprentice, and your name will be, ahhh…Brunor. That means golden-brown, after your hair. Will that do?"

"It will," she replied. "Brunor of the Ravani, apprentice kaffa-peddler. If only my esteemed ancestors could see me now!" This brought a smile to Hallagond's face, and they were both in reasonably good spirits as they approached the gates of Al-Muniqui's stronghold. When they explained their errand, they were admitted at once.

Hallagond was taken before Al-Muniqui's chief tradesman, the one who actually bought and sold goods. Fabric-merchants often made stops here on their way to the great markets of Castalan and Dûn Bennas. Al-Muniqui's brocades had been offered in the Sandstone marketplace during the festival. Gaelen had seen them there, and they were very dear to purchase, but they were undeniably beautiful. Hallagond had explained that it took many weeks to produce a single yard, and one mistake would ruin the perfect, ornate pattern. It took weavers of unsurpassed skill to create such fabric.

The tradesman was polite to Hallagond and to Brunor, his apprentice. Gaelen kept her eyes downcast, handing the parcel of kaffa to Hallagond before bowing and taking her leave. She had a task to perform.

She did not attract attention as she strolled about the compound. The dwellings were clean and well kept, painted white; some were ornately decorated and gilded as well. It was obvious that whoever lived here was prosperous.

Gaelen wondered how in the world she would find Nelwyn, though she could sense her cousin's presence. The settlement was larger than she had imagined; almost like a very small city. Al-Muniqui employed many men, and those men had families. He kept many slaves as well. One thing was certain—the large, elaborate dwelling in the heart of the settlement looked like a palace. *That must be where Al-Muniqui lives,* thought Gaelen. *That's where I'll find Nelwyn.*

As she approached it, she heard the click-click of busy looms working under the practiced hands of the weavers in a nearby dwelling, and she was drawn there for the moment. Gaelen had seen weavers at work, for many of the Elves of the Greatwood were skilled in this art, but few could rival the industry or the artistry displayed before her now.

She watched in fascination as the weavers wove gorgeous patterns of iridescent silk before her eyes. She was drawn especially to the woman who worked the largest loom, as the pattern she was creating was impossibly ornate. This, clearly, was the Master Weaver. Gaelen bowed before her, and as Bint Raed looked up from her work into the bright eyes of an inquisitive She-elf, her heart leapt. She knew the truth at once; this was another of the Immortal Ones. Though the face and hands were browned, the eyes were unmistakable.

To Gaelen's astonishment, the weaver whispered to her in the Elven-tongue. "You are akin to the golden-haired one, to Nelwyn of the Greatwood?"

Gaelen was unsure of what to think. This woman, whose grey eyes were unlike those of the Ravani, had called Nelwyn by name, and had spoken Elvish. In Gaelen's experience very few of the sutherlings knew any Elven-speech at all, yet this woman seemed practiced. Gaelen did not know how to reply.

Bint Raed saved her the trouble. "I know where your friend is. She is well, but is being held prisoner. My name is Bint Raed, I am also enslaved to Al-Muniqui, and I hold no love for him. Does that aid you in replying to my question?"

Gaelen nodded; it did, indeed. "Where is Nelwyn? Is she where I might slip in and speak with her?"

Bint Raed shook her head. "No, she is always under watch when I am not present. But I can carry a message to her, if you like."

Gaelen looked furtively around before replying. "Carry this message, then, and may the aid of Aontar go with you. Tell Nelwyn that her friends are here, and that we are working to free her. I will remain in the settlement for a day or two while my associate does his bargaining. I will need to know where Nelwyn is being held and what I must do to set her free. Then my companions and I will come for her as we may. Tell her that Gaelen will aid her, and that Galador is at her side. Can you remember all that?"

Bint Raed nodded before returning to her work. Gaelen was still in awe of her skill, as she gazed for one more moment at the gorgeous multicolored brocade. "That is amazing. I have never beheld the like of it," she said.

Bint Raed's voice was quietly resolute. "Someday soon I hope to never look upon it again." Gaelen took her meaning, knowing that it was not only Nelwyn who would be seeking freedom when the Company put their plan into motion.

Hallagond and Brunor enjoyed the hospitality of Al-Muniqui's people that night, housed in a small, clean dwelling with plenty of food and wine. They would be leaving at first light to rejoin their friends. Gaelen told Hallagond what she had learned, but it was not enough. She needed to find Nelwyn and see for herself what they would be facing when they came for her. She donned her black garb so she would not be easily seen in the dark streets, and stole quietly out into the night. The palace was guarded, but the guards were not expecting intruders, and their attention was somewhat lax at this late hour. Gaelen easily stole past them, for she made no sound at all and was concealed by her dark clothing. Once inside she had little to fear, for most of the household had gone to their beds.

Gaelen picked up a vessel from beside one of the doors; if anyone noticed her she could pretend to be a serving-woman. There was a foul smell coming from the vessel, which turned out to be a chamber-pot in need of emptying. Gaelen was disgusted, but the chamber-pot would prove to be an excellent addition to her disguise. She set her sharp hearing to work as she crept quietly through the shadowed halls.

She was rewarded as she passed one of the doors, for she could hear voices inside, and there were guards standing by. She heard

Bint Raed's voice, as well as the deep voice of a man speaking the common-tongue. His frustration was evident.

"I am pleased that you have found a companion in my Master Weaver," he said. "Soon you will relax and be happy here. It's not the worst place in the world to spend the rest of your life, is it? You cannot deny that you have been well treated. I will return tomorrow, for tonight I am weary, and I trust you will choose to speak to me then. Good night, my golden bird."

Gaelen lingered just a moment too long. A large, bearded man wearing very ornate purple robes bustled from the chamber, startling her. She gasped and took a quick step back, but alas, she stepped on her black robe and nearly fell, dropping the chamber-pot. Unfortunately, it was made of clay, and it shattered in spectacular fashion.

Gaelen cried out in alarm as the man exploded with rage. "You stupid, worthless creature…see what you have done! You will clean this immediately, so that no trace remains, or I will have you flogged. Hurry up, you stupid cow!" Gaelen knew to bow before him at once, and she prostrated herself so that he would not look her in the eye. He responded by kicking her viciously in the ribs, eliciting a surprised cry of pain.

It took her a moment to regain her breath as she remained prostrate before him. He gave her another half-hearted kick before returning to his own chambers, for he was too weary to concern himself with punishing her properly. This was well for both of them, for Al-Muniqui did not realize that Gaelen carried four blades concealed upon her person, and had he kicked her again she might not have been at all shy about using them, guards or no guards.

As the heavy, ornate doors to the chamber were pulled closed, Gaelen stole a glance inside. She beheld Bint Raed and Nelwyn, who seemed whole, if a bit pale and dispirited. Gaelen winced, holding her bruised ribs. *Galador will be very glad of this news, and should he elect to place a shaft in one of that cruel man's evil, black eyes, I won't stay his hand.* She had accomplished her purpose. There was a window in Nelwyn's chamber, and Gaelen thought she could now tell how to find it from the outside.

Her ribs throbbed as she made her way back into the night air. She needed to return to Hallagond, but first she made her way to stand beneath the window that she supposed was Nelwyn's. Ornate iron bars would block escape or entry, but she knew Nelwyn would be able to hear her. She sang a well-known Sylvan prayer-chant in a quiet, haunting voice, and Nelwyn heard, knowing at once that it was Gaelen. She sent Bint Raed to the window, for her tether would not allow her to reach it, instructing her to throw down a token—a hair-ornament that she wore always. Galador had given it to her, and he would take comfort in it. Gaelen took the golden ornament, bowing quickly in acknowledgment before disappearing into the dark.

"Why did you not *kill* him? You had every chance to free Nelwyn in that moment. Surely you could have dealt with him and two guards!" Galador stood before Gaelen, his hands clenched, his eyes alight with passion. "He kicked you hard enough to bruise your ribs... if you were a mortal woman he would have broken them. You did not deserve such treatment. He deserves to die for his cruelty! How could you stay your hand? Why now, of all times, did you display *restraint?*"

Rogond stepped between them. "You don't know what you're saying. Would you have her lose her composure and risk everything, including your beloved? If she had acted upon her indignation, it would have meant disaster for all. We would have lost any chance of ever rescuing Nelwyn, and while she might not have been killed, Gaelen surely would have."

Gaelen reached out to Rogond, gently guiding him from between herself and Galador. "Peace, Thaylon," she said. "Allow me to explain it to him." She turned to Galador. "I know you are distraught, and so I will overlook your lack of concern for my welfare. Know now that I have never before endured such flagrant abuse and humiliation, but I did not act because I would not risk Nelwyn's freedom, not even to restore my own pride." She smiled wryly at him. "I shall have to content myself with the fact that I did not clean up the mess I made. With luck, the stench will linger in the hallway for a while in remembrance."

Then her tone grew serious. "You had better master yourself if you want to be of any help at all. This compound is well protected, and these people know how to safeguard what they believe is theirs.

If you would aid Nelwyn, you must allow Hallagond to guide us. I stand ready to act on his bidding. You must do the same." She turned to Hallagond and smiled. "After all, we must admit, so far he has proven to be extremely useful!" As usual, her observation was correct, and could not be denied.

13
The Unlucky Moon

"We'll need a diversion," said Hallagond. "We know now where Nelwyn is being held, and it will take all our wits plus a good measure of luck to free her. We must occupy Al-Muniqui and his people with other things."

"Yet there are only four of us. What diversion could we provide that will distract so many?" asked Galador. Having been thoroughly chastened by Gaelen, he was now quite willing to do whatever Hallagond suggested, within reason.

"I may have a workable plan," said Hallagond, "but it will be fairly tricky and will involve further information-gathering by our stealthy Wood-elf. We must play on their deepest fears. Nothing is as diverting as the fear of losing your life and the lives of your family, and it has not been that long since the Plague devastated these lands. I suggest we turn that to our advantage."

"How do you propose we do that?" said Rogond. "It seems an invitation to ill fortune, using such a terrible thing to one's advantage."

Hallagond shrugged. "Then propose an alternative if you will. I'll do whatever works."

He went on to explain the plan, and even Rogond had to admit that he had no better suggestions.

"You are certain that none will die because of this?" he said.

"I cannot be certain who will die, Rogond, including ourselves," Hallagond replied. "But what I'm proposing will not directly result in anyone's death. I must ride to the Chupa to obtain what I require; I doubt they will have it in the Neela. I will need to ride swiftly… perhaps I could avail myself of one of the other horses?"

"You can ride Réalta," said Galador, eliciting a rather surprised look from Rogond. Galador did not often allow another to ride his proud animal.

Hallagond looked over at Gaelen. "I suppose you will want to go along and make certain that I don't run off and abandon you," he said.

To his surprise, she shook her head. "No, I trust you. I know you will honor your life-debt, for you are still a man of honor. Besides, I also know that you realize the extent of my tenacity, and that I will hound you unto death if you disappoint me." She smiled as she said this, but he took her meaning.

"Then I shall leave at once, for the moon is waxing and I can ride swiftly in darkness," he said. "It will take several days, even mounted on Réalta. By the time I return, it will be a week or more."

"You underestimate Réalta," said Galador. "You will never have ridden so swift an animal."

"Indeed," said Rogond. "We shall be expecting your return in five days, not seven."

"Provided my errand is successful," said Hallagond. "I may not find what I need in the Chupa. If not, we will need to make another plan. I may bring others to aid us, but that will take time."

"What others? There are none in the Chupa who are our friends, except El-morah and his family," said Gaelen.

"I know people there, though I would not necessarily call them friends," replied Hallagond. "But, speaking of El-morah, I will need to purchase a rather large quantity of kaffa—I need it for our deception. Do you have gold that I may give for it?"

"One of our companions, a dwarf, remains in the Chupa. He may have a little," said Rogond. "Just explain our situation to El-morah. He will want to aid us in freeing Nelwyn, but make certain you explain your plan so that he will understand fully his involvement in it. Do you take my meaning?"

Hallagond did. After a brief parley with Galador, he took the provisions needed for the journey, mounted Réalta, and galloped off toward the Chupa oasis.

Réalta more than lived up to Hallagond's expectations. He gained the Chupa after two days of hard riding. Though Hallagond would have appreciated a day or two of rest, he had no time to spend in pleasantries. He would go to El-morah, and then to another man of his acquaintance from whom he hoped to purchase something very unusual. This was essential to the plan, and it was lucky that this man was here, in the Chupa, for there were very few who could provide such an item.

His name was Mikla the Poisoner, and he was known by the darker element of the Ravi as the man who could provide "any poison for a price." His wares were sought after not only by those wishing to do harm to their enemies, but also by Shiva, the healer. Many poisons have medicinal properties when given in lesser amount.

Hallagond walked into Mikla's dark dwelling, with its countless flasks, vials, and bubbling elixirs, but did not see anyone there. "Mikla, reveal yourself. You have a paying customer!"

A dry, papery laugh sounded from a dark corner, followed by a bout of wheezing. Mikla's health was none too good of late, no doubt from countless hours of exposure to the acrid vapors of his dreadful compounds. Rumor had it that he was already half-mad from them.

"Paying customer, you say? That is not the reputation of you or your fellows, Al-amand. Show me the payment so that I may judge for myself."

Hallagond held up his purse, shaking it to reveal a few coins inside. "This is only a down payment," he said. "When the deed is done, I will return and pay you more than you could hope for."

"Of course you will," said Mikla in a silky, sarcastic voice. "What is your need?"

Hallagond spent the next several minutes explaining, and, to his relief, Mikla had the very elixir he desired. Yet the cost would be high for such a quantity. Hallagond used all his skill at persuasion to convince Mikla to trust him. When he had finished, the old man laughed again.

"Al-amand, your skills at beguiling hapless merchants have improved. Alas, I am immune to your charms."

"I thought as much, but though I have no more gold to give, I do have a thing that is perhaps more valuable to one such as yourself." Hallagond brought forth a small packet of dark brown hair, Galador's hair, and handed it to Mikla.

"Strands of hair? And why should this interest me?"

"Because it is of the Avinashi, they who never venture into these lands and would never give their hair to one such as you. I believe Elven-hair is of use in the making of some of your talismans, is it not?"

In truth, Elven hair has no medicinal properties, but the important thing was that Mikla believed it did. His eyes grew round and bright as he removed a single strand from the packet and held it over a candle-flame to test it. The hair curled slightly, but did not singe. Mikla wrapped one end around his finger and pulled with all his might, but the hair would not yield.

Mikla smiled—men would pay dearly for a talisman containing a single strand of Elf-hair, in the hope that wearing it around the neck would confer some of the disease-resistance that had so blessed its previous owner. There was enough hair in the packet to provide many talismans. Since the Plague, the demand was understandably high.

"I will admit that this has some value," he said. "Yet it does not cover the cost completely. You will need to return and pay what you owe, but as I am truly generous I have decided to trust you." Mikla's eyes never left the packet of long, silken hair—it was worth a fortune in the southern markets.

Fair enough," said Hallagond. "I will return and compensate you properly when our plan has been carried out. As always, no word of our transaction is spoken to anyone. Agreed?"

Mikla nodded and bowed, sending himself into another bout of wheezing, as Hallagond left the shop with his precious, dark elixir.

After he left Mikla's establishment, Hallagond made his way back toward the House of El-morah, taking a less-traveled path. There were those in the Chupa that he would avoid if possible, including Haifa, to whom he owed an extensive amount of money. He had already gone to the dwelling of Estle, the half-sister of his friend Azori, to inquire as to whether Azori and his band had come to the Chupa as expected, but Estle was not at home, and Hallagond had no time to spend in searching for her. He made his way toward El-morah's house, trusting that Réalta had been fed, watered, and rested, for it was his intention to leave at sunset. As he approached, he heard a deep, growling voice from behind him.

"Tuathan! It's about time you returned. Bad enough that you left me here, but now you return and do not even seek the company of your friends?"

Hallagond turned to regard a very short, stocky figure walking briskly toward him. *Ah. This must be the dwarf my brother referred to.* "Hail, Fima," he said. "I am pleased to meet you, but you've been addressing the wrong Tuathan. I'm Rogond's brother; they know me here as Al-amand."

Fima stopped in his tracks, his long white beard waving gently in the dry breeze. He looked up at Hallagond and blinked. "Are you, indeed?" he said. "Well, now I see that you are not Rogond. You are older, and the desert has left its mark on you. Yet the resemblance is undeniable!" The dwarf bowed low. "Fima, son of Khima, and I am extremely pleased to meet *you*," he said. Then he drew himself up and fixed Hallagond with a wry expression. "Do you have any notion of how long and how far we have come in search of you?"

Hallagond muttered under his breath. "Apparently just far enough, regrettably."

"Eh? What's that?" Fima asked.

"Nothing," replied Hallagond. "I'm sure you want to know what's happening with your friends. Walk with me and I will enlighten you, but then I fear I must be away. My brother and his friends are awaiting my return."

When Hallagond had explained the nature of his errand to Fima, and told what had befallen, the dwarf was understandably unhappy. "All is as we feared, then. I must return with you and aid you! Any who put their hands upon Nelwyn shall feel my axe upon their necks."

Hallagond quite believed him. The old dwarf was bristling and red-faced; he had regained at least some of his strength and would have made a worthy ally.

"I'm sorry, Fima, but I must ride hard. They are expecting my return in two days. You would burden the animal, and if you are like most dwarves of my acquaintance, riding swiftly is not among your talents. Remain here, and rest assured that your friends will come for you when this matter is resolved." He clapped Fima on the shoulder as he spoke, for the dwarf was a stout friend and Hallagond could not help but like him.

El-morah was suspicious of Hallagond at first, as he knew him by reputation. Such a quantity of precious kaffa was worth a small fortune; how did El-morah know that Hallagond wasn't simply taking advantage for his own profit? Yet Fima had vouched for him, and he had been granted permission to ride Réalta by Galador, which indicated a high degree of trust. Besides, the plan seemed well-conceived enough to actually work.

"Rogond and I will find some way of compensating you, El-morah," said Fima earnestly. "Do not fear."

Réalta would bear an even greater burden on the return journey, for in addition to Hallagond he carried more than fifty pounds of El-morah's finest kaffa. This was nearly half his reserve—the rest would need to last until he made contact with his secret supplier.

As Hallagond rode away, El-morah and Fima went back inside to find Mohani busily brewing a fresh batch. "We still have plenty of less costly blend," she said to her husband. "We will save what remains of the better stuff for those who appreciate it."

He smiled back at her. "A sensible plan," he said. "But you will need to bake ever-more-wonderful cakes to make up for it, or our profits may dwindle."

"Not to worry," said Fima, his blue eyes twinkling. "When my friends return, Gaelen will sing for your patrons. If she does, you'll have more than this dwelling can hold, and folk will talk about it for years to come." He sighed and looked back toward the path Hallagond had taken. "I pray that Nelwyn returns with them."

"I will drink to that," said El-morah, pouring himself a hot cup of the better kaffa as well as one for Fima. Others could drink the lesser blend. They raised their cups together, for they were folk of worldly ways and discriminating taste.

The Company was first alerted to the return of Hallagond by Eros, who called to Réalta long before he came within hearing or sight. "His senses are keen," said Gaelen, patting Eros' strong neck in admiration. Finan seemed to take exception to this, pinning his ears at Eros and snorting.

Rogond was amused. "Your battle-mount has a jealous nature, Gaelen. You had better not show affection to Eros in his presence, for it would seem that he desires all of your attention."

Gaelen turned to her proud animal, shaking her head. "Finan, Eros is my friend. I fear you must bear it if I pat him, for I will show affection to my friends if I please." Finan seemed not to hear her, but continued to threaten Eros, switching his tail back and forth, his nose slightly wrinkled. Eros ignored him.

Réalta came into view a few minutes later; he was weary and had been trotting for many miles, trying to conserve his strength. This was a trick he had learned from Eros, who, though he could not match Réalta in speed or grace, would spend less energy and nearly always outlasted him.

Hallagond raised his right arm, indicating that his errand had been successful. He vaulted from Réalta's weary back and handed the reins to Galador. Then he rested by the fire as Gaelen brought him food and drink.

"I met your friend, the dwarf," he said. "Looks like he'll soon be strong enough to travel with you again."

"Well, that's the best news I've heard in a while," said Rogond, examining the large package of kaffa. "El-morah has made quite a sacrifice. We must make sure it is not in vain. Tomorrow we will begin our task to free Nelwyn, and then we must find a way to repay this generosity."

"Indeed," said Gaelen. "Hallagond, tell me again how we are to proceed. We must understand all elements of the plan…I do not wish to make any mistakes tomorrow."

Hallagond nodded and called Galador over to listen with them. The moon was rising in the eastern sky; it would be full in two or three days. Gaelen hoped that it would prove to be a most unlucky moon for Al-Muniqui. Her bruised ribs reminded her to make certain of it.

Hallagond hoped that this would be the last full moon beneath which he would endure his brother's company, while Rogond hoped it would be the first of many. Galador prayed that his beloved would be at his side ere it began to wane. The Company sat in silence, the golden orb reflected in their eyes, and kept their own thoughts until morning.

Al-amand, the kaffa-peddler, and Brunor, his young apprentice, were admitted into the settlement as the sands warmed under the sun of early afternoon. They carried a cargo of great worth—a large amount of the finest kaffa, to be paid for by Al-Muniqui's trade-master. It then would fall to Brunor to deliver the packages to the buyers, which numbered three. The largest quantity went to Al-

Muniqui's household, and the other, smaller lots had been purchased by his two full-witted brothers. The trade-master's eyes widened when he saw the size of the parcels. "Al-Muniqui's captains will be quite happy…their master likes to keep them alert," he said.

Hallagond smiled. "Very wise of him. I'd make sure they have a good supply, and there will be no one falling asleep at his post, that's certain." The trade-master chuckled back at him, for they were two men-of-the-world. Hallagond slipped two gold pieces into the other man's hand, just to make certain of his welcome.

Gaelen took the kaffa to the brothers first. It was fortunate that "Brunor" did not need to speak, as each package was accompanied by a note of explanation from the tradesman. She merely handed the parcels to the weary, careworn women who came forth to collect them, and retreated without a word.

When she left the courtyard of the eldest of Al-Muniqui's brothers, she beheld a man tied to a stake, forced to stand in the full sun, apparently not long destined to remain in the world. He was an old man, thin and in very poor condition; his body was bruised and battered, and his eyes held no life. Gaelen had been strictly instructed by Hallagond not to take any notice or make any comment upon anything she saw happening around her, but she truly didn't understand such cruelty being practiced by one man upon another. She stopped in her tracks, turning to the man-servant who led her from the courtyard, addressing him in the common-tongue.

"Who is that man, and what was his crime?"

The servant was shocked that a stranger would ask so bold a question, but he could not fail to answer; after all, Gaelen was masquerading as a free tradesman, and was therefore his superior. He dropped his eyes and answered in a halting voice, for his use of the common-tongue was limited. "He is a servant. He disobeyed. The wrath of Al-qamadan is swift and just, and this punishment is deserved. Take no notice."

The bound man moaned once more in his misery, tearing at Gaelen's heart. She approached him as the man-servant followed behind, admonishing her.

"It is the will of Al-qamadan! You must not interfere!"

But Gaelen saw only the hopelessness in the tethered man's eyes, the longing for comfort and release from pain. She drew forth her water-skin as she drew nigh him, taking his chin in her hand that she might offer him a mouthful. It was better than nothing.

The servant grabbed her arm. "It is *forbidden!* You must not interfere with this man's fate!"

As she gazed into the hopeless eyes of the unfortunate old man, Gaelen saw that she need not disquiet the servant further. She sighed with frustration, and a deep sadness took hold of her. No one deserved to be treated in this manner, certainly not by those of their own race, those who held power over them.

The servant shrank back from the fire in her eyes as she began raving at him in Elvish. "Do you people not know that this is wrong? Why do you not rise up and strike at your tormentors? Are you so weak and dispirited that you will let them torture you and take your lives without a struggle? I cannot understand." She appeared to be on the verge of drawing a blade until she came to herself, shaking her head.

The concept of helplessness was one she did not grasp well, for she had rarely known what it means to be truly powerless. "I'm sorry. This is not your doing. Please…say no word of this. I will take my leave of you now."

She left the courtyard, bowing before the surprised and relieved man-servant, heading toward her final destination, which was the Al-Muniqui's palace. She would have her gentle cousin spend no more time in such a place.

The sun went down that evening, and Gaelen knew she had not much time before moonrise. She needed to accomplish her purpose before then, as she would be difficult to see in the twilight shadows. She had to speak with Nelwyn, and she had formed a rather risky plan that would allow her to do so.

A ledge ran above Nelwyn's window; it was only about a foot wide, but it would easily support Gaelen's weight. She would gain the ledge using her bow, a specially barbed arrow, and some of her own hand-made rope, then climb down to the window so she could tell Nelwyn of the plan. Luckily, the window was on the western side of the palace. Fortunately, the moonlight would not reach it until many hours had passed, for it would reveal Gaelen to any who passed by. This would be difficult enough.

She gained the ledge by anchoring her arrow in the wall above it and using a slender cord tied to the shaft. After climbing up, she coiled the precious cord about her waist and made her way along the ledge a few feet at a time, freezing in place when anyone passed by. The carved walls of the palace aided her, as she could blend in more easily among the intricately rendered figures of birds, beasts, and Al-Muniqui's ancestors. She made no sound. This was not difficult for one who had spent so many centuries surprising the unwary—she was unrivaled among her people in this regard.

She listened carefully at the window, hearing only the voices of Nelwyn and the weaver-woman, Bint Raed. They were speaking in the Elven-tongue, and Gaelen thought it likely that they were alone. There was a small shelf into which the window-bars were set, and Gaelen drew a deep breath before taking on the tricky task of leaping down onto it, grabbing the bars to keep from falling to the courtyard below. Her face was bathed in the warm light of the chamber as she looked inside.

Nelwyn, hands still tethered, took food and drink with Bint Raed. Their hopes had risen considerably, and they appeared to be in good spirits. Nelwyn knew that her friends would not fail her. Al-Muniqui had come to her each night, trying to sway her to his way of thinking, but she still refused to speak to him. His patience was wearing thin.

Soon now, Bint Raed had warned, he would try to take her by force. "I hope your friends are swift in their rescue, for I know Al-Muniqui, and he will not long stand for your treatment of him." Then she gave a tiny yelp of surprise as a pebble struck the back of her head, tossed in by Gaelen to attract her attention. "Who's there?" she said, approaching the window with caution.

"It's Gaelen Taldin, Nelwyn's cousin, or Brunor-the-apprentice-kaffa-peddler, whichever you would prefer. I need to have words with Nelwyn. Listen carefully, both of you."

The sound of her cousin's voice thrilled Nelwyn almost beyond description. "Are you well? What of Galador, and Rogond, and Fima? When will you come to liberate me? What must I do?"

"For now, be silent and listen" said Gaelen. "Everyone is fine. You will need to endure two more days of captivity. You must not drink any dark, hot liquid that is served to you. Do you understand?"

"Why not?" asked Bint Raed, who was very fond of kaffa, especially with breakfast. As Master Weaver, it was one of her privileges.

"In two days, when the moon has come into full phase, the people of the settlement will appear to sicken. They will suffer from a slow poison that has been placed in the kaffa, but they won't know it. They will fear a return of the Plague, and the household will be locked down. The guards and servants will be unable to stop us, and we will rescue you then," said Gaelen. "Only Al-Muniqui's supply has been poisoned, but it will be enough that the people will most likely panic. I would imagine he will serve kaffa to many of his guests; the sickness will appear widespread before all is ended."

Bint Raed was concerned, as many of the people were blameless, and she would have no harm come to them. "Will these people that sicken…will they die?"

"Not of this poison," said Gaelen. "But after what I've seen, I wouldn't put it past them to kill each other to protect themselves. The poison will sicken them for a few days, but it will not in itself cause death. You must both be ready, for when the time comes we will act swiftly. You'll know when we come for you."

"Al-Muniqui loves his kaffa. I would imagine the guards won't be allowed to share it," said Bint Raed with a worried glance at the door.

"Probably not, but their officers will," said Gaelen. "We have it on good authority."

"Who thought of this plan? It seems odd, but…inspired," said Bint Raed. "The people will be thrown into chaos, and they will take little notice of you. This sounds like a plan hatched in the mind of a man, not an Elf."

"Indeed," said Gaelen, looking meaningfully at Nelwyn. "We have found Rogond's brother. The plan is of his design—he is proving quite useful. I can say no more at present." Her gaze flickered toward the door...she had heard something.

"Someone is coming. I must leave you now. Take courage; only two more days, and you will be free." With that, she disappeared, leaping down from the window-ledge after first making sure she would not be observed. She landed lightly on her feet, though her teeth rattled a little on impact. She gathered herself and disappeared, leaving no trace behind, just as Al-Muniqui entered Nelwyn's chamber.

This time he brought gifts to try to convince her to speak to him. Once again he would leave frustrated, threatening, as he had every night, that his patience and generosity were reaching their limit. Nelwyn and Bint Raed hoped that they would both be rescued before he decided to take Nelwyn whether she spoke to him or not.

As Gaelen made her way back through the darkened settlement, she had to admire Hallagond's ingenuity. Because of the delayed nature of the poison, no one would make the connection between the kaffa and the sickness. The elixir had no taste or odor, and it did not sicken for two days, so the man employed by Al-Muniqui to taste all his food and drink would feel no immediate effects. The signs were very much like those of the Plague; a dead feeling in the hands and feet, followed by a dark purple rash. Victims would weaken and be unable to eat or drink anything, and they would take to their beds. Unable to speak clearly, their tongues would swell and their fevered words would make no sense. Though the effects would appear suddenly, and would be unpleasant, they would fade in a day or two. It was essential to strike while the distress of the people was greatest.

When the first victims of the poison began to sicken, the rumors spread quickly. Al-Muniqui's household was particularly hard hit, and no one was allowed in or out. The few healers who were not ill had mysteriously packed their belongings and left by dark of night. Wayfarers and traders would be turned away, at least until the extent and nature of the sickness became known. People were terrified, and the wails of the frightened as well as the ill filled the streets. Oddly, very few of the servants and slaves had been taken; it was mostly the privileged who felt the cold hand upon their necks.

As Hallagond had instructed, Galador and Rogond came to the gates at the full moon's rising, garbed as desert wayfarers, leading their horses. As they approached, the sentinels called out to them to come no closer.

"This is a place of sickness. Turn back, if you would live"

Rogond stepped forward, with Galador behind him. "We know of your plight," he said, "for we have followed this illness from a neighboring oasis. We are healers of renown. My friend here cannot suffer from any sickness, and he has offered his services. Are you sure you would decline them?"

Naturally, they were admitted at once.

"Our Chieftain and his family are in grave need of you," said the gatekeeper. "No doubt you will be handsomely rewarded."

One of the men took hold of Rogond's arm; his fear evident. "Is it the Plague?" he asked. Then he spoke in a hushed voice. "I have not been myself since early evening…I have some pain, and… and I think fever. I have a young wife and son. They would be lost without me."

Rogond looked back at him with gentle reassurance. There was nothing wrong with the man's body; only in his mind. "Don't be afraid," he replied in a soothing tone. "You do not have the look of death about you. Go home and rest, for you are weary. My friend can work miracles; even the Plague flees before his hands. You'll be all right." Rogond could see the relief in the young man's eyes, and he almost felt shame at bringing such fear among these people.

"May the blessings of heaven go before you," said the sentinels, bowing low and spreading their hands palms-upward before them. Rogond and Galador bowed solemnly and made their way toward the center of the Settlement, where their friends awaited them.

Galador and Rogond were admitted into the palace without hesitation, for the Chieftain and his family lay in the grip of a dire illness, and the newcomers were reputed to be healers of renown. They were promised great reward if they would save Al-Muniqui from death.

Hallagond and Gaelen, known only as kaffa-peddlers, would have to find another way inside.

A rear entrance led to the palace kitchens, and it was unguarded, as most of the guards who were still healthy were otherwise occupied. Gaelen paused to look around the large, well-appointed kitchen, liberated two ripe, sweet fruits from a basket, and tossed one to Hallagond.

"Remember, don't drink the kaffa," she said playfully, looking out into the courtyard, where the first rays of the full moon were beginning to appear.

Now it was time to find Nelwyn and Bint Raed. They carried their weapons in plain view, and Gaelen had made no attempt to disguise herself, shedding the raiment of "Brunor" the moment she gained entry into the palace. Silent and purposeful, she strode down the corridor with her blades at her back, her bow in her hand and a fierce light in her eyes. She met only a few folk, and they did not oppose her. They shrank back from her strangeness, thinking she must have been a delusion brought by fever. Hallagond had only to follow after her.

She took one wrong turn, but quickly corrected her course, moving without further error to the chamber of Nelwyn. Unfortunately, there were two undeniably healthy guards at the door. Gaelen knew that she could take them quickly using her bow, but she held nothing against these men, who had done nothing to harm Nelwyn. They were simply doing their lord's bidding. She waved Hallagond back and crept toward them unseen.

"I will give you one chance," she said, startling both of them as they turned to find her standing not twenty feet away. "Lay down your weapons and depart this place. First unlock the door, for we will free our companion. Your master is ill and dying—he will have no further need of her. I can draw this weapon and release it in the blink of an eye. Obey me, or breathe your last. Your master is in no condition to punish you, so why not live to fight another day? Go down to the kitchens and treat yourselves to a meal. Sleep well this night. Just unlock the door and walk away."

The two guards looked at one another, the fear in their eyes evident. Yet there was something else there as well, though Gaelen was uncertain of its nature. There was fear, but not enough of it. These men knew something that she did not.

"Obey me, *now!*" she cried, sending one shaft flying, then drawing another before the guards could react. The shaft grazed one just to the outside of his wide-open right eye, and came to rest quivering in the door behind his head. Both guards froze as though made of stone.

"This time *I will* strike your eye if you do not obey within the count of five," said Gaelen. "I'm growing impatient. If you will not do as I ask, I will shoot you both and unlock the chamber myself. One….two….three…."

She was interrupted by a cry of alarm from Hallagond, and by the ring of clashing blades.

Galador stood over the prone body of Al-Muniqui, his strong hands clenched, his expression veiled. The wretched man had taken to his bed, and was now lying in a miserable knot among the fine brocaded sheets, his dark purple robes soaked with sweat. He mumbled words of supplication, though they were difficult to understand, as his senses were addled and his tongue was thick in his mouth.

Galador did not feel pity for this cruel man who had taken Nelwyn. Even though Gaelen had reported that Nelwyn was in good health and seemed to be in fair spirits, both Gaelen and Galador had felt the despair she had sent out to them many days ago. Galador looked down upon the helpless man, this man he hated, knowing that he would now have to bring him comfort.

Al-Muniqui gazed up into Galador's bright eyes, and they did not comfort him. He had looked into Nelwyn's eyes long enough to recognize that this tall healer was another of her race, and he was afraid. "Keep him away from me," he called to his attendants. "He is another of the Immortal Ones. I cannot bear to look upon him…I wish now that I had never set eyes upon any of them. *Keep him away!*"

The attendants looked over at Galador, who did not reply. Rogond stepped in to reassure them. "Your master is fevered, and does not know what he is saying. It is true that my companion is Avinashi, which is why he cannot get the sickness. If it were not so, we would not be here to aid you. Step back and allow him to accomplish his purpose. If all goes well, your master will soon be himself again."

Galador mixed up a concoction that Hallagond had given him; it was a simple mixture, but it would dull the effects of the poison and allow for a speedy recovery. "Give him some of this. It will bring him around by late tomorrow," said Galador.

The attendants worked to comply, but Al-Muniqui would not swallow the remedy. "I tell you, he is bent on vengeance! He is trying to poison me! The light of his eyes burns my soul...I will not drink of his poison! Get it away!"

They held down the raving man as Galador poured the elixir down his throat. The wretch gagged and spat and struggled, but eventually they were successful. Galador stood erect again, wiping spittle from his face.

"He will sleep now. Take me to the next unfortunate in need of my ability," he said. *At least this fool regrets his association with Nelwyn...I'll have to take what satisfaction I can from that simple fact.*

A cry of alarm from Hallagond had distracted Gaelen, and her attention wavered for just a moment. The guards took advantage, springing toward her with fierce yells, swords flashing, intending to cut her down. She let her first arrow fly; it killed the one nearest dead as stone, straight through the right eye. He blocked her as he fell, and the other was upon her before she could draw another shaft. He was large and formidable, and she just managed to duck under his blade, hearing the clash of steel in the corridor behind her.

Apparently it had been time for the guard to change, and the replacements had come upon Hallagond unaware. He was now fending off two very adept swordsmen, slashing and ducking, calling upon his considerable skill. *First Bezaltor, and now this,* he thought. It had been long since he had faced such a challenge, as he normally did not place himself in such a position.

Gaelen fared better, for her adversary was in need of sleep; the guards who had not become ill were weary and overtaxed. She had relatively little difficulty with him despite his size, for she was agile and quick, and he could not touch her. She finished him with a quick thrust beneath the left arm as he raised his blade. He gasped in surprise, falling next to his companion.

She then ran to the aid of Hallagond, who had suffered a slash to the left forearm that was bleeding rather badly. If things had gone on as they were for much longer, Rogond would have lost his brother for good. Yet the guards had not reckoned on Gaelen, who shot one in the throat, allowing Hallagond to take the other with a thrust to the heart. "Your life debt is becoming ever more compelling," she said, retrieving her arrow as he stood before her, trying to catch his breath. "Come now, and help me unlock the door! We may have been heard."

"You will need the large, squarish key…quickly, quickly!" said Bint Raed from behind the door. She had heard the commotion, and knew that her freedom was at hand.

Hallagond found the keys on the belt of the guard Gaelen had shot in the eye, even as she struggled to retrieve her arrow. "There's no time for that," said Hallagond, fumbling with the keys until he found one that was large and squarish.

"They who waste arrows will want them," was the calm reply. "Just get that door open, will you?" Then she called to Bint Raed and Nelwyn: "Make ready! We must fly from this place, and I will need to raise the alarm. That is the signal for our other friends."

Hallagond succeeded in opening the heavy door, whereupon Gaelen ran to her cousin and embraced her. Nelwyn wept, for she had once thought that all was lost and they would never see each other again.

Bint Raed shook her head. "There is one small difficulty, and that is with Nelwyn's tether. Only Al-Muniqui holds that key."

"Not a problem," said Hallagond. "Step back, Gaelen…I would rather not injure you." He swung his bright blade, cleaving the tether with three strokes that notched the steel post it was fastened to. Nelwyn was free, though her wrists were still bound with iron. "If you will give me a few minutes, I can get those off…I think," said Hallagond.

"We don't have many minutes to spend here," said Bint Raed, looking anxiously up and down the corridor. "If anyone heard you…"

"It's all right," said Nelwyn. "I can run just fine."

"You women-folk go on, then," said Hallagond. "I will raise the alarm to attract their attention, and then let them chase me for a bit before I elude them. You go on, Gaelen, and make certain all are kept safe." He flashed a broad, rather wicked grin. "Don't worry… I'm fairly good at this sort of thing. I have had some practice while traveling among thieves and bandits."

"Yes, no doubt we women-folk should leave everything to you," said Gaelen. "That's why I have needed to save your life on two occasions now." She looked with concern at the wound on his arm. "Can you cope with that?"

"What…this? It's not bad—barely a scratch."

"Well, then keep safe, O Practiced Bandit. We shall meet at the appointed place."

Hallagond bent over one of the dead guards, the one Gaelen had shot in the throat, and drew forth a small horn that would no doubt raise quite a noise in the echoing confines of the palace. Then he ran back the way he had come; he wanted to put some distance between himself and Nelwyn's chamber before he raised the alarm. Once he was satisfied with his location, he lifted the horn and blew one long, loud blast upon it, waited a few seconds, and then blew another series of shorter notes. Of course, he had no idea whether these sounds would have any special meaning, but he knew two things for certain. The horn was meant to summon aid in case of trouble, and everyone in the palace was certain to hear it. He began to make his way back down toward the kitchens, and freedom.

Galador was administering aid to Al-Muniqui's head wife when the alarm sounded. The guards left her chamber, all save one, to attend to whatever the trouble was. They couldn't imagine what it could be—after all, no right-minded man would venture here and risk illness. Perhaps one of the guards was fevered, and had imagined enemies attacking the palace. That would explain it.

Galador and Rogond straightened, rising to their feet, for it was now time to rejoin their friends. Galador took heart, for the alarm meant that Hallagond and Gaelen had succeeded in freeing Nelwyn. Either that or someone truly *had* raised the alarm.

"I shall need to return to my pack-animal and replenish my supply of ingredients for my remedy," Galador told the guard in the chamber. "I was unaware that so many were in need. I will return shortly."

"Your assistant may leave and fetch what is needed," replied the guard, a tall, burly fellow who was obviously taking no nonsense. "You are to remain here with the sick until they are well."

"Of course," said Galador, inclining his head courteously as Rogond picked up a copper brazier and struck the guard from behind, knocking him senseless. As they turned to leave the chamber, Rogond comforted Al-Muniqui's head wife, whose eyes were now round with terror. "You will be fine in a few days. You have nothing to fear from us, my lady. Rest well, and don't be afraid." She looked at him with an expression that seemed torn between relief and confusion, as he followed Galador through the doorway.

They had arranged to meet at the stables; the horses had already been laden in preparation for leaving the settlement in a hurry. Gaelen, Nelwyn, and Bint Raed arrived first, despite the fact that Bint Raed had insisted on taking a short side journey to the weaving-shed. There were items that she could not leave behind. She returned with a rather large, soft bundle.

Gaelen shook her head. "You can't carry all that, for the horses will need to be swift."

Bint Raed would not be moved. "You would curse me forever if I left this behind. It's not heavy." She immediately set about the task of adding it to Faladinn's burden. He did not appear to mind.

It would have been difficult to accomplish a speedy escape with two extra riders; the Company only had five horses, and only Eros, Réalta, Malvorn and Finan could be ridden. But Gaelen had already located Gryffa, Nelwyn's mount, among Al-Muniqui's horses. Nelwyn was fond of Gryffa, and they all knew him to be a worthy mount; he was courageous and surefooted, if somewhat temperamental. Gaelen had stolen in earlier, untied him, and allowed him to make his own decisions regarding his captivity. He stood waiting beside Réalta, nickering at Nelwyn as she approached.

Nelwyn reached over and playfully ruffled Gaelen's hair, an act that caused her cousin to cringe back and shake her head in disgust.

"You thought of everything, didn't you?"

"Not quite," said Gaelen, looking to her gear. "Otherwise, I would have stolen in to the Chieftain's chambers and found the key to those manacles. And while I was about it, I could have cut his throat while he slept, thus saving us all the trouble of avoiding him later. It would serve him right for kicking me!" If she lived forever, Gaelen would never forget the savagery of that gesture. She sensed that Al-Muniqui's comfortable world was about to fall down around him, and she would waste no time in feeling sorry for him when it did.

The three of them spent the next several minutes looking anxiously toward the palace. Sharp-eyed Nelwyn first beheld Rogond and Galador making their way toward her, emerging into the moonlight, but it was Gaelen who noticed the tiny shadow atop the wall. She cried in dismay and pointed toward a single archer, who even now appeared to be drawing on Galador!

Gaelen knew that their only hope was Nelwyn's bow. The shot was long, and the archer was well protected atop the wall; only his head, shoulders and arms were exposed. There was a strong breeze out of the north.

"Nelwyn, only you can make this shot. Remember when I practiced with Wellyn? I have brought your bow…quickly, we must work together!" Nelwyn's wrists were still bound, but there was nothing wrong with her eye. Gaelen bent Nelwyn's longbow as her cousin crouched behind her. Nelwyn made a very tiny correction and held her breath, signaling Gaelen to release. In what was clearly a miracle of good luck, the shaft struck the archer's right arm. He would not draw his bow again for a while.

In a few moments they were reunited. Nelwyn embraced Galador as though she would never let go, throwing her manacled hands over his head. He was completely unmanned, his face buried in her golden hair, hugging her fiercely, as Rogond and Gaelen exchanged worried looks.

"Where is Hallagond?" asked Rogond. "I thought he was with you."

"He sent us ahead—it was he who raised the alarm," said Gaelen. "He insisted on doing it alone, without any aid from us women-folk, as he put it. Oh, and his life-debt has grown deeper thanks to my bow."

"You will release him, nevertheless," said Rogond. He was now very worried, looking back toward the palace. But Hallagond was nowhere in sight. They could hear shouts and wails; Gaelen hoped that Hallagond would be all right. She really did not relish trying to get him out of another difficulty.

They were on the verge of starting back to look for Hallagond when he suddenly appeared beside Malvorn as though out of nowhere. He startled Nelwyn; had she been able she would have drawn her bow on him. He shot a wry look at Gaelen and Rogond. "You really didn't think me foolish enough to cross that open courtyard, did you? The moon is bright. I would have been a clear target for any archer atop the wall."

"Well, thank the stars you didn't waste any more time in getting here," said Gaelen with a slightly crooked smile. "We must fly from this place before they try to stop us." She mounted Finan without another word. "I will not release you from your life-debt until we return to the Chupa, Hallagond. You must ride with us until then." She turned and started toward the gates.

Nelwyn and Galador were mounted as well. Bint Raed rode behind Nelwyn, who was her friend. The Company rode toward the gates of the settlement, calling out to the gate-keepers to open them. Rogond raised his arm to the man he had spoken with earlier. Knowing Rogond to be a friend, and knowing of no reason why he should not do so, the gatekeeper opened the heavy gates to the wide sands that lay under the bright golden light of Al-Muniqui's very unlucky moon.

14
Some Debts Repaid

The Company rode swiftly for several hours, placing as much distance between themselves and Al-Muniqui's stronghold as possible. It soon became clear that no immediate pursuit was forthcoming, which puzzled everyone except Hallagond, who simply shrugged it off. Gaelen and Rogond had expected to be fighting off Al-Muniqui's forces by now, and they asked Hallagond about it. "This is the third time I have expected pursuit and found none," said Gaelen.

"You forget—they think they are in the grip of a dreadful pestilence. They have far greater worries than coming after us. Most of them don't even know what's happened yet. I'm not concerned." He reined in his mount, and they all stopped for a breather. He then displayed his usefulness by working Nelwyn's manacles open with a stout pin of steel—apparently there were few locks that could foil him—and she felt truly free for the first time since Sajid's treachery.

Malvorn regained his breath as Eros rolled briefly in the sand, lurched to his feet, and shook himself before attempting to rub his head on Rogond. "I know, old fellow. You've been sweating under that bridle, and you've got an itch," said Rogond, reaching obligingly underneath the headstall with strong fingers. Eros was so delighted that he nearly knocked him over.

"If they are rested, we should move on before the sun rises," said Gaelen, swinging up on Finan. "That is, if Nelwyn and Galador can tear themselves away from one another long enough..." She hadn't fully realized how much joy could be had from saying those simple words, and she smiled, turning her mount back to the deep desert.

Nelwyn and Galador were lost in the relieved joy that comes with being reunited at last. Bint Raed likewise reveled in her liberty, for she had not felt the free air in many, many years. The only member of the Company that seemed disgruntled was Malvorn, who struggled to keep up with the swifter horses, burdened as he was by Hallagond, who was a large, heavy, and somewhat unbalanced rider at present.

His left arm had been badly slashed during his encounter in the palace, and had received only minimal attention. He pulled up, slowing Malvorn to a walk, as he felt shaky and light-headed.

Gaelen turned Finan about almost without touching him, for they were developing so close a connection that she had only to think of where she wished to go. She cantered back to find Malvorn standing head down, with Hallagond weaving slightly in the saddle.

"*Aiyah!*" she cried, even as Rogond rode up behind her. They both went immediately to Hallagond's aid, though he tried to wave them off. He was soon lying under the waning moonlight on the sand among some tall stones, his feet propped on Bint Raed's mysterious bundle.

"He hasn't eaten, and he is nearly exhausted from running and fighting," said Gaelen. "We need to bind his arm and get some food into him. Then he'll need rest."

"Look who knows so much about healing," muttered Hallagond as Rogond gave him a long drink of water and honey. The color was coming back in his face and his gaze was reasonably clear as Nelwyn examined his arm, yet he moaned in pain and would not keep still.

Gaelen extracted a small silver flask from a leather pouch on her belt, holding it to Hallagond's lips. "This is very precious, and there is only a very small amount of it. I have brought it all the way from the northern forest. Take one sip, Tuathan, and one only."

Hallagond took a very small quantity of liquid from Gaelen's flask. A tingling sensation filled his mouth and throat as he swallowed it. It was warm, yet it felt refreshingly cool, filling his body with a pleasant sensation. He felt sleep taking him gently into its dark embrace, and he was briefly dismayed. "What sorcery is this?" he mumbled, his eyelids drooping. "What have you given me, you pointed-eared harpy?"

Gaelen didn't much like being called a harpy, but she brushed it off. "Sleep, if you would be healed. Dream of that which brings you joy." She recapped the flask, after first wiping the rim rather pointedly in front of Hallagond, and replaced it in her pouch.

Hallagond's eyes rolled back in his head and he was soon dreaming very agreeable dreams.

"What is that elixir?" asked Rogond, but Gaelen did not answer. "It's water of moon-flower, isn't it?"

"Yes, it's moon-flower. I thought it could be useful." *I dare not tell him the real reason I brought this…if Gorgon should somehow prevail, or regain the use of his mirror, I will die rather than aid him.* The herb itself was poison, but the water in which it grew could be distilled into a powerful elixir, such that a few drops could subdue the strongest man. A few too many drops would kill. With the aid of the moon-flower, Gaelen would die painlessly, filled with blissful visions, and be of no use to her enemy.

Rogond knew she was holding something back, and he thought he could guess where her thoughts had turned. "Gaelen, you must promise not to use that elixir until we have tried everything else," he said softly. "Not unless there is no other way. Promise me."

"Unless there is no other way," she repeated. Then, after a long moment of quiet, she nodded. "I promise."

Nelwyn attended to Hallagond's arm as Bint Raed looked on, occasionally offering advice. Nelwyn would learn much from this woman of the southland, as would they all. She had offered to guide them for as long as she could. Nelwyn would ever be her friend, as would everyone else in the Company, for she was intelligent, knew much of the ways of the southlands, and would prove to be a stalwart companion. Bint Raed was no fighter, but she had skills that would prove valuable. She would never need to lift a weapon if the Company could help it.

Hallagond slept until mid-afternoon of the following day. He awoke to the sound of Elvish singing; he had heard it several times during the night. Gaelen was joyful at the successful completion of their quest, and she had poured forth her happiness in song. She sang especially for Hallagond, thinking to aid him in healing, for without him they would not have succeeded.

"Stop that noise," he muttered, turning his head away and pulling his cloak over his face. "Didn't I say that your tongue is not welcome in my ears? That includes singing as well." Though he grumbled, he had to admit that he felt wonderful. The waters of the moon-flower bring pleasant dreams and restful sleep…Hallagond felt as though he never wanted to truly be awake again.

Gaelen and Nelwyn laughed at his growling, and Gaelen continued to sing, but instead of the beautiful words she simply sang "Eh-ya-la…la-la-la…"

Nelwyn turned to Rogond. "Hallagond is well enough to travel, though he will not wish to. I would suggest that we begin to make our way when the sun sets." Rogond agreed. In the meantime they would eat, drink, and rest.

Gaelen, who needed no rest, offered to ride back a short way toward the settlement and scout for pursuers. She did not like being idle, and this delay in the open desert with nothing to occupy her was bothersome.

"There will be no pursuit," mumbled Hallagond, who was still only half-awake. "I would expect they are seeing to their own affairs today, and will have more than enough to occupy them."

This comment brought puzzlement again to the minds of Rogond and Gaelen. "Why say you so?" asked Rogond, but his brother either had fallen asleep again, or was pretending to have done so.

"Stay here then, Gaelen, and lie with me," said Rogond. "I know that you do not need rest, but I have seen precious little time with you, and I will rest better with you in my arms. Come, and let us share our love."

Nelwyn and Galador kept the watch together, as Bint Raed and Hallagond rested beneath the shade of stones.

Bint Raed slept peacefully; she would no longer need to dream of freedom, for it was hers at last. Hallagond enjoyed the last of the effects of the moon-flower as he strayed from one pleasant vision to the next; not even the strongest liquor could rival it. Not far away, Rogond Thaylon, his brother, slept contentedly with his beloved in his arms. Gaelen stretched and sighed, her fingers straying to his ever-lengthening beard, entwining and playing in the soft curls, for even though she was happy in Rogond's embrace, she could not keep still.

As Hallagond had predicted, they gained the Chupa with no interference from anyone. El-morah and his family were both surprised and pleased to see them alive and whole. They were delighted to meet Nelwyn, and they offered space beneath their own roof for the Company to rest and keep their valuables.

Fima was nearly overcome with joy at seeing his friends again, especially Nelwyn, for she was as radiant as ever. He covered these feelings by growling and blustering at her. "How could you have been so careless as to let Sajid take you? You had best take better care in the future, for I shall be angry if you so frighten me again."

Nelwyn embraced him, kissing the top of his soft leather head-covering. The dwarf closed his eyes and patted her arm gently, for he had feared never to see her again.

"My friends," said El-morah, lifting his cup. "I drink to your return and rejoice with you. Yet I would caution you, for though you have prevailed over your enemies, you have made several here in the Chupa that must now be avoided. Please, do nothing to place yourselves in further jeopardy."

Hallagond nodded. "I understand. Yet there are a few debts that must be paid while we are here, including those owed to you and Mikla. I'm not yet certain whether a certain She-elf has released me from a life-debt, for she saved my life again in the palace. If she has not, then I must learn how I may repay her so that I may be on my way. I have matters of my own to attend to."

Rogond did not react openly to this, but Gaelen perceived his dismay. Despite their recent cooperation, at least one of the brothers could scarcely wait to be separated from the other. She could not comprehend this—Hallagond had no other kin, he had not long been aware of his brother's existence, yet now he would turn from Rogond rather than embrace him. The idea of shunning one's close kin, when they had done nothing to warrant it, seemed strange and unnatural.

When Hallagond rose and went out into the night, Gaelen followed after him, for she would understand. She called out to his rapidly retreating back. "Tuathan! Stand and face me, for there are things I would say to you."

Hallagond turned toward her, an expression of annoyance on his face. "Do not call me that here. I do not wish to call attention to my heritage, and if you had learned anything at all from your time in the Ravani you would know it. Here, I am Al-amand. Remember it!"

Gaelen bowed before him. "You're right. I should have known better, for you would not be reminded of your heritage were you in the Ravani or not. Very well, Al-amand, Forsaken Man of Tuathas, hear what I have to say. You are hereby released from your debt, even though, as you pointed out, I did save your life again and could hold you further if I wished. But your brother has asked, nay, has *insisted* that you be released, so I suppose that means you are free to go and get on with your wasted life. I would ask only one thing of you ere you leave us, and I believe after such a long and arduous quest to find you that you owe me a response."

She looked hard at him, trying to read his expression. When he did not try to interrupt her, she continued: "Why do you so wish to hurt Rogond? Why can you not embrace him as your family, and give him the courtesy and respect that he is due? Why can you not love him as your brother, when it is so obvious that he wishes only to aid you? Your lives will be brief enough without bringing such sorrow. Imagine yourself in his place! His heart was filled with hope and joy upon learning that he has a brother, yet your fondest wish is to be rid of him forever, and he knows it. Why would you hurt him so?"

Hallagond sighed. "I have long known that your people are not at all shy about speaking whatever is in your minds, and you take forever to do it. Do you spend years perfecting the art of tedious, meddling sanctimony? In some respects you are more skilled in this than you are with your blades. I thank you for the release of my debt, but I would rather keep matters related to my brother to myself, if it's all the same to you."

Gaelen bristled at him; she had heard quite enough of his high-handed censure. "*Save* it, elder son of Diomar! It is only my love of Rogond that prevents me from demonstrating skill with my blades right now. It's obvious that you'd rather not share your motives, but answer me if you can find the words. I wonder whether you even understand what drives you. Answer me if you can, but do not answer falsely, for I shall know it. When I'm not practicing being tedious and meddlesome, I am perfecting my skill at detecting lies in the eyes of men!"

Hallagond was weary of her, yet she was right; he probably did owe her an explanation. He looked at her as she stood before him in the moonlight, knowing that she would not relent. Despite the fact that telling Gaelen of his dark history was the last thing Hallagond wanted to do, he sighed, extending a beckoning hand.

"Come with me, Gaelen Taldin, and you shall hear. Then I must ask that you truly release me, and not trouble me further with such bothersome questions. I must also ask that you share none of what I will say to you."

"I cannot promise that," said Gaelen, "for if revealing your words would bring understanding and comfort to Rogond, then I will reveal them."

Hallagond smiled darkly at this. "Then I need not fear, for nothing I will say to you will be of comfort to Rogond. On that you may rely!" He looked hard at her. "Do you still wish to learn?"

"I do."

"Very well, then." He led her to a dark, lonely alcove behind an empty dwelling. Once he was satisfied that they were alone, he began. "I…I got into a bit of trouble in the north," he said. "It was a bad time, and I did something very foolish. I cannot give any specifics."

"That's not good enough," said Gaelen. "You'll have to do better than that."

Hallagond sighed, and she could hear him grinding his teeth. "Once, back in the northern lands, I was a Captain of Rangers, in command of a company of twelve good men. I made…a bad decision."

"What sort of bad decision?"

Hallagond thought for a moment. "One that makes me unfit to go among brave and honest men." He looked back into the darkness, from which Rogond soon emerged, walking quietly up from behind. Apparently, he was looking for Gaelen.

Her eyes did not stray from Hallagond's, though she knew she had heard all she would from Hallagond for the moment. "This is not yet ended, Al-amand," she said quietly. "We shall speak of it again upon another time."

Not if I can help it, thought Hallagond, though he nodded in assent. He would not meet her gaze, and she knew that he had no intention of giving her any further enlightenment. Rogond had unwittingly interrupted her attempt to aid him, and that was regrettable, yet Hallagond had convinced her of one thing: if this situation could be fixed, she would not be the one to fix it. The healing of this deep hurt would need to come from within. She hoped that somehow the

Company could remain with Hallagond until that occurred, for he was a man worth redeeming, and she would see his faith in himself restored.

The following morning, Gaelen, Galador, Rogond, and Nelwyn sat together, enjoying the hospitality of Mohani, who was serving Nelwyn her first taste of kaffa. Gaelen had not managed to fully acquire the taste, and as she watched her cousin's expression she knew that this view would be shared. Rogond loved kaffa, as did Galador; they could drink the bitter fluid even without benefit of adding sugar to sweeten it.

Gaelen and Nelwyn shared quite a different view of the dark, sweet koka, however. Gaelen still had some that Mohani had given her, and now she shaved a large bit off into her kaffa-mug, watching as it slowly melted away. She held the cup to her lips, tasted of it, and smiled. Now she was on to something!

"Try adding some of this," said Mohani, offering her powdered spice that turned out to be a mixture of cinnamon and nutmeg. Gaelen was very pleased with the result. She handed the vessel to Nelwyn, who tasted of it, but gave it back immediately; it still was not to her liking.

Gaelen shrugged, and sat cradling the warm mug in her hands until she had finished it. The kaffa began to affect her shortly thereafter, and she grew very bright-eyed and restive. "The sun has been up for hours," she said. "Where are Hallagond and Fima? If we do not rouse them soon, the day will be half over. There is much that needs doing. Shall I go and fetch them?" Her expression indicated that she would enjoy the task of turning Hallagond and Fima out of their beds, for she had never understood the desire of healthy mortals to sleep so much.

Rogond, who had a much clearer understanding, admonished her. "I think it would be unwise for you to perform the task, Gaelen, as you would get far too much pleasure from it. Hallagond shared a bottle of brandy with Fima last night, and I would expect neither is in the mood to be roused by an energetic Wood-elf who is presently under the influence of dancing goats."

"Ah. I see," said Gaelen, looking over at Nelwyn, who was finishing one of Mohani's wonderful cakes. "Drunkenness is a common excuse for lying about all day among both men and dwarves, apparently."

Rogond smiled. "It is not merely an excuse, Gaelen. I doubt that either of them will be pleased with the state of their pounding heads or aching bodies this morning. I shall go and try to rouse them, for I know that Hallagond wanted to take care of certain affairs today."

Gaelen, who would not suffer harmful effects from drinking, shook her head. Why did men drink if it made them ill?

Hallagond finally appeared as the morning waned into mid-day. Rogond and Galador were replenishing their supplies, while Gaelen and Nelwyn had gone out to exercise the horses. Fima, who had never been an early riser and who was presently suffering from the effects of the previous night's indulgence, had declared that he would not be joining anyone in anything today…at least not until suppertime.

El-morah served Hallagond a large mug of his most excellent kaffa, laced with a small amount of sweet liquor that tasted rather like rum. "It is said that a small amount of liquor will aid in banishing the after-effects of a large amount," he said.

Hallagond scowled at him. "You're far too cheerful this day, innkeeper," he said, rubbing his hand across his red-rimmed eyes.

"One of the tasks that I perform for my customers is listening to their woes," said El-morah with a knowing look. "It would seem that you had sorrows to drown last night. If you would unburden yourself, I would listen."

Hallagond liked and trusted El-morah, but he would keep most of his troubles to himself. "Thanks, kindly host, for your concern. My life has been thrown into disarray with the appearance of my brother and his friends, nothing more. I am trying to determine how best to proceed from here. The She-elf has released me from my life-debt, so I may now go on my way. I only need to decide where to go, I suppose."

"You would truly abandon your brother, after he has come so far to find you?" El-morah was incredulous, for family was a thing he valued above all else.

"My brother wishes to take me back to the northlands with him, and I have sworn never to return. Rogond will not accept that I have become a man of the Ravani. He still belongs in the northlands, and I would prefer that he return there as soon as possible, taking those Elves with him."

El-morah shook his head. "You are not just a man of the Ravani. You are Al-amand, companion of Azori the bandit. Your reputation is unsavory; you and your friends have done some dreadful things. Perhaps your brother would see you redeem yourself? He has said that you are a good man in your heart, and I believe him, for I also see this in you."

Hallagond shrugged. "It matters not to me what any of you see. My actions have spoken for the kind of man I am." His eyes narrowed as he looked sidelong at El-morah. "Once, a long time ago, I actually cared about what happened to others, but I have since learned that there is no benefit in it. I care now only for my own comforts. If that She-elf had not claimed a life-debt, I would have left them all to their fates. I do not care for Elves; I never did before, and I don't now. I would escape their bright gaze as soon as I may, but I have a few errands first. When I'm ready, I will face the unpleasant task of confronting my brother so that he will know my inclinations, and stop trying to pursue me. I look forward to that as I would to being buried neck-deep in an anthill."

El-morah shook his head again. "As host, my task is to listen, and not give advice," he said, "but I am finding it difficult to keep silent."

"Well, I will not keep silent," said Mohani, as she approached from behind her husband. Apparently, she had overheard at least part of Hallagond's declaration. "This path you are taking is wrong. Your brother is a kindly soul, and he has your best interests at heart. I expect he could be very persistent. I don't think you will put him off so easily, and make no mistake…Gaelen loves him, and I believe she could be somewhat unforgiving, so have a care how you trample him."

Hallagond looked at Mohani as though she were an interesting insect that he had only just discovered. "Do you think I have cause to worry about my safety? Do I need to watch my back, or have someone taste my food before I do?" He chuckled softly as Mohani's face reddened. "My thanks for the warning, but I am not afraid of any avenging She-elf, especially that one. She is all talk and bravado—she certainly would not do harm to Rogond's only surviving brother. Now, if you will pardon me, I have business to attend to. You dispense excellent kaffa, and I feel renewed. It's a pity that the same may not be said of your advice, but my thanks are given to you anyway." He drew forth three pieces of silver and laid them on the counter.

El-morah took one as payment for the kaffa, but he pushed the other two back toward Hallagond with a chilly expression. "Save these, northlander, for our advice comes without charge, particularly to those not wise enough to listen. We would never take advantage of such a man. I hope you don't find your confrontation with Rogond too unpleasant, Forsaken One." He turned from Hallagond then, returning to the back room to aid Mohani in the preparation of food for their evening meal.

Hallagond shrugged, pocketed the two silver pieces, and went out from El-morah's house. He sensed that he had estranged both the innkeeper and his wife, but this did not dismay him, for he had so intended.

"Tuathan!"

Hallagond winced at Nelwyn's bright, clear voice calling out to him as he made his way to the abode of Mikla, the poisoner. Apparently the Elves had returned from their morning ride, and now Nelwyn walked with Galador through the streets of the oasis, for she had not as yet truly explored it. "Wait for us, and we will walk with you," she said, as he turned to regard her striding briskly toward him with Galador at her side.

Both Elves bowed before Hallagond in greeting, but he did not return the gesture. He was in a less-than-charitable mood this morning, and Nelwyn heard this in his voice as he addressed her: "I have spoken with your cousin about this, and I will now say the same to you. Obviously it has not occurred to you that I have taken the name Al-amand because I do not wish to call attention to my northern heritage. You have just called this to the attention of everyone in hearing. Northmen are not well thought of here. Never refer to me as "Tuathan" again. Do you understand?"

Nelwyn's bright expression changed immediately, and she was chagrined. "I'm sorry," she replied in a small voice. "I did not realize…"

The look on her face made him immediately regret his reprimand, and the look on Galador's face convinced him that he should make it up to her. "It's all right…you didn't know any better. I apologize for growling at you." He smiled warmly at her. "Will you forgive me?"

Nelwyn smiled back at him and nodded, although Galador's expression might still have been described as glacial. Hallagond explained his errand, and offered to take them to meet Mikla, promising a most entertaining experience.

Nelwyn was delighted; she would be most pleased to inform Gaelen that she had seen such wonders. The two cousins occasionally shared a sort of rivalry as to which of them had the more interesting day.

Mikla's place was at first rather frightening to Nelwyn, with its bubbling flasks and strange smells, but it proved to be all that Hallagond had promised. Mikla nearly expired on the spot when he beheld Nelwyn and Galador. He had never before seen Avinashi; many thought them to exist only in legend, and now two of them were standing in his very establishment. He nearly choked to death from wheezing, and both Elves were alarmed.

"Are you all right?" asked Nelwyn, gazing at Mikla with the greenest eyes he had ever seen. He could not yet speak, as he was still wheezing, tears streaming from his eyes, his face purplish-red. He held up one hand in a gesture of dismissal, as Hallagond translated.

"It will pass. Wait a moment...he'll be all right." Amused, he spoke softly to Mikla. "What do you think of my visitors?"

Mikla managed to take a couple of breaths without coughing, and turned a jaundiced eye on Hallagond. Yet he was quite suitably impressed. In another few moments, he had recovered enough that he could speak.

"Why have you come, Al-amand? Is it your intention to pay your debt to me?" He was eyeing Nelwyn's hair with longing.

"It is. I have brought you a token of great worth, though the gold I bring is perhaps not the gold you desire."

"That is most likely true," the old man replied. "Yet the gold I desire is unattainable, unless of course your friend would part with it, which would be a thing beyond hope, I expect."

Hallagond smiled at Nelwyn. "Perhaps not," he said. Then, to the surprise of everyone present, he spoke to the Elves in their own tongue. "This man's skills are responsible for your freedom, at least in part. Without his elixir we could not have done what was done. He wants you to give him some of your hair, as it is valued here as a talisman to ward off sickness. I paid for his services in part with Galador's hair earlier, though he did not know it. What is your will, Nelwyn? Will you part with a small quantity?"

"What do you mean, you paid with my hair?" said Galador, his expression torn between surprise and dismay. He was very vain of his hair, and could not imagine how Hallagond had acquired it.

"My hands are skilled, Galador, and my touch is light. I can pick the pocket of any man in the Ravani; I have done so on many occasions in order to survive. You were distracted, and did not even feel the touch of my blade. Don't worry; no one will notice, and it will grow back. Was it not worth Nelwyn's freedom?"

This reply, of course, was well chosen, for Galador could not argue with it, though Hallagond could see that he was distressed at this invasion of his person. "You might have asked me, and it would have been given willingly," he growled under his breath.

Hallagond bowed slightly in acknowledgment. "Fair enough. I will do so in future. Nelwyn, what say you? If you give him what he desires, it will spare our gold, and we need that to repay El-morah. I would like to give him something extra for his trust and trouble."

Nelwyn nodded, extending her right hand to accept Hallagond's blade. She reached back behind her head, cut off a long lock of hair, and offered it to Mikla, who stood in disbelief, milky brown eyes wide, toothless mouth half-open. Nelwyn's hair caught the sparse light of the dwelling and sent it back in rays of spun gold. It was worth a fortune, and Mikla accepted it with reverence, carrying it back into his private chamber with such care that one might have thought it as fragile as cobwebs. When he returned, he held out a small phial made of blue glass.

"Here is a token in acknowledgment of your generous gift," he said to Nelwyn. "It is a fine oil to scent your hair. A mere drop will last for days; it is made of many things from faraway places. May you enjoy it, and think of Mikla." He bowed as she accepted the token, and then waited expectantly for her to try it.

She opened the blue phial and held it to her face, breathing in the fragrance. Her expression was more than satisfactory, for here were mingled essences of flowers and fields, of woodlands and riverbanks. Many were familiar, and yet some were not. It was a green smell, a fair and wild scent that brought to mind deep forests and spring meadows. Nelwyn loved it.

Hallagond had never seen Mikla so transported. He was obviously pleased that his gift was acceptable. Later, Hallagond would speak of this to Nelwyn. "I believe he was so smitten with you that he would have thrown himself into a fiery chasm had you wished it."

Galador scoffed at this notion. "Nelwyn needs no man-made scent to enhance her attractiveness."

Hallagond smiled inwardly; it was enough that Nelwyn enjoyed the fragrance. Galador would never complain about it again, for he would deny her nothing.

As Nelwyn had hoped, Gaelen was more than impressed—and not a little envious—when she learned of the adventure. "It certainly outshines my afternoon, which was spent caring for the horses," she said. "Gryffa's feet required attention, and they all needed a good and proper currying. Yet I enjoyed myself, even though my day has not been particularly interesting so far."

Nelwyn took the scented oil that Mikla had given her, placed a tiny drop on her fingertip, and stroked it through the silken mop of Gaelen's hair, which the desert winds had made even more disheveled than usual. It was in need of trimming, as Gaelen now had to shake her head frequently to keep it out of her eyes.

"What *is* that?" she said with wonder, as her senses perceived the fragrance. "It smells like…like the Greatwood, and…perhaps Mountain-home, at least in part."

"It is Mikla's gift, that is all I know," replied Nelwyn. "He did not explain where it came from."

Gaelen scowled, though her eyes were playful. "I'm not certain I would put any elixir in my hair that came from one known as 'the poisoner.'"

Rogond came in then with Fima, who had finally emerged from his chamber and was looking for a meal. The Company, now seven in number if you counted Hallagond and Bint Raed, would feast together for what Hallagond hoped would be the last time. Soon he would summon Rogond to a private conversation, after which he expected to be taking his meals alone.

After they had finished their meal, Gaelen and Rogond went up onto the roof of El-morah's establishment, from which they had a fine view of the sunset. The wind was out of the north, and Gaelen scented the air briefly before settling down beside Rogond. She sensed that he wanted to air some concerns with her, and she kept silent, waiting.

At last he spoke: "You went out after Hallagond last evening, and you were alone with him for some time. He was in a foul mood when he returned, and sought refuge in a brandy bottle. What did you say to him?

Gaelen would keep nothing from Rogond, for he knew her well, and she was not a very adept liar. "I asked him why he is so anxious to leave the only family remaining to him, and why he seems to have little regard for one who has endured such hardship to find him." She looked away from Rogond, hoping that he would not be angry with her.

"Did you, indeed? And what did you learn?" he replied, not at all surprised by her actions. He knew that Hallagond's lack of regard for him bothered Gaelen, and that she would not long suffer it without at least trying to get to the bottom of it.

"You are not angry?"

He smiled. "No, Gaelen, I am not angry. I have only been truly angry with you when you deserved it. Now I am merely curious. What did my brother say to you?"

"He asked me not to reveal it," she said in a thoughtful tone, "yet I did not make that promise, and some things I shall reveal. Hallagond endured some terrible trial in the northlands…one that all but destroyed his faith in himself. The horror of it haunts his dreams. He did not elaborate, but I could tell that he holds himself to blame, and now believes that he is unworthy of respect. That's why he has fallen into disrepute…because one so stained with failure is unfit to go among honest men." She looked hard at Rogond. "I released him from his life-debt. There is nothing holding him now…he is planning to leave very soon, and when he does I fear we will never find him again. I know that must dismay you. I'm sorry."

To her surprise, Rogond was not dismayed. "Don't worry, Gaelen. I have been expecting this, and I still have a card to play." He chuckled softly. "My brother won't be getting rid of me so easily. I knew he would be difficult, and I did not expect him to embrace me and allow me to lead him back north like a lamb. I made a promise to my father and I will do all I can to keep it. Still, I do hope it doesn't take too long, for as you have repeatedly and correctly pointed out, our mortal lives are brief enough."

Gaelen was intrigued. "What card have you to play?"

"It was you that gave me the idea," said Rogond. He explained his plan, and Gaelen could not help chuckling.

"Well, he's going to hate me all the more. Still, it should work, at least for a little while," she said. "It's a simple plan. I like it."

"Tomorrow we shall see," said Rogond, as he pulled her over to lie with her head in his lap, so that she could more easily observe the brightening of the stars.

Rogond went looking for Hallagond at mid-morning. According to El-morah, he had not come down to breakfast, and Rogond did not find him in the sleeping-chamber that he shared with Fima. The dwarf had appeared at an uncharacteristically early hour, drawn to the smell of honey-cakes baking in Mohani's oven. "Hallagond was already gone when I awoke," he said. "I am surprised he has not eaten…his appetite is almost as healthy as mine." He shot a worried look at Rogond. "I do hope he has not left us, for I find him likeable. It would be a good thing if he would travel with us, though he does not seem to get on particularly well with the Elves. Pity, that."

"A pity, yes, but not surprising," said Rogond. "Recall what Turan told us. Hallagond has always had more of an affinity for dwarvish folk. And since most dwarves and Elves are like oil and water…"

"That they are," said Fima. "It would seem that your brother has discerning taste. Luckily, you seem to get on equally well with everyone, Rogond. Thank heaven for that, or this would not have been a tranquil journey!"

Rogond took breakfast, to the surprise of Fima, who did not understand why he did not go looking for Hallagond at once. "Are you not fearful that he has left us?"

Rogond swallowed a mouthful of cake. "How would he leave us? He does not have a mount here in the oasis; his horse remained at Bezaltor."

"He can always buy a horse, you know," warned Fima, his silvery eyebrows lowered in disapproval.

"He could, if any of quality were to be had. He has a fondness for a good horse; he nearly died of shame at having to ride Malvorn." Rogond chuckled at the memory of his brother's expression as he rode the laboring pack horse.

"He might take one of our own horses…have you thought of that?"

Rogond gave Fima a look suggesting that perhaps his friend's brain had been addled by the desert sun. "And which of them do you suppose he might take? Eros? Finan?"

"What about Nelwyn's horse, or Galador's?" Fima never referred to the horses by name, for to do so might imply that he found them anything other than troublesome.

"The horses are presently under Gaelen's watch," said Rogond, to which Fima replied, "Say no more."

Rogond was correct; Hallagond had not left the Company as yet. The past evening he had gone to Haifa's tavern, for he heard there was a game up and he wanted to join in. While there, he had spoken with Haifa, who expressed the opinion that Hallagond's luck couldn't have gotten any worse.

"Your brother found you in spite of all our efforts. It is regrettable. He does not fit well into these southern lands, for he is proud and does not use good sense. He does not respect our ways as you do. I have forbidden him to return to my establishment."

"That's certainly understandable," said Hallagond, eyeing Haifa's bandaged right hand. "Yet I intend to show him his own folly. Just be patient and indulge me if you can, and I will make certain he has no reason to remain. If he comes here with me, please do nothing to discourage him. I will reward your forbearance."

"Hmph! You ask much of me, Al-amand. Just make certain he leaves and takes his friends with him. That is all I ask."

"Then that I shall do," replied Hallagond. "You need not fear him or his friends. Now, if you'll excuse me, I have some ill-gotten gains to wager." This he did, winning a small amount of gold before losing it again. There were those in the Chupa more adept than he. He had spent some of his winnings on drink, however, and when the establishment closed at sunrise, Haifa's men found him underneath one of the heavy tables. They shrugged and dragged him out into the alleyway. He did not awaken, but lay on his back with his mouth open, snoring loudly. After making the prediction that there would be fewer flies troubling the folk inside the tavern tomorrow, Haifa's men laughed and left Hallagond to sleep off his drunkenness.

While at Haifa's, Hallagond had learned several things of interest. A man had come into the tavern with news of dire goings-on near the Neela. It seemed that two of Al-Muniqui's brothers had tried to take the palace at the same time, and in the ensuing conflict all three had perished. The information of greatest interest was what happened after.

Apparently the surviving brother, Waddi, had been thought feeble-minded, but was not. He was actually bright enough to know that his brothers were dangerous, and had feigned his affliction so that he could live in peace. Although he did not desire leadership, it was now thrust upon him, and there was every indication that he would rule with a much kinder hand than Al-Muniqui had done. He had already adopted his brothers' wives and children as his own.

Hallagond had suppressed a smile. *That's three fewer contemptible taskmasters in the world,* he thought. *They thought to take advantage of the situation, and it was their undoing. Now, it seems, the meek will inherit their empire.* He would tell no one in the Company except Bint Raed, for it would cheer her. He had resolved to find Estle, and see whether she knew the whereabouts of Azori and his companions. Then he would leave, fine horse or not.

Now he was awakened from his drunken slumber by the tickle of flies in his beard and the prodding of his ribs by the toe of Rogond's boot. He closed his mouth, startling several of the flies that had come to rest there, nearly choking on them as they fluttered and buzzed in alarm.

Rogond waited for the sputtering and groaning to subside as Hallagond came to himself. It was fortunate that the alleyway was narrow and fairly dark even in daylight, for Hallagond could not have endured the sun in his eyes. He squinted up at his brother with a bleary expression that rapidly turned into a snarl. "What do you want? Can you not see that I was sleeping? Thanks to you, I am now awake and in considerable pain. You had better have good cause for disturbing me."

As Rogond looked down at his elder brother, it seemed that Hallagond truly looked like the pathetic, unwashed, unsavory wretch he proclaimed himself to be. Rogond, who was not prone to excessive drink, looked at him with wonder. "You are absolutely disgusting. You need a bath, and a good ration of strong kaffa. When you have regained your senses, I would speak with you on a matter of some importance."

Hallagond continued to snarl up at him. "And what makes you think I want to regain my senses? If you had left me alone to sleep this off I would have been happier. Why can't you cease meddling in my affairs? So long as we are speaking plainly, allow me to say that I did not ask for your aid, and I do not desire your company. I don't wish to speak with you concerning matters of importance, or anything else. I neither love you nor want you. Are we clear on that point?"

Hallagond's words stung Rogond's heart, yet he persisted, for his brother truly needed his aid whether he knew it or not. "Come on, and let's return to El-morah's. You can be made clean, and be fed and rested. Then we'll talk."

Hallagond placed his head in both hands as though in unspeakable pain. He groaned miserably. "What part of 'I do not desire your company' did you not understand? Go home, Rogond. For the love of heaven, *go home!*"

"For the moment, my home is where you are, Hallagond," said Rogond with a smile. "*Wherever* you are! Get used to it. Since you will not come with me, I will tell you now that you might understand. I owe you a life-debt, and I must remain until it is repaid." He smiled wickedly at Hallagond, who was staring at him with his mouth open. "Careful, my brother, or you will catch still more flies this morning."

Hallagond's eyes narrowed, for in that moment he truly hated Rogond. "A life-debt," he growled. "The harpy put you up to this, didn't she?"

"Speak no ill of her in my presence," said Rogond, who was finding it very difficult to love his brother in that moment.

"Then I had better not speak of her at all, for I will say only ill of her. She has deluded you into loving her, and she keeps you now on a short tether. You fawn around her feet like a dog, yet when your back is turned her contempt for you shines like a beacon. No Elf will ever regard you as an equal. You are a fool!"

Hallagond knew that Rogond had been raised among Elves; Fima had told him so. He knew just what to say to infuriate and hurt his brother. Rogond's face reflected this as he stood over him. Hallagond still lay in the dirt, though he had propped himself on one elbow.

"Get up, you worthless wretch," said Rogond slowly. "Let's discuss this in a tongue that is familiar to you."

Hallagond smiled. "You would take out your frustration on me when I am thus impaired and helpless? I'm sure the Elves would shake their heads in shame, yet they always expect the worst from you, I'm sure. You cannot escape the burden of your mortal heritage. I'm afraid you have given your heart above your station, my hapless little brother."

"You have just talked yourself out of a thrashing, for I have realized that I should not soil my hands, despite the fact that I would derive great pleasure in wiping that drunken smile from your face. Your words are chosen to hurt me, and you have chosen them well, yet I know they are untrue."

Hallagond looked slyly up at him. "That's right, *Thaylon*, keep telling yourself that."

"You won't rest until I have wrung your neck, will you?"

"It would be a better fate than living with you."

Rogond took a deep breath and stepped back. "Very well, then. It is regrettable that you would prefer death to my continued presence, but I still owe you a life-debt. Therefore, I shall remain until the debt is repaid. If you want to kill yourself, you will need to find another way to do it."

Hallagond's expression grew thoughtful at once, as he mulled Rogond's words over in his mind. "Another way…" he muttered.

Then he smiled briefly before struggling to his feet. This act took several minutes, as he was most unsteady and his head was pounding. He made several failed attempts before he finally succeeded. Rogond did not offer to aid him.

Hallagond turned and staggered back into the tavern. Rogond followed after him, for he suspected that his brother was up to something. Hallagond slumped in a chair at a corner table and waited, casting a conspiratorial look at Haifa.

Haifa had taken Hallagond's reassurance, therefore, when Rogond followed his brother into the tavern, Haifa did not interfere. Rogond sat with his back to the wall on the opposite side of the room, his expression wary, his hand never far from his sword-hilt. A serving-woman asked if he wanted drink, and he politely declined. Hallagond already had a now half-empty ale tankard before him.

Rogond was uneasy; he would have felt better had Galador been present. He looked back to the table where his brother now sat with a woman; apparently she knew Hallagond well. They spoke for a time, and then the woman rose to her feet and moved behind him, massaging his neck and shoulders. She had already drained the remainder of his ale, telling him that he should drink no more today, an act that earned her a disapproving scowl.

Rogond began to grow weary as the afternoon wore on. *Is he going to waste the entire day here? To what end?* Rogond began to worry. Gaelen would surely come looking for him soon, and she would not be welcomed. In fact, he wondered why Haifa suffered his presence in the tavern. He kept his weapon at the ready, just in case. *He warned me never to come back in here. Perhaps he is merely waiting for reinforcements. My brother is up to something...that is certain!*

All the patrons in the tavern grew quiet as the largest man Rogond had ever seen lumbered in, accompanied by three others who were either relatives or friends. The big man was as tall as Rogond, but much, much more broadly made—he weighed more than Rogond and Hallagond put together. He was filthy, and the light of his eyes was mean and unintelligent. He called for an enormous flagon of drink, settling onto a low bench, apparently reserved for him, that groaned beneath his weight. All the tavern's other patrons were careful to distance themselves from him.

Ah. Right on time, thought Hallagond. Estle had gone out to take some air; he would not risk her safety, and his opportunity was at hand. He rose with little difficulty, for though his head still pained him and his judgment was still muddled, he was steadier on his feet. He approached the man and settled himself on the other side of the same table. No one, including Rogond, could imagine what he was doing.

"Hello, my large and impressive friend," said Hallagond. "I would like to buy you a drink, will that be all right?"

The large man grunted malevolently, but he nodded assent, and at a word from Hallagond his flagon was refilled. He was not bright enough to be suspicious. Hallagond looked over at Rogond and winked.

"Drink up, my friend. May you soon consume enough that you forget both your ugliness and your stupidity. Tell me...are you the only one in your family endowed with such attributes, or are the womenfolk as ugly, misbegotten, and stupid as you are? That would certainly be an intriguing and revolting sight."

The large man's expression grew quite black, and Hallagond wondered about the wisdom of his plan. If he had not been muddled by drink, he would never have started down such a path. He steeled himself for the inevitable result, hoping that his brother was paying sufficient attention.

Haifa could not believe his eyes. Hallagond had just insulted Hassan the Giant, an ill-tempered man who was not accustomed to being insulted. What in the world was he playing at? Haifa ran out from behind the bar, trying to prevent the inevitable. "Please, please," he cried. "Calm yourselves, my friends, or take this matter outside. You will destroy my beautiful tavern. Please, let there be no fighting in this place today." He approached Hallagond, who sat impassively before him. "What are you doing? Do you wish to end your life at his hands?"

Hallagond looked over at Hassan, who was flexing his great fingers in preparation for welcoming Hallagond's neck into them. *That will be for my brother to decide.* "I just wanted to find out whether anyone so obviously dull-witted would be able to stand up and breathe at the same time," he replied.

Without further warning, Hassan roared like a bull and lunged at Hallagond, swinging at him with fists the size of large hams. Hallagond made very little effort to defend himself as one of the blows connected with his shoulder, knocking him halfway across the room. He lay in a daze, blood trickling from a gash in his forehead where it had hit the floor. Hassan roared again and lumbered over to where Hallagond lay.

Rogond was now on his feet, a shocked and dismayed expression on his face. He drew his sword, realizing he would now have to save his brother's life, but Hassan's three cronies surrounded him at once.

Hassan the Giant stood over Hallagond, growling. This sort of behavior was outside his experience. It was easier when they fought back, at least a little...yet now the upstart was insulting him again! It made no sense.

"You think that blow was of any consequence?" said Hallagond, his words clearly understandable, though he was dazed. "I have taken harder blows from women. Your sister, for example."

Hassan raised his arm again, and Hallagond winced in anticipation of what might be his last encounter with this man's fist. *You'd better get over here and save me, Rogond, and I mean now!* He still had made no move in his own defense.

Yet it was not Hallagond who suffered the next blow. A bright dagger came seemingly from nowhere to lodge in Hassan's right shoulder, causing him to bellow and drop his arm, as Estle leaped into the room, two other blades in her hands.

At the same time, Rogond engaged Hassan's cronies, all three of whom had rushed at him with drawn swords. Hassan pulled the dagger from his shoulder with a groan, casting it at Estle. It whistled past her ear as she moved to avoid it, calling to Hallagond.

"Are you hurt? Get up, Al-amand…get up and fight!"

Rogond fought hard against the three sutherlings, while also calling to Hallagond. "Are you whole? Get up, if you can!" Hallagond was still sitting half-dazed on the floor, actually unable to defend himself for the moment.

Estle had distracted Hassan, but now she would need to contend with him. The hulking giant drew a huge, heavy scimitar, and rushed at her. She was quicker and more agile than he, but the sight of him terrified her. She knew that he could crush her to the ground in an instant, and she cried in dismay.

This was too much for Hallagond, and he rose from the floor, drawing his own sword to aid her. The ensuing struggle was brief, but intense. It ended with the death of Hassan, who fell with Estle's remaining dagger in his eye.

Meanwhile, Rogond was tiring, for he fought against three foes. Hallagond and Estle came to his aid; they succeeded in gaining the tavern entrance, felling one of Hassan's cronies as they did so. "Come on!" cried Rogond. "We must escape from this place before more of this man's companions appear."

Estle shook her head. "You have no notion of what you have just done, either of you. Hassan and that other man have large families. We cannot remain in the Chupa—it is no longer safe. I must now leave with you, for they will blame me for this, and will kill me on sight. Whatever madness you have done has just cost me my home." She looked hard at Hallagond, who would not meet her gaze. "I hope it was worth it," she said, her voice as cold and bitter as a hard northern winter.

El-morah and Mohani were dismayed and sorrowful upon hearing Hallagond's tale. They knew and liked Estle. She had been a regular visitor at the inn, for she was fond of kaffa. "My friends, I regret we must say goodbye to you now," said El-morah. "The Chupa will no longer be safe. You will need to gather your belongings and leave at once, before Hassan's family can exact vengeance…I fear you can never return to our hospitality. We will aid you in your preparations, and we are grieved that you must leave us, but leave you must. We will not meet again in this place."

"Yet we may meet again in another," said Rogond. "I'm sorry to have brought trouble...we will leave straightaway." He bowed, and went to see to the preparations. The Elves had been collected and told of what had befallen, and they were making ready. Fima was especially saddened to leave Mohani's children behind, for he had grown very fond of them.

Hallagond had suffered some damage from Hassan's great fist; he was still a little dizzy and did not move with his usual confident grace. Fima aided him in collecting and securing his few possessions.

Estle was furious, though she did not yet know which of the brothers to turn her wrath upon. She went back to her dwelling, packed some of her belongings, and returned, leading a smallish chestnut gelding with a flaxen mane. Like it or not, she was part of the Company now.

Estle and the Elves regarded one another in silence. Rogond and Hallagond were not speaking, either. Rogond pulled Fima up behind him, bracing himself for the inevitable grumbling, but it did not come.

Bint Raed had elected to ride with the Company, even though she most likely could have stayed in the Chupa. She sensed the pall of apprehension and dismay that had settled over her friends; they did not want to leave the oasis under these circumstances. Finan sensed their disquiet, and pawed the ground continuously until Gaelen bade him stop.

"Farewell, my friends," said El-morah. "May the powers of heaven guide you, and give you safe passage to whatever your fates hold. It has been a great gift to know you. Farewell."

Rogond rode forward and bowed, presenting El-morah with a gift; it was a wonderfully carved pipe that he had brought from the Greatwood, and El-morah had admired it. "Think of your friends when you enjoy it," he said with a slightly wistful smile. He turned and began to ride westward, not knowing as yet where he would go.

With the exception of Hallagond, each member of the Company presented El-morah and Mohani with a small gift. Nelwyn and Galador, who were mindful of the role their friends had played in freeing Nelwyn, each gave a rather large lock of hair, which El-morah gravely accepted, even though he had not the slightest idea of what to do with it. Bint Raed gave a beautiful band of hand-woven silk. Gaelen, who rode up last, seemed particularly unhappy at their parting. "I have nothing to give you, my friends, for I have nothing of worth that I can spare. Yet I will always remember you, and you will ever have the gift of my friendship. I pray that it pleases you." She bowed before them as Finan stood with his head lowered, his expression somber.

Mohani spoke then to Gaelen: "Do not be troubled, for your gift of friendship is of great worth. I will add your names to my prayers, and I will always remember your song. Farewell, little wild spirit. Take care of Rogond, and safeguard him from his wayward brother.

I suspect this whole affair is of his making."

"Hush! You know of no such thing," said El-morah, yet Gaelen saw in his eyes that this was also his belief.

She would reserve judgment until she heard the tale. She did not reply, but turned her head so that El-morah and Mohani would not see the sorrow in her bright eyes. Then she rode away from those good people, never to return.

15
The Fire-cloak

The Company rode to the southwest, following Hallagond. There had been some discussion of going back to the Neela, but the idea was abandoned once Estle pointed out that Hassan's people would expect it. It was many days' swift travel to the next oasis, yet Hallagond knew the way, and since no one else could offer a better plan, they followed him. He was feeling so guilty and foolish by now that he would have done nearly anything to aid them.

Bint Raed still rode with Nelwyn, which was all right, for Gryffa was a stout fellow and bore them easily.

"Are you ever going to show us what is in that bundle that is of such almighty importance?" asked Gaelen, referring to the goods Bint Raed had brought from the weaving-shed. "If we cannot eat or drink it, you should probably have left it behind."

Bint Raed laughed. "That would be a most costly meal! It is of great worth. One should not love too well their own works, but I labored over it for many years, and it was nearly completed. I could not leave it."

"So, are you going to show us, that we might marvel at the wonder of it?" asked Gaelen. She was of curious mind, and had already seen examples of Bint Raed's artistry. "It must be fabulous, if years of your labor went into it."

"And so it is," said Bint Raed with some pride. "Few now have the skill to produce such things—the secret of their making was never widely known. The women of my family have passed the knowledge down over many generations, and when Al-Muniqui discovered that I had such abilities, he demanded that this thing be made. He never received it, and now I bring it because I sense there will be a need for it."

"So, what *is* it?" asked Gaelen again. She was on the verge of stamping her feet with impatience.

"You are drawn to it, aren't you?" asked Bint Raed. "There is something about it that you cannot resist. I have seen you place your hand upon the cloth that covers it, as if it calls to you."

Gaelen shrugged, feigning nonchalance. "I am driven by curiosity, nothing more," she said. Yet the bundle *had* called to her, in a way.

Bint Raed smiled. "When we stop to rest I will show you what I have brought. Let us speak no more of it...you must be patient until then." Gaelen was satisfied; she could wait a few more hours.

"I miss El-morah and Mohani already," said Nelwyn. This sentiment was shared by everyone. The Company had taken precious little rest since leaving Dûn Bennas, and El-morah's house had been a safe and comfortable haven. Rogond had told the tale of the incident in Haifa's tavern, and as a result no one was actually speaking to Hallagond for the time being.

Estle had been particularly indignant. "You set up that entire, insanely reckless incident in the hope of escaping a *life debt?* Never mind. Don't answer...I would rather not hear your voice ever again!"

When the drink finally left Hallagond, he was utterly chagrined. The Company had shown him nothing but good will, and he knew that any one of them would fall defending him. In spite of his reckless behavior, they still allowed him to guide them. He smelled of drink, sweat, and filth. His hair and beard were unwashed and oily, and he bore an ugly gash on his forehead that would probably leave an equally ugly scar. Yet the Elves did not scorn him, though he noticed that Gaelen in particular strove always to remain upwind of him.

He now felt an unfortunate sense of obligation to make certain that the Company at least found another safe haven, since they had been driven from the Chupa by his foolhardiness. There was a shortage of safe havens in the Ravani; it would probably be some time ere they found one.

He shook his head, knowing that this would not be a pleasant journey. Estle had already indicated that, had she known the nature of Hallagond's predicament in the tavern, she would have let Hassan finish him. "It would have served you right. What a colossally *stupid* plan that was! Only drink and temporary derangement could have excused it." Estle was rather direct in her dealings with people.

"I'm sorry. I thought it was a good idea at the time," he said. "Somehow, I expected a much different outcome. Wouldn't be the first time..."

"I'm sure," said Estle. "But now we all must live with the consequences."

The Company made camp in the shelter of great stones so that they might rest during the heat of the day. Gaelen had not forgotten Bint Raed's promise, but she kept silent while Bint Raed slept. Nelwyn offered Shiva's healing salve to Hallagond, and for once he did not resist or complain; it was best to mind his manners for a while.

Fima, who liked Hallagond and still trusted him, spread out his map, bidding Hallagond to examine it. "So, where are you taking us?" he asked. "Can it be found on this map?"

Hallagond studied Fima's map with interest, desperate to be useful in some way. "This is incomplete," he said. "Here...let me add a few things." Fima, who tried always to be in possession of ink, quill, and parchment, drew them forth. Hallagond then drew several new features onto the map. "This is where we are going. I don't remember its name, but there is water there." He gave the ink and the quill back to Fima. "I must sleep now. My head still aches, right along with the rest of my body, and I'm weary." He drew his hood over his head to shade his eyes and was soon asleep.

Estle kept to herself, as though determined to remain outside the Company. She had been told tales of Elves, and most were not flattering, hence she expected them to be haughty, arrogant, and cold-natured with little regard for men. *Because they are immortal, and we are not. It's the same as with very wealthy men who have inherited their fortune and done nothing to earn it. How dare they feel superior!* She curled up in the shade, and tried to take rest.

Rogond sat at the base of a tall stone, his long legs stretched out before him, having fallen asleep with his head at an odd angle. Gaelen gently slipped her arm behind his head, straightening his neck and settling him into a more comfortable position.

Hallagond had awakened, for he found it difficult to sleep soundly in the open desert. He observed Gaelen as she tended Rogond, and he saw then that she truly loved him—never was a man treated with a gentler, more loving hand. There would be no scorn of men in her heart. Hallagond was saddened for a moment...did she not realize that Rogond would die, and that she would not share his fate afterward? Surely, Rogond knew this truth. Their love must be strong indeed, to endure in spite of the certainty of such a painful and final separation. Hallagond sighed. His brother was a fool to make such a choice, but he was, for now, a happy fool.

When Gaelen was satisfied that Rogond would not awaken with a stiff neck, she left him, springing lightly up onto the ridge of stones that surrounded them. She paced slowly back and forth like a cat, keeping her eyes trained back the way they had come. Hallagond knew that her vigilance would not fail, and he was soon asleep again.

In the lands near Tal-ailean, far to the north of the rocky shelter where the Company rested, Gorgon Elfhunter observed three young Wood-elves, who were searching for one of their companions. *Search well, you vermin. You won't like what you find...*

They finally did find their friend, standing horrified at the flayed, ruined body that swung slowly from its tether. None of them had ever seen such a sight before, yet it was not the worst sight they would see. Gorgon purred deep in his chest as he readied his weapons. *Look on the bright side. The sight of your companion won't haunt you for long.* They were trying to cut the body down, and didn't hear him coming.

The Company had made good time during the evening hours. They decided to stop and rest to save the horses, as Hallagond had estimated that they were less than a day from their destination.

Gaelen and Nelwyn had gone hunting by moonlight, and they brought back many strange and interesting creatures for Fima's roasting-coals. The dwarf had insisted on making a fire against the chill of the desert night; he had noticed that when the large, thorny desert plants died, their flesh fell away to reveal a woody skeleton beneath. This would burn as well as firewood, for it was surprisingly hard and dense. He had already made himself a beautiful walking-stick with it, nearly dulling one of his small axes, for the wood was like iron. It burned for a long time and made excellent coals.

Now his eyes widened as the Elves laid their gifts at his feet. Desert animals are mostly active under the moon, not the sun, and Gaelen and Nelwyn easily caught those that were unwary. Here was a very large lizard, some smaller lizards, and an assortment of soft-furred animals that looked rather like rats with very long, furry tails and large hind feet. Here was a huge hare with very long, black-tipped ears, which delighted Hallagond, for according to him they were fine eating (if a bit stringy). Gaelen was especially proud of her catch, for the animal was swift and it had been difficult. It turned and zigzagged, flying across the sand with great speed, and she nearly lost it. They had also encountered several snakes, but they left those strictly alone.

"You need to be wary of the lizards, as well," said Hallagond, prodding the big one with the toe of his boot. "Some of them are venomous, and you do not want to be bitten by any of them."

"I do not want to be bitten by anything," said Nelwyn. "But why is it such a dire thing to be bitten by a lizard?"

"They have a black bite, and even a tiny wound may fester so badly that death may result," said Hallagond. He had seen a man die from such a bite, raving with fever and stinking of decay.

"Now, of course, *you* don't have anything to fear. Your life-force will banish the agents of disease...you have no idea how fortunate you are!"

"I have every idea," said Gaelen, remembering her experiences with Rogond and Thorndil.

Estle and Hallagond aided Fima with the meal; lizard was a dish new to him and he had not the slightest notion of how to prepare it.

Bint Raed did not relish the sight of lizards being prepared for cooking, and had gone to sit alone under the moon. *Perhaps this would be a good time to approach,* thought Gaelen, kneeling down beside her. "Will you show me now what you are carrying? I would truly like to see."

"I will," replied Bint Raed with a slightly enigmatic smile. "In fact, I intend to give it to you. I owe you my life and my freedom, and you will appreciate this work more than will any of your friends." She moved to her small pile of belongings, taking the soft bundle in both hands. Then she sat upon the sand, bidding Gaelen do likewise, and revealed a thing the like of which no Elf of the Greatwood had yet seen.

"What is it?" Gaelen's voice was still and quiet, yet alive with wonderment. "It looks like...like tiny flames in the dark. Almost like water that smolders and burns. What *is* it?"

"It is a fire-cloak," said Bint Raed proudly. "And though its brilliance is barely discernable in the dark, in the sun it appears as living flame. I have been laboring on this one for nine…no, the better part of ten years. I give it now to you, for you possess the spirit best suited to wear it."

Gaelen lifted the fire-cloak, letting the fabric run through her fingers like liquid silk. "This feels alive in my hands," she said. "It is light, yet heavier than it would appear to be, almost like…like metal."

"And so it is" said Bint Raed, "at least in part. Fire will not touch it, and it will turn the harsh sun aside. It will even turn a blade or a dart, provided they have not much power behind them. Look now, and see." She drew forth a blade, draping the fire-cloak across Gaelen's thigh, and pressed the sharp blade down. The fabric locked together under the pressure of the blade, and would not allow it to penetrate.

Gaelen was fascinated. "So, this is almost a form of very light armor," she said, continually running her fingers over it, watching how it caught the light and sent it back in flickering rays of orange, scarlet, and gold.

"After a fashion, yes," said Bint Raed, "although it will not turn a well-directed blade or arrow. But neither will armor protect you from the sun, or from fire. This will turn both flame and smoke. Such a garment is worth a king's ransom, and I am pleased that you will wear it, and not Al-Muniqui. He was not worthy of it, which is why I have been reluctant to finish it. Now I am rewarded, for it will have an excellent home. Please accept it, and keep it close at hand. One day it will save your life, of that I am certain."

"You say it's not finished…it looks finished to me," said Gaelen.

"It would have needed a few more inches to really fit one as tall as Al-Muniqui. For you, it's fine!"

Gaelen flushed, unsure of how to react to Bint Raed's generosity. "But why have you chosen me for it? Why not give it to Nelwyn, with whom your friendship is close? Why not to Rogond, who is of your race? I do not understand."

Bint Raed smiled. "I have my reasons. Just accept my gift and be glad. You are a fire-spirit, Gaelen; I have read this in your eyes. Nelwyn is a water-spirit, and is not as suited to the fire-cloak. It called to the one who will wear it best. In doing so, you will be able to endure terrible hardship. You might even save the Company from death one day. Will you now accept my gift, little Fire-heart?"

"What terrible hardship? What death? " asked Gaelen, her eyes wide.

"You ask too many questions," said Bint Raed. "Will you accept my gift, or no? I give it not lightly, but I do give it willingly. Do you accept?"

Gaelen looked down at the fabulous cloak, knowing that she could not refuse it. It had called to her, just as Bint Raed had observed, and if she needed it to save the lives of her friends, she had no choice. "I accept with thanks, though I say it with some trepidation, for your dire foreshadowing has unsettled me. I will keep it safe, and wear it only when needed."

"That is wise, for many will covet it," said Bint Raed. "You will be a fearsome vision clad in such a garment, mounted on your fiery horse, shooting deadly arrows at people. They will cover their faces from dread at the sight of you!" She smiled at Gaelen in the darkness.

Gaelen smiled, though she already thought herself quite fearsome, with or without a fire-cloak. "I would like to show it to my friends before I tuck it away…do you think that would be all right?"

"Of course. It won't hurt that they know you have it," said Bint Raed. "But then you should put it away until the need arises."

Gaelen nodded at Bint Raed, folding the beautiful cloak carefully before tucking it away. It did not want to be folded, slipping this way and that, but she finally subdued it. "The fabric has a mind of its own," observed Bint Raed. "If you think it is difficult to fold, you cannot imagine the effort it takes to create! It fights you every step of the way. Some days I would struggle just to weave a single row, and there are many hundreds of rows in the hood alone. Take good care of your gift."

"I will," said Gaelen respectfully. She knew that Bint Raed was right, for she had seen her own fiery aura, as well as Nelwyn's gentle, liquid blue-white one. Bint Raed had declared Nelwyn to be a water-spirit—how was it that she held such insight? Gaelen did not know.

"Come on, you two, and prepare to feast well tonight! Your catch is nearly ready," called Fima. "I have been informed that no one may eat until all are present, and I'm hungry, so let's not delay."

Gaelen bowed, taking Bint Raed's right hand and touching it to her forehead in acknowledgment of her indebtedness. Bint Raed smiled and returned the bow, and then rose and moved to the fireside, where even now a wonderful meal of roasted hare (with a side of roasted lizard) was being served to all.

In the morning, when the sun glinted red-gold upon the sand, Gaelen drew forth the fire-cloak, gasping as she beheld its brilliance for the first time in daylight. She needed to introduce this fabulous garment properly to her friends, and so she called to Finan, donned the cloak, grabbed her bow and quiver, and swung aboard.

She cantered up to Rogond, Hallagond, Fima, and Estle, who were putting out the campfire after breakfast. She gave a war-cry and halted her fierce battle-mount, who stood briefly but dramatically on his hind legs. Then she sent a shaft into the sand at the feet of Rogond who, though he knew she was playing, still took a step back from her. She was a sight that might have given pause to the fabled warriors of old.

"See what Bint Raed, the unrivaled artisan, has seen fit to give to me! Is it not the most fabulous cloak ever?" Gaelen, who almost never adorned herself, was feeling quite impressive and radiant in that moment.

Estle, who made it her business to be unimpressed with Gaelen, smirked and snorted. "Yes, it is certainly fabulous. Especially if you want to be an obvious target for your enemies, or if you wish to frequent certain shady districts of portside towns and sell your favors there!" She turned from Gaelen and went to secure her pack, walking briskly past Nelwyn and Galador, who had heard Gaelen's war-cry and had come to investigate.

Gaelen refused to be chastened, but turned Finan about on his haunches so that all her friends could see the cloak to full effect. "Bint Raed has told me that this cloak took ten years to make, and that it will turn fire and smoke aside. She has also said that we may one day have need of it. I shall not wear it again until that day, but I wanted to show you." She slid down from her mount and removed the cloak, unfastening the golden clasp, which was made in the shape of a winged dragon.

She placed it carefully in her small leather bag. It stowed in a very small space, but it was heavier than it appeared, so she tied it to Finan's harness. She had acquired a light leather pad covered with a red-and-gold-tasseled tapestry, secured with a girth, a breastplate in front, and a strap that ran around Finan's tail behind. It could not be properly called a saddle, as there was neither a tree nor stirrups, but it provided a place to secure her belongings, and it protected her from the sweat of the animal. Soft and well fitted, it would not gall Finan if kept clean.

She turned him back around to face her friends, who appeared to be most suitably impressed. Hallagond, in particular, seemed almost stunned. He stood with his mouth open, his eyes distant, lost in his own thoughts.

"Hallagond, you may as well close your mouth before you trap something winged and bad-tasting," said Gaelen. "As experienced a man of the world as you are…have you not seen an Elf wearing a fire-cloak before?" She laughed good-naturedly at him, though her smile faded when she saw that his expression did not change.

The Company traveled ever to the southwest, moving slowly toward the sea. Bint Raed and Hallagond had guided them well, but as they drew farther from the lands he knew, Hallagond deferred more to Bint Raed. They didn't really seem to know where or why they traveled, they just moved between one water source and the next.

They experienced the wrath of the desert sands as a windstorm overtook the oasis where they were sheltering. Thankfully, they were not in the open desert, for such a storm might have finished them—Hallagond had seen wind-driven sand strip the skin from a man's body. He did take advantage, however, by hanging Fima's steel pots out in the wind. With no water available to clean them they had become dirty and blackened, but when the storm passed they had been polished to a clean, bright finish.

Due to his constant efforts at being helpful, everyone's attitude toward Hallagond had mellowed with time. However, there were tensions evident elsewhere. Estle did not get along especially well with any of the Elves, particularly Gaelen, and took every opportunity to cast sarcasm at her, thinking her prideful without cause and annoying without equal. Gaelen refused to be baited, ignoring what was said of her, which only confirmed Estle's assessment of her arrogance.

Estle had grown up a woman in what was definitely a man's world, and her life had been hard. She had battled always for respect, and now she demanded it. In truth, if Estle had been able to think clearly about why she scorned Gaelen so, she would have realized the truth of it. Hallagond had grown to like Gaelen, and often sought her company. She was capable, and in possession of many abilities, and her youth and strength would not fade. Estle had seen Hallagond cast admiring looks at Gaelen as she rode or practiced with her weapons. The Elves' lack of physical hardship was infuriating, and Estle knew that they were well aware of their superiority to men in this regard. Gaelen probably thought herself too good for the likes of Hallagond, despite her evident affection for Rogond. Estle was determined to remain unimpressed with Rogond also, for he comported himself more as an Elf than a man, at least the men in her experience. His manners were far too refined, and he was far too clean.

Although Estle did not yet fully admit to herself that she still desired Hallagond as more than friend, she resented his attentions to Gaelen, and would not rest until she had forced the Elf to acknowledge her scorn.

That day finally came. The Company had encountered a merchant caravan and were availing themselves of supplies. The merchants were only too happy to sell their wares, and they had some interesting goods from trade cities on the far southern coast. Their descriptions of those strange lands made Gaelen long to visit them and see the wonders for herself. She looked over at her cousin Nelwyn. "They say there are great forests there…trees as tall as hills, where no light reaches the floor. How I would long to see such a sight again."

Nelwyn nodded and turned away, her eyes filled with tears. This journey through desert wastes had been hard on her, for she was a child of the forest and always would be. She would never be truly at peace anywhere else.

Gaelen placed a comforting hand on her shoulder. "Don't worry. One day we will leave this forsaken waste behind, and return to our green country. You will feel the rain upon your face again." Nelwyn nodded, a single tear flowing down her face as she thought of that day. It could not come soon enough.

Estle overheard Gaelen's comment, and rounded on her. "And precisely *which* forsaken waste are you referring to? It could not possibly be my beautiful desert, *my home*, where I was born and raised. Even you would not be so ignorant and rude as to suggest such a thing, although I can fully understand why neither of you would be happy here. Why don't you go back to the forest right now, so that you can live easily in lands where water falls every day from the sky, and food literally drops into your hand? These lands are too hard for you! Go home."

Nelwyn turned to face Estle, who saw her tears for the first time. "You know nothing of me or of my home, woman of Tal-fásath!" She turned and left them to be alone with her sorrow.

Gaelen's eyes glittered as she faced Estle. "You would not last long in the Darkmere. There are enemies in the northlands that you cannot even imagine! Here, it seems the only things you need fear are those of your own kind. That is one difference between your lands and mine."

"Ah. Well, we could test that opinion, couldn't we? I'm not afraid of you, Gaelen Taldin! You would not have survived in the Ravani without our aid. Admit it. You and your friends would have died long ago if not for the generosity of Ravani-folk."

"That is true, yet I have yet to see much generosity in certain of them," said Gaelen. "Although, with one notable exception, the women-folk have been worth knowing. For the most part they realize that respect cannot be demanded, and must be earned."

"Yet I will demand it, for I *have* earned it," said Estle with a slight curl of her lip. "And I will not suffer your scorn of my race, you who understand so little of the ways of men. You profess to love Rogond, yet he is more alike to Elves than to real men. For example, I have never seen him cast his eyes upon another woman, and that is most unnatural in a real man. It makes me wonder whether he is of a normal masculine disposition in that regard." Estle glanced sidelong at Gaelen, and her eyes glittered maliciously. "I have seen him look with greater admiration upon Galador!"

Estle knew this would ruffle Gaelen, and so it did. "You are making it ever harder to earn my respect," she said, throwing back her powerful shoulders and drawing herself up to her full height. She was not as tall as Estle, but her demeanor more than made up for it.

"You think I care at all?" Estle replied. "At last I see and hear the truth from you, and my thoughts concerning you are confirmed. I will not vie for respect from one so arrogant. Go home, that you may live again like a bird among the tree-tops, preening your beautiful feathers and telling yourself each day of your superiority. Fly away home now, and leave these hard lands—and hard men—to those who understand them."

Gaelen, who was not used to tolerating any disrespect of either Rogond or herself, felt hot blood rising in her face. She hated Estle in that moment. She flexed her fingers, wishing that they held a weapon so that she might take the infuriating smile from the woman's face.

Estle, who felt more than capable of dealing with an angry Wood-elf, sensed her advantage, and pressed it harder. "You want some of me? Come, then, and take it!"

The confrontation might have turned into a battle had not Hallagond chosen that moment to intervene. "What's this, then?" he asked, stepping between the two combative females. "What has so upset you that it's worth fighting over? Well, whatever it is, it ends now, for both of you. We cannot afford such displays of female temperament. Make friends, or…or I shall be forced to *sing* until you do." Hallagond was like to Rogond in singing ability—he lacked any vestige of it.

"Ah. I see that you are still glaring at each other, and have not yet become friends. Well, you have brought this on yourselves…I am no longer responsible." He threw his head back and, to the dismay of all in hearing, began a tuneless bellowing that might have been mistaken for cries of pain.

"Stop it, Al-amand. We cannot be friends, but we will not come to blows. Let that be enough for you...please!" begged Estle, wincing as Hallagond hit another horrible quavering note.

"Sorry, not good enough. Shake hands and part as friends, or the singing continues."

Gaelen looked over at Estle. "I suppose I cannot really shoot him, can I?"

Hallagond merely threw his head back and sang louder. Everyone in the caravan was now staring at him with a pained expression.

"Oh, very well, be *silent*, already!" growled Estle, extending her hand to Gaelen, who took it in a grip that was crushingly firm. Estle returned it in kind; neither would give the slightest hint of discomfort as they strove to turn the other's hand to jelly. Each spoke in a tongue they knew the other would not be understood—Gaelen in Elvish, Estle in Ravani.

"This is not ended, you prissy, dainty, prudish, worthless excuse for an Elf. I would not shed a tear if you were to leave and return to your precious trees right now! Stay away from Al-amand if you know what's good for you."

"It's taking all my self-control to hold back from breaking your fingers, you weakling! You had better watch what you say of my beloved, or else keep watch over your shoulder. And by the way, you are unclean and your smell offends me."

These things were said with smiling faces, but Hallagond, who understood the words, became silent. These two were far from being friends, but this was the best he could ask right now. Besides, if he did not stop caterwauling soon, the men of the caravan might shoot him to save themselves.

One thing was certain—Estle was unhappy with his friendly attentions to Gaelen. He smiled inwardly. *So that's how it is, is it,* he thought to himself, after Estle and Gaelen had exchanged black looks, broken contact, and departed. Hallagond had long admired and liked Estle, and he knew that she enjoyed his company, but now it seemed that there might be something more growing in her heart. He would wait and see, and pay no more extra attention to Gaelen for the time being.

The Company followed the caravan to the next oasis, a journey that took nearly five days. Rogond noticed that Hallagond seemed unusually quiet and somber; typically he was of a much more cavalier demeanor, with a ready smile and a bright, if occasionally wicked, sense of humor. Now he appeared to be lost in serious thought. Estle tried to distract him, but he was preoccupied, and paid her little heed.

On the evening of the third day, Rogond moved to his side. "Something troubles you, my brother," he said. "It has done so for some time, and I am becoming concerned. What has turned your mood so grim?"

"It doesn't concern you."

"Any matter that troubles you concerns me," said Rogond in a calm but earnest voice. "Talk to me, brother, and unburden yourself. This mood came on you when you first beheld Gaelen's fire-cloak. Why has such a thing dismayed you?"

Hallagond drew a deep breath. In truth, this matter did concern not only Rogond, but all in the Company. He could no longer keep it to himself.

"It was not merely the sight of the fire-cloak, but the sight of Gaelen *wearing* the fire-cloak that unsettled me. Many months ago, I dreamed of a horror so real that it terrified me, yet when I awoke I could remember none of it. It has been coming back slowly, bit by bit. The sight of your face brought some of it back, for you were a part of my dream. Gaelen was there as well, and she was wearing the fire-cloak. There was a terrible battle, and…and a Great City. A dreadful host assailed it, all clad in red and black. Their hands were stained with the blood of innocents, and Darkness went before them. That was frightening enough, but there was something more. I cannot now fully remember it, but it was horrible…some fierce black warrior with strange, golden hair. It was immense, and nothing could stand against it. It spoke, but I cannot recall what it said." Hallagond looked over at Rogond to see that his brother's sun-browned face had gone quite pale. "This has meaning to you, doesn't it?" he asked in a low voice.

"It might. This warrior...was it very tall and broadly made? And when it spoke, did it make your skin crawl?"

"As I said, brother, it was immense. None could stand against it. I remember the hair—it was most disquieting. It did not seem to belong on such a being as that."

"Was it like to the hair of Elves…long, and silken?"

Hallagond nodded grimly. "Yet there was nothing Elven about the rest of it," he said. "Tell me, my brother, what does it mean? Is this a thing we need fear? If so, how may we avoid encountering it?"

Rogond looked into his brother's eyes, his expression at once fearful and resolute. "I believe that you have seen Gorgon Elfhunter. He is definitely a thing to fear, yet I cannot imagine him traveling to this place. He has no love of sunlight, and the desert would not be at all to his liking."

Hallagond drew in a sharp breath. "By the Sun-and-Stars...you know much of this! You are truly unsettling me, Rogond."

"Hush. Lower your voice. You don't understand the half of it. Say the wrong words in too loud a voice, and we will have no hope of avoiding the Elfhunter, for once Gaelen suspects that he has returned, she will immediately take up his trail. Nothing will sway her from it. He is our sworn enemy, and she has made it her life's quest to bring about his ending. She has sworn that she will not return home until he lies dead at her feet."

Hallagond snorted in disbelief. "Gaelen? *Our* Gaelen? Are we discussing the same undersized She-elf? She thinks to defeat the creature I beheld in my vision?" He shook his head. "I had thought her to be of practical mind, but I see now that she has taken leave of her senses if she thinks she can prevail against such a warrior. Talk about false hope!"

"She nearly succeeded the last time," said Rogond quietly. "And although there were many of us working to defeat him, we had also to deal with his army. Many tried, but our undersized She-elf was the one who laid him low."

Hallagond was intrigued. "You must tell me the tale," he said. "For in so doing you will both entertain me and aid me in understanding the nature of my dark dream."

"Would that it proved to be only a dark dream; it seems to have the markings of a prophecy," said Rogond. "Our Company will tell you the tale, for many took part in it. But in return, you must tell me why you forsook your name, your home, and your people. Something drove you to do it, and I would know of it that I might understand. That will be a private telling, between brothers. Will you agree?"

"Why must everything have a price?" said Hallagond.

Rogond looked around at his brother with some dismay, for he thought he heard a quaver of profound sorrow in his voice. "This is a deep and festering wound, isn't it? It has nearly taken your heart. It has taken a long time of trying to convince yourself that you do not care, but you do...you always will. You need to make yourself free of it. Have you ever told the tale to anyone before?"

"I haven't," said Hallagond, "and I cannot. Please do not ask it of me."

"You must unburden yourself one day, brother, and when you come to know it, I will be there to listen. Our Company will share the tale of the Elfhunter, and ask only your promise that when you are ready you will share your tale with the one who shares your blood. We are all that remains of the line of Rosalin and Diomar—we must defend our own. I would release you from that which plagues you. Do I have your promise?"

Hallagond rode along in silence for a long moment. At last he spoke. "When I am ready, I will tell you my tale. Perhaps then you will hold me in sufficient disregard to leave me alone."

Rogond sighed, knowing that his brother might never be ready, but he was glad to have exacted the promise nonetheless.

That evening there began a long recounting of the tale of Gorgon Elfhunter, and the Company's adventures. Many had a part in the telling, for each brought forth different insights and experiences. Only Galador drew back; he had never liked revealing anything of himself before an audience. "Someone must keep the watch," was his simple yet effective excuse.

The Ravani merchants gathered each night to listen. They were riveted by the tale, for they had not heard of such things before. The real storyteller, of course, was Fima, and he never tired of it. Rogond noticed that their pace had slowed, and they stopped more often, because the merchants did not wish to part from the Company until the telling was complete. When they reached the oasis, they settled in for a stay of many days.

The merchants shook their heads, their long, dark beards wagging, as Rogond told of Gorgon's presumed escape in the Barrens. They clucked in sympathy as Rogond described his and Galador's frustration at losing their enemy. Yet when Rogond told them of Gaelen's lighting of the maglos, and the burning light that would blind and torment the creature for a long time to come, they cheered in approval. One actually approached Gaelen and clapped her on the back, which was highly unusual for sutherling folk. To touch a strange woman in such a manner was strictly forbidden. Apparently, in that moment he regarded Gaelen more as a warrior than as a female.

"Where is Gorgon's mirror now?" asked Hallagond, who sat always with Estle, and was presently sharing a fine dish of dates dipped in thickened cream from one of the dromadan cows.

"It is in safekeeping," replied Fima. "I will say no more."

"May we not look upon it? I have never seen such a thing before," said Estle, who had been drawn into the tale with everyone else.

"I would prefer that it remain hidden," Fima replied, "for it is beautiful, and there might be those tempted to take it unto themselves. That would mean disaster, for we would not be able to rest assured that the creature had not regained it."

"Do not fear, Fima," said Gaelen grimly. "If Gorgon ever touches the mirror again, I will know it. He is far away, and at present can do no harm to the Company. Show them if you will."

Fima was surprised at this response, but he nodded, rising from his seat by the fire and moving behind a nearby tent. There he reached down into his leather jerkin, found the hidden pocket there, and drew forth Gorgon's mirror. He did not know that Gaelen had followed him, and now took note of where the mirror could be found. This had been in her plan, for if she ever needed to locate it she would waste no time in searching for it. She feared that one day this need would be on her, and she would have no time then to waste.

She spirited herself back to the fireside before Fima returned. Rogond looked over at her with some suspicion, for he had felt it best that she not know of the mirror's whereabouts. Gaelen would not look directly at him, but tossed her cloak around Nelwyn and herself to keep back the cold.

Fima held the mirror aloft for all to see, though he did not open it. The beautiful golden casing glittered and flashed in the firelight, and the sutherlings were quite impressed. Gaelen's blood chilled in her veins as she beheld it, for although it had been a long time since she had looked upon it, she sensed that it had lost none of its power. As she stared hard at the mirror's golden housing, she called out to Gorgon, and he perceived, even across the vast distance that separated them.

Here is your property, Dark Horror. I know you are abroad again, and I know you can hear me...you have been listening for a while now. Keep on coming, then, if you have the strength of heart. I will be waiting. Your fate is waiting for you.

She closed her eyes, as a wave of sickening dread came over her. She thought she heard harsh, ill-natured laughter drifting on the wind, but then she realized it was only in her mind.

Fima finally finished the tale, to the dismay of his audience. He looked around at their disappointed faces, knowing that they had not enjoyed such fine entertainment in a long time. They knew almost nothing of Elves, and now they had been treated to descriptions of the great Elf-realms of the north, stories of great forests and rivers, and mountains covered in snow and ice. Fima almost hated to see the tale end as much as they.

"How ever did you come to be in this place?" asked one of the men of the caravan. "How came you to be so far from your home, and why? Surely you have had many adventures on your way to finding our caravan. Will you not share them?"

Fima's eyes grew wide with excitement at the prospect of more tale-telling. "You cannot imagine the perils we have endured, nor the trials we have faced," he said, his eyes alight with enthusiasm.

Rogond looked hard at him, clearing his throat and scowling. It would not do to tell them everything; it was best to not bring certain matters to the attention of these Ravani-folk. Fima would just have to disappoint them. The dwarf nodded in understanding, his face falling a little as he turned back to his expectant listeners.

"Ah, my friends, I am afraid that we must all be moving on. My father, who was a fine storyteller himself, in fact a much better one than I, told me once that a tale should always end while the listeners are still hoping for more. This story will have to wait until another day."

Hallagond rose and moved behind Rogond before leaving the gathering to return to his resting place. "Very wise, my brother, very wise," he said.

Later that night, Gaelen sought out Bint Raed, for she would ask something of her. She approached quietly as Bint Raed sat alone in the moonlight, and sat down beside her.

"Why have you come, Gaelen Taldin? There is something that you would know. Ask, and I will answer if I can."

Gaelen paused for a moment, admiring Bint Raed's insight. There was much to admire about this woman. "I have come to ask why you are leading us on this path. We moved out of reach of Hassan's folk long ago, so there is some other purpose at work here. Are you trying to get to the Silver City? If so, why not simply tell us? Then we may choose."

Bint Raed smiled. "One thing I will never need worry about, Gaelen Taldin, and that is discerning what is in your mind, for you make your thoughts plain to all."

"There is no time for veiled thoughts," said Gaelen. "Each day we draw farther to the southwest. Just tell me…are you drawing us to the Citadel? If it's true, I don't mind, for I care not where we go so long as it is not near any Elven-realms. That I must not do until my enemy is defeated at last."

Bint Raed looked over at her with a mixture of admiration and sympathy. "I know what it's like to leave your home," she said, "and I cannot imagine the path that will lead to the downfall of this enemy. He sounds fierce...and terrible! You alone I judged to be worthy of the fire-cloak, and that should encourage you, yet none can know who will be left standing when he finds you at last."

She looked hard at Gaelen then. "I will answer your question if you will answer mine. You have said that you want to lead him away from Elven-realms. Are you calling him to follow after you?"

Gaelen's eyes widened as she turned to Bint Raed. "That's a bold question. I'm afraid my thoughts in such intimate matters are not yours to know…and you need not answer my question, for I believe I know the truth of it already. I have said nothing to Rogond, but I think that for all our sakes you must. He should at least know what forces drive the Company."

"Perhaps so, but also he should know that you are drawing that horror ever-closer. You have likewise unintentionally answered my question, for you did not deny it, and you most certainly would have were it not true." Here her gaze softened as she placed a gentle hand upon Gaelen's shoulder. Gaelen stiffened, but did not move away. "I cannot imagine what you have endured, and my blood freezes at the thought of what is yet to come, but know this: I am your friend. I will not sit in judgment of you or of your motivation, and I will keep your counsel."

Gaelen chuckled softly, shaking her head. "I thank you for your confidence in my ability to meet my enemy. Now I will simply have to prove you wrong." She lifted her head, and turned her right ear to the wind. "Nelwyn is coming," she stated simply. "We should speak no more of these matters, for they will unsettle her. Yet I'm glad of your friendship; you should know that it is returned. However, as I believe I now know the answer to *my* question, you should tell Rogond of your plan to return to the Silver City as soon as possible."

Bint Raed nodded, patting Gaelen's shoulder, as Nelwyn appeared and sat beside them. Had Gaelen thought long about it, she would have realized that speaking to Nelwyn of Gorgon's likely return would not have unsettled her, for she already knew that it was so.

The Company remained in the oasis for three more days, and they learned several things of interest. Chief among them was the rumor of a great, savage army, made up of warriors of various races, that had been wreaking havoc upon all in their path. According to the rumor, they left none alive that they encountered. They had come out of the southeastern lands, and were now working their way slowly westward. There were no survivors to tell of them, only those who had met with the aftermath of their passing. These tales were terrible, and Bint Raed was understandably fearful.

"Did you say they were moving west? Are you certain?" she asked.

"That is certain, though they are a large force, growing ever-larger, and they move not swiftly, but linger for a time around each water-source. None draw near enough to observe them and live to tell about it, so I have been told. At any rate, they have definitely been moving toward the sea, leaving only destruction and death in their wake."

"If they cannot be observed, then how does anyone truly know of them?" asked Rogond. "For example, you have said that they are mostly sutherlings and easterners, and that their numbers grow larger. If they kill all in their path, how do they grow larger? How is it that such things are known?"

"One may tell many things in the aftermath of a battle," was the calm reply. "That they are growing larger is easy to see, for they now cut a wide swath through the desert that is impossible to miss. Though no bodies have been found, there have been items of clothing and broken armaments such as the sutherlings and easterners use." Here, he smiled at Rogond. "You are welcome to try and approach them to confirm the rumors, if you wish."

Rogond shook his head. "No, thank you. I meant no disrespect," he said.

"This army…does it have a name?" asked Hallagond. "And the garments that have been found…are they of any special nature or coloring?"

"They are known simply as the Scourge," the man replied. "I have heard little concerning the nature of the garments. Few in these lands even know of them, and I pray that they do not learn. This is a terrible enemy, and so far none have had the power to stand against them." He lowered his voice, and Gaelen noted that his hands shook a little as he spoke. "They show no mercy to their victims. Make no mistake…they are capable of great evil. They thrive on the pain and suffering of others. Do all that you may to avoid them...their cruelty defies description!"

Gaelen and Nelwyn looked meaningfully at one another. They had quite enough dark enemies to deal with.

"Don't fear, my friend. It is always our aim to avoid pain and suffering. We thank you for the warning," said Gaelen. She looked now into the eyes of Bint Raed, knowing that her new friend was afraid for her beautiful homeland. *I don't blame you,* she thought, knowing only too well the dread that comes from putting one's own people at risk. The Company's course might well cross paths with the Scourge, and there was now a genuine risk of leading them to the Silver City, which would be a great shame indeed.

16
The Silver City

Bint Raed took Gaelen's words to heart, and in the morning she went to speak with Rogond. He had just finished sharpening a spear point and had started on a sword blade, nodding toward her in acknowledgment. She sat down beside him, drawing a deep breath. "Gaelen came to see me last night," she began. "She told me that you and the rest of the Company are wondering why I have been directing you as I have. Is this so?"

Rogond paused in his rhythmic stroking of steel upon stone to meet her gaze. "It is so," he said. "I have been wondering, but I assume there's a good reason for your choice to lead us here. You seem honest and steadfast, with a generous allotment of common sense. We all trust you. Is there some reason we should not?"

Bint Raed shook her head. "I don't believe so, yet there's a motive behind my actions…some might consider it self-serving. Gaelen urged me to come and explain to you, so that the Company may choose its path."

"What self-serving motive?" said Rogond, putting aside his sharpening-stone to give Bint Raed his full attention.

She drew another long breath and looked away. "I am not originally of the Ravani desert. I come from a fair city on the far southern coast. We call it the Citadel, but it is also called Dûn Arian, the Silver Fortress. Its history is both impressive and unique. I left it long ago because I wanted to see the wide world—a fool's errand, as it turned out. I was caught and sold into bondage after only a few years' wandering. I saw nothing appealing in the wide world, I have had quite enough of it, and I wish more than anything to return home. I've been leading the Company there because I can't make the journey alone, and there is no one else in whom I may trust. And now I hear of this terrible army making its way westward—straight toward the Citadel. Someone must warn them! I know this was not in your plan...I'm sorry."

Rogond pondered for a moment. "Don't be concerned, for you have done no harm to the Company. You have guided us well, and this place we're in is not a bad one. We are far enough away from Hassan that we need not fear. Put your mind at rest, and lift up your heart." Bint Raed looked gratefully up at him as he continued. "The Silver City…how far distant is it?"

"Very far, I fear...hundreds of miles from here. And they are difficult miles. It will not be easy to persuade your friends to accompany me over such an arduous path." She hung her head. "There is something else, Rogond—we of the Citadel are sworn not to reveal its location to any but the most trustworthy. The City has stood alone for nearly five hundred years, and for much of that time we welcomed any who would enter. But not all who came into our midst were of good heart, and eventually we became fearful of those who would destroy our way of life. We have worked long to preserve who and what we are, and to safeguard our legacy we are now somewhat wary of strangers. I am uncertain of how you would be received."

This set Rogond back for a moment. "But, we are trustworthy, none more so," he said. Then he remembered his brother. "At least for the most part…your people would have nothing to fear."

"I know," she replied. "Once I could have assured you that you would all be welcome, but it has been a long time. I don't even know for certain that the Citadel still stands. And I don't know how things may have changed in the many years I've been away."

Tears started in her eyes as she said this, and Rogond could almost feel the heart-wrenching desire to see her home again. "I understand your quandary, yet it must be dealt with," he said. "All in the Company must agree to this course, especially since it is long and difficult. Will you tell us the tale tonight?"

"I will," said Bint Raed. "I can assure you none will have heard it before. When I have finished, if you are not intrigued, then I will go on alone. I truly hope you will agree to accompany me, for my chances as a lone woman making that crossing are small indeed, and I am neither young nor strong. Yet I will attempt it, for at this point in my life I have resolved to see my home again, or die trying."

"Tell your tale then, and let's hope it will not come to that," replied Rogond, knowing that some members of the Company were fond enough of Bint Raed that they would never allow her to risk her life alone. He rose to his feet and stood before the little weaver-woman, offering one of his large hands in a gesture of reassurance. She took his hand and was comforted.

"Tonight you will hear the tale of the Silver City, where the glory of the lost realm of Tuathas still resides," she said. "We need to put some miles in before then, for it is a long tale, and you will not wish it to be interrupted." She smiled at him. "This is a great gift I will give to you, Rogond, for that which you thought lost will be found."

Rogond lifted both eyebrows at her. "Well, I'm certainly intrigued already. Until tonight, then." He bowed before her, put away his weapons, and went to assist Gaelen, who was seeing to the horses.

The Company gathered that night beneath the nearly-full moon. They had been promised a tale of great significance, and were prepared to be both enlightened and entertained. It was always a treat to hear a good story, and Fima, as always, had his ink and parchment ready, for he tried always to record what he heard. This evening's fare would surpass all his wildest expectations. This tale was not fiction, it was *history*. Rogond and Hallagond took special interest, as Bint Raed would bring forth a missing piece of the lost history of the Tuathar. They sat side-by-side, their nearly identical grey eyes bright with anticipation, as Bint Raed began to speak.

"I know you're likely to be familiar with the founding, waxing, and downfall of the great realm of Tuathas. You've learned of the ill fate of Duinar the Asarla, who was overcome by the wrath of the fire-mountains, and of the small remnant who escaped. I'm sure you know that the survivors founded the City of Dûn Bennas, as well as smaller settlements in the northlands. But you might not know of the fate of a ship that set sail from a different mooring, under the command of Salasin, the greatest lore-master of that time."

"I know of Salasin," said Fima. "He was thought lost in the cataclysm. Are you saying that he was *spared?*"

"There is no doubt of it," replied Bint Raed. "When it became known that the fire-mountains would arise in wrath, and that the doom of Tuathas was likely, Duinar the Asarla thought he could quell the mountain and spare his beloved realm. He assured his people that all would be well, and so it would have been, but the eruption was far more extensive than Duinar or any of his scholars had predicted, and he was overwhelmed. It is said that he died trying to stem the flood of molten rock that buried the capital city and set the forests aflame."

Everyone in the Company shuddered as they tried to imagine such a terrible thing, and even Bint Raed paused and bowed her head before continuing.

"Yet there were those who had prepared. The fire-mountains had arisen before, and when they first began to rumble, there were some who doubted the ability of Duinar to hold them back. They prepared ships so that some of their people might escape, and they loaded their animals with provisions and things precious to the people, as though to leave Tuathas. Many of their friends scorned them, for they obviously did not display the proper faith in Duinar, who had been sent by Aontar and was therefore infallible...alas that it was not so. Lore-master Salasin counted himself among them, for he had feared such a catastrophe for many years, and he knew what it would do to his beloved manuscripts and works of art.

As the ships prepared to bear the doubters from the realm, Salasin was dismayed, for even though he was offered a place on one of them, there was little room for the writings and artworks and other things precious to him. In his mind, the knowledge of Tuathas was its most vital and precious asset. Men could be replaced sooner than knowledge could be acquired.

Therefore, though Salasin was no mariner, he prepared his own vessel, placing into its hold as many of the writings and works of beauty that he could manage. You see, to Salasin, these things were more important than the lives of men. Yet many additional lives were spared because of him, for he carried nearly three score and ten of the most able and intelligent men and women of Tuathas, those who had not found places on the other ships.

"When the terrible doom fell upon Tuathas, Salasin escaped even as the others also set sail, though he was delayed. He left from a separate harbor, and was blown by a different wind. His ship was nearly lost in the dreadful rising of the sea, and those on board were helpless to guide it. It came ashore far from the lands that received the others—those who founded Dûn Bennas.

When Salasin's ship made landfall, only forty souls remained alive. The entry into the harbor that now guards the Silver Fortress can only be made during a tempest of wind and high water, for it is blocked by rocks that are impassable otherwise. There would be no turning back, for the ship was no longer seaworthy. Luckily, many of the great stores of writings and beautiful works were spared."

Fima was trembling with excitement, and Bint Raed could see that she would have no trouble in convincing him to go with her. "So...this place was founded upon written lore of Tuathas that was thought forever lost? I had heard rumors of such a place, but thought little of them."

"Yes, and most of those treasures still survive today, or at least they had when I left. Of course, the people have added treasures of their own making since then. When Salasin realized that he and his people could never leave their new home, they decided to build a Great City. This took quite a lot of time, for there were few people to do the building. Yet more came, and bit by bit our numbers grew. Salasin lived to be very old, though he died before the City was truly completed. Of course, it has grown since then, but at the heart of it is Salasin's great Library. It may be the most complete storehouse of the wealth of knowledge of Tuathas still in existence. That is Salasin's legacy." Bint Raed looked around, quite pleased to see the excited looks on the faces of the Company.

"This Great City...what is it like now, and what is its name?" asked Hallagond. This had opened up a whole new world for him.

"It is called Dûn Arian," said Bint Raed, who then spent the next several hours describing the City and its populace in detail. The people were very diverse, and all were welcome provided they obeyed the laws of the City and showed the proper respect for and devotion to learning. Much of the bloodline of the original founders remained; nearly all of the present families could trace their lineage directly back to Tuathas—but there were contributions to all families from other cultures and races. There was Ravani and Anori influence, as well as many others that had enriched the mixture.

"What about Elves? Are there Elves there?" asked Nelwyn in a hopeful tone.

"Alas, they have not made their way so far southward," said Bint Raed, to Nelwyn's obvious disappointment. "I wouldn't doubt that you three have already traveled deeper into these southern lands than any others of your kind." Nelwyn was crestfallen, but Bint Raed knew just how to cheer her.

"A great coastal forest surrounds the City, and the trees that grow within its walls are said to be among the tallest in the world. There are birds and flowers and fruits, and green things everywhere, and water aplenty...the sweetest and coldest you will ever have tasted." At the mention of tall trees, Nelwyn forgot all about her disappointment.

"The Citadel of Dûn Arian is a haven for all that is enlightened and fair," said Bint Raed. "There is music, art, science, and the study of numbers. Of course we are profoundly devoted to history and lore, as well as to poetry and philosophy. There is something to delight each one of you.

For all these years we have remained safe from enemies, guarded by the rocks and the harbor to the west, and the hard desert and hills to the east. Yet now I fear for our safety, for the Scourge is said to be making its way westward. I must return home, and soon, or my people will not be warned. They will never expect such an invading force, and the City may fall. That's why I have been leading you there."

"Completely understandable!" cried Fima, who found the thought of such savages destroying the lost lore of Tuathas unthinkable.

"Perhaps so," said Bint Raed, "yet you must now choose. I intend to return to my home and warn my people of the approaching Scourge. You are being taken farther and farther from your homelands. This will be a long journey, and it will not be an easy one. There are many perils to be faced, yet the reward will be great should we succeed in gaining the City. You must decide whether to go with me or not. You must tell me by tomorrow night. Then, if you decide against it, I shall leave you."

She sighed looking around at her companions. "I know that I should not try to sway your thinking, but know that regardless of your decision I will be trying to return home. My chances are very poor of making it on my own, and I need your help. Consider well." With those words, she turned and left them to their own counsel.

It was nearly dawn when Estle found Hallagond sitting alone; she had gone looking for him, sensing his disquiet. At first he did not appear to notice her, sitting upon the sand with his chin resting on his crossed arms, which were laid upon his knees.

"Are you all right, Al-amand?"

She wanted to place a hand upon his shoulder, but thought she might startle him. He was not particularly fond of being touched, preferring to maintain his distance, and in that he was more like the northern folk. Sutherling men stood very close together, and were constantly touching and embracing and kissing one another.

The Elves were even more distant. Estle smiled inwardly as she thought of Galador being thrown into a group of enthusiastic sutherling men, being kissed and embraced and surrounded until he could no longer bear the impropriety of it. Of course, Gaelen and Nelwyn would not need to bear such good-natured smothering, for to touch a woman not your own wife was strictly forbidden. *Probably a good thing for the sutherling men*, thought Estle, for they would not long intrude upon Gaelen's intimate space and survive.

Hallagond did not acknowledge Estle's question at first, for he was deep in his own thoughts. All at once he seemed to come to himself, and his eyes lost their faraway look. "What do you want, Estle?" he asked. "Have you come to share counsel, or to give it?"

She hesitated for a moment before replying. "To share, if it will aid you," she said. Estle had ever been his friend; she had come to his aid more than once, and he trusted her.

"Very well, then," he said. "When they ask you which course you will take, what will you tell them? Will you go your own way, or will you follow the weaver-woman?"

Estle sighed. "To explain my choice, I must reveal some of my past. I have never told you much of my history, for we have stayed away from matters of personal nature."

"Yes, and I have always appreciated your respect for my privacy," said Hallagond. "Yet I would know your thoughts in this matter, if you would share them."

"You are my friend, Al-amand, and I will not keep secrets from you, for I know you will respect them and safeguard them. The truth is that the Silver City was known to me before. My mother spoke of it when I was little. I wondered at first whether she was merely telling a tale to amuse me—a tale of a fair, enlightened realm where all things were good and beautiful—but then I saw in her eyes that it really existed. My mother knew of the Citadel because…because it was her home. She left it for love of a man, a Corsair, who was not welcome there. She could not return and face the disgrace of it, and so she never did. She died when I was young. Part of me has longed to find the Silver City ever since."

"Your father was a Corsair? Long had I suspected as much, especially when I look at your two half-brothers, Azori and Azok, but you are different from them, Estle. Your mother's nobility has left its mark on you...you have the eyes of the Tuathar." Hallagond looked deep into Estle's beautiful eyes; they had seen much of the ugliness of desperate men who had fallen from grace. *Does she not deserve also to behold beauty?* "Then you will go with the weaver-woman?" he said, his deep voice gentle and soft.

"I cannot help but feel that I am fated to do so. When Bint Raed began to tell her tale, it was as if she spoke only to me. My feet have been set on this course for a reason. You are at the heart of it; if you had not insulted Hassan I would not have been driven here." She smiled. "Obviously, your stupidity was driven by the hand of destiny, and I suppose I owe you my thanks." She kissed him lightly on one bristly cheek. "I wonder what it would be like to kiss an Elf? I have never touched my lips to the face of a clean-shaven man, though I suppose it would be similar to that."

Hallagond smiled in the dim light of dawn. "Have you ever kissed the face of a young child? I suppose the skin of Elves is similar, though if you decide to try it, I would suggest you avoid using Gaelen as your example," he said.

"Ha! As if I would lower myself to touch her," said Estle in mock indignation. She grew serious, turning to Hallagond and placing her right hand upon his arm. "You have not said what your course will be. Will you go with us, or will you turn aside? Your brother will not leave you in either case—that is certain."

Hallagond's forehead wrinkled, his eyebrows drawing together in an expression that looked almost like a man in pain. "I also would see this great sight, and it would be most enjoyable to learn more of the history of my people, but I don't know where my path should turn."

"Never have you known such things," said Estle gently. "Would you not remain with your friend Estle, who would rather not face this difficult journey without you? If we are fortunate enough to gain the City, I would share the wonders with you. I truly have no one else I can call friend, except my brothers, and I do not know whether I shall ever see either of them again. Will you not go for my sake?"

"You don't understand," he said, and the dread in his voice gave her pause. He turned to her in earnest, taking her right hand. "What I would say to you now you must not reveal. Do you agree?"

Estle nodded, dismayed by his urgency.

"Long ago I dreamed a terrible dream, more real than any in my experience. I was shown many things...much of death and of grief. It pains me even to recall it, and for a long time I had forgotten, but it has been slowly coming back. Estle, I saw the silver towers of Dûn Arian in my vision, and the City was burning. I heard the screams of the people as they died."

She felt him tremble as he said these words. "Was there anything more?" she asked.

"Yes. My father and brother came to me, and my brother said that I failed to turn the tide of destiny because I turned from it. The City fell because of me…because of my weakness." He looked hard into her eyes. "Do you not see why I am having a difficult time with this choice?"

"Yes, I see. It *was* a terrible dream, Al-amand, but a dream only, and though they are sometimes meaningful, they do not always come to pass. It's difficult to interpret this one, but it seems to me that you were meant to go with us to warn the people of the Scourge. Perhaps if you do not go with us, we will fail. If that happens, the Scourge will burn the City. Does that not seem most likely?"

"Perhaps it does, to those who know little of my history," said Hallagond bitterly, "for they would assume that I would aid in the defense of the City. They would not understand that my misguided and unwarranted pride has brought about the deaths of those nearest to me. They would not know of the shame I bear."

Estle soothed him with her hands and her voice. "They who truly know you know better. There is strength in you, though you would hide it with a veil of doubt. When I look upon you, I see a sad, strong man who has been made wiser by circumstance. I don't care what has gone before, or what terrible thing lurks in your past. Al-amand, you are not forsaken, for…for I love you. I have tried to deny it, but my heart has known it for a while now. I love you, man of Tuathas, and will stand by you. No shame can change that. Go with me to the Citadel. Your friends need you, and I would not leave you. Please go with me, that I may attain both of the desires of my heart. Do not make me choose between them."

She knew that he had not expected a declaration of love from her. He sat in silence, looking at the ever-brightening horizon.

"Have you nothing to say?" she said at last, in a steady voice that belied the fear in her heart. "Will you not answer?"

"You do not know all that I must consider," he said. "I beheld something else in my vision, something I have revealed to no one save Rogond. Gorgon Elfhunter is being drawn to the Company, somehow."

Estle's eyes grew round with fear. The tale of Gorgon had unsettled everyone who heard it, and she had no desire to ever cross paths with him.

"How do you know this?"

"Because he was there, standing in witness to the burning of the City. He warned me not to stand in his path. I don't know whether it is my destiny to thwart him, or to aid him unwittingly. I don't know what to do." They both heard the horses stirring, chortling at Gaelen as she approached them with their breakfast of boiled barley.

"Soon the others will be gathering to make their intentions known. I need to ponder this matter, at least until then," said Hal-lagond.

Estle knew he could sense her disappointment, feeling it in her hands, noting the sag of her shoulders out of the corner of his eye. "Know this," he continued. "Although I must keep my own counsel for the moment, you have aided me greatly. Know also that my heart will never leave you, even as my head will deny it. Take no dismay from my words as yet." He gave her a tentative smile, which she managed to return, even though they were both unsettled by what they had heard, and dreaded the choices before them.

Gorgon stood beside the Ravani road, his pale eyes squinting painfully at the horizon. The Vixen had called him here; no doubt she thought to lure him into harsh lands that would weaken him with the sun and the lack of water. "You think you've outsmarted me, don't you?" he whispered. "You think I lack the courage to chase you to the ends of the world? How foolish you are." He shifted inside his dark armor, which was heating up alarmingly. "I will travel by night," he muttered. "Darkness will be my friend, and I can hide from the sun."

Can you? Gelmyr's sarcastic voice raised the hair on the back of Gorgon's neck, though he did not actually see the Elf this time. *I certainly don't see many hiding places around here!*

"What would you know about it? Go away!"

You're afraid of the desert. You doubt your ability to cross it, which is one of the smarter thoughts you've had in a while. Ha! I don't blame you…nothing but heat and dry, you slimy creature of the cold and dark. Good luck, I say!

Gorgon roared into the empty air, then drew his blade and sank the edge of it into the stump of his left wrist. The pain brought back his resolve. It reminded him that Elves felt real pain—pain that he inflicted on them—and he had nothing to fear. The pain was about the only thing that would make Gelmyr go away once he appeared.

He stood in silence for a few moments, hoping the wretched Elf had left him alone again. He turned slowly around, seeing no one, hearing nothing but the wind hissing over the sand. He gave a satisfied grunt, licked the blood from his arm, and went to find shade.

"What do you want, Gaelen?" muttered Hallagond, thinking that an encounter with her was the last thing he desired at that moment. "You're not as stealthy as you suppose, you know. I heard you approach."

She lifted her chin in mock hauteur. "I was not attempting to be stealthy, Hallagond. Even if you would try to avoid me, I would find you. If you tried to run, I would catch you. There's no need to creep up on you unaware." She hunkered down before him in the sand; he was still sitting where Estle had left him.

He tried to look past her, but she kept shifting such that he could not avoid her gaze. At last he quit trying. *Where are Azori and Azok when I need them?* "I say again, Gaelen, what do you want?"

She hesitated for a moment. Hallagond didn't want her assistance, and had most certainly not asked for her advice, yet she needed to speak her mind. "Regrettably, you are on the verge of having to listen to more meddling sanctimony," she said. "Just know that it is well-intentioned. I realize you're struggling with the choice before you, and I promise to waste very little of your time."

"I've heard that before," growled Hallagond, "and you have since wasted quite a lot of my time. But the pressure of having pent-up opinions that you haven't aired might very well damage you, so say what you have to say."

Gaelen spoke her piece, and then left Hallagond to his thoughts. As he looked after her retreating back, he knew several things that he had not known before, and he now understood her a lot better. He knew that he had several friends among the Company, and that he could count her among them. And though he would not have predicted it, she had aided his choice. Gaelen was caught up in a dark fate of her own, even as he was, and his vision had made it clear that their paths would be woven together. Neither of them could know what the outcome would be. Hallagond stood upon legs that were shaky and stiff from sitting cross-legged on the sand, and then moved to join his companions. He hoped Fima had not eaten all of the breakfast sausages; he would need strength for the journey ahead.

The Company gathered solemnly around Bint Raed, and each made clear his or her intentions, beginning with Fima: "I have studied nearly every manuscript in Mountain-home, and have availed myself of the storehouses of lore in Dûn Bennas. Now I learn of another treasury of the lost writings of the Tuathar, and you ask me whether I desire to go there? I ask you, what other choice could be made? I will not rest until I have seen this great sight for myself."

Bint Raed smiled at him. "This is of no surprise to me, Fima Lore-master, for I saw this in your eyes last night. You are aflame with desire for learning. You will be most welcome in my City."

Estle stood forth next. "My mother spoke of the Silver City that was her home. I have always desired to see it. Now I will go with Bint Raed to safeguard it." Her eyes never left Hallagond's as she returned to her place, as though she could hold him with her gaze.

"How do you choose, Gaelen Fire-heart?" asked Bint Raed. "My city needs such warriors to defend her. Will you aid her?"

Galador smiled at this unwitting-yet-appropriate insult. No Elf enjoyed being compared with the legendary Aincor Fire-heart, viewed by many as the most disastrously stubborn, willful, selfish being ever to breathe Alterran air.

Gaelen took no offense. Everyone had expected her to leap to the defense of the Citadel, for she would surely not resist the offering of a new and preferably dangerous adventure. But she simply took one step forward, speaking to Bint Raed in a quiet voice. "You have said that there are no Elves in Dûn Arian. Are you certain?"

Bint Raed nodded. "Reasonably certain," she said. "There were none when I left years ago, and I do not know how they would have gained it since."

"Then I will go with Rogond Thaylon," she said. "I will follow wherever his choice leads him." Galador looked at her in surprise, as did Fima.

Rogond was not at all surprised. Gaelen would not take the responsibility for harm that might come to the folk of the Citadel should Gorgon follow her there—she would defer to Rogond's choice. Rogond was not sure that Gorgon would follow through these hard desert lands, where the heat and sun would not be his friend. He was a creature of shadow and darkness, of cool, damp mountains and underground deeps. Gorgon's strength came at least in part from the suffering of Elves. Surely the mere promise of vengeance upon one lowly Wood-elf could not sustain such a sun-hating creature across a thousand miles of desert, no matter how much he despised her. *Still...Gaelen and Gorgon share an unbreakable connection, and their hatred for one another is strong. There is real danger.*

He stepped forward. "I owe a life-debt to my brother Hallagond, and as such I cannot separate from him until that debt is repaid," he said. "But all should know that I would choose to follow Bint Raed to the Citadel, for it is worth safeguarding. A Ranger goes where he is most needed, and I am needed now to aid Bint Raed."

He paused for a moment, looking earnestly into his brother's eyes. "I cannot allow what has happened before to change what must happen now, and in the time to come," he said.

All eyes turned then to Hallagond.

"What will your course be, my brother?" asked Rogond in a very quiet voice. "Will you aid us, or will you turn from the only family you have left?"

Hallagond looked from Estle to Gaelen to Rogond. He drew a deep breath. "You seem to think I'm having difficulty with this decision," he said, as a crooked smile appeared on his face. "If you think that you're all going off without me to this storied realm, where a man could expect to live in comfort for the rest of his days, then think once more. I would taste the fruits, drink of the water, and languish in comfort as surely as any of you. You may count me among your companions, weaver-woman." He stepped forward to stand beside Estle, whereupon Rogond and Gaelen joined him.

Nelwyn and Galador looked at each other and shrugged. "We want to see the forest," they said simply.

Bint Raed cautioned them all: "Be aware that this path may be the hardest one you have ever taken. We will need to prepare for it, and prepare well. I will guide you to a place where we can make ready." Tears welled in her eyes. "You cannot know how grateful I am for all of you. May our journey be successful, with none of the Company lost. May we find the Citadel as fair as when I left it."

"Let's all drink to that," said Fima, passing around a flask of strong liquor that he had concealed on his person, so that everyone could have a share.

When Estle met Hallagond the next morning, she was shocked to see that he was clean-shaven. "So that you may answer your question without annoying Galador," he said. At first she stood staring at him with her mouth open. Then she burst out laughing, for Hallagond's face was brown only to the level of his upper lip. Below that, it was fish-belly white. When he caught sight of his own reflection, he could not help but laugh along with her. After all, it was only hair. It would grow back. "Well? Aren't you going to kiss your Elf?"

"Perhaps later," she said. "The sun is up, we have a journey to make, and I'm not ready to leave yet." Before she returned to her preparations, she leaned over and gave him an affectionate peck on the cheek, which pleased him a great deal.

The Company settled into its new purpose. It had been difficult not knowing where their paths would turn, merely wandering from place to place with no true direction, searching for someone that they might not find in lands they did not know, guided by a man they did not remotely trust. Once they had found Hallagond, things had improved.

Now they were focused on the single task of making their way to the Citadel to warn the people of the approaching Scourge. They absolutely trusted their guide, Bint Raed. Each had a compelling reason for traveling to the City—Fima to avail himself of the library, Nelwyn and Galador to see trees as tall as hills, Estle to see the home of her mother's people. Rogond wanted both to aid the Citadel and to take Gaelen to a place where Gorgon would be unlikely to follow. Gaelen wanted to lead Gorgon away from Elves, but where she would have assistance in defeating him.

Though he had joked about wanting to see this legendary land of leisure, Hallagond was still uncertain, but he took comfort in being with the Company. Their acceptance of him was reassuring. He would not leave Estle, at least not until the desire of his own heart became clear.

At Bint Raed's direction, they would now make their way to the desert city of Mumari, the last reliable water-source before beginning the difficult crossing to the Citadel. Here they would combine all their resources to purchase supplies, including dromadin. Horses could not carry enough on their backs, and they required too much water and feed.

Gaelen bristled at this, thinking Bint Raed meant to leave the horses. "I will not leave Finan behind," she said. "If we must buy more dromadin to carry food and water for the horses, then we shall."

"I would never suggest otherwise," said Bint Raed. "In fact, we will need to purchase another horse that I may ride; no horse should bear two riders on this journey."

Fima blanched at the thought of having to ride and control a horse by himself.

"Do not fear, Fima Lore-master," said Bint Raed with a smile. "We'll lead you on one of the dromadin. I think you will find the view quite interesting."

"Hmmm....no doubt of it," said Fima with a rather unconvincing smile.

He had been trying to add to his map, but had long since run off the edge of the parchment. He had turned it over and continued on the reverse side. "So, where is this city we are going to?" he asked Bint Raed. She studied his crude but effective rendering with interest before taking the quill and drawing in the city of Mumari. She sketched a couple of the tall, brush-like trees to indicate water there. Fima smiled. "Very good," he said. "Now can you draw the Citadel?"

"Only if you provide me with another parchment, unless you do not mind inaccurate distances," she replied. "On this parchment I can draw about two-thirds of the crossing, but no more."

"Oh, we cannot have inaccuracy—this map is for posterity. I intend to take it back north with me some day. Wait until Lady Ordath hears of my adventures! Not even she will have the knowledge that I will have gained. Ha! I'll see if I can locate another parchment."

As he searched, Bint Raed drew in as much as she could on the back of his original map. He returned with a new parchment in his hand, his smile fading quickly as he looked over her shoulder. "The dreadful mountains...great salt wastes...fire-sands...winds of death...plains of dire thirst? What sort of horrible place are you leading us into?"

"I told you the crossing would be difficult," she replied. "And just because those things are on the map does not mean we're going to travel through them. I wouldn't blame you for having second thoughts, if your courage wavers."

Fima drew himself up importantly and set his jaw. "The courage of a dwarf *waver?* Obviously you have never known many dwarves. I am more concerned for the safety of the rest of the Company. Elves are more delicate than they appear, you know. I wouldn't let a simple thing like...like fire-sands keep me away from that library!"

Bint Raed smiled at him. "I will never doubt you, Lore-master. And we are planning on avoiding the sands, if we can."

"Well, of course we are," said the dwarf. "But in the future it would be best that you not draw little death's-head symbols all over the map. It might discourage the others."

Bint Raed bowed and took the fresh parchment from his hand, and then sat down before a flat rock, spreading the parchment before her so that she could draw the remainder of the map as best she could recall it. "When we get to the City, you will find maps that are very accurate; some gave their lives to make them."

This was not encouraging, and Fima held some dread in his heart. Though he had joked about the delicacy of the Elves, he was not so certain of his own strength in making the crossing. He had found the journey quite taxing enough already, and things were now expected to get much worse. Fima was old, and was nearing the end of his lifespan. The poison Sajid had given him had taken some of his vitality; he was not the same now as he had been.

He drew a deep sigh. There was nothing to do for it now…he would find this great storehouse of lore, or die in trying. *A fitting end for a lore-master*, he thought, because once he learned of the existence of Salasin's library, he could not live happily until he had gained access to it.

Gaelen and Nelwyn had left the group and ridden ahead to scout the way, when Nelwyn noticed something dark upon the sand in the distance. "What's that?" she asked Gaelen, pointing to the darkness on the pale sand. They reined in their mounts, peering into the bright sun, Gaelen shading her eyes with her hand.

"I cannot tell from this distance," said Gaelen, her nose in the wind. "But I think it is something not long dead. The black is probably vultures or ravens…it's moving, anyway."

Nelwyn turned to her cousin. "Should we investigate, do you think?"

Gaelen considered. "I don't know why we should, but something compels me to do so, even though it will take us out of our way." Nelwyn, who felt the same compulsion, agreed. The Elves approached with caution; it took a while to cross the distance, and they both wondered why some dead thing would warrant so much of their attention.

As they drew nigh the dark object, all became clear. The ravens flew up, disturbed in the midst of feeding, when Gaelen approached. Finan was agitated, snorting and pawing the sand, shaking his head.

"Why does he act that way?" asked Nelwyn, who had rarely seen Finan agitated without cause. "Surely he has smelled death before."

"I'm certain he has," replied Gaelen, who was now close enough to get a good look at the thing in the sand. "He's upset because he already knows who the dead one is, and knows him as his enemy."

"What do you mean?" said Nelwyn as she rode closer. She looked down upon the small, ravaged object on the sand, and her eyes grew wide. She could not find her voice for a moment. When she did, she whispered a single word:

"Cuidag…"

Even in its half-eaten state, Sajid's head was recognizable to those who knew and hated him. The burn mark on his neck was still there, and he was not long dead. Someone had buried him up to his neck in the sand while he was still alive, even as the Company had found him long ago, only this time they had treated him with even greater cruelty. A half-full water-skin lay just out of reach of his cracked, fevered lips.

Gaelen shook her head slowly. "Well, Treacherous Guide...no tender-hearted Ranger to come to your aid this time, alas! I do believe Rogond would have dug the pit that buried you with his own hands this time. You have done much evil since we released you. My only regret is that someone else had the pleasure of placing you back where you belonged."

Nelwyn's blood burned hot in her face. She had endured more humiliation than anyone at Sajid's hands. "I share that regret," she said, her hands clenched upon her bow. She looked over at Gaelen. "I had once thought to spare the suffering of any living soul, yet upon Sajid I would have wished a long and terrible ending. This is darkness in my heart that I don't know how to remedy."

"There is the remedy," said Gaelen. "Look upon your enemy and be glad. He is vanquished. The ravens have taken his eyes, so I cannot read them, but I know he suffered greatly. His evil is ended. That should gladden your heart."

"Suffering should not gladden the heart, Gaelen, no matter how we might wish it," said Nelwyn. She was having some difficulty coming to grips with her dark feelings. "This is like…like eating something rich and sweet, but poisonous. The taste is irresistible, but the poison sickens your soul."

"There is only one remedy for such poison, and that is the sight of your vanquished enemy, that you know will bring no more evil among good-hearted folk. You are no better than the rest of us, Nelwyn… even the most lofty desire vengeance. No one is above such feelings. You are fortunate to have lived so long without tasting of this fruit."

Nelwyn looked at Gaelen, her eyes filled with tears. "I weep not for my enemy, but for the end of my innocence," she said. "How do you deal with such feelings? They twist like a knife in my heart."

Gaelen nodded, her expression cold. Her innocence had fallen long ago. "Here is how I deal with them," she said, mounting Finan and galloping some distance from Sajid's head. She charged it, drawing her bow, yelling a war-cry, releasing the arrow as she passed. The shaft disappeared into the sand just behind the oily tangle of Sajid's hair. She wheeled around and galloped back to stand before Nelwyn.

"I told him once that I would place a shaft between his worthless ribs, and I have now done so. I know he can never hurt me or my friends again, and I will pay no more heed to him than if he were a squashed spider beneath my feet. Try it and see."

Nelwyn did so, but she aimed for his throat, and the shaft struck with such power that the skull came partially away from his neck, lolling sideways onto the sand. She rode up to Gaelen, breathless with spent effort.

"Well?"

"I don't feel better. The spider is dead, and my arrows are pointless." She drew a long breath. "Nothing but a waste of good arrows."

"I intend to retrieve the arrows. Tell me what troubles you."

Nelwyn considered for a moment. "I just wish that…ah, it is nothing. It's not important."

"You'll have to do better than that," said Gaelen. "You can keep nothing from me, and you know it."

Nelwyn's eyes glittered. "Very well, then. See the true nature of your reputedly gentle, forgiving cousin! This wretch brought more humiliation to me than I thought I could bear, he does grievous harm to my friends—my family—and yet he dies alone, with no one to bear witness to his final loss of dignity. I didn't just want him dead; I wanted him shamed beyond words, even as I was. I wanted him to pay, and…and I wanted to *watch* him pay!"

"Bint Raed has said that you are a water-spirit," Gaelen answered. "Water may be just as destructive as fire when it is aroused to wrath. Your feelings are understandable, but ask yourself how you would have felt witnessing his end. I'm sure he babbled and pleaded with the ravens even as they plucked out his eyes. They do not wait for death to come to the helpless. What would you have done then?"

Without another word, she vaulted down from Finan's back and approached Sajid, pulling her arrow from the sand. "Leave mine," said Nelwyn. "I will never touch it again."

Gaelen nodded, swinging back aboard Finan, turning him back the way they had come. "We must tell the others what we have found. They will want to know."

Nelwyn did not answer, but stood for a moment, pondering Gaelen's question. *What would I have done? I would have put him out of his pain…no matter how much I hated him.* She turned and followed Gaelen back to rejoin her friends.

It was no surprise that Galador, Rogond, and Fima all wanted to bear witness to Sajid's remains. Rogond told the tale, and the entire Company loathed Sajid by the time they drew nigh what was left of him.

Rogond was first to approach. "A sad and undignified ending, to be sure. I'm certain he wishes that he had yet been alive when Nelwyn's shaft struck him; it would have taken him from his pain." He turned to regard Galador standing alone, his finely chiseled, strong face stony, his grey eyes expressionless. "Do you not wish to look upon your enemy, who is vanquished?"

"No, I do not," said Galador, "for I regret that he is dead by someone else's hand. Farewell, Cuidag. May you enjoy carrying your foul, deceitful head as you scuttle through whatever eternal torment awaits."

Galador had said all that was needed. Sajid's name was never spoken again by any of them. Rogond's final thought as he mounted Eros was that, in spite of the terrible trials put upon the Company, Sajid had unwittingly aided them. Without his treachery they would not have been led to Hallagond, and might have come to even more terrible trials in a fruitless search for him. Rogond inclined his head slightly to Sajid's remains in acknowledgment of this unwitting aid, but as he rode away he doubted it would be enough to save his enemy's wretched soul from darkness.

They approached the city of Mumari at dawn of the following day. It was a welcoming sight, with red dwellings built from stone carved from nearby ridges, the ever-present, odd trees that told of water, the streets just coming alive with colorful people. "I am looking forward to a bath and a good meal," said Estle as she rode beside Hallagond.

"I would agree," put in Gaelen. "It will feel so good to wash the dust from my face."

Estle gasped in mock horror, peering at her. "Oh, no, Gaelen… you mean to say that our desert dust has actually clung to your Elven face? How very *mortal* of you! I cannot see evidence of it, but surely you would be able to feel each and every grain of dust, unaccustomed as you are to its presence. We must find you some wash-water at once!"

Gaelen laughed. "Yes, and when I have finished with it, I will give it to you. It will do to strip the first layer of dirt from your poor, mortal self. After that you will need more...a *lot* more." She rode ahead as Estle grumbled, for her chestnut was not swift and could not vie with Finan, therefore she was left to mull over a thousand clever retorts. No matter; she would keep them for future use.

The people of Mumari were a varied and interesting lot. They seemed to be accepting of strangers, especially those with wealth to spend. Over the next few days the Company spent everything they had, selling all they could spare to buy what they needed. Only those things most precious to them would be kept. Yet when all was ended, it still would not be enough.

"We'll need more than this to provision ourselves," said Bint Raed. "Is there nothing more that we may use?" She had already sold the remainder of the fabric she had brought from the weaving-shed. Though it had brought a good price, she had been mildly disappointed that it wasn't more.

"We still need to purchase a horse, for Bint Raed must ride on her own. Malvorn will need to be traded, for he will not make the crossing. I worry also about Eros," said Gaelen.

"You're probably right about Malvorn, but you needn't worry about Eros," said Rogond. "Bint Raed says that our pace will be slower and less taxing to the horses because of the dromadin. She also said that one of the advantages of using dromadin is that they provide large areas of shade, especially when they are draped and laden. Eros can ride beside them in the heat. He'll be all right."

That still left the question of acquiring another horse for Bint Raed. Gaelen and Nelwyn went to the only horse-provider in the city; his prices were high and his stock unimpressive. "I do have one new animal, just acquired from some travelers who passed this way recently," he said, hoping to tempt them. "She is in rather poor condition, so I did not show her to you earlier, but she is improving and I think she may be to your liking. Come and have a look."

If the Elves had any hope of acquiring this animal for less money because of her poor condition, that hope vanished the moment Gaelen beheld her. "*Siva!*" she cried. "I have found you, my friend, my beautiful lady. Come here to me!" The sad, rather boney grey mare lifted her proud head, knowing Gaelen at once. She gave a soft whinny and trotted squarely up to stand before Gaelen, who stroked her face and rubbed her ears, to her delight. She appeared to be a different horse, a fact that was not lost on the horse-provider.

"As you can see, she is a fine animal. It appears that you two are already acquainted." The smile died on his lips when he saw the look in Gaelen's eye as she turned to face him.

"How did you acquire her? She was stolen from me, and not purchased, thus you have no right of ownership. We found the thief dead in the desert. This animal must be restored to her rightful owner."

"You are obviously not from these lands," said the merchant, "or you would know that what is found in the desert becomes the property of the finder. I paid good money for this mare, and I will not give her away."

"I will give you what you paid, plus some for your trouble, but no more," said Gaelen, as though that should settle the matter. "You should take it, and be done. Either that, or you will give her to me willingly. If you do not believe it, wait and see."

"What are you doing, Gaelen?" whispered Nelwyn. "We dare not make enemies of these folk...you must not raise your hand to them."

"I will not need to. He won't want to keep Siva once I have finished with him. Let's see if he will be reasonable."

The horse-merchant looked sidelong at Gaelen. He decided to try to bluff her. "I'm sorry, but this horse is rightfully mine. You want her, I own her. If you want her, you must pay. Ten gold pieces and she is yours."

Gaelen had lived among the Ravani-folk long enough to know that this was exorbitant. "Very well, I see you will take me for a fool, and will not be reasonable. Now you force my hand."

She turned to the grey mare standing placidly beside her, and spoke to her in Elvish. "Siva! That man is my enemy! He is *our* enemy!" Siva did not hesitate, flying at the merchant with her teeth bared. He vaulted over the rail just in time, as she aimed a deadly kick in his direction. She turned to face him, pacing back and forth, her head high, her ears flattened, her silky grey nose pulled into several fierce-looking wrinkles.

"She will do the same to any others who try to purchase her; I will make certain of it," said Gaelen calmly. "Now let's be reasonable, and begin again. You bought an animal that was stolen, and should not have come to you in the first place. I will compensate you for your loss, but that's all I will do. Do you agree?" She spat into her right hand, as she had seen the Ravani-folk do, and then extended it. The merchant drew a deep sigh, but another menacing look from Siva decided him. He spat into his own right hand, and slapped his palm down upon Gaelen's. This sealed their agreement and he would not break it.

Gaelen turned then to Siva. "Stand down, and come to me." Siva's ears came forward and she returned to stand beside Gaelen, who drew forth what few coins she still possessed and gave them to the merchant.

After counting them, he actually returned one. "I paid very little for the mare," he said, "and when I make a bargain, I honor it."

Gaelen bowed before him. "Then perhaps my cousin and I will do you a favor. We have talents in the taming and training of horses that may be of use to you. I offer my skills as a token of good will."

"A *female* horse-breaker? Never mind…I accept," said the merchant. "There is always a need for a horse-breaker. Come back at sundown and I will have a task for you."

Gaelen and Nelwyn left with Siva; Bint Raed would have a worthy mount indeed. They would make a friend of the horse merchant before all was ended, and when Hallagond heard their tale he nodded in approval.

"Well done, Gaelen," said Fima. "You are learning. You're far from being a shrewd bargainer, but you are learning."

Nelwyn laughed. "No, her bargaining was done more, ah… directly, I would say." She could not forget the sight of the startled horse-merchant vaulting over the rail just in front of Siva's teeth.

"Of a choice between shrewd and direct, I suppose I must choose direct, for I doubt that I shall ever be shrewd," said Gaelen, to which all would agree.

Gaelen and Nelwyn returned to the horse merchant at sunset, whereupon they spent several useful hours lending their skills as they could. They tended lame legs and bruised feet, as well as difficult temperaments. They brought Malvorn with them, requesting that the merchant, whose name was Makkbah, trade for a desert-bred animal that Hallagond could ride.

"His coloring is unfortunate," said Makkbah, eyeing Malvorn and spreading his hands. "There are many who believe that animals colored black have been marked as unworthy. He will be difficult to sell, as I will need to find a buyer who does not hold this belief."

Nelwyn was examining the only likely candidate in the yards, a chestnut with very high white legs and a glaring white face that was blistered by the sun. "What about this one? With those awful white legs he will not bring much. Is it not also your belief that such an animal is of little worth?"

They all knew this—white markings would burn and peel in the sun, and white legs were especially disastrous. They would become so irritated from dust and sweat that the horse might become lame. Nelwyn thought she could cope with this; the gelding was strong and looked as though he could carry Hallagond with no trouble. She turned to Makkbah. "What say you? Our worthless black horse traded for your worthless white-legged one?"

Makkbah considered, looking Malvorn up and down. The horse was travel-worn, but he was strong. And there were buyers who would accept him regardless of color, for aside from a bit less heat-resistance it would not affect his ability to work. The white legs, on the other hand, might well make the other horse very lame...already he was showing the signs. "Very well," he said. "But I will have you and your companion working for me until dawn, in addition. Do you agree?"

Gaelen looked over at Nelwyn in approval. This was a good trade.

In the morning they led their new horse back to their encampment, and presented him to Hallagond. "I think you should call him Talba, for his white feet," said Gaelen, or perhaps Derrin, the red?"

"I like Derrin," said Hallagond. "But how will I keep his poor skin from cracking and blistering in the sun? He already has scars on the back of his ankles, with more coming."

"Bint Raed can weave a shield for his face, and we can use Shiva's salve," said Gaelen. "I can purchase ointment to aid him; he will stay sound as long as we use it. Nelwyn has made a fine trade, don't you agree?"

Hallagond swung onto the red horse's back and rode him for a short distance to try him out. "He seems stiff, Gaelen," he said as he dismounted.

"Not to worry. The salve will soon put him right. He'll run swiftly and well in a few days, you'll see. Now at least our band of horses is in order."

Even with Nelwyn's good trading and the return of Siva, the Company would need more provisions than they could afford. Folk in this place were more frugal than in the Sandstone. Gaelen favored them each night with beautiful singing, but she received very little for it other than enthusiastic applause. They would need to find another way.

Hallagond drew forth his last few coins, asking that Gaelen, Nelwyn, Fima, and Estle give theirs as well.

"I'm going to try to grow this at the gaming tables," he said. "I know some of you don't approve, my prudish brother Rogond in particular, but this is a skill I may lend to the greater good."

"Sounds like a good excuse to me," said Estle. She would enjoy an afternoon of watching Hallagond test his ability, and she followed him to the gambling-house.

It was typical of such establishments, thick with smoke and the smell of drink, ringing with voices that were both cheerful and ill-natured, yet neither Estle nor Hallagond expected to find what awaited them. They stood frozen in their tracks as a familiar voice greeted them from behind, followed by the equally familiar laughter of a dozen rough men.

"I was wondering how long it would be before you found your way in here!"

Hallagond turned to see Azori and Azok, the bandit brothers, lifting their tankards to him and smiling sinister smiles.

Estle, who had not expected to see either of her half-brothers again, was astonished and not a little alarmed. What were they doing here? What would this mean to the Company? Even as she smiled and moved to embrace Azori, she wondered. They would all find out soon enough.

"Ah, Al-amand, I see your taste in traveling companions has improved," said Azori good-naturedly, drawing Estle into his lap over her mild protestations. "What in the name of heaven happened to your beard?"

"What are you *doing* here?" asked Hallagond.

"We followed you, of course. A man has only one sister, after all," said Azori, placing a full tankard in Estle's hand. "You really think I would allow you to run off into the barren wastes with her, and not pursue you? What an absurd notion."

I had forgotten how devoted he is to her, thought Hallagond. Azori may have been unscrupulous, pitiless, and thoroughly dangerous, but he was fiercely loyal to his family.

"Do you know the tale of how we came to be driven here?" asked Hallagond.

"Something about Hassan the Giant, and your insulting *his* sister, I believe," replied Azori. "Most unlike you, Al-amand. Whatever could you have been thinking? It must have taken quite a lot of drink to allow you to be so foolish. At any rate, I have come to inform you that I have fixed things with Hassan's family. You may return to the Chupa if you wish."

"How did you fix them?" asked Estle, afraid of what she might hear.

Azori grinned at her. "My teeth are bigger than theirs."

"No doubt," said Hallagond, glad that he did not number among Hassan's relatives. Azori was a force to be reckoned with—he was worth three ordinary men in a fight. And Azok, his brother, was even more formidable, though less intelligent. It was small wonder that Estle handled herself as well as she did, with these two instructing her.

"So, that's settled then," said Azori jovially, refilling his cup. "We'll return home as soon as we are ready to make the journey. I'd like to remain here for a few days and regain my strength, not to mention avail myself of the wonders of this fair city."

Estle knew what that meant; Azori and his men would stay long enough to pick as many pockets and gamble for as much gold as they could before moving on. She looked over at Hallagond, whose expression indicated that he wasn't happy with this unexpected complication of his life.

"Nothing is settled," she said, pulling herself free of Azori's possessive grip. "Do you hear me? *Nothing.* You want to go back? Do it, then—the sooner, the better!" She walked briskly through the doorway, wondering what in the world she would do if Azori decided to take her with him whether she liked it or not.

Hallagond took the bridge of his nose hard between his thumb and forefinger, trying to quell the headache forming behind it. *Azori loves his sister, but it's more than that. He's up to something—he's always up to something.*

17
The Crossing Begins

It fell to Estle to break the news of Azori's presence to the Company. Her friends reacted with varying degrees of dismay, wondering how this sudden appearance of a group of criminals would affect their plans.

"Well, he *is* my brother, and I love him," said Estle. "He usually behaves himself where I am concerned."

"I'm sure," said Rogond. "But what about the rest of them?"

"They respect Azori, and they fear him," said Estle. "I wouldn't worry about them."

"Your eyes tell a different story," said Gaelen. "You seem light-hearted and unconcerned, yet you are holding back. Tell us what we need to know, not what you think we want to hear."

Estle sighed. "Very well, since you insist. My brother is a bad enemy, and he has no sense of humor where I'm concerned. If he decides to take me back with him, he will. Should he decide to follow our Company, believe me, you will not prevent him. That's the hard truth."

"He will stand to gain nothing from following us," said Galador. "We travel a hard road."

"He would gain access to the Silver City!" cried Bint Raed. "That must not happen."

Estle looked hard at Bint Raed. "Forgive me, but my brother's band of thieves will have little impact compared with the Scourge. I'm thinking your well-kept secret City will be secret no longer in any case. Here is something else to consider—Azori is very wealthy, and good to have as an ally should there be trouble along the way. We might actually turn this event to our advantage. Can we agree to at least keep an open mind for now?"

"We can," said Gaelen, "but we don't have to be happy about it."

Hallagond spent the next several days at the gaming-tables on the pretext of increasing the Company's wealth so they could acquire provisions for the journey. It was helpful to have Azori around. He would stand behind Hallagond's opponents and intimidate them, for he let it be known that neither he nor his brother Azok would tolerate any underhandedness. "While I am of a moderate temperament, my brother is not," he said. "I would surely hate to be caught cheating and have Azok learn of it... truly, he is a humorless fellow!" This strategy ensured that Hallagond was the only one cheating with any regularity, except for Azori himself.

Estle convinced her friends that the best way to allay their fears concerning Azori's men was to get to know them. "They're really not all that bad," she said. "Some of them are quite intriguing, hailing from various faraway lands. They have asked to be introduced to you, and I have promised you will let them come to your evening fire...tonight."

"I just love it when people promise that I will do things," Gaelen muttered. "Perhaps you should speak only for yourself the next time."

"My apologies. You said you'd keep an open mind. I would have thought you willing to try to make this bad situation better," said Estle.

Rogond put a hand on Gaelen's shoulder. "They will be welcome."

The bandits were an interesting, if unsavory, lot representing several races, including four Anori easterners, five sutherlings, one northlander, and, of course, Azori and Azok. It was an interesting demonstration of tolerance—most sutherlings did not get on well with easterners, and so on—these men were united under the purpose of taking from others while doing as little real labor as possible.

The evening circle grew from eight to twenty, with the bandits sitting around one side of the fire and the Company around the other. Introductions were made and tales were shared, as they would be for several nights to come. Those who did not tell tales entertained the assembly with feats of strength, agility, and skill at arms.

Although they showed proper appreciation for the attributes of Azori's men, the Elves remained politely passive and silent. They did not wish to gain the attention of such less-than-honorable fellows, especially when the wine and ale began to flow.

As the men drank they grew loud and discourteous, making comments in various tongues that neither the Elves nor Rogond would understand. The shadowy looks and gestures directed at Gaelen and Nelwyn said all that was needed. Estle was not made the object of such comment for fear of the wrath of her half-brothers, but even she felt uncomfortable at such times.

The Elves, who did not enjoy the company of drunken men, would take their leave, preferring to sit alone beneath the stars. Rogond would bid goodnight as well, for though he knew that she could look after herself, he did not wish to leave Gaelen alone.

Hallagond spoke with Azori one evening, when the wine had flowed very freely and the bandits had gotten quite out of hand. "Can you not control them? My companions are refined, courteous folk, and it pains me that they cannot suffer your company. They have interesting tales to tell, and they have become my friends, in a way. Can you not at least suggest that your men remain civil?"

Azori looked curiously at Hallagond as though he had recently sprouted a third eye in the center of his face. "My, my…aren't we in possession of delicate sensibilities these days! Not so long ago you would have been one of those most in need of civility. Tell me, Tall One, what is it that has changed you? Is it the association with the Elves? I'm surprised they tolerate you at all. Perhaps it's the influence of your brother, for he is about as true-hearted and idealistic as anyone I have met. What a deluded dunce! I'm surprised you haven't managed to teach him how real men behave."

Hallagond felt a surprising, momentary twinge of outrage in Rogond's behalf, but it passed quickly. He smiled at Azori. "My brother was raised among Elves, and it will take a while to undo what they have done. Give me a little more time. I'll bring him around."

Azori was amused. "There'll be no bringing *that* one around, Alamand. Save your breath."

Hallagond smiled wryly back at him. "You underestimate me. Why, only last week I nearly had him convinced to enter the gaming-house...he almost set foot inside the door! But then he remembered that he had not washed himself in nearly a day, so he rushed back to rectify it. After all, his little She-elf must not think him unclean!"

"Waste of water, if you ask me," said Azori, stretching his powerful arms and yawning, releasing quite an impressive quantity of unwashed man-stench. "I'm very glad that I don't need to impress anyone but myself, since I'm quite favorably impressed with myself already!"

Hallagond reflected that Azori was likeable under three conditions: if you were not his enemy, if you had nothing he wanted, or if you had something he wanted but he considered you to be more formidable than he cared to cope with, which was rare.

Azori's expression grew serious. "You are returning with us, of course…along with Estle? I'm afraid she has taken a fancy to you, and if you do not return, then she may not. That would displease me greatly, not to mention Azok would not take it well at all. I think you need to come back to your real friends before these folk exert too great an influence." He clapped Hallagond on the shoulder. "Just think on it, is all. You're free to do as you choose, as always."

Hallagond understood Azori's meaning clearly, and it wasn't making his choice any easier. *Is he threatening me? Of course he is. He says I am free to choose, but if Estle stays with me, and I go with Rogond, what will he do then?* He decided it was better not to think about it.

On the following evening, one of the easterners stood forth to tell a tale. His name was Ikari, and he was of undetermined age, for he had the smooth features typical of his folk. His eyes were black and difficult to read, and there was an air of mystery about him that he tried always to perpetuate. He dressed entirely in black, and was often accompanied by a glossy black crow that sat perched on one shoulder. Named Karatsu, it was clever and raucous with an unusual fondness for shiny objects. Ikari had taught it to steal such objects and return with them, whereupon they would be traded for a favorite treat. He had gained a few very valuable trinkets that way.

This night he shared his people's view of the creation of the world, a story involving four dragons: Earth, Wind, Fire, and Water. They spawned the Elves, who were named Ashahi, or Beings of Light, and the Demons of Darkness, named Osha, presumably Ulcas. The Osha sometimes assumed other forms, including those of Ashahi, thus it was difficult to tell which were truly good and which were only pretending.

Men were created last, with the intention that they should hold dominion over the world. They were given special abilities by the four dragons. Those who received enlightenment from the dragons of wind and water were especially perceptive; they could see through disguises and expose the demons. Ikari looked meaningfully at the Elves. "I am such a man. I can see through any veil of deceit." Then he turned to the remainder of the circle. "Can any of you know for certain that these are *truly* Beings of Light?"

"Do you dare suggest that we are anything else?" asked Galador, rising to his feet. He had heard quite enough of this nonsense. "Your tale would be far more impressive if the dragons conferred the ability to see into the hearts of men, and tell which were true and which were given over to darkness. One certainly cannot tell it from their smiling faces."

Ikari's hand strayed to his waist, toward a hidden dagger, and this did not escape Gaelen's sharp eyes. "Stay your hand, Anori-man!" she said in a loud, clear voice. She already had a blade in her hand.

"No one will cast a blade at anyone this night," said Azori in a commanding tone. "Not in front of my sister. This will remain a friendly gathering…or *else!* I have promised Estle that we will all behave ourselves, and therefore, Ikari, you must apologize for insulting the Elves. Galador should acknowledge his quick temper, and apologize to Ikari for interrupting him. Go on now, both of you."

Nelwyn laid a soft hand on Galador's shoulder, whispering in his ear. "Go on, my love, and make peace with him. I know why you are so dismayed, but you must make peace for the sake of the Company. Your friends will not think less of you. When you have finished, we will take our leave and roam the starlit sands together."

Galador rose and reluctantly approached Ikari. They stood like a pair of large cats—each appeared to be ready to spring upon the other. "My apologies for offending you," said Ikari, his black eyes devoid of expression. "Surely you can understand why I find it difficult to trust one such as you."

The Elves had long warred with Anori-men, some of whom had been known to ally themselves with Lord Wrothgar. Galador had not forgotten it. "I regret interrupting your tale," he replied in a tone that was most unconvincing. "Pray continue, so that others may enjoy its conclusion." Ikari bowed stiffly, and resumed his telling, but Galador would not stay to hear it.

The following morning the Company breakfasted together, all save Hallagond. Estle had gone looking for him, returning to report that he was ill, and not in the mood for breakfast. The past night's tale-telling had gone on well into early morning, but by then the only ears still sober enough to hear were those of Gaelen, Rogond, and Estle.

Fortunately, Fima had fallen asleep while he was still only lightly intoxicated, snoring softly beside Gaelen, from whom he had extracted the promise to record any tale that he missed. "I don't think you will find much of worth there," she told him as he passed her a plate of sausage and a tasty little cake made with honey and nuts.

He perused her notes with some interest. "I don't know which is more entertaining...your outlining of the tales or your commentary on the ones telling them." He turned the page. "Nice renderings. I would suggest we keep these to ourselves, as they are somewhat unflattering."

He handed the parchment to Rogond, who smiled at the wonderful sketches Gaelen had made of Azori's men. One was depicted with the ears of a jackass, and another with a pig-snout. Apparently, the story being told at the time had not held her interest sufficiently.

Estle looked over Rogond's shoulder, smiling at the drawings. She had to agree with Gaelen once in a while. Estle was a rough woman, but she rarely drank to excess; it took her wits and made her vulnerable. She didn't like it when Hallagond drank so much. He had managed to remain sober for a long while, until last night. Her thoughts were troubled—was he reverting to his old ways? *Does this mean he will return to his old life among the bandits, and not make the crossing to the Citadel? If that is his choice, could I leave him behind?*

Estle knew that Hallagond was torn by shame, that he harbored a dark thorn of guilt in his heart for something he had done in the past. He would not speak of it, but she could see it sometimes. She heard it in the false bravado he cloaked himself with—saw the pain in his eyes when she asked him about his life in the north. The arrival of his overly-honorable brother and his "perfect" companions hadn't helped...they had made things worse.

She knew that he had come to the desert to hide—to lose himself. Now Rogond had forced him to try to "find" himself. It wouldn't surprise her if Hallagond ran away again, and following Azori would be the perfect way to do it. *What will I do then? He has drowned himself in a drunken stupor…this does not bode well.*

Unfortunately, Gaelen chose that particular moment to comment on Hallagond's "illness."

"I would suggest that he needs medicine, but I suspect he has had too much of it already," she said, winking at Fima.

"There is no denying that, Elf," said Estle in a chilly voice. "Yet you do not know what drives him…you do not understand the battle he fights. I am fighting now, too—I fight for his life. You will have to help me fight for him if you want him. There is no humor in this situation."

"He drinks far too much," said Gaelen. "There is a remedy for that."

"Not an easy one," retorted Estle. "Words from the mouth of a Wood-elf, who could drink a whole cask of wine and not feel it, no doubt. Tell me, Gaelen, have you ever been drunk in your life?"

"You should see her after she has been at the honey-jar," said Fima helpfully.

"I'm serious," Estle snapped. "Have you ever felt real sorrow, or genuine shame, or profound regret? Until you have, you cannot understand the need to drown them with drink."

You cannot possibly fathom the sorrow and regret I have felt, thought Gaelen, placing her breakfast-plate calmly on the ground. "This is not about me, or the nature of drink. You are fearful of losing the one you love. You do not wish to abandon your quest, nor would you leave Hallagond, for you genuinely fear for him should he turn from this path. I understand—I have observed men long enough to know that there are many reasons to drink, with different results that are hoped for. You're right…this is a moment of crisis for him. Yet have faith, for he has been called to a higher purpose. He will not turn." Even as she spoke the words, she prayed that they were true, for should Hallagond turn from the quest he would force a nearly impossible choice upon Rogond.

"And who is this Elf, who concerns herself with my choices?" came a bleary voice from behind. Hallagond had joined their circle after all, and now he sat down beside Fima with some effort. He picked up Gaelen's breakfast plate, eyeing it with interest.

"So, you were not as ill as we supposed," said Fima in a jovial voice that was far too loud.

"Please, my good dwarf," whispered Hallagond, wincing. "My ears will be somewhat sensitive for a while this morning." He paused in his perusal of Gaelen's breakfast. "What are you all staring at?"

His eyes were red, his face filthy and covered with stubbly dark whiskers, his hair uncombed and matted. *Actually, you look terrible, but it is very, very good to see you,* thought Gaelen. She wanted the matter settled then and there, addressing him with her customary directness. "What is your choice, then? Will you return with your bandit friends, or will you come with us to the aid of the Silver City?"

Hallagond took a mouthful of sausage and cake. "I said I would go with you…do you doubt my word? I told you before, I very much desire to see this place of comfort, where people have such an easy life that they can afford to spend each day in endless studying. Sounds like the perfect place for a lazy sod like me." He looked sidelong at Rogond. "Besides, I can't let my innocent little brother face such hardships without me, not when he is so woefully unprepared to deal with them." He took another great mouthful of food, as though what he had just said was of no consequence.

Estle knew better. "What will you tell Azori?"

"I would sooner ask that question of you, for he expects you to return with him as well," said Hallagond. "Truly, I'm surprised he went to all this trouble, though I know that he and Azok love you and would die to protect you. I expect you are the only thing they would die to protect, other than themselves."

"You will both need to speak with him, then," said Gaelen, who apparently held the mistaken idea that she was still part of the conversation. Both Estle and Hallagond looked at her curiously for a moment. "Is that not so?" asked Gaelen, "Or were you planning to spirit yourselves away by dark of night, without telling him?"

Hallagond and Estle went silent for a moment before bursting out laughing. Hallagond immediately regretted this, holding his aching head with both hands, but he could not help himself.

"Oh, yes! We'll surely be able to escape notice with our caravan of dromadin and our beaming scarlet Elf wearing her fire-cloak," said Estle.

"Are you quite finished?" asked Gaelen, after the laughter subsided. "I ask you now, when will you tell Azori? I will go along to aid you, if needed."

This set Estle to laughing again. Hallagond, unfortunately, was beginning to look rather green. "Oh, thank you, Gaelen. You'd be of *great* help, I'm sure," said Estle, rolling her eyes.

Gaelen did not take notice; she was staring in fascination at Hallagond's face, which was now the color of grass in late autumn.

"Come, my brother, before you treat these Elves to a sight that I doubt they will have seen before," said Rogond, helping his brother to his feet and half-dragging him behind a nearby dwelling, apparently just in time. Fima began humming considerately, but it was not enough to prevent the strange, deep liquid belching sounds from reaching them. It sounded like someone had thrown a small pot of stew onto the ground, which, in a way, someone had. Gaelen and Nelwyn looked at each other and shrugged. Men did many things that were disgusting.

"To answer your question, Gaelen, I don't know when Hallagond is planning to inform Azori, and though I appreciate your offer of aid, it will not be needed," said Estle.

"If I'm not mistaken, we plan to remain here only a day or two longer," said Gaelen. "You will need to make peace with your brothers before then." She turned to leave, but looked back over her shoulder just in time to witness Estle making silly faces at her back.

Gaelen suppressed a smile. "As for the answer to your question of whether I am capable of feeling the effects of too much wine, it depends," she said.

"On what?" asked Fima, who had never witnessed real drunkenness in any Elf, and did not think it possible.

"It depends on the wine," said Gaelen, just before she retreated to the horse-yards, pausing first to collect what still remained of her breakfast.

Hallagond spent much of the day sleeping and regaining his strength. When he came to the fireside that evening, his friends were relieved to see that his face was of normal coloring and, in fact, he looked quite hale.

"I am nearly starving," he said enthusiastically, lifting the lid of an enormous iron pot that was simmering over hot coals. What he saw transported him with delight. "Laffas! I have not tasted this in months. What perfect nectar for a starving man."

"I'm glad you approve," said Estle, who was one of the few that could actually prepare the dish properly. "Regrettably, you'll need to starve for a while longer, as it is not yet ready. The peppers have not yet turned black enough. Have some flatbread while you wait."

Hallagond sat down between Fima and Bint Raed, who handed him a small piece of leathery flatbread made from wheat, barley, and sunflower. It tasted delicious, though it would be easy to break one's teeth on it. Dromadan milk was very rich, and made beautiful creamy butter. Hallagond was soon quite content to wait for his favorite dish.

Estle declared the laffas ready to serve just as Gaelen and Nelwyn appeared. "And where are our bandit friends?" asked Nelwyn, secretly thankful that they were nowhere in evidence. Estle looked meaningfully at Hallagond.

He nodded before answering. "They have decided to leave us to ourselves tonight. I asked them if they would not mind feasting on their own, giving you and your friends a rest from their no doubt well-intentioned but perhaps excessive…ah, enthusiasm."

"You mean their drunken riot?" said Galador.

Hallagond ignored the comment. *He had better find his good humor somehow, for things are about to get a whole lot worse in his orderly, courteous world. Better to allow him to enjoy a last meal in peace.*

"Let's all eat of this wonderful laffas. Estle went to a great deal of trouble to make it." He picked up a large clay bowl and moved to stand by the iron pot, waiting.

Estle served him a heaping bowlful, and he happily returned to his place beside Fima. "What, exactly, *is* that?" asked the dwarf, peering curiously at the dark, steaming concoction.

"It's a kind of Ravani pepper-stew," he replied. "Not for the faint-hearted, though, I warn you."

Fima began looking around for a spoon, but found none.

"No, Fima…you eat laffas like this, with your fingers," said Hallagond. "Let it cool for a few minutes before you try." He demonstrated, using the three middle fingers of his right hand, scooping a quantity of the lumpy, blackish-red stew into his mouth, whereupon he closed his eyes with pleasure.

Everyone had now been served; it remained only for them to taste the laffas. The Elves would not use their fingers, preferring instead to use their flatbread as a scoop. Gaelen sniffed at her bowl, wrinkling her nose as the heated vapors assailed it. "This is very, very spicy," she said.

"Yes," said Estle, "it contains six different kinds of peppers, all of which I was lucky enough to find here. It also has many different lentils and beans, rice, and three different meats. It will both warm you and fill you quickly. Try it!"

The three Elves looked at one another, lifted their flatbread in unison, and simultaneously took a bite. They chewed thoughtfully, savoring the taste, and finally swallowed it. They looked at Estle, who had been expecting them to choke on the searing hot spices. "This would taste fine, were it not completely overpowered by the peppers," said Nelwyn.

"Indeed," said Gaelen. "Why do men seek to prove their mettle by consuming spicy-hot foods? I have never understood this. Far better to develop discriminating taste than to paralyze the inside of your mouth and throat with pepper. Though this is by no means unbearable, and there is an undercurrent of very fine flavor."

"True," said Galador, looking over at Estle. "I expect it is an acquired taste."

Estle rolled her eyes heavenward. If she had hoped for a significant reaction from the Elves, she would be denied. Fima, however, would not disappoint her. Neither would Rogond or Bint Raed. Their eyes and noses were streaming, and they were gulping water even as they asked for a second helping.

Rogond looked over at his brother, who was likewise drinking large amounts of water. "A good thing your stomach has settled since this morning. This would be a lot more painful coming back up."

"Indeed," said Hallagond. "Bringing up laffas would be no laughing matter." He was rewarded for this terrible comment by having at least three pieces of flatbread thrown at him.

Once they had partaken of food and drink, the Company turned their attention to Hallagond, who had risen to his feet. "I have something important to tell you," he said. "Although it is perhaps not the best news, you must remain of open mind, for some good will come of it, I'm sure."

He swallowed in a dry throat, wondering how to break the news to them. He had gone with Estle to see Azori not two hours earlier, and the meeting had not exactly gone as he had hoped. He winced inwardly, remembering the expression on Azori's face as his sister told him everything he didn't want to hear.

"We need to talk," she had said.

"Well, what is there to talk about?" said Azori, patting the cushion beside him. "Sit down, then, and we'll talk, though my mind is made up already concerning you."

"That's what we need to talk about," said Estle, folding her arms. "If you don't mind, could you ask your…um, 'associates' to leave us alone? I feel somewhat vulnerable with them lurking in dark corners."

Azori dismissed his men with a wave of his hand. "All right, we're alone. So talk."

Estle forced herself to look directly into his dark eyes, though she dreaded his reaction to her next declaration. "I am not returning to the Chupa with you."

Azori lifted one side of his mouth in a sort of sneering half-smile. "Of course you are."

"No, I'm not! You don't own me, Azori, and I won't have my actions dictated by you. You've tried to rule my life since I was a child, and I've never liked it. In fact, it's your fault that I don't have a husband and a house full of children…as soon as a man finds out that I'm your sister, I never see him again."

Azori sniffed. "Is it my fault none of them have been worthy? I have kept you safe all these years, and I should think a little gratitude would be in order."

"I will not debate this with you…I haven't the time," she said. "But know that I intend to go with my friends, and you can't stop me. If you or your men take after any of them, I will never speak to you again. I mean it, Azori. One hair on any of their heads is harmed, and you're dead to me."

Azori sighed. "There's no need for such dramatics."

"I'm not being dramatic. I'm through with you and your attitude of ownership. From now on, I make my own choices, and if you want to be a part of my life, you *ask* permission."

Azori's face reddened and his eyes grew blacker than ever. In the dim light, they almost looked reptilian. He turned to Hallagond, as if noticing him for the first time.

"Why are *you* here?"

"Estle asked me to come, just in case her resolve wavered or you couldn't hold your temper."

"Did you put these ideas into her head?"

Hallagond stared back at him. "Estle has her own ideas, Azori. Her thoughts are not all put into her head by men, and certainly not be me."

Azori turned back to Estle. "You are absolutely convinced that you won't return home with me?"

"I may return one day, but for now I choose to follow my friends."

Azori thought for a moment. "Well, I can't exactly fault you for bring stubborn, as it is a family trait." His eyes had returned to their normal warm brown, to Hallagond's relief. He sat in silence for a moment, as though unsure of his next move.

"I knew that one day you would defy me, though I had hoped it would not be this day in particular," he said. "But not to worry…I have come up with a solution."

He turned to Hallagond. "And I will hear no argument."

Now, Hallagond stood before his friends, having gained their undivided attention.

"Very well then… I shall tell my news now." He turned to Estle. "May I have some water, please? Thank you. Now, then, my news. Yes. Any minute now."

"Get on with it, won't you?" growled Fima, who did not like to be kept waiting. "What have you to say that is proving so difficult?"

Hallagond stood perfectly still and silent, as though frozen, for a moment. At last he began. "I have spoken with Azori, declaring my intention to go with you to the Silver City. Estle has done the same." He paused and looked around at his friends.

"Well, we knew that, didn't we? That's certainly good news," said Fima. "Why did you seem so hesitant to tell us that?"

"Because he isn't finished," said Gaelen, a look of dawning dread in her eyes. "*Are* you?"

"No, Gaelen, I'm not," said Hallagond. "Azori and Azok will not allow Estle to make such a dangerous crossing alone. They insist on going with us, at least for a while." For a few moments there was no sound to be heard, save for the quiet crackling of the fire and the chirping of a few lonely crickets.

The stunned silence was broken first by Gaelen. "Azori and Azok…the bandits. The thieving, drunken *bandits.* Right?"

"No, he means Azori and Azok the kitten-vendors," said Nelwyn.

Rogond was aghast. "Do you truly need me to list the five hundred reasons why that is a *bad* idea? I had better begin at once. One: Azori and his men are bandits. Two: We are leaving the day after tomorrow. Three: They do not have provisions for the journey. Four: Galador and that easterner despise one another. Five: I'm sure the people of the Citadel will have enough difficulty accepting strangers who are *not* in the company of a group of criminals. Six…"

"All right," said Hallagond. "I know all of these things. If you would prevent Azori from traveling with us, I will welcome any suggestion as to how to prevent him. And while I'm at it, let me offer a few reasons why this could actually benefit the Company. One: Azori is quite capable of provisioning himself and his men in a day. Two: He is very wealthy at the moment and will make certain that we all have ample provisions. Three: He is highly experienced in both desert travel and in desert warfare. Four: We may need him and his men to defeat the Scourge, for they are fierce fighters. Five…"

"Here is the biggest point on Rogond's list, Hallagond," said Gaelen. "Azori and his men are not trustworthy. They are as likely to run from the Scourge, or even to join with them, to save themselves."

"My brothers are not of the same lofty character that you would find trustworthy," said Estle, her cheeks flushed with hot blood. "But I know them. They would defend me to the death if they had to."

"And when you lay dead before this terrible army, they would have no other reason to resist," said Gaelen gently. "They will do what they must to survive, no matter the outcome."

"Again, worthy friends, I would welcome any suggestions as to *how* to prevent Azori from going wherever he will," said Hallagond.

All eyes turned to Estle in that moment, for everyone in the Company knew that Azori would never undertake the crossing were Estle not with them.

Galador shook his head and rose to stand beside Hallagond. "As much as it pains me to say it, I'm afraid we have no choice. We all know that Estle is the reason Azori's men would follow us, but if she remains, I believe Hallagond will also. If Hallagond remains, so then will Rogond, at least until his life-debt is paid. I will not leave Rogond, and neither will Gaelen. Nelwyn and Fima will not leave their friends either, and we cannot allow Bint Raed to attempt the crossing alone. Therefore, at least for now, we shall be forced to endure the company of Azori and his bandits."

Hallagond sighed. "I'm sorry for this, my friends, but I must tell you…I'm relieved that Azori has chosen this course, rather than several others available to him. Think on that for a moment." He returned to his place by the fire, as the Company pondered his words. Azori did have several other choices open to him, all of which involved violence done to the Company.

"How reassuring," muttered Fima. "At least he will wait until we are far from the city to kill us."

"He may try," said Gaelen, "but at least we'll see him coming."

"One thing is certain," muttered Galador. "I will not walk the same path as that easterner. They may follow us, but they may not walk beside us so long as he is with them."

Hallagond nodded. "I'm sure Azori will understand, and I don't think the easterner will object to walking a separate path from the Elves, either."

Azori and his men set about the task of provisioning themselves for a journey that would take a very long time to complete. All in the

Company were uneasy as they went about their final preparations, though Azori tried his best to open friendly relations with them. After all, this would be easier if they did not at least openly despise one another.

One of the sutherlings, named Hattaras, knelt beside Gaelen as she applied a healing ointment to Hallagond's new horse, Derrin. "I see you have some ability to help the lame ones," he said, admiring Gaelen's technique as she stroked the animal's legs. "That is an important skill, especially where we're going. I wish you would teach me how to stroke legs so effectively."

Apparently, Hattaras did not suffer from the same reluctance as most sutherling men, for he threw a companionable arm across Gaelen's shoulders quite unexpectedly.

She stiffened, clenching her teeth. "Take your hand from my shoulder, please. Were I not reluctant to startle this animal, I would do it for you."

Hattaras did not withdraw his arm, but spoke to her again. "Now, now, little flower...do not be so unfriendly. We will travel together for many weeks, you and I. Why not make the best of it? I mean nothing unseemly; I am simply extending a friendly hand."

"The last person who called me 'little flower' ended up dead in the desert with his head taken off," she replied. "Keep your friendly hand to yourself, or you will lose it." Derrin sensed her disquiet and began to move restively about.

"Ooh, this flower has thorns," said Hattaras, removing his arm. He laughed at Gaelen, who looked sidelong at him and rose to her feet, stroking Derrin's neck to calm him.

"We leave tomorrow at dawn," she said. "Once on the path I will neither speak to you nor acknowledge that you exist, except perhaps in the heat of battle when need is on you. I expect you to likewise refrain from speaking to me again. If you touch me, you will lose your hand. Do you understand what I am saying to you?"

Hattaras laughed again, to Gaelen's surprise. She was accustomed to having her threats taken seriously. "It would not be the first time, little flower," he said, showing both a gap-toothed smile and the empty left sleeve of his robe, for he had lost one of his hands already. He held up a very lifelike wooden replica, which he then re-affixed to his left wrist before leaving her to stare after him in dismay. How in the world had they been saddled with such a burden?

"No matter," she growled. "There are only twelve of them, and I have many arrows." Hattaras had smelled rather strongly, and she would wash away all trace of him ere she left in the morning.

Quite an impressive caravan stood assembled near Mumari's main water-source, a large pond that was fed from below ground. Animals were allowed to drink only from troughs lined up along one end; since the Plague, people were not allowed to bathe in the water directly, but they could take it from the pond and bathe in their own homes.

The group that set forth in the early morning light comprised twenty people, fifteen dromadin, and twenty-one horses. Nine of the dromadin carried nothing but water, and four carried nothing but food for people and animals. The other two carried everything else. The water was contained in skins and in light casks that were very, very well sealed.

Before they left, Gaelen and Nelwyn had given all the animals a ration of salt to encourage them to drink their fill before departure. They had filled up on hay and water all night; now that hay would act as a sponge, holding water in their guts for as long as possible.

Azori was in quite a congenial mood as he mounted his dark bay mare; she was adorned with scarlet and gold tassels, and Azori cut quite the figure with his dark beard and piercing gaze. He rode up to the Company as if to cheer them, flashing a white-toothed grin. "Why so somber, my fine friends? You will be happy to know that my men all washed themselves and combed their hair and beards last night. That's the good news—the bad is that it will be our last opportunity for many weeks. Ha! Might as well enjoy life, my friends, for it might end tomorrow. Let us be away!"

Azori's men were in the mood for adventure, for they answered to no higher cause. They had been told of the Silver City, and it sounded like a rich fruit ripe for plucking. The Company was of a far more sober mind, having been cursed with a group of bandits as traveling companions.

"Since only Bint Raed knows the way, you would think they would allow her to ride ahead," said Nelwyn as she made her way calmly beside Galador.

"That would assume they are capable of allowing clear thinking to rule their actions," said Gaelen, as she rode past.

"Slow down! You are not thinking clearly yourself, or you would save your mount," called Nelwyn as her cousin drew farther ahead. Gaelen turned Finan about and cantered back to her.

"I need to let him out for a while; he's excited. He will expend more energy in arguing with me. He senses a battle on the wind."

Finan had energy to spare. He was compact, but mighty, and he maintained on very little. Gaelen knew what she was doing. She allowed her little horse to run ahead and enjoy his freedom for the moment. She knew he would outlast all the others, except perhaps for Faladinn, the Kazhi-horse.

Bint Raed was not an accomplished rider, but Siva bore her well and without complaint. She had received one small surprise the day before, as Gaelen instructed her: "Whatever you do, don't take hold of her mane unless you wish to ride swiftly." Regrettably, Bint Raed lost her balance and gave in to the natural impulse to grab Siva's mane. The horse shot out from beneath her like a flaming silver arrow, leaving Bint Raed to sit in the sand and wonder what had just happened.

Nelwyn and Gaelen ran to her aid. When they saw she was unhurt, Nelwyn began to chuckle. "You should have seen the look on your face," she said.

Gaelen brushed the sand from their friend's posterior. "I told you not to grab her mane. Let's see if we can provide an alternative."

From that day on, Siva was fitted with a strap that ran across the front of the saddle. "Grab that, if you have the need," said Gaelen. In addition, Gaelen plaited Siva's mane so that it would be out of the way of Bint Raed's hands.

On the evening before departure, Bint Raed spread out their makeshift map and explained the path that would be taken. "First we will travel straight south, to the northern edge of the Mountains of Dread. We will skirt around the mountains to the west, crossing the salt wastes, which are vast and deadly—we'll need to save as much water as we can for that. We'll take this route here…where it is not as wide. The fire-sands and the pit-traps must be avoided if possible, but I fear we cannot miss them entirely. Let's hope that luck is with us. We are likely to encounter fierce lightning and wind-storms in this area, but there is no way to avoid them. If we are caught in the open, it will likely be the death of us. Finally, we must cross the Fire-mountains and the Plains of Thirst. Our survival there will depend on the amount of water we have been able to find and conserve. Once we gain the Salt Wastes, we may not find any wholesome water until we reach the Brown Hills."

She looked at the pale faces around her. They had not actually realized how daunting this challenge would be—one minor mishap could lead to a catastrophe. If they lost even one of the dromadin, they would most certainly not all survive.

Azori looked at Hallagond. "Are you certain you will go on this fool's errand, and not return with me to the nice, comfortable Chupa? You could change your mind, you know."

"Estle and I are going to the Citadel, Azori. I'll take good care of her. Why don't you and your men go back to the Chupa?"

Azori laughed. "Because I would never see my sister again. She is our only family, Al-amand. Having recently found your brother, I should think you would understand."

"At one time I would have willingly *given* you my brother, Azori. In fact, I would have paid you handsomely to take him off my hands, but no more," said Hallagond. "I do understand, but I can't help but question the wisdom of throwing your lot in with ours. Is there no other way?"

Azori looked wryly at him. "You used to consider yourself part of my lot."

"I know," said Hallagond, "but my brother is part of their Company. And, like it or not, so now am I."

"And so is Estle," said Azori. "She thinks I'm just meddlesome and domineering, but she doesn't know that my efforts have prevented some bad things from happening to her over the course of her life." He shook his head. "She has no idea."

Hallagond smiled. "She has *every* idea. And you have saved my neck on more than one occasion. You can be a staunch ally when it suits you." He gave Azori a worried look. "I'm just not sure about the rest of them."

"None will dare to defy me...or Azok. They will find their manners before long, or I will deal harshly with them, and they know it. Now, stop worrying. Just adapt as you always have. That is the desert way."

Now it looked as though they would all need to do a great deal of adapting. Fima sat perched upon one of the dromadin, and he was uncertain whether he felt better or worse about it. At least he had been able to talk to Rogond while riding behind on Eros, although admittedly his comments had been limited to "Arrgh! Slow down! Oh, my poor backside, are we there yet?" and so on. Rogond might have questioned whether such an exchange constituted a conversation, but he still missed Fima's presence behind him.

Now the dwarf struggled to become accustomed to the motion of the dromadan, which was very different from that of a horse. At first it had made him rather ill, and for a moment he imagined he must have gone nearly as green as Hallagond. Those feelings passed once he learned to keep his eyes fixed on the horizon.

The dromadin were not at all like horses; they made strange noises and had rather temperamental natures. When they were truly angry they ejected a stream of fluid that was among the foulest-smelling substances imaginable. This they did mostly at each other, but an unwary person might still find himself in the way of it. Once in the open desert they stopped this foolish behavior, knowing perhaps that wasting precious fluid was ill-advised.

The caravan moved steadily forward, stopping to rest whenever shade could be found. They traveled with greater speed in the cool, starlit darkness, and at such times the Elves would sing together as they rode. They took turns leading the string of dromadin, a task they proved very good at, for they befriended the strange animals quickly. Gaelen and Nelwyn insisted on naming them all.

Bint Raed told stories of the Citadel as they rode, frustrating Fima, who was too far away to hear. He insisted that she repeat the tales when they stopped to rest. They learned many things from her. The Citadel had never been overtaken by any invading force, either by land or by sea. The Corsairs had attempted it, only to have their ships destroyed by fierce seas and terrible rocks guarding the harbor. They had not tried again since. Only the lost would approach from the east, across such a terrible, barren waste with no water for weeks in any direction. The occasional souls who found their way would never leave…why would they? Most who tried probably died in the attempt, unless they knew the way.

"If there is a way out, why do we not use it as the way in?" asked Gaelen. It seemed a sensible question.

"Because any way in from the north would take too much time, months that we do not have," said Bint Raed. "And it is not an easy passage in any case—the north is guarded by nearly impenetrable forest. There are sicknesses and dreadful beasts that lurk there. The way we are going is the right way."

"The Citadel is the gift of Aontar to Lore-master Salasin, as his reward for safeguarding the beautiful works that men had created in praise of the Light. Now it is the responsibility of the people not only to preserve what had been created before, but to create new works of greater beauty, and to explore and learn new things to enrich the mind. We have received enlightenment, and it must not be quenched. The Citadel must not fall."

The Company traveled for many days, and at first they were lighthearted, as is the tendency at the beginning of a journey when thoughts are of adventure and far horizons. But soon they settled into the business of survival, and the tales grew less, though the Elves still sang beneath the stars. Azori's men kept apart from the Company, as Azori had promised.

The Mountains of Dread had been visible for some time, and as they drew nearer it became possible for the Elves to see the whitish tops of the peaks. "There—on that tall one…is that snow?" asked Nelwyn hopefully.

"It certainly looks like it," said Gaelen in an excited tone that was immediately flattened by Bint Raed.

"It's not snow. To make snow, there must be water. The Mountains of Dread are capped with white ash...they sometimes throw great plumes of it into the sky. We must pray this doesn't happen while we are too close."

"That I will most certainly do," said Nelwyn, the disappointment heavy in her voice. *The journey to the Citadel has truly begun…and we will see neither snow, nor rain, nor tall green tree until it had ended. I wonder whether any of us will survive to behold the towers of Dûn Arian, with their gleaming spires of silver.*

18
A Savage Land

As the Company drew nearer to the Mountains of Dread, they beheld a barren, disheartening landscape that put all thoughts of a pleasant journey aside. Not that they had actually held any such thoughts, but the sight of those tall, white-capped mountains had called familiar images to mind, with perils that were known and understood. Here the mountains were stark and lifeless; they had blanketed all the lands about in a layer of fine, white ash and rock. There was no sign that anything grew, or had ever grown, near them. A pool of fetid water bubbled ominously as the Company passed—the foul smell coming from it stung their eyes and noses. A sort of yellow crust surrounded it, and the brownish-yellow film over the water was broken by bubbles of vapor rising through it.

"Sulfur!" yelled Fima, as his unhappy dromadan snorted in distaste. "Alas that we cannot collect some. It's a very useful substance in the right hands."

"We dare not get that close to the edge, for the approach may give way beneath our feet. We don't know the extent of solid ground surrounding the water, and one who fell into that pool would never come out again," said Bint Raed.

Nelwyn looked over at the horrid, evil-smelling mire and shuddered. "That would be the worst ending imaginable," she said. "I cannot think of the foul creatures that must live here."

"Nothing lives here," said Galador.

There were no further words from anyone in the Company, yet Azori and his men were not dismayed as they rode past the pool. "Ah, my friends! Here is water in which you may wash yourselves. My men have decided to forego the pleasure," bellowed Azori, as his companions laughed. The relative cleanliness of certain members of the Company had become a source of amusement, and many had hoped to see even the Elves unwashed and filthy by journey's end.

All at once, the Elves lifted their heads. They felt dread from an unknown source—a very deep and primal fear. The very earth seemed charged with dark energy. The horses and dromadin appeared to feel it, too. Gaelen looked at Nelwyn's wide eyes and pale face, calling out to all in hearing: "Mind your beasts and yourselves! Keep alert, and *hold fast!*" No sooner had these words been uttered than the ground began trembling, and a low rumble, almost too low to be heard, pressed upon their ears. The horses were frightened and struggled with their riders, as the dromadin bellowed in dismay, planted their feet, and refused to move. An acrid plume issued from the mountaintop, together with a quantity of ash. It drifted down like evil snow upon the surrounding land.

A moment later, an upheaval of steam and foul water issued from the pool. The travelers were thankful to be upwind of it, or they would have felt the caustic yellow spray burning their skin and eyes. In a moment the danger had passed, and the earth was still again, but the bravado had cooled for many in those few moments.

"Let's put as much distance between ourselves and those mountains as we may," said Bint Raed. "From what I've heard, that was only a small sample of their displeasure."

"Ah, what a pity that we must leave…I was so hoping to make this my permanent home," said Fima, urging his dromadan to walk as quickly as it would.

"Yes," Rogond shouted back. "Such a wondrous place, where you can pick up all the sulfur you need from the very ground…a pity indeed." He looked over at Gaelen. "You will let us know if you feel anything else, won't you, my love?"

"I will if I am able," Gaelen replied grimly, "not that it will make the slightest bit of difference."

They kept their beasts moving for many hours, until the dromadin decided that it was time to rest. They were practical beasts, seldom finding urgency in anything. When they felt the need to rest they simply stopped and folded their legs beneath them, lying upon the ground. Fima dismounted thankfully, even though the sight of the occasional wisps of steam issuing from the still-far-too-nearby mountains concerned him. Yet the earth seemed to have quieted, at least for the moment. "Don't worry, Fima," said Rogond. "The dromadin would not take rest if they felt anything amiss."

"Besides, we will go no farther until they decide the time is right," said Estle. "They cannot be moved once they have elected to stop." She had observed this behavior many times when merchants tried to persuade their animals that the open desert was calling to them. The dromadin had decided that they preferred the oasis, and neither whips nor angry shouts nor pleading could move them until they were ready. Dromadin were wonderful builders of patience among men.

Now their own beasts lay placidly upon the ash-covered ground, chewing slowly and thoughtfully with their dark eyes half-closed. They had the longest lashes of any beast in the world, no doubt to serve as sunshades. Finan moved alongside one of them, his small body shaded by the larger animal, and dropped onto his belly to lie beside it. He dozed as Gaelen went to procure water for him and herself; thirst would be the normal condition of everyone during this journey.

The dromadin used very little water considering their size, and the horses had learned that they would rarely be allowed to drink their fill, but enough water had been carried that none would face terrible hardship so long as nothing unforeseen happened.

Gaelen carefully refilled her water-skin from one of the larger vessels; she spilled not a drop of it, ensuring that the vessel was tightly sealed again. Then she moved to lie beside Finan, sharing the water with him. Finan took the end of the vessel in his mouth, curled his pink tongue around the narrow spout, and sucked the precious water down in measured swallows. Gaelen allowed him to have ten of these before attending to her own thirst.

"The dromadin will rest until it is fully dark," said Bint Raed. "We might as well sleep until then."

"Interesting that they moved through the heat of the day and stopped as the sun began to wane," said Hallagond. "I would think they would rather rest while the sun is high, to conserve strength and water."

"They know what they're doing," replied Bint Raed, "for the ash takes in the heat of the sun, such that it is uncomfortable to lie upon during the full heat of the day, but cools quickly when the sunlight fades."

"I know one thing," said Hallagond, "The glare from this ash has nearly blinded me. It's almost like traveling on snow. How much farther does it extend?"

"Probably at least another day's journey," said Bint Raed. "And we must devise some way to deal with it, because it will be the same when we cross the Great Salt. The animals have built-in sunshades for their eyes, but we do not."

"I have a remedy," said Azori, who had approached them and overheard. "Here is a gift from me to your Company." He drew forth a pot of black ointment and demonstrated its use by smearing broad swatches underneath both eyes. "The black will absorb the light," he said. "It will be of some help, but you should keep your faces veiled as much as you can to shield your eyes further."

They all availed themselves of Azori's gift, bowing before him in gratitude. He smiled at the Elves, who were unused to smearing things upon their faces and were somewhat inexpert at it. Gaelen sniffed curiously at the little pot. "What is this?" she asked Azori. "I cannot place the scent, though it is not a foul one."

"It's made from the blackened remains of inquisitive Wood-elves who ask questions about the nature of gifts," replied Azori with a smile. "If I told you, you might not make use of its benefits. Just accept your gift and enjoy it." Gaelen bowed before him; the point had been taken. She smeared two black marks on her cheekbones, to Azori's delight.

"Now we are all a fine group of blackened travelers," he said. "We are united by our dark marks. Ha!"

He turned and went to rejoin his men, who were sitting down to a light meal. Rogond followed their example, and began passing out flatbread and dried, salted meat to the Company. "I believe you may have brightened Azori's day," he said to Galador as he chewed his dry bread and meat. "He has been wanting to see something black on the skin of an Elf for many days now. I have often wondered how it is that your folk never seem to get truly dirty...I've seen Elves emerge from the heat of a battle without so much as a smudge on their faces. Do you have some magic that prevents it?"

"You have asked me this question before, Tuathan," said Galador. "I had no answer for you then, and I do not have one now. But I have noticed that, if Elves have a tendency to avoid dirt, men seem to attract it."

They continued on past the mountains, making their way toward the Great Salt. There was very little of note that occurred, except on one dark night when they were astonished to see a fiery glow in the sky over the receding mountains. They heard a distant, booming rumble, and their beasts turned their heads briefly back before continuing on. Gaelen turned Finan around, staring at the ominous orange glow, tensing as a bright plume lifted into the heavens. A dark cloud seemed to spread across the stars, moving toward them. Bint Raed rode up to stand beside her.

"Thank heaven we are far away. Had we stood near to that eruption it might have taken us all."

"What is that darkness blocking the stars?" asked Gaelen in alarm.

"It's a cloud of ash," said Bint Raed. "Your stars will be dimmed for a while, for the ash will hang in the air for a long time ere it settles. But be of good cheer, for whereas the stars will not be as brilliant, the sunrises most certainly will be."

"I have never seen a mountain on fire until now," said Gaelen, awed by what she had seen.

"When the sun rises, you will see the sky on fire," said Bint Raed, "and you may yet see another fire-mountain before we reach our journey's end."

"One is enough, really," said Gaelen, though she was intrigued.

Bint Raed had been right about the sunrise; it was the most brilliant the Elves had ever beheld. Hallagond explained that such fiery red skies were seen only when a large quantity of dust or ash hung in the air, and that such things were brought on by storms of wind, as well as by the belching of ash by fire-mountains. "Let's hope that the sunsets are of a more ordinary nature," he said grimly. "Our path lies to the west, and the sort of storm that enflames the evening sky is exactly the sort we hope to avoid." Hallagond knew there would be windstorms, but they would hopefully not be of the sort that would kill.

The land about them was stony, with tall rocks and ridges, so there was some shade. Bint Raed spoke very little to her companions for the next few days. She was trying to concentrate on the speed, direction, and distance traveled so that she could keep her bearings. It was important that they cross the salt plains where they were not as wide, for they represented terrible heat and thirst, and the salts were hard on the feet of both the horses and the dromadin. "We will rest very little in the crossing," she said, as the plain could now be seen as a wide, featureless expanse of white with only the occasional ridge of stones. These looked like dark ships upon a flat, pale sea.

"It almost looks like a lake filled with water," said Nelwyn, who naturally knew better.

"So it was, long ago," said Bint Raed. "Actually, it was more like to an inland sea than a lake. There are a few creatures that make their home here. I have been told of snakes and lizards, but I have never seen them. It is an odd creature that can live where nothing grows."

"Indeed," said Nelwyn with a shiver. She was not looking forward to traversing the Salt.

They sheltered in the shade of stones for the last time before the crossing would begin; they could not long linger in such places, for the shaded areas were alive with horrid black gnats that fed on blood. The horses could not bear it—swarms of the tiny insects blackened their ears and nearly drove them mad. Gaelen reached back behind one of her own ears to crush her tormentors, and her hand came back wet and sticky with blood. She moved back into the sun with Finan, for the gnats would remain in the shade and would not follow.

She decided that it might be a good time to test the heat-turning properties of the fire-cloak. She drew it forth from her bag; it shimmered and flashed, seeming glad of its freedom as she draped it across Finan's head and neck, drawing part of it across her own head and shoulders. The result was both immediate and impressive. The sun was turned by the cloak so completely that even the ground that it shaded became cooler. Gaelen and Finan were much more comfortable.

"Does that thing actually help?" asked Estle, who was red-faced from the heat. Her fair complexion did not serve well, and she was in some distress.

"It does," replied Gaelen, who was by now feeling quite guilty about it.

"Good. At least *some* of us are comfortable. I'm relieved to see that garish garment has a use other than in calling attention to oneself."

"Would you care to share it?" asked Gaelen, offering Estle a place under the cloak. "I am now quite cool, and have no further need of it for a while. At least try it and see if it will aid you…your face is red, and I fear the heat is robbing you of your strength. Come then, if your pride will allow it."

"How kind of you to allow me to share space with your horse," said Estle, though she appreciated the gesture more than she would have Gaelen know.

"Actually, Finan trusts very few of your race, and I doubt he would allow you to share space with him," said Gaelen. "He will need to do without." She called to Fima, Nelwyn, and Rogond; four people could shelter beneath the cloak without hardship. Gaelen stood with Galador, who would take his turn with Hallagond and Bint Raed. The bandits were camped on the other side of the ridge, which was just as well. Gaelen didn't want them to know of the existence of the fire-cloak.

No one would ever forget the crossing of the Salt. The hard west winds raised fine, white grit, bringing discomfort to eyes, lungs, and unprotected skin. When the wind calmed, the heat was terrible, and there was the ever-present glare. At night the salt gave up its heat quickly, and though the travelers donned extra garments, they shivered in the chill. Fima was profoundly affected by these extremes, for he was old and had not held full strength when the journey began. Now he grew weaker by the day, though he tried to hide this fact from his friends.

They did find water once—topped with a layer of bubbly reddish slime—nestled in a ridge of rock that projected above the white plain like a dragon's backbone. The crusted salts gave way beneath their feet, leaving tracks that would likely remain for months. "Our enemies could easily track us here," growled Gaelen, who was not happy about it. She was very worried for Fima, and her good humor was wearing thin.

"Lift your heart, Gaelen, for only an enemy that was completely mad would follow us here," said Nelwyn, trying to cheer her. "We needn't worry about being tracked. Who in their right minds would venture here without dire need?"

Against all expectations, that question was about to be answered, as Azori cantered over to their group. Ikari's black bird, Karatsu, had returned from his morning flight carrying a gold button in his beak. This could mean one of two things—either the remains of someone's caravan could be found nearby, or there was presently a caravan passing nearby. The bandits wanted to follow the bird and see for themselves, as they anticipated gaining wealth from their fellow travelers in either case. Karatsu never flew more than a few miles from his master, thus it would be a short diversion.

"I would rather not bother, but it will help my men in keeping their good humor," said Azori. "It shouldn't take long. Besides, you look as though you are all in need of rest. Why not take some while my men investigate?" Without waiting for approval, he cantered back to his own group, and in a few moments the Company observed Ikari and another of the easterners, two of the sutherlings, and Azok following Karatsu, who flew south toward a distant ridge of stone, calling loudly. Their task was simply to investigate, and if there was no opposition they would bring back whatever valuables they deemed worthy. They had promised not to take either food or water from living folk.

"Just don't make enemies…we can't afford them!" said Rogond, shaking his head.

Hours passed, and the travelers rested until they beheld a small, black speck in the southern sky. They roused themselves, expecting the imminent return of Azok and his party, but they did not appear.

Azori came to parley with the Company. "I am becoming quite concerned," he said, and his face showed it. "It's not like the bird to return without Ikari, and Azok would not fail to return unless he had fallen into dire need. I fear he may have been taken...the bird is quite agitated. I must ride out and learn what has befallen, and I would ask your aid."

"How may we assist you?" asked Rogond, who respected Azori's obvious natural leadership and concern for his men.

"I will need one or two to accompany me. I dare not go alone along such an unclear path," said Azori. "Will any of your Company agree to this task?"

"You seem to forget that Azok is my brother, as well," said Estle. "I would aid him if I can."

Azori smiled at her and nodded. "Is there anyone else?"

"The purpose of this errand is to learn of your brother's fate," said Gaelen. "You will need someone who can travel unseen and unheard, and can slip in among enemies unnoticed. Your people may have been surprised by some enemy that has either killed them, or holds them captive. Is this not your belief?"

"It is," said Azori. "Are you offering your service, tree-dweller?"

Gaelen shrugged. "You will need someone who can approach unnoticed. In this Company, that will be me."

"But, you do not understand Ravani-speech," said Estle, who was uncertain whether she wanted Gaelen along.

"That does not matter...you will be there," said Gaelen. "You can translate what is said. Much can be learned without benefit of words."

"I'm satisfied with that," said Azori. "It would be best if there were only a few of us. Our aim is only to gain news, and not to attempt rescue."

At first, Rogond resisted the notion of having Gaelen go off into the desert with only Azori and Estle to safeguard her, but Hallagond spoke to him aside. "They are only going after information. It's important that they remain unnoticed, and if there are too many it will be more difficult. Gaelen can take care of herself. Even if she cannot, Azori and Estle are two very fierce fighters. Azori could take on both of us and most likely prevail. He will protect her."

"You don't understand," said Rogond, his face drawn with concern. "She can be reckless on occasion; she sometimes imagines her abilities to be greater than they are."

"So you say, brother, yet I have heard the tale of the Elfhunter, and of your adventures. She is still alive today, and that must count for something."

"Yet these are not her lands, and she may encounter people and things that she is ill-equipped to deal with," said Rogond. "I would feel a lot better being at her side."

"Put your fears away," said Hallagond. "Azori loves nothing more than his own life, but he also loves Estle dearly. He will not place his sister or your beloved in jeopardy, for to do so would threaten his own well-being. He will discover the truth of what has befallen Azok, and then he will return." He looked hard at Rogond. "Do you not trust Gaelen to keep her word? She has sworn to return to you."

Rogond did not reply, but went to aid Gaelen in making ready. She clasped his hand, promising to return as soon as she could. Then she bade farewell to Nelwyn, Galador, and Fima before riding away with Azori and Estle.

They had gone only a few miles when they saw smoke curling from behind a small rise. Azok's band had left a trail that was easy to follow, and it was a safe bet that Karatsu had led them there. Azori, Estle, and Gaelen dismounted, commanding the horses to stay where they were, and crept in to investigate.

Gaelen did not care for the scents she was picking up on the wind. "There is only death here. I sense no living being." She moved quickly to within sight of the sad remains of some unlucky travelers' caravan. Someone had made quick work of these people, and there were a few bodies, but Azori's men were nowhere to be seen.

There was no sign of living folk. The caravan's water supply had been taken, as well as any food that they carried, but very little else. There were two dead dromadin and several dead horses; the rest had no doubt been seized by the enemy. Many tracks of horses and dromadin led away from the caravan; obviously, the invaders had taken captives. Two of the dead horses had belonged to Azori's men.

Azori was grim. "They have been taken, but not killed, or the enemy would have left them behind."

"Yet there is a lot blood on the ground," said Estle, "Too much to be explained by these few bodies. I would say that the fighting was fierce, and many were wounded."

"I agree," said Gaelen. "All signs indicate that your friends have been taken captive, along with the people of the caravan. Perhaps we should follow and see what may be done?"

"We cannot return with so little knowledge," said Estle, who was beginning to fear the worst for Azok. "We should at least find out where they have been taken, and by whom. Yet the extent of these tracks would indicate a number of enemies. I doubt there will be anything we can do."

"I must know what has happened," Azori declared, whistling for his mare. They followed cautiously, riding under the sun and the moon, until they came within sight of a spectacle that exceeded all of their wildest imaginings.

Gaelen smelled the encampment long before she drew within sight of it, wrinkling her nose in distaste. *"Arrrah!* There is a great foul stench on the wind! We may be nearer to the enemy than we supposed, and a force that would produce such a reek must be vast indeed. Could we have come upon…the Scourge?" She turned to Azori and Estle. "This is not going to have a happy outcome. You both know it."

Azori nodded. "I know. Yet we must do what we may in our brother's behalf. We should conceal the horses and continue on foot."

Though it was dark, the moonlight soon revealed the men set to keep the watch. They were well armed, but they were not expecting enemies in this deserted place, and their attention wandered. Azori, Estle, and Gaelen managed to circumvent the guards, moving carefully from shadow to shadow, creeping silently like cats in the darkness.

They moved to within sight of the huge encampment, and as the first light of dawn began to redden the salt, they came to appreciate the extent of their enemy. Row upon row of scarlet tents, scores of black banners, thousands of spear-points, smoke from a few cook-fires, hundreds of dromadin, and uncountable numbers of horses and men appeared before their astonished eyes. This army stretched as far as they could see back to the southeast, and it was on the move. Azori, who had once served as a spearman himself, could not imagine the difficulty in moving such a huge force across such a terrible, waterless waste.

"We will need to get inside the encampment," said Gaelen, "and for that we shall need to disguise ourselves. It's a good stroke that we are all reasonably tall."

"A pity you did not bring your fire-cloak," said Estle. "You could have blinded them."

"Hush!" said Azori. "We need to move from this place, and begin to make our way in. Gaelen…do you think you can obtain garments for our disguise?"

"I will give it my best effort," she replied. "It's early and they are not as yet fully aware. We should find a better hiding-place."

They made their way to a stockpile of supplies, discovering a sledge loaded with casks and covered with a heavy drape, beneath which they could all remain safely hidden. From there, Gaelen spirited herself to a nearby tent. Her companions tried to keep sight of her, but it was difficult. Apparently she did not find what she was looking for, and they saw her roll from beneath the tent wall and move on to the next. Then they lost track of her.

When more than an hour had passed, Estle began to worry. "Perhaps she has been taken captive. She has been gone a long time, and I cannot find her. Should we do anything?"

She was startled by the sudden appearance of Gaelen beneath the canvas drape. She carried garments for their use, having already disguised herself, and her eyes were bright with triumph at having met the challenge before her. She had certainly proven her worth to Azori.

"What took you so long?" growled Estle. "I was beginning to worry."

"Never mind...just put these on, will you? I am sorry they're not cleaner; it seems these men don't care whether their enemies can smell their approach."

"I would say they have few enemies, only victims," said Azori as he donned the red and black garments. Soon their identity was hidden such that they could all walk freely, provided they did nothing to attract attention.

Gaelen gripped Azori's arm. "I have seen your friends, and many other unfortunate captives," she said. "I know where they are being held."

Estle was surprised. "How did you find them so quickly in such a vast place?"

Gaelen looked away for a moment. "I was drawn to their cries. They are in a bad way...your brother Azok has been wounded, and they have done nothing to tend him. I fear he will not live long."

"I'm not surprised," said Azori. "He would have fought like a dragon before letting them take him."

"There is something else," said Gaelen. "From what I could see, the captives have been fettered by cutting the cords behind their knees. They won't be escaping, that is certain. There are women and young children who could do no harm." She shook her head in disgust. "These are cruel people."

Azori nodded. "We must find Azok as quickly as we may," he said. He looked over at Gaelen, seeing the truth in her eyes. Azok and the others would never be free again. "I know I can't save my brother, but perhaps I can take away his pain. Lead on."

They drew nigh the captives as the morning brightened. Apparently the Scourge brought along an army of flies, thousands of fat, black ones buzzing all around everywhere. A stink pervaded the place, dank and rotten, that was quite new in Gaelen's experience. It grew stronger as they drew deeper into the encampment.

Nearly twenty unfortunate souls had been tethered to poles; Estle could hear some of them crying as she drew near. Three or four had been bound to each pole, and none could stand on their ruined legs. There was the smell of blood; none of these people had received any attention since they had been taken. They were filthy, terribly thirsty, and in pain—the cries of the children were especially difficult to hear. The women tried to comfort them, but they could not.

Azok appeared to be unconscious, his head lolling over with his eyes not quite closed. The sight of him wounded Azori and Estle to the heart, for though he was a rough man, a thief and a murderer, he was their kinsman and they cared for him. Azori looked into the eyes of his half-sister. "He is wounded unto death. I can take his pain away quickly," he said, drawing forth a bright dagger from beneath his red robes.

Regrettably, Azok was destined to live just a while longer, for a group of perhaps twenty men chose that moment to address their captives. They bore sharp blades and mattocks with them, and several wore aprons of leather stained black with blood. The flies gathered in even greater numbers, drawn to the smell.

"Well, we had best get on with it," said one in a voice that was almost cheerful. "The fresher they are, the more acceptable the meat will be. Remember, we must keep our great force well fed if we are to prevail against the Silver City." He strode up to the first pole, where two men and two half-grown boys had been tethered. Without a word, he struck them with the mattock to render them senseless, cut them down from the pole, dragged their bodies onto a heavy, oiled canvas, and began to cut them into pieces as their friends and family stood aghast.

To the horror of Azori, Estle, and Gaelen, the men moved from pole to pole, first bludgeoning and then dismembering their shivering captives, all the while commenting on the quality of the meat that each would provide. The screams of the terrified children were almost too much to bear, and the smell of blood and the buzzing flies sickened poor Estle. She became very pale and unsteady on her feet as she struggled with herself. Her throat had closed and was now wide open, her gorge threatening to rise at any moment. Saliva filled her mouth, and she swallowed hard, trying to gain control.

Gaelen gripped her arm. "Steady, proud maiden of the Ravani... turn away from the spectacle if you must." The genuine concern in Gaelen's voice, together with the shared horror in her eyes, brought Estle back to her present situation. They could not afford this squeamishness now. To her relief, Gaelen saw the life coming back into Estle's eyes. "Well done," she whispered, squeezing Estle's arm. "Now you must steel yourself, for your friends are next in line for the bludgeon."

The butchers walked up to the pole where the bandits were tied. For the first time, Gaelen noticed that Ikari was not among them, nor had they found his body in the desert. She wondered what had become of him.

One of the sutherlings began pleading for his life. "Please, fearful menace, be merciful! I am a worthy warrior, and I can aid you. Only let me live, and I will serve your cause until the end of my days." Gaelen couldn't blame him, though she was strongly reminded of Sajid.

"Keep quiet," growled the butcher. "Your cries will not aid you. It's obvious that our captains have deemed you unworthy, or they would not have ordered your fettering. You will never move upon your own legs again, and I'm afraid we have little use for a warrior that must crawl into battle." His fellows laughed cruelly as the butcher raised his mattock.

Azok had been roused by the screaming of his fellow captives, and he was now listening with some interest despite his pain. He knew his time had come.

"No…no...do not kill me!" cried the sutherling. "What if I were to tell you that I have information of interest to you? I…I can lead you to the rest of our party, and they have gold…lots of it!"

The butcher hesitated for just a moment, and Gaelen's heart leapt into her mouth. This man was on the verge of betraying them all! She drew her own blade, hoping that Azori could explain her actions, but Azok saved her the trouble. His hands were tied behind the other man's head, and he snarled, grabbing the sutherling first by the hair and then by the throat, crushing it with the last of his strength. The sutherling's life ended, and the angry butcher then turned his mattock upon Azok, bashing his skull in with several lethal blows.

Azori looked into his brother's fading eyes, seeing no sign that he had been recognized, before the three of them turned from the spectacle and made their way back. Azori and Estle kept their eyes downcast so as not to call attention to their tears.

When Azori, Estle, and Gaelen had gained enough distance from the encampment, they removed their foul garments and made their way back to the horses, who thankfully had not strayed. By now it was mid-day, and all were hot and thirsty. The horror of what they had witnessed had unnerved them, and they needed rest—even Gaelen of the Greatwood. She had neither wept nor truly lost her nerve until she came face to face with Finan. When he saw her, he knew of her need, placing his head over her shoulder so that she could embrace him.

She wept for the terrible sights she had seen, and for the suffering of those she could not help. Ulcas were known to eat their captives; certainly it was quite usual for them, but Gaelen had never known men to stoop to such measures. Neither she nor Estle would ever forget the cries of the children, or the sacrifice of Azok. Gaelen would view Azori and Estle with a more appreciative eye from that day on.

Finan stood patiently, waiting for Gaelen to finish weeping. She was quite unsteady, and she lay down upon the hard salt, sleeping for the first time in a long reckoning, as Finan stood over her.

At last they roused themselves, ate and drank, and mounted their horses. It would soon be dark, and their friends would be very worried by now. By the time they approached their own encampment, it was nearly dawn. Gaelen gave a warning-call that many in the Company would know; it would not do to come on them unaware.

By this time there was only one encampment, for all had joined together. Azori smiled as he beheld Galador sitting around the same small fire as the sole remaining easterner, whose name was Okami.

They appeared to be getting to know one another, although it was unlikely that either would ever call the other "friend."

Rogond was alarmed at the haggard faces before him. He embraced Gaelen, and she shed silent tears as he held her.

Azori's men were understandably dismayed as he sat among them, shaking his head, a grim, haunted look in his eyes. They knew that their comrades would not return. Karatsu, it seemed, was not overly dismayed; he had already taken up with Okami, sitting placidly on his shoulder, occasionally fluffing his feathers against the chilly night air. Everyone sat in the circle, waiting for someone to begin the tale of what they had seen. At last, Azori spoke:

"We found the Scourge, and they are terrible."

For the next several hours, Azori, Gaelen, and Estle tried to describe what they had seen. Hallagond held Estle, trying to comfort her, for she wept again at the mention of Azok.

Bint Raed wept in fear for her homeland. The butcher had mentioned the Silver City directly; it was obviously their goal. "Our citizens will have no notion of how to deal with such folk; they will try to reason with the Scourge, even as it camps on their doorstep and prepares to take the lives of all within. This enemy will have no use for knowledge and learning—they will loot the library of its golden treasures before burning it to the ground!"

Fima's dread was evident in his weathered face, as he sat wheezing by the fire. The dust and salt had settled in his chest, and breathing was increasingly difficult. Rogond despaired, for he knew they were still many weeks away from anyone who could heal Fima, and that the environs would be unwholesome until then. The Company might well be grieving for the loss of its lore-master before long.

When the tale had been told, it was decided that the Company would move on as soon as all were rested. Bint Raed wrung her hands, stating that there was no time to waste. In the meantime, Azori's men asked to have a private parley with him. They talked for several hours, and their voices and faces were grave.

At dawn the Company prepared to continue the journey, rousing the dromadin and the horses. Azori approached Hallagond as he checked the seals on the water-casks. "My friend," he said, "There's something I must tell you, and a choice that you must make. My men do not wish to continue on this course, and neither do I."

This surprised Hallagond, and he stopped his labor to turn and face his friend. "I do not make this choice lightly," Azori continued, "but these lands have already surpassed any level of hardship that we expected, and we believe this enemy is far beyond your enlightened city. Neither I nor my men signed on for such a task. I have lived a hard life, and have witnessed great evils that men do unto men, but this was new to my experience. Having seen it, I do not wish to see any more."

Hallagond's dismay showed in his face. He would miss Azori as an ally, particularly his skill in battle. "Are you certain you will not come with us, and aid us? You may yet avenge your brother's death," he said.

Azori laughed. "You don't understand, do you? This is an enemy far too powerful for you or me to exact vengeance upon. Do you know why I have lived as long as I have? Because I know when I'm outmatched. Why not come back with us? You will live longer."

"I have sworn to aid the Company," was the calm reply. "And I must protect Rogond. A man has only one brother, after all."

Azori's eyes darkened with grief as he spoke. "Yes, a man has only one brother. Azok and I have lived our lives thinking only of our own comfort. It's too late for him to live an easy life, but I intend to, and I will ask Estle to return with me."

"She will not go," said Hallagond, "for she is bound by a similar promise. And once she gains the fortress of Dûn Arian, I doubt she will ever leave it. I would suggest you say your farewells."

Azori nodded, for he knew that Hallagond was right. "Well, I'll ask her all the same. You have sworn to protect her, Al-amand. Remember that. If I hear otherwise, I shall return and flay you alive!"

"I am not Al-amand anymore. My true name is Hallagond, and that means "Tall-stone". I am forsaken no longer."

"Well, then guard yourself, Tall-stone," said Azori. "Take care of my sister, if you would stay alive." He clapped Hallagond on the shoulder. "I must go now and speak with her," he said, "but I expect to be disappointed."

Azori left with his men a short while later. They decided to travel north to the coastal city of Fómor, where they would find welcome.

Though it would be a long journey, once they reached the northern edge of the Salt there would be water at intervals along the way. They left the extra dromadin with the Company, taking only two with them. "Take them as a gift from me, and be glad," said Azori, "for you will now have seven fewer men and eight fewer horses to provide with water. You are now much better provisioned for the rest of your journey."

Estle wept when Azori departed, for she feared that she had seen the last of her brother. At least he would never need to face the Scourge. Given his self-serving nature, that would have asked far too much of him.

She took comfort in Hallagond and, strangely, in Gaelen. Their hearts had softened through shared trials, and although they would still poke and prod at one another with sharp words, there was no longer any malice behind them.

Gaelen rode beside Nelwyn, flanked by Galador and Rogond. Hallagond led the dromadin, riding beside Estle and Bint Raed. Fima still slumbered; he had become so accustomed to the motion of his dromadan that he often slept for hours while being carried. As a precaution, he used a sash to secure himself to the saddle.

The Company continued to make its way across the salt basin, knowing that it was even more important to reach the Citadel so that they might warn the people of the Scourge. Everyone hoped that there would be enough strength in Dûn Arian to prevail over the looming darkness. If not, they would all fall victim, and not one of them wanted to consider the horror that would be waiting if they did.

19
Trials of the Road

Because they now had more water and provisions, the Company could travel faster and with more efficiency than before. They did not take the extra supplies for granted, because they knew that even a small unforeseen circumstance could drain their reserves quickly. Still, they saw no harm in allowing everyone to drink their fill at least once.

Rogond became ever more worried for Fima, who was now plagued by a deep cough that would not abate.

"It's this accursed salt and dust," Fima grumbled. "It will fade once we're clear of this place. Bint Raed...how much farther is it across the Salt?"

She smiled up at him. "Only a few more days."

"That's what you said two days ago," Fima muttered under his breath, wishing once again that he had never left Mountain-home.

Nelwyn rode up beside the dromadan that bore him. "Take heart, Fima Lore-master, and think of the reward at the end. This library is just waiting for your ready mind and eager hand. Think of it! You will be privy to secrets that no others of your people will have ever known... or my people, for that matter."

Fima smiled down at her. "Ah, Nelwyn, you seem to know exactly the right words to lighten my heart. Even Lady Ordath may not know of the history of this realm. Just wait until I see her again, and tell her of it. Ha!" This last remark sent him into a fit of coughing that turned his face red and made his eyes water.

Gaelen drew Bint Raed aside. "Fima won't last very much longer in this place. We should try to make better time."

Bint Raed understood, but she could offer no reassurance. "We may escape the Salt, but the rest of the journey will tax him no less," she said quietly. "The dust will remain. And we still must contend with the winds near the fire-mountains. At least he's riding high on that dromadin; the dust is always worse nearer the ground." She sighed, obviously worried. "I only hope I have not led you astray. If my path wasn't well chosen, it might finish us all."

Gaelen shrugged. "If that is so, then at least the Scourge is also on an ill-fated path. Maybe it will finish them, as well." She smiled at Bint Raed. "Take courage. I'm certain you remember the lay of these lands better than you realize. I am not concerned."

Three days later they reached the end of the Salt, and the lands that stretched before them seemed less forbidding. They were of a more familiar character, with rolling terrain and ground that was both rocky and sandy. A ridge of hills could be seen in the distance, and the Company was thrilled to see what looked like grey-green, brushy, gnarled shrubs dotting the landscape. Here and there they would find and collect the dead skeletons of those shrubs, which were covered with wicked, sharp thorns. Soon there would be enough to build fires at night against the cold. The air was still dusty, but it seemed clearer than that of the salt waste. Fima's breathing appeared to be a little easier, though he still coughed far too often.

Gaelen had just spotted a depression in the sand some distance away when Finan dropped his head and made for it, ignoring her effort to bring him about. She allowed him his freedom, for she had learned that he was seldom diverted without cause. He slid down into the bottom of the depression and began to paw at the sand, bobbing his head, his long, black forelock waving in the dry breeze. Rogond had followed behind upon Eros, who snorted and tossed his head before sliding down after Finan, pawing right alongside him. The sand beneath their busy feet turned darker...it was wet! A few more minutes, and they were standing in water up to their ankles. "Do not let them drink until the sand has settled," warned Rogond. "It will make them very ill otherwise. Hallagond has told me."

Gaelen smiled at him. "Your brother is coming around nicely. He could have gone with Azori, but he chose to stay with you. He truly is a fine man, and you can be proud to claim him as your kinsman."

"I don't think he remains on my account. He stays for Estle."

Gaelen laughed. "Then it's a good thing Estle wants to see the Silver City so badly, otherwise they might both have left with Azori." She leaned forward, resting on Finan's neck, stroking him. "I would say that Finan has earned an extra treat. There is enough water here that we may all clean ourselves, plus fill a few of our empty casks."

It seemed their outlook had brightened, until Bint Raed rode up with Estle, looking in alarm at Gaelen and Rogond. "You haven't let them drink, have you?"

"No…we are waiting for the sand to settle first," said Gaelen, tightening her hold on Finan's head-collar. "Why do you ask?"

"Come up out of there, both of you. That water is not safe!" Eros was reluctant to leave the water, for it felt wonderful on his tired legs, but he listened to Rogond. Finan squealed when Gaelen legged him back up to the level without so much as a sip.

"There are poisons that lie beneath the sands here," said Bint Raed. "They leach into the water that rises from under the ground. You dare not drink of it, for over time it will kill both man and beast. I'm sorry I did not think to tell you this before, but I didn't expect you to find water at all, and it just didn't occur to me." When she left to return to the caravan, Gaelen stood looking at Rogond for a moment. Then she turned her puzzled horse and cantered back to the group. Apparently she had decided to forego even washing in the poisoned waters, which was wise. Finan did not understand, and kept trying to turn back.

"Never mind, Finan; you deserve to be praised for finding the water, even though it's unsafe. That isn't your doing...it's the fault of this horrible place! One day we will ride back to the Great Forest, and you will never want for water again." She stroked his neck, turning to look rather wistfully back toward the northeast. "There are tall trees there, Finan, and wonderful plains of green grass where a horse may run for hours upon soft turf, and he will never go hungry, for the grass grows ever at his feet. You probably cannot even imagine such a place, can you my friend?" She took a deep breath. "Someday, I shall take you there."

That evening, Hallagond and Fima built a small fire, and the Company gathered for what would be the first of several disappointing talks with Bint Raed. "It has occurred to me that you truly do not know these lands, and you don't understand what is in store. Gaelen and Rogond might have been poisoned by bad water had I not noticed them. I don't wish to dishearten any of you, for you have met every challenge and none have faltered. But you must understand what lies ahead. These are bad lands. It will take at least a fortnight to gain the far side of the fire-mountains." She looked around at the weary, resigned faces of her friends, and sighed.

"The three chief perils yet to be faced are of earth, wind, and fire. The earth will trap you in three ways—in tar pits, in sand pits, or by hurling stones down upon you in the mountains. The wind may blow so wild and fierce that the sands will strip you of your flesh if you are caught unaware, and even without such ferocity it will raise the dust to choke you. The fire is perhaps the kindest ending; we need worry about it only when crossing the mountains. There are storms that happen there, often in dark of night, where lightning strikes will end your lives quickly. These storms bring wind, but no rain...and the lightning shakes the stone mountainsides such that great rocks may fall upon our heads."

Gaelen turned toward the distant hills. "I can hear thunder," she said, "and I can see a flickering glow over the hills yonder."

"This will be more impressive as we draw closer," said Bint Raed, "for those are not the fire-mountains. You will not see those until we have crossed that line of hills. *Then* you will see something! The fire-storms happen not every night, but from what I have read they are common enough that we are certain to be caught in at least one."

"How is it that you are so familiar with these lands?" asked Hallagond. "I mean…I know you must have traveled them once, but who in his right mind would frequent these places long enough to gain so much knowledge of them?"

She smiled at him. "When I was young, I held a special interest in what was known of faraway lands, for I greatly desired to travel to them. I have always had a special fascination with maps. I read the old records of Tuathas, and of Eádros, the Realm of Light, but though such tales were captivating, they didn't seem *real*. I knew they didn't exist anymore, and I wanted to learn about real places. I was especially fascinated by such terrifying and formidable lands as the ones we must now traverse.

I never wanted to come here, but I still wanted to know all about it. It has been the friend of Dûn Arian, for it has protected us from invasion over land throughout our history. As you have said, Hallagond, what enemy would frequent such a place? Yet there are those of the Citadel who would learn all they can no matter where they venture. Those brave souls did venture here, and made it their business to explore and record all they could. I loved reading of their adventures! Many did not return home, but, thankfully, their written journals were brought back."

"It sounds as though your people are afflicted with an unfortunate curiosity," said Gaelen.

"Well, that's certainly something you would understand and know about," said Galador. He turned to the others. "I could elaborate, but I will refrain for now."

"Let me bring your attention back to the moment," said Bint Raed. "You must not eat or drink anything here, hunt any beast or bird, or disturb any living creature. Things here are unwholesome in general, with venomous bites and poisonous flesh. These are hard lands, and they make for short lives."

"Hmmm…a fortnight, you say?" Fima was downcast. He knew that his strength waned each day, and the prospect of a fortnight in such a place did not exactly fill him with optimism.

"Do not be disheartened, my good dwarf," said Gaelen, who probably loved Fima more than she did any living soul save Rogond and Nelwyn. "Your folk are the hardiest in all of Alterra. You will reach the library with enough strength to spare, and you will spend countless happy hours studying and learning there. I swear on my life that I shall do all in my power to aid you."

Fima smiled at this, but he could not resist toying with her. "Oh, no, Gaelen…please do not make such an oath. The last thing I would wish for is to owe you a life-debt! After all, look at what happened to Hallagond."

"I would prefer to not dwell upon such thoughts, if it's the same to you," said Hallagond, with gruffness in his voice that didn't match the humor in his eyes.

Tomorrow they would resume their grim journey, suppressing all curiosity. They would keep their eyes fixed on the course ahead, and yet would remain wary of everything around them. There would be no time spent in playfulness—all effort would be expended in putting as much distance behind them as possible.

When they crossed the hills, they were treated to their first sight of the fire-mountains, and that night they witnessed the incredible spectacle of a distant fire-storm. It was as though the mountains knew of their approach, and would bid them a spectacular but sinister welcome.

In the land between the hills and the mountains, everything seemed to change. The heat of the day was lessened, but the nights were truly cold, and they shivered around their small fires, each keeping company with his or her own. Rogond and Gaelen, Nelwyn and Galador, Hallagond and Estle, all shared their cloaks and the warmth of their bodies, as well as the love that grew in their hearts. Bint Raed and Fima were likewise united in their frailty, for neither had seen youth in many a year, and both were mortal. They told interesting tales, and their friendship grew. Fima learned much concerning the founding of the Citadel, and Bint Raed learned of the realm of Mountain-home, and of the Great Wars in the northlands.

"Do they have good things to eat in the Silver City?" asked Fima wistfully on one especially cold evening, after he had finished his third meal that day of flatbread and dried meat. The water from some of the casks was beginning to taste stale, and though it would not harm them to drink it, it had lost some of its appeal.

Bint Raed warmed to the question at once, and all in the Company were rapt at her descriptions of the bounty they would feast upon once they gained the Citadel. She described some of the treasures that could be gained from the deep waters, speaking of strange creatures filled with sweet meat, and deep green ocean plants that chewed like salty leather but made wonderful soup when boiled. She told also of great fishes that could swallow a man whole, and others that would tear hapless mariners to pieces if ill fortune took their vessels into the deeps.

Galador had seen the vast waters long ago, and he had never forgotten them. He looked forward to standing once more upon stony shores and hearing the call of the sea in his ears. He had last looked upon it not long after the ruin of Eádros; he had traveled there from the Monadh-ailan, standing in awe upon the rocks, looking out over the waters that stretched before him without end.

Bint Raed's words tantalized them, but speaking of wonderful food and drink is not nearly as satisfying as actually eating and drinking it. The Company grew silent, bundled against the ever-rising wind for another long night.

As they drew nearer to the mountains, the risk of high winds increased. When these blew across the lowlands they carried sand and choking clouds of dust, dismaying even the dromadin. They flattened their ears and folded their long legs beneath their bellies, refusing to rise from the sand and move on. The Company tried as best they could to keep the sand and dust from their eyes and nostrils. Breathing of it was ill-advised, and some, like Fima, had already suffered harmful effects. Everyone huddled together beside the dromadin, using them as shields, hoping that all their belongings would not blow away.

According to Bint Raed, these winds could get much worse—no living thing could survive them in open lands. She had read the accounting of one brave party that had survived such a storm; apparently they witnessed the painful and unpleasant end of a comrade who didn't make it to the shelter of rocks. His clothing and flesh were literally stripped from his bones by the screaming, wind-driven sand. This did nothing to encourage the Company, and they began always to look for rocks that they might escape to.

They approached the foothills of the Fire-mountains at last, asking Bint Raed whether the killing sands would follow beyond them. "I don't know the answer to that," was the solemn reply.

A strange odor hung in the air; it was picked up first by Gaelen, who described it as being rather like pitch. "It is no doubt one of the many tar-pits that dot the lower elevations of these mountains," said Bint Raed. "Do you recall the black smoke we noticed two days ago...how it still burns? It is the smoke seen when one of the tar pits is set afire by a lightning strike. Remember, no rain comes with these storms, and the tar is very easily struck alight. It will burn for a long time when that happens."

She smiled at her friends' expressions of horror. "Whatever you do, don't set your feet into anything black and sticky."

The Company shuddered; this warning was entirely unnecessary. Soon the black rivulets of tar were everywhere, and they made it more difficult to move forward, for even a narrow ribbon would mire the feet of man or beast.

"How did this come to be here?" asked Rogond, who held some fascination for such things.

"We do not know," said Bint Raed. "This is the only place our people have encountered it. We do know that sometimes the tar flows up from beneath the ground, and there's also black oil. Alas that is it far from the City, across the Plains of Thirst, or we would have made use of it."

"Alas, indeed," said Rogond with a sigh. He had forgotten about the Plains of Thirst.

They climbed ever higher, making for a low pass across the mountains. They gained it as the sun went down before them; soon they would begin the long, slow way back down into the flat plains beyond. "That did not seem so difficult," said Nelwyn, with some pride. "In the north we have many sets of mountains, and we have crossed the tallest among them. They are much more formidable than these. Gaelen and I have made that crossing twice—once even in winter!"

"Each place has its own perils," replied Bint Raed. "See now, how the clouds gather to mock us? No water will they give, but they will soon spawn a fire-storm, and those are always more fierce near the mountaintops, which is where we are now. We must find shelter for the night."

That night would prove to be one of the longest since the journey began. It started with the building of the clouds above their heads, bringing a sense of foreboding. The ground felt strangely warm as they sheltered beneath a large overhang of rock. Bint Raed explained that to be in the open was to invite being struck by lightning, and now they all crowded together as they saw the first flash of fire snaking across the darkening sky. Sometimes it traveled among the clouds, and at such times it was beautiful, but when it struck the ground it shook the mountains.

Rogond could feel Gaelen's heart beating hard and fast. Neither she nor Nelwyn had ever liked lightning storms—a very sensible attitude in a forest-dweller. He tried to calm her, but she would not be comforted.

When the storm struck with its full force, it was a cataclysm of noise and light that shook the mountain. A mighty bolt struck the cliff-face above the Company, breaking loose a huge chunk of rock and earth, sending it down upon them. Though it missed their sanctuary, the force split the very ground where they were sheltering. Part of the overhang broke loose and fell into a great rend that had suddenly appeared in the rock. Two of the dromadin fell with it. The Company struggled to keep hold of their beasts and keep track of their friends, calling frantically, trying to be heard over the roar of the wind and the crashing rocks and thunder-claps.

Fissures opened in the mountainside, issuing forth steam followed by rivulets of black oil. These spread all around them as they tried to find one another and re-group. The Company now stood on opposite sides of a great gap in the rock—Gaelen, Hallagond, and Rogond on one side, Nelwyn, Galador, Estle, and Bint Raed on the other. Except for the two unfortunate dromadin, all the animals were accounted for.

"Where's Fima?" asked Gaelen, clutching Rogond's arm.

"I have not seen or heard him, though I have been searching," was the reply. They began calling to Fima with no success.

"I didn't see him fall," said Gaelen, fighting back tears of panic. "He may be trapped, or hurt so that he cannot answer. I don't know what to do…what should we do?" She looked to Rogond and Hallagond, hoping for guidance, but they had none to give.

"Just keep calling," said Rogond at last. "He is bound to hear us."

"Yes, Gaelen, keep calling to him," said Hallagond, who wanted very much to be of help. "The worst of the storm has passed, I think."

But just when Hallagond thought their lot was improving, he was proven wrong by a fire-bolt that struck the mountainside not a hundred feet from him. It nearly knocked him down, raised every hair on his body, and terrified the horses. As if that wasn't bad enough, it ignited one of the streams of black oil, sending flames and odorous black smoke billowing into the air, fueled by the high winds.

"We must get away from that raging fire at once," yelled Hallagond. "If the wind shifts it will cut off our escape. We dare not stay here."

"But, we must find Fima! I will not leave without him," cried Gaelen.

"Nor will I," Rogond shouted, and the two of them resumed their frantic calls to their friend, who would now have to answer over the sound of wind, thunder, and fire, if he were able.

"There he is!" cried Gaelen, pointing straight into the wall of flames. "I saw him on the other side of the fire. He is lying at the base of the rock, and he's not moving. No, wait…I think he *is* moving after all. How could we not have seen him earlier?" Now that she knew where to look, it seemed as plain as day.

Fima had been roused by the heat and smoke, both of which threatened to take him in a few minutes. He had nowhere to run to, and they heard him cry in terror as the flames drew nearer. This cry was drowned by a fit of coughing as the black smoke nearly engulfed him. His friends did not know how to aid him, and they cried out in frustration, for he would surely be lost.

Gaelen broke free of Rogond's grasp and ran to Finan, who quieted as he felt her touch. She grabbed the fire-cloak from her pack, praying that it would do as Bint Raed had promised. Before Rogond could stop her she wrapped herself in it, pulled the hood down over her face, and ran toward the flames. She drew back for a moment—this would take all the faith and courage she could muster. She gathered herself and sprang into the fire, calling the name of Farahin Ri-Elathan in a loud and terrible voice.

The next few minutes lasted nearly a lifetime for Rogond. There was no sign of Gaelen or Fima, and he heard no cries. The wind rose higher and the flames rose with it. None could survive that inferno, and Rogond stood helpless, screaming the name of his beloved as his brother looked into the fire, his face a mask of horror as though lost in a black memory.

If Rogond never received any gift in his life again he would be content, for the sight of Gaelen struggling back through the flames with Fima in her arms was a greater blessing than he could ever have hoped for. He cried out with relief and ran to her aid. Both she and Fima were in a bad way; they had nearly been overcome by the heat and smoke, but they were most definitely alive.

"Her boots are on fire!" cried Hallagond, who set himself to the task of putting out the smoldering leather of Gaelen's old, worn favorite boots. They were covered with black oil, and he could not extinguish them—she would not be able to salvage them this time. Hallagond removed them as quickly as he could, but her feet and legs had already blistered. "We must get away from here," he yelled at Rogond, who nodded in agreement. They bore their friends to relative safety, with the horses and dromadin following.

As if it could sense that all in the Company had learned their lesson about underestimating the Fire-mountains, the storm abated. Soon, it had gone.

The Company worked their way around the barriers separating them, and they were soon reunited. Fima was still unconscious. Nelwyn wept as she tried to clean the black ash and soot from his face. His beautiful white beard had been badly singed, with large sections of it frizzled away. His breath rattled in his chest and whistled in his throat, as though he could barely draw air. He showed no evidence of burns other than reddening of his face and hands, for dwarves are quite fire-tolerant.

Gaelen, on the other hand, was not resistant to fire. Although the cloak had served her well, there was still the matter of her swollen, blistered feet and legs. She cried as Rogond tended them, biting down hard on the collar of her leather jerkin. It had been difficult to secure the fire-cloak around both herself and Fima, but she had managed as best she could. Still, her right hand had been exposed to the flames, and had been badly burned. It was hard for her to bear the pain of it.

"Where is that wonderful ointment?" asked Galador, recalling the good it had done for Hallagond's wound.

"There's not much left," said Rogond. "We dare not use it, for it burns when applied, and I don't think she would withstand the pain. These wounds are too extensive."

"What about that dark elixir she carries? Perhaps a drop or two of that wouldn't hurt," said Hallagond. "It certainly took my pain away, and gave me a long, restful sleep filled with pleasant dreams. It might aid her."

Rogond drew forth the small silver flask from the pack at Gaelen's belt. "Gaelen, Hallagond is right. You should have a small sip of this, so that you can rest. We are taking good care of Fima." He held the flask to her lips, and she took a very small sip of the dark fluid. The pain left her eyes almost at once, and she sagged down onto the sand.

Hallagond was worried, as she appeared to be dead rather than asleep.

Rogond smiled. "It's the eyes, isn't it? I'm quite accustomed to the tendency of Elves to keep their eyes open even when they are resting, but for most it takes some getting used to. She's not truly at peace here in this place, and so her eyes remain open. I don't blame her."

"So, is she still partly aware, then?" asked Hallagond. "When she gave me that elixir, I was dead to the world. Nothing would have roused me."

"Yes, she is still aware, and I would say nothing that I did not want her to hear. She took a smaller amount than you did, probably because she wants to be able to rouse herself quickly should need arise."

"But she can't walk on those feet, surely...and she can't pull her bow with blistered fingers," said Hallagond.

"Yet she can still ride, and she can wield a blade with her left hand. You are about to witness something miraculous, Hallagond. She will heal quickly so long as nothing else happens to take her spirit." With those words, Rogond covered Gaelen with his cloak and left her to see to Fima, whose need was greater.

Hallagond remained with Gaelen, his grey eyes moist, many emotions turning in his head. He whispered to her, for he knew she could hear him: "That was a most courageous act. You are the most true-hearted and valiant of friends. I once faced the same, but I failed my test...I'm not sure that even a fire-cloak would have made any difference. My brother is a fortunate man to have your heart, for a great heart it is. Rest well, little Avinasha. I will watch over you." Gaelen closed her eyes, and he knew she had heard him.

Estle and Nelwyn were examining the fire-cloak with wonder. Other than the bright finish having been dulled by a coating of black soot, it had taken no damage. "So, this is more than just a garish garment. I know it reflects the sun, but it actually turns fire and smoke," said Estle, fingering the cool, bright folds of the curious fabric. "It must be rare indeed. I have never even heard of such a thing."

"Thank the stars it worked," said Nelwyn. She then addressed Bint Raed, who sat nearby. "You knew this would be needed. We owe you a great debt, Master Weaver."

Bint Raed's face was deadly serious. "Thank the stars, indeed. The cloak had never been tested. It took great faith for Gaelen to throw herself through a wall of flame on my word alone. I don't like to think of what would have befallen if the cloak had failed."

Nelwyn smiled at her. "Gaelen knew better. She trusts you with her life, as have we all."

"Still, I might have tested it first," said Bint Raed.

"You forget who you are speaking of," said Estle, laughing. "Gaelen seems often to act on faith...mostly in herself, I'm thinking."

"Yes," replied Bint Raed. "It's one of several ways in which you are alike." To this, Estle would no longer argue.

Fima did not come around until long after sunrise. He reeked of burning oil and soot, and immediately began coughing. The deep, liquid rattle in his chest was very distressing. When he finally spoke, he could barely manage a croaking whisper; the fiery-hot air and smoke had taken its toll.

"How is it that I'm still here? I was helpless, and there was no aid anyone could give. My friends could not find me. How is it that I'm *here?*"

Gaelen had found Fima unconscious; she could barely see him through the choking, foul-smelling blackness that engulfed him. She had lifted him with some difficulty, for he weighed more than she did. She had then wrapped the fire-cloak around both of them, keeping the hood across her face, and struggled back through the wall of fire. He had not been aware of his own rescue.

Nelwyn told him the tale, placing the fire-cloak in his hands. He looked at it with wonder; as with Estle, he had not truly appreciated its properties. "So, this is what allowed Gaelen to come for me," he said.

"That, and a lot of faith," said Bint Raed. "She did not know the cloak would work as well as it did. She must love you dearly, Fima Lore-master. Rest now, and take some water. Gaelen has vowed that you will reach the Citadel alive, and we must now make certain her effort has been well spent."

"Take me to her," said Fima. "I would thank her for my life, and see that she is well."

"She is resting. This act took much of her strength," said Nelwyn. "There will be plenty of time later." She covered Fima with his own cloak and left him to rest. He was faring better than they had hoped, though he coughed up black soot for many days.

Gaelen recovered quickly, and within a week her skin was almost fully renewed. Fima grumbled endlessly concerning the fact that he now owed her a life-debt, and he made her promise to release him from it should he ever pull her from flaming death. She gave him her solemn oath that she would release him should he save her from any form of death whatsoever, including that caused by excessive weariness from listening to dwarves grumbling endlessly about life-debts. "True friends do not owe life-debts, Fima," she said. He stopped reminding her of it after that.

Hallagond was very solicitous of Gaelen while she was healing, and she now had both brothers attending to her every need. The entire Company treated her with reverence, as though she had done something very heroic, and she accepted their attentions even though they made her uncomfortable, saying: "Any of you would have done the same."

They started across the plains of thirst, a journey that Bint Raed estimated would take another fortnight, telling them that when they reached the end of it there would be kinder lands, and only about a week's travel to the mountains guarding the eastern approach to the Citadel. Thankfully, they still had plenty of water despite the loss of their two dromadin.

The Company was encouraged, and all felt certain they would succeed in completing the journey, yet Fima's breathing was now quite labored. Bint Raed was not faring well either; she was pale, and tired quickly. The long hours of riding across the hot, dry plains taxed both of them, and thus they needed to rest more often.

During one of these periods of rest, Gaelen noticed Hallagond standing alone on the watch. She approached, offering to stand the watch with him, for there was a question she would ask. "Ask away," he replied, "Though I think I've guessed your question. You want to know about the test that I faced, and failed."

"You have told me some of it already," she replied, "but I believe the only way to be free of such a burden is to set it down. Will you not let me help you?"

His face drew briefly into an expression of anguish before becoming a mask of stone. "If only it were as easy as that," he said. "The sight of you emerging through that wall of fire brought everything back. I could not have done what you did to save your friend, though I had the choice once, and I turned from it. I didn't even have the courage to come to terms with my own failure...I ran from it because I could not face it."

"Then face it now," said Gaelen. There was no accusation in her voice, no judgment of him in her eyes. "You need tell no one save Rogond. I believe that was your promise to him?" She saw the look of surprise flash briefly across his face. "Rogond keeps nothing from me. Surely you know it by now."

"Summon him here," said Hallagond, "and you shall hear of my shame. I'm weary of running."

Gaelen went immediately to find Rogond, lest Hallagond waver in his resolve. The three of them sat at the base of a ring of large stones, having set Galador to the watch.

Hallagond began his tale, his voice and eyes cold and without expression. "There was once a young Ranger, who was strong, fleet-footed, and skilled in battle. He was also proud, and overconfident, and did not believe that any ill fortune would ever befall him. His friends, Rangers all, had made him their captain, and why not? He was the tallest, the cleverest, and the boldest among them. His plans did not fail. He began to believe that he was blessed, and that it was his destiny never to be defeated, but to bring grief to his enemies and praise to his own name. His pride grew with each victory.

But then, his acts turned to recklessness driven by overconfidence, and a few of his forays against the enemy didn't end so well. This surely could not be through any fault of his, and he resolved to prove it to himself and everyone else by arranging an attack on a group of Anori bandits, who had been of a particularly troublesome nature in the lands he was set to defend."

Hallagond sighed, dropping all pretenses. "I thought nothing of it. I knew this man, this bandit captain, was a clever enemy, but I underestimated him. One of the other Rangers—my best friend at the time—tried to warn me. His name was Tomas, and he was one of the fiercest fighters I've ever known. We'd served together through countless forays, and I always admired him for his courage, though not often for wits. He warned me that the bandits had a reputation for trapping and killing anyone who came after them. He told me my plan was risky, and it could end badly if all did not go as intended. It was the first time he had ever questioned my authority.

When he tried to turn the others against the plan, I…I grew angry. I was supposed to be in command, and I couldn't tolerate a supposed friend undermining me. I drove him out of the group, warning him to not show his face among us again. In my anger, I called him a traitor and a coward. Yet he followed behind, hoping to be forgiven, for he was still my friend."

The words came harder for Hallagond now as he struggled to control the grief in his voice. "The bandits were fierce fighters, and their chieftain was very clever—as it turned out he was cleverer than I was. My plan was a spectacular failure, exactly as Tomas had warned. My men…my men were trapped against a stone cliff by a wall of fire, as their enemies had intended. All except me."

Hallagond's voice went very quiet, so that Rogond could barely hear him. "Do you know what it's like to burn to death? I think I do." A tear blazed a trail through the dust on his face, his jaw muscles working. "The fire burned so hot that I could not aid them. All I could do was stare at them as my strength, my will, drained out of me. I heard a sound behind me and turned to behold my friend, Tomas, the one I had named a coward, rushing up from behind. A great, wooly bear of a man, Tomas. We both stared in horror, hearing the screams of our comrades, seeing the anguish in their faces as the flames took them. There is no other sound like it.

I just stood there, helpless—I could not believe what was happening before my eyes. But Tomas, the one I named a coward…he didn't just stand there. He cried a terrible cry, wrapped himself in his woolen cloak, and leaped in to try to save at least one. Alas, my last sight of him was as a flaming torch; his cloak had not protected him for more than a few seconds. All the while, the Anori were laughing at us…laughing!"

Hallagond shuddered, wiping his eyes with the back of one hand, like a child. "They all died," he said, his face expressionless. "Every one of them. I heard the laughter of my enemies as my friends screamed in their agony, and I could do nothing. I knew that I could not save them. To pull them from the flames would have prolonged their lives by a few hours of agonizing torment at most." He looked up at Rogond. "Nelwyn said that being mired in that foul pool we passed near the Mountains of Dread would be a terrible death, but I know of a worse one."

Gaelen and Rogond remained silent, for they sensed that Hallagond had not finished. After a moment he spoke again, his voice choked with the shame welling up within him. "I wanted in that moment to die with them. It would have been fitting...after all, I was their captain. I should have been the first to suffer, and the last to find release, for it was *my* pride that placed them in harm's way. My friend, the one I named 'coward,' died trying to make a difference to them, but I…I just stood there. Even when I knew they would all die, I could not cast myself into the flames to join them."

He looked at Rogond as though pleading for his life. "I wanted to, but I could not. Do you believe me?"

Rogond was torn between shock and horror. He did not answer at first.

"My brother, I ask you once more, do you believe me?"

Slowly, the shock faded from Rogond's face to be replaced with deep sorrow. "Yes, my brother," he said gently. "I believe you. And you cannot hold yourself to blame for failing to take your own life in such a terrible way. Your friend must have thought he could aid the others and escape—alas that he could not. You knew the truth of it. Pulling them from that hell would not have helped them."

Hallagond spoke in a small, quiet voice. "I have lived for so long with the weight of these deaths," he said. "I could not bear the pain, and so I ran from it, drowned it with drink, dulled it with weed… yet it remains. I still hear their screams, still hear the laughter. It will always remain, and I will never be free of it." He began to weep, his head in his hands.

Rogond wanted to embrace his brother, to comfort him and tell him that all would be well, but he did not. Hallagond needed to grieve openly; the poisoned thorn must be withdrawn. Rogond just sat quietly by, waiting.

Finally Hallagond grew weary, and he stopped weeping. He looked into his brother's eyes. "Will you now shun me, as I have shunned myself? I know that would be my desire if I were you."

"I will never shun you," said Rogond. "It is my great joy to have found you, and it is my great desire to return you to the northlands. I will never shun you."

"I cannot return," said Hallagond. "The northlands are my home no longer, for I'm not the man I was, and never will be again."

"No," said Gaelen, speaking for the first and only time. "You are a much better man now."

It took the Company nearly three weeks to cross the plains of thirst, because of the need to rest Fima and Bint Raed. Gaelen had wrapped Fima in the fire-cloak because it turned the heat, but also because it would shield him from the dust and allow him to breathe more easily. He was very ill now; he would not eat, and had to be coaxed even to drink water, for the mere act of swallowing would send him into a violent fit of coughing that was truly alarming.When it abated, he was so exhausted that he would not move for hours. He lay shrouded in the brilliant fabric; the soot had blown away in the wind, and the cloak shimmered brightly again. It seemed to be almost a living thing. *You think I will tolerate that foul blackness? I am a fire-cloak! My light remains undiminished.*

The cold nights taxed Fima, for the fire-cloak did nothing to warm the air. At such times Gaelen would sing to him, wrapping his woolen cloak around him, while Estle boiled a small quantity of water into which she had placed dry sage-leaves that she had collected earlier. Their vapors aided Fima, who was instructed to hang his head over the basin while breathing as deeply as he could manage.

Eventually he became so weak that he could no longer ride, so they fashioned a litter and bore him on it. He was not aware of his surroundings, and was too ill to comment on them, but they all knew that his own helplessness grieved him.

Bint Raed had not fared much better. She had lost a great deal of weight, and now could ride only a short while without tiring. Hallagond, Estle, and Rogond seemed hale enough, yet Gaelen noticed that they appreciated the extra rest. The Elves, of course, were tireless, but even they looked travel-worn.

Because their pace had slowed, they used water quite sparingly, and they debated the notion of killing several of the dromadin, who were no longer needed to carry the dwindling provisions. Gaelen and Nelwyn objected to this notion, contending that the dromadin had served faithfully and well, and they were part of the Company.

"Finan does not mind short rations, and neither do I." She and Nelwyn had become attached to the dromadin, who would now be sacrificed only as a last resort.

Their journey was uneventful, except for the remains of a caravan that had attempted the crossing and failed. The dried, sand-blown carcasses of several dromadin were found lying together, still wearing their fine harness, and still carrying goods upon what was left of their backs. Bint Raed sorrowed when they came at last upon the bodies of men struggling toward the west, having finally collapsed from heat and thirst.

"They were lost," she said quietly. "They did not mean to come this way. They probably became bewildered in a sandstorm, and could not find their bearings again."

"What a pity that they came so far, only to fail now, when they were so close," said Hallagond. He had been moved especially by the sight of two dried collections of flesh and bone that had once been living beings. One was shrouded in black cloth, and it held the other, much smaller, in its arms. "Rest, mother, and sing to your child, for you will never thirst again," he said.

The wind shifted at mid-day so that it was out of the east, and Gaelen tested it, her body tense. The worry in her face attracted the attention of Nelwyn at once. "The wind is speaking to you, isn't it? What does it tell?"

"It tells that the Scourge is moving ever-westward, though they are not near to us. We must do all that we may to make better time."

Gaelen called the Company together, and told them of what she had learned.

"How far away do you suppose they are?" asked Estle with a small note of alarm in her voice. Except for Gaelen, only she had seen the dreaded army with her own eyes.

"They are a very great distance from here—we have been moving much more swiftly than they have. Such a large army takes a long time to get anywhere. We're nimble, and they are not. That great stench will carry a long, long way. What I can't figure out is how they are managing to get such a large force across this waste. Their course has crossed even more desert than we have, and they could not possibly carry enough water."

"Are you certain it is the Scourge?" asked Hallagond.

Gaelen frowned at him. "Are you taller than a dwarf? Of *course* I'm certain! There is some foulness about that army that I have never encountered before. I don't know its origin, but it's vile, and I don't expect to find it anywhere else." She turned and began to make ready to move on. "We dare not linger," she said. "None of us can afford to go on our own feet. One of us must bear Fima with him on a horse. It will do us no good to arrive at the Citadel if we don't have time to prepare for battle."

"He can't even hold up his own head, Gaelen," said Rogond, somewhat surprised that she would even suggest taxing her dear friend so.

"He won't need to if you steady him," said Gaelen. "Even if Eros must walk slowly, he walks more swiftly than we can. It will tax your strength much less than bearing that litter."

Rogond had been sharing the burden with Hallagond and Galador. It had been difficult bearing Fima through the deep sand, and the rocky ground was not much better. Rogond's boots were nearly worn through. He nodded to Gaelen, and readied himself for the task. Nelwyn sat beside Fima, telling him that although he must now ride, Rogond would bear him gently and he need not fear.

Gaelen steadied Eros as Fima was lifted into Rogond's strong arms. "You must walk carefully, Eros, and never argue with Rogond, for he will have his hands full. I know you will see your task done." She stroked his light golden face, and worked a tangle out of his long, black forelock, somewhat distressed to see that it had been reddened by the desert sun. Eros dropped his head and nuzzled her as though this was nothing to make a fuss about.

It was not long before they drew within sight of the tall, brown hills. A good thing, for the last few days had taken much of their strength. They had nearly run out of food, and had enough water for perhaps three more days. The animals suffered from the lack of water; some would not long survive. The hills were nothing like the tall, forbidding crags of the north, but they were daunting enough for the Company.

"Will we need to cross them, or is there a pass through them?" asked Gaelen.

"There is a pass, but we must travel south to find it," said Bint Raed. "The hills are formidable, and we do not have the strength to traverse them. I have brought us north of where I wanted to be." She shook her head slowly, her skin wrinkled and dry from sun and lack of water.

"Never mind," said Nelwyn. "At least you know where we are, and what we must now do. We are not lost, thanks to you."

"Yes, and it's a good job that you did bring us north, otherwise we might have experienced a much more unpleasant encounter with our enemies," said Gaelen. "Yet it distresses me that they seem to be more directly on target than we are."

"There is only one explanation for that," said Estle. "Someone from the Citadel leads them."

This notion shocked Bint Raed. "I would never imagine such a thing...our people are sworn to keep the secret of the Silver City from any that are not trustworthy. We would never betray it!"

"So all would like to believe, but there are forces in the world that may corrupt even the most steadfast, and the threat of death is a strong incentive for treachery," said Galador. He knew much of such things, having seen the result of evil and corruption during the course of his long life. "What other explanation is likely? Even if your folk did not so intend, it is possible that one they thought trustworthy was not so. It is not all that difficult to be beguiled."

Bint Raed turned from him, her dismay apparent, as Nelwyn tried to reassure her. "Never mind…it doesn't matter how the Scourge is being guided. What matters is that we will reach Dûn Arian long before they do, and your people will be warned." Nelwyn could see that this was not the only thing troubling her friend. Bint Raed was literally shaking with sorrow, though her eyes were dry. "What is it?" asked Nelwyn. "What has so distressed you?"

"I'm so…tired. Tired and weak and in pain," said Bint Raed. "I knew the journey would be difficult, and I knew that at my age I would never make it alone, yet even with your aid I don't know if I will live to see my home again. That is a sorrow I cannot bear. We are only a few leagues north of our goal, but those few leagues might well be the death of me." She wept, though she was so dry that no tears came forth, as Nelwyn held her.

Gaelen approached them, and her eyes were sad. "Nelwyn, the time has come for last resorts. We will do what we must do." She walked over to one of the dromadin, the weakest of the lot, a young male that Nelwyn had named Ortan. She stroked his thin, bony neck as he lowered his head to greet her, closing his large, soft eyes with pleasure. She whispered to him, telling him of how strong and brave he was, and how faithful. He would surely be rewarded in the Eternal Realm, where no burdens need be carried and there was neither thirst nor hunger. Then, in the blink of an eye, she cut his throat. He seemed not to feel it, looking around in a puzzled way when his legs suddenly grew weak and he collapsed on the sand. Gaelen took the water-rations he carried, distributing them among the other beasts, and moved to Bint Raed.

"Drink, most worthy woman of the Citadel. Drink your fill. Ortan needs no water now."

Gaelen would do the same to two more of the dromadin ere they reached the pass at last; the journey took five more days, and the beasts were on their last legs. Hallagond had suggested that perhaps some of the horses might be considered for sacrifice, as they drank more water considering their size, and were not as valuable as the dromadin. Gaelen would not hear of it. "We have more dromadin than we need to carry supplies, but the horses carry the Company," was her terse reply.

The way into the pass was interesting, and Hallagond commented that it was as if someone had arranged the hills so that the pass would remain hidden to all but the most diligent. The brown, barren hills were staggered such that one needed to be directly in line with the pass to see it, and even then it was difficult, for the hills behind obscured it. When Bint Raed pointed it out, all were astonished, for it was a wide path, yet they would not have found it.

When they rode through it they saw before them a changed land. The ground was stony, but there were green things growing up from the rocks. "*Trees*, Nelwyn! Real trees…look, there!" cried Gaelen, pointing to scattered olive-trees and sage shrubs that grew in ever-increasing numbers.

Finan found a flowing spring amid the stones; it was only about a hand's breadth, but it was deep and clear. "Bint Raed…is this water safe?" asked Gaelen, who was so thirsty that her throat ached at the sight of it.

"Yes, Gaelen, it's safe," whispered Bint Raed, "That is a seep from far beneath the earth. Man and beast may drink of it without fear."

"Here, then, fill your dry throat with this," said Gaelen, bringing her a skin with some of the spring water. Then she moved to her friend Fima, to offer him what he would take.

Finan drank his fill, lifted his head, and shook himself. *Ahhh! Now that was good water. It was almost worth being so thirsty to enjoy it.*

They rested by the seep for an hour, and all in the Company drank of it save the beasts; the seep was slow to fill, and so they were given the last of the water they carried. It would take quite a while to fill their casks. Eros was envious. *So, why did they let you drink of it?* he asked Finan, who was being rather smug about it.

Because I found it, is why! Finan replied with a toss of his head, licking his lips to make clear to Eros that it was very tasty water indeed. Eros turned his tail to Finan, and would not acknowledge him further.

The wind had turned again so that it blew from the west, and Gaelen was nearly beside herself, for she could smell trees, water, and all sorts of wonderful scents, overlaid by a salty tang quite unlike that of the salt desert.

"Ah, Gaelen...that is the sea," said Galador. "I cannot detect it as yet, but so it must be."

Gaelen was very excited; she could not wait to tell Fima, for she was reasonably certain that he had never seen the ocean. She tried to rouse him, speaking enthusiastically into his ear. "Fima…Fima my friend! I have tasted the scent of the sea! It's not far now, soon we will gaze together upon its wonders. Surely it will rival any sight you will have seen before. Fima…?"

The dwarf did not move, nor did he appear to respond to her question, and Gaelen despaired. Then she heard him whisper through what was left of his formerly luxuriant silver moustache.

"Don't be so sure…I have seen sights much more wonderful than any Elf could fathom…yet I would enjoy your delight and amazement, for you are young, and have not my...experience…"

Gaelen smiled at his description of her as "young and inexperienced". Fima had probably seen two hundred years at least, yet she was many times his age.

"My friends!" said Bint Raed, who had felt some of her strength return with rest, water, and hope. "Behold the great cliffs that guard my City from the sea!"

Beautiful, tall cliffs, banded with pink, azure, and grey, ran in a continuous line along the coast. As the Company drew nearer, Galador pointed to a gleam of bright white and silver, and they knew they had found their destination at last! As Rogond looked through Thorndil's glass, he was reminded of a rendering depicting the city of Tallasiar, which was lost in the fall of Tuathas.

Gaelen and Nelwyn agreed that the City was a beautiful sight, but their thoughts were elsewhere. "There is a forest nearby, Gaelen! I have seen birds and other signs that tell me so; the nights are getting warmer, and the air is heavy with moisture," said Nelwyn, who could hardly contain her excitement. "I will never need gain the Citadel, if only I may rest among tall trees again.

Gaelen smiled back at her, tapping the end of her nose with one finger. "I need no further sign than this," she said. "I have caught the scent of forest, even over that of the sea. We shall soon walk in the green shade, my friend."

They approached Bint Raed. "Is there anything to fear within the City?" asked Gaelen. "There are trees there, and Nelwyn and I greatly desire to see them. Our mounts have been watered, and they are eager. May we not ride ahead and see this great sight?"

"I wouldn't advise it," said Bint Raed, "for the forest lies on the other side of the cliffs. There's nothing but rocks and scrub until you reach the Great Gates. Do you not wish to approach together, as a Company, after all these days of hardship?"

Gaelen took her meaning. "So, you believe we *may* have something to fear?"

"I honestly don't know. It has been long since I set foot inside the walls, and I don't know what might have changed. Our people have always been suspicious of travelers, as we see so few of them. It would do to be cautious."

"I would agree," said Rogond. "Look now to the walls, yonder." He indicated the distant cliffs, where they could now see immense gates set into walls of stone, and the gates appeared to be opening.

"There are horsemen coming," said Galador. "Perhaps twenty of them. We have been seen."

Rogond raised Thorndil's glass, handing it then to Hallagond and Estle.

"They are well armed," said Galador as the horsemen drew nearer. "They ride well. We should keep our weapons ready."

"Yet there is no hostility in their manner or in their faces," said Gaelen. "We are a small and ragged group. Surely they hold no fear of us." She turned to Bint Raed. "What is the usual method of dealing with strangers who approach the City?"

Bint Raed shook her head. "I cannot say, for I have never witnessed any," she said. "Yet it is clear that some have been welcomed, for our people represent races that were not among the original founders. Our city was built upon and enriched by the hands of those who would once have been called strangers."

"I would guess that they will deal with us according to our intent," said Rogond.

Bint Raed agreed. "You must be certain that our intent is abundantly clear," she said. "My people have little experience in warfare, for they have not faced a real enemy in untold years. The City has kept herself well protected. They may well be afraid of such well-armed, experienced warriors as yourselves, and you must not be seen as threatening. Leave your blades and your bows alone for the moment."

"We will soon have an answer to Gaelen's question," said Estle, "for they are approaching with all speed. See the one bearing the banner? What is that device upon it?"

"It's the emblem of the City of Salasin," said Bint Raed, "a black raven bearing a silver lamp in its talons, upon a field of blue. A seven-rayed star shines over its head."

"Why a raven?" asked Hallagond. "There is little nobility about them."

"Ah, that is where you are wrong," said Fima in a croaking whisper, lifting his head briefly from the crook of Rogond's left arm. This proved to be too great an effort, and he sagged back down. "Ever have our people been allied with ravens, and relied upon them for news. Great birds they are, filled with wisdom. It's no surprise that a lore-master would choose one as the emblem of his House."

"You refer to the stinking black carrion-birds that fill the air with their horrid croaking and cawing?" asked Hallagond. "I was unaware that they could bring news of anything, except for the location of those dead and dying." He shook his head in disgust.

Fima coughed and rattled and sputtered for a few moments before he could answer, opening his watery, red-rimmed blue eyes to scowl sardonically at Hallagond. "You obviously have mistaken ravens for crows," he said. "Only ignorance can excuse you...ravens are nothing like them. If you are ever fortunate enough to encounter one, you will see the difference. Ravens are much larger, and some can speak the tongues of men. Yet they speak only to the wise, thus you may not be fortunate enough to hear it."

Hallagond started to retort, but Rogond stayed him. "Save your breath, my brother. He is asleep again."

"We have plenty of ravens in the north," Hallagond muttered. "I know the difference."

"Look to yourselves, all of you!" said Galador. "The riders are here."

The Company was surrounded in a few moments.

"You will please dismount from your horses," said a tall, brown-skinned man who rode beside the standard-bearer. He had brown hair and light brown eyes, and was clad in blue robes. He was obviously a person of some importance. Blue cloth was the most difficult to produce, as true blue dyes were rare.

Bint Raed rode forward. "I am a citizen, and as such should not be treated as a stranger. These are my friends, and are worthy allies. They pose no threat to us or to our people."

"What is your name, citizen?" asked the tall man, who obviously did not recognize her. "Tell me your name, and those of your father and mother, that I may know you."

"I am Bint Raed, daughter of Raenien and Hasta Nimblejack. I have been gone a long time, but I still remember you, Colin Al-jaseem."

The man's eyes widened. "You were thought lost, weaver-woman. The world has not been kind to you these many years."

"The world has not been kind to any of us recently," she replied. "Our journey has been very difficult. We have faced the mountains of dread, the storms of fire, and the plains of thirst to bring news of a terrible enemy that will soon threaten the City, and have nearly killed ourselves in doing so. One of our Company lies near death, yet you will now waste time asking us to dismount, when you should be guiding us to the High Council? The ways of our people have changed if you would now treat such a ragged band of travelers, who have drawn no weapon, as threatening."

All heard Bint Raed's words, but the horsemen were now staring in wonder at the Elves. "Of what race are these?" asked the tall man, indicating Gaelen, Nelwyn, and Galador.

"They are Elves, of course," replied Bint Raed, as though this was a common occurrence and he certainly should have known it. "A dwarf travels with us also, and these two men are of the Tuathar, men of the kindred of Alduinar." She indicated Estle. "This worthy woman of the Ravani is the child of one of our citizens, as well. Now, do you still insist upon inconveniencing our Company, or will you now conduct us to the City so that we may care for our friends and deliver our news?"

"Forgive me," said the man, inclining his head toward her. "We cannot help but be suspicious of any who approach, until we understand their nature and intent. Of course, we will conduct you." So saying, he turned to his men, speaking to them in a language that actually appeared to be a debased form of Elvish, yet there were many elements of other speech intermingled with it. It was a tongue unique to the folk of Dûn Arian, and had arisen over five centuries of isolation. Fima would have a fine time delving into it, if he lived.

"Come with us, please," said the standard-bearer, bowing courteously to the Company. He was not as tall as the other, and he was dark haired and grey eyed. Rogond returned the bow, asking that they be allowed to ride slowly on account of their friend, Fima. The standard-bearer assented, conducting the Company slowly and carefully to the Great Gates of the Silver City.

20
The Legacy of Salasin

The massive wooden gates appeared to be set into the very cliffs on which the City stood. These cliffs extended in either direction as far as could be seen, and the City nestled atop them like a fabulous bird, the white walls and silver-tipped spires of the watchtowers glowing in the light of late afternoon. It was built on four levels above ground, and one below.

The Company did not have time to marvel at the beautiful stone courtyards or majestic fountains just yet. They would first be taken to a place where they could rest before being presented to the Council.

Fima was taken to the Citadel's physicians, and his friends were assured that he would receive the best care that could be given. Bint Raed accompanied him, for she was very weary and in need of healing. The others were shown to comfortable chambers where they could attend to their own needs. Soon all were washed and refreshed, full of food and drink, and wearing fine, new clothing that had been provided for them.

Word had spread quickly among the citizens that strange and wonderful folk had come among them—Elves and men of the line of Alduinar. This was not entirely true, for Rogond and Hallagond were descended of the people of Alduinar, but not of Alduinar himself. Naturally, the people were curious. They could be seen gathering in the courtyards and corridors nearby, hoping to catch sight of the Company.

Estle sat with Nelwyn, waiting for Rogond, Hallagond, and Galador to accompany them to the Council. When they appeared at last, they did not resemble the same weary travelers of hard desert lands.

Rogond and Hallagond had been transformed into elegant beings who would not have been out of place sitting at the hand of King Hearndin or Lady Ordath. Combed and washed, dressed in fine clothes, and well rested, they truly did look like brothers. Rogond was taller and less weathered than Hallagond, who still sported a neatly trimmed beard, but they could not deny their kinship. Galador, needless to say, was immaculate.

When Hallagond beheld Estle, her transformation amazed him. She was radiant—her freckled ivory skin glowed, her soft hair shone with the touch of scented oil. She was among the most beautiful women Hallagond had ever beheld.

"Where is Gaelen?" asked Rogond, for he did not see her.

"She was here a short while ago. She lingered rather long in the bath, and when I saw her last she was putting on her old clothing that she brought from the Greatwood," said Nelwyn, who was attired in a simple wrap of off-white linen. "Perhaps she is still resting on the veranda...why not go and have a look?"

She's up to something, thought Rogond. He didn't care for the thought of Gaelen attired in her old, drab hunting gear. He took notice of a fine-tailored black linen tunic that had been laid out for her, but she was nowhere to be seen.

Galador, obviously vexed, declared that he had no intention of waiting around until Gaelen decided to appear. "If they summon us to the Council, I will go without her," he said.

"That will not be necessary," said a cheerful voice from beyond the veranda. They all turned to observe Gaelen's tousled head hanging downwards from the overhang, her cheeks rosy, her eyes bright. She turned a graceful somersault, gripping the roof support for a moment before dropping lightly down onto the polished hardwood floor. In her hand she held a long, green branch of copper-veined beech, no doubt akin to one of the most common and beloved trees in the Greatwood. She handed it to Nelwyn, who took it with wonder. "For you, my cousin, with promise of things to come!"

"Exactly where have you been, my fine hunter-scout?" asked Rogond, who was intending to sound stern, but failed.

Gaelen drew one of her long knives and began nonchalantly cleaning her nails with it, humming to herself. "Oh, nowhere in particular...I was just practicing the stealthy arts and suddenly found myself among very tall trees. Imagine my surprise!" She looked quite pleased with herself.

"I suppose you think you're frightfully cunning, don't you?" said Galador. "May I remind you that we still do not know how these people will receive us? They won't know what to think with you sneaking about all over the City. We need to earn their trust, not make them suspicious. Once again, you are thinking only of yourself."

"They did not take notice of me, Galador. Don't be concerned."

"Hmmmph. So you say," replied Galador, who was far from convinced.

"Be as surly as you wish. Nothing could dampen my spirits right now," said Gaelen, smiling and nearly bursting with suppressed energy. "I truly feel like myself for the first time in a long reckoning."

"Why does that statement fill me with foreboding?" said Hallagond, whereupon Gaelen startled Rogond by leaping into his arms.

She flung her hand dramatically across her eyes. "Ah, proud Aridan! Lead, and I will follow. Bear me whither you will, to whatever destiny...so long as it is not back across that desert. I give my fate into your hands." She went completely limp in his arms, and he struggled to manage her, sinking to one knee in the effort to avoid dropping her.

"Ah, my brother...she has brought you to your knees," said Hallagond. "Better it should be you than me. She has unbalanced you!"

Rogond set Gaelen down, straightening and smiling at Hallagond. "You have no idea."

Nelwyn was already sitting beside Gaelen, her excitement evident. "Tell me of the trees!" she said, and for the next few minutes they spoke happily together in their own tongue.

"Just like Elves, to speak of wondrous things in a tongue that only they can understand," said Estle. She wanted to learn of the forest, as she had never been afforded the chance to walk among really tall trees.

"We're sorry, Estle. Come and join us," said Nelwyn, offering a place on the floor beside her. "We shall speak with words known to all."

"Make sure they're small words," put in Hallagond.

"Why? Are you planning on joining us?" said Estle, nudging him in the ribs as she passed by. She then ignored him, sitting with Gaelen and Nelwyn, listening as they described the great forest that was their home, wishing in spite of herself that she could one day walk with them in a place where all was cool and shaded, bright waters flowed, and the blue skies were hidden by a stately vault of deep green.

At last their thoughts turned back to their friend Fima. "We should go and see how he is getting on," said Nelwyn. "I did not care for the thoughts I read on the faces of the healers when we left him."

Gaelen nodded. "One of us should always be with him; he must know that his friends are near."

Estle shook her head. "I can understand why you care for him, as he is very likeable, but I thought Elves and dwarves did not get on well. At least, that's what I have been told."

"Fima is no ordinary dwarf," replied Nelwyn. "Wait until the Council hears that he is Lore-master to Lady Ordath! They will never want him to leave."

"And you…are you, well…ordinary Elves?" asked Estle. Gaelen and Nelwyn began laughing good-naturedly.

"Yes, on the whole I would say we are quite ordinary," said Gaelen. "We are Wood-elves...that means our lands were never graced by an Asarla. Hence there are many who consider us less enlightened than the High-elves, or even the men of Tuathas. We dwell in and defend the forests of Alterra, which are much-beloved."

"Is Galador a Wood-elf?" asked Estle, for she didn't really see much difference between them, but Nelwyn and Gaelen looked at her with wide eyes.

"Good heavens, no, he is not!" said Nelwyn. "He is High-elven, of an ancient line of Eádram. He was born during the First Reckoning."

Estle sat with her mouth open for a moment, trying to imagine living for thousands of years. "You would think he might have had sufficient time to develop a sense of humor," she said.

"Truly," agreed Gaelen, winking at Nelwyn.

"Oh, he has a sense of humor," said Nelwyn, who would love Galador until the End of Days. "You just need to look through the right glass to see it."

Nelwyn would go back and stay with Fima, leaving Rogond, Galador, Estle, Gaelen, and Hallagond to stand first before the High Council. If Bint Raed had recovered, she would stand with them; Nelwyn would send her. Gaelen wanted to go with Nelwyn, for she was very worried about Fima, but she had seen the enemy, and her tale needed to be told.

The men sent to conduct the Company to the Council were tall and well made. They bowed courteously, speaking to Rogond in the common-tongue. "Please, our Ministers are most eager to hear your news, if you are ready to provide it."

Rogond bowed in return. "We are at the service of the Council, and stand ready to aid the people of Dûn Arian. Our news is of grave importance."

One of the men stepped out into the hallway, extending a beckoning arm, and the Company followed him to the Chamber of the High Council, taking note of the many wonders along the way.

The city was filled with carvings, paintings, and great stone likenesses rendered by the most skilled artisans. A beautifully-appointed courtyard welcomed all visitors to the Council Halls, with wonderful, clear fountains and dark green ivy that made cool, living mats against the white stone walls. In the center of the courtyard stood a huge stone likeness of the great Tuathan scholar Salasin, the founder of the Citadel. By the time the likeness was made he had been an old man, yet still straight and strong, his renowned wisdom evident in his aged face. Yet his eyes seemed cold.

Rogond looked into those cold stone eyes, reflecting that such a man might well deem written lore more worthy of saving than human life. *Fima is also a dedicated lore-master, but he would never choose parchments over the lives of his friends. I suppose we cannot fault Salasin too heavily, because he managed to safeguard not only the written lore of Tuathas, but the blood of her people as well.* Rogond was excited to be meeting representatives of a heretofore unknown branch of the Tree of Men.

The Hall of Council was simple and austere. No decorative objects distracted the eye, and no gurgling fountains drew the attention of the ear from matters at hand. The white walls and floor lightened the hall, which had no windows, though part of the roof was open to the sky. The High Council sat at the far end on a raised dais with a heavy, curved table before them. Papers and parchments, representing the day's business, had nearly obscured the table-top, but all was put aside as the Company approached.

Gaelen felt uncomfortable in this place, as there were no avenues of escape other than the front doors, and she had been required to go in without her weapons. Her nearly-new boots still creaked every now and then, a fact that drove her to distraction. It would be several more weeks until they were properly broken-in.

Rogond looked into the incredulous faces of the Council, knowing that the sight of two Elves and two northmen standing before them was perhaps the last thing they had anticipated this day. But such wise, learned councilors would surely welcome them. Had not the people already done so? They would doubtless be thankful for the warning the Company had to give, though it would no doubt dismay them. Rogond approached them with confidence.

The High Council included three women along with six men. They had always numbered nine, so that no vote could be evenly split down the middle. Salasin had declared that, since nine was the highest number that could be expressed by a single numeral, it symbolized the unity of purpose of the High Council.

Although a Lord presided over them, his vote carried no more weight than any other. Decisions were made by the body as a whole, and while the Lord could overrule them, he rarely did so. He sat in the center of the group of nine, with four flanking him on either side.

Estle, who had lived her entire life among sutherlings, had never viewed women in such positions of authority. She wondered whether a woman had ever sat in the center seat.

Gaelen saw the situation somewhat differently as she looked into the eyes of the council-members. She faced a difficult task. These people would have trouble imagining the sort of evil they faced, and would no doubt underestimate the gravity of their predicament, as they would not have faced such a thing before. Gaelen knew, even from her limited experience, that weapons and warfare were not among the skills they valued. How long since they had truly defended the City? Salasin had ensured that it could be defended—the design of the gates and the outer walls made that clear—but Salasin understood the nature of the evil that had roamed Alterra. He had lived in a time when real enemies threatened, and real battles were joined. His descendants had been sheltered from such things. Gaelen stole a glance at Galador and Hallagond, and saw the same concern in their faces.

The Company bowed before the Council, who rose from their seats and returned the gesture before making introductions. Rogond could hear the diversity of the people in their names. Some had Elvish roots; others suggested Tuathan, Ravani, or even Anori derivation. The councilors varied in age as well as in gender, but all were old enough to have acquired experience and skill.

Apparently, each member governed a separate concern. For example, one was introduced as being responsible for waters and forests, another for creative pursuits, and a third for the healing arts. Gaelen was relieved to hear that at least they did have a Minister of Defense. She looked long and hard into his eyes. He had seen battle; of that there was no doubt, and she was encouraged. She wondered how long he had been in the Citadel, for she could hear in his speech that he had been born elsewhere. Other councilors were introduced as the Minister of Omens, the Minister of Farms and Fisheries, and the Minister of Lawful Affairs.

Hallagond whispered to Estle aside. "Notice that they have no Minister of Trade, though they do have one who governs commerce within the City."

"How would traders ever find this place, and why would they choose to travel here?" replied Estle. "The citizens must make all these fine things from materials that are found here. What a jewel this place must be!"

The Lord introduced himself last, giving his name as Salastor IV. Salastor I, one of the sons of Salasin, had ruled the City upon his father's death. It was said that they were much alike, and Salastor's name had been taken by three other Lords. Salastor IV was a noble man with heavily silvered dark hair and a neatly trimmed beard. He reminded Rogond of King Hearndin, only less careworn. His only badge of office was a seven-rayed silver star bound to his brow, signifying that he was also the city's Chief Lore-master.

Gaelen hung back behind Rogond and Galador with her arms folded and her chin lifted, her expression alert and watchful. She would say nothing unless requested, but she would carefully observe the Council that she might learn how best to address them.

Rogond introduced himself and the others of the Company. "I am Rogond Thaylon, son of Diomar of Dûn Bennas, and this is my elder brother, Hallagond. This worthy woman is called Estle, and she hails from the eastern Ravi-shan, but her mother numbered among your citizens. She has seen the face of your enemy. This Elf is called Galador, originally of Eádros, and this is Gaelen Taldin of the Greatwood Realm, who has likewise looked upon the enemy that slowly approaches from the east. Three of our companions could not be here to stand before you. One is a dwarf, Fima of Cós-domhain, now Lore-master to Lady Ordath of Mountain-home. He lies in your Hall of Healing with one of your citizens, Bint Raed the weaver. Gaelen's cousin Nelwyn, a Wood-elf of the Greatwood, watches over them."

"Why have you come?" asked the tall, grey-bearded Minister of Lawful Affairs. "We have been told that you bear news of great value. Is that the only purpose of your errand here?"

"It is," said Rogond, "though Bint Raed wanted to return to her home, and Estle wanted to see the land of her mother's kin. But our urgency lies in the news we bring. Will you hear it now?"

Salastor nodded, his expression somber. "Tell your tale, man of Dûn Bennas. We cannot help but take said tale to heart, when such a rare and distinguished Company stands before us. Never before have the Elàni set foot within our walls, nor have we set eyes upon dwarven-folk. Tonight we will try to find ways to welcome you properly, but first you must tell us of the urgent matter that brings you into our presence." He leaned forward expectantly, as all eyes and ears fixed on Rogond.

In an earnest voice that rang with the clarity of his Elven upbringing, Rogond spoke of the Company's journey, and told the Council of the Scourge. When he had finished, he surveyed the faces of the councilors. What he saw did not comfort him, though he had expected them to have some difficulty grasping both the reality and the enormity of their peril.

He saw perhaps two who might have believed him—the Minister of Defense and the Minister of Omens. She, in particular, seemed ill-at-ease, and Rogond wondered whether she might possess the gift of premonition. It might not have been the first time she had considered the likelihood of such a threat.

The other seven councilors were looking at the Company with various expressions of polite dismissal and disbelief. It was obvious from their demeanor that they wondered whether Rogond had spent too much time wandering under the desert sun.

"Forgive me," said the Minister of Commerce, "but how would such a large force survive such a crossing? The lands to the east are nearly impossible to navigate even with the lightest of burdens. How would such a great army make its way here? Never has any done so since the City was founded nearly five hundred years ago. We are not aware of advancements in the world outside that would make this burden any easier. Why, and how, could this happen now?"

"I wonder how such a force would find its way here from so far to the east," Salastor mused. "It's unlikely they would even know that we exist, much less be able to find the hidden way. Our citizens are sworn to never reveal the City to any outsiders."

"Yet we are outsiders, and we are here," said Hallagond.

"You are here because one of our citizens led you here," Salastor replied. "She must think you trustworthy. She knows also that if we do not find you so, you will not be allowed to leave."

Salastor took notice of the spark that kindled in Gaelen's eyes as he spoke these words. She would brook no restriction of her freedom, or stand for any interference with events leading to the downfall of Gorgon Elfhunter. She kept silent, waiting.

Estle stepped forward, bowing before Salastor. "I have seen the enemy," she said, "and although I don't know what guides them, or how they are managing the crossing, I know they are on their way here. The enemy encampment is vast; for all we know, there are pockets of it all the way back to some great inland water source. They are moving slowly, but they are moving, and theirs is a savagery that you cannot imagine! Never have I seen such cruelty and disregard for life. Please, take heed of Rogond's warning."

"What do the Elves have to say?" asked the Minister of Lawful Affairs. "It is said that they do not deceive. What is their stance in this matter?"

Galador bowed, addressing them in a deep, soft voice. "Rogond has spoken true, but I don't believe he has adequately conveyed the dire nature of your peril."

"You have seen this army, Gaelen Taldin," said Salastor. "Speak, if you would enlighten us."

Gaelen did not bow before him, as she was still unsettled at the prospect of being confined to the Citadel. Yet she looked directly into the eyes of the Lord, and spoke what was in her heart. "First, let it be said that Elves *are* capable of deceit, though perhaps not so easily as men, and you must not think otherwise. Second, the Company has spoken only truth. Debate and doubt our words at your peril, for you will waste valuable time."

She drew a deep breath, knowing that her next words might offend them, but they had to be said. "In my experience, when men try too hard to decide upon a course of action, they choose no course at all. I look around at this peaceful, well-ordered realm that has stood so long unchallenged, and I wonder whether you are even capable of mounting an effective defense. We are here to assist you, but make no mistake—you do not command me. I answer only to Ri-Aruin of the Greatwood Realm, but I will aid you if I can."

There was some murmuring from the onlookers as Gaelen spoke these words, and Salastor did not smile, though there was humor behind his eyes. "We appreciate your candor," he said, "and your point concerning time spent in debate is well taken. Yet we would learn more of this enemy. Have you anything to add to what is now known?"

Gaelen then told of what she had seen, and she spared no detail. Several in attendance turned pale as she described the Scourge in fearful words, and the haunted look in her eyes was unsettling to all who took notice of it. When she had nearly finished, she turned to the Minister of Omens. "You have seen this, haven't you? I can read it in your eyes. There is one more thought that I would share. There is something hidden in that encampment that I did not see...some great weapon of which we are unaware. I don't know what leads me to that conclusion, but I know it's true. Even the Company does not know the full extent of this threat."

She turned back to Salastor. "You have now been given the gift of forewarning, along with the services of those well-versed in the arts of war. I would suggest you take these gifts to heart." Then she bowed before him, for she had read his thoughts in his eyes, and they had reassured her.

Salastor would not allow her to be held against her will; his trust in the Company was growing rapidly. With luck, he would make certain that his people would begin preparations at once. She suspected that he would have no trouble convincing at least four of the others, and that was enough to sway the decision.

Salastor looked back to Rogond. "You have given your message, and it has been heard. Return now to your quarters and rest, for tonight we shall feast long and well in demonstration of our gratitude. You have endured incredible hardship on this journey, and we shall do all in our power to ensure that you have few regrets. We hope that you will choose to stay with us, at least for a while. My people are very excited to meet you and to learn from you."

His gaze moved back to Gaelen. "The task of the Council is to decide upon a course of action. When we begin to make definite plans we will need your advice; for example, I would like to hear your estimation of when you expect the Scourge to arrive here." His eyes swept over the Company. "You will all be needed in this effort, for you are right—this is an enemy outside our experience. We are a peaceful people, and I fear it will take some convincing to arouse the populace to the idea of warfare. We have always preferred reason to taking up arms." He shook his head. "I am loath to even consider what must be done, what actions we will be forced to take, if you are correct."

"My lord," said Hallagond, "from what Estle and Gaelen have told me, I fear there will be no reasoning with the Scourge. Your people may not like the idea of war, but war is coming.You have a lovely jewel here. Your City has everything anyone could want. The Scourge takes whatever it wants, and it is bent on taking your City from you. Surely the people will not wish to lose their home and their lives."

"Indeed," replied Salastor, "but comfort often gives way to complacency, and we have been comfortable for a long time. Those committed to peace may be incredibly stubborn." He looked back at Gaelen, who was standing with her arms folded once more. "We may have need of your plain-spoken form of persuasion."

"Then we will simply have to convince them," said Gaelen. She had decided that she liked Salastor, and her mouth tugged in a half-smile as she bowed before him, turning then to follow her friends from the Hall of the High Council.

This place is not at all to your liking, is it? Well, you can't say I didn't tell you so!

Gorgon had not heard Gelmyr's silky, sarcastic voice in several weeks. *The heat and the light are no friends of yours. The She-elf is leading you here, and we both know it. She thinks the desert will finish you, and with any luck she will be right.*

Gorgon rumbled deep in his throat. "For once I agree with you, Èolo. Yet I will track her, and I will find her. These lands have no power over me that I cannot endure. I am overjoyed that she has chosen to call me to her; it will make things all the easier. I follow her by choice. She holds no sway over my actions."

Gelmyr's laughter stung his ears then—it seemed that the Elf found the entire situation to be utterly hilarious. *You are so deluded! She is leading you into a land where Elves do not venture, and where there are none whom you may prey upon. She knows that this is what sustains you. Have you not realized it, or is the sun beginning to affect your brain already? She is far, far away from here, across terrible wastes. Your father's folk could never attempt this...they would run shrieking from the very idea of it!*

"She does not know what sustains me," growled Gorgon unconvincingly. Gelmyr was correct; he did not wish to remain long in a land where Elves did not walk unwittingly into his grasp. For one thing, it was the killing of Elves that supported his faith in himself and in his purpose. Gelmyr would not plague him unless he wavered.

"Besides…how do you know that there are no Elves in the south? Perhaps there are many of them. How would *you* know?" Gorgon smiled wickedly, barely exposing his strong, sharp yellow teeth.

I know it only because you know it…you have sensed this long ago. You know that I can express no thought that is not also in your own mind, but let's not stray from the discussion! How ironic, O Dark Dread, that it is your mother's people, those you have sworn to destroy, that have given you the gifts that will allow you to survive in this place. Without the strength and stamina of Elves, you would have shriveled already. Just one more reason for your poor mother to regret giving birth to you. Ha!

Gorgon could not argue with Gelmyr, for he knew that he would not even be able to venture forth under such bright sun were it not for the blood of Brinneal. Elves tolerated harsh sunlight even better than men did, though they did not care for it. The starlit darkness was more to their liking, and to his. He had already experienced the brilliant desert stars; they had mesmerized him in much the same way as they had the Elves. The ability to appreciate the stars was a gift he had received from Gaelen.

"My armor will shield me, and I shall travel by night. I need little water to sustain me, and my resolve is strong. Try to dissuade me, and you will fail."

Why would I try to dissuade you? It is my belief that you will die out here, you pathetic, misbegotten lump of scarred flesh! You think you're so formidable? Just think on this: while you are off chasing down that She-elf, there are many others in the north who would now exact vengeance upon you, including the Lord of Black Flame Himself. You can never return there without peril, and your quest to eliminate the Elàni is ended. She has beaten you!

"*No!*" roared Gorgon, swinging uselessly at the apparition that appeared to be sitting beside him. "It has not ended. It can *never* end!" His outraged cry echoed across the sands for miles in every direction, though no one was there to hear it.

The Company arrived back at their chambers to find a man and a woman awaiting them.

"Please," said the man. "Your friend Fima is in very grave condition. If you do not come at once, you may not see him again while he is alive. We will conduct you." Naturally, all were dismayed, especially Rogond and Gaelen. They followed the healers to another level of the Citadel, where the Halls of Healing gleamed clean and white in the bright sunlight.

"Why is this place set apart?" asked Gaelen. "Do not your people need the comfort of belonging when they are ill?" She had noticed that the Hall was separate from any other structure; there was even a wall around it.

The woman looked puzzled by such a question, and Rogond answered. "Places of Healing are separated to prevent the spread of sickness. I wonder…did the Plague find its way here?" He asked the man who walked beside him, and was relieved to learn that no serious pestilence had ever assailed the Citadel. Its isolation had protected it. If Rogond had thought long about it he would have guessed, for had the Plague withered the populace, that same isolation would have prevented recovery. There would have been few citizens to welcome them, if any at all.

He had heard the stories. People became so fearful of disease that they even killed those of their own who fell ill rather than risk themselves. Often the sick were forced into confinement under terrible conditions, where they died miserable and neglected. It was wise to hide any infirmity from even your friends and family for a long time after the Plague had passed. Rogond hoped to never be faced with such a choice, for he knew what it would be. He would surely perish—he could not turn from those he loved while they were in need. *And then there was the aftermath, when people were blamed and persecuted. I heard they were burned alive…* He shuddered, and put such thoughts from his mind.

They were conducted through a labyrinth of corridors until they reached their destination—a plain, white chamber. In the center stood a stone platform with a soft mattress laid upon it, and Fima rested there. Nelwyn sat beside him, and her eyes filled with tears as soon as she saw Gaelen in the doorway.

The Senior Healer, a very capable and learned woman with a kind voice, called Rogond back into the corridor to explain Fima's condition.

"Your friend has a deadly lung ailment brought on by the dust and salt…perhaps some poison in the air? We have little knowledge of his kind, but it is apparent that he is of advanced age. Because he suffered such deprivation of rest and water during the crossing, he has been weakened to the point that he cannot recover. His lungs are filling up as we speak; soon he will not be able to draw breath at all. We have done everything within our power already…this is a death watch. I know he is your friend, and I wish that we could do more. I'm sorry."

Rogond bowed his head. "I'm sure you have done what you can," he replied. "He was poisoned some months ago, and has not been the same since...may the soul of Sajid the Spider walk forever headless and in shame." The healer nodded solemnly before turning to see to her other duties.

When Rogond went to Fima's side, one look at him said all that was needed. He had wasted even further, his skin was slack and sallow, and he was very pale. His eyes sank into dark sockets, turning his formerly ruddy, lively face into a skull-like mask. Were it not for the struggle to draw breath, he would not have moved at all. There was the smell of approaching death about him.

Rogond did not wish to relate the healer's sad tale within Fima's hearing, but it would not be needed—the dark path upon which their friend now walked was plain. He was too weak to swallow food or water, and Nelwyn told that he had roused himself, and had spoken to her, though his voice had been only a whisper for he could make no sound.

"What did he say to you?" asked Rogond, hoping that perhaps the dwarf had been complaining about something. At least then they would know that he still held on to his spirit.

Nelwyn shook her head, tears filling her beautiful eyes again. "It's all right, my love," said Galador, laying gentle hands upon her shoulders. "Tell us. Rogond needs to hear it."

Nelwyn drew a deep breath, composing herself. "He said that he would soon go to his fathers, and that he would walk once more with Khima, who was a greater lore-master even than himself. He said that he hoped he would learn of great mysteries in the Halls of Fior. He said to say goodbye to each of you, for he feared he would not be able to do so." She turned to Gaelen. "He said...he said he was sorry he would not stand with you to defeat Gorgon. He referred to you as the 'little Wood-elf' again."

Nelwyn expected this last to bring forth tears in her cousin, but Gaelen was not looking at her—she was focusing on something else entirely. She looked down at Fima, placing her hand upon his chest.

"He has given up," she said softly. "He could find the strength to stay with us, if only he would. He has convinced himself that this is his time."

Suddenly, all became clear to Gaelen; there was still a course of action they had not taken. She turned to Nelwyn with a determined expression. "Did you say that he mentioned learning of great mysteries?" Nelwyn nodded, her eyes brightening with renewed hope. She had already guessed Gaelen's thoughts.

"What are you on about?" asked Estle, who could not imagine anyone being hopeful at this point.

Gaelen turned to Rogond. "He's stubborn enough to battle this affliction if we can convince him that he must. Now that we are safe in the city walls, he believes his journey has ended. We must persuade him otherwise by reminding him of what he truly loves the most. Lift him up, Aridan, and follow me."

"Take us to the library," she said to the confused attendants who had been keeping watch at the doorway. "Quickly, and no arguments! We have very little time!" Gaelen was obviously in no mood for debate. Knowing that Fima's ailment was not the kind that would spread, the attendants shrugged, bowed, and led the Company to the vast storehouse of the lore of Salasin, which was his greatest legacy.

They took Fima into the heart of the library, ignoring the puzzled looks from the scholars assembled there. "Lay him on the table," said Gaelen, sweeping several parchments from it with no respect whatsoever. She was preoccupied, and had not the time to care. Rogond placed Fima gently upon the heavy oaken table as several scholars gathered around them, staring curiously at the dying dwarf. They had never seen such a sight before.

Gaelen rounded on them: "Bring us something of great rarity, the like of which a person living in the world outside will never have seen. You may save his life!" The scholars were confused, and did not move.

"This dwarf is Lore-master to Lady Ordath of Mountain-home. Please do as Gaelen asks," said Rogond. That set them into action at once, for the name of Lady Ordath was well known in the Citadel. A person such as Fima would be a great treasure in the eyes of the scholars.

Gaelen whispered into Fima's ear, pleading with him to only open his eyes and see the wonders around him ere he left them forever. She tried to describe the library, tried to tempt him, but he did not respond. For the next several minutes Rogond, Nelwyn, and Gaelen all tried to rouse him, but it seemed they had come too late.

"It was a fine idea, Gaelen. Perhaps he truly is beyond healing," said Estle, trying to comfort her.

"He is *not* beyond healing," replied Gaelen, nearly shaking with frustration. "He could remain if he wished to badly enough, I just *know it!*' She turned to Fima, and, to the surprise of everyone, took him by the shoulder and shook him quite hard.

"Rouse yourself, you weakling! I have had quite enough of your indolence. Show some resolve, you sorry excuse for a lore-master! Here are wonders beyond your imagination, and yet you lie there and will not even open your eyes and *look* upon them? My people are right about dwarves after all. You are not nearly possessed of the fiber you claim if you would leave these wonders now. I'm most certainly glad that I do not have to face Khima, and explain to him that I let all this slip away without even making an effort! I would…I would *disown* you. Open your eyes, you lazy iron-mongering…ummm… you lazy iron-mongering *git*! What shall I say to Lady Ordath when next I meet her?"

Gaelen was literally shouting at him by this time, tears flowing from her bright eyes. She did not enjoy saying such things to her beloved friend, but she was determined to say them. If she could restore his spirit, she didn't care if he ever spoke a civil word to her again.

To the wonder of his other friends, Fima drew a deep, shuddering breath. It sounded as if it had been taken through a vessel of water, but it was definitely a breath. He opened his sunken blue eyes. Though they were surrounded by wells of dark purple flesh, there was a spark in them that was encouraging to see.

"Gaelen…look! He has opened his eyes," whispered Nelwyn, who could hardly believe it.

Gaelen now assailed the scholars again. "Tell him what you have brought. Show him," she commanded, in a voice that could not be denied. "Convince him that you have the answers to mysteries that he does not know. *Tell* him!"

As the scholars described the wonders of the library as only true scholars can, Fima's passion for learning and knowing took hold of him. While he was still very ill, he seemed to come to life before their eyes, reaching down within himself and finding his resolve. He coughed weakly, stirring his arms and legs, trying to turn onto his side so that he could see better. Rogond moved to aid him, but Gaelen stayed him.

"Do not aid him yet…he can do this himself." She held a weathered volume of leather before his eyes that was hundreds of years old. "See, my friend, this says it is the recorded annals of the Citadel from its founding." She opened the volume and began to read, occasionally interjecting such remarks as: "Surely you did not know that," and, "You did not know of *this*, either!"

Fima's eyes brightened especially when the scholars told him of the vault wherein all the original manuscripts of Salasin were stored. It was sealed to prevent damage by the sea-air, and one needed to wear special gloves to handle any of the items in it. At last, however, he grew weary and closed his eyes. Though every breath still sounded as though it could be his last, he had found his resolve.

"He is sleeping," said Gaelen, who was worn out from the effort she had made. "I'm satisfied that all has been done here that can be. We should return him to his place, and rely on the skills of the healers from here."

Estle looked with wonder at Fima; it seemed now that there might be hope for him after all. "Do you really think he will live?" she asked Gaelen.

"I'm not a healer, but it is my belief that stubborn will can overcome affliction, and he is among the most stubborn of beings. We'll see." She turned to Rogond. "I do hope that he will still consider me to be his friend after those terribly discourteous things I said to him."

Rogond smiled. "What things?" he asked. "He won't remember them; he will only remember the promise of exploring the wonders of the library. You will always be his friend."

Gaelen shook her head. "You think he won't remember every insulting *word*? That has not been my experience with dwarves."

As she walked away, Rogond smiled to himself. It had not been his experience, either.

21
The War Council

If Gaelen hoped that Fima would not remember the insults she had given, and that she would not hear about it from him, she hoped in vain. The first words issuing from his mouth when he regained enough strength to speak were directed at her.

"The eloquence of Elves continues to astound me," he murmured in a sort of croaking whisper. "A git, am I? Iron-mongering, yes, I could see that, but…a *git*? You must have delved deeply into your repertoire of excoriations to come up with that one. I stand in awe of your vocabulary." He was still coughing, and he would not breathe easily for weeks, but having set his will to remaining alive he would do so. One day he would leave Alterra despite any desire, but that day had not yet come.

Gaelen was too overjoyed to be dismayed, though she knew that he would tease her for a long time to come. She sighed inwardly and prepared herself.

A very large task loomed before the Company, and they could ill afford to spend much effort in worrying about Fima. Salastor had called a war-council, and at first he had requested only Gaelen and Estle, for they alone had actually seen the enemy. They sat before a large table with a fairly detailed map of the region spread upon it, and tried to pinpoint where they thought the Scourge had last been seen. Neither Gaelen nor Estle held much skill in the use of maps, but they remembered many details of their journey. From their recollection it was possible for others to retrace their course.

Gaelen had seen more of the encampment than had Estle, and she tried to describe the vastness of it. Those present at the war-council had difficulty visualizing such an extensive army, and their faces betrayed their skepticism, thinking that she was surely exaggerating!

Salastor's advisors questioned her, and some adopted a tone and manner that were almost condescending, yet Gaelen was unconcerned, for she saw no such patronizing expression in Lord Salastor, nor in the Minister of Defense, a man named Talishani

Ali. He posed an important question that was shared by nearly everyone present.

"Will we have sufficient time to prepare for this siege, I wonder?"

Gaelen set herself to the question, for her other senses provided insight in addition to what she and Estle had seen. Fima might have chided her for her lack of spoken eloquence, but she was very adept at interpreting the language of scent. Based on the rapidity with which the Company had outdistanced the stench, she knew that the Scourge had been moving relatively slowly. The City had some time to make ready.

Gaelen estimated that the Scourge moved at about one-third the speed of the Company, but they moved on a course that was more direct, and the Company had been forced to slow down once they reached the Fire-hills. It had taken nearly thirteen weeks to make the crossing from Mumari, and it had been almost seven weeks since they had encountered the path of the Scourge.

"The Fire-hills will slow them down, surely," said Estle.

Gaelen was uncertain, her eyes and voice grim as she remembered the last days of the journey. "If Azori and his men had not chosen to leave us when they did, so that we had extra water, the Plains of Thirst would have finished us. We nearly ran out of reserve as it was. We would have lain down beside that dead caravan, and joined them." She shivered, recalling the sight of the remains of the woman with the child in her arms.

She turned now to Ali. "I believe that for every day of travel the Company made, it will take between two and three days for the Scourge. They will not simply march up before the Gates; they will camp for a while until their force is gathered and made orderly. We have at *least* seven weeks, but I would guess it will be a lot longer before they engage us."

Ali nodded. "From your description, I believe they will take closer to three months. Each time they stop to rest they lose more time, for it takes many hours even to spread the word through such a vast encampment, never mind moving it forward. We may have even more time than you know. The Fire-hills will impede them, and they will not be in a hurry unless they suspect that we know of their approach. If they have made it this far, the Plains of Thirst will hold little hardship for them."

"I just cannot fathom how it is that they are supplying such a vast force with water," said Estle. "They surely could not carry it with them."

"Of that, I do not know," replied Ali. "I truly can't fathom it either. Yet, somehow, it must be so. At any rate, it is fortunate that you came to warn us when you did, as we now have a fair amount of time to make ready."

Gaelen's eyebrows lowered and her bright eyes narrowed, remembering the condescending looks from some of the Council. "Indeed. From what I have seen, we'll need every day of it."

Now the Council called upon the rest of the Company, for they would begin to plan their defense. Galador, Rogond, Hallagond, and Nelwyn were summoned. Bint Raed was still resting and regaining her strength; she did not need to attend the Council, for she knew little of warfare.

Unfortunately, most of the men sitting at the Council-table knew little of it, either. Some were historians and scholars; they could provide insights from what they had read concerning fortifications, but they had no practical experience.

Fortunately, the original designers of the Citadel had kept an eye toward possible attack by an eastern enemy. The Great Gates, set into tall walls of solid stone, were an example. Archers could be positioned on the battlements atop the wall; fortunately this art had not been lost. There were many fine archers in the City, though few would ever have drawn their bows on a living man. Gaelen and Nelwyn shook their heads. They knew well the difference between aiming at a stationary target and bringing down a swift-moving enemy.

The first session of the war-council was distressing to Rogond, Hallagond, and Galador, for they saw men of little experience debating matters of which they had little knowledge. Hallagond, in particular, was quickly driven to point this out. Yet when asked about his own experience, he had to admit that no one in the Company save Galador had participated in any situation that was even remotely similar to the one they now faced, and he was chastened.

When several hours had passed, all were given food and drink, and they rested from the debate. Galador approached Ali, who sat alone with his meal.

"May I join you?" he asked.

"You are free to sit with anyone you choose."

"Gaelen believes that you have seen battle," said Galador. "She said she has read it in your eyes. Now that I look upon you, I see that it is so. How does a man of your experience come to be here?"

"You mean, how would an old, battle-scarred warrior come to live in a city devoted to peace?" said Ali, setting down his meal and looking hard at Galador. "I see that you also have lived through some hard conflict, and I will spare you the details of my personal history, but know that I am a refugee from a now-dead realm. Our people had been winnowed by the Plague before being felled by an enemy army. My record as a defender is none too fine of late, yet I'm the best we have to offer." He shook his head. "If this force is as great as it is reputed to be, my knowledge will not be enough. I hope your people can aid us."

Galador looked around him to behold two Rangers, two Sylvan hunter-scouts, and Estle...it was not much to put forth against the Scourge.

Ali smiled wryly at him. "Don't fear, my fine friend. We always have your sage advice, and you might be surprised at how resourceful our folk can be once they stop talking and are moved to action. Never undervalue the power of men standing in defense of their homes. Besides," he said, lifting his plate and cup once more, "one must die of something eventually."

Galador returned the smile, but he did not find this sentiment to be especially comforting.

After a bit more debate, the Council disbanded for the day. Rogond, Hallagond, and Galador would go with Ali to the armory and take stock of the weapons stored there, and Nelwyn would return to stay with Fima. Gaelen requested leave to roam about the City, for she wanted to work out the lay of things.

Salastor inclined his head to her. "The Company had been afforded the status of honored guests. You may go wherever you wish…the Citadel and her people are at your service. Just be sure to return to your chambers before sunset. Tonight we feast in your honor. It has been three days since your arrival, and we have yet to welcome you properly. Tomorrow we shall return to business, but tonight there will be singing, dancing, and the telling of tales."

Rogond understood his strategy—no doubt rumors were flying all over the City by now. A welcoming feast was to be expected, and would put people's minds at rest until Salastor and the Council decided what their course would be.

Estle approached Gaelen as she made ready to go out into the city. "Would you like some company?"

Gaelen looked at her in surprise. "I had not expected any, but my errand is not of any urgency, and you are welcome."

"I just thought you might need some assistance," said Estle with a grin. "You're quite the object of curiosity among these folk. You might need me to ward them off."

"If you were not with me, I could evade them," said Gaelen. "If I do not wish to be noticed, I will not be." She lifted her hood, concealing her ears and shading the light of her eyes.

Estle shook her head, chuckling. "I'm afraid they will see through that disguise, Gaelen. You will never appear to be anything other than what you are. You simply can't help yourself, alas."

"Hmmm…so you say," replied Gaelen, then her eyes suddenly grew wide as she looked past Estle's shoulder toward the balcony beyond. "What in the world is *that*?"

Despite an inner feeling that she should not do so, Estle turned toward the balcony. After all, they would no doubt see many strange and wonderful things here. Naturally, there was nothing there, and when Estle turned back around, Gaelen was nowhere in view. Estle had not heard a sound from her.

Oh, I do so hate it when she does that. "All right, Gaelen, you've made your point. Gaelen…? All right, now, the joke has ended. Reveal yourself, or I shall be forced to leave without you." She took a deep breath. "Very well, then, I suppose I shall leave you to your fate. It'll serve you right if you're swamped by well-meaning folk, whereas I will be free to roam unfettered, for they will take little notice of me. Have it your way."

She turned and made for the doorway, keeping all her senses trained rearward in full expectation of an ambush from behind. Therefore, when Gaelen dropped down immediately in front of her, she was startled nearly out of her wits. Without thinking, she grabbed Gaelen and tossed her over her shoulder. Gaelen rolled lightly onto her feet, shaking her head and smiling.

"I see your brothers trained you well," she said. "The look on your face was worth it. Now, let's go first and see Fima. I would ask if there is any errand he would have me do. Also, I would have Nelwyn come with us...she will want to see the trees."

"These weapons haven't seen use in a long time," said Hallagond, lifting a sword from the rack and examining it. "They all need sharpening, and they are actually rusted. Why have you not kept them oiled?"

"We have," replied Ali. "Yet the salt air defies our efforts, which admittedly have been somewhat lax. It's difficult to prevent steel from rusting and pitting with time."

"Indeed," said Rogond. "Many of these will need to be carefully tended and re-worked, as they could not be trusted against an armored foe."

"It is as I feared," said Ali, shaking his head. "Naturally, I am responsible, for the defense of the City is my duty. Yet it's not easy to convince folk to expend effort in such pursuits when no enemies threaten them. We have many fine smiths here, but their works have been directed elsewhere." He looked over at Galador, who was examining the rusted blades with a somber expression. "Ah, my friend, let me show you a sight that will cheer you. Metal fares not well beside the sea, but wood and hide and cane are only made stronger! Come with me."

He led them into another part of the armory, where archery stores were kept. Here were hundreds of fine bows. Most were designed for hunting, but some were powerful and capable of long range.

Galador examined them with wonder. They were made of a wood that he didn't recognize, but it was very straight-grained and strong.

"The strings are fashioned of sinew blended with fibers of tuaga trees," said Ali. "They are incredibly durable. Before we make our bows we submerge the staves in the harbor for several years. When we draw them out and dry them properly, the wood wears like iron and will never decay, yet it remains resilient. Try it and see." He handed an arrow to Galador, who strung the bow with some effort, then pulled it and sent the arrow into a target set against the far wall. The shot went high, but the arrow nearly disappeared into the target with the force of it.

"Are your archers strong enough to pull these?" he asked Ali in wonderment.

"Some are, and more can be made so. The smaller bows are very accurate, require less power, and are in fine shape."

"Show me," said Galador.

At the end of their time in the armory, they had come to know several things. More arrows were needed, though many were already available and in good condition. Many would no doubt be lost, however, in training additional archers, for they would be most vital in defense of the city walls. The forges of the Citadel would now have to be turned from their peaceable pursuits toward the making of blades and spear-points. Most of all, the people would need to be trained, as few in the city would ever have seen battle. Ali turned to his companions, holding forth his right arm so that it extended into the center of the group.

"I shall need your aid," he said, "you and the others of my folk who understand such matters. Will you give the promise of your service? Without it, we will surely fail."

"We may even fail with it," said Rogond. "Yet I will promise to serve the people of the Silver City." He extended his own arm, placing his right hand upon Ali's clenched fist. Hallagond and Galador both did likewise.

"Then I name you captains in the army of Dûn Arian," said Ali, "and I give you leave to order my people as you will. You answer only to me, and to Lord Salastor. He and I will deal with the others of the Council, those who do not believe such measures are necessary. We shall meet each day and plan our strategy. Agreed?"

All four warriors nodded in assent. They were now united in their resolve to defend the City, in their mutual respect, and in the bond of friendship.

Gaelen, Nelwyn, and Estle had gone to view the western side of the city, where they could look out over the blue water and the vast coastal forest. This expanse of emerald foliage was the most beautiful sight imaginable to Nelwyn, who trembled with anticipation at the thought of roaming the dark green depths.

Gaelen was also quite taken with the harbor and the flat seas beyond. The smell of it tantalized her...so full of life!

As for Estle, she simply stared in awe at the great, dark purple horizon. The idea of waters stretching without end was nearly beyond imagining. "Some of my ancestors were mariners," she said softly. "They called the sea their home. I would very much like to know more of it…I do not believe I have ever seen anything so beautiful, or so powerful. It frightens me."

"You shall have the chance to learn of it, I'm sure," said Nelwyn. "These folk will know much of the ways of the sea, and they will be eager to share their knowledge with you. You'll be sailing in no time." She indicated several vessels of various sizes that dotted the calm waters of the harbor. In the distance they could see the great, sharp rocks guarding the entrance, and they could hear the roar of the wild seas beyond.

"Enough talk," said Gaelen, shouldering her small pack. "Let's be on our way. There's exploring to be done—I will not rest until I have wetted my feet in the water *and* climbed the tallest tree in the forest." She leaped lightly down from the wall on which she had been standing and sprang away. It took Nelwyn and Estle a few minutes to catch up with her.

They spent several hours exploring the shores of the harbor, venturing into the shallows, taking notice of the bitter saltiness of the water. They found shells and parts of sea animals that had died and washed up, and also some live crabs and small fish. Gaelen was fascinated by the number of armored creatures. "In the northlands such armor is rare, although the fish still have scales," she said.

"It is ironic...with so much water at your feet, you could still die of thirst," said Nelwyn. "This water is undrinkable. I believe the sea could be a lonely and deadly place to the unwary."

"Or just to the unlucky," said Estle. "I have heard stories of mariners whose ships were disabled, who drifted for many days and nearly perished from thirst. Yet if they drank of this water, they went mad and died very quickly. Those tales were brought back by the living; most were not so fortunate."

"I'm ready to enter the forest now," said Gaelen. "Estle, will you come with us, or will you stay by the water?"

Estle was not yet ready to leave the harbor. "I will remain here and listen to the sea," she said. "Come back for me, and we'll return together. Don't stray too far. Remember—we must be back before sunset."

Gaelen and Nelwyn promised to return for Estle, and they did so, but they lingered long in the forest as only supremely contented Wood-elves will. Estle was annoyed. "You're late! Now we will be hard pressed to return by sunset, and we would need to run swiftly. It's a lot harder running uphill!"

The people of the Citadel had done a fine job preparing the welcoming feast. Few in the Company had witnessed such pageantry, and they were nearly overcome with the splendor of Dûn Arian at the height of her flowering. Dûn Bennas was a larger city, but it had been in the grip of winter, and the people still remembered the Plague. They had seen shadows of war and hardship that had yet to dim the Citadel.

The celebration was made even more special by the presence of the Elves. Estle had noticed that when she walked the streets with Gaelen and Nelwyn, the people would not approach, but kept a distance with their eyes lowered in respect. Elves, it seemed, were among the most highly regarded of beings here, and the fact that none had ever set foot inside the City only increased the mystery and esteem surrounding them.

That esteem had its roots deep in the early origins of the human race. Men had always sought enlightenment from the Elves, learning of music and art, of languages and lore. The Elàni were the wellspring from which the love of learning could be satisfied. Hence, in a city founded upon devotion to learning, Elves were revered by many.

Rogond and Hallagond were likewise treated with the greatest respect, for they were of the people of Tuathas, distant kin of the Citadel's founders. Word had somehow spread that they were of Alduinar's line, which was untrue, but so long as the rumor persisted they were regarded as visiting royalty.

The celebration lasted until sunrise. Clouds moved in at midnight, obscuring the stars, but not even the Elves minded. The feel of the rain and the scent of the forest more than made up for it. The food was some of the best they had ever tasted, and the wine and ale were quite acceptable. The Company sampled many delicacies from the sea, to their delight. There was honey as well, but neither Gaelen nor Nelwyn would touch it. They wanted to keep their wits about them.

Salastor had insisted that all in the Company should be outfitted in the finest raiment, and they were resplendent as they sat beside him. The entertainment continued all night long, and included dancing, singing, and story-telling. Visitors to the Silver City were very rare, let alone such distinguished ones, and the citizens put forth the warmest of welcomes.

Rogond knew that he could not allow these happy, peaceful people to be set upon and destroyed, yet he wondered whether such untried metal could withstand the heat of the forge. These gentle-natured folk had not been tempered by hardship. Rogond hoped they could be made to understand what lay before them.

At midnight, Salastor rose and bade the people listen as he introduced the newcomers and made them officially welcome. He declared that they were to be afforded every privilege while in the City, for they had journeyed long and across great, hard lands to warn the people of their enemy. "My people, as of this day, the City is at war for the first time. Preparations must begin at once, and the support of everyone will be needed. Our efforts will make the difference—will we lose our City, or will we defend it? It will be for us to choose." The people took the news fairly well, despite the fact that many among them had not cared for what they had heard. Some of those who cared the least for it were people of influence, and they were already wondering how they could discredit the Company's warning.

There was very little astir until noon of the following day, for the night's feasting had kept many folk in their beds until the sun rose high above them. Gaelen and Nelwyn had gone to the immaculate stable-yards to see to their animals, who needed to be fed in a timely way even if one had been out feasting all night. When Finan saw Gaelen he called to her, shook himself, and then stretched his forelegs out before him, arching his back like a cat. Gaelen's care had transformed him into a glowing red, glossy creature with a long, ebony mane, well-muscled and sinewy, bright-eyed and proud of bearing.

Horses were of great value in the Citadel, and new blood was always welcomed, for it was rarely encountered. Most of the animals now present were in some way descended from those few that had found their way in from more northern lands. Like Finan, Gryffa, and Siva, they were fine of limb, small in stature, and hardy of wind and heart. There were only about three hundred horses in a City where the people outnumbered them tenfold. As a result, relatively few could ride. The animals were used in farming and in the transport of goods, but some had been trained as cavalry mounts, and these were stabled in Salastor's yards. They were ridden mostly to ward off the occasional civil unrest. Although peaceful protests of city affairs were common, such disagreements sometimes became unruly, and the mounted guard was invaluable in quelling any disturbance.

Now there were four fine new stallions present in the compound, and the Master of Horse was very pleased. How fortunate that they had arrived at just the right time of year, for the days were growing longer and the open mares would soon be coming into breeding condition. The Master was already planning to keep the new stallions quite busy.

Gaelen and Nelwyn decided to go for an early ride on the sandy shores of the harbor, cantering easily along in the shallows. Finan was frightened by the foaming water at first, for he had never seen such things, but he trusted Gaelen. Gryffa, who came from Mountain-home, was accustomed to wild waters. The chilly salt water would take heat and swelling from Finan's forelegs, which had both seen grievous injury on a time. They still swelled and grew stiff unless cared for. This would be so until the end of his days.

It was obvious that the sea provided much of the livelihood of the City; fishing vessels and nets clustered around each of the four long piers extending into the harbor. Nelwyn had noticed vegetable gardens and some crop fields, but these were relatively few. The fields had once been mighty forests, and the soil was thin, although the abundant rains and moderate temperatures made for excellent hay. The livestock were fed dried seaweed as well, and they maintained on very little. Dried seaweed is an acquired taste that Eros, in particular, learned to relish after a few days. The forest also provided some good fodder, especially for the dromadin, who could eat plants much too tough for the horses to manage.

The Elves returned to the yards, cooled and curried their mounts, and then moved to each of the other horses, giving them bits of dried cake saved from the last night's feasting. Finan stood with his head in the air. *Do you see this fairest of beings, who brings good things to eat and shares them willingly? She is mine, and the rest of you can only dream of such things. Enjoy her generosity while you may.*

For the next several days, the Council was engaged in making their plan to improve the store of weapons and to train the people in their use. They would also begin to fortify the path in through the hills, laying traps and pits to impede the enemy army. Gaelen and Nelwyn would oversee the making of arrows and the training of archers. Galador was set to the task of planning fortifications; Rogond and Hallagond would assist in the refitting of steel blades.

There was a very dark-skinned man named Seti, who had been an ivory-trader upon a time. His lands were far to the south and east of the Citadel. He had wandered here when a storm waylaid him from his normal trade-route.

Hallagond, who knew something of these folk, was drawn to him at once. He learned that it was nearly impossible to cross the Great Salt to the south of where the Company had traversed it, and thus the ivory traders skirted far to the east. To Seti's surprise, Hallagond spoke a few words of the far-southern speech—Rogond was not the only son of Diomar with a flair for languages.

Seti flashed impossibly white teeth at him. "I was blown here like a bird at the mercy of winds, and I have made this my home ever since. It's wonderful to hear some of my own tongue again. I hope you will find me useful, for I am skilled in digging and provisioning deadly pits, which we use in my lands for trapping and killing large, fierce beasts. Now they will trap mounted soldiers, impaling them on sharp stakes within. We can dig them as deep as we wish, but the bigger they are, the harder they will be to hide."

"Let's also take some lessons from the Fire-mountains," said Galador. "There are stores of oil and pitch that may be set aflame to confound our enemies. The smoke will spoil their aim at our archers atop the walls, who will be far above the fray."

"Just be certain the wind is right," warned Ali, "or you will spoil *our* aim as well. Our own cavalry should not worry about being struck by friendly arrows. The fire-lines must be well away from the gates."

Galador nodded. "So they will be."

The plan was to make the relatively narrow way in through the Brown Hills as treacherous as possible, so that the Scourge would be forced to choose the only path not blocked by fires or pit-traps. Channeling the enemy forces through such a narrow way would allow the archers to concentrate their efforts to greater effectiveness. Galador and Ali surveyed the area with Seti, and they laid out the design of the barricades.

When Galador returned that evening, Gaelen and Nelwyn were waiting for him. "What plans did you work out today?" asked Nelwyn. She had spent her day aiding the Citadel's archers, among whom she had already achieved exalted status. Galador explained the intricacies of the plan, sprinkling salt upon the table and tracing the barriers on it. Gaelen was strongly reminded of the fire-pits in the Barrens, when the Elves of the Greatwood strove against the small but formidable army of Gorgon Elfhunter.

"These traps and barriers are all to the good," she said, "yet it is the gates themselves that trouble me. There was a scent, nay, a *stench* that hung over the Scourge's encampment. I did not recognize it, but it was dank and fetid, and for some reason I know it is significant. I have long held the feeling that something approaches other than just a savage army; something against which we may not prevail, for we are not anticipating it. I don't know how I will make this plain to Ali, but I believe we must build an inner wall of great strength behind the City Gates. This wall must be of stone, and it must withstand great force." She traced the Great Gates on Galador's salt-map, and drew a curved wall behind them.

Galador shook his head. "Ali is having a difficult enough time convincing his people to put forth even the present effort. He will not take kindly to putting this plan before them, for these people believe their walls and gates cannot be breached. Even if they all agree, is there time and resource enough to do this?"

"I don't know, but someone will need to convince them," said Gaelen. "If the Scourge is aware of Dûn Arian, they know it is defensible. Why besiege it, if they cannot win?"

"If it distresses you, then speak with Salastor and Ali about it," said Galador. "But I expect the people here will not take it seriously, for many are already skeptical. It is proving difficult to unite them in a common purpose."

"They think too long, and act not enough," said Gaelen. "Exactly the trouble with too much reading and studying; they have grown soft and complacent as lambs with no enemies to threaten them." She wrinkled her nose in an expression of disgust.

Gaelen had lived every day of her life with her senses turned to a potential encounter with trouble, and she did not understand. "I will regret dying in defense of a City of a thousand sheep," she said bitterly. "I can't wait to stand before my beloved in the Eternal Realm. I'll just explain that the quest to slay Gorgon Elfhunter was prevented by the Scourge, because the Citadel folk were too blind to lay proper defenses and too deaf to listen to those with insights they do not possess!"

"Try to hold on to that passion when you speak with Salastor, won't you?" said Galador, chuckling and shaking his head. He had no idea of the reaction this would kindle in her.

"You think this is amusing? That doesn't surprise me. Go on and plan your little traps and fires, and wait for the *real* threat to arrive. If even my own friends will not listen to me, then...then I shall go out into the forest and await my death in pleasant lands, away from fools!" She stormed out of the chamber, grabbing her bow and quiver as she did so, ignoring Nelwyn's calls at her back.

Galador stared after her, puzzled. It was not like her to lose her temper and her good humor so easily. "What's the matter with her?" he said to no one in particular.

He received his answer from Nelwyn, who was now quite dismayed. "She's angry because she truly believes the City will fall if the people do not heed her warning, and you have just told her that she's wasting her effort. You should know better than to make fun of her when she has mentioned both Ri-Elathan and Gorgon in the same breath! She was of very serious mind to have done so. You've wounded her confidence, and I'm surprised you would treat her with such lack of consideration. You will sit beneath the stars alone this night, unless you can convince Ali or Hallagond to join you!" She turned from him, ignoring his attempt to explain himself, and went to find Gaelen.

As she was leaving, she brushed past Rogond, who chose that particular moment to arrive. He did not say anything, but there was an unspoken question in his eyes as he looked at Galador, who simply shook his head, turned, and went out toward the veranda, where he fully expected to remain in solitude until sunrise. At the last, he turned back toward Rogond, who was staring after him with an expression of puzzlement, and spread his hands. "Truly, am I not generally reasonable and even-tempered? Is the moon in a phase that brings female wrath upon my head? If so, may it pass quickly."

Rogond nodded in understanding. "Have you seen Gaelen?" he asked, innocently enough.

"She is suffering from the effects of the same moon, and has gone into the forest. I would leave her there if I were you. She made it quite clear that she wished to be alone with her thoughts." Rogond raised both eyebrows, nodding slowly and deliberately. Sometimes, solitude was best.

Gaelen decided to ignore Galador's admonition, and very early the following morning she went to Salastor, requesting leave to speak with him, as well as Ali, on a matter of importance. She was admitted at once. Salastor was just beginning his breakfast, and he invited her to join him while they awaited the arrival of Ali. Gaelen liked Salastor; he reminded her of Hearndin, the King of Dûn Bennas. Both men seemed to be wise, worthy of great respect, and of a kind nature.

"Please, take bread with me, Gaelen," he said, as a fully laden breakfast-plate was set before her. She had not eaten since noon of the previous day, and this was reflected in her eyes, but she pushed the plate away.

"Forgive my discourtesy," she said, "but the counsel I would give is of great importance, and based on your response I may be better served if I am not lulled by food and drink." She looked away, trying to firm her resolve, for she really did not know what she would do if Salastor and Ali discounted her.

"Personally, I am more persuasive when I have eaten well, and my strength is not lessened by hunger," said Salastor, taking a great bite of food to illustrate his point. Gaelen did not appear to be moved by it.

"I have less need of food than you," she said. "My strength level is quite sufficient at the moment, yet I thank you for your concern." As she said this, her eyes betrayed her again, moving over the plate of food with longing.

"Then please eat with me because I dislike eating alone," said Salastor, smiling warmly at her. "Your resolve will be just as firm, I'm thinking. Try the fish—it is especially excellent this morning." He interrupted his own repast, looking hard at her. "Surely you would not deny me the simple pleasure of your company; not when you have counsel to give. I will seriously consider any warning you would bring, Gaelen. Be assured of it. Now will you join me?"

That was enough for her, and she politely consumed four delightfully flaky pieces of fresh, white fish—the best she had ever tasted. She finished with a piece of fine, dark bread soaked with butter and cream, and was quite content until Ali arrived, looking a little disheveled. It was still very early in the morning.

"What is the nature of this meeting? I was told there was some dire counsel that could not wait. What has befallen?" he asked, his dark eyes worried.

"Gaelen has asked to see us both," said Salastor. "Sit down and compose yourself for a moment. Have something to eat." A plate was set before Ali, but, as with Gaelen, he did not partake of it at first.

"Thank you, but I would rather come to know the nature of Gaelen's revelation," he said, looking earnestly at her. His trust in her had been plain from the beginning.

Gaelen gathered her wits, mustered her resolve, and told Salastor and Ali of her fears. She told them of the need for the second wall behind the gates, despite not knowing exactly why it was needed, though a new thought had occurred to her. *Could it be that I know what this stench means because…because Gorgon knows it?* She kept this unpleasant speculation to herself.

She despaired at the stunned looks on their faces, for even as she heard her own words, she thought they sounded foolish and ill-advised. Surely now they would dismiss her. Tonight they would talk of her foolishness with all-knowing smiles, and the City would be lost.

"How certain are you of this?" asked Ali. There was no disdain in his voice, only concern. "If you are certain, then I believe we must convince the people to act. They won't be too pleased about it."

Gaelen drew a deep breath and looked Ali directly in the eye. "I am reasonably certain," she said. "In my experience one cannot be absolutely certain of anything. Yet consider this: if I'm wrong and you build the wall, then you may have wasted time and effort, but if I'm right, and you do *not* build the wall, there will be no defense. Which is the greater evil?"

"This thing you ask is not small," said Salastor. "It will take a great deal of time, and will place a hardship upon my people. You need to understand this."

"I'm no builder, and I probably do not fully appreciate the extent of the task," said Gaelen. "But I would ask again…which is the greater evil?"

"It is said that Elves are very insightful, and some have the gift of seeing into the future," said Ali. "Does this number among your gifts, Gaelen Taldin?"

"Not usually. But I have been known to possess insight," she replied. "And that strange stench means something. Of that I am absolutely certain." *Gorgon knows what it means…and it means we need a wall of stone.*

No one spoke for a few moments, as Ali and Salastor considered. Then Salastor spoke: "We shall weigh this matter carefully, Gaelen. For my part, I'm convinced that we must prevent the greater evil. Now we must craft our proposal to the people, and convince them it is in their best interests to put aside all their other affairs to build a great wall. That will not be an easy task. Some believe the threat of the Scourge is exaggerated; others wonder if it exists at all. To be frank, there are those who do not trust you or your Company. They wonder whether you have some dark purpose in being here."

"What dark purpose could we possibly have?" asked Gaelen. "How would building the City's defenses benefit us? What ulterior motive would it serve?"

"All I can tell you is that some of our people are suggesting it," said Salastor. "Some have even proposed reasoning with the enemy, and these ideas have followers. They may be difficult to convince."

"Can you not simply order them?" asked Gaelen, who served a king in the Greatwood without question.

"We are a people dedicated to the free exchange of ideas and respect for the views of others," said Salastor. "I'm afraid I will have to persuade them."

"If you will allow it, I will aid you," said Gaelen. "The time has come for the people of the Silver City to hear of the savagery that will soon approach their gates, and I am one of very few who has seen it with my own eyes." *And I am the only soul in Alterra to have looked at it through the eyes of Gorgon Elfhunter.*

The war-council was reconvened and informed of Gaelen's insight. They reacted predictably; a few scoffed, but most did not. One who sat upon the council was the Citadel's Master of Numbers. He was very clever at designing structures, and he wondered whether there might be another way. "What about heavy steel bracing, such that the gates cannot break?" he asked.

"Steel may not break, but it will bend," said Gaelen. "It has to be stone…tall and thick such that it cannot be moved."

"You say your insight is based on some strange *smell* you encountered?" said another man, who had been introduced as a master builder. "Ridiculous. What in the world could the enemy be carrying? A stinking battering-ram? We do not have the time to build such a structure. Our people are unused to such heavy labors."

"Forgive me," said Gaelen, "but they had better get used to them. They face a long and difficult trial."

"You ask much of them, She-elf," said the man darkly. He did not care for her directness, and was of the opinion that she did not show proper respect. "You are a stranger here, and do not understand our ways."

"I ask only that they not lie down and die," she replied. "There is no time for debate. You must act, for your enemy draws near. What path will you choose?"

Ali turned to the master builder. "I am not in any way ridiculous," he said, "and I trust her. Whether the Scourge has a stinking battering-ram or something far more dire, we must be ready. I say we vote."

"Will you favor this plan, or no?" said Salastor. "Choose now. For myself, I say yes."

The vote was called, and most stood in favor beside Ali. Yet those who had voted against the plan were muttering about the foolishness of "Ali's folly." Ali was undaunted.

He turned to the Master of Numbers. "You are charged with the design of the wall. Remember that it cannot be completely closed until all of our own defenders are back inside." Then he turned to the others. "We have a new task before us, and the people must agree. You must prepare for it, and you must continue to perform all the other duties with which you are charged."

With those words the Council disbanded for the day, knowing that they had a monumental task before them and precious little time to achieve it.

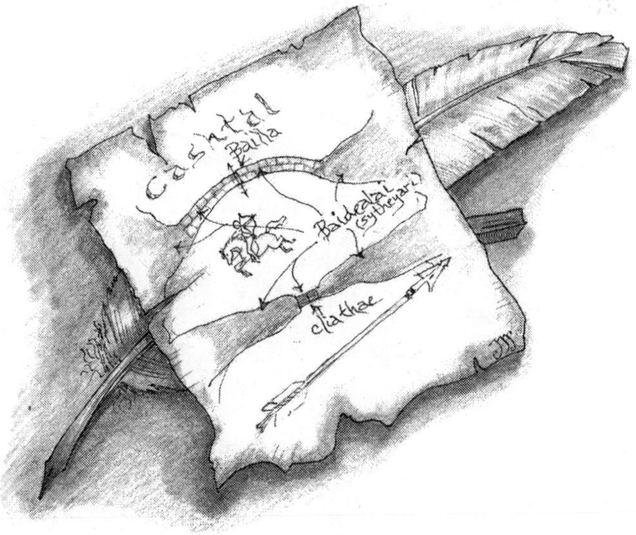

22
Ali's Folly

Every stonecutter and mason in the Citadel had been summoned and told of the plan, which would require untold hours as well as a small army of laborers. They set about the task of carving heavy blocks of stone from the nearby cliffs and moving them to within easy reach of the gates, but until the design of the wall was completed they could not set them into place. Fortunately, a number of blocks had already been cut and stacked for use in a planned expansion of the library, but the wall would require many, many more. Horses and men worked day and night with little rest.

The Master of Numbers called upon his best builders to help craft the wall. It was a clever design, with blocks set over and around a small, steel-braced doorway through which the mounted defenders could ride. It would be massive—nearly seventy feet tall and over twenty feet thick—and no force of men could have moved it. The Master Builder shook his head, whistling through his dark mustache. "This requires more like three years, not three months," he muttered.

The wall would be set into the living stone of the cliffs, and it would be well over two hundred feet long. There would be battlements surmounting it where archers could release their arrows in relative safety, even if the gates were breached.

Gaelen stood with Ali, as the Minister of Commerce tried for the last time to convince them that the gates would withstand any attack. "They are crafted from the strongest timber—nearly seven feet thick—as old and strong as the City itself," he said.

"They are impressive, but they have not been asked to endure such a trial as they will face," said Gaelen simply.

"And what trial, short of an impossibly large battering-ram, could possibly shatter them?"

"I don't know, but we had best be ready for it," she replied, in a voice that was maddeningly sure. They would never convince her otherwise. She quirked a smile at Ali. "If I'm wrong, neither of us will ever hear the end of it."

"If you are wrong, I shall rejoice anyway," said Ali, "for it will mean that the Scourge does not wield enough power to smash the Great Gates. No doubt we will both be thrown from the top of our own wall. I have heard them calling it 'Ali's folly' already." He shook his head in disgust. "So be it, then."

With the construction of the wall underway, Gaelen had set herself to a new task. She worried that there might be places along the tall cliffs where the Scourge might gain access, and she wanted to scout along them and make certain they could not be easily breached. The ones flanking the City were over two hundred feet tall and nearly vertical—no one could scale them. Any attempt would be met by a storm of arrows. There was no way to gain the top save by flying there, but Gaelen wanted to be certain. She spent the next fortnight in careful examination of nearly four miles of rock formations, both from the top and from along the base. Each night she returned to Rogond, who had been spending his days in training the City Guard, improving their skills with the sword and the spear. Some were quite skilled already, and they would fight well, but there were many in need of improvement.

The forges ran day and night, and the streets resounded with the sound of hammers upon steel. Fletchers and arrow-smiths had little rest, for Lord Salastor had ordered thousands of new arrows. Nelwyn and Galador had been of great help in this, as well as in training the City's archers.

Hallagond and Estle spent much of their time together. Though the preparations seemed to be going well, Hallagond was worried. "We need more seasoned battle-commanders," he said. "We can train the rank-and-file, but we need men of experience to direct them. I don't know where we will find such men in this place."

Estle shook her head. "I expect that every man of experience has already been called upon," she said, "and there are precious few of them. I almost wish Azori and his men were here. They would have been of great help, if they had not all been thrown into prison by now."

Hallagond's face brightened, as a thought struck him. "Do they even *have* a prison here?"

"Of course they do. Well...they must have! I don't know," said Estle. "Even the enlightened may stray from lawful paths."

"Let's find out at once, and then I will want to go there," said Hallagond. "Where battle commanders are lacking, rogues may serve."

"Oh, the Council will surely be as enamored of that idea as they are of Gaelen's useless wall," said Estle. "In my opinion, the effort used in building 'Ali's folly' would have served better elsewhere."

Hallagond had heard this opinion from her before. It wasn't that she didn't trust Gaelen, it was simply that she considered the Elves much too driven by visions and vague mysticism. She preferred things she could see and touch. She did not believe it possible that any object large and heavy enough to smash the gates could be transported across hundreds of miles of open desert.

What Estle didn't know, what no one in the Citadel knew, was that the object was approaching the City under its own power.

The Scourge had indeed been guided by someone who knew the Citadel very well. He had been a citizen once, although he had been born elsewhere. Neither his name nor his situation was of importance, only that he could lead the Scourge right up to the Great Gates. Once the City had been taken, he had been promised a reward and a position of influence there. He had been told that he would want for nothing. Of course, the Scourge's commanders intended to kill him the moment they reached the City. It was his just reward for betraying his own people, in their opinion.

He had painted a most attractive picture of the prize that lay within the City walls—the spoils would be fine beyond compare! He had warned that the Great Gates were as thick and solid as tree-trunks, and would be very difficult to break down, but this concerned the commanders not at all, for they possessed a thing that no gates made of wood could possibly withstand.

Gaelen had sensed it in the Scourge's encampment...a stench that, though unfamiliar, had triggered in her an undeniable feeling of foreboding. When she first passed through the City gates, she had marveled at their impressive construction, yet the feeling of foreboding grew. Listening to the war-council had made everything clear—the Scourge would break down the gates, and the City would be defeated by something their forces would not withstand. She did not know precisely what it was, or how she knew of it, but she was certain the City would fall. Without the new wall, all would be lost.

Rogond and Nelwyn wondered how it was that Gaelen, who was not normally given to premonition or to mysterious insight, held such certainty. It was just as well that they did not know, for if Gaelen was right, and the new wall held, the City would have been saved by none other than Gorgon Elfhunter.

When Gorgon had finally confronted Gaelen in the Barrens long ago, he had drawn forth his mirror, hoping to see himself through her eyes. This action had mesmerized and bewildered them both for a few moments, and much had passed between them. Many of the insights and perceptions held by each were given to the other, and though neither was truly aware of them, these thoughts now lay deep within. Therefore, when Gaelen first detected the stench of the thing in the encampment, she perceived its nature, even though she did not truly understand it. She knew these things because Gorgon knew them—this stench was not unfamiliar to him.

There were many foul and oppressive odors in Lord Wrothgar's black pits, but this one was distinctive. It smelled of rotten meat and sulfur, with a dank undercurrent that reminded Gorgon of the foul musk given off by serpents when they are caught and struggling for their lives.

This made some sense, as the beasts that gave off such a reek were akin to serpents, though they were much, much larger. Even as younglings they would dwarf a horse, and when fully grown they could lay waste to nearly any force of men or of Elves. Yet they grew very, very slowly; the one that moved now with the Scourge was hundreds of years old, and it had not yet come into full maturity.

How dragons had come to be in the lands of the Ravani desert, so far from their usual home, was not known. There must have been others that traveled there, even during the Time of Mystery, and this one was the spawn of their descendants. It was apparent that they had roamed the desert lands for many generations, because they had been altered over time, and were now quite different from their few remaining counterparts in the north. The Great Worm Lokai this one had been named, and he was of masculine gender—a fearsome creature with many weapons, including venom issuing from his tail-spines and teeth.

He was winged, but would never be able to fly, as his leathery grey wings had been reduced to simple-but-effective cooling devices. Normally carried quite flat against the body, they could be extended over the back to provide shade. When the dragon was moving he would sometimes rear up on his hind feet, aided by the huge wings, and raise great air-currents to cool his belly. This was an impressive and fearsome sight, for the animal would stir up a storm of whirling dust and sand about himself, often adding a short blast of fire from his ugly, shovel-nosed snout.

Lokai was mostly a dull grey in color, with scales roughened like those of an adder, but his belly-scales were bright salmon-pink and as smooth as glass, though they were rarely seen. Wisps of fetid steam rose from his mouth and nostrils. Despite the wings and fiery breath, he appeared more akin to a large lizard, and was neither clever nor especially swift. He was, in fact, quite unintelligent when compared with the fire-drakes and winged dragons of the northlands. This was a good thing for the Scourge; otherwise they could never have kept what little control they had.

When Azori, Estle, and Gaelen had gone into the Scourge's encampment, the dragon had been resting and they had not seen him. He could, by wriggling his body and wings, raise a layer of sand over himself, rendering him nearly invisible. When they observed the butchering and dismembering of the helpless captives, they had assumed from the remarks made by the butchers that the flesh would be consumed by the army. In fact, the Scourge took captives only to feed them to Lokai, whose appetite seemed to wax and wane with the moon. The dragon would not eat for several weeks, and then he would demand daily feedings requiring the sacrifice of at least twenty human lives, sometimes more. The Scourge did not stoop to eating the flesh of their own kind, although that knowledge would have brought little comfort to the Citadel. Lokai would feast very well should the defenses fail.

The Scourge took excellent care of their dreaded weapon, for he was useful in many ways. They used the venom to tip their blades, arrows, and spear-points, such that a small wound would bring agonizing death. Lokai's immense strength could be harnessed to draw an enormous sledge, upon which countless water-barrels were carried.

But perhaps his most valuable talent was in the ability not only to find water, but to burrow deep into sand, shale, or rock to obtain it. It was through the efforts of Lokai that the Scourge had been able to cross the desert wastes, and there were now several new, deep water-holes scattered behind them.

Lokai had been found as a hatchling and raised among evil men—he knew no other master. The Scourge took strength and confidence from the dragon's presence, even though he often killed their own warriors, for he was ill-tempered and unpredictable. Their war-cry, translated, was: "The Great Scourge comes. Our foes wither in flames!"

The creature was coming into his prime, and no weapon would dent his armor. Even his cruel, yellow eyes were covered with thick, glass-like shields that protected them from the windblown sands. His teeth were as long as sword blades, and his claws were enormous, deadly spades that could tear into solid rock. He appeared to be invincible.

Those unfortunates who drew the unhappy task of caring for Lokai lived greatly shortened lives. Often the dragon would crush them, or snap them in two as they yoked and harnessed him, but by far the most perilous task was the harvesting of venom, either from the tail-spines or from the mouth. Only the rear fangs held venom, and in order to collect it one needed to encourage Lokai to bite down upon a huge wooden pole held by two trembling attendants. This was usually accomplished while the beast was feeding. The post enraged him and he would lash his head from side to side, venom dripping from the fangs in the back of his mouth. At this point, the collector would leap forward, grab the hand-hold on the wooden post, climb in between Lokai's jaws, and gather the venom in a large, copper vessel. Needless to say, this position was not envied. Fortunately, a single collection would treat many weapons. The Scourge had lost many collectors, for if Lokai managed to vent a blast of flame while some unfortunate was still in his mouth, that unfortunate would die horribly.

Without Lokai the Scourge's army would not have seemed nearly as fearsome, though it would still have been quite fearsome enough for those whose lives it had ended. At any rate, it was a good thing that the people of the Citadel worked day and night to build "Ali's Folly", and that Gaelen Taldin had acquired more from Gorgon Elfhunter than an undying hatred of him.

Now the Scourge moved closer to the Citadel, pacing itself according to the whims of Lokai. It was the dragon that decided when they should move on, and how swiftly. Sometimes, when water had been found, Lokai would linger for a time, burrowing beneath the sand during the heat of the day and emerging by night. When he decided that he was ready to move westward, he would rouse himself, dragging the water-sledge, for as long as the darkness lasted. Lokai seemed to know when there would be long stretches of waterless waste, and these he crossed with tireless ease, stopping only to shelter from the worst of the midday sun. Although the Scourge had its own two-legged commanders, Lokai truly led them.

When the winds shifted and came out of the west, the dragon could taste of the air by waving his broad, slippery blue-grey tongue slowly to and fro. The tongue would disappear back into the beast's mouth, and he would rise from the sand, straightening his massive forelegs and giving forth a loud snort of steam. Lokai was on the scent, and the Scourge's war-lords contemplated killing their Citadel guide right then, for they guessed that he would no longer be needed. They smiled to his face and grinned wickedly at his back, at last deciding to leave him alive until they actually gained the City, just in case.

The people of the Citadel scoffed at "Ali's Folly" because they were expecting an ordinary army of men and weapons. They could defend themselves very well if besieged, for they had control of the resources and would outlast any invaders, but they couldn't imagine the existence of Lokai. If only the wooden gates stood in the way, the beast would turn fire, wind, venom, and incredible brute force upon the City. The stone-cutters might have grumbled as they set about their labors, but the lives of all the people rested in their hands, though they did not yet know it.

Ali was planning additional defenses with his lieutenants when he was interrupted by Hallagond, who had come on a matter of some importance. Ali immediately made him welcome.

"Ah! Hot oil-cauldrons to be set atop the walls, I see," said Hallagond, examining Ali's latest drawings in approval. "An excellent idea. And who is to be in charge of them?"

"Broca will command them," said Ali, indicating one of the men who stood by. "It was his suggestion."

"I thought Broca was going to see to the direction of the archers atop the north wall," said Hallagond. "He is one of your most capable men."

"And so he is. He will need to serve for both—my other men are to be occupied elsewhere. A pity, but there you are. Nelwyn is to command the archers atop the gates, and Habib is taking charge of the south wall. As Supreme Commander, I must be able to go where I am needed most."

"Who will orchestrate the launching of the catapults?" asked Hallagond.

"That has not been decided," said Ali with a hint of frustration in his voice. He was running out of experienced people, and Hallagond knew it.

"What if I told you there were several fine, battle-seasoned men wasting their talents in lying about within these very walls? And what if I also told you that I have arranged for you to meet with them?"

"First, I would ask if you have been standing too long in the midday sun, and then, having learned that you were not addled, I would kiss both of your feet simultaneously in gratitude," said Ali with a vague but discernable smile. "Yet I fear there are no such men in the City."

"But there are, Worthy Commander," said Hallagond. "You will merely need to overlook a few, ahh… past transgressions. I have been to your prison, where I found at least six men who will serve your needs. You need only determine how to convince them to aid you."

Ali sighed and shook his head, never taking his eyes from Hallagond's. "You don't understand...people here are not imprisoned unless they pose a grave threat. These men are undeniably dangerous, and their treachery is of the highest order. We dare not ever release them. But, just because I am curious, do you have a list of their names?"

"I do," replied Hallagond, handing it to Ali with a flourish. When Ali read the names, he laughed.

"I intend no offense, but you truly do not perceive the absurdity of this notion. Not one of these men could ever be trusted with freedom—violent murderers and rogues, the lot of them! We're very glad the walls that hold them are strong. Two are Corsairs, the only survivors of a shipwreck at the harbor-gates. We tried to welcome them among our folk, but their true nature surfaced quickly. They robbed and killed several of our citizens before their evil deeds were discovered, and these other four are no better. Lord Salastor will never permit the release of any of these fine gentlemen. We will need to find another way."

"Will you not at least speak with them?" asked Hallagond. "I do take your point, but you have no one else of experience. I have some knowledge of the sort of men these are...they're incredibly useful in a fight."

"I will not ask how you acquired such knowledge," said Ali with a wry look, "but I'm afraid these prisoners might be just as useful to our enemies, depending on which direction the wind took at the time. They have no loyalty to us—after all, we threw them in prison. It was a worthy thought, Hallagond, but I must insist that you pursue it no farther."

"Yet the time may come when dire need is on us, and we have nothing else," said Hallagond. "Just remember that these men will fight to save their own lives, and I doubt the Scourge will care to spare them. Keep this thought in your mind." With that, Hallagond and Ali agreed to speak no more of the matter, and they resumed their planning. Hallagond stayed the rest of the day, for his opinions were both respected and needed.

In the Healing Halls, Fima the dwarf was responding well to the care he was receiving. He insisted on spending part of each day in the Library, borne there on a litter until he could walk the way himself. Lord Salastor had ordered that he be shown every courtesy, and that the scholars attend his every wish. Of course, he spent nearly as much time teaching as he did learning, for he knew of places and events that the scholars could only imagine.

The folk of the Citadel soon learned to love his earthy sense of humor and his sharp-witted but good-natured banter. He was a treasure of great worth. He plumped back up very quickly on fine food and drink, but his white beard had been so damaged by fire that he had to cut off most of it to even it out. This pained him; Grundin's folk cherished their beards as a mark of maturity and experience. Fima, however, had spent enough time in the world and had gained enough wisdom to be able to separate his mind from the hair on his chin, and he shrugged it off. After all, even Elves could sometimes be wise, and they had no wisp of a whisker at all. His snowy-white eyebrows had been singed as well, but they had grown back already.

Gaelen and Nelwyn went to see him as they could, spending hours relaxing with him, reading aloud as he dozed by the window in his chamber, or singing to him as he wished. The scholars were surprised at the fondness held by this dwarf and these two She-elves, for such friendships did not exist in lore.

"I will not be able to come and see you for a while, Fima," said Gaelen on one pleasant afternoon as she sat with him in the Courtyard of the Scholars.

"And why not?" asked the dwarf. "Though I am not dismayed, for I have plenty to occupy my time other than the entertaining of a Wood-elf." Gaelen smiled inwardly at this contention, which was so obviously untrue.

"Because I am going away from the City for a while," she said, "if Lord Salastor and Rogond will allow it, that is."

"Hmmm..." said Fima, lowering his eyebrows at her. "If you are worried that Rogond won't allow it, it must be foolish and dangerous. How very typical of you."

"I don't consider my errand to be foolish or especially dangerous," she replied, "but it is necessary. Someone should scout back to the east and determine how near the enemy is to the City. I'm the only one here who truly knows how to read the language of scent, thus only I can determine their location without coming within sight of them."

"Surely an army of that size can be heard before it can be seen," said Fima. "There are others who could perform this task, and they know these lands better than you do."

"I'm certain that the Scourge raises quite a dust-cloud as well," replied Gaelen, "but you have just proven my point. They no doubt travel by night, when their dust cannot be seen, and those who pay little heed to the subtleties borne upon the wind have no notion of how far a scent will carry. I will smell them long before I hear them, if the wind is right. My hearing is far superior to that of mortal folk, as well. You know it. Besides," she added with a slight shiver, "They will have advance scouts ranging far from the main body of the army. Even I dare not come within sight of them."

"Rogond won't approve of this, Gaelen," said Fima. "And I see no advantage in it, either. You must at least take someone with you who knows these lands."

"Oh, I intend to," she replied, "if any experienced scout can be spared. Nearly everyone is busy preparing our defenses. I may need to trust to my own instincts."

"That, and pray the wind blows from the right direction," growled Fima. "If you are seen, things will go all the harder for the City. The Scourge will know they have been anticipated. I expect Lord Salastor will not approve of your plan either."

Gaelen threw a sardonic half-smile at him. "Perhaps not, but I will go in the guise of one of the enemy warriors. I still have those red-and-black garments, though they are now much cleaner than they were when I acquired them. If I am seen, I will not arouse suspicion, and I will disappear quickly. Lord Salastor need not fear." She patted Fima's shoulder affectionately. "If I don't come tomorrow, you will know that I have gone," she said. "Don't fret over me, for I will return."

Fima shook his head. "At least take Nelwyn with you. She will not want you to leave without her."

Gaelen sighed. "And then Galador will go. Both he and Nelwyn are needed here. I am apparently not essential to the defense effort, as I have been assigned no duties as yet. This knowledge, if gained, will be vital; it is the best way to use my abilities to aid the City."

"I'll make a small wager right now, if you are willing," said Fima. "You will not be going on this scouting foray if Rogond has anything to say about it. If I win, you must promise to aid me in translating a difficult manuscript that was set down by the Lore-master of Tal-ailean. If I lose, I will buy you a large pot of honey. Do you agree?" He held out his strong, gnarled hand, and Gaelen took it. She would accept that wager, for she had already decided that Fima would lose.

Even if he didn't, she wouldn't mind. She would enjoy aiding him in translating the manuscript anyway.

As it turned out, Fima was soon required to obtain a large pot of honey. Despite the fact that Rogond did not care for the idea of Gaelen's traversing miles of open desert alone, he did trust her to take care of herself. Lord Salastor and Ali wanted to know how much time remained to make ready, and they thought Gaelen's plan could work. She left the City at sunset a few days later, mounted on Finan and leading Faladinn, who bore enough water for at least a fortnight. She carried a very detailed map, with last known water-sources clearly marked. Gaelen could find her way. *What would we have given for this map when we came here from Mumari?* she wondered. *Almost anything, I expect.*

She sang as she rode away, and many in the City paused in their labors to listen. Rogond stood atop the gates and watched her go, knowing that if she did not return he would just as soon throw himself from them.

Gaelen had never been in a lonelier place than the open desert, and she found herself talking to Finan even more than usual. She was well-provisioned and knew where she was going, so she did not have the constant worries of the prior desert journey, but the vast emptiness depressed her. At night things were better—she could hear desert creatures calling in the dark, and the enormous star-filled sky delighted her, though it was almost overwhelming.

She moved steadily forward, hour by hour, enjoying the cool darkness. She knew that Finan could see as well as she did, and her thoughts focused on her task. *Rain…I have seen much since you sent me back. I'm here, and I haven't forgotten my purpose. I promise to stay until my oath is fulfilled…if I can. I wish you could be here to see the stars. They are like nowhere else…I wish I could share them with you.* She looked to the east, where the faint glow of morning had begun to make its way over the horizon, and drew Finan to a halt. It was time to test the wind again.

Gorgon Elfhunter looked at his own right hand in dismay. The skin had blistered and peeled, and now it hung in dry, lackluster folds.

If he didn't find water soon, he would die. His armor had grown heavier as his strength had waned. Worst of all, Gelmyr taunted him without mercy. He struggled through the sand, grinding his teeth, tasting salt, dust, and grit on the back of his tongue.

One foot in front of the other…one foot in front of the other…

He had to keep moving. There would be water on the other side of the ridge…full of sand and covered with a layer of slime. If he could only reach it, it would save his life.

You'll be lying down to die soon, won't you? Gelmyr's rotting, leering face loomed over Gorgon's right shoulder. *I almost wish I had water to give you, as I'm really not ready to say 'goodbye,'* he said.

"There will be water soon enough," Gorgon muttered, waving at Gelmyr as though he were an irritating fly.

"You'd better hope so," said Gelmyr, who, naturally, was unaffected by Gorgon's attempt at deflecting him. *"I don't believe I've ever seen you look this bad. Such a pity…"* His tone indicated that he didn't think it was a pity at all.

Gorgon squeezed his eyes shut and kept walking, heading relentlessly for the rocks and the scant pool of scum-topped water he knew would be there. He had already found water once, and his instincts would not fail him.

He knew these things because Gaelen knew them. She had been here before.

Gaelen returned in about a fortnight, and her news was grim. Though they had not yet crossed the Fire-mountains, the Scourge would arrive sooner than she had predicted. She looked at the new wall in dismay.

"Why has this not come nearer to completion?" she asked Ali, who spread his hands in apology.

"The builders decided they were being overworked for no good cause, and now refuse to labor for more than a few hours a day despite all entreaty from Lord Salastor and the Council. They're not the only ones—I have been having difficulty convincing the people on many fronts."

Gaelen nearly panicked. "The wall won't be finished in time if they do not task themselves now. If even a small part remains unfinished, all is lost!" Her eyes narrowed. "Someone on the Council is behind this. I would suggest that we call them together, and the builders as well. They need to be made to understand." She went to her chamber to wash the desert from her body, and to prepare herself.

At the insistence of Lord Salastor, the Hall of Council was packed nearly full. Builders, smiths and ironworkers, stonecutters—everyone deemed vital to the plan—had been summoned. The Council of Nine sat in their usual places, awaiting the arrival of Gaelen. The Company, including Fima and Bint Raed, stood behind them.

"Where is our bold scout, Rogond?" asked Salastor. "The people are becoming restless, and their labors await them."

"She is coming," Rogond replied, even as he heard the unmistakable sound of hooves upon stone. A moment later Gaelen rode in, the crowd parting back before Finan, who made his way forward to stand before the Council. He dropped gracefully to his knees and bowed before them, as Gaelen drew her short-sword and offered it hilt-first to Lord Salastor in a symbolic gesture of loyalty. He took it from her, and they both bowed in acknowledgment, then Finan rose to his feet and swept around to face the anxious crowd.

Gaelen's fire-cloak glittered and flashed in the torch-lit hall as she spoke to the people, pacing back and forth upon her fiery war-horse. Her voice and his footfalls were the only sounds to be heard. Estle could not help but smile at Gaelen, who was certainly making herself as fearsome and impressive as possible.

"Hear me, Ye People of Dûn Arian! Your enemy approaches, and yet you doubt the need to make ready. I am now charged with revealing to you the nature of the doom that will stand before your gates. Hear me and be afraid, for your need is dire and your City will fall if you do not heed the warning. Listen to my tale, and listen well!"

Finan stood on his hind legs, snorting fiercely as she spoke these last words. As if on cue, distant thunder rumbled, and a hard rain began to fall, hammering the rooftops so that Gaelen nearly had to shout over the noise. Her voice was powerful, and her words compelling; none would doubt her sincerity.

"I saw helpless captives...many of whom were women and children just like your own wives, sisters, daughters and sons! They had been mutilated, tortured, and left to face the cruelest possible fate. Imagine your own mother pleading for her life as a man bludgeons her to death, drags her body from you, and hacks it to pieces. Then imagine that man commenting that her flesh will be tough and stringy and perhaps he should *cook* her first!"

Gaelen took note of the crowd's dismay, knowing she had their full attention. "Now imagine a child, barely old enough to walk, screaming in pain and fear and confusion, while another man grabs him by his ankles, swings with all his might, and cracks the little one's head against the stones." She punctuated this by cracking a flat strap of stiff leather against one of the supporting columns. Everyone in the Hall jumped.

Gaelen's eyes darkened. "He's dazed, but not dead. They start slicing off his limbs while he is yet alive. There'll be no need to cook him, though...he's no bigger than *this one* is!" She drew her blade and pointed toward a little blue-eyed boy being carried in his father's arms. The boy buried his face against his father's neck, whimpering piteously. *Right on cue*, thought Gaelen, noting the horrified expressions on the gentle people of the Citadel—the father's face was ashen.

"This is what approaches your gates, and those gates will not stop them. I *know it*! Do not doubt the need for this new fortification, or your people will be the next ones torn and eaten. You may have not even a month to safeguard yourselves. Do not listen to the counsel of the foolish! Pay heed to Talishani Ali, who is wise."

At this, the crowd began to talk amongst themselves. They were horrified by the pictures Gaelen's words had painted, and her bright eyes held no deceit. She looked like the Warrior-elves of old, clad and mounted as she was.

Estle stepped forward, turning first to the Council and then to the crowd. "I have seen these things also," she said. "Gaelen's words are true, although any description of the savagery in that encampment cannot help but fall short of the reality. You face a terrible enemy." She looked over at Gaelen, who, she had decided, was now her friend. "I know it's difficult to accept the need for such great labors based solely on the intuition of Elves. At first I did not accept it, scoffing right along with the rest. But I have since asked myself—why would Gaelen urge us into such a task without need? She has nothing to gain, whereas we have everything to lose. I have seen the dread in her eyes. I'm no stone-cutter, but I will aid in the building as I can."

At this, the Minister of Commerce, who had not been in favor of the wall from the beginning, stood and addressed the people. "Our gates have withstood all challenges, and they have never fallen," he said, though it was difficult to be heard over the excited muttering of the crowd. "Now we are asked to complete this impossibly huge wall in so little time? It cannot be done! It is not necessary that it be done, and I will not aid in seeing it done, for it is folly. A waste of time, effort, and resources." He turned to Gaelen. "What proof have you that the gates will fall?"

Gaelen had no proof other than her own dark intuition, which she had no intention of speculating upon in public. She was silent for a moment. But then another voice was heard, from the Minister of Omens, who rose to her feet, her face pale save for two spots of high color in her cheeks.

"The Elf needs no proof, for I also have seen a…a force under the enemy command. I cannot see it clearly, but there is no doubt that it comes. If only the gates stand before it, the City is lost. Build the wall, my people, or we are all dead."

She turned to the Minister of Commerce. "You have been undermining this effort from the beginning, choosing to ignore the words of one who has seen the enemy, and who has risked all in coming here. You would place your own desires above the welfare of your people, and you are not worthy to sit upon this Council if that is so. Your actions bring shame upon our ancestors." She sat down again, but did not drop her gaze from the now furious Minister of Commerce.

Lord Salastor held up his hand. "Peace, my fine Councilors. All may voice their opinions and be heard. Have you anything to say?" He looked at the assembly, who sat in silence. "Then I would now ask the people to vote on their desire—will they set their efforts into completing the wall, or will they not? They must choose, and then agree to abide by the choice. What say the people?"

A great cheer went up, indicating the crowd was in favor of the vote. "Very well, then," said Lord Salastor. "Who among you will agree to the task of completing the wall? Please raise your arm that we may count you." He then asked the same of those who did not agree. To the dismay of the Minister of Commerce, the vote was nearly five-to-one in favor. Apparently Gaelen, Estle, and the Minister of Omens had made their argument.

As Gaelen rode past the Minister of Commerce, she looked him in the eye. "If the City falls, there will be no more commerce." He looked away, having finally taken the point.

That evening, Rogond went to find Gaelen, who had gone out onto the cliffs facing the sea and was now watching for the approach of another storm.

Is it spring already? He had lost track of the seasons in the endless heat and dry of the Ravani. He wondered whether Gaelen would ever see another season in the Greatwood when she turned to face him, having heard him approach. He drew quietly beside her, placing a loving hand on her back before taking her into his arms.

"You made quite an impression on them today," he said softly. "Riding Finan and wearing the fire-cloak was a nice touch. Now they are making plans to resume work at full strength and effort. That should cheer you."

She nodded, nestling into the valley between his right arm and his strong chest. "Then tomorrow I shall join them in the labor," she said. "I have no other task, and while I know nothing of wall-building, I can take direction and I have strong hands. We shall need many strong hands before all is ended."

Rogond held her, feeling the warmth of her body against his own. "I shall labor beside you," he said, "for our time together may be dwindling. I fear the Scourge may prevail, even if the wall is completed." He felt her tense in his arms as he said those words, and he immediately regretted them. He decided to try to distract her. "Did you receive insight during your time alone in the desert? Did you speak with your beloved, who waits for you? I know you sometimes seek guidance from him. Were you enlightened?"

Gaelen did not answer immediately, and he felt her tremble. She held Rogond more tightly, looking up at him with wide eyes, in which the approaching lightning now flickered. "I cannot speak with Rain, but I believe that he can hear me when I'm alone and my thoughts turn toward him. I did ask for insight, but whether I received any remains uncertain. I won't know that until I face dire need, I expect.

"Yet you *have* received insight, Gaelen, which is why we build the wall," said Rogond quietly. "I believe I know from whence that insight came. Gorgon is coming toward the City, isn't he? He has somehow communicated with you that the wall must be built, for he would save you for himself. Is that not so?" He braced himself for her response to this bold, deeply personal question.

Gaelen simply shook her head. "How little you understand," she said. "I do have a sense of my enemy, and you're right...I wish that he *would* come here, within range of my bow and my blades. At least I'd know that he was far from the Greatwood. I may have gained some insight from his dark history, for I seem to have knowledge of things I never knew before. But you're wrong if you think that I have shared any thought directly with him. *At least, not that I know of...not lately...* "If that creature ever tries to invade my senses again, I won't allow it. I'll die first."

The bitterness in her voice dismayed him, and he tried to reassure her. "Then surely that will never happen. I regret mentioning Gorgon to you, and won't do so again." He stroked her left ear as he said the words, but she did not relax.

"A storm is coming," she said simply. "We should not be atop the cliffs when it breaks."

She pulled from his grasp and stood on her feet, stretching up on her toes as the wind rose about her. She turned back toward him, her hair whipping across her face, looking like some wild spirit from the first days, before the coming of men. Her cold eyes glittered in the light of the approaching storm—there was none of the usual warmth and love she held for him.

"Keep your regret, Rogond," she said. "You should not regret the mention of Gorgon, for I shall face him again soon enough. But never again suggest that I share anything with him other than hatred."

Her eyes softened when she beheld the consternation in his face. "I'm sorry, Thaylon. I never mean to hurt you. Sometimes my words seem to be chosen for me, and are not as I would wish. Please forgive me." She turned and ran back to the shelter of the White Pavilions before he could reply.

He stood for a few more moments upon the cliffs as the storm rose about him, knowing that her spirit would only be at peace upon the death of Gorgon, until the winds and lashing rains forced him to follow where she had gone.

No rain fell upon the scarred, dark flesh of Gorgon Elfhunter. After finding the water, and drinking deeply of it, he had removed his heavy armor and spent many hours recovering his strength. He had barely survived, his mind lost in feverish delusions, as he lay on his back and moaned, hoping the water would restore him. *Why do you hate me? I am innocent...and yet they all hated me. It is not my fault that I am what I am. You made me this way...you made me what I am.*

The water slowly seeped through his desiccated body, bring life and vitality, restoring his awareness. He wept for a while without knowing why, but soon regained enough strength to drink again. The water was foul and full of minerals, but it was among the finest things he had ever tasted.

He sat now beneath the fiery desert stars, wondering how they could be so impossibly bright and beautiful. Had there been any living soul bold enough to ask him about it, he would have denied such feelings, but there was no living soul, bold or otherwise, for miles in any direction. Gorgon could sit and wonder at the stars to his heart's content. Even as Gaelen denied the existence of any bond between them, so did Gorgon. But unlike Gaelen, whose healing would only be accomplished upon the death of her enemy, Gorgon's only hope of salvation lay within her, and in the bridge that she had made between the Darkness and the Light.

Gorgon didn't want salvation—he had scarcely even entertained the notion of it. What he wanted was vengeance, to prevail over Gaelen and every other Elf who drew breath. When they were vanquished, there would be no more troublesome diversions, no more unwanted insights, and no more conflict within. Deep within his black heart, he knew that he would both celebrate and regret the time of her passing. He did so enjoy looking at the stars.

True to her word, Gaelen worked beside the stone-masons whenever they needed her, despite the opinion of Galador that her talents would be better used elsewhere. "You could show these fletchers a thing or two," he said, as he rested briefly from his own labors one afternoon.

When it came to the making of arrows, Nelwyn was the better of the two cousins at fashioning the shafts, but Gaelen was the undisputed master fletcher, matching and shaping the feathers perfectly, binding them in exact spirals so that they would never come loose. Arrows crafted by Gaelen not only flew straight and true, but they spun as they flew, making them more effective when they struck their target. None in the Citadel could match her skills, which had been perfected over a thousand years of practice.

"We need large quantities of arrows. We don't have time for elegant fletching," said Gaelen. "There is no more important task before these people than the building of the wall, and therefore, I am most needed here. No quantity of arrows, regardless of the quality of the fletching, will make the slightest difference if this wall is not completed."

"Enough arrows will make a difference in any battle," said Galador. "Nelwyn was wishing you would go and aid her; she trusts no barb that has not been fletched by her cousin Gaelen. She also asked for some help in training the City's archers."

"Train them how? You draw, you aim, you loose. It's as simple as that. Skill with a bow can only be gained with practice, Galador. Nelwyn knows this as well as anyone. The citizens can run their own archery practice."

Galador laughed good-naturedly at her. "I will tell her," he said. "Though I doubt she will care for the notion. I would stay and aid you in moving mortar and stones, but alas, I am called to other tasks. Ali has commanded me, and I am a captain of the Citadel, after all."

"How unfortunate that Ali prevents you from laboring beside me…I know that fills you with dismay. Tell Nelwyn that moving stones makes for strong shoulders, which gives steady and tireless aim," said Gaelen, smiling back at him. "Look what it has done for me!" She flexed her arms and shoulders provocatively.

As if by prearrangement, Rogond arrived looking rather worn out; he had been working alongside Gaelen for many days now. He had not shaved, and he was stripped bare to the waist, revealing several scars upon his shoulders and chest. He brought a water vessel to Gaelen, and she drank gratefully. This was hot work.

He brightened when he beheld Galador. "Ah! My friend! Come to aid us at last?"

"What? And become unkempt and dusty, not to mention hot and tired? I think not," said Galador, as Ali approached from behind.

"Hail, Talishani Ali," said Gaelen, raising her hand to greet him. "Our friend Galador was just lamenting that he could not stay and aid us in building the wall; he said that you had commanded him to be elsewhere. It is such a pity to disappoint him so."

Ali did not reply at first, looking with some confusion at Galador, who was now delighting Gaelen with an expression of barely concealed dismay. "Perhaps some messenger has misspoken…I have given no tasks to Galador this day. He's free to do whatever he is called to do."

"What a relief for him," said Gaelen, looking sidelong at Galador. "All the same, you had better reassure him. I know he would make certain you can spare him before he sets about this labor."

Ali had perceived the joke, though his face was serious as he turned to Galador. "You are free to remain here for the entire day if you choose, with my blessing. It looks as though your friends could use your strong hands. Enjoy your freedom this afternoon; only be advised that I may ask you to work even harder tomorrow to make up for it. There should be great progress made on the wall today, with your efforts added."

He bowed to Gaelen and Rogond, and last to Galador. "Forgive me, but I must see to another task. Farewell, my friends; I will see you at supper tonight. I'm sure you'll have hearty appetites."

"Come, Galador! Let's get dirty!" said Gaelen.

"Indeed. I'm delighted at the prospect," was the chilly reply.

The Company reassembled that evening around the supper-table. Ali joined them, and they dug into the meal as though it would be their last. Hallagond couldn't resist taunting Galador; he had never seen the Elf eat so much at one sitting. "That's what comes of hard work," he said.

"And what were you doing all day, might I inquire?" said Galador through an uncharacteristically large mouthful of roast lamb and potatoes. He paused and looked around to see Gaelen and Rogond staring at him with identically bemused expressions. They had never seen such a sight, either.

Galador drew himself up in a dignified manner, and swallowed hard. Suddenly it was as though he had never lowered himself to touch food in his life. "I ask again, Hallagond, what undoubtedly vital and important task occupied your time?"

"Actually, Estle and I were making plans of our own today," said Hallagond. "She decided that I needed a respite from battle preparations. The sea was calm, the west winds were fresh, and the white sands were warm beneath our feet." He looked hard at Galador as though daring him to say anything about it.

Galador was not put off in the least. "I hope you enjoyed the respite. Tomorrow is another day."

"Let's drink to tomorrow, then," said Fima, raising his glass. He was getting stronger by the day—the clean air of the Citadel was working wonders. The sight of his friendly face, eyes twinkling with their old good humor, filled his friends with joy. "I, for one, wish you had come to fetch me when our tall friend got his first taste of the quarry. After all, stone-building is an art at which my people excel. I might have given him helpful advice."

"Indeed," said Ali. "If you are strong enough, my good dwarf, I will set you to aiding our builders tomorrow. Not with labor, but with experience and wisdom." Fima nodded, casting a rather sly look at the Elves. It would be enjoyable to be set in a position of authority over them, if only for a while.

"Never mind, beloved," whispered Nelwyn, turning to Galador. "Tonight I shall wash the dust from your feet, comb your hair, and soothe your weary shoulders with oil. Tomorrow I shall work beside you, whatever your task."

Galador smiled. There were benefits to this sort of hard labor, after all.

The next morning, Gaelen and Rogond returned to the building of the wall. Through their efforts, and those of countless others, it looked as though the task might actually be completed before the Scourge arrived. It remained to be seen whether "Ali's Folly" would be enough to withstand the fury and power of Lokai, or whether Gaelen's estimation of the need had been sufficient. After all, she was only a Wood-elf, and knew little of such things.

23
The Enemy at the Gates

As the eve of the battle drew closer, the Company grew more restive and anxious. The preparations would not take very much longer—the citizens were making every effort. The City was nearly ready, but all within it shared a feeling of unease. The Minister of Omens had thoroughly unsettled them with her pronouncements of some unknown terror approaching as if on dark wings.

Gaelen stood in the shallows of the harbor, sitting astride Finan, allowing the cool currents to draw the heat from his legs. They had both worked hard this day, galloping and maneuvering in preparation for the battle to come. Finan was a superb archer's mount; he could sense when Gaelen drew her bow, lengthening his stride and remaining suspended long enough for the release. She almost never missed a target while riding him. She leaned over his neck, rubbing it with gentle hands, tracing an old, ragged scar with her fingers as he dropped his head and closed his eyes with delight.

I would dread this conflict all the more were you not with me. You are the finest horse ever born. I promise to keep you safe if I can, but we both know that we may fall. I love you with all my heart. Let's take care of each other when the time comes. Finan sighed with pleasure as she continued stroking him, but when he felt her tears on his neck he lifted his head in concern.

Gaelen would tell no one, but she was afraid of the battle to come. This was not just an army of savages; they had some fearsome terror under their command. What of Rogond, and his suspicion that Gorgon was somehow sending her these insights? What if it were true? She wept long that night, alone and unheard by anyone except Finan, who would have comforted her if he could. Gaelen needed more reassurance than he could give.

Galador and Nelwyn tried to take heart in their embrace, spending as much time together as they could before the storm broke. Galador found comfort in the fact that Nelwyn would be in a relatively safe position atop the wall over the Great Gates. He would ride out with Rogond and Hallagond, along with Gaelen and the rest of the mounted warriors, trusting Nelwyn to safeguard him from above. She, of course, had vowed that no enemy would come near him if she could help it.

Fima feared for the safety of the vast treasures contained in the library, and he had worked with the other scholars to relocate all the irreplaceable volumes and parchments in a central vault deep beneath the main level. When the time came he would barricade himself inside with the other elderly scholars; no enemy would gain entrance without feeling the wrath of his axe. Fima would defend the legacy of Salasin to his last breath.

Bint Raed had settled in quite happily, but of course she knew that this happiness might soon be lost. She worked with the City's tailors, using her talents to construct garments of green and gold that could easily be told apart from the red and black of the enemy.

Rogond's anxieties were torn between Gaelen and Hallagond. There was something astir in his brother's mind that was unsettling—rather like a young horse thinking of taking flight. Hallagond seemed uneasy, often filled with false cheerfulness, and it worried Rogond. At such times he would convince himself to take a deep breath, and trust in his brother as well as in his beloved. Gaelen, of course, would not falter. And, he told himself, neither would Hallagond. Even as he paced the wall, Rogond reminded himself that no one can truly know the heart of another, and that whatever Hallagond was destined to do, he would do.

Estle had likewise felt this false cheerfulness, but unlike Rogond she knew the cause of it. Hallagond was dismayed that Ali had forbidden him to enlist the aid of the six battle-seasoned prisoners who even now languished in captivity. The people of the Citadel needed their skills and experience—they were going into battle with few capable captains to lead them. Hallagond was not nearly as prideful as he had once been, but when he was right, he knew it.

Now he sat with Estle under a cloudy night sky. Soon the clouds would clear, but for now he enjoyed the misty dampness and the fresh smell left behind by the rain. Estle shivered a little in the damp, and Hallagond pulled her close, wrapping his warm, woolen cloak around her shoulders. Sometimes he believed that she was the only person in whom he could confide, for she alone truly knew and understood him. She accepted him as he was, and that was a great comfort. He turned his eyes to hers, and spoke in earnest.

"Did you mean what you said…do you care for me?"

She was surprised by the question. "Do you think I would make such a declaration lightly? Of course I care for you. Yet you have not made your own heart clear in this regard, and I'm still waiting."

These words were met by a long silence, until finally Hallagond continued. "I must tell you some things that have been gnawing at me…can I trust you to keep them secret?"

She sighed. "You can trust me. What have you to say?" It looked as though she would have to wait still longer for Hallagond to declare the desire of his heart. Because she loved him, she would wait.

"Ali is wrong in not allowing me to carry out my plan with respect to the prisoners. He needs men like them...they understand the sort of decisions that must be made in battle, and are not afraid to make them. If I can spend a little more time convincing them, they will fight for the City to save their own lives. Ali's fears are without cause. All our lives hang in the balance—at least he should allow me to try my plan."

"Yet he seemed adamant," said Estle with a note of worry in her voice. "You're not thinking of going against orders, are you? That would be a mistake. Ali might throw *you* into prison before all is ended, and then we will not have you to aid us. Please, whatever you're thinking of doing, think again. You might very well be right, and Ali might be wrong, but he is the Citadel's commander, and he truly knows these men. You don't."

"Since what day did you become so law-abiding?" asked Hallagond, somewhat surprised that Estle had not immediately stood in support of him. "I thought you would remember that sometimes we must do what we think is right, despite edicts from authorities."

"That's Al-amand talking," said Estle, looking directly into his eyes.

"Perhaps," said Hallagond, his voice betraying no hint of his disappointment. "But I would remind you that Al-amand will not stand by and watch someone embark on a foolish course, even if that man is a friend, or an authority. I intend to try my plan, Estle, for it is the right plan. We need those men beside us. I believe I know how to convince Ali."

"Why do those words fill me with dread?" said Estle.

"Just trust me. Only promise that you will tell no one of my intent," said Hallagond. "Now, come closer that I may warm you, and properly show my gratitude. Let's speak no more of these matters." They spoke no more of them, or of anything else, until the breaking of dawn.

Gaelen returned to Rogond at first light, having spent the night alone with no one but Finan to share her fears. She had done this because she needed to choose her course carefully, with her own intuition to guide her. The opinions of others, even well-intentioned and thoughtful ones, could confuse and distract her. She loved Rogond, and he now kept her heart, but she would not allow him to sway her. He possessed a maddening tendency to make her consider alternatives.

"Why did you go out from here last night, Gaelen? I was…I was wondering." Rogond knew better than to suggest he would restrict her freedom, and he also knew it irritated her when he fretted over her safety. In her mind, such worrying suggested that she could not take care of herself. She allowed him to embrace her, snuggling down into his strong arms, resting her head in the hollow beneath his chin, but she did not answer immediately.

Rogond was a patient man, and he knew that she would reply in her own time. He smiled inwardly as he recalled recent words of his friend Fima, on a day when he had been most exasperated with Gaelen.

Ah, Rogond, think on this: only one man in the world could have captured her heart, and that man would need both a loving spirit and a patient nature. Just think of the higher level of forbearance you have achieved since you met her. Soon you will have such skill and diplomacy that you could arbitrate the affairs of the Mighty, and you owe it all to our little Wood-elf. There's a shining crystal inside the difficult grey stone. Ha!

Now Rogond held his difficult Wood-elf in a gentle embrace, feeling her truly relax at last, asking no more questions of her.

"I went out with Finan last night; I wanted to soak his legs in the harbor."

"Was there no other reason?" *It doesn't take all night to soak Finan's logs.*

"I wanted to think," she continued, with a slight smile. "It's something I do once in a great while."

"Indeed? And what thoughts came to you that you would share?"

He felt her tense again. "You will not like them," she said.

"Tell me, then, and I'll decide whether I like them," he replied, stroking her hair to reassure her. "It won't be the first time. Tell me, if you will."

"I will ride out with Nelwyn, and we'll set up a scouting-post in the desert. When the Scourge appears, we will take stock of their forces, for they will be much more apparent when the army is moving than when they're encamped. Then we will return swiftly, so that the City has time to prepare. We still don't truly realize what faces us...it might be helpful to know before it gets here."

"What difference will it make?" asked Rogond, who, as Gaelen had predicted, did not like the notion at all. "Whether the Scourge numbers two thousand or ten thousand, the City is as prepared as it can be."

"There are things moving with that army, and don't ask me how I know it! I must find out what that dank smell is. I fear we will need time to make ready…time we may not have. At least if Nelwyn and I can bring it to light we'll have a short while, which will be better than nothing."

"What if Galador won't agree to let Nelwyn ride out with you?" *I expect he'll care for this idea as much as he would enjoy being staked to an anthill while listening to a revered High-elven chant being performed by Hallagond.*

Gaelen stiffened, and Rogond could almost feel the hair on the back of her neck standing erect as he said these words. She had always resented Galador's interference in Nelwyn's choices. "Nelwyn is her own person, and governs her own affairs. At least, that's how it *used* to be."

"Now, Gaelen, be fair," said Rogond, trying to soothe her. "She attends to Galador's wishes out of love. She wants to avoid causing him grief. I'm sure you can understand that."

Gaelen's voice still held a slight edge, but she relaxed back into his embrace. "I suppose I can, yet love should not seek to take away freedom."

"Yet love will seek to protect from harm. You know that Galador will die to protect Nelwyn, even as you would."

Gaelen sighed. "Why can he not understand that Nelwyn and I have faced untold peril for years unnumbered before she ever heard the name 'Galador?'" Gaelen sometimes longed for the days when she and Nelwyn had roamed the Greatwood together, and the hardships they had faced, while challenging, were familiar.

"He knows this, Gaelen. I'm just reminding you that your desires and Nelwyn's are not the only ones involved. She may not be riding out with you."

"Then I shall ride alone."

"I'll ride with you," he said, knowing that she would carry out any plan once she had decided it was necessary.

"You're needed here, Captain of the Citadel," she said with a smile. She felt his disappointment in his embrace, and turned her gaze upward to look in his eyes. "Be not dismayed, Thaylon. I will return to you. It takes only one set of eyes to learn what must be learned, and but one swift mount to return with the news. Take heart. Do you not know that I always wish to be at your side? Yet I am a hunter-scout; I must do what I was meant to do, and wait for our reunion. We shall fight then side by side, but tomorrow we will be parted until the Scourge approaches the gates."

"Tomorrow?" Rogond felt a sudden dread take hold of his chest and squeeze it. He had not expected her to leave so soon.

"They had difficulty with the Fire-mountains," she said in a distant voice, "and it has slowed their pace, but they will now gain speed across the Plains of Thirst. Our scouts must be in place very soon now...and you must make certain the wall is truly complete."

He could not imagine how she knew such things, but he had learned never to doubt her. He said nothing, but held her until they parted. She went to find Nelwyn to ask for her aid, but he sat brooding for a while longer, seeking answers to many questions that he could not resolve. After a time, he rose and went out into the City, making his way to the Hall of Council to seek enlightenment from the one person who might be able to provide it.

The Scourge had indeed had difficulty with the Fire-mountains. Lokai would have nothing to do with the troublesome task of carting their water supply over such an obstacle, nor did he care for lightning-storms, for he was not immune to their effects. He was, of course, resistant to fire, but a well-placed lightning bolt shooting through his vast bulk would, at the very least, stun him quite thoroughly. Were it not for the services of their newly acquired dragon-master, the approach to the City might have ended right there.

The Scourge had found such a master in the person of Ikari the Anori-man. Formerly a bandit of Azori's band, Ikari had fought viciously along with his companions, but like them he had been overcome. When his enemies had stripped him of his fine, black robes, they had seen the dragon-design across his back and shoulders; it was very ornate in red and black, green and blue. They knew it at once, though it was as rare as the men deemed worthy to bear it. It saved Ikari from being crippled, and later dismembered and thrown to the dragon, particularly once he had demonstrated his impressive abilities. Ikari had knowledge of dragon-lore that few in Alterra could rival, and when he first beheld Lokai he was nearly overcome, weeping with both joy and awe. He had thought never to set eyes upon one of the Great Ones. He stood before the beast's huge, ugly snout, trembling as it lowered its head, fixing its malevolent, muddy yellow eyes upon this man who dared stand before it.

The man was either stupid or frozen with fear, and Lokai really did not care which. He extended his tongue just far enough to taste the air, and decided to make a meal of him, thrusting his great head forward. The man tensed and leaped aside, barely evading the huge, sword-like teeth.

Not yet, Great One...not yet... Ikari began chanting in an odd, buzzing monotone, swaying back and forth in rhythm, as the dragon's eyes followed the hypnotic movement, blinking in dull surprise.

Ikari was terrified, and his pale face showed it. After all, he had performed this chant only in front of smaller beasts—cold drakes, mostly—never before a real dragon. But he had practiced it for many hours over days, months, and years. As he kept chanting for several minutes without being eaten, he gained confidence. The chant was mesmerizing; the peculiar buzzing quality lulled anything with scales, including snakes and lizards. Ikari had risked his life many times, practicing on the huge, deadly snakes of his homeland, and the venomous cold-drakes of the eastern isles.

Lokai wavered, and his head sank onto the sand. The hard, clear eye-shields drew across his now rather unfocused eyes. The vertical pupils, like those of a cat, yawned wider just before the dark blue leathery eyelids dropped down over them. The fearsome beast exhaled a long plume of steam as it fell into slumber. The dragon-master had beguiled it.

Black-clad Ikari stood alone before the sleeping Lokai, and there was no sound to be heard from the fearsome warriors of the Scourge. From that day on, Ikari was elevated to a status he had never enjoyed before, and was promised great power if he would join with his enemies. He had gone to Azok, who was tethered miserably to a pole with the other less talented captives, and told him that he had chosen betrayal. Azok replied that he could understand Ikari's choice, and then spat in his face anyway.

Later, when the dismembered parts of the unfortunate prisoners were brought for Lokai to feast upon, Ikari recognized Azok's powerful quarters and limbs, and he bowed slightly as they disappeared into the mouth of the Great One. He smiled sardonically at the memory of Azok and Azori, whom he had once thought mighty. The true power was here, in the person of this Great Beast, and Ikari commanded it.

Were it not for the small black figure that sat now just behind Lokai's enormous head, the crossing of the Fire-mountains might have presented an insurmountable difficulty. Yet Ikari knew the ancient dragon-speech, leaning over and whispering into ear-holes so large that he could almost have climbed into them. Lokai remained stubborn for a time, but eventually Ikari convinced him, offering promises of food and comfort, water and blood, even the flesh of Elves. The dragon had tasted Elf-flesh only once before, and he had never forgotten it. Ikari smiled wickedly as his beloved, magnificent Lokai began to move forward at last. Soon, he thought, Galador would have yet another cause to hate him.

Hallagond made his way down to the Citadel's prison and asked to speak with each of the six men that he had placed on his list of potential allies, selecting the two whom he deemed most suitable. Then he went to see Ali, who was standing atop the nearly-completed wall. As he approached, he heard Galador giving praise to the great depth and sturdiness of the wall, striding confidently back and forth upon it as Gaelen and Nelwyn stood by.

"Your people have done well," he said, with a furtive look at Gaelen. "However, it's a good thing I was here to assist in the building, otherwise you might not have made such progress."

Gaelen, who had labored for countless hours, perceived the joke. "Yes, and it's a good thing we made the wall as tall as we have, so that when I push your cocky self from it you won't suffer much at all," she said, winking at Nelwyn.

Though Hallagond would have preferred to speak with Ali alone, he had no time to waste. "Forgive me for interrupting," he said, "but I have a matter of interest to Talishani Ali. Here are the histories of two men who have offered to serve, but have not yet come forward because…ahhh, circumstances have prevented them. Take a look. They seem as though they might be useful to our defense force."

Ali scowled at Hallagond, taking the parchment from his hand. "I thought I made it clear that I have already searched the City, and have found every suitable man within it," he said. "Do you doubt my diligence?"

"Not at all," said Hallagond, bowing. "Yet there may be those few who escaped your notice somehow. Just have a look."

Ali had some difficulty at first, for Hallagond's handwriting was not as neat as it could be and some of the characters were unfamiliar. His brow furrowed, but then his eyes brightened with interest.

"Well? What do you think of them?" asked Hallagond.

"They seem experienced, but why was I not made aware of them until now? Why have they not come forward?"

"As I said, circumstances have prevented them," said Hallagond. "Would you not agree that we are in grave need of their services?"

"I would, if what is written here is the truth. Yet I would know the names of these two fine officers, whose services are so gravely needed," said Ali, who by now had guessed he would not be receiving any news that he wanted to hear.

"They are Ishtar Al-khamal and Haleck Visili," said Hallagond quickly, trying to avoid wincing in anticipation of the inevitable response of Ali. There was naught but silence for a moment as the powerful commander's face grew dark.

"And you believe what they told you, if I understand this writing," said Ali. "They obviously left a few things out. It may interest you to know that they are each responsible for several murders of innocent citizens. Do not continue on this path, Hallagond. Get it out of your mind!"

"Actually, they both proclaimed their innocence," said Hallagond, which naturally displeased Ali even further.

"It means nothing that guilty men deny their guilt," he said. His dark eyes had grown rather flinty.

Galador attempted to intervene before Ali became truly angry. "Hallagond does not always think before speaking. Keep that in mind." He turned to Hallagond. "What has set you on this course? I realize you relate better to thieves and bandits than the rest of us do, but surely you know that Ali is right. We cannot have our lives turning on the trustiness of brigands."

"Fine," said Hallagond. "Then let's have them turn on the directives of trustworthy people who have not the slightest notion of what they're doing." He bowed to Ali. "My apologies—I shall withdraw my efforts and abandon them. I do hope that the few battle-seasoned warriors standing with us do not fall too quickly."

He looked over at Galador. "I appreciate your drawing attention to my unsavory history. After all, Ali must know the kind of man he is dealing with."

Hallagond was obviously disheartened and angry, and Galador had done nothing for his good humor. He turned and began to walk away, leaving the parchment behind.

Ali called after him: "Hallagond, we do appreciate your efforts. Know that I understand and take your point. But this path, while it does hold some promise, could result in disaster, and I am unwilling to take the chance. Let that be the end of it."

Hallagond raised his hand in acknowledgment, but as he continued walking his resolve was undiminished. *This won't be the end of it. Not as yet.*

Rogond had gained the Hall of Council, and had requested an audience with the Minister of Omens. He was shown into a well-appointed chamber where birds sang, and water gurgled and played as it flowed from many small fountains. Soon a tall woman with very long, greying hair entered the room. He remembered her name was Maji, but as he bowed before her he addressed her as "Minister".

"Why have you come?" she asked. "Do you seek enlightenment?"

He looked into her gentle, light brown eyes, but had some difficulty holding her gaze, for his request was a bold one and very personal.

"Indeed...I have come seeking enlightenment, but I don't know whether such a request is reasonable," he said. "I would never seek to offend you, yet there is great dread that grips my heart, and I would know the truth of it if I can."

"Your beloved would place herself in jeopardy, and you are concerned for her?"

Rogond looked up in surprise, his own grey eyes wide. "How...how could you know that?" he whispered, not really intending her to hear.

She smiled. "It is the only thing that makes sense. There's no great insight here, Rogond. I was named Minister of Omens because I sometimes possess the gift of foresight, and I am adept at reading what signs we are given. But I am also favored with the ability to see what lies beneath the actions of men, and predict their future course. You desire only to safeguard your beloved; it is very clearly told by your actions."

She called for food and drink to be brought to the chamber. "Sit down, bold soldier, and partake of food and drink with me...I am no one to fear."

"Never had I thought so," said Rogond quietly.

Maji laughed. "Of course you hadn't. Then eat and drink with me, and tell me of your trouble and why you seek my aid," she said. "Then we shall see what may be done."

By the time Rogond had finished, he was more relaxed around Maji, but some of his trepidation remained. He truly did not know what to make of this likeable, pleasant woman who somehow managed to fill him with quiet dread.

Then it came to him—it was not Maji he feared, but what she might reveal. Having asked for her aid, he would now need to suffer whatever insight she provided.

She finished her small meal and reached out toward him, taking both of his hands in her own. "This matter is not one that I can address alone," she said. "Do you really wish to know the truths you seek? Consider carefully, for once given, knowledge cannot be returned, whether it pleases or dismays the learner. Do you still wish to learn?"

"Is it true that events known through foresight may then be prevented?" said Rogond quietly. "It has always been my belief."

"I cannot say," replied Maji shaking her head. "But if that is your belief, then you must act upon it. Yet you should know that, although there are some ways in which we may alter the outcome of things, there are other avenues of destiny that cannot be altered despite all efforts. That, at least, has been my experience, and it is my belief. Come, now, if you would learn, for I will take you to one who will enlighten you."

Maji led Rogond down a long passageway ending in a heavy, carved door with a very ornate brass handle. This she opened with little difficulty despite its weight, revealing a curved stairway of stone. Rogond followed her upward to another doorway, this one of polished brass with a beautiful hammered design that appeared to be a map of the heavens.

A large and intricate sunburst stood prominently in the center. Maji pressed her long fingers against four of the rays, and Rogond heard a quiet "click" within the door, which now swung open to reveal a dimly-lit chamber. The smell of marwani-weed hung heavily in the air.

"Who enters the Chamber of Aryiah, the seer?" said a quiet but powerful feminine voice. Rogond looked around for the source, but the voice seemed to be echoing from all points of the room at once.

"It is I, Maji, your friend. I bring one who would seek the benefit of your insight."

"Step forward, that I may look upon you," said the voice.

Rogond wished that he could know from whence the voice came, but he supposed it did not really matter. A shaft of sunlight beamed down from an eight-sided window in the vaulted roof; it was the only source of light in the room apart from a few candle-flames. "Step into the light," said the voice.

Rogond did so, and for the first time he detected a dark figure gliding silently around the perimeter to face him. He heard a sort of low, humming chant that was somewhat disturbing; it sounded strange and otherworldly to his ears. The figure swayed in rhythm with it; there was no doubt now where the voice was coming from.

"What is your errand, North-man?" said the voice at last.

He did not reply immediately, looking instead at Maji as if asking whether it was appropriate to answer. Maji nodded encouragement, and Rogond turned back to the figure in the shadows. "I have come to seek enlightenment, for the fate of one whom I love is uncertain," he said.

More chanting and swaying followed, but the tone of the chanting changed, becoming deeper and more resonant. "The fate of everyone is uncertain, North-man. Why do you risk coming here? Do you not know that sometimes it's better not to know?" This was followed by a sound that might have been laughter.

"My concern for my beloved sometimes overrules my good sense," he replied, peering into the shadows. Again, the sound of the strange laughter was heard.

"Come then, and learn what you may," said the voice, as the figure came forward. Rogond beheld a slight, willowy woman dressed all in black gauze. Her skin was very dark, but one could only tell it from her hands, because her face was veiled. Rogond could not see her features through the veil, and he wondered how she could see through it. She extended her right hand, touching his sleeve, and guided him to a place near the wall.

"Wait here," she said, and turned back to Maji. They drew forth a small table and set it in the center of the shaft of light, placing 3 large cushions upon the floor around it.

"Come, Rogond," said Maji. "You shall sit upon Aryiah's right hand, and I upon her left." The veiled figure lowered herself gracefully onto the center cushion, placing both of her elbows on the little table, her fingers extended as if beckoning them, whereupon Rogond and Maji sat in their appointed places beside her.

"Maji appreciates my gift even though it is sometimes unsettling. I do not go forth from this chamber except to my balcony...few in the City have ever looked upon my face."

She drew back her veil, and Rogond was startled at the sight of her blank, cloudy orbs, set into an ebony face that might have been comely but for the terrible scarring upon it. "When I displeased those who had fostered me, they branded me with hot iron. Having looked upon me, North-man, do you still wish to know what I can tell?"

She took his left hand in hers, her skin smooth and warm, like dark, polished wood. He was overcome with compassion for her, for the loneliness and uncertainty of her life, and she felt this in him.

"Do not pity me, Tall-stone," she said. "I did not ask for this fate to be handed to me, yet it has been. I am no longer afraid, for Maji has been very kind, and I have proven my worth to the City. Now, let us see what we may. Give me your other hand."

Tall-stone...that's my brother's name, thought Rogond, extending his right hand. She took both together, surrounding them with her own.

"You are trembling," she said. "Do not be fearful."

She turned her blank eyes to the sun, and did not move at all for many minutes, chanting rhythmically, as Rogond felt a great wave of relaxation sweep over him. His eyelids drooped, and he grew quite calm. When she finally released him, he did not know it at first.

"Come back to me, North-man," she said. "The stars have revealed all that they will for now, yet they have told me some things of interest."

Rogond was now wide awake, his face drawn with worry. "The stars have told you? But, my lady, the sun is high and there are no stars to be seen."

"Not by you," she replied with a cryptic smile. "Yet the stars are always shining upon us. I, who cannot see the sun, can read the stars by day or by night, for they speak to me."

"And having spoken, what did they tell you?"

Aryiah drew a deep breath. "You wish to know whether your beloved's desire to ride out and await our enemy is ill-advised. You fear it will mean the death of her."

Rogond nodded. "It seems to be a dangerous path. Do I need fear for her?"

"Not from that path," said Aryiah. "It is her destiny to die in battle, defending those whom she loves."

Rogond felt a blade in his heart. He had not truly wanted to know how Gaelen would die, only that she would not die on the watch. "And I...will I fall beside her?" he asked, praying that it was so. He would not wish to live a day without her.

"I'm sorry, Thaylon," said Aryiah. "The stars have said that your fate will be quite different. You will not die with a blade in your hand. Such will be the fate of the Elves alone among your Company." She turned her pale eyes to his. "All of them."

"This is an ill fate!" muttered Rogond. "How could this be? If I fight beside them, and the battle turns ill, then surely I will fall with them. My courage will not waver! Surely, you are wrong."

Aryiah shook her head. "The stars do not reveal whether you fight beside them when they fall, or whether the conflict that looms now before you will be their last. And I can learn nothing by desire...I can only reveal what I am given. It is your task to give meaning to it, for I cannot. But I have learned much of you, Tall-stone. You have given your heart to one who will someday leave you forever. You did this in full knowledge, but my words have made you truly realize it for the first time. Someday, you must face this parting."

"I understand," said Rogond, though he was greatly discomfited and now wished he had never come. He wanted very much to divert his thoughts from the day he most dreaded. "I thank you for allowing me to see that Gaelen will return from her scouting foray. Now I can let her go without such fear in my heart."

"I am glad to have reassured you. Was it worth the new fears I have engendered in your heart?"

For a long moment, Rogond was silent. At last he spoke in a broken voice: "It is my greatest wish to die beside Gaelen, and now I learn it shall not be so. That is a source of great sorrow, but I asked for your enlightenment and I knew all might not be as I wanted to hear."

"Yet I have not said you will not die beside her, only that you will not fall beside her in battle," said Aryiah. "It may not be this battle that claims her; you might be long dead when she falls before an enemy. Remember, there are many possibilities."

She drew the veil back over her scarred face. "I asked about the Scourge, and about the battle to come," she said, "but I learned nothing. Not even the stars can predict that outcome, for it turns on the actions of so many. Seeing into the fate of your Gaelen is much simpler, for she will ever make her own destiny." They both smiled at this, together with Maji, who had heard Gaelen's impassioned speech in the Hall of Council.

"One thing I did learn," said Aryiah, "is that Gaelen's wall is not ill-advised. Your beloved has gained some insight that guides her, though I sense it is much different from mine…darker and more sinister. I believe she may know from whence it comes."

Rogond looked hard at the veiled face of the seer. "Did you see… did the stars reveal anything of a Dark Warrior? A terrible enemy filled with evil?"

"Not at this time. You must leave now, North-man, for I am weary and I must take rest. Go to your beloved, and be with her while you may. Your time together will be brief enough in this life, and you will have none in the next. Go to her."

Our time will be brief enough in this life, and we will have none in the next, thought Rogond. *I knew that…and I chose her anyway. I don't need a seer to tell me. I wonder whether she really did not see Gorgon, or whether she would even tell me if she had…*

He started to ask her again, but Maji silenced him.

"Hush. Ask nothing more of her, for you will receive nothing. Come, now, and let us return to the light." She took his hand to lead him from the chamber, but Rogond was still watching Aryiah intently. She had trembled visibly at the mention of a Dark Warrior. She had seen something, and it had filled her with the same dread held by all who looked upon the face of Gorgon Elfhunter.

Gaelen and Nelwyn left the following day, taking two of the Citadel's best scouts with them. In three days other scouts would join them, replenishing their provisions, sending the first two back. Only Gaelen and Nelwyn would remain constant on the watch. When the Scourge appeared, they would first take stock of them, and then return with all speed to warn the City.

"Safeguard yourself, my love, and make certain that the wall is fully completed," said Gaelen, embracing Rogond with some fervor.

"Be sure to come back to me, so that we may ride out and face this fate together," said Rogond, returning the ardent embrace. He did not want to ever release her, and she finally had to gently suggest that if he did not, the Scourge might soon come upon the City unaware.

Galador watched the departure from atop the wall, having said his farewells already. Nelwyn rode beside Gaelen, and they seemed almost lighthearted, though he knew they understood the seriousness of their errand. Though Galador was unhappy with this arrangement, he did not dissuade Nelwyn from following her heart's desire. He was finally learning that the tighter he held on to her, the more likely she was to fly from him.

Hallagond and Estle had come to see them off, but Estle held far greater concerns. Hallagond had not given up his plan to enlist the aid of the prisoners Ishtar and Visili. He might well earn the wrath of Ali, who had made it quite plain that he wanted no further consideration of the idea. After the scouting party had left, Hallagond made his way back to his own chamber with Estle following.

"I'm going to try my plan," he said. "Will you aid me?"

"I will not!" said Estle. "This is a mistake, and you know it."

"Have it your way, then," he said, the disappointment in his voice evident. "At least promise you won't go to Ali and tell him."

Estle bristled at him. "You think I would do that? Do the cold winters in the northlands affect the brains of the men who dwell there? I love you, you foolish man! That is exactly why I will not aid you in this…this folly! Why can you not see it?"

"Perhaps I have insights into the hearts of men like Ishtar and Visili because I have been down much the same path. They are said to be murderers...do you know how many men I have killed?"

"I can only guess," she replied. "Yet I know you would not take the lives of innocents."

"I didn't know the guilt or innocence of all who fell to my hand," said Hallagond. "Yet I know some who were innocent. I have made some great errors in judgment before, my fine lady, and good men died as a result. I am no better than Ishtar or Visili, yet Ali trusts me to aid him. He needs these men and their abilities." He drew a bottle of fine brandy from beneath his cloak.

"Good idea. I might need a large dose of brandy before resolving to commit acts that will result in my being thrown into prison," said Estle in a sarcastic tone.

"Oh, no…this isn't for me, but for the guards in the keep," said Hallagond with a crooked smile. "My brandy I carry in a separate container. This bottle has a fair dose of Gaelen's dark elixir; that should send them into a fine, deep sleep."

"How did you get hold of Gaelen's elixir?" asked Estle in some astonishment.

"Well, I am a pickpocket, am I not?"

"Of course, but not even you could accomplish such a feat with an Elf, especially *that* one. Now tell the truth."

"All right. She gave it to me last night, when I told her I was having trouble sleeping for worry over the coming battle. She made me promise to take but one drop; of course, I took quite a number of drops, apologizing and explaining that my hands were shaking and I spilled a small amount. She seemed satisfied with that."

"Hmm. Just naïve enough to think the best of you, I suppose," said Estle. "I'm surprised that she did not detect the lie in your eyes."

"She was preoccupied," said Hallagond. "Now, if you don't mind, I have things to do."

He turned and left her to stare after him. This would not end well, and she would aid him if she could. She followed him down the corridor, hoping that his plan would not result in shared imprisonment with Ishtar and Visili, rather than gaining their freedom as Hallagond hoped.

The guards, who knew and liked Hallagond, were still reluctant to partake of the bottle with him, as they were at their posts and it was not permitted.

"Why the festivity, Hallagond? Is there some occasion that warrants this fine gift?"

Hallagond smiled back at them, trying to think of something they would not be able to resist. "Ahhhh…well, yes, as a matter of fact, there is. I am…I am betrothed!"

"Truly?" said the Captain of the Guard, who had admired Estle and was now quite pleased. "May we assume your fine lady Estle is the lucky one?"

"Yes, indeed," said Hallagond. "I wanted to share my happy news, and it seemed a small nip of fine brandy would be a harmless and appropriate way to do it." Then his tone grew serious. "After all, none of us knows whether any will be alive to witness this union, as we stand on the eve of battle. But, if you would forego the courtesy of joining me in a small toast…"

"Say no more," said the Captain. He turned to the others. "Well, don't just stand there...bring glasses!"

The small toast turned out to be a series of enthusiastic toasts to nearly everything and everyone, resulting in the draining of the brandy-bottle. It wasn't long before the guards were all snoring in contentment; they hadn't suspected a thing.

Now it would be left to Hallagond to free Ishtar and Visili, having already exacted their promise to serve the Citadel's army without question. He unlocked their cells, intending to lead them to the chamber of Ali, where they would swear fealty to him. They would kneel with bowed heads, inviting Ali to strike them dead if he would.

This would take courage, but both men were weary of imprisonment and they were willing. They had also been quite concerned about their fate should the Citadel fall to the Scourge, for they would be taken easily as they sat helpless in their cells. Aiding the City was the only way to assist in saving their own lives. They knelt now before Hallagond, promising to give their best in carrying out the plan.

Ishtar, a short, stocky man, was bearded and dark-haired. There was an air of good humor in his deep brown eyes, reminding Hallagond a little of Azori. Visili, by contrast, was pale, with blue eyes and thinning grey hair. His chiseled face bore a proud nobility that Hallagond had detected from the first. Neither man was in good fighting form due to long confinement, but they would soon come around now that they were free. Both were highly experienced, having seen enough of battle to lend great value to the City's efforts.

Hallagond took down two cloaks from their pegs in the guardroom, and soon none would notice the three men making their way quietly toward the house of Ali as twilight fell.

"We must accomplish our task before the changing of the guard," said Hallagond. "We only have about an hour's time now, so we must be swift."

"Ah, my friend, that is where you are *right,*" said Ishtar, suddenly bringing his hand down hard on Hallagond's neck, sending him into darkness.

Estle had followed behind, but she kept a great distance so that Hallagond would not notice her. She shook her head as she observed him stealing away from the prison with the two brigands in tow, and had followed as she could, but it was difficult in the twisting maze of streets and alleyways. Now she came upon Visili crouching over Hallagond, who apparently had been rendered senseless.

She drew her blade and rushed forward, thinking Visili to blame. "Stop what you're doing and back away from him, or you die at this moment!" she said, her grey eyes ablaze. Visili was alarmed and backed away, his hands open to show that he held no weapon.

"Put down your blade. I am not your enemy, or his."

"What happened? Where's the *other* one?" asked Estle, who did not lower her blade as yet.

"He has gone…he intends to provision himself quickly and leave the City," said Visili. "You must go after him. I cannot, as I may be recognized." He drew a deep, frustrated breath, "Do you not understand? If Ishtar escapes, Ali's full wrath will come down upon us. You must prevent him, if you can. Go now! I will tend your beloved."

Estle was angry and fearful, and her next words were hard. "He is not my beloved…he is a *fool!*" She turned and went in pursuit of Ishtar, to save her beloved fool if she could.

Hallagond soon came to himself; his neck ached and his head was swimming, but he was unhurt. When Visili explained what had happened, Hallagond groaned. "So, she says I'm a fool? Well, she's right."

Visili did not doubt it, though he was grateful for his freedom.

"Hallagond, we must pursue Ishtar, until he is either recaptured or lies dead at our feet. He must not be allowed to escape, for I have little doubt that he will reveal Dûn Arian to ears that should not hear of it. Like it or not, it is our problem to repair."

"Do you actually think he will make the difficult crossing alone?" asked Hallagond miserably.

"Ishtar is a survivor. I wouldn't take the chance."

Unfortunately, Ishtar was a lot more like Azori than was good for any of them. Now Hallagond would be forced go in pursuit. *I'll need to catch him before he can leave the City, otherwise I'll have to chase him down.*

He could only imagine what his friends would think of him, deserting them on the eve of battle. And what of Rogond? His brother would not understand the reason behind it; he would only know that Hallagond had departed the City, just when he was most needed.

"Sorry to disappoint you again, my brother," he muttered as he followed after Visili, who at least seemed to be trustworthy. "It appears that my judgment is correct only half the time."

He couldn't imagine what Estle would do to him when next he saw her, yet for a moment he was quite overcome with concern. What if she came upon Ishtar alone? Such a man wouldn't hesitate to hurt or even kill her. At first the thought chilled his blood, but then he thought upon it again, and decided that it would be Ishtar, not Estle, who would be in need of aid.

Hallagond's mischief was discovered at the changing of the guard. It was not difficult to piece together what had happened; the empty brandy bottle and the sleeping guards explained it all. They would not rouse easily, and it would be awhile before their tale could be told. It was clear that someone had given them a sleeping-draught, and then had released the criminals Ishtar and Visili. When Ali was told, he understood at once, calling Rogond, Galador, and Fima before him. Neither Hallagond nor Estle could be located.

"I have turned out the City Guard and have informed the Minister of Lawful Affairs," said Ali, his face as dark as a thundercloud. "The guilty ones will soon be found." He turned to

Rogond. "I would like to know where your brother Hallagond is at this moment."

"I don't know," was the honest reply. "I haven't seen him since Gaelen and Nelwyn left for the frontier."

"If it please you, Ali, may I see the brandy bottle?" said Fima with a worried look. Ali handed it to him courteously; he knew Fima was not to blame. "This was a very fine brandy," said the dwarf, examining the bottle and handing it back to Ali.

"Well? Is that all you have to say?" growled Ali. Fima had obviously noticed something of significance.

"For the moment, it is," Fima replied, his blue eyes glowing with the desire to ask Ali if there was anything he intended to do about it.

"Very well. It is of no consequence, for our people will soon locate those responsible and bring them before me. But you should know that they will be pursued if they have left the City. We cannot allow folk of such obvious low character to escape and betray us."

"Have a care, Ali," said Rogond. "Hallagond is not of low character, despite what you're thinking."

"Who said anything about Hallagond?" said Ali in a cold voice.

"Obviously, you suspect him," said Rogond. "My brother is a man of honor. He will never betray the City."

"Then why does he set criminals free, and leave on the eve of battle? Is he so proud that he would risk everything to prove himself right? Is he a coward, fleeing before the storm?"

"I did not think him so misguided," answered Rogond. "I will stand by him until I know otherwise."

Though Rogond's words were resolute, his heart was troubled. Ali left the three friends trying to piece together what had happened. When the guards finally regained their senses and told their tale there was no doubt—Hallagond had betrayed the trust of those he was set to protect. When the City Guards reported that neither of the prisoners had been found within the city walls, and when it was further discovered that three dromadin had been taken, the truth was undeniable. The fugitives had left the City, taking paths that only those familiar with her design would know, and they were by now well away. Ali ground his teeth in frustration. He could ill afford sending men to pursue them, for the enemy was drawing near the gates, and none could be spared.

Gaelen and Nelwyn stood, as ever, side by side.

The east wind lifted their hair, stirred the deep sand about their feet, and brought with it the scent of the enemy army moving relentlessly toward them. Gaelen closed her eyes and shuddered—they were close, now.

This was the scent of a thousand unwashed bodies, of sweat and blood and rotting carrion. There was a sharper undercurrent there as well, and Gaelen knew it for what it was. Men gave off this scent whenever their darker passions were high—fear or pain or savage lust for battle.

Finan stood by her side, turning his sharp senses toward the northeast. The wind blew his long, dark forelock back from bright eyes filled with the reflection of brilliant desert stars. He snorted, and Gaelen turned to him, stroking his scarred neck and shoulder. *What have you heard?*

She trained her own sharp ears toward the advancing army, but heard only the wind hissing over the starlit sand. Closing her eyes, she took in one more draught of the chilly, dry air. Then she opened them again, looked into the earnest face of her cousin Nelwyn, and gave her appraisal.

"By first light, they will be here."

Rogond stood with Galador atop the tallest spire and trained his keen grey eyes to the northeast. The time of battle was near—they could both sense it. Rogond knew that this would be the largest and most fearsome host he had ever engaged, and he drew a deep breath, hoping he would prove worthy at the end of it.

Such was not so with Galador, who had seen strife far greater and more wearisome than this, as he had fought in the Third Battle beneath the Banner of Ri-Elathan, and had witnessed the downfall of Wrothgar. Yet he dreaded this upcoming conflict even more, for he had a reason to survive it.

His beloved Nelwyn stood with Gaelen on the eastern frontier, and he feared for both of them. They were capable, certainly, and their skill as hunter-scouts was beyond question. Though he still considered Gaelen prone to recklessness, he had learned to trust her. He suppressed a shudder, his dark hair blown back from his strong face.

In spite of their looming fate, Galador was now glad that he and Nelwyn had not remained in the Greatwood. They had since come into many adventures, but now he wondered whether they might all have come to the end of the road. The Scourge was large, strong, and savage, with no real vestige of honor left to it. There would be no mercy shown, no quarter asked or given.

Now their own small forces stood ready, awaiting the frenzied return of the scouts. The size and nature of the enemy army would then be known, and there would be some time to modify the defense plan, if needed, in preparation. Galador and Rogond would join the ranks of the Citadel's cavalry, riding out to meet the mounted riders of the enemy, taking as many as they could before falling back to the safety of the walls. Their foes would not expect this, and would rush headlong, following them right into the sights of the archers standing shoulder-to-shoulder atop the battlements. It was hoped that the archers would repel the enemy long enough for their mounted comrades to regain entrance through the enormous gates, re-securing them before too many of their foes could enter.

In the meantime, the archers upon the battlements would strike with deadly accuracy before the enemy could truly prepare to mount any assault upon the walls. Lured within range before they were ready, the Scourge would have to fall back and re-group. They would, of course, have archers of their own, but they would be vulnerable in the open, whereas those of the Citadel would be well protected on the battlements. The enemy would fall back, waiting until their war-machine was in place before moving on the City.

Then the siege would truly begin.

Galador sighed as Rogond reached out to him, placing a steadying hand on his shoulder. "Don't worry, my friend, they will not fail. You will see Nelwyn again, and then we will face our greatest test." Galador knew he was referring not just to the perilous task of their mounted warriors, but to the outcome of the war itself. This was more than a struggle between armies. All that was good, fair, and enlightened grappled for its very survival against that which was evil, savage, and ignorant.

Galador smiled back at his tall friend. "I look forward to the day when we may all lift our glasses and toast of victory. You will have earned your place among the most worthy warriors of your race. Gaelen will look upon you with great pride, as she does even now. You have nothing to fear from the betrayal of Al-Amand; there is enough strength and honor in you to serve for both. Your father would be very proud of the man his younger son has become."

Rogond nodded, still keeping his gaze to the east. "Let's not mention Hallagond now, my friend...we have a task before us that is daunting enough. We'll see it done, or none survive. I'm going back down to see to Fima. Will you stay and keep the watch, and alert me if our scouts are seen?"

"That I will," Galador replied, patting his silver horn. "Make certain the horses are ready, won't you?" Then he paused for a moment. "Are you certain that all is well with Fima? He's still not strong, you know. I would hate to lose him, though I will miss his axe."

"His axe may yet come in handy, Galador. I'm not certain we can hold off the enemy, and keep them from the lower halls. Fima knows his duty, and he has accepted it. He will not waver."

The wind shifted in the hours just before dawn. It now turned to the south, blowing both the scent and sound of the enemy away from the scouts. *Well, it really doesn't matter so much*, thought Gaelen. *We'll need to wait until the enemy is well in sight so that we can get a good look before retreating to the Citadel. We have an excellent vantage point, but the enemy forces will have to get close enough to be counted and evaluated—maybe too close for comfort.* Two of the Citadel's best scouts stood beside her; they were superb horsemen, and she was glad of their company.

As predicted, the first sight of the Scourge came at first light, as the black, starry sky gave way in the east to indigo and deep purple. The scouts took the horses back down into the hollow behind them, commanding them to stay until called for. Then they waited, still and silent, as the approaching army drew nearer, the sharp eyes of the Elves trained on their enemies, taking stock of their numbers and of the weapons glinting faintly in the light of the rising sun.

The wind had shifted back toward them, and now another scent was evident—the one that Gaelen most needed to identify—unwholesome, dank, and rotten.

The enemy host was large and well equipped, but not remarkable, and at first the scouts' confidence was high. Yet as the eastern sky grew rosy and the sands came alive with early morning light, they beheld the source of the strange scent for the first time. It took the breath from their bodies and the courage from their hearts.

An enormous grey dragon moved with the Scourge, fanning its wings occasionally and lashing its short, powerful tail. The Scourge's forces gave it an understandably wide berth. Gaelen looked over at her cousin, noting the despair in her face. "A dragon. They have a dragon. *Now* I understand." The despair was replaced by determination as they nodded to one another—it was time to begin the long ride back. But they could not tear their eyes away from the dragon, which was unlike any they had ever imagined. Misshapen, bloated, and monstrous, it moved inexorably toward the west, mesmerizing them until long after they should have been away.

One of the Citadel scouts grabbed Nelwyn's arm. "Forgive me... but they are getting too close. We must fly now if we are to escape them."

Gaelen and Nelwyn knew that signs of their presence would remain in the sand, and then the pursuit would begin. They had to keep out of the range of enemy archers, and they would be in the open nearly all the way back. They mounted their restive animals and rode as though the demons of darkness flew at their backs.

Rogond made his way down to the deep halls, and thence to the vast inner chambers where all of the most valuable written lore had been moved to keep it from the enemy. It was a massive collection that had taken weeks to secure.

In the midst of it, glowering from under his snowy eyebrows, axe at the ready, stood Fima the dwarf. He was surrounded by the Citadel's scholars, and Rogond knew they would die rather than allow the enemy even to set eyes on the lowliest parchment. Fima's talents were of much greater use in this place than as one of hundreds upon the battlements, where Rogond felt he would almost certainly fall. Fima was a fierce fighter, but his recent illness would sap his strength, and his age would work against him. Here, in this cool underground place, he was in his element.

Rogond called out as he stood before the heavy doors, and heard a faint reply from within. A few moments later the doors opened to reveal Fima's weathered face. His bright eyes twinkled when he beheld his friend, though his expression was set and determined. Rogond stepped inside, marveling at the enormous store of written lore that lay now before him.

"In a few minutes they will barricade you inside. Are you certain you have everything you will need?"

"I have food and water enough for many weeks, and I have my axe, which is the most important of my needs," said Fima.

"I pray your axe remains idle, yet I'm relieved that you have it. The knowledge of the Citadel will not be taken easily."

"Indeed not, for the Scourge will only destroy it…knowledge is of no use to such a people. I hope the wall holds, but I'm ready if it doesn't." He patted his axe. "I'm not so sure about the rest of them," he whispered, eyeing the scholars with some disdain. "I suspect their only experience with combat has come from reading about it."

"Regardless, I pity the fool who first pokes his filthy head inside this chamber," said Rogond. Then, with a last farewell, he left Fima to his task. As he turned and looked for what might be the last time upon the old dwarf, Fima called out to him.

"Keep safe, young Tuathan, and try to safeguard our little Wood-elf. May we all meet again and share tales of victory. Thank you for preserving my honor...I know what you have done, why you have set me here. You were right to do so. This is my place, and here I shall prevail, or die."

"You were set here because the fire of knowledge burns hot within you, and you are sworn to guard it. For no other reason were you chosen," said Rogond. "I shall look out for Gaelen as I may, but I fear we shall all need looking after before it ends. Farewell, my stout-hearted friend!"

The sand flew from under the feet of the horses as the four scouts galloped toward their destination, but they knew it was still a fair distance away, and the first shouts of their pursuers could now be heard. Gaelen's heart sank—these people were superb mounted fighters, and were skilled with the bow. It was said that to be struck by one of their arrows was death, for they were tipped with a deadly poison. If she were the enemy, she would have her archers aim for the horses, as they, too, would fall to the deadly darts. On foot, the scouts would be helpless. She risked a backward glance under her left arm, dismayed to see a dozen mounted archers that even now strove to draw within range. She urged Finan forward, and he responded. He would not fail her.

Nelwyn bent over Gryffa's neck as the man riding next to her suddenly gave a cry, his mount falling hard into the sand, a deadly arrow lodged in its hindquarters. They could not stop for him, and rode on, their right arms raised in salute to the courage of their comrade, their faces grim. It would be such with any who fell, as all had agreed. The horse screamed in pain and struggled, thrashing about for a few moments, until the venom did its work. The fallen scout crouched behind the convulsing body of his dying animal and waited, an arrow nocked to his bow, for death to overtake him.

Three scouts now flew recklessly through the hill-pass, leaping over the stony ground. They could see the distant Citadel, gleaming white with spires of silver glinting rose-red in the early morning light. A deadly shaft tore through the sleeve of Gaelen's tunic—she cursed silently, wishing that she could send it back to them. Thankfully, it did not pierce her flesh. Finan ran with his tail and his head high, his ears flattened with effort, nostrils wide and red.

Galador's heart leapt as he beheld Nelwyn's golden hair flying back from Gryffa's neck. He blew a short blast on his silver horn, and called down to the guards in the courtyard.

"Open the gate!"

Rogond sat mounted on Eros, who stood placidly, for he had learned not to waste energy on the eve of battle. The Ranger tried to follow his example, but his emotions were high. He gripped the shaft of his spear tightly as he looked toward the gate, imagining the desperate flight of his beloved Gaelen, longing to see her bright, fierce eyes as she passed through. She would tell what she had seen, and then he would ride out with her and engage the enemy, to whatever end.

He looked up at the tower, knowing that Galador and Réalta would soon be joining him. He patted Eros, and it calmed him somewhat, as he reflected upon how the Company had come to this place, and how it was that they now faced death together in the defense of these peaceful, enlightened people.

The Great Gates drew open, and the three remaining scouts rushed headlong into the courtyard. Rogond rode up to Gaelen, who sat breathless upon her panting, steaming horse, and waited for her to compose herself. Her news was grim—he could see it. At last she spoke words that chilled his heart.

"We need a bigger wall."

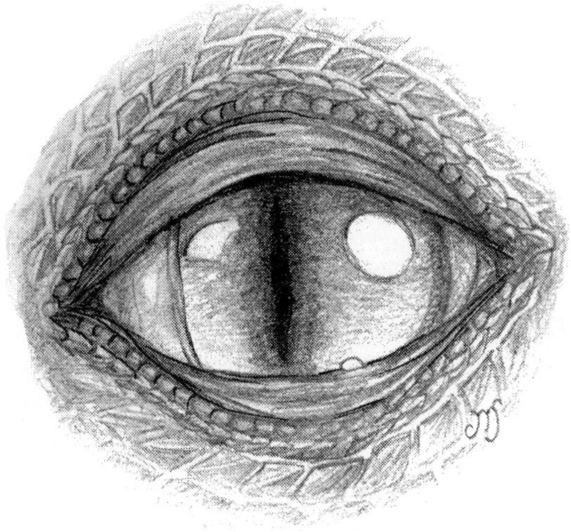

24
The Battle Is Joined

"What do you mean, we need a bigger wall?" asked Rogond. "Why? What have you seen? What...bigger than *this* wall?" He indicated the massive structure at his back.

Gaelen shook her head. "What I have seen is going to change everything about the way we engage this army. We have thought that all we need do is withstand the siege within the safety of walls, but once this battle is joined it will continue at fever pitch until our enemy's great weapon lies dead. Where is Ali? I would prefer not to explain this twice."

"Lies *dead?* What do you mean?" said Rogond with dismay.

Ali was heading toward them, having already been informed of the dragon by his own scout. Clearly, the defense plan would need to be changed. As with all desert dragons, Lokai was no climber, but he was most certainly a digger, with claws that could work through the wall, or even the hard rock beneath it, with time and effort.

Ali was understandably disheartened by the news that a huge dragon would soon approach his gates. "Apparently it cannot fly, and that's a good thing, but the wall will not withstand it for long. How does one kill such a beast?"

He obviously hoped that one of these northerners would have some knowledge that he lacked, but only Galador had ever beheld a dragon before, long ago and from a great distance. There would be no enlightenment from any of them.

Nelwyn had gone to her place atop the gates; she plied her archer's skill in deadly fashion and had managed to pick off many of the enemy's advance riders. The Scourge's main cavalry could be seen approaching in a cloud of dust, as the defenders had anticipated. Their own small mounted force, including Gaelen, Rogond, and Galador, would now ride forth to lure the enemy within range of the city's archers, most of whom still remained hidden.

"Where is Hallagond?" asked Gaelen, for she did not see him waiting with the others.

Ali growled into his beard as Rogond shook his head, saying: "Hallagond will not be joining us as yet, Gaelen. He has...other concerns at the moment. I would explain, but..."

"We have no time now," said Gaelen. "We must ride forth to lure their mounted warriors. Otherwise, they will not draw near enough." At this, she and Galador turned to line up with the other defending riders as the Great Gates slowly began to open.

Rogond, who had been taken with a sudden inspiration, lingered for a moment. "Send word to Fima and the other scholars sequestered in the underground keep," he said. "Surely there is enough dragon-lore stored there to find some answers. Set their busy minds to work." Ali nodded, his scarred face set with grim resolve. "There will be a way," said Rogond, just before turning to join his friends on the front line.

"Remember—keep to the center path!" cried Ali, as Galador blew his silver horn. The small but determined group of defenders rode toward their approaching enemy, gathering speed as they went.

The captain of the Scourge's riders lifted his curved ram's horn to sound the attack. It was obvious that all was as the traitor had promised; only a few archers stood atop the city walls, and this was but a small force of mounted fighters. The traitor had told that the people of the Silver City were peaceful, and felt little need for a standing army. No enemy had ever really engaged the City in war. What few forces they had resembled civil police more than an army; they would surely not be battle-ready.

With the surety of one who has been given inside information, the Scourge's captain urged his men forward. First they would crush this pathetic defense, for it would make the task of subduing the City that much easier. Alas that three of their scouts had evaded pursuit, for the commander would have preferred to take the City entirely unaware, but he was unconcerned. It would require time to mount a defense—time that would not be given. He chuckled as he rode with his thousand cavalry; they outnumbered the Citadel's mounted force ten to one. He counted about twenty skilled archers visible atop the battlements, and these would need to be reckoned with, but twenty archers and a hundred mounted peace-keepers? Not much of a challenge against a thousand seasoned warriors armed with envenomed weapons.

He stood in his stirrups, giving a great battle-cry that was answered by his men, and the Scourge's first wave flew toward the gates.

When Gaelen heard the enemy battle-cry, she felt Finan surge forward. He was already weary from his frantic rush back to the City, but he was the hardiest horse she had ever ridden. She and the other defenders would not long engage the Scourge's cavalry—only long enough to convince them that their effort was genuine before retreating to the gates, luring the enemy within range of three hundred archers who crouched now behind the battlements.

Nelwyn had done her task well. These archers, though not battle-hardened, would shoot patiently and accurately, for they were well protected. Each would need to take only two or three of the enemy to decimate them.

The overconfidence of the attackers was apparent, and Gaelen smiled to herself. *That overconfidence must be preserved…it will be their undoing. We should appear to be either reckless or suicidal, a logical result of having been thrown into the fray on a moment's notice. A battle-cry might aid in that illusion…*

She stood in her own stirrups and held her bow aloft, looking first at Galador and then at Rogond. "*Fire-heart!*" she shouted in a booming voice, shrugging and smiling at Galador as Finan charged ahead. The rest of the cavalry, who knew the name of Aincor Fire-heart well, followed her example. It seemed as good as anything for the moment.

Rogond was amused as he, too, shouted the name of Fire-heart. Yet he was less caught up in the excitement of the charge, for he knew that some of the valiant who rode beside him would be lost in those first few moments of engagement. They would all be hard put to survive long enough to retreat.

He wished that his brother had not abandoned them, yet he still held faith. Hallagond would not betray his trust; there had to be some other explanation. Rogond could not bring himself to believe otherwise. He put Hallagond out of his mind as he rode beside Gaelen, his dark spear in his right hand and his bright sword in his left, and concentrated on the task before him.

Ishtar knew his way around, and he had quickly stolen enough provisions to make his escape. A clever man, he knew that the citizens would not waste energy in looking for him, as they had much greater concerns approaching their gates.

He stole a dromadan and made his way through the winding streets to a doorway that few in the city knew about; it led beneath the first level to a small gateway on the northern side of the City. From there, one could access the outside world through a hidden cleft in the cliff-face. It served as a sort of emergency escape in case the City was hopelessly beleaguered, and was always under guard. The ones set to watch it were not expecting trouble from within.

"What is your errand?" asked one of the guards, immediately becoming suspicious. Folk on legitimate errands did not use this tiny gateway. "Commander Ali has ordered that no one is to depart the City without leave." Ishtar put on a jovial, friendly expression as he approached the wary guardsmen.

"Have you news of the battle?" he asked, felling one of them with a blade hidden in his right sleeve before leaping on the other, snapping the man's neck with a vicious twist of his strong hands. He took the guards' provisions and made his way quickly out into the darkness, leading the now well-laden dromadan, thinking he had made his escape.

Hallagond and Visili had caught up with Estle while she was still in the City. They took two dromadin, provisioning them lightly, for they would rely on speed to catch Ishtar quickly before returning to the City to face punishment. They didn't plan to be gone long. Hallagond was a superb tracker, and so, as it turned out, was Visili. With two such relentless hounds on his trail, Ishtar would surely fall, and neither of his pursuers had any intention of bringing him back alive.

Once he caught up with Ishtar, Hallagond intended to kill him quickly and with no regret, for he would try to regain the trust that had been placed in him. He would never run from failure again.

"You had better make room for me," said Estle. "I won't be left behind! You'll get into even greater mischief if I don't go along to watch over you."

"We only have two dromadin," said Hallagond.

"I can ride with you, and Visili can carry everything else," said Estle. "Ishtar is no lightweight, and he has a heavy load of provisions. It's no good arguing with me."

Although this irked Hallagond, he accepted it, secretly glad that she was beside him. He would have been worried for her safety in the upcoming battle otherwise. Besides, she was a trusty traveling companion, and she made excellent biscuits. *The fact that I actually love her has little to do with it...*

Visili, as it happened, was not a bad fellow. He had made some poor choices in his life, and one of those, a very poor choice indeed, had resulted in his having been thrown into prison. Yet he was a clever, skilled warrior, and possessed many useful talents. Hallagond had recognized leadership in him, together with experience in warfare, and that combination was most desperately needed by the Citadel forces. Hallagond shook his head. How could he have been so right about Visili, yet so wrong about Ishtar?

When he found the guards slain at the north gateway, Hallagond was further chagrined. It was his fault that they would not return to their families in the morning. He wanted to take a few moments to write an explanation of what had happened, so that everyone, particularly Rogond, would understand. But in the end, he just covered the dead men respectfully and went on his way. There was no moon tonight, and he would need all the time available to track Ishtar, for he would see him dead as soon as he could manage it. He would explain himself in person...if he survived.

Nelwyn's bow sang its favorite song, felling any Scourge rider that drew within range. Most of the City's forces were still hidden; the riders had not yet come close enough to spring the trap. Nelwyn, who was in command of the archers, had instructed them to wait until the word was given, and then to use great care lest they take down their own riders.

Rogond's spear was red with blood, for he was very adept at striking mounted riders as they passed. His sword found plenty of good use, also. Gaelen preferred the bow for mounted combat, choosing the small hunting bow she had brought from the Greatwood. A dark, curved weapon well suited to the task, it had taken five enemy riders already. Yet the goal was not to kill so many, but to lure them within range of the City walls. When Galador sounded the retreat, the defenders turned back toward the gates and rode as fast as they could, knowing that this was probably the most perilous time for them. The enemy would now shift to their bows, and the riders retreating before them would make easy targets.

None of the Scourge riders were aware of Seti's deadly pits. These had been set to the left and right of the central path to the gate, because otherwise it would be too easy for one of the City's own riders to blunder into one in the heat of battle, falling upon the sharp stakes. The defenders would retreat in a relatively narrow line, avoiding over a hundred well-hidden pits that would take many of the enemy riders, who would approach in a wide swath.

Now the defenders rode as fast as they could back toward the gates, hoping to avoid being taken from behind. Nelwyn's sharp eyes fixed on any who would draw their bows on her friends; they would not live long enough to threaten them if she could help it.

A shaft tore through Galador's cloak, and he winced as it grazed his arm, but thankfully his flesh was not pierced. Still, the welt that it made burned like fire, and would trouble him for several days after. He did not wish to imagine what death from the venom would be like.

"Open the gates," yelled Ali. "Stand by the passageway!" He referred to the iron-clad archway through which the Citadel's forces could retreat to safety behind the new wall. If the gates were breached later, they would give the signal to collapse the archway so that the Scourge could not do likewise.

The pits had taken many unfortunate horses and riders, and the Scourge quickly learned to narrow its ranks. The opening of the gates encouraged them, and they rode hard, thinking that they would be poorly defended. Yet when they drew at last within easy range, three hundred archers appeared out of nowhere atop the battlements, raining deadly arrows down upon their unprepared attackers. The first volley decreased the number of foes by one quarter, and the next two saw only half of the riders still standing.

The captain knew then that he had been lured into a disaster, and he tried to rally his men to retreat before it was too late, but they had been thrown into confusion and were now attempting to save themselves by shooting at the archers on the battlements. Their darts were well-placed, and several of the defenders fell despite their protected position, but the Scourge had no hope of prevailing against the storm of arrows that continued to claim them. A few of the enemy riders actually gained the gates, only to be dispatched by the remaining mounted defenders.

As the Great Gates swung closed again, the captain looked upon them with his dying sight as one of Nelwyn's arrows tore through his throat. Darkness claimed him quickly, but not before he held one last thought—soon the main body of the Scourge's army would arrive, and even these impressive wooden gates would not stand long before the onslaught of Lokai.

A great cheer went up from the archers as their arrows chased the pathetic remainder of the Scourge's cavalry back toward the east, and this was echoed by most of the onlookers and surviving riders. Yet Ali silenced them quickly. "This is only the first wave," he warned. "You have done well, and you should be encouraged, but know that we face a much greater peril. The Scourge has a dread weapon that travels with it, and we do not know how such a threat may be conquered. We must not celebrate too lustily as yet. Look to your weapons and replenish your arrows. We will send forth gleaners to retrieve those already spent and to recover any survivors."

"Do so quickly then," said Nelwyn. "The dust raised by the army can be seen already; they are passing through the hills and will soon arrive here. Are the fires ready?" She referred to the fires intended to ignite the arrows that would set the oil pits ablaze.

"Yes," said Ali, "and the advance guards are in place to ignite those that are beyond the range of arrows. Between the pits and the fires, the way will be made quite narrow, and that should unbalance our foes. They will not expect any of this, I'll warrant."

"The fires will aid us," said Nelwyn, "yet I doubt the dragon will be dismayed by either our fires or our traps!"

Ali was undaunted. "This is most unusual for a commander to say, but I almost hope they breach the gates. I want to see the look on their faces when they encounter the wall."

In the courtyard below, Gaelen embraced Rogond, thankful that they had not been sundered. Yet there was little time for such things. "You have seen this dragon," said Rogond. "You and Nelwyn should go down to Fima and the scholars, and aid them in determining how it may be defeated. You must go at once, for you will be needed when the army arrives."

Gaelen smiled at him. "When they see what's left of their cavalry, I doubt they will mount an attack until they are ready. They will not be lured close quite so easily the next time. And the dragon moves by its own will, I expect." She tossed her head, shaking her hair from her eyes. "We have a little time, but you're right—once that monster gets here there will be no rest until it lies dead." She embraced Rogond again before turning to find Nelwyn, whereupon they would make their way down to the Scholar's Keep.

"Ishtar draws farther ahead of us, Hallagond," said Visili, shaking his head. "And he is moving toward the hills. I wonder if he knows we're following him, and thinks it likely that we'll lose the trail in the stony hills. Ishtar is very clever, and he may yet elude us."

Estle sighed. "And while we waste time and energy in this pursuit, our friends are no doubt engaged in pitched battle, one in which we are desperately needed. Just let the wretched man go. What harm will come of it?"

Hallagond did not reply, for he was weary of explaining his actions. He knelt beside Visili, examining the signs left by Ishtar's dromadan. "You're right," he said grimly. "He has gained ground since yesterday."

"Do you truly believe he'll survive, traveling alone through these hard lands?" asked Estle, who obviously didn't think this likely. Again, Hallagond did not respond to her question, but made ready to continue following Ishtar's trail.

Visili moved to stand beside Estle, and spoke with her aside. "He believes that, if there is any chance of gaining the company of other men, Ishtar will not only survive but will bring new enemies to threaten the Citadel. For that reason, he must be stopped. Hallagond must undo what he has done, for he will not have peace until then. You, of all people, should know this."

Estle knew Visili meant to be kind, but she was still angry and frustrated with Hallagond, and did not want to admit that Visili was right. She grew more restive with each passing hour, for she knew the City needed as many able hands as could be mustered. Impatience was a trait she occasionally shared with an Elf named Gaelen.

She growled under her breath. "He thinks he can undo what was done simply by tracking down Ishtar? Ali will most likely lock us all away when we return…provided there's a City left to lock us up in. We should go back at once, and aid them as we may. They may delay our punishment until the war is ended, at least. What must they think of us? I can just imagine what the Elves are saying right now."

Her voice took on a sort of patronizing simper that was most unflattering. "Oh, isn't it just like weakling men to run off when they are most needed…but we shouldn't be surprised, after all, they are not so noble as we are." She shook her head in disgust. "May their hair be infested with fleas."

Estle envied the Elves their beautiful, flowing hair that never seemed to become untidy; even Gaelen's windblown mop fell more-or-less into place with a shake of her head. Estle's own hair was curly, and in the sea air it had puffed out around her head like a wooly corona. It tangled terribly in the wind, and she had tried various ways to tame it, to no avail. Hence she was rarely seen without a bright silk scarf tied around her head, which made her look rather roguish, as Corsairs often wore such headgear. Hallagond found this alluring, but Estle would have preferred the flowing, care-free tresses of the Elves. We always want what we do not possess.

Her disgruntled thoughts were interrupted by Hallagond. "I am moving on now, Estle," he said. "You know that I can't allow Ishtar to escape. Will you join me, or no? If you would return to the City take one of the dromadin with you, but please leave most of the provisions. I shall have need of them. Take Visili with you if you wish; I can handle Ishtar alone."

"Do you even *care* whether I leave you?" she asked, her face reddening. "I came along so that I could aid you, and I would still aid you—the only way I will turn back is if you do. I admit that I'm concerned, because this pursuit is taking us farther and farther from matters at hand, and still you will not *listen*."

To her surprise, he reached for her right hand and took it gently. "Estle, I would rather cut off my own right arm than have you leave me, but I don't rule your actions and never have done so. Come with me, or return as you will, but know that I care for you in either case. I fear we may not see each other again if you leave, and I would declare my heart first. You want me to say that I love you? All right—I do. So choose now, and know that I will hold no ill will toward you. I must see this wrong made right. I am responsible for setting loose a potential threat to the City, and I alone must rectify it."

He stood before her, disheveled but proud, a warrior both of the Ravani and of the North, so winsome in that moment that Estle knew she could never leave him. He was a fine man, and her heart had been given.

"Well, perhaps not quite as romantic as I might have wished, but it will do," she said.

Visili smiled and shook his head. Their intrepid band of hunting hounds would remain, and perhaps now Estle would cease her nearly incessant grumbling and growling, a possibility that would not dismay either of her companions.

Deep beneath the City, Fima and the scholars worked their way through the vast stores of written lore, trying to find anything that could aid the defenders in defeating Lokai. Gaelen and Nelwyn made their way in, as the entrance had been unblocked earlier and the chamber would not be re-sealed unless the Wall was breached. Fima was happy to see his two beloved friends, and was relieved to learn that none in the Company had yet fallen. "So, you survived the first onslaught, I see! Well done," he said. "But now we have a task before us, and we need your aid." He called out to an aged man sitting at a table with a great volume opened before him.

"These Elves have seen the dragon. Ask your questions of them."

"Excellent," said the man, turning back to a marked page. "This volume features a series of identifying characteristics of various beasts, arranged in a very orderly way. We can follow the clues like pieces of a puzzle." He looked up at Gaelen and Nelwyn. "Now, then…which of these applies to our beast? Scales diamond-shaped and keeled, go to 6. Scales not as above, go to 9. Well? Which is it?"

Gaelen and Nelwyn looked at each other. "What, exactly, does that mean?" asked Nelwyn.

Gaelen snorted. "It means this man doesn't realize that we managed to view the dragon from a very great distance. The only reason we got even a decent look was that it stood upright for a moment. It's of no use asking about the shape of its scales."

"Fine. Perhaps you could not take notice of the shape of the scales, but surely you could tell if they were keeled," said the scholar with a frown. "Did the creature have a roughened appearance, or was it smooth and shiny like glass?"

"It was rough-textured, and the color of lead," said Nelwyn helpfully.

"Ah. Well, that is of some help. All right…now, how did it stand upright? Is it winged?"

"All dragons are winged," said Fima. "Move along."

"Fair enough," said the scholar. "Let's see now…ah. Here is the next couplet…tongue bluish, forked, and less than thrice the length of a man, go to 12. Tongue red or pinkish and greater than thrice the length of a man, go to 20." He looked up at the Elves as though he actually expected them to know this.

"We have no time for such ridiculous nonsense," said Gaelen. "We have wasted enough of it already. Fima…is there a book here with *pictures*? Perhaps we will know the creature if we see a depiction of it."

"Here is such a volume," said an eager voice from another table. They turned to view a small, thin-faced, nervous little man wearing olive-green robes.

There was indeed a book with pictures of various dragons, cold-drakes, and fire-drakes. The little man delighted in turning the pages for the Elves to see, as he was the only one specially gloved to handle them.

Regrettably, the Elves soon concluded that none of the beasts in the book really looked like the one they had seen. Nelwyn shook her head. "It's probably unique to these southern lands, and this book is one of the original ones brought from the north," she said. "It's no wonder we do not see that beast here."

"If we do not find a way to kill it, we are lost!" said Gaelen, whose patience had worn thin long ago.

"Kill it, you say?" said the little man looking up from his manuscript. "There is a way in which all drakes are vulnerable, and may be killed, regardless of type."

"There is?" said Gaelen. "What is it, and why, in the name of heaven, did you not reveal it earlier?"

"I was told to find out what sort of dragon it is, not how to kill it. There is a spot in the roof of the mouth where a well-placed arrow or spear can penetrate. It is thought that the beast uses this area to tell the nature of what it scents upon the air with its tongue. It's a soft spot that goes straight into the creature's brain, but it takes a mighty dart to penetrate all the way through, so said missile must be thrown from very close range." He leafed through the book until he found a drawing of the roof of a dragon's mouth, showing the place quite clearly. "See? Here is an excellent depiction of it." To his horror, Gaelen reached out and tore the page away.

Fima winced and groaned as a collective gasp went up from the scholars. The sound of ripping parchment was not one that they were accustomed to hearing within those walls.

Gaelen regretted her action, but she knew it was necessary. "We shall need this. I'm sorry…I will return it if we survive the battle. If not, there will be nothing to return it to." She bowed before the outraged scholars, and she and Nelwyn bade farewell to Fima before returning to the task at hand.

Fima turned to his companions. "Don't just stand there with your mouths open…let's get these works back in order and pray we don't lose the entire collection to the enemy."

The scholars spent a few more moments in stunned silence. Then they called for the chamber to be re-sealed immediately, lest any more pages be torn from their precious, irreplaceable manuscripts.

Gaelen took the parchment up to the battlements, showing the spot to the archers stationed there. If the gates fell they would move to stand atop the wall, and might be in a position to send forth a shaft into Lokai's great mouth.

"A killing shot will need to be made at very close range. It's no good otherwise," said Nelwyn. "Yet the beast is large enough that we may well be presented with the opportunity."

Lokai was nearly a hundred feet long from head to tail, and though not normally inclined to raise his belly from the ground he could do so by using his wings. His hind legs were powerful enough to move forward with great force, but they were not designed for an upright stance. Any clear shot given to the archers would be a brief one.

"Those of us who fight from the ground will also try to strike this spot," said Gaelen, "but the enemy warriors will distract us, and it will be very difficult to draw near enough to the beast without being trampled…or worse. The dragon's efforts will be directed at bringing down the wall, so you will face it most directly. Remember this drawing, and remember it well!" So saying, she passed the parchment down the line once more before retrieving it, for she would also share it with the waiting horsemen below.

The Scourge's army had drawn at last within sight of the City, and the news the Commanders were given was not as expected. They had thought to be reunited with their cavalry, who had ridden ahead to visit whatever damage they could upon the unprepared Citadel. Instead of a thousand confident riders they found but fifty who could still stand, and they were full of tales of the unexpected resistance they had encountered.

"Bring the traitor," growled the Commanders. "We should thank him properly."

They caught him trying to escape toward the City, hoping to be admitted. He knew the people would know him, and would not leave him to die. Nor would they kill him outright in any case. They might throw him into prison for life, but that would be a far better fate than the Scourge would unleash on him. Unfortunately, the Scourge's scouts caught him and bound him with cords, taking him before the Commanders.

"It would seem your information has proven unreliable," said one. "As a result we have now lost nearly a thousand of our mounted warriors. What have you to say?"

The traitor cringed. "They must have been warned a long time ago, somehow. My information would have been entirely reliable otherwise. Someone else has warned them of your approach. You cannot blame me for it."

"All right, then," said the Commander. "We don't blame you." He turned to his lieutenant. "Take him to Lokai that the beast's appetite may be awakened," he said, his eyes narrowing. "Spare him no pain."

Hallagond had some trouble tracking Ishtar in the dust and stony ground of the Brown Hills, and he despaired, for if he truly lost the trail there would be no regaining it. The winds were rising, making everything more difficult, and he was losing hope.

"What's that in the distance?" asked Estle, pointing toward the northeast. "Vultures?"

"I can't tell if they are vultures or ravens," said Hallagond. He squinted into the morning sunlight. "Bad luck we don't have the Elves here—I have missed Nelwyn's keen sight and Gaelen's sharp nose."

"Do you see any harm in heading there?" asked Estle, for she too was becoming frustrated trying to keep to Ishtar's trail. "Vultures or ravens are drawn only to dead things; perhaps Ishtar has killed again. We truly don't have a trail that we are certain of, and we are moving so slowly now that we're unlikely to have one again. I believe the vultures are a sign that will draw us to the trail."

"And if not, we'll lose Ishtar for good," said Visili.

"We have lost him already, I fear," muttered Hallagond. "Very well then, let's see what the birds are so excited about."

They drew cautiously within sight of the group of vultures—huge ugly black things with wrinkled, naked heads and necks and tiny, malevolent yellow-green eyes. Hallagond spent one of his arrows, bringing down one of them, whereupon the remainder lifted ponderously into the air. Inherently patient creatures, they would not risk themselves. As Hallagond, Estle, and Visili drew nearer, they beheld a disturbing sight. Their search for Ishtar had ended.

The fresh remains of a dromadan and a dead man lay before them; the vultures had been at both, but not for long. The dromadan had been torn apart and partially devoured by something large and fierce; no vultures could have done such damage. Ishtar had been carved with a blade; there were signs of struggle throughout the area.

Hallagond tried to piece together what had happened. Apparently something had come on them, probably by night, and had leaped upon the hapless dromadan, twisting its slender neck with such force that it broke. Then it had pulled Ishtar down after a fierce fight. There was some blood in evidence, but the windblown dust had covered much of it.

Estle could not imagine a creature capable of tearing a healthy dromadan to pieces. "Whatever it was, it had sharp teeth," remarked Visili, shaking his head. "And, in order to twist the dromadan's neck like this, it must have had *hands*. That's what really worries me."

"One thing is certain," said Hallagond, we don't want to encounter it ourselves. I no longer need worry about Ishtar. We must make our way back with all speed, and we must be careful not to lose our way. With luck we will arrive home in time to aid our friends, if any remain."

"The Scourge has not yet fully engaged the City," said Estle. "We would see the smoke from the oil-fires. Let's make haste!

They turned about, Visili lingering for a moment to say a prayer for the soul of Ishtar, who would have need of it.

"Here they come; they're on the move at last," said Galador, training his sharp eyes to the east. The Scourge had waited for over an hour before finally advancing. "I still cannot see the dragon." He turned to Nelwyn, who stood beside him. "You are certain this was not a flight of imagination? There were no honey-jars among your provisions, were there?"

"One could wish for that to be true," said Nelwyn grimly, "but he would wish in vain."

Her eyes widened, and she pointed to the horizon. "There! You see that great plume of steam? The Worm is moving closer, and it is aroused. We will lay eyes on it soon enough." She turned to Galador.

"I shall have need of your powerful bow here on the battlements, and I'm relieved you will stand with me, for I fear the task of slaying the creature will be ours to bear."

She shivered, and Galador placed a hand on her shoulder to steady her. "Calm yourself, beloved," he said gently. "All will be well."

Nelwyn turned determined eyes to him. "You think I tremble with *fear*? How wrong you are. Is this what the lust for battle feels like? I cannot wait to engage my foe and slay him. I would see every one of these evil warriors cast into darkness, and their fearsome drake with them!"

Galador was surprised to hear such words from Nelwyn, spoken with such fervor. "Well…try to hold onto your battle-lust, so long as it doesn't muddle your thinking or spoil your aim," he said, "but save most of it for the enemy. It will tire you if you cannot be calm until the battle is joined."

"Don't worry…it won't spoil my aim," said Nelwyn, her green eyes flashing. "At last I understand what Gaelen has been talking about." She smiled at Galador, whose expression told that he was a little fearful of this change in her.

"Don't be dismayed, Galador, you still have your beloved Nelwyn beside you. Yet my blood is up now, and my arrows will fly fast and true once the enemy arrives."

"Just be cautious," said Galador gently. "You Wood-elves seem to lose all restraint when your blood is up. Remember to wait until Ali gives the word."

Nelwyn frowned at him as though she resented the very suggestion that she would act rashly, and he smiled back at her.

Down in the courtyard, Gaelen prepared Finan to ride forth again. She wrapped a strip of thin, elastic deerskin carefully around each of his lower forelegs. These would support the old injuries, allowing Finan to remain longer in the fray without pain. When she had finished, she coated the entire assembly with melted beeswax mixed with a flexible resin; the wraps would need to be removed with a blade.

"They are coming!" yelled Galador to Ali, who had been looking to the small archway that had been built at the base of the new wall. This was now the only way in or out, and was guarded by a heavy door of iron. The cavalry, under the command of Rogond, would ride through and engage Lokai only if it appeared that the dragon would somehow manage to defeat the wall, for if that happened all would be lost. A determined company of foot-soldiers stood by as well, knowing that their deaths were assured if the Scourge breached the great stone barricade, since the enemy outnumbered them a hundred to one.

Nearly every able-bodied citizen had been given a weapon and at least marginally trained in its use—the people were now as ready as they could be. They learned quickly once inspired, and they possessed great heart and fine spirit, but, despite all efforts, they would not stand long against such brutality. It takes more than weapons to make a warrior.

Eros drank long and well, took a bite of the salt-lick, and shook himself. He was ready. Réalta stood by; if the cavalry was called out, Galador would no doubt ride with them, but for now he stayed on the battlements with Nelwyn.

Rogond had clad himself in chain mail and a blackened steel breastplate that would turn an envenomed blade. The armor, though old, was still serviceable; it had been kept in oil for many years. Any artisans skilled in its making had long since passed, and their skill had not been kept alive, for it was no longer valued. Rogond wondered whether there would be a revival of this art should the City prevail.

Gaelen had drawn in a sharp breath when she first set eyes upon him, for he looked like a King of Tuathas. His breastplate bore the beautifully hammered images of the Great Lights of the World—sun, moon, stars, and the lamp of knowledge—plated with silver and gold. This was a symbol Gaelen had seen elsewhere; it was the Great Seal of the Tuathar. Rogond had no doubt chosen this regalia because of his northern heritage; the other breastplates bore the raven-crest of Salasin, and were being put to good use in protecting his people.

Gaelen wore no armor, for she would have none. She had attired herself in the red-and-black garments of the Scourge, thinking to confuse them, for the archers on the battlements knew her mount and they would not slay her. Beneath this she wore the fire-cloak over her usual attire; she would die wearing the vestments of a hunter-scout of the Greatwood. Rogond had tried to convince her to wear a light mail-shirt, but she would have none of it. Such things would slow her down with their weight, and would spoil her flexibility and her aim. Her short, dark bow would have little rest; two quivers were affixed to Finan's breast-plate with nearly forty arrows in each.

Some of the bold riders had already been lost in the first assault, and an air of hopelessness hung about the others as they made their preparations, for they knew they could not possibly prevail against the dragon. Yet Gaelen's words cheered them as she rode easily back and forth among them; she wanted to keep her mount moving so he would not become stiff from standing idle. She sounded so confident that they all took heart.

"My friends, be encouraged," she said. "For you are dauntless, and have proven your skill. You have the better horses, and the defenses of the City are behind you. Plus, you have three Elves among your number! You will prevail, and your friends will be avenged." She laughed lightly as she rode.

"Will you call upon the name of the Fire-heart again?" they asked, smiling at her as she passed.

"Most certainly. It worked the last time, didn't it?" She began a lusty rendition of one of the songs she had learned from the sutherlings, in their tongue. It was a rowdy, unseemly chant that was usually heard through a haze of alcohol, but it raised the hopes of the men as they joined her, laughing at the sound of such earthy lyrics sung in Gaelen's sweet voice.

Lord Salastor stood on the eastern watch-tower; from there he could observe the progress of the battle. Gaelen's singing carried to him on the wind, and he smiled. He wore his own armor beneath his long, grey cloak; it had been well kept for many generations. He had never worn it, not even in ceremony, for the people had decided that such attire was out of place in a City devoted to peace. He would engage the enemy only if they breached the wall. If that happened, he would die fighting beside his people. He would not wish to witness the fall of the City to such a Scourge.

Nelwyn and Galador were the first to sight the great, grey bulk of the approaching dragon. Behind it moved the army, marked by a vast dust cloud rising high into the air. The Scourge would not pass gently through any lands; the swath they left behind would be visible in the dry, stony ground for years to come.

"It's even larger than I expected," said Galador. "I hope the wall will withstand it, as I now see that the gates will almost surely fall. Gaelen's insights were right all along."

Soon the dragon drew close enough to be seen by all the City's forces, and no one spoke of "Ali's Folly" ever again.

The Scourge had taken some losses during the approach to the City, and the Commanders reflected ruefully that their enemies were even better prepared than they had thought at first. The surviving cavalry warned of great pits dug into the earth and hidden, but many of their warriors were lost in these before the army learned to narrow its ranks sufficiently. Even when the pits were discovered by the first victims, others were driven into them by the inexorable force of the ranks behind them.

"Keep to the path taken by the riders!" cried the Commanders, for this path was safe. Archers had loosed great flaming torches, igniting oil-fires, and this apparently was a signal for hidden scouts to ignite others that stretched all the way back to the Brown Hills.

The way was made narrower, and the oil-fires now blocked the retreat. They sent black clouds of smoke high into the air, but these did not spoil the aim of the Citadel's bowmen that had been set along the approach, and they sent many shafts into the enemy forces as they passed. They were well hidden, dressed in clothing that blended perfectly with their surroundings, courtesy of Bint Raed.

As they heard the screams of the men impaled at the bottom of Seti's deadly pits, the Captains were dismayed, but not unduly. They had begun with ten thousand men, and they would still have nearly eight thousand when they gained the gates. Then the dragon would have the City, for most of its defenses lay outside the walls. One could dig pits and build fires, and could even train archers and lay elegant plans to keep the Scourge from breaching the City, but it took far more effort to turn a nation of peaceful sheep into a formidable fighting force. The Commanders would have their prize when the gates fell; or so they thought as they drew nearer, their ranks gathering safely behind their fearsome ally.

Lokai lifted his broad snout into the air and tasted it, tantalized by the hundreds of strange scents wafting in from the west. The wind was out of the east at the moment, and he was frustrated, but the closer he drew to the City gates, the less the wind would matter. Lokai was still young, but nearly mature. His male gender was not apparent to his human escorts, for the worms of the southlands were alike to the eye, though the females tended to be larger.

The dragon could not speak, but he could understand at least some of what was said to him, particularly when the words were spoken by one trained in the use of dragon-tongues. Ikari was such a man, and although Lokai neither loved him nor needed him, he did heed Ikari's words, which had promised great reward should the City be taken. Lokai had little to fear in the upcoming battle; none had ever prevailed against him, despite their weapons and their valor.

During battle he had always feasted well. He preferred the flesh of those still living or very recently killed, enjoying the warmth and vitality of their flesh before it became truly lifeless. He had ever preferred two-legged prey; the younger and more unspoiled the better.

The dragon-keepers had discovered that Lokai preferred fresh, dismembered captives that had been stripped of all annoying clothing and ornaments. If there were no captives available, Lokai would select his own prey from among the Scourge's own ranks, which explained their fervor in taking captives, at least in part. He would help himself to an occasional hapless man who strayed too close, hence he was given a very wide berth. Such a man would be honored, for it was considered a sacred duty to provide for the Great Lokai, but it was an honor that none would envy.

Ikari spent nearly all his time perched behind Lokai's head, just rearward of the great, swollen venom glands, clutching the leather straps of the harness. From there he could lean forward and speak so that Lokai could hear him, telling of all the wonders that awaited them.

When he was promised Elf-flesh, Lokai grew especially keen. He had tasted of it long ago, when three Elven mariners had been swept to the far southern coast by a storm, and had been taken captive to be sold as slaves. Lokai, who was then much smaller, had come upon their caravan by night. He and his human caretakers had slaughtered the lot of them, and Lokai had devoured all three of the Elves, who were bound hand and foot and provided little resistance. Their meat was the finest he had ever tasted, as the flesh of Elves is incorruptible, remaining as pristine as on the day of their birth. Lokai had desired it ever since, and Ikari had promised that at least three of these delicacies were waiting behind the Great Gates. Lokai would never forget the scent and taste of Elf-flesh.

The southern worms, though not large compared with the great northern ones, were much more heavily made, hence they could not fly. Designed for burrowing, they had short, broad necks and legs, and wide, flattened snouts with a hard ridge of bone at the tip that resembled a spade. Their thick, powerful tails bore short, sharp spines at the end. These broke off frequently and were replaced, the cast-offs highly prized in the making of weapons.

Lokai was not graceful or beautiful, but he was incredibly strong. His skull, two feet thick and hard as steel, encased a tiny brain. His body measured nearly fifty feet in length, and his tail thirty. He could sweep a mounted rider to the ground, crushing both man and horse with a single stroke. His great head came equipped with very powerful jaws, and, of course, Lokai was a dragon and he could breathe fire. He drew his huge, heavy body up before the gates, exhaling a plume of steam from his flattened nostrils.

His smallish, muddy yellow eyes darted to and fro as he considered the task before him, his thick, blue-grey tongue unfolding slowly from his purple-lined mouth, sliding wetly to and fro. He heard Ikari whispering to him in the dragon-speech, telling him that sweet water and Elf-flesh were his for the taking, and that he should not be denied.

Galador stood with his bow nocked and ready, looking down at the horrific creature, knowing that it had enough power to defeat them if all did not go as planned. He noticed for the first time the small, lean figure, clad now in dark grey robes, perched behind the beast's head. Hatred surged within him as he recognized Ikari.

"*Traitorous easterner!*" he shouted, loosing a shaft at Ikari, who ducked behind the impenetrable skull of Lokai and was unhurt. Nelwyn turned to Galador and lifted an eyebrow, remembering his admonition to wait until the word had been given.

Ikari was undaunted, and he smiled up at Galador. "There, my beautiful Lokai! There stands your delicacy. Show him your power, my love, my life… show him you are *mighty!*"

Lokai heard Ikari's words, and his attention now focused on Galador. He unfurled his leathery wings and roared, fanning the air to lift his body from the ground, standing tall upon his hind legs. He blew a blast of flame that swirled in the wind he had created, forcing the archers to crouch behind the battlements until it passed. Not a few were singed by the heat.

Below in the courtyard, Gaelen and Rogond waited with the rest of the ground forces. They could not see what was happening outside the gates, but they could hear. Gaelen turned to Rogond as they heard Galador's challenge, and Lokai's answer—the blast of flame shooting over the battlements.

"I hope to never hear Galador call me reckless again," said Gaelen. "He had just better *not.* If he survives, I shall forever call him the son of Aincor!"

Rogond shook his head. "Well, then let's hope you both survive, and that I'm still here to restrain Galador when you do," he said. "From what I'm hearing now, I believe the battle is joined."

Rogond was correct. After his fearsome display, Lokai had decided that his next order was to smash the gates, and he had set himself to the task, backing slowly away and tilting his great skull forward. He rushed at the gates with about half his strength, testing them, smashing his heavy head and body against them. They stood firm, and Lokai knew they would require more effort to bring down, but he would have smiled if he had been capable of amusement, because he could feel their weakness.

Ali gave the word, and the archers sent a volley of arrows at Lokai as he backed up again, digging in with his powerful hind claws for purchase, launching himself at the gates. This time the cliffs shook with the force of the strike, and Lokai felt the gates give just a little. Ikari clung grimly to Lokai's harness, flattening himself against both the arrows of the defenders and the debris that had begun to fall down upon him. The force of the impact had nearly torn his arms from their sockets.

The Scourge had by now drawn up behind their champion, and they readied themselves, cheering each time Lokai struck the Gates.

As soon as they were breached, the red-and-black tide would sweep through them, and neither the fires nor the pits would be of any use. The archers were many, and they were deadly, but Lokai would manage them as well. The Scourge knew they had little to fear.

The dragon gathered himself for another effort; he had yet to employ his wings in the charge, and he now did so. It was enough this time to splinter the massive tree-trunks that served as bolts for the gates, and they sagged inward as more stones from the cliff-face rained down upon Lokai. He shook his head; this last blow had dazed him a little and he took a moment to collect himself. With a final charge the gates crashed into the empty space between the outer battlements and the wall, and Lokai rushed in behind them expecting to be unchallenged, free to roam the City and wreak his havoc upon the people. Behind him, over a thousand men and two hundred horses charged in while sharing the same presumption.

The sight of the massive wall standing behind the outer courtyard and set into the cliffs was not at all in keeping with those expectations. The Citadel's archers now surrounded the enemy, as there were many atop the wall as well as those still standing upon the outer battlements. Lokai took some of them with fire, and the Scourge's archers managed to claim a few, but there was far more blood on the stone below. It was not at all desirable to be trapped in such an enclosed space with a disappointed Lokai.

The dragon blinked dully at the wall at first, as if he did not understand why it was there. Ikari had recovered his wits; the fall of the gates had shaken him, but now he leaned forward and spoke to his fearsome mount. "Do not be dismayed; this will also fall before you. Be not discouraged, for you are mighty!"

Lokai shook himself, nearly unseating Ikari, and considered his next plan as arrows peppered his scales harmlessly.

"Stop aiming at the dragon! Aim instead for the enemy below," shouted Ali, echoed by Nelwyn. They had moved to the top of the wall, along with Galador. A hundred red-and-black bodies already littered the stone, and many more joined them as the Scourge attempted to retreat. Attacking now was no good; they would need to wait until the wall was breached. Soon, Lokai and Ikari stood alone among the living in the courtyard, the remainder of the army having moved out of range of the archers.

Ali wanted to give the Scourge something else to think about, and now he called for the catapults. Six had been built, but two had failed during testing. Now the other four hurled great boulders high over the cliffs and down upon the enemy. Even more effective were the gigantic brush-balls that had been impregnated with pitch and set ablaze; these fragmented spectacularly and left burned, blackened bodies in their wake.

The Scourge answered with equally fearsome weapons; they brought up great, mounted crossbows that took three men each to load and release. These sent forth missiles that were as giant spears bearing thick glass globes filled with wicked steel barbs soaked in dragon-venom. These were quite deadly, killing anyone stricken by the flying projectiles that issued forth on impact. One managed to shatter in the middle of the north battlement, killing nearly thirty of the archers assembled there, including Broca, their captain. Another landed amid the unfortunate foot-soldiers, killing many and forcing the others to crowd forward in order to shelter among the cavalry behind the back of the wall.

Death by dragon-venom was most unpleasant, and there was nothing to be done for the victims as they writhed upon the ground. Gaelen and Rogond, who stood near to this horror, were unnerved by it, and Gaelen almost saw the sense in wearing chain mail. She was glad that at least some parts of Rogond would be protected.

Lokai, meanwhile, had decided to test his strength against the wall. He threw himself at it in much the same way as he had the gates, crashing into the stone with such force that those standing upon it were shaken, but it was very thick and would not be moved. The second all-out attempt resulted in the ignominious and no-doubt-disappointing death of Ikari, for his arms finally tore loose of the harness and he was flung over the beast's head. He cried in dismay, holding a brief image of solid stone rushing toward him, with time for only one last thought. *This was a bad idea…* His body landed at the base of the wall like a bundle of rags.

The dragon roared in frustration. He would not be able to bring down the wall as he had the gates; it was too thick and too strong.

Slowly he lashed his massive tail, considering, and then began to climb. "Bring the oil...*now*!" cried Ali, as large cauldrons of very hot oil were brought forth and poured down upon the dragon as he lurched upward. This enraged him and he belched a blast of flame that ignited a few of the unlucky souls manning the cauldrons, as well as the remaining oil. Unfortunately for Lokai, it also ignited the oil that now covered most of the top of his head and shoulders. The flaming oil was very irritating and he could not rid himself of it, and although Lokai was naturally fire-resistant, he was not fire-proof. Eventually, his skin would burn.

The enraged dragon was now determined to scale the wall, and he made a great effort, but with his very short legs he was no climber. He tried using his tail and his wings to assist in lifting his heavy bulk upward, but this resulted only in his claws losing their purchase, and once he actually fell over backward, exposing his glistening pink belly-scales.

The last cauldrons of oil were poured down upon him as he struggled to turn himself over, and Nelwyn sent a flaming arrow into the midst of it, setting his belly afire. He rolled over very quickly, being as he was highly motivated, extinguishing himself by rubbing his underside against the stone. Still, the irritating oil tormented him.

Nelwyn, Galador, and Ali had hoped to goad Lokai into exposing the inside of his mouth to Galador's powerful bow. When the beast roared there was a relatively clear view of it, and they had discovered that Lokai could not roar and breathe fire at the same time. He was certainly roaring now, but his head was not turned toward Galador, who could not get a proper shot.

Lokai had finally realized that climbing was not the way. If he could not topple the wall by force, or scale it, he would claw his way under it. Given time he would almost certainly succeed. As he began to employ his enormous, spade-like claws on the stone, neither oil-cauldrons nor arrows, flaming or otherwise, would distract him from it. He worked furiously, and large chunks of the wall began to fall away beneath his busy claws and formidable snout.

Ali knew that there was but one choice now, and his hopes sank as he and Galador made their way down to the waiting cavalry, to inform them that their time had come.

Hallagond could not dismiss the undeniable feeling of foreboding that had come over him as he made his way back to the City. The smoke from the oil-fires told him that the battle had been joined, and now he, Estle, and Visili traveled in haste to bring aid as they might. Hallagond doubted Ali would expend the effort of throwing them into prison until afterwards. He rode up alongside Estle, who was urging her dromadan with all speed. They were now quite close to the cliffs, but they were riding in from the north and the City could not be seen. She bore the provisions, for Hallagond and Visili rode together upon the other dromadan.

"There is something unsettling in the air," said Hallagond. We are being observed, perhaps even followed. I fear the follower may be the one responsible for the brutal death of Ishtar, in which case I would not wish to guide him to the hidden entrance. I would stop for a while to see if we can lure our stalker in and trap him. Estle, you should go on and aid our friends in their time of trial. Visili and I will follow when we know the nature of our pursuer, and have dealt with him. Will you agree?"

Though Estle was anxious to return to the City, she did not like the idea of being separated from Hallagond. "Did you see what was done to that dromadan? What must a being that could do such a thing be like? You could not prevail against it, even with Visili to aid you. You haven't seen any pursuers, so let's just outrun them, if they even exist. I don't wish to part from you under these circumstances…you might be in grave danger."

"That's precisely why you should ride ahead, Estle. At least one of us must survive to tell our story and restore some of my respectability. Ali must know that I did not forsake him out of cowardice. My brother must know that his faith in me was not in vain. Please… do this thing for me. I swear to you that I will return and aid the City, but I must take care of this matter first."

He could see from her expression that she required further convincing. "Estle, I have lived my life independently for far too long to be swayed in my thinking now. You and I are two very stubborn people, and we both know when we are right. You're right in thinking that our friends in the Citadel need our aid, and I'm right in knowing that someone is following us and must be dealt with. Neither of us is likely to yield, so let's indulge our mutual stubbornness. Do what you must do!"

He reined in his dromadan and began to head for the shelter of nearby stones. From there he would be able to watch after Estle's track; if anyone followed her, he would know it. He would wait and deal with whoever was shadowing them, hopefully in little time.

Estle stopped for a moment, considering his words. He was right; they both knew what they had to do. She raised her right arm briefly to his back, and he turned as though he could sense the gesture, returning it. *If you have underestimated this danger and get yourself killed, I'll never speak to you again!* She smiled, knowing she would see him again. Hallagond might fall in battle, but he would not be taken so easily as had Ishtar.

25
The Sons of Diomar

Gorgon Elfhunter had come upon Ishtar by night. It was a good thing, too, for the desert crossing had nearly finished him. He had needed all of his considerable strength, but once he had crossed through the Brown Hills he had found shade, rest, and water. He was nearly starving when he came upon Ishtar.

By the time his hunger was sated he had eaten nearly one-quarter of the good meat on the tough, stringy dromadan. He had then gone briefly to ground, concealing himself in the shelter of the cool rocks, hunkering down in his dark armor and covering himself with his very dusty grey cloak. He needed time to digest his huge meal before continuing.

When Hallagond and his companions came upon what was left of Ishtar and his animal, Gorgon observed them unaware. His hearing and sense of smell were very acute, and none save the Elves could match his eyesight in darkness. *I know the tall one...his scent is like the other one—the Ranger. This must be the long-lost brother he spoke to the Vixen about. How marvelously encouraging! He'll lead me to the rest of them...to the Vixen!*

"It would appear that my luck is changing for the better, wouldn't you say, Èolo?" Gorgon addressed Gelmyr, who, naturally, was not there to torment him. "No answer to that, have you? I'm not surprised. You only have answers when my resolve wavers...otherwise you are afraid to confront me! Ha! I expect I shall not look upon you again, not that I shall grieve, for I shall not miss you."

He gathered himself and prepared to track Hallagond's party from a distance. He must not alert them, for if they discovered him he would need to kill them all, and that would not serve his purpose. He would follow them to this place—the great City—that had been spoken of, for he sensed that the answers to all his needs lay within its walls.

When Hallagond and Visili sent Estle on ahead, Gorgon smiled to himself. It was so obvious that they were lingering behind to trap him, and he would have laughed out loud had he wanted to risk being heard. Rather than allow this to happen he moved beyond their sight, though night was coming on and they would never see him, trusting to the wind and to his very great stealth and tracking abilities to follow the woman unaware.

There was a battle raging—apparently the City was besieged. Gorgon knew that to accomplish his purpose he would need to wait until that battle was either won or lost, otherwise Gaelen and the others would be distracted and he would not fully taste of his revenge. It occurred to him that, should the City be taken, this undeniably savage and undisciplined host of men would interfere with his just revenge. He was briefly dismayed, resolving to do all in his power to prevent it.

Gorgon would fight for the Citadel, not caring that he strove now in defense of the Light. He cared nothing for good, nor the injustice of the slaughter of innocents, nor the defense of enlightenment. He cared about two things only: one was the regaining of the simplicity of his life's purpose, and the other was the achieving of that purpose. He wanted to return to his life before the mirror, when the killing and tormenting of Elves drove him and sustained him. To do that he would need to rid himself of the one who had opened up the Elves' world to his all-too-regrettably-curious eyes... the Vixen must die by his hand.

When his strength had nearly left him during the crossing, he had drawn upon the familiar imaginings of her ultimate fate. He had dreamed of killing her, as well as the others of the Company, in many vile and painful ways. These imaginings had aided him in regaining his resolve to defeat the desert, and no red-and-black clad rabble would deny him the chance to see them come to pass.

Visili was alerted to a strange sound, rather like one of the small, big-eared foxes that roamed the desert lands farther to the north—a sort of high-pitched, barking cough. He was immediately suspicious and went for his weapons, but Hallagond stayed him. "Do not be dismayed," he whispered. "I believe I know what is making that cry; at least I *hope* I do."

Visili was unconvinced. "It is not as it seems. A man makes it, not a beast. I have heard bandits use such signals to one another. We are beset!" He gripped his blade more tightly, peering into the darkness, opening his eyes very wide as though it would help.

Hallagond laughed. "I know that sorry, lame impression of a bat-eared fox, Visili, and you are right. A more detestable bandit never roamed the Ravi-shan. But this bandit is a friend, at least I thought him so." He called to the darkness, giving an equally unconvincing response. His voice was far too deep to do it properly.

Almost immediately, a familiar voice was heard in reply. "Lame, am I, Tuathan? Not nearly so lame as you. What *was* that noise you made? It sounded like someone had nearly suffocated a cat." A powerful, bearded man stepped into the dim light of Hallagond's small fire.

"Hello, Azori. It is good to see you, too."

"Enough pleasantries," said Azori with a dark gleam in his eye. "Where is my sister?"

"She has gone on to the Citadel. The City is beseiged, and Estle would defend it. I, too, would join in the fight, but I sensed you following me and stopped to intercept you, in case you were an enemy."

Azori laughed. "If I were an enemy, you most assuredly would both be dead now," he said, whistling for his men. There were two loyal ones who had returned with him; the others had gone on to Fómor.

"I am very happy to see you," said Hallagond, who was relieved to be dealing with Azori, and not with whatever had killed Ishtar. "The City will be very glad of your skills in battle."

"I don't understand why you are out here, if the City is besieged," said Azori. "It would not have anything to do with the poor unfortunate we found murdered in the hills, would it?"

Hallagond did not mind explaining his actions to Azori, because his friend would understand them. "This worthy man is Haleck Visili. I, ahh, secured his release from prison so that he could aid in the defense. Regrettably, I also liberated a man who proved to be untrustworthy. I was tracking him, and someone else saved me the trouble of dealing with him."

"Some*thing*, I would say," said Azori with a grim shudder. Then his face brightened with good humor. "Ah, Hallagond...you haven't changed much with all this time spent in civil company, although I notice you are cleaner than usual, and you have trimmed your beard." He shook his head and clucked in disapproval. "So you liberated two criminals from prison, and found it necessary to hunt one of them down? That is a typical average of fortune for you, I would say. You were nearly always half right, at least."

"I have answered for myself," said Hallagond, "but why have you returned? I would not expect that being hopelessly outnumbered in a grim battle would be at all to your taste. You have said so several times."

"I should think it would be obvious," replied Azori. "A man has only one sister. I made my way north, reflecting on the fact that I had left her in the care of a man who is generally right only half the time, and I grew concerned. I have returned to safeguard her. Let's be on our way. I would hate for the battle to be over before I can join in it."

Five men rode back toward the Citadel, all rogues and bandits guilty of many misdeeds, but they were all superb fighters and Ali would be very glad of them.

When Hallagond gained the City he was unopposed, and he quickly climbed one of the watch-towers that he might decide his course. What he saw unnerved him; he had not known about the dragon, and the sight of it was terrifying. The Cavalry had not yet ridden forth, but the beast was beginning to tear at the wall, and Hallagond knew they had little time. He felt a pair of eyes upon him, and looked across to the other watch-tower to see Lord Salastor standing there. The two men bowed to one another in acknowledgment, and then Hallagond made his way back down to his waiting allies to see what could be done.

"The Scourge is preparing to set their great crossbows loose upon our archers," he said breathlessly. "How may we prevent them? They are out of range of our weapons."

"Did I not see six catapults?" asked Visili. "Why have they not been trained upon the crossbows?"

"You saw only four that will work," said Hallagond. "These folk have no experience in their use...only what they could learn from writings." He paused, puzzled. "I was not aware that you could direct a catapult. I thought you just loaded it and let it fly."

"One can, and I have done," said Visili. "Where is the line of crossbows?"

Rogond and Gaelen stood by the iron door that would now be opened so that they could ride forth, probably to their deaths. Eros called to Réalta; his friend stood near the back of the line with Galador astride him. Ali rode up on his dark red mare, making his way to the forefront, and Rogond spoke to him as he passed. "You ride to your doom, Talishani Ali. You are the commander of the Citadel's forces. Are you certain you would leave them without their leader?"

"I would not ask my most worthy captains to ride into the storm were I not beside them. I once told Galador that one must die of something eventually, and I reckon my time has come. I have left Nelwyn in command of the archers, but the City will stand or fall based on what we can manage. If the dragon tears through the wall, no commander will be needed, regardless. I ride with you."

"You need more riders, and here are four very worthy ones," said a voice from behind. Hallagond and his three bandit friends had ridden forward with Galador to stand behind Ali, Rogond, and Gaelen.

"I have made certain there will be no trouble because of my actions," said Hallagond, "and I beg forgiveness. Allow me to prove my worth to you now."

Ali's eyes narrowed for a moment, yet Hallagond's desire to aid the City seemed genuine, and he was gravely needed. "Very well, Forsaken One. Be forsaken no longer, but ride out and die as a captain of the Citadel. You and your friends are welcome."

Ali gripped his mare's mane as she snorted and tossed her proud head; she was seasoned and ready for battle. Gaelen's mount, Finan, responded with a loud snort of his own as Gaelen completed her disguise, donning the black head-covering that would conceal her face.

"Try not to shoot me by mistake, won't you?" she said to the assembled riders. They chuckled at her—they would know her no matter her raiment. Her eyes widened for a moment as she remembered the page of dragon-lore that Hallagond and Azori had not yet seen. She pulled it from her robes, handing it to them. "Here is your target," she said. "Make certain your aim is true."

Even Eros shifted his feet restively as he awaited the signal from Rogond. As the men stood by the iron doors, Hallagond turned to his brother. "So, we fight together at the last...the two sons of Diomar. Let's go and hunt a big lizard!" With a grinding sound of iron upon iron, the way was made open, and the cavalry gave a great cry, riding down the passageway into the path of the dragon.

It would be their task to distract Lokai from his efforts at breaching the wall, and hopefully to slay him. Each man knew how this might be done, for all had seen the parchment with the depiction of the vulnerable place in the dragon's mouth. The riders wouldn't have much time, especially given the new wave of mounted Scourge warriors who now rode into the fray.

The lives of the Citadel's riders rested in the hands of the remaining archers. Nelwyn prayed that Gaelen, disguised as a Scourge rider, would not be taken by friendly arrows. She ran from one end of the wall to the other, calling for the archers to aim with care as the enemy poured through the gateway. The first volley found its mark, and fifty savages were taken from the fight. Nelwyn was thankful for the many arrows remaining to her as she took aim again.

One hears tales of great battles told around evening fires and in great halls, and it would seem that they are fought long and hard, but in truth, the telling of the tale probably lasts longer. Pitched battles are over quickly, unlike sieges, which may last for years. Ali's riders engaged the dragon for perhaps twenty minutes that seemed to last a lifetime.

It was a good thing Lokai was not especially swift or agile, though he could turn very quickly on occasion. The riders darted around him, trying to avoid his tail and his fearsome head. Many were unlucky on both sides of the conflict; Lokai did not discriminate, crushing or burning Scourge riders as well as defenders.

Rogond readied his spear; it was probably the weapon best suited to killing the dragon except for Galador's bow. If someone did not kill it soon, Rogond knew his friends would never survive. He prepared himself for the mightiest thrust of his life, if only the beast would open its mouth.

He rode up before it, brandishing his spear, calling upon the name of his father in a loud, booming voice. Eros trembled, but he trusted

Rogond, and he charged straight at Lokai's head. The beast swung its powerful snout, striking the great horse with a glancing blow. Eros screamed in terror and pain as he was flung aloft to land hard upon his side, stunned and unmoving. Rogond was thrown aside as well, feeling his shoulder collapse painfully just before his head struck the stone, sending him into darkness.

Gaelen's disguise had served her well; she had taken twenty Scourge riders unaware, and none had attempted to shoot her as she rode among them. The archers knew the difference, and their way had been made easier by the catapults, which now seemed to be aimed more-or-less directly at the troublesome crossbows of the enemy. These were now under constant bombardment, and they could no longer be effectively used, which was a good thing for the Citadel's archers.

Both captains Broca and Habib had fallen, and this had thrown the remaining archers into disarray. Nelwyn was hard put to rally them until a tall, grey-haired man suddenly appeared on the south end of the wall with Estle beside him. The man began ordering the archers, gathering them under his command. Nelwyn would now need to concern herself only with those on the north end.

Who was this man? Nelwyn was certainly thankful for his presence on the battlements, but it did not occur to her that Visili did not know that the Scourge rider upon the bright bay horse was not an enemy. Visili was a fine archer himself, and he drew his bow upon Gaelen, his arrow finding its mark as she rode beneath him. She had seen Rogond's fall and was riding to aid him, calling out his name.

Gaelen was struck from behind just inward of her left arm. It was a killing shot, and she fell hard, hitting the stone as Rogond had done. Nelwyn's arrow fell from her hands as she saw the downfall of her cousin, and she gave a terrible cry of grief. Hallagond and Azori also witnessed Gaelen's fall, and Hallagond turned as if to aid her.

"No good, my friend. She's gone," yelled Azori. "You can't afford such a distraction…fight on!"

Hallagond shook his head. It was a great pity.

Rogond had somehow managed to escape trampling as he slowly regained his senses, although at first he had no notion of where he was or why he was in such pain. Then, the roar of the dragon reminded him as he struggled to his feet. Realizing that his right arm would no longer serve, he gripped the spear in his left, preparing to stand as he could against the dragon. It was then that he saw Gaelen lying with an arrow in her back, as brave Finan stood over her body, his head lowered, ears flattened, defending her to the last.

The Scourge was not faring as well as expected. Apparently someone in the City had figured out how to direct the catapults, and they were striking with much greater accuracy. Though the dragon was holding its own, it was tiring—the fiery blasts were losing some of their power. The Scourge's commanders kept sending riders and foot soldiers into the fray, only to have them taken by the Citadel's archers.

Now there was a new terror to be faced. The captains heard this clamor long before they saw it, for the ranks of men behind them had been thrown into a panic—something about an army of huge, armored creatures winnowing their forces like wheat.

In the rear of the ranks, Gorgon Elfhunter had caught the Scourge unaware. He roared, surprising them as he charged forward, a bright sword in his right hand and a long, curved blade strapped to his left arm. Immense, dark, and powerful, he swung the blades with deadly precision, cutting his enemies down with practiced skill. Their blades and darts would not pierce his armor; they were not designed for such things. He could cut them down as he wished, displaying a disconcerting tendency to take their heads, which was the form of death they dreaded the most.

Except for Lokai, Gorgon was no doubt the most terrifying sight they had seen, and they were soon completely unnerved and disorganized. Gorgon roared again, displaying long, sharp teeth that had never belonged to any two-legged creature of their acquaintance. What little courage they had deserted them, and they turned and fled back toward the safety of the hills.

Rogond knelt beside Gaelen, sorrowing at the sight of the feathered barb that had surely killed her. He made as if to withdraw it, expecting a struggle, for it appeared to have gone deep. To his surprise, it came away easily through the red and black outer garments, at least four bright folds of the fire-cloak clinging to the point. The last and deepest fold had not been penetrated! He turned her over gently with his one good hand as she took a painful, shuddering breath. She was alive, but she had taken damage from both the arrow and the fall, and would not awaken.

Rogond tried to drag her away as Finan flung his head in the air and screamed in challenge; the stone floor trembled as Lokai made his way toward them. Rogond's one arm was useless and he had to lay Gaelen down, clinging grimly to his spear, knowing that his left arm did not have the skill of his right. Yet if Gaelen would die now, he would die with her. *It would seem the stars were wrong…*

Hallagond rode to the aid of his brother, leaping from his horse as the dragon drew nigh them. He knew what needed to be done; he just prayed that he would have the courage to do it. "I am here to aid you, my brother. Do not hinder me," he said. He drew a blade, cut through Gaelen's disguise, and removed her fire-cloak. Then he turned to Rogond, who did not as yet grasp what he was about to do. "Give me your spear; you are not as adept with your left arm, and I am at full strength," said Hallagond. "I must face this thing now, or it has all been for nothing. Take care of your beloved."

The fear in his eyes was evident, but there was also resolve, and Rogond did not try to stay him as he took the spear. Hallagond stood now behind Gaelen's valiant little horse, wrapping himself in the fire-cloak, determined to pass the test this time. Finan charged forward, defying the dragon, rearing onto his hind legs, but alas, he met with a blast of flame and was knocked aside as Eros had been. Rogond was thankful that Gaelen had not seen it.

Hallagond now stood alone, gleaming in the bright metallic folds of the cloak, praying that it would protect him, as Lokai prepared to assail him. The dragon opened its mouth, sending forth a torrent of flame that engulfed Hallagond. Rogond cried in despair, for his brother fell to his knees, surely burned to death.

The dragon closed its mouth as, against all hope, Hallagond struggled to his feet. His right arm was burned, but the fire-cloak had passed the test—it had turned even dragon-fire. Lokai blinked twice in dull disbelief and drew a deep, hissing breath, intending to send forth another blast. But as the fearsome mouth opened wide, Hallagond hurled the now-flaming spear straight into the dark purple folds of the vulnerable spot. With a screaming roar, the dragon threw itself backward, toppled sideways, and crashed to the ground, thrashing briefly before lying still and dead. The Great Worm's long life of killing and devouring had come to an end.

The Scourge's stunned captains witnessed the death of Lokai, knowing that they now held no hope of taking the City. They truly had thought the dragon could not be defeated. Now they were in disarray, with only about half their original force remaining. Without their terrible and revered guardian they had lost their unified purpose, and were only a collection of poorly organized savages armed with swords and light bows. Lokai had given them their power, and they knew it. And now, there was a new threat—some dark, unknown creatures attacking from the rear of the ranks.

Gorgon was beginning to tire as the Scourge finally sounded the retreat; he had taken over a hundred of the enemy, and since they were now in full rout he was no longer needed. He still managed to kill about six more as they passed before turning to make his way back to his sanctuary in the hills. There was fresh water, and a dark place where he could rest until the furor subsided. He stopped beside the headless body of a freshly-killed warrior and slung it across his shoulder to feast upon later. The flesh of men was not his favored source of nourishment, but it would serve, and at least this one would not stare back at him. As an afterthought, he also took the man's bread ration. He would be lying in wait for a while. He knew Gaelen was still alive…he could feel it. He could also tell that she was unconscious, which was so much the better for him. The battle had taken all of her attention, and he expected the aftermath would, as well. She would never see him coming.

The Scourge had been defeated, and the City secured. The Great Wall would remain as both a monument to the battle and as a defense in case an enemy army ever threatened the Silver City again. But now, there was much of sorrow to mar this victory, as some in the Company were only just discovering. Many of the losses had yet to be measured.

Azori had been wounded unto death, as had Ali. Both were taken to the healers at once, but there was no remedy for either of them. Hallagond had suffered burns, especially to his right arm, for he had needed to expose it to hurl the spear. He was in great pain as they led him away. Eros, though badly bruised and shaken, had taken no lasting damage; his sturdiness had served him well. Rogond's shoulder was broken and battered, and he would lose the use of his right arm for a time, but he would heal. All were exhausted; even Nelwyn and Galador found that much of their strength had left them. Gaelen's body would heal, for the fire-cloak had saved her life, but the same could not be said of her heart.

She found Finan where he had fallen. He had been burned, and some of his bones were broken such that he would never get up again. Gaelen knew this as she drew nigh him, just as surely as she knew that he had fallen defending her.

He was breathing hard and fast, for he was in great pain. She laid a soft hand over his large eye, and he closed it as she spoke to him in a gentle voice. "Rest well, my brave Finan. You have saved my life, even as I saved yours. You have earned your place among the valiant. Never was there a finer friend." Finan shuddered with pain, and groaned as he tried to rise—it would not do for him to lie helpless upon the ground when there was a battle to fight. "No, my friend," said Gaelen quietly, soothing him with her wonderful touch. "The battle is over, and you have won it. Be at peace, my beloved." She looked into his left eye and read the pain within; it wrenched her heart and she began to weep.

She noticed a tall shadow that fell across Finan's body as Galador appeared, deep sorrow in his eyes. He drew his blade. "Let me take him from his pain," he said. "He is beyond recovery."

Gaelen looked up at him with bright eyes. "Know that I appreciate your offer of aid, Galador, but do not mistake my tears for weakness. This is my task, and I alone must do it." She drew forth the silver flask of dark essence that she had brought all the way from her home in the Greatwood. It was her last defense against Gorgon's power; without it, if she had to take her own life, she would end painfully. Yet Finan was in pain right now, as he lay before her. He had stood over her, and shielded her. There was no other choice. She worked her arm beneath Finan's head and lifted his muzzle from the ground, poured the entire contents of the flask into his mouth, and stroked him gently as it took effect. She looked up at Galador.

"He will drift away from pain…into a realm where all visions are happy ones," she said. "And then, he will die."

Finan stood in grass up to his knees, even as Gaelen had promised. There was water, and cool shade or warm sun on his withers as he desired, but no flies came to bother him, not in this place. He heard her singing as she approached, his black head-collar in her hand, calling to him. He ran toward her, his tail raised high, and no pain assailed his limbs, for it was as if they had never been damaged. She haltered him, and they rode for hours over the soft grass, until at last they came to another place that was familiar, and he heard another voice that he had not heard in many, many years.

Rama! Rama, my favorite mount, my handsome friend, how I have missed you. Come, now, to me. Finan halted and turned toward the voice, as Gaelen slid down from his back. She led him toward the glowing figure of a young man dressed in royal hunting-garb, and Finan knew him at once. He had found his Prince at last!

Take care of him, said Gaelen, *for he is my friend.* With that she handed him to the Prince, who bowed before her. As his beloved Gaelen began to fade, only one thing would mar Finan's ultimate joy…she was crying.

Finan drew his last breath peacefully and without a struggle, and now lay still upon the stone. Gaelen stroked his neck one last time, her eyes full of pain. "Finan, oh, Finan...who now shall I tell my troubles to?" She grew pale and swayed slightly, for she was hurt, and Galador grew alarmed.

"Come, little one. I will bear you to a place of healing. You can rest with Rogond there." He felt her shudder with pain as he lifted her, but she did not resist. He bore her to the healing halls, which were filled with the casualties of battle. The healers had never been faced with so many, and they were overwhelmed.

Both Ali and Azori had been laid low by the dragon—Azori by the venom and Ali by fire. He had been burned so badly that he had no sensation in much of his body, which was a mercy. If some of his men had not seen him fall, they would have known him only from the design of his boots. His beautiful mare had fallen beside him. He lay in a private chamber swathed in silken bandages, awaiting the end. Though he suffered terrible thirst, and was in some pain, he was still in his right mind. It was perhaps a gentler fate than Azori would endure.

Hallagond had been given herbs to lessen the pain of his burned arm, which had been treated with ointments and wrapped, but was still most unpleasant. He sat now with Estle beside Azori, who writhed upon his bed, froth bubbling from his mouth, his eyes wide but unseeing as the effects of the deadly venom tormented him. There was no healing to be done.

Estle was nearly beside herself, and Hallagond could not blame her. "He is my brother...I should take away his pain, but I can't... Lord of Light help me, I can't just kill him," she said. It was not easy to see a hard, strong man like Azori in the grip of such a bad death.

Hallagond looked over at Gaelen, who sat in the shadows, her face a mask of sorrow. "Gaelen...can you give him your elixir? At least then his pain will end."

"I'm sorry. I have no more dark essence...it is gone. I'm sorry," she replied, so miserable that no one said any more of the matter.

Nelwyn, who liked Estle and Hallagond both very much and would do anything to aid them, sat helplessly as Azori's life ended slowly and unspeakably. Were it not for his great strength he would have died already.

Then Nelwyn remembered a story Fima had told long ago, about a dragon and Fesok the Iron-beard. That dragon had venomous tail-spines, and when Fesok had been poisoned and was certain to die, he took the blood of the dragon, which cured him. Nelwyn had been taught that dragon's blood was deadly poison, yet Fima had assured her that it had cured Fesok of the venom. Could it be that this would actually work?

She looked back at Gaelen, whose expression had become thoughtful. "Are you thinking what I'm thinking?"

"Go now, Nelwyn, go at once!" said Gaelen. "We have no time."

Nelwyn ran out of the chamber on her desperately important errand, pausing to grab a glass flask in which she could collect the dragon's blood. She made her way back to the battlefield and the huge, dead bulk of Lokai, wrinkling her nose against the stench of him. Kneeling beside his enormous pink belly, she worked her blade between the thick, glass-like scales until a quantity of thick, dark red blood oozed forth. She caught the flow in the flask, praying that it would be sufficient, and hurried back to the healing-chambers.

Meanwhile, Fima had been summoned. Gaelen had told him of Nelwyn's errand as soon as he had appeared, but rather than encouraging her, he had paled. Dragon-blood is normally quite a deadly poison, and because of a tale he had told, they were on the verge of poisoning Azori with it.

He looked into Gaelen's eyes, reading the openness and trust in them. She would believe nearly anything he told her. "It *will* work, won't it, Fima?" she asked.

"What are you on about?" said Estle. "Dragon's blood is poison. You can't give such a thing to Azori…you'll kill him!"

"He's dead already, with or without it," said Hallagond quietly. "Tell us, Lore-master, does this idea have any merit?"

Fima looked at Gaelen again. He could not dash her hopes, not after all the trial she and her friends had endured, but neither could he lie to her. "Gaelen…have you ever heard of artistic license?" Her brow furrowed and she shook her head. He had to allow her some hope, even if it was false. "Gaelen, remember that ordinary folk are not like the Iron-beard. Even if the tale I told you was true…"

"Yes, *if* it was true," put in Hallagond. He had borne witness to several of Fima's tall tales, and his hopes had already fallen into his shoes.

"… *even* if it was true," Fima continued, "Azori is not Fesok. And much time has passed; the venom has had time to act. What we are attempting may not work. Do you understand?"

At that moment, Nelwyn appeared with the flask of dark blood in her hand. "You must save Azori, Fima. He does not deserve this terrible fate. Many have fallen today undeserved...we must not let Azori add his death to theirs. We know the cure may not work, but you must try." A strangled cry from Azori decided them all. Fima's remedy might well kill Azori, but at least he would suffer no more pain.

Fima's hands trembled as he carefully poured a small amount of the thick blood into a cup. "But, I don't know how much to give him...I know nothing of ministering healing to a man. How would I know such things? What if I give him too much, or not enough?"

Gaelen noticed the tiny muscle over his left eye—it twitched uncontrollably when he was very distressed. "There is no time to be certain, anyway," she said. "No one will blame you. Don't kill him with your fear of failure…do what you must!"

"Just be guided by your wisdom, Fima," said Nelwyn gently. "It's the best we have."

As it happened, Fima's remedy worked. Azori would not die on that day, though he might have preferred to. The cure was most unpleasant, first sending him into a hard, shaking fit. Then it locked all his muscles up as though he were a marble statue. His hands clenched so hard that Fima feared he would break his own fingers, and he could make no sound except a thin, reedy whistle as he struggled to breathe. At last he collapsed into a limp, exhausted heap, and they all thought he had left them, but his heart was still beating.

Estle wept again when the pain finally left Azori's face the next morning. Her half-brother was a thief and a rogue, but he had fought like a lion and she loved him. Fima was so relieved that he did not even boast about it, at least not immediately. The healers were quite impressed, adding the remedy to their writings. Gaelen insisted on naming it "Fima's dragon-cure."

Regrettably, Talishani Ali died in the night, to the sorrow of all. He had been a fine man. Though he could only speak in a rasping whisper, he told his attendants that he had been wrong about Hallagond, and that without Visili's efforts the battle might have been lost. When Hallagond was told of this he sorrowed most deeply, and did not speak to anyone until the following day.

Lord Salastor had declared that a ceremony would be held for the fallen. They would be laid to rest at the base of the wall that had saved the City, and a great stone memorial would be erected there to honor them. But Hallagond insisted that Ali's body be burned, for it was his belief that men of honor are released by fire, and not buried in the ground. Hallagond himself lit the pyre on which his friend had been laid, and the people sang songs of valor as the flames rose high into the night.

Now was the time for rest and healing of body and spirit. The City would never be the same again; one cannot face the reality of such evil and not be altered by it. The Company took comfort in being together. Fima was especially solicitous of his wounded friends, and helped them whenever possible. He marveled at the story of Hallagond and the slaying of Lokai.

Estle cared for Hallagond, changing the dressings on his burned arm twice daily. He tried not to show how much this pained him—mostly without success—and his arm would be forever scarred, but he didn't mind. The beautiful designs upon it, marred beyond hope, were reminders of Al-Amand, and he would never be forsaken again. This time he had faced the fire; he had passed the test.

He found Rogond sitting with Gaelen upon a late afternoon not long afterward, as they rested together and looked out over the sea. The rains had moved on, and the sky was clearing as he sat beside them.

"Well, my brother," he began, "I suppose now I shall remain here. Will you stay beside me, and fight for the City if the need ever arises again?"

Rogond smiled at him. "I will for the moment," he said, "but I don't know where my fate will turn."

Hallagond drew a deep breath. "I owe you a great debt, and I'm sorry for my early treatment of you. It seems that Al-Amand did not wish to give in so easily, and I don't know whether he ever would have were it not for your little hunter-scout. Her words were well chosen upon a time. Because you are both very special to me, I think you should be the first to learn of my betrothal."

"That is fine news," said Rogond.

"I would have my little brother standing beside me, if he will agree," said Hallagond.

"Truly?" said Gaelen, lifting her head. "And what does Azori think of this idea?"

"Azori will stand with Estle, and release her to me," said Hallagond. "I'm not sure he entirely approves of anyone being wedded to his sister, but he said I'm probably the one person he wouldn't feel compelled to kill."

"Well, that's something at least," said Rogond. "Of course, I will agree. The two sons of Diomar should stand together on this happy occasion."

"They will ever stand together," said Hallagond, reaching out with his one good hand to clasp Rogond's one good hand in friendship.

So, will you two brothers kiss each other now? Should I avert my eyes?" said Gaelen, who knew full well that Hallagond was uncomfortable with such displays of sentiment, and therefore could not resist teasing him. "And I would caution you both against this annoying habit everyone seems to have adopted. I am not little. Not a little Wood-elf, nor a little hunter-scout, nor a little anything! I am an Elf of the line of Tarfion and Gloranel, and I am over a thousand years old, so stop calling me 'little!'"

"My apologies," said Hallagond. "You're right, Gaelen. You may be undersized, but you are not little. Never again will I call you so."

26
The Company Is Reunited

Nearly a month had passed since the Scourge had been routed, and the people of Dûn Arian were already hard at work renewing their homes and their hearts. The carcasses of the enemy had been gathered and piled up for burning; the fires lasted three days, sending columns of smoke into the air that could be seen for miles. Visili commented that they could probably even be seen by what was left of the Scourge.

He had been quite mortified upon learning that he had shot and nearly killed Gaelen, and had apologized to her at once. "I did not know you," he said. "I very nearly committed a great wrong by mischance, and I am truly sorry. I hope you will forgive me."

Gaelen shrugged. "I'm just thankful it wasn't a head shot," she said. "You did not know differently; there's nothing to amend. I suppose it was not the best idea disguising myself, but as I managed to claim more than twenty foes I suppose it was worth a little pain."

Rogond lifted his eyebrows at this. Gaelen had suffered more than a little pain as a result of Visili's arrow; had his shot been only a bit more powerful it would certainly have killed her. It had broken at least one of her ribs and bruised her left lung as well as the overlying muscle.

Her bruises were fading and could now barely be seen, except across the left side of her back where the arrow had struck her; this would take some time even for Gaelen to heal. Rogond had been very thoroughly battered himself when Lokai had flung him across the courtyard, and now his bruises were in a very ugly state of greenish-black. Gaelen tended him each day, gently massaging the muscles of his right arm to aid him in maintaining his strength, for he could not move it due to the shattering of his shoulder. He was looking forward to many more weeks of this gentle treatment.

Azori had fared well once "Fima's dragon-cure" had banished the venom from his body, and he was now amusing himself by teasing Hallagond incessantly about the perils of being wedded to his sister. If she ever complained of unhappiness, Azori would have no choice but to kill the one responsible. He shot menacing, fierce looks at Hallagond whenever possible, but they were false.

Estle was in on the joke briefly; one evening at feast she had remarked that she thought she might be unhappy. Azori drew a deep sigh, rose to his feet, and addressed Hallagond. "It would seem that my sister is unhappy. Regrettably, I must now take you outside so that I may kill you without disturbing the feast of these other folk. Come along quietly, now." Hallagond rose and followed Azori outside, after rolling his eyes at the ceiling.

Inside the hall the feast resumed, until a terrible cry was heard from Hallagond. A few moments later, Azori reappeared, wiping imaginary blood from his blade. He sat down at the table, looking around at the horrified expressions on the faces of the citizens. "What?" he asked innocently, and resumed eating.

"Azori," said Estle, "did you kill Hallagond?"

"Naturally," said Azori through a mouthful of pastry.

"Oh, dear. Now I suppose I shall need to look for someone else to marry, since we have been planning a large ceremony, and all. I wonder if any of these fine gentlemen would be interested?"

There were nine other men at the long table, but, save for Rogond, they all seemed suddenly to be needed elsewhere.

Nelwyn and Galador had recovered quickly from their weariness, and they aided greatly in the restoration of the Citadel, as did Fima. "It would be a great honor to have a dwarvish craftsman design the memorial," said Lord Salastor, and Fima accepted the task with proper solemnity. He also aided in the restoration of the materials to the Great Library, which was now where he spent much of his time. Gaelen had saved the page that she had torn from the volume of dragon-lore, and one afternoon she came into the Library to find a rather chilly reception awaiting her as the scholars clustered protectively before the doorway to the inner archives. She recognized the little easterner with the olive-green robes, and approached him, bowing respectfully, holding out the parchment so that he could take it from her.

"This is battle-weary, and not in the same condition as when I acquired it, but I return it now. Please know that it may have saved the lives as well as the lore of the City. I admit and regret my earlier discourtesy, but I truly had no other choice. I bow humbly before you all, and ask your pardon." She bowed somewhat stiffly due to the hurts she had taken, as the scholar took the battered parchment from her. He took notice of the sweat and blood that marred it now, and wondered.

"This should not be returned to its place, where it may not see the light of day," said Fima. "It should be set apart as a reminder that, although all writings are worth preserving, there are times when some are worth sacrificing. I will set to work crafting a vessel for it at once." To this, no one would argue. They did agree that the page should be copied, however, so that the volume could be restored.

Gaelen felt a little better after returning the parchment, but she was still melancholy. She missed Finan; the fallen horses had been gathered and burned, but separate from the enemy. Gaelen had not witnessed this, nor did she care to. She felt as though a part of herself had been torn away, and would be so for a long time to come. Bint Raed had cheerfully returned Siva to her, and Gaelen was glad of it, but it was not the same. She did not allow herself to grieve openly for Finan until one day when she was tending to Rogond; she looked down at the silver brooch on her cloak and suddenly gave a heart-wrenching moan, looking around helplessly before bursting into tears. Rogond was alarmed until he realized what had come over her; she clung to him until her grief was spent.

Everyone now looked forward to the marriage of Estle and Hallagond. Lord Salastor had arranged for all in the City to rest from their labors on the day of the ceremony, and there would be a great feast in honor of the event. Everyone in the Company had some part to play in the preparations; Bint Raed had worked day and night to weave a beautiful silver and grey fabric for Estle's gown, and there was enough to make a sash for Hallagond. Nelwyn had gone out into the forest gathering flowers and vines to make garlands, for it was springtime in the City and there were plenty to be had. Gaelen had gone with her, but she was not adept at such things, and left the making of the garlands to Nelwyn.

Rogond and Azori would play important parts in the ceremony, as would Gaelen, who had been asked to sing. Nelwyn and Galador would bear the ceremonial garland that would entwine Hallagond and Estle. Lord Salastor himself would preside, but the words would be read by Maji, the Minister of Omens.

It seemed that Fima had no part to play, and he was feeling rather left out. He and Hallagond sat with Visili one evening, sharing a flask of wine, when Fima asked about it. "Why have I not been given a task in preparing for this great day? Surely there is some service I may provide, some contribution that I can make?"

Hallagond clapped Fima on the shoulder. "My stout and learned friend, you already made the greatest contribution when you saved Azori's life. Estle would have been devastated had her brother been lost, and were it not for you he certainly would have been. Rest assured that your contribution was of the utmost importance."

"It's not the same thing, and you know it," growled the dwarf, refusing to be placated. "Surely there is something else that I may do?"

Hallagond shrugged. "Planning the ceremony is not my task," he said. "Ask Estle."

"Hmmmph," said Fima, pouring himself more wine. "I suppose I had better ask her, but if she cannot come up with something I will simply have to think of it myself."

Fima did so, and for the next several days he could not be found in any of his usual haunts. Finally he emerged, looking somewhat careworn as though he had been working very intently at something. He called Estle and Hallagond together, telling them that he had prepared a small contribution to the ceremony. "I once possessed such skills," he said, "but I am no longer practiced. I hope these are worthy, and are to your liking." With a flourish, he revealed two beautiful golden rings; they were very nearly perfect, and he had engraved them himself.

"You once said that the sound of Elven-tongues was unwelcome, Hallagond. I hope that is no longer true." He proceeded to read the engraving, which was in High-elven. Then he translated. Estle's ring read: *I give my heart to Estle, and shall never forsake her.* Hallagond's ring, though larger, was identical except for the inscription: *I give my heart to Hallagond, who shall never again be forsaken.* Fima shuffled his feet, complaining that the words had barely fit on Estle's ring, but he had managed it.

"These are beautiful, and very, very special," said Hallagond. "We will treasure them always. You are quite the romantic, aren't you?"

"Well, actually, I had some help from Rogond," said Fima, blushing furiously. "Now *there* is a romantic!"

"So, how did he end up giving his heart to Gaelen?" asked Estle. "She is about as romantic as a plate of hard cheese." Hallagond laughed along with her, but both he and Fima knew differently. They had seen the tender side of Gaelen Taldin, and knew the truth of it.

The day of the ceremony drew near, and the spirits of the people were lightened. The weather was unusually fine, as if the whole world was looking with favor upon the union of Hallagond and Estle.

On the day before the ceremony, Gaelen had gone out into the forest to escape the last of the preparations. She had little use for such things, and was secretly thankful that she and Rogond had bound to each other in secret. Their union would never be recorded anywhere but in their hearts.

She had been in a dark mood for some reason, troubled by a feeling of uneasiness—a vague tingling in her fingertips—as though something needed her attention…an enemy approaching, or someone in need. This confused her, for she had expected to be happy on this day when two of her friends prepared to celebrate their greatest joy. Tomorrow she would stand beside them and lift her voice in tribute to their love…it was a great honor in her mind. Why, then, was her heart so empty?

She sat heavily upon the mossy ground, trying to take solace in the fresh, green smell of late spring in this strange-yet-familiar woodland, lying back and looking up at the impossibly tall canopy. She felt herself drifting away into a waking dream…no, she could not allow it! She had to remain vigilant. But her heart was so weary.

The vague tingling in her fingertips became a sharp burning as icy water filled her veins and she began to tremble. Something had happened! She jerked upright and leaped to her feet. *Rogond…where is Rogond? He is dying, and in pain…something terrible has befallen him!*

She flew back to the City, rushing headlong into Rogond's chamber, but he was not there. She ran to the market, and to the Hall of Council. By the time she got there, she was screaming his name.

The Council was not in session, but Lord Salastor heard her cries and came forth to aid her. He found her still calling for Rogond in a panicked voice, looking around as if wondering where to look next.

"Gaelen! What has so dismayed you?"

"I must find Rogond at once! Something has happened. Do you know where I may find him?" She was nearly breathless by now.

Salastor did not know, but Galador and Fima had heard her cries and ran now into the Hall.

"Gaelen, Rogond is fine. We just left him...he is down in the armory," said Galador.

"Fine. Then I shall go there." Without another word to any of them, she turned and made her way to the armory as swiftly as she could manage. She found Rogond tending to his blades, and ran to him at once, tears of relief starting in her eyes. He was whole; no ill had befallen him. Yet as he held her, confused and frightened by her sudden, panicked appearance, her eyes grew wide again. *Who, then, if not Rogond?*

"Where is your brother?" she cried, tears now spilling from her eyes. She looked around in alarm, as though seeing and hearing things that were not there. Then, she wailed piteously and wrenched away from him. "Gorgon is here…Oh, *no*…Hallagond…he has been taken!" Without waiting for Rogond to react she ran from the chamber, moving so swiftly and unerringly through the winding paths of the City that he had no hope of catching her quickly. At last she came upon a sight that would haunt her until her dying day.

It was hanging at the end of a blind alleyway, just visible in the waning light of late afternoon. The smell of blood and offal and the buzzing of flies announced it long before she beheld it; the body of a tall man, pegged to the wall and suspended with cords tied beneath both arms. Hallagond…was *this* how Gorgon would announce his return? The familiar foul reek still lingered after him, and Gaelen knew his handiwork, for she had seen it before. One thought filled her horrified mind. She had called this monster to herself, and now he was here!

Gaelen did not rush up to the body, for she dreaded what she would see, yet she had to be certain of its identity. The slow dripping of blood upon the stone floor was the only sound to be heard, other than her shallow, terrified breathing and the hammering of her heart. The body was all but unrecognizable, yet the eyes were intact and open; death had not been long upon them.

With an almost overwhelming sense of relief, she realized that the eyes were not Hallagond's, for although they were grey, they were not the same. This man was older…much older. Still, she knew these eyes. *Who, then, has paid this terrible price?* She could not yet bear to ask him.

There was no clothing or ornament upon the body, nothing to identify it other than a few remaining tangled locks of long, greying hair. But then, Gaelen noticed a small, blood-soaked bundle laid at the feet of the corpse. She reached down to take it with shaking hands. Rogond, by now, had come up from behind her and was staring at the scene in horror. Galador and Fima were right behind him.

"Stay back," Gaelen warned, opening the bundle. She stared at the contents for a few moments, and uttered a cry as she recognized the object inside. There was also a parchment, with a message written in a hand that she had seen before. The blood used in the writing was not man's blood; it was darker, yet it smelled vaguely Elven.

Gaelen dropped the bundle to the floor, fury rising in her face as she now turned her attention to the dead eyes of the man hanging before her. She looked hard into them, and read the unspeakable pain of this tormented soul's last hours, the force of it causing her to cry out as though in pain herself. She heard Gorgon's hated voice inside her head: *The time has come for us to dance. Thou hast called me to thee, and now I have come. I call thee out to face thy destiny.*

She shuddered and mastered herself, caressing the face of the man with bloodied hands. "I'm sorry, my friend...alas that you have found us again, even as you said you would. This is a grim reunion. Please forgive me. I would do anything to restore you."

She gave herself completely over to hatred and thoughts of vengeance, backing away from the corpse, preparing herself for the only course of action open to her uncomplicated nature. She would not stop to explain to Rogond or anyone else, for there was a task before her, and she would see it done.

Rogond approached the terrible display before him, and picked up the bundle where Gaelen had dropped it. He knew the object inside at once—a carved wooden pipe, lovingly oiled and tended, that had belonged to one very well known to him. "Thorndil… however did you have the bad luck to be here?"

The Company had been reunited at last.

"What does the parchment say?" asked Galador. Rogond could not reply, for he was stunned by what he had seen, and was trying to make sense of it where there was little sense to be made. Fima read the words aloud, taking the note gently from Rogond's nerveless left hand.

"My name is Gorgon Elfhunter. I have returned. I call upon the Company to face me, or I shall eliminate you one by one. You must send Gaelen Taldin forth, or I shall prey upon your citizens until you do so. You are warned."

Fima shook his head. There would be no celebration of joy tomorrow. The Company now faced a conflict of a different kind, and either Gaelen or Gorgon would lie dead at the end of it, as might they all. They had underestimated the Elfhunter, and let down their defenses. Thorndil had struggled across unspeakable hardship to find them and reunite with them, only to meet with the most horrific ending imaginable. Fima closed his eyes.

"How could such a terrible misfortune have come to pass?"

After the battle, Gorgon had remained concealed in his cool sanctuary, emerging only by night. He had witnessed from afar the burning of the bodies of the dead, and he wondered why the Citadel's forces had not pursued the remnants of the enemy army, but he was glad of it. The rabble had potential; one day Gorgon might turn them to his purposes, but for now it was clear that they would pose no threat until they could find another fearsome power under which to unite.

In the meantime, he made plans of his own, smiling as he did so. Gaelen Taldin, his mortal enemy, was living her last days within those walls. He had sensed no distress in her for a while now; she was relaxing and lowering her guard. He had been very careful to keep his thoughts hidden from her. This had been a relatively easy task, since her attention was divided along many paths. She must not sense his presence until he was ready.

Thorndil, a guide, and another companion had finally approached the City not long after the battle ended, drawn to the smoke rising from the burning pyres of the dead. Gorgon had attacked and killed the guide and the companion, but had spared Thorndil, for even though he had been worn down by the hardship of the journey, Gorgon still knew him. It was nothing short of miraculous that Thorndil had found his friends as he had sworn to do, and it was a wonderful stroke of luck for Gorgon. Now he would arrange a display that would almost certainly bring the Company forth to face him.

He crippled and bound Thorndil, holding him captive for several days, sharing food and water with him, although Thorndil would touch none of Gorgon's food at first.

"Please, Aridan, eat and drink and save your strength, for you will have need of it," said Gorgon in a tone that was almost hospitable. "I know you will not eat the meat, but the bread will surely sustain you, will it not?"

Thorndil saw the sense at last, for starvation is an unpleasant form of death. If he kept his strength, perhaps he could lull Gorgon and strike him unaware.

Alas, he was never given the chance. On the afternoon of the day before the ceremony was to take place, Gorgon approached Thorndil and offered him a last meal. He had actually bothered to roast the meat this time, and Thorndil recognized it as bird-flesh, eating it thankfully along with the last of the bread. Perhaps he would strike the creature tonight, for his strength was returning. After Thorndil had eaten, Gorgon had turned to him, and had spoken to him in a deep, menacing voice.

"Now, Aridan, the time has come for us to dance. You must serve my purpose, and to do so I must cause you pain. You should know that I hold no grudge against you, and that I respect you as a worthy adversary, but you are a most unlucky old man. Please understand that I hold no ill will toward you, but I must now bring as much pain upon you as possible."

Thorndil tried to hold on to his courage, for he knew enough to know that inflicting pain was something that Gorgon was very, very good at. But in the end, despite his valor, he was reduced to pleading with his tormentor.

Just like all the rest of them, thought Gorgon, as he worked his unspeakable atrocities. He repeated the same words, over and over, each time he set his blade to the flesh. "Thou hast called me to thee, and now I have come. I call thee out to face thy destiny." He knew that when Gaelen looked into Thorndil's dead eyes, she would hear these words as clearly as if Gorgon stood beside her, together with helpless wails of agony.

"What's to be done now?" asked Galador, trying to bring Rogond back to the moment. "Should we go after the creature? He is not long gone."

"Where is Gaelen?" asked Fima. She was no longer in the passage.

The three friends looked at one another, cursing their lack of awareness. They all knew of Gaelen's tendency to recklessness, and it was quite possible that grief and guilt had now unbalanced her.

"I must find her at once," said Rogond in a tone of barely concealed panic. "Galador, pursue Gorgon if you will, but take others with you. *Many* others!" He gripped his friend's arm. "You know the difficulty in tracking him. Do what you can, but safeguard yourself. He is bent on taking all of us!"

"Just find Gaelen before she does something…something the Fire-heart would do," said Galador, for once finding no humor in the comparison. "Gorgon is counting on her impulsiveness to drive her out to him. We must not let that happen!"

Rogond and Fima went looking for Gaelen, hoping to find her before Gorgon did.

Gaelen could afford no more grief for Thorndil; she gathered herself and made her way back through the city streets. She went directly to the wonderful quarters she and her friends had been given, not surprised to find Fima's in disarray. She searched his belongings, and searched again, but did not find what she was looking for. She clenched her hands, suppressing the urge to cry out and strike the bed-post in frustration. *Where else could it be?*

She looked around, shaking her head, for the dwarf was given to untidiness, except, of course, when he was in the Library, where nothing would ever be misplaced. Of course! It had to be there.

Fima and Rogond searched the streets, calling Gaelen's name, visiting all her usual haunts, having alerted the Minister of Lawful Affairs that she had gone missing. He set a watch on all the gates in case she tried to go out after Gorgon, and discovered the dead guards at the small north entry.

So, that was how he got into the City, thought Rogond, marveling at Gorgon's dark talents. *He invaded the Citadel in broad daylight, spirited a large body that was dripping blood everywhere deep within, and left undetected. At least, that's what we're all thinking…we're all thinking he left his message and departed, but what if he has not left the City at all? What if he is lying in wait for Gaelen, stalking her?*

Rogond could not banish the terrible thoughts of what Gorgon would do if he caught her; his horror was replaced by a fury that he could barely control. Broken shoulder or not, if his beloved died at the hands of this black monstrosity, Rogond would rip the creature apart no matter his size. He would say no word to anyone, keeping his wrath hidden behind stony silence as he ran.

Gaelen tried to appear unconcerned as she entered the dim, silent halls of the Library. The scholars had forgiven her earlier discourtesy, but they had not forgotten it, and they still did not trust her. She made them uneasy, particularly when her blood was high as it was now; they could practically feel the heat of it as she passed. She approached a group of the senior scholars. She had often seen them engaged in debate with Fima, and inquired as casually as she could as to whether they knew the whereabouts of his leather jerkin.

"Why do you ask?" said one in a tone that indicated it was none of Gaelen's affair where Fima left his things.

"Because he asked me to fetch it for him," she replied, trying her best to deliver a smooth and convincing lie, a talent she had not developed to very great extent. "Please…I have little time. Fima wants his jerkin, and he will grow impatient if I do not bring it at once. He will chide me for days. Will you not aid me?"

The scholar hesitated, and then directed her to a small chamber behind him. There she found several of Fima's things, including his jerkin. Apparently, this was his private reading-chamber, given to him in acknowledgment of his station as Lore-master to Lady Ordath. Gaelen suspected that he actually slept here on occasion. She lifted the jerkin and bowed, thanking the scholars for their aid before making her way out into the City.

She shrank back into the shadows, for she did not want to be found—not until she accomplished her purpose. She would face Gorgon, but not in the way he had intended.

She ducked into a deserted alcove where a small fountain was set, turning Fima's jerkin wrong side out, exposing the hidden pocket. Fima had actually stitched it shut so that her blade was required to open it, but the object she needed was still safe inside. Once she touched it there could be no delay, for Gorgon would know, and she could not risk alerting him. She had no notion of what would happen as a result of her next action, and her heart filled with dread, yet she now called forth her hatred and grief to banish it.

"Prepare yourself," she whispered, not knowing whether she addressed Gorgon or herself. "Dark Horror, the time has come for us to dance."

She faced an unknown fate, hoping that all would not turn to ashes, as she reached into the pocket, gasping at the unpleasant surge of power emanating from Gorgon's mirror…she had never touched it before. She drew it forth, flipped open the golden cover, and with neither a pause nor another word stared as hard as she could into the misty depths of the glass.

GLOSSARY of NAMES

With aid to pronunciation:

Aincor (INE-cor): Elf of the Èolar, a great scholar and warrior, known as the Fire-heart. He was among the most skilled and passionate of his people, but he was prideful, and his reckless acts bore terrible consequences. It is unflattering to be compared with him in terms of willfulness. He produced two sons, Asgar and Dardis. Name means "fire-heart." (ain-fire, cor-heart)

Ainrath (INE-rath): The Elves" name for Redruin, the Fire-drake. Name means "fury of fire."

Airan (EYE-rahn): Lord Airan, Elf of the Eádram that founded the realm of Tal-sithian. From airith (noble).

Aiyah! (EYE-yah): Elvish expression, translated as "Attend me!" It is also an expression of alarm (Pay attention! Look to yourselves!).

Al-amand (AL-amand): Name taken by Hallagond for use in the southlands, it means "the forsaken one."

Alduinar (AL-dwee-nar): Ruler of Tuathas at the time of the Third Uprising. He successfully repelled Kotos' forces, and was a good friend and ally of the High King. His name means "worthy guide."

Al-hamad (al-HAH-mahd): youngest brother of Sheikh Al-Muniqui.

Al-Muniqui (al-moo-NEE-kee): Sheikh and ruler of wealthy sutherling clan; his family was known for weaving beautiful brocaded fabrics. He is the eldest of four brothers.

Al-qamadan (al-KAH-mah-dahn): Eldest brother of Sheikh Al-Muniqui, Al-qamadan is the second-born.

Alterra (Al-TAIR-ra): The World That Is; the Realm in which these tales take place. From terra (earth) and alta (being).

Amandir (AH-mahn-deer): Elf of Tal-Sithian, spouse of Brinneal. His name means "artful one." From aman (artful).

Ambros (AHM-bros): Great River of Western Alterra, it is formed by the Eros and the Brocca in the north. From ambra (great) and ros (river).

Anori-men (Ah-NORI-men): Men that dwell in the eastern regions of Alterra. They are fierce fighters, have golden skin and dark brown eyes, and are slight of build. From anoir (east). They are also known simply as "easterners."

Aontar (Ay-ON-tar): The One Lord of All, the Creator.

Arialde (Ah-ree-AL-deh): Lady Arialde, the Asarla that founded the Tal-sithian with Lord Airan. She is the only known female Asarla, and is the keeper of the Stone of Léir. From arialdas (beautiful).

Aridani (Ah-ree-DAHN-ee), sing. Aridan (AH-ree-dahn): Men. Name means "Those that fade." From "aridas" (fading).

Arrah! Elvish expression of disgust, as when encountering something foul or distasteful.

Aryiah (Ah-RYE-yah): Dark-skinned, blind Seer of Dûn Arian, Aryiah is possessed of strange and wondrous abilities. She is an unsettling character, for one never knows the nature of what she might reveal.

Asaad (AH-sahd): Evil, controlling religious leader of the Sandstone Oasis. An old man, Asaad controls his followers with fear and intimidation. He has many assassins at his command.

Asari sing. Asarla (Ah-sah-REE): Immortal beings endowed with great knowledge, sent to enlighten the Children of Aontar. They were generally of the Light, but could be turned. Name means "Teacher."

Ashahi (Ah-SHA-hee): Eastern, or Anori, name for "beings of light." It was believed that Elves were Ashahi, but that many were beings of darkness (Osha) that were only pretending.

Astor (AS-tor): Lore-master and chief of the Library of Dûn Bennas. His name means "of great worth."

Avinashi (ah-vee-NAH-shee): Ravani name for Elves, it means "immortal ones." (Sing. fem. avinasha, sing. masc. avinashan)

Awani (Ah-WAH-nee): Dwarf in Ravani-speech; it means "Stunted one."

Azok (AH-zok): Second-in-command and brother of Azori, brother of Estle

Azori (ah-ZOR-ree): Leader of Hallagond's band of thieves, brother of Estle.

Ballali (bah-lah-LEE): Repressive cult of the Sandstone oasis, led by Asaad. The Ballali are very dangerous to anyone that disagrees with their very restrictive set of beliefs.

Bezaltor (BEZ-al-tor): Settlement of the Ravani known for its slave-market.

Bint Raed (Bint Rah-YED): masterful weaver-woman held by Al-Muniqui, she was originally a citizen of Dûn Arian. Her name means "daughter of Raenien."

Brinneal (BRIN-nee-al): Golden-haired Elf of the Èolar, she moved to Tal-sithian after the fall of Tal-elathas. She is the mother of Gorgon Elfhunter and the spouse of Amandir. Name means "beautiful young maid."

Broca: worthy commander of Dûn Arian, killed in battle.

Brocca: The river in the north that, along with the Eros, gives rise to the Ambros. It is as wild and turbulent as the Eros is smooth and gentle. From broca (restive).

Brunor (BROO-nor): Name taken by Gaelen when she disguises herself as Hallagond's apprentice. It means "golden-brown." From bruna (brown) and or-(golden).

Capellion (Ka-PELL-lee-on): Master of Horse in the Greatwood realm. His name means "horse master." From capella (horse).

Castalan (CAS-tah-LAHN): Coastal city near the mouth of the Ambros, it is known as a center of trade from the south. It is the home of Harsha, the wine-merchant.

Castor (CAS-tor): Wealthy slave-dealer of the Ravani. He often trades at Bezaltor.

Chupa-jul (CHOO-pa-JUL): Oasis settlement, home of Estle and the House of El-morah. The name means "hidden water."

Cós-domhain (Coss-Dome-Ha-EEN): Great Dwarf-realm, known as the Realm of Caverns. Ruled by Lord Grundin. From cós (cavern) and domhain (domain).

Cuidag (KWEE-dahg): Name given Sajid by the Company, it means "Spider".

Cúinar (COO-ee-nar): Sylvan Elves, Wood-elves. Considered to be of lesser stature than High-elves, they did not have the benefit of Asari influence. They inhabit and defend the Forest Realm of Greatwood. Examples are Gaelen and Nelwyn. From cúin (silent).

Dardis (DAR-dees): The second son of Aincor, a highly talented and inventive artisan and lover of learning. Unlike his father, Dardis was of gentle temperament and was revered especially by the dwarves. He was apprenticed to an Asarla named Léiras (the far-sighted), who taught him of the making of things that could be endowed with magical properties. It was Dardis that made the mirror given to Gorgon Elfhunter; he also created the Stone of Léir. He was killed on the eve of the Second Uprising.

Darkmere: The name given to the Great Forest Realm (Greatwood) when Wrothgar's power began to grow there. The Elves refer only to the southern part of the Forest as the Darkmere, but others make no such distinction. See also Dominglas Forest.

Dergin (DER-gin): Ranger, friend of Rogond and Thorndil. He is named for his red hair. From der- (red).

Derrin (DER-rin): Red horse purchased for Hallagond, Derrin has four white legs, which are a liability in the desert. His name means "The red."

Dessa (DESS-sa): River that marks the southern boundary of King Hearndin's influence. It means "southern."

D'hanar (Dah-NAHR): The ruin of Tal-elathas. It is now an evil place inhabited only by dark beings. The name is dwarvish for "land of darkness."

Diomar (DYOH-mar): Northman, sire of Rogond. His name means "The proud," from diomas (proud).

Dominglas Forest (DOME-een-glas): The vast woodland occupying approximately one-third of the northern lands of Alterra. In the north dwell the Sylvan Elves, and in the south Wrothgar has made his new, Dark Tower. From domhain (domain) and glas (deep green). See also Greatwood, Darkmere, Aruinnas.

Dona (DOE-nah): Name given Elraen by Gaelen, it means "one who is miserable." From donar (misery).

Dromadan (pl. Dromadin): Desert-dwelling beasts used by the Ravani-folk, often in place of horses. They are a type of camelid.

Duinar (DOO-ee-nar): Asarla who founded the northern realm of Tuathas. He appeared to be very old, with a long snow-white beard and a lined, weathered face. He was slain during the cataclysmic rising of the Fire-mountain that destroyed Tuathas and all lands near it. Name means "guide."

Dûn Bennas (Doon-ben-NAS): City of Men founded by the Tuathar, located in the southern tip of the Monadh-ailan. Name means "white fortress." From dûn (fortress) and bennas (white).

Dûn Arian (Doon-AH-ree-AHN): Largely unknown City of Men founded by the renowned scholar Salasin, located in the far southern lands. Also known as The Citadel. Name means "fortress of silver." From dûn (fortress) and ariant (silver).

Eádram (Ay-AH-drahm): High-elves, Elves of the Light that were never beguiled by the dark Asari. Examples are Galador and Lord Airan of Tal-ailean. From eádra (light).

Eádri (Ay-AH-dree): The Evening Star.

Eádros (Ay-AH-dross): Elven-realm, greatest of the Eádram. It was lost in the War of Betrayal, destroyed by the Dwarves of Rûmm.

Elàni (El-LAN-ee): Elves.

Elathanar (EL-ah-tha-NAR): Elvish name for Dûn Arian, it means "place of wisdom."

El-morah (El-MOR-rah): Kindly host of the kaffa-house in the Chupa-jul oasis, he and his family are friends of the Company.

Elraen (EL-ray-en): Elf, lost and taken to Wrothgar, who is no longer in her right mind. The name means "Star-elf," from elàn (elf) and réalta (star).

Elwyn (EL-win): Sylvan Elf, mother of Nelwyn. Name means "Elf-maiden." From elàn (elf) and wyn (maid).

Elysia (Eh-LEE-see-ah): Eternal Elven-home that has been provided to house the spirits of the Elàni after death. It is a paradise separate from the afterlife of men. From elàn (elf).

Èolar (AY-oh-lahr): High-elves that achieved the highest level of learning and skill, but were deceived by Wrothgar and his dark Asari. They were mostly lost during the second uprising. Examples are Aincor, Dardis, Magra, and Ri-Elathan. From Èolas (knowing).

Eros (EH-rohs): Sturdy, intelligent dun horse of Rogond. Also a smooth-flowing, gentle river that gives rise to the Ambros in the north. From eran (soft, easy).

Estle (ES-tle): Hard-bitten but endearing half-sister of Azori and Azok, the bandit brothers, Estle is forced to join the Company. Her mother was a citizen of Dûn Arian. She is beloved of Hallagond.

Faladinn (FA-la-deen): small, plain horse, given to the Company by the Kazhi. His name means "hill pony".

Farahin (FA-ra-heen): Given name of Ri-Elathan. Name means "welcome rain," from farath (welcome) and hin (rain).

Farath-talam! (Fa-RATH TAH-lahm): Elvish welcome, it means "you are welcome among us," or "welcome to our realm."

Farin (FAH-rin): Dwarf of Cós-domhain, eminent craftsman and maker of Rogond's ring.

Fayalah (FYE-ah-lah): Wife of Hari, the horse-provider of the sandstone.

Fesok (FES-ok): Legendary dwarven hero, known as "The Iron-beard."

Fiana (Fee-AH-na): Wood-elves" name for the constellation Orion, also the clear stream that flows from the Linnefionn. Name means "huntress."

Fima (FEE-ma): Dwarvish Loremaster, originally of Cós-domhain and now serving Lady Ordath in Monadh-talam, he is a good friend of Rogond.

Finan (Fih-NAHN): desert-bred bay horse, rescued by Gaelen, he becomes her favorite mount. His name means "The fair."

Fiona (Fee-YO-na): Elvish name for the constellation Orion, it is named after Fiona, the Huntress.

Fior (FYOR): The Dwarves" name for Aontar. Name means "The Maker."

Fioran (FYOR-ran): King of Dûn Bennas, felled by the Plague. His nephew, Hearndin, rules at present.

Fómor (FOE-mor): Southern coastal city, ruled by the Corsairs. It is not a place for either the faint-hearted or those of upstanding character (such as Rangers and Elves).

Gaelen (GEH-lehn): Sylvan Elf of the Greatwood, daughter of Tarfion and Gloranel, cousin of Nelwyn. Name means "daughter of valor." From gael- (valor, feminine).

Galador (GAL-ah-dore): High-elf, formerly of Eádros, beloved of Gwynnyth and later of Nelwyn. Friend of Rogond. From gal- (valor, masculine).

Galdor (GAL-dore): Beloved of Elraen, he was slain in the Greatwood while grieving for her after she was lost.

Gelmyr (GEL-meer): Èolarin Warrior-elf of Monadh-talam, friend of Magra, slain by Gorgon. He "appears" in Gorgon's mind, taunting him, whenever Gorgon doubts himself. From gal- (valor, masculine) and mirys (graceful).

Gilien (GIL-lee-en): Bright, cold stream near the northern mountains, it means "bright maiden."

Gloranel (GLOR-ah-nel): Sylvan Elf, mother of Gaelen. Name means "Bright tree", from glora (bright light) and nellas (tree).

Gorgon (GORE-gun): Dark but mighty perversion brought into being by Wrothgar, he is also known as the Elfhunter. From gor- (dark) and gundas (horror).

Grundin (GROON-din): Dwarf-lord, ruler of Cós-domhain. Grundin was very wise and reasonably open-minded, and he could trace his lineage back directly to the Five Founders. Name means "Solid-as-stone."

Gryffa (GRIF-fa): Chestnut horse ridden by Nelwyn, his name means "The red."

Gwynnyth (GWIN-nith): Beloved mortal woman, lost love of Galador. Her name means "blissful."

Habib (Hah-BEEB): Worthy but ill-fated commander of Dûn Arian.

Haifa (HYE-fah): Unsavory tavern-keeper of the Chupa oasis.

Haldur (HAL-dur): Master armourer of the Greatwood Realm.

Hallagond (HAL-la-gond): Older brother of Rogond. His name means "Tall stone" from halla (tall) and gondas (stone).

Halrodin (HAL-roe-din): Hunter-scout of the Greatwood, friend of Gaelen, slain by Gorgon. His name means basically "Tall-tree," from halla (tall) and rodo (trunk of a tree).

Hamad: (Ha-MAHD): Eldest son of Hamir.

Hamadir (HA-ma-deer): Sire of Hamir.

Hamir (Ha-MEER): Merchant of the Ravi-shan, friend to the Company. He is the head of a large family.

Hari (HA-ree): Horse-merchant of the Sandstone settlement.

Harnien, or **Harnen**: Dwarf-realms that lie beneath the northern mountains. They were founded in large part by the descendants of Rûmm, also known as the Rûm-harnen.

Harsha: Wine-vendor of Castalan, friend to the Company.

Hassan the Giant: Very large and ill-tempered inhabitant of the Chupa oasis. He appears in a rather memorable encounter with a drunken Hallagond.

Hattaras (HAH-ter-rahs): Sutherling, a member of Azori's band of outlaws. He has only one remaining hand.

Hearndin (HERN-deen): Present King of Dûn Bennas.

Ikari (Ih-KAH-ree): Anori easterner, member of Azori's band of outlaws. Ikari has a pet crow named "Karatsu," and he is a member of a rare dragon-cult. He despises Galador.

Ishtar Al-Khamal: Known simply as "Ishtar," he is imprisoned as a criminal in Dûn Arian. Hallagond releases him in the belief that his battle-experience will aid the City. He is of Ravani heritage, and somewhat resembles Azori.

Jao: Scholar of Dûn Arian, he is an easterner that proves to be very helpful in the battle-preparations. His name is pronounced "Jow."

Kaffa (KAFF-fa): Sutherling drink, akin to coffee, highly prized and very costly when of fine quality.

Kamal (Ka-MAHL): Sutherling employed by Radeef to deceive Rogond by directing him to Fómor.

Karatsu (Ka-RAHT-soo): Tame crow belonging to Ikari.

Kazhi (Kah-ZHEE): Short, stocky, good-natured people of the eastern stone-desert. They are nomads of a strong horse culture, and are generally hospitable to well-meaning strangers. They are a type of Anori-folk.

Koka: Dark, bittersweet material relished by the people of the Ravani. It is most likely akin to chocolate.

Kumri (KOOM-ree): Odd-tasting but powerful liquor of the Ravani; it is made from fermented mare's milk.

Laban-fuath (la-Ban-foo-ath): The great evil bog surrounding Tur Dorcha in the south of the Darkmere. Name means "Terrible mire." From laban (bog) and fuath (terrible).

Laffas (LAH-fahs): A sutherling pepper stew that is difficult to prepare and not for the weak of stomach, it could probably take the tarnish from silver and the rust from iron.

Lamas (LAH-mahs): Young son of Hamir, and a fine singer.

Léir (Stone of Leh-eer): Great crystal made by Dardis and presently located in Tal-sithian, in which one may behold visions of the future or of the past, and gain enlightenment. It derives much of its power from the grieved and bitter spirit of Shandor, the Asarla, who is entrapped within. Kept by Arialde, it must only be used in her presence (léir-far sighted).

Liathwyn (Lee-ATH-win): Elf of the Eolar, mother of Ordath, espoused to Shandor the Asarla, with whom she founded Monadh-talam. Her name means "Blue-eyed maiden." She relinquished her spirit after the Second Uprising. She was kin to the High Kings Ri-Aldamar and Ri-Elathan. From liath (blue).

Linnefionn (Lin-neh-fee-YON): The very large, very deep and very clear Lake in the center of which is located the Elven-realm of Tal-sithian. The Lake is generally shrouded in mist and cannot be seen by unwelcome visitors. Name means "clear lake." From linne (lake) and fionn (crystal-clear).

Lokai (LO-kye): Fearsome, ugly dragon of a rare desert variety. Lokai cannot fly, but he has many fearsome weapons, including venom and fire.

maglos (MAG-los): Soft, white metal discovered and refined by the dwarves, it reacts violently when exposed to water. It is most likely akin to sodium or magnesium. Name means "mighty light," from magra (mighty).

Magra (MA-gra): Mighty Èolarin Elf-lord, second-in-command and kinsman of Ri-Elathan. Name means "mighty." Magra was very tall and strong, and had golden hair. He was related to Liathwyn, and hence to Lady Ordath.

Maidrin (MYE-drin): Name given to Gaelen by Gorgon, it means "fox."

Maji (Mah-ZHEE): Minister of Omens in Dûn Arian, she is a woman of great insight and vision.

Makita (Mah-KEE-tah): Head of the clan of Kazhi-folk encountered by the Company.

Makkbah (MAHK-bah): Horse-merchant of the Mumari oasis.

marwani (Mar-WAH-nee): Herb that is frequently used in the southlands for its mood-enhancing and mildly intoxicating properties when dried and smoked. It is used as a medicinal herb rather than for recreation in the north, as it is difficult to obtain there.

Mikla (MEEK-lah): Man of the Chupa oasis, known as "The Poisoner". He can provide any poison for a price.

Mohani (Mo-HAH-nee): Spouse of El-morah, the proprietor of the kaffa-house in the Chupa oasis. Her name means "beautiful." She is small, comely, and capable.

Monadh-ailan (Monath-EYE-lan): The Verdant Mountains; gentle, coastal peaks that run along the sea, they are inhabited by folk of many races, notably the Wood-elves of Tal-ailean. Name means "green-mountains". From monad (mountain) and ailan (green).

Monadh-hin (Monad-HEEN): The Great Mountains, largest of all mountain-ranges in Alterra, they are a daunting obstacle for travelers. Snow-covered in winter, they are shrouded by clouds year-around. Name means "peaks of rain," from hin (rain).

Monadh-talam (Monath-TAH-lahm): Elven-realm presided over by the Lady Ordath. Hidden among tall peaks of the Monadh-hin, it is also known as Mountain-home. It is perhaps the greatest of remaining Elf-realms, and holds great stores of written record. It is a place of healing, study and enlightenment, and is home to folk of many races. Name means "mountain-realm." From monad (mountain) and tal- (realm).

Mumari (Moo-MAH-ree): Small desert settlement and last outpost on the way to Dûn Arian.

Neela-jul (NEE-la-Jool): The Neela Oasis, a fair place with good water. Unsavory folk are not welcome there. The name means "blue water" in the sutherling speech.

Nelwyn (NEL-win): Sylvan Elf of the Greatwood, daughter of Turanen and Elwyn, younger cousin of Gaelen. Name means "Tree-maiden," from "nellas" (tree).

Okami (Oh-KAH-mi): Anori easterner, a member of Azori's band of outlaws.

Olaf the Unfortunate: Rough, savage northman who competes for the prize in the Sandstone during the Festival. He will do whatever is necessary to win, but he more than meets his match in Sajid. His name "The Unfortunate" is well-earned.

Ordath (OR-dath): The Lady Ordath, very powerful overseer of Monadh-talam. She is the product of a union between a powerful Asarla (Shandor) and an Elf of the Eolar (Liathwyn). She is a great healer and protector of Monadh-talam. Name means "Treasure-of-the-land". From or- (golden, gentle) and –dath (of the land).

Osha (OH-sha): Evil spirits of Anori lore, these pretended to be good spirits. Elves were often viewed as Osha masquerading as beings of light.

Quarinar (KWAH-ree-nahr): People of Tuathas that did not hold sufficient faith in Duinar's ability to quell the Fire-mountain that destroyed it. They were the only people that escaped the Cataclysm. There is some question as to whether their lack of faith lessened Duinar's power, and hence the descendants of the Quarinar carry some guilt with them. From quari (to doubt).

Radeef (Ra-DEEF): Very unsavory horse-trader from whom Gaelen acquires Finan; he orchestrates the deception of Rogond for a price.

Raenien (RAY-nee-en): Master weaver descended of Tuathas, mother of Bint Raed.

Rashid (Rah-SHEED): Pleasant young sutherling hired by the Company as a translator while in the Sandstone.

Ravi-shan (RAH-vee- SHAHN): The southern desert region of Alterra. Name means "Sun-country." It is also known simply as the "Ravi" or even the "Rav." The people are known as "Ravani" or Ravani-folk." From sutherling Rav (sun) and shan (realm, land, country).

Réalta (ray-AL-ta): Swift and beautiful grey stallion, favored mount of Galador and companion of Eros. His name means "Star."

Redruin (Red-ROO-een): Fearsome Fire-drake featured in a tale, told by Fima, involving an encounter with the legendary dwarvish hero, Fesok the Iron-beard.

Ri-Aldamar (ree AL-da-mar): Second High King of the Eolar, brother of Liathwyn and sire of Farahin. He was killed by a dragon during the Second Uprising. His name means "most noble ruler." From ri- (ruler), aldos (high, noble) and –amar (great, majestic).

Ri-Aruin (ree-AR-oo-een): Ruler of the Sylvan Elves of the Greatwood Realm. His name means "King of the forest". From ri-(ruler) and aruinnas (forest). (note: the prefix "ri" was not adopted by the Sylvan Elves until the death of Ri-Elathan. Prior to that time it was reserved only for the High King.)

Ri-Elathan (ree-EL-a-than): Last High-elven King, Ri-Elathan left no one to succeed him. He was arguably the wisest of all the High Kings, and was both feared and beloved, but he lived a very lonely and arduous life. Beloved of Gaelen Taldin, he was killed during the Third Uprising. His given name was Farahin. His name means "King of Wisdom." From ri-(ruler) and elathas (wisdom).

Ri-solas (Ree-SO-las): Elves" name for the midsummer festival, it means "king sun."

Rogond (ROE-gond): Man of the Tuathar, born during the Plague Year and fostered by the Elves of the Verdant Mountains. Name means "Treasure within the stone." From or- (golden, gentle) and gondas (stone).

Rosalin (ROS-a-lin): "River-beauty."Woman descended of Tuathas, mother of Rogond. From Ros-(river) and –aille (beautiful).

Rûmhar (ROOM-har): Dwarves. Their speech is known as Rûmhul. From Rûm- (to delve).

Rûmm (RHUM): Ancient and Great Dwarf-realm, known as the Deep Delving, which was lost in the War with the Eádram. From Rûm- (to delve).

Rûndiam-har (Roon-dee-ahm-HAR): The Book of Mystery, an accounting of what is known of the time before the First Reckoning begins. From rûndiam (mystery).

Sajid (Sah-ZHEED): Ne'er-do-well of the Ravani. Little is known of him, other than having been branded as a criminal.

Salasin (SAH-lah-seen): Chief Lore-master of Tuathas, he was prominent among the Quarinar. He founded the City of Dûn Arian after the Cataclysm, having been carried there by great waves, bearing much of the library of Tuathas with him.

Salastor (Lord Salastor): Present Lord of Dûn Arian, and her chief Lore-master, he presides over the High Council. He is descended directly from Salasin, who founded the City.

Scourge: the: Fearsome, savage army that is presently sweeping across the Ravi-shan. It is made up of fierce warriors, gleaned from Plague survivors, and is a very dark and dreadful enemy. Scourge warriors wear red and black garb.

Seti (SEH-tee): Good-natured former ivory trader, now living in Dûn Arian. He aids in preparing the City's defenses.

Shadowmancer: Wrothgar, the Dark Power of Alterra. He is thought by many to be an extremely powerful, black sorcerer, hence the name " Shadowmancer." The name has also been applied to Lord Kotos, but in these tales it refers specifically to Wrothgar.

Shandor (SHAN-dor): Arguably the most powerful of the Asari, he loved Liathwyn, an Elf of the Èolar, and together they founded Monadh-talam. He actually challenged Wrothgar in battle, and defeated him during the Second Uprising. He is the sire of Lady Ordath. When Liathwyn relinquished her spirit and went to Elysia, Shandor withdrew from the world, eventually seeking refuge in the great stone crystal of Léir, which is presently in the keeping of Lady Arialde, the Asarla of Tal-sithian. Shandor was the only Light Asarla to leave his protected realm and go forth to Battle. His name essentially means "great spirit."

Shiva (SHEE-vah): Healer of the Chupa oasis.

Siva (SEE-va): Silver-white horse ridden by Gaelen, her name simply means "grey."

Sundahi (Soon-DAH-hee): Trustworthy guide arranged for by Harsha. Regrettably, the Company never encounters him.

Tal-ailean (Tal-EYE-lee-ahn): Elven-realm located in the Monadh-ailan. It is inhabited by various small, secretive groups of Cúinar known as the Elàni-ailan (green-elves). From tal- (realm) and ailan (green).

Taldin (TAl-deen): Name given affectionately to Gaelen by Ri-Elathan, it means "walks unnoticed, stealthy." From taldin (unnoticed).

Tal-elathas (tal-EL-a-thas): Ancient realm of the Èolar, it was the greatest center of invention and discovery that has ever been. At one time there were no less than three Asari that resided there; they were Leiras, Baelta, and regrettably, Kotos. It was destroyed by Wrothgar's army when Kotos betrayed the Elves, aided unwittingly by Baelta. From tal- (realm) and elathas (wisdom).

Tal-fásath: The Elves" rather unflattering name for the Ravani desert, it means "realm of barren waste," or, "land of terrible loneliness." From fás (lonely, barren) and tal- (realm).

Talishani Ali (TAL-ih-SHAH-ni Ah-LEE): Battle-seasoned Minister of Defense in Dûn Arian, he commands the City forces during the Battle. He is a worthy and likeable man; Hallagond, in particular, admires him. He is usually called simply "Ali."

Tallasiar (TAL-ah-SHAR): Western city of the lost realm of Tuathas, it was reputedly very beautiful. Dûn Arian is said to resemble it in design.

Talrodin (TAL-roh-deen): Hunter-scout of Greatwood, friend of Nelwyn and brother of Halrondin. He was slain by Gorgon. His name means "Strength of the realm," from tal-(realm) and rodos (as the trunk of a tree).

Tal-sithian, (SITH-ee-ahn): Green forested island in the Linnefionn; the Elven-realm of the Lord Airan and Lady Arialde. From sithion (deer). It means "realm of deer roaming."

Tarfion (TAR-fee-ohn): Father of Gaelen, spouse of Gloranel, twin brother of Tarmagil and elder brother of Turanen. Tarfion was probably unexcelled as a hunter-scout, and he gained the King's favor upon saving the life of his son, prince Aruin. Name means "hunter of the realm." From fiona (hunter) and tar-(of the realm)

Thaylon (THAY-lon): Given name of Rogond, it means "Trustworthy." From thala (to trust).

Thorndil (THORN-deel): Northman, ranger and friend of Rogond, companion of Belegund. His name means "Piercing gaze, eagle-eyed." From thorn- (to pierce).

Tréigim (TREY-geem): High-elven word meaning "forsaken."

Tuathas (TOO-ah-thas): Greatest of all Realms of Men, Tuathas alone possessed an Asarla. Because of this they were more enlightened than other men, and were nearly as fair as the Elves. It was destroyed during an eruption of one of the great Fire-mountains that bounded it, and very little of the realm survived. From "Tuath" (north).

Tuathar (TOO-ah-thar) sing. Tuathan: Men of the northern realm of Tuathas, lost in the rising of the Great Fire-mountain. Name means "northman," from tuath (north) and aridan (man). They are more enlightened than other races of men.

Turanen (TOOR-ah-nen): Younger brother of Tarfion and Tarmegil, father of Nelwyn and spouse of Elwyn. An unparalleled archer, he was slain in the third uprising. Name means "glen-bowman." From tuag- (bow) and ranen (glen).

Tûr Dorcha (Toor DOR-ka): Wrothgar's stronghold in the Darkmere, it means "Dark Tower."

Ujaalah (oo-ZHAA-lah): Ballali High Holy Day that corresponds to the Summer Solstice.

Ulcas (UL-cas), sing. Ulca: Evil servants of Wrothgar, their origin is unknown, but they are undoubtedly perversions of other races, as Wrothgar is incapable of true creation. They are varied, and some are quite formidable in battle, but most can prevail only through sheer numbers. All are ugly. They dislike sunlight and live in dark places, particularly beneath mountains.

Undaalah (oon-DAH-lah): Ballali High Holy Day that marks the Winter Solstice.

Upani (oo-PAH-nee): Unsavory oasis known as the Darkwater.

Visili, Haleck (Vih-SEE-lee): Criminal, imprisoned in Dûn Arian, freed by Hallagond, and later redeemed. Visili appears to be of northern descent.

Waddi (Wah-DEE): Good-hearted third brother of Al-Muniqui, he feigned feeble-mindedness to protect himself from his ambitious relatives. He succeeded Al-Muniqui as chieftain.

Wellyn: (WEL-lin): Son and heir of Ri-Aruin of the Greatwood, and very dear friend of Gaelen. His name means "courageous, one who is brave."

Wrothgar (ROTH-gar): Evil being of Alterra. Also known as the Shadowmancer and the "Black Flame". Name means "Dark Fury." From wroth (fury, wrath) and gor (dark).

About C.S. Marks

C.S. Marks has often been described as a Renaissance woman. The daughter of academic parents, she holds a Ph.D. in Biology and has spent the past two decades teaching Biology and Equine Science. She is currently a Full Professor at Saint Mary-of-the-Woods College in west central Indiana.

She began writing shortly after the untimely death of her father, who was a Professor of American Literature at Butler University. A gifted artist, she has produced illustrations and cover art for all three books. She plays and sings Celtic music and a few examples of her songwriting may be found within the pages of Fire-heart. She enjoys archery, and makes hand-crafted longbows using primitive tools.

Horses are her passion, and she is an accomplished horsewoman, having competed in the sport of endurance racing for many years. One of only a handful of Americans to complete the prestigious Tom Quilty Australian national championship hundred-mile ride, she has described this moment as her finest hour.

Website: CSMarks.com

Facebook: Facebook.com/Alterra

CSMarksTwitter: Twitter.com/CSMarks_Alterra

Goodreads: https://www.goodreads.com/author/show/521676.C_S_Marks

C.S. Marks Mailing List Sign Up: http://eepurl.com/st8Vj

Books by C.S. Marks

Tales of Alterra (The Elfhunter Trilogy)

Elfhunter

Fire-heart

Ravenshade

Alterra Histories

The Fire King

Fallen Embers

The Shadow-man

Undiscovered Realms

Outcaste

We hope you've enjoyed reading Fire-heart. Please consider leaving a review on Goodreads and your point of purchase.

Where to Find C.S. Marks

The Author's Website: CSMarks.com
Facebook.com/Alterra.CSMarks
Twitter.com/CSMarks_Alterra

Stay up to date with what's happening with C.S. Marks by joining the mailing list. You will receive exclusive teasers and be the first to know when a new book has been released.

Sign Up For the C.S. Marks Mailing List at

CSMarks.com